A Cruel Wind

A Cruel Wind

A CHRONICLE OF THE DREAD EMPIRE

GLEN COOK

NIGHT SHADE BOOKS
SAN FRANCISCO & PORTLAND

ISBN: 978-1-59780-104-1

Third Printing

Night Shade Books
Please visit us on the web at
http://www.nightshadebooks.com

Contents

GLEN COOK: GODFATHER OF MODERN HEROIC FANTASY

Glen Cook doesn't suffer fools easily. I mean this as a compliment, not a slam. It's an attitude that permeates his fiction as well: this sense of no-bullshit, no-compromise. Despite having written innumerable series, Cook still writes for himself first and foremost, and isn't willing to compromise his vision. As Cook himself has said, "I work in series because I can't tell a story in one book, usually. There's always more to tell. A series allows you to tell a larger story, usually. I enjoy world building."

Over the past twenty-five years, Cook has carved out a place for himself among the preeminent fantasy writers of his generation, with classics such as the Dread Empire novels, The Black Company novels, and the Starfishers series. His work is unrelentingly real, complex, and honest. The sense of place that permeates his narrative and characters gives his "fantasies" more gravitas and grit than most fictions set in the here-and-now. The people in his novels tend to be deeply flawed—struggling to do what's right but not always able to stick with it due to circumstances or simply human nature. As Cook says, "That's life. We all face it every day. And most of us don't live up to the talk we talk. How much more so when the stakes are life or death?"

If Cook is sometimes overlooked on the roll call of great fantasists, it may be because the genre is currently overshadowed by the over-emphasis on cross-genre work and new literary movements. But Cook has always created cross-genre fiction, if on his own terms. The Black Company novels, for example, combine the intensity of Viet Nam-era war fiction with the classic quest of heroic fantasy, while his Garrett detective series combines magic and noir mystery to excellent comic effect. He has also written the ultimate submarine novel in space, *Passage at Arms*. (Although long out of print, it is well worth seeking out. The claustrophobic evocation of what it might be like in close quarters on a spaceship remains one of Cook's great achievements.)

As the excellent fantasist Steven Erikson has written, "The thing about Glen Cook is that he single-handedly changed the field of fantasy—something a lot of people didn't notice and maybe still don't. He brought the story down to a human level, dispensing with the clichés and archetypes of princes, kings, and evil sorcerers. Reading his stuff was like reading Viet Nam war fiction on peyote."

But well before Cook's Black Company series, there was the Dread Empire trilogy, Cook's first major work.

I still remember the first time I read *A Shadow of All Night Falling*, the first in the Dread Empire trilogy. I had long since read the Tolkien books, the McKillip Riddlemaster series, and, earlier, the Narnia books. Then I'd tried reading Terry Brooks and David Eddings and a few others, and had been turned off of heroic and quest fantasy as a result.

Only a few months later, in Book Gallery, a used bookstore in Gainesville, Florida, something caught my eye in the mass market paperback SF/Fantasy section: the cover of *A Shadow of All Night Falling*. It didn't look like all the other heroic fantasy covers. I read the description on the back of the book:

> *Across the mountains called Dragon's Teeth, beyond the chill reach of the Werewind and the fires of the world's beginning, above the walls of the castle Fangdred it stands: Windtower. From this lonely keep the Star Rider calls forth the war that even wizards dread, fought for a woman's hundred-lifetime love. A woman called Nepanthe, princess to the Stormkings...*

That didn't sound like the same-old same-old, either. So I read the prologue and it didn't read like anything I'd read before. There were suggestions of worlds within worlds and plots within plots. It was a true prologue, not one of those fake cliffhanger-type prologues. The prose was spare and tight and not given to melodrama. The idea of the Star Rider was presented in pragmatic and yet mysterious terms. (Ironically enough, the same day in the same bookstore I picked up Edward Whittemore's *Jerusalem Poker*, which would be another of my major influences—it too had a stylized cover and an amazing prologue.)

As I read the rest of the novel, I realized Cook was a true original, creating his own unique approach—one that would increasingly be from the eye-level/foot-soldier level, one that could be blunt and bloody, but also include a very sophisticated view of societies and of people. The Western, Middle Eastern, and Far East influence worked well and made the story unique.

In short, I loved the book and quickly bought and read the other two initial volumes: *October's Baby* and *All Darkness Met*. I found myself drawn to characters like Nepanthe, Mocker, and so many others. These people came off the page in a fascinating way. Mocker in particular—I loved that character, his complex motivation and his basic humanity.

There was also a talent Cook had for micro- and macro-level action and plain-spoken dialogue that made the stylization of much of heroic fantasy look flat and false. Not to mention that the series grew ever more complex as it progressed, with *All Darkness Met* demonstrating an amazing ability to juggle storylines, characters, and subtle intrigue.

What also struck me was just how weird and alien these books were—they didn't evoke the twee fussiness of Tolkien or the kind of fey detail of McKillip at all. Instead, they put me in mind of the best of the *Weird Tales* writers, and of icons like Jack Vance or Fritz Leiber—another unique writer who knew how to get at the strangeness of the world.

At the time, I was about eighteen or nineteen, just learning about the craft of writing, completely wet-behind-the-ears. From a writer's perspective, the Dread Empire trilogy was a goldmine. Like the Whittemore books I found at the same time, Cook's work explored both the complexity of history and the grim reality of its situations. Through the Dread Empire I learned how you could place characters in a historical context much larger than the individuals involved without relegating character to the background. Cook taught me that moral and immoral acts have consequences in fiction, some of them tragic. He also taught me a lot about how to inject specific detail into the fantastical. And more than anything else, Cook taught me that characters in a fantasy world have it just as tough as we do in real life. (Not to mention my excitement in reading the subsequent Dread Empire novels—*The Fire in His Hands, With Mercy Toward None, Reap the East Wind,* and *An Ill Fate Marshalling*—which share the attributes of the first three books while expanding on the characters and milieu. It's really hard not to be reduced to a fanboy writing about all of this, to be honest.)

Ever since that first encounter, I've found Cook's novels not only entertaining and exciting, but often moving and complex. In *Passage at Arms* and the Black Company novels, I can see the echoes of those first Dread Empire volumes—in the ethical and moral complications, in the no-bullshit approach. And given that I've seen so many authors fall prey to their own success, I find it invigorating and a great example that Cook, after so many years, hasn't budged an inch in his approach. He's still producing great work and he's still doing it on his own terms.

I don't know if anyone can imagine my delight and joy at being able to provide an introduction to a body of work that has been so inspirational to me. Or my envy for those of you for whom this is your first encounter with Mocker, with Nepanthe, with the Star Rider, and with so many other amazing characters. I hope you find as much in Cook's work to savor as I did, picking up that first battered paperback in Gainesville so many years ago.

Jeff VanderMeer
Tallahassee, Florida
May 2006

(Both quotes by Glen Cook taken from his *Green Man Review* interview with Robert M. Tilendis.)

A Shadow of
All Night Falling

Contents

PROLOGUE:
SUMMER OF THE YEAR 994
AFTER THE FOUNDING OF THE EMPIRE OF ILKAZAR
HUNT'S END

A blue-lighted room hollowed from living rock. Four men waiting. A fifth entered. "I was right." The wear and dust of a savage journey still marked him. "The Star Rider was in it up to his ears." He tumbled into a chair.

The others waited.

"It cost the lives of twelve good men, but they were profitably spent. I questioned three men who accompanied the Disciple to Malik Taus. Their testimony convinced me. The Disciple's angel was the Star Rider."

"Fine," said the one who made decisions. "But where is he now? And where's Jerrad?"

"Two questions. One answer. Thunder Mountain."

Denied a response, the newcomer continued, "More of my best agents spent. But word came: a small old man and a winged horse have been seen near the Caverns of the Old Ones. Jerrad took pigeons. Birdman brought one in just when I got home. Jerrad's found him, camped below the mountain. He's got the Horn with him." His final remark was almost hysterically excited.

"We'll leave in the morning."

This Horn, the Horn of the Star Rider, the Windmjirnerhorn, was reputed to be a horn of plenty. The man who could wrest it from its owner and master it would want for nothing, could create the wealth to buy anything.

These five had fantasies of restoring an empire raped away from their ancestors.

Time had passed that imperium by. There was no more niche it could fill. The fantasies were nothing more. And that most of these men realized. Yet they persisted, motivated by tradition, the challenge, and the fervor of the two doing the talking.

"Down there," said Jerrad, pointing into a dusk-filled, deep, pine-greened canyon. "Beside the waterfall."

The others could barely discern the distance-diminished smoke of the campfire.

"What's he up to?"

Jerrad shrugged. "Just sitting there. All month. Except one night last week he flew the horse somewhere back east. He was back before dark next day."

"You know the way down?"

"I haven't been any closer. Didn't want to spook him."

"Okay. We'd better start now. Make use of what light's left."

"Spread out and come at him from every direction. Jerrad, whatever you do, don't let him get to the Horn. Kill him if you have to."

It was past midnight when they attacked the old man, and could have been later still had there been no moon.

The Star Rider wakened to a footfall, bolted toward the Horn with stunning speed.

Jerrad got there first, gutting knife in hand. The old man changed course in midstride, made an astounding leap onto the back of his winged horse. The beast climbed the sky with a sound like that of beating dragon's pinions.

"Got away!" the leader cursed. "Damned! Damned! Damned!"

"Lightfooted old geezer," someone observed.

And Jerrad, "What matter? We got what we came for."

The leader raised the bulky Horn. "Yes. We have it now. The keystone of the New Empire. And the Werewind will be the cornerstone."

With varying enthusiasm, as their ancestors had, the others said, "Hail the Empire."

From high above, distance-attenuated, came a sound that might have been laughter.

ONE: THE YEARS 583-590 AFE
HE IS ENTERED IN THE LISTS OF THE WORLD

While hooded executioners lifted and set the ornately carven stake, a child wept at their feet. When they brought the woman, her eyes red from crying and her hair disheveled, he tried to run to her. Gently, an executioner scooped him up and set him in the arms of a surprised old peasant. While the hooded men piled faggots around her calves, the woman stared at child and man, seeing nothing else, her expression pleading. A priest gave her the sacraments because she had committed no sin in the eyes of his religion. Before withdrawing to his station of ceremony, he shook brightly dyed, belled horsehair flails over her tousled head, showering her with the pain-killing pollen of the dreaming lotus. He began singing a prayer for her soul. The master executioner signaled an apprentice. The youth brought a brand. The master touched it to the faggots. The woman stared at her feet as if without comprehending what was happening. And the child kept crying.

The farmer, with a peasant's rough kindness, carried the boy away, comforting him, taking him where he wouldn't hear. Soon he stopped moaning and seemed to have resigned himself to this cruel whim of Fate. The old man dropped him to the cobbled street, but didn't release his hand. He had known his own sorrows, and knew loss must be soothed lest it become festering hatred. This child would someday be a man.

Man and boy pushed through crowds of revelers— Execution Day was always a holiday in Ilkazar—the youngster skipping to keep pace with the farmer's long strides. He rubbed tears away with the back of a grimy hand. Leaving the Palace district, they entered slums, followed noisome alleys running beneath jungles of laundry, to the square called Farmer's Market. The old man led the boy to a stall where an elderly woman squatted behind melons, tomatoes, cucumbers, and braids of hanging maize.

"So," she said, voice rattling. "What's this you've found, Royal?"

"Ah, Mama, a sad one," he replied. "See the tearstreaks? Come, come, find a sweet." Lifting the boy before him, he entered the stall.

The woman rifled a small package and found a piece of sugar candy. "Here, little man. For you. Sit down, Royal. It's too hot to tramp around town." Over the boy's shoulder she asked a question with a lifted eyebrow.

"A hot day, yes," said Royal. "The King's men were witch-burning again. She was young. A black-hood had me take her child away."

From the shade beside the old woman the boy watched with big, sad eyes. His left fist mashed the rock candy against his lips. His right rubbed the few tears still escaping his eyes. But he was silent now, watching like a small idol.

"I was thinking we might foster him." Royal spoke softly, uncertainly. The suggestion closely skirted a matter painful for both of them.

"It's a grave responsibility, Royal."

"Yes, Mama. But we have none of our own. And, if we passed on, he'd have the farm to keep him." He didn't say, but she understood, that he preferred passing his property to anyone but the King, who would inherit if there were no heirs.

"Will you take in all the orphans you find?"

"No. But this one is a charge Death put on us. Can we ignore Her? More-over, haven't we hoped through our springs and summers, into our autumns, hopelessly, when the tree couldn't bear? Should I slave on the land, and you here selling its produce, merely to bury silver beneath the woodshed floor? Or to buy a peasant's grave?"

"All right. But you're too kind for your own good. For example, your mar-rying me, knowing me barren."

"I haven't regretted it."

"Then it's settled by me."

The child took it all in in silence. When the old woman finished, he took his hand from his eyes and set it on hers in her lap.

Royal's farmhouse, on the bank of the Aeos two leagues above Ilkazar, blos-somed. Where once it had been dusty within and weathered, tumble-down without, it began to sparkle. The couple took coin from hidden places and bought paint, nails, and cloth for curtains. A month after the child's arrival, the house seemed newly built. Once-crusty pots and pans glistened over the hearth. Accumulated dirt got swept away and the hardwood floor reappeared. New thatch begoldened the roof. A small room to the rear of the house became a fairy realm, with a small bed, handmade cabinet, and a single child-sized chair.

The change was marked enough to be noticed. The King's bailiffs came, reassessed the taxes. Royal and the old woman scarcely noticed.

But, though they gave him all love and kindness, the child never uttered a "thank you." He was polite enough, never a bother, and loving in a doleful way, but he never spoke—though sometimes, late at night, Royal heard him crying in his room. They grew accustomed to his silence, and, in time, stopped trying to get him to talk. Perhaps, they reasoned, he had never obtained the faculty. Such afflictions weren't uncommon in a city as harsh as Ilkazar.

In winter, with snows on the ground, the family remained indoors. Royal taught the boy rustic skills: whittling, the husking and shelling of maize, how bacon is cured and hung, the use of hammer and saw. And chess, at which he soon excelled. Royal often marveled at his brightness, forgetting that children are no more retarded than their elders, just more innocent of knowledge.

Winter passed. The child grew in stature and knowledge, but never spoke. They named him Varth, "the Silent One" in their language. Spring came and Royal began working the fields. Varth went with him, walking behind the plow, breaking clods with his bare feet. Soon shoots sprouted. Varth helped with the weeding, planted stakes for the tomatoes, and threw stones at birds threatening the melons. The old woman thought he would make a fine farmer some day. He seemed to have a love for tending life.

When summer came and the melons fattened, the tomatoes reddened, and the squash grew into green clubs, Varth helped with the harvesting, packing, and the loading of Royal's wagon. The old woman opposed his return to Ilkazar, but Royal thought he had forgotten. So he went with them to market, and a good day they had there. Their crop was one of the earliest in, their produce was exceptional, and Ilkazar was out in force, seeking fresh vegetables. Later, when tomatoes and squash were common, they would be spurned in favor of meat.

The old woman, from her usual place in the shade, said, "If for nothing but luck, the adoption was wise. Look! When they can't get melons they take tomatoes or squash."

"It's early in the season. When the stalls are full and there's produce left for the hogs, things won't look so bright. Do you think we could get a tutor for Varth?"

"A tutor? Royal! We're peasants."

"Castes are castes, but there're ways to get around that. Silver is the best. And we've got some we'll never use otherwise. I just thought he might want to learn his letters. Seems a pity to waste a mind like his on farming. But I wouldn't get involved with anyone important. The village priest, maybe. He might take the job for fresh vegetables and a little money to tide his wine-cellar between collections."

"I see you've already decided, so what can I say? Let's tell him, then. Where's he off to now?"

"Across the square watching the boys play handball. I'll fetch him."

"No, no, let me. I'm getting stiff. Mind you watch the tomatoes. Some of these young things are dazzlers. They'll steal you blind while you're trying to get a peek down an open blouse. Those painted nipples…"

"Mama, Mama, I'm too old for that."

"Never too old to look." She stepped between empty tomato crates, past the remainder of the squash, started across the square.

Soon she returned, disturbed. "He wasn't there, Royal. The boys say he left an hour ago. And the donkey's gone."

Royal looked to the corrals. "Yes. Well, I've got a notion where he's gone then. *You* mind the sly young 'prentices from the wizards' kitchen."

She chuckled softly, then grew grave. "You think he went back where…"

"Uhm. I'd hoped he wouldn't remember, being so young. But the King's lessons aren't easily forgotten. A death at the stake is a haunt fit for a lifetime of nightmares. Have some candy ready when we get back."

Royal found Varth about where he expected, astride the donkey, before the King's gate. The plaza was less grim than usual, although, apparently, the boy hadn't come to see the leavings of executions. Looking small and fragile, he studied the Palace's fortifications. As Royal entered the square, Varth started for a postern gate. The sentry there was a gruff-looking, middle-aged veteran who stopped him and asked his business. He was still trying to coax Varth into answering when Royal arrived.

"Pardon, Sergeant. I was minding my stall too close. He wandered away."

"Oh, no trouble, no trouble. They'll do that. Got a flock of my own. What's in down to market? Woman was talking about going."

"She'd better hurry. The melons are gone already. The tomatoes and squash will be soon."

"Look for me this evening, then. Save a squash and a few tomatoes. I've a craving for goulash. And mind where that donkey wanders. He has a likely lad aboard." He offered Varth a warm parting smile, sincere in its concern.

Varth betrayed no emotion as Royal led the donkey away. But later, as they pushed through the twisty alleys and the old peasant asked, "Varth, would you like to learn the cleric arts?" he grew ecstatic. Royal was surprised by his intensity. For a moment, indeed, it seemed the boy might speak. But then he settled into his usual stolidity, revealing only a fraction of his inner joy.

So, after the last squash were sold and the three returned to the farm, Royal went to visit the parish priest.

Time passed and the boy grew until, at an age of about ten, he was as tall as Royal and nearly as strong. The old couple were pleased. They cared for him like a precious jewel, giving the best of everything. In a land where disease, hunger, and malnutrition were constant companions of the poor, he had the gift of an excellent diet. He grew tall in a land where tall men were rare.

His learning, under the tutelage of the priest, went well. He learned to write quickly, often used notes where another would have spoken. The priest was impressed with his ability. He refused all payment except the occasional gift of produce. He insisted that the teaching of an eager student was ample reward. He soon took Varth to the limits of his own knowledge.

As it must, sorrow one day entered the house by the river above Ilkazar. In the fall, after a last load had been sold at market, the old woman suffered a seizure. She cried out and went into a coma, never to waken. Royal grieved, as a husband of long-standing will, but accepted the loss in his stoic way. She had had a long, full life, except for her barrenness, and in the end had even had the pleasure of rearing a son. Moreover, Royal was pleased to see Varth equally stricken by her passing. While he had seldom been demonstratively affectionate, neither had he been disobedient or disrespectful. His mind simply dwelt away, as if in a shadow world where life couldn't reach him.

As farmers have always done, and will always do, Varth and Royal buried their dead, then returned to working their fields. But the peasant was old, and his desire to live had failed with the death of his wife. Early in the spring, with the first crops planting, he joined her quietly in the night. Varth thought him sleeping till he shook him.

Varth wept again, for he had loved Royal as a son should love a father. He went to the village, found the priest, brought him to say the burial service. He worked the farm to the best of his ability and finished the season. At market he often sold cheaply because he refused to haggle. Then, having worked the summer in memory of his foster parents, he had the priest sell the farm and began a life of his own.

Two: Autumn, 995 afe
Down from the Mountains of Fear

Ravenkrak was an ancient castle built so deep within the Kratchnodian Mountains, on a high peak called the Candareen, that few people down in the settled lands knew that it existed. Yet seven people who followed a winding mountain trail would soon put the name on countless pairs of lips. Six were called Storm Kings by those who knew them not. Their destination was the capital city of the northernmost of the Cis-Kratchnodian kingdoms, Iwa Skolovda.

At their head rode Turran, Lord of Ravenkrak. Behind him, eldest, cruel-faced and graying, Ridyeh came, then Valther, the youngest brother, who was quite handsome. Next came stolid, quiet Brock and his twin, Luxos. Luxos was tall and lean as a whippet; Brock was short and heavily muscled. Jerrad came last. His sole interest in life was the hunt, be it for a mountain bear or a dangerous man. Six strange men then.

The seventh was their sister, Nepanthe, the last-born. Her hair was black and long, a family trait. She rode proudly, as befit her station, but hers was not a conquering, militant bearing. She rode not as the virgin mistress of Ravenkrak, but as a sad and lonely woman. She was uncommonly beautiful in her waning twenties, yet her heart was as cold as her mountain home. But her aloofness, here, was caused by opposition to her brothers' plans.

She was weary of their plots and maneuvers. A week earlier, braving eternal damnation, she had summoned the Werewind to seal the passes through which they now rode, in order to keep her brothers home. But she had failed, and now they no longer trusted her left behind.

The party approached Iwa Skolovda's North Gate nervously. They were dead if recognized. A feud as bitter as blood, as old as the forests, as enduring as death, existed between Ravenkrak and the city. But their entry went unchallenged. It was autumn, a time when northern trappers and traders were expected with summer pelts for Iwa Skolovda's furriers.

They rode to the heart of the town, through thick foreign sounds and smells, to the Inn of the Imperial Falcon, where they remained in hiding for several days. Only Turran, Valther, and Ridyeh dared the streets, and that only by night. Days they spent in their rooms, honing their plans.

Nepanthe, alone and lonely, stayed in her room and thought about things she'd like, or things she was afraid, to do. She slept a great deal and dreamed two repeated dreams, one beautiful, one dreadful. The bad one always grew out of the good.

In the first dream she rode out of the Kratchnodian Mountains, south, past Iwa Skolovda and Itaskia, to fabulous Dunno Scuttari, or the cradle of western culture, Hellin Daimiel, where a beautiful, intelligent woman could make herself a place in the sun. Then the dream would shift subtly till she was afoot in a city of a thousand crystal towers. She wanted one of those towers as her own. Warmth flooded her when her gaze touched one in particular—always emerald—and she was inexorably drawn. Both fear and eagerness grew as she moved nearer. Then, at twenty paces, she laughed joyously and ran forward.

Always the same. Nightmare then came roaring from the dark dominions of her mind. Touch the spire—it was a spire no more. With a roar like a fall of jewels, the thing crumbled. From its ruins a terrible dragon rose.

Nepanthe fled into a dreamscape that had changed. The city of crystal towers became a forest of angry spears, striking. She knew those spears meant no harm, yet she feared them too much to question the cause of her fear.

Then she'd awaken, perspiration-wet, terrified, guilt-ridden without knowing why.

Though her nights, because of the dreams, were anything but dull, Nepanthe was bored by day. Then all she had to occupy her mind was the dreariness of her life at Ravenkrak. She was weary of gray mountains snow-shrouded and ribboned with rivers of ice, and of continually howling arctic winds. She was tired of being alone and unsought and a tool for her brothers' lunatic plan. She wanted to stop being a Storm King and get out in the world and just be.

Finally, there came a night, their fifth in Iwa Skolovda, when the Storm Kings set things in motion. Under a cloudy midnight sky, with intermittent moonlight, the brothers left the inn. Armed.

Valther and Ridyeh ran toward the North Gate. Turran and the others ambled to the Tower of the Moon, an architectural monstrosity of gray stone from which city and kingdom were ruled.

In cellars, in dark places, rough men met and sharpened swords. This would be a night for settling scores with Council and King.

Valther and Ridyeh neared the gate and its two sleepy guardsmen. One growled, "Who goes?"

"Death, maybe," Ridyeh replied. His sword whispered as he drew it from its scabbard. The tip stopped a hair's breadth from the watchman's throat.

The second guard swung a rusty pike, but Valther ducked under, pressed a dagger against his ribs. "Down on the pavement!" he ordered, and down the man went, pike clattering. The other followed quickly. Valther and Ridyeh bound them, dumped them in the guardhouse.

Ridyeh sighed. "When I saw that pike coming down…" He shrugged.

"The gate," Valther grumbled, embarrassed. Grunting, they heaved the bar aside, pushed the gate open. Ridyeh brought a torch from the gatehouse, carried it outside, wigwagged it above his head. Soon there came sounds of stealthily moving men.

A giant of a man with a red beard emerged from the darkness, followed by sixty soldiers in the livery of Ravenkrak.

"Ah, Captain Grimnason," Ridyeh chuckled. He embraced the shaggy giant. "You're right on time. Good."

"Yes, Milord. How're things going?"

"Perfectly, so far. But the end remains to be seen," Valther replied. "We've got the hardest part to do. Follow me."

Arriving as Valther and Ridyeh were opening the city gate, Turran and the others found the door of the Tower of the Moon held by a single guard. Politely Turran said, "Bailiff, we're Itaskian merchants, fur traders, and would like an audience with the King."

The watchman inclined his head, said, "Tomorrow night, maybe. Not tonight. He's tied up in a Defense Council meeting. And isn't it a bit late?"

"Defense Council?"

"Yes." Lonely posts make men eager for company. This watchman was no exception. Leaning forward, whispering, he confided, "Ravenkrak is supposed to be stirring up the rabble. One of the men thought he saw Turran, the chief of the mad wizards. Old Seth Byranov, that was. Probably looking through bad wine. He's a souse. But the King listened to him. Huh? Well, maybe the old fool knows something we don't." He chuckled, clearly thinking that unlikely. "Anyway, no audiences tonight."

"Not even for the Storm Kings themselves?" Luxos asked. He laughed softly when the old man jerked in astonishment.

"Brock, Jerrad, take care of him," Turran ordered. They bound and gagged the man quickly. "Luxos," Turran called, holding a ragged piece of parchment to torchlight and squinting at it. "Which stair?" He held a plan of the tower that had been put together for Valther by those men sharpening swords in cellars.

"The main if it's speed we're after."

Turran led the way. They met no resistance till they reached the door of the council chamber at tower's top. There another bailiff tried to block their way. Leaning forward to look at their faces, he discovered the naked steel in their hands. "Assassins!" he cried. He scurried back, tried to close the door. But Brock and Turran used their shoulders, burst in over his sprawling form. Jerrad offered him a hand up after planting a boot on his sword.

Councilmen panicked. Fat burghers threatened to skewer one another as they scrambled for weapons while retreating to the farthest wall. Their ineffectual guardian joined them. The King alone didn't move. Fear kept him petrified.

"Good evening!" said Turran. "Heard you were talking about us. Come now! No need to be afraid. We're not after your lives—just your kingdom." He laughed.

His mirth died quickly. The Councilmen still kept their weapons presented for battle. "Ravenkrak must have this city!"

"Why?" one asked. "Are you reviving a feud so ancient that it's hardly a legend anymore? It's been centuries since your ancestors were exiled."

"It's more than that," Turran replied. "We're building an Empire. A new Empire, to beggar Ilkazar." He said it seriously, though he knew that to his brothers the business was more a game, chess with live players. For all their planning and preparation, he and his brothers hadn't devoted much thought to consequences or costs. Brock, Luxos, Jerrad, and Ridyeh were playing out Ravenkrak's age-old fantasies more for the excitement than from devotion.

Nervous laughter. Someone said, "A world empire? Ravenkrak? With a handful of men? When Ilkazar failed with her millions? You're mad."

"Like a fox," Turran replied, pushing his dark hair back. "Like a fox. I've already taken Iwa Skolovda. And without blood lost."

"Not yet!" A Councilman shuffled forward, sword ready.

Turran shook his head sadly, said, "Take care of the fool, Luxos. Don't hurt him."

Luxos stepped up, smiling confidently. His opponent's certainty wavered. Then he made a lunge that should have slain. But Luxos brushed his blade aside, launched his own attack. Steel rang on steel three times. The Iwa Skolovdan stared at his empty hand.

The lesson wasn't lost on the others.

Turran chuckled. "Like I said, we're taking over. We'll do it without bloodshed if we can. But we can hold a festival for the Dark Lady if you want it that way. You there. Look out the window."

A sullen fat man did so. "Soldiers!" he growled. "What're you doing?"

"I told you, taking the city."

Deep-throated rage sounds came from the Councilmen. They started forward...

"Tower's secure, Milord," said a bass voice from beyond the doorway. The red-bearded captain led a squad into the chamber. He glanced at the bewildered Councilmen, laughed, asked, "What should I do with them?"

"Lock them in their own dungeon till Nepanthe's secure. Where's Valther?"

"You want me?" Valther entered, panting from the climb up the stair. His face was flushed with excitement.

"Yes. Collect your revolutionaries. I want to start organizing the new administration tonight. And get our troops out of sight as soon as we can."

Valther departed.

Turran continued, "Ridyeh, take a squad and get Nepanthe. I want her moved in here before sunup."

Ridyeh nodded, left.

Turran's captain led the Councilmen off to their cells. Then the Storm Kings sat down with the King of Iwa Skolovda and dictated his abdication announcement.

Nepanthe came. The men from the cellars brought their sharpened swords. She became their Princess and they her army and police—though no Storm King trusted them. They had proven treacherous already.

Nepanthe took to her role, played it better than her brothers expected. She didn't approve of the conquest, had risked much to prevent it, yet, when forced, plunged into the act with a will. This was a squalid, festering city unlike any in her dreams—she feared there were none that marvelous—but, at least, Iwa Skolovda provided a shadow of an answer to her needs. She would take what she could from her stolen moment of glory.

The deposed King announced his abdication formally at noon next day, though the city already knew and seemed disinclined to resist. People seemed to think nothing could be worse than the fallen government, so corrupt had it been.

Because he didn't want to flaunt his power, to aggravate historically based animosities, Turran led his soldiers back to Ravenkrak, leaving just one platoon, commanded by Grimnason's lieutenant, Rolf Preshka, to be Nepanthe's bodyguard. The other Storm Kings remained, to help their sister establish her administration, but they worked impatiently, looking forward to their next easy conquest.

Nepanthe stood at a window in a dark chamber of the Tower of the Moon, alone. She looked out on a garden bathed in moonlight. It was almost morning. Her black hair, flowing over her shoulders, shone from recent brushing. Her dark eyes danced, searching the garden. Her lips, full and red when she smiled (so rarely), were pulled into a tight, pale line as she pondered something unpleasant. An almost permanent frown-crease rose between her brows. Suddenly she drew out of her slouch, turned, began pacing. Her walk was graceful but asexual. Despite her beauty, she seemed unfeminine, perhaps because she had lived too long in the company of hard men, perhaps because she was always afraid. The evil dreams came to her every night now. But Ravenkrak, not her dreams, haunted her at the moment.

They were, she thought, making a game of conquest, just as they had during childhood. But they were grown up and it was a real world now, a world they hardly knew. They had lived too long in droll, dead Ravenkrak. It had done things to their minds. A mad castle, she thought, up there on the highest of the high peaks, brooding in a land of knife-backed ridges and permanent winter. It just sat there crumbling away, its inmates occasionally attacking Iwa Skolovda. Poor city! Yet there was the old score to be settled… Their ancestors, the Empire's viceroys in Iwa Skolovda, had been driven into the Kratchnodians when the Empire fell apart, and nearly every generation since had taken its stab at reestablishing the family suzerainty over the former Imperial province of Cis-Kratchnodia. Fools' dreams took the longest to die.

Turran, as always, played the general. But what had he for armies? Ha! A few hundred men, of whom only Redbeard Grimnason's renegade Guildsmen were fit for combat. Yet she pitied the cities of the west. They would fight, and Turran would smash their ancient walls and venerable castles with the Werewind. Never before had there been such command of the Power in the family. A way of life would end. A microcosmic culture, Ravenkrak's, would fall because its people had to play their game. She grew increasingly angry as she considered the yet-to-die.

Without realizing it, she was making the same arrogant assumptions she despised in her brothers. She hated their bold confidence, yet could not herself conceive of anything but victory on the battlefield of witchcraft.

"Will the idiocy never end?" she asked the night.

Certainly it would, someday, if only when Lady Death's couriers called her name. There would be an end: victory or defeat. Yet in either she could see no escape from the cramped, exclusive society of her home. Death seemed the only path to real freedom.

Oh, so terribly, she wanted done with this wearisome business of life. Her brothers didn't understand. They were little fishes happy in the waters of their little happenings. They didn't recognize the frightened child, the wondering, eager, world-curious child, hiding in Nepanthe's mind. But Nepanthe didn't understand Nepanthe either—least of all those fears that by day hid behind her fiery temper and by night ruled her dreams.

The dreams had changed during her stay in Iwa Skolovda. The pleasant part remained fixed, but, as she reached a tremulous hand for the emerald spire... Tower dissolves, dragon rises, she runs into strange land. Into the forest of spears, but no longer alone. On every hand, in graceful thousands, cats, twisting and dodging; spears leap from the earth and stab. Struck, cats accept the shafts with joy. Most make only token attempts to escape. Horrified, Nepanthe runs. To her sorrow, she always escapes alone.

Alone. She was always alone, even in the center of a city, at the heart of a kingdom.

Her dreams so troubled her that she fought sleep. Now, thinking of the horror, there was nothing she wanted more than to be able to cry. She couldn't. Ravenkrak had weathered her tenderer emotions; even anger and hatred were growing pale. Soon she'd have nothing but the terror of her lonely nights.

Slowly, methodically, she cursed. Across her lips passed every abomination, every blasphemy, every obscenity heard during a life spent in the company of hard men. The moon passed the western horizon. Stars faded. Dawn came before she finished. And when she was done she was left with nothing. Nothing but fear.

But, for just a moment, childhood memory stirred. The daydream about the strange knight who would come to rescue her from the Candareen.

That memory was as bad as the dreams. It made her question what that innocent child had become; almost a harlot, letting her brothers prostitute her for the advancement of their game. Daily she was forced to endure the indignity of being ravaged by the eyes of the human trash her brothers had given her to rule. A curse on them all, and especially on her brothers for being too lazy to handle their own administration.

When she finally surrendered herself to her bed, she whispered a formal prayer:

"May the Gods Above, or the Gods Below, or any Powers here present, cast down, disperse, and render unto destruction the agents of destruction, the Storm Kings of Ravenkrak."

One night, in the highest chamber of the Tower of the Moon, six people gathered, waiting for Turran. Five waited with disinterested patience, but Nepanthe...

"Blood!" she swore, her small fist striking the table in inelegant pique. "Will that sluggard never get here?"

"Patience, Nepanthe," Ridyeh pleaded. "What's the hurry? The weather's terrible since you abused the Werewind. We'll wait, no matter how long."

She bridled at the reference to her past failing, but said no more.

"Just a bit longer," Valther said. "He'll be here soon."

And Turran arrived within the hour. Head cocked, eyes appraising, a smile his only greeting, he stood a moment at the door, studying his family. He was the tallest of the seven and had a heavy, muscular body massing almost two hundred pounds. His eyes and hair were those of the family, black and shining. There was something about him, a charisma, that made people, especially women, want to forward his plans. He was a dreamer, though he dreamed less complexly, more grandly than Nepanthe, of leading victorious armies. He was handsome, pleasant, lovable, potentially a great leader—and more than a little mad.

"How're things going?"

"Perfectly," Ridyeh replied. "Our victory is written in the stars. The earth should be shaking." Turran frowned. Subdued, Ridyeh continued, "You're late. What happened?"

"The weather." Turran settled into the one free chair. "There's a permanent storm over the Kratchnodians. Result of Nepanthe's experiment. It's getting more powerful, too. Had a hell of a time getting back. We've got to fix it."

Nepanthe didn't miss his sarcasm. "You damned men!" she sputtered. "Always so lordly... Now we're all here, let's get on with the foolery. What's your news, Turran?"

"Ah, always the same, aren't you Nepanthe? Always rush-rush-rush. Well, it seems the world could care less what we do in Iwa Skolovda. Brock," changing the subject, "is there any wine? It's been a hungry ride."

"Is that all you've got to say after keeping us waiting so long?" Nepanthe demanded. "Just: 'Give me something to eat.'"

Turran's reply expressed an anger long held in check. "We've put up with your pets too long, Nepanthe. What you did with the Werewind won't happen again. I'll warn you once: you'll be treated the way you behave."

She missed the danger-sound in his voice. "What can you do? Lock me in the Deep Dungeons so I don't spoil your idiot scheme?"

The unanimity of their nods bought her silence. Shocked, she listened as Luxos, who often defended her, said, "If it's the only way, I'll take you Downdeep myself."

"And throw away the key," Valther added, the only brother to whom she felt really close.

She was overwhelmed. Turran's madness had infected them all. And she knew they made no idle threats. She shut her mouth and kept it that way.

"Valther, what's happened here?" Turran asked. Intelligence was Valther's responsibility.

"We hold the Tower, the symbol of power. For the time being the people are satisfied. The shadow of Ilkazar doesn't disturb them as much as it did a few generations back."

Turran grew thoughtful. Finally, he asked, "Nepanthe, can we trust you if we leave you here alone?"

Not risking anything, she merely nodded. Anyway, Valther's men would be watching every minute. What *could* she do to ruin their game?

"Good. I want to go home, work with the troops. We'll leave in the morning, come back in time for a spring campaign. You take care. If you get an urge to sabotage things, remember the Deep Dungeons. Think about living there till this's over. My patience will be short for a while."

Nepanthe shuddered. The Deep Dungeons were places of slime and stench and horror far beneath Ravenkrak, supposedly haunted, so long abandoned that no one living knew them in their entirety.

"Valther?"

"Yes?"

"Will you get the sending gear ready? I stopped by Dvar's embassy on the way. I don't like their attitude. They won't recognize our sovereignty. We'd better make an example of them. Show our power early."

An eager blush colored Nepanthe's cheeks. At last something interesting was going to happen. She enjoyed manipulating the Werewind.

(Aerial elementals haunted the high range, powers that ran with and sometimes controlled the Kratchnodian storms. Lowlanders, who thought in terms of ghosts and demons, called these the Wild Hunt, believing them to be malevolent spirits in search of souls to drag into their own special Hell. The Storm Kings knew better. During the generations following their flight after the Fall of the Empire, the family had learned to control the elementals, and thus the weather that followed them—especially raging wind. The Werewind.)

That evening, while people enjoyed a pleasant winter's evening in cities like Itaskia, Dunno Scuttari, and Hellin Daimiel, Iwa Skolovda's tributary Dvar groaned under the attentions of an unnatural storm. All night it raged and, when it passed on, Dvar lay under fifteen feet of snow. As her savaged people dug out, the Storm Kings rode north toward Ravenkrak.

THREE: AUTUMN-WINTER, 995-996 AFE
OUT OF THE MOUTH OF A FOOL

A man called Saltimbanco, better known as Mocker elsewhere, sat by Prost Kamenets's Dragon Gate, his plot of muddy earth besieged by unwashed, half-clad children. They all giggled at him, or demanded a trick. The obese pseudo-philosopher, pretend-wizard, despairing of driving them away, tried to shout over their clamor while mopping floods of sweat from his dark face.

"Hai, Great Lord," he called to a passing traveler, "have your future told! Fare not forth from glorious Prost Kamenets without hearing what Fates hold in store. This unworthy obesity is known as great necromancer, your future to foretell. But a single korona only, Lord, and potent cantrips enfold your person. A single korona and your worthy self is made proof against every evil spell."

The traveler spat in the general direction of the fat man and passed on, out the Dragon Gate. His gaudy chariot rolled beneath smoking, putrid braziers of incense, past statues of winged lions and ugly gargoyles, between the two titanic green stone dragons, Fire-Eyes and Flame-Tongue.

Saltimbanco, casting his voice, cursed the traveler through the teeth of one of his collection of skulls. Ignoring his language, the children squealed with delight. They called their friends. The fat man continued, directing invective at himself for having attracted more of the rowdy brats. His large brown eyes, squinting angrily, were as baleful as those of Fire-Eyes at the gate.

He began a lengthy black invocation calling for thunder, lightning, fire from the sky to fall on the precocious urchins. Nothing happened. His magic was false, though impressive—and the children knew him a fraud.

"Pshaw!" Saltimbanco snorted, fat lips tight in a brown face as round as a melon, "Pshaw!" Speaking to himself, he muttered, "Mighty, generous, wealthy Prost Kamenets, my mother's prize carbuncle! Three cold, miserable, rainy days sitting by famous Dragon Gate, and no shekels. Not even one little, very corroded copper cast this humble, helpful soul. What kind of strange city this? No profit here, unless spittle and dung be measured in shekels and talents. Saltimbanco, O closest and flabby, friendliest friend of my heart, time comes to travel on, to seek great greener pasture on other side horizon. Maybe more superstitious realm where people believe in gods and ghosts and powers of mighty necromancer. Self, would travel to fabled kingdom of Iwa Skolovda.

"Woe!" cried the fraudulent wizard, his belly shaking as he answered himself. "So far! This corpulence is in no wise able to walk so far! Large, well-fed student philosophic should perish of overexertion before marching of twentieth weary mile!"

Seeing his lazy nature would want convincing, his adventurous half marshaled its most potent—and least truthful—argument. "And, obese one, what dread future transpires should harridan wife of self discover recalcitrant husband returned to ungrateful Prost Kamenets? Reddest murder right in heart of filthy streets!" He paused for a moment of contemplation. Beneath his brows, he examined the watching children. They had fallen silent, hung on his words. They were ready.

"Moreover," said he to himself, "man of tender feet, it is not meant that self should walk many miles on long path to Iwa Skolovda. Cannot we, being of many talents and supported by this loyal band of younglings, perchance purloin some worthy transport?"

His face brightened at the suggestion of theft. He answered himself, "Hai! When stared in face by fangy-toothed necessity, this obesity is capable of all things. Wife? Hai! What a horrible thought!" He was silent for a long moment, then looked up, selected a half-dozen youngsters, motioned them closer.

Loungers by the Dragon Gate, of which there were ever hosts ready to fleece unwary travelers, were treated to an unusual spectacle the following morning. A fat brown man in an ornate racing chariot, emblazoned with the arms of a powerful noble family, hastily fled the city. Behind the chariot ran a pack of laughing, ragged children. Behind these, hotly pursuing the vehicle but hampered by the youngsters, were a dozen pikemen of the city watch. Then came a band of professional thief-takers, anticipating a considerable reward from the chariot's owner. Lastly, too late to have hopes of being in at the kill, came an aging beauty wailing like a Harpy deprived of prey (Mocker, too, had wailed at her price for playing his mythical wife).

The cavalcade thundered through the gate and north, the fat man laughing madly.

Presently, having lost the thief, the disgruntled pursuers returned. Out in the countryside, a laughing fat scoundrel trotted his new chariot up the road to Iwa Skolovda.

As soon as safety was apparent, Saltimbanco began vacillating. Each wayside spring was an excuse for loitering. The first inn he encountered had the pleasure of his windy custom for much of a week—till the landlord suspected deviltry and threw him out. He didn't really *want* to go to Iwa Skolovda, though he wasn't consciously aware of it.

Later, Saltimbanco stopped in for a talk with the owner of a prosperous farm. The farmer thought him feeble-minded, but considered that an advantage in the business of horse-trading. He got Saltimbanco's chariot and horses for three pieces of silver and a bony, pathetically comic little donkey. This beast appeared ridiculous beneath Saltimbanco's hugeness, but seemed not to notice the load. He plodded stolidly northward, unconcerned with his new master's foibles.

The farmer left the trade laughing behind his hand, but so did Saltimbanco. He had back the money spent in Prost Kamenets, and a donkey besides. And the donkey would be half what he needed to make his Iwa Skolovdan entrance both noteworthy and innocent. Looking the part, he began building a reputation as a mad, windy, harmless fool.

He started by giving scores of moronic answers to questions asked him in the villages he passed, then demanded payment for his advice. He became righteously indignant if that payment was not forthcoming. The common people of the valley of the Silverbind loved him. They paid just for the entertainment. He laughed often, to himself, as Iwa Skolovda drew nearer and nearer.

His movement north was so slow that his fame advanced before him—which was what he had in mind. Soon each village prepared improbable questions against his coming. (Usually dealing with cosmogony and cosmology: the Prime Cause, shape of the Earth, nature of the sun, moon, and planets. Sometimes, though, serious requests for advice came, and those he answered more than usually madly.) When, almost two months after leaving Prost Kamenets, he at last passed Iwa Skolovda's South Gate, his reputation was made. Few thought him anything but the lunatic he pretended—and this was the foundation of his plan. Without it he couldn't succeed, would never see the pay for the job he had been hired to do.

A week after his auspicious and feted arrival, after he had taken suitably odd lodgings in a poor quarter of the town and had converted them into a weird temple, the fat man said to himself, "Self, should begin work." On a cold, blustery morning he entered Market Square on his donkey, searched the stalls till he found one belonging to a farmer met in the country. "Self," he said to the peasant, "would borrow empty box."

"Box?" the mystified farmer asked.

"Box, yes, for pulpit." He said it deadpan, but with enough intensity to convince the peasant some high madness was involved. The farmer grinned. Saltimbanco smiled back—secretly congratulating himself.

"Will this do?"

Saltimbanco accepted and examined an empty field lug. "Is good, but short. One more?"

"If you'll return them."

"Self, offer most sacred promise."

A low mound of rubble, remains of a fallen building, rose at one end of the square. There, precariously, Saltimbanco set up his boxes, mounted them, bellowed, "Repent! Sinners, end of world, mighty doom, is upon you! Repent! Hear, accept truth that leads to forgiveness, eternal life!" Nearby heads turned. Suddenly terrified, heart hammering, he forced himself to continue. "Doom comes. World nears time of killing fire! O sinners, yield to love offered by Holy Virgin Gudrun, Earth Mother, Immaculate, that would save you for love! 'Give me love!' she says, 'And life forever I return.' " He continued with a great deal of nonsense delineating the path of righteousness Gudrun demanded of her lovers if they were to achieve her grace and dwell with her in her place called Foreverness. He followed up with a little hellfire and brimstone, listing the fearsome tortures awaiting those who didn't enter Gudrun's love. A good deal of his adopted father's love-me-or-else, why-do-you-hurt-me-so, you-cruel-little-child went into his interpretation.

At one time this mythology had been widespread in the Lesser Kingdoms, especially Kavelin, but was centuries dead. Neither Saltimbanco, nor any who heard him, had the slightest notion of what it was really all about. Yet success attended him. His fiery oratory and threats of present doom attracted attention. Then a bit more. Soon a full-blown crowd had gathered. He grew increasingly cheerful and confident as, more and more, the curious came to see what was happening. Half an hour after beginning, he had three hundred enthralled listeners and had forgotten his fears completely. Once he hit his second wind, he played the mob's emotions with considerable skill.

The final result of the speech was what he desired. He saw it in their faces, in smiles hidden behind hands, in cautious, agreeing nods by those closest, people who didn't want to hurt his feelings by disagreeing with self-evident insanity. His own smile of joyous success he kept carefully internalized. They had decided him a harmless and lovable screwball, the sort who wanted watching lest he catch his death of forgetting to get in out of the rain.

He also achieved success by bringing himself to the attention of Authority. In the crowd there were men of a sort he had seen in other kingdoms, too average, too disinterested, too carefully attentive beneath that disinterest to be anything but spies. Storm King spies, who would be very much interested in any large gathering. Nepanthe, their Princess, had proven cunning politically. She had made certain her followers, proven traitors once, couldn't escape suffering if she fell. Their names and deeds would be made painfully available to any successor government—and they would die. They *had* to support her, take deep interest in anything which might foreshadow a movement to bring their Princess to ruin.

They were the shadow men who backboned the government Valther had built for his sister. Attracting their attention lay at the root of Saltimbanco's plan. Everyone, especially them and their mistress, had to think him a harmless clown.

"What do you think?" one shadow man asked the other.

"A clown with a new act. I imagine he'll end up asking for money."

And at just that moment, Saltimbanco did so, proving himself less than wholly concerned with his listeners' souls. He smiled to himself on seeing the spies' knowing nods. He was safe for a while.

Day after day, week after week, he continued his idiot's speeches, moving about the city so the greatest numbers might hear him. He spoke on a different subject each day, parlaying the philosophical nonsense of centuries into a mad but innocent reputation. In time he gathered a following of young enthusiasts who appeared at all his harangues. Those he feared. Would they taint his political neutrality? The young being the political idiots they were, and denied any other place of meeting, might be using his speeches as cover for some clandestine activity. But time showed his fears groundless. These were no activists, just bored youngsters enjoying themselves.

Because he was enjoying himself hugely, and making a fortune from donations, the weeks slipped away rapidly. Spring was but a month distant when he decided the city was ready for his *magnum opus*, a long-winded and, to the people in the street, laughable oration praising the Princess Nepanthe—for the political weather was growing more treacherous daily, and the woman faced increasing popular opposition. Daringly, the speech was to be presented on the steps of the Tower of the Moon.

Because most Iwa Skolovdans thought the speech a new high in his career of idiocy, Saltimbanco felt certain they would place him where he wanted. Indeed, they turned out in record numbers. When he reached the Tower, astride his patient donkey, he found a vast crowd waiting. They cheered. A nervous, redoubled Tower guard eyed them uncertainly.

The soldiers relaxed when they spied him. They now assumed nothing but storms of laughter would be raised. Saltimbanco prayed he would incite no insurrection.

Ponderously he mounted the steps leading to the Tower entrance, lifting the skirts of his monkish robe like an old woman about to go wading. His ears told him his audience would be warm before he spoke a word.

He stopped five steps below the soldiers, turned, launched upon flowery rivers of praise dedicated to Nepanthe. Soon the crowd was roaring delightedly.

Nepanthe sat in the shadows of her lonely chamber, mind in a stupor. A dark mood was on her. She cared not at all for the world, had but one foot in the realm of consciousness. The dreadful demons of her dreams now pursued her even by day. She could sleep only when she fell from exhaustion. This coming out of Ravenkrak had worsened things, not, as she had hoped, made them better.

Dimly, as through a sound-baffling curtain, the roaring reached her. *The Werewind?* was her first startled thought. Then: *Those're human voices!*

She went to a window overlooking the street, walking stiffly, not unlike a woman twice her age. From a shadow she looked down on the crowd, awed. She had never seen so many people in one place. A thrill of fear brought her fully awake. She backed from the window, hands at her throat, then turned, ran. She seized a bell-cord and rang for her guard captain.

He was awaiting her summons, knocked before she finished ringing.

"Enter!" she commanded, trying to mask her panic.

"Milady?"

She ignored the amenities. "Rolf, what're those people doing?" She waved an unsteady hand at the window.

"A fool's making a speech, Milady."

"Who?" she demanded. She was certain she sounded terrified. But, if she did, he gave no sign of having noticed. He waited with the merest hint of a curious expression. "Let's listen," she decided.

They went to the window and stood, but could hear little over the laughter of the crowd—though Nepanthe thought she heard her name spoken several times. Timidly, little-girlish, she asked, "Why do they laugh so?"

"Oh, they think him a great clown and fool, Milady." Rolf chuckled as he leaned on the windowsill.

"And you, too, eh?"

He smiled. "Indeed. Iwa Skolovda's needed him for a long time. Too staid."

"Who is he? Where's he from?"

"There you've got me, Ladyship. Because he has the ear of the people, we've tried to find out. All we know is that he rode in some time ago, after preaching in the villages to the south. There's some evidence he was in Prost Kamenets before that.

"After arriving, he spent several days alone, then started the speeches. He's a folk-hero now. I'm sure he's harmless, Milady. The people just gather to laugh at him. He doesn't seem to mind. He makes a good deal off them."

So. He did see my fear, she thought. *And now he's trying to reassure me.* Aloud, "What's he talking about? Why such a huge crowd?"

The soldier suddenly seemed distressed. He tried to hedge.

"Come, come, Rolf. I heard him use my name. What's he saying about me?"

"As your Ladyship commands," he muttered. Plainly he feared losing his position as her captain. "His speech is in praise of yourself, Milady."

A spark blazed in Nepanthe's eyes, a mote of fire that could easily become anger. "And for that they call him a fool?" The anger waxed, spread from her eyes to her brow. "Why?"

Rolf's manner made it obvious he wanted to be elsewhere. He hemmed and hawed, shuffled, glanced at ceiling and floor, mumbled something inaudible.

"Captain!" Nepanthe snapped. "Your reticence displeases me!" Then, in a more kindly tone, "When was the last time I punished a soldier for expressing an opinion, or for carrying bad news?"

"I can't remember. Milady."

"If you think carefully," she whispered, looking toward the window, "you'll remember all punishments have been for breach of discipline, not for performing duties which discomforted me. Now, speak up! Why do the people laugh when this man praises me?"

"They despise you, Milady."

A cold wind seemed to blow through the room. Indeed, swift-coming clouds in the north promised a winter's storm.

"Despise me? But why?" There was a hint of hurt behind her quiet inquisition.

"Because you're whom you are," he replied gently. "Because you're a woman, because you're in power, because you overthrew the King. Why do men despise their rulers? For all those reasons, and maybe more, but mostly because you're from Ravenkrak, get of the old foe, and because the ousted Councilmen, that you foolishly freed, keep inciting them." The cold wind sighing round the Tower, down off the Kratchnodians, seemed as much spiritual as real. Chilling.

Would the reverberations of the Fall never cease? Ilkazar was dust, but echoes of the fury of her collapse still beat upon her scattered grandchildren. The shadowy wings of hatred still drifted across their lives like those of searching vultures.

The people still roared below.

"Tell me, Rolf—honestly—aren't the people better off since I came here? Aren't the taxes lower? Don't I care for the poor? Haven't I replaced a corrupt, lazy, indifferent government with an incorrupt, efficient, responsive one? Haven't I repressed the crime syndicates that were almost a second government before I arrived?" She shuddered, remembering ranks of heads on pikes above the city gates. "What about my subsidies for trade with Itaskia and Prost Kamenets?"

"All true, but such things don't mean much to fools, Milady. I know. I was raised here. Your reforms have won support among the small merchants, the artisans, especially the furriers, the guildsmen, and the more thoughtful laborers. All the worst victims of the old government and syndicates. But most of the people refuse to be fooled by your chicanery. And the rich, the crimebosses, and the deposed Councilmen, keep telling them that's what it is. And, irregardless of programs, you're a foreigner and usurper." He grinned weakly, trying to make light of the matter.

But the cold still filled the room.

Nepanthe eased Rolf's nerves with one of her rare smiles. "Foreigner, ergo, tyrant, eh? Even if their ingrates' bellies are full for the first time in years? Well, no matter. Their opinions don't concern me—as long as they behave."

She thought for a moment. Rolf waited silently, ignoring the pain his remarks had caused. Finally, she said, "I remember the words of an ancient wise man, in one of the old scrolls at home. He wrote, 'Man is wise only when aware of his lack of wisdom,' and went on to point out that the masses are asses because they're ignorant to the point of knowing they already know everything worth knowing."

Rolf said nothing in response, seemed unusually thoughtful—perhaps because she was being unusually verbose... She jarred him back with a change of subject.

"Does this man make a habit of talking about me?"

"No, Milady. It's something different every day and, begging your pardon, always something idiotic. Far as I know, this's his first political venture, though it's hardly controversial."

The cold wind blew, gathering strength with time.

"Give me some examples."

Rolf, back on safe ground, relaxed, chuckled, imparted a bit of high nonsense. "Just yesterday he claimed the world is round."

Nepanthe, who knew, was startled into wary curiosity. "Another example!"

Without a chuckle, Rolf hurriedly said, "The other day he claimed the sun was just a star, only closer. Skaane, the philosopher, challenged his claim. They had a real madman's debate, with Skaane claiming the Earth revolves around the sun..."

"What'd he say the day before that?"

Rolf could maintain only a minimal air of sobriety. "Something religious, something about every seventh rebirth of the soul being into the animal with a nature most closely approximating the individual's. His donkey, he claims, is Vilis, the last King of Ilkazar."

A ghost of a smile played across Nepanthe's lips. "Go on."

Rolf grinned. He had remembered an excellent example. "Well, the Earth's changed shape since last week. Then it was a big boat floating on a sea of Escalonian wine, the vessel being propelled by a giant duck paddling in the stern. He was drunk that day, which's maybe why he saw the universe as a sea of wine."

Another of those rare smiles broke across Nepanthe's face. "Bring him here!"

"Milady, they'd storm the Tower if we stopped him now!"

"Well, wait till he's done."

"Yes, Milady."

She crossed the chamber to a northern window. The snow-topped Kratchnodians loomed in the distance. The north wind muttered, threatening snow.

Saltimbanco recognized the importance of Rolf's appearance the moment he came out the Tower door. Five minutes later his mad speech rolled to a hilarious conclusion. In a quarter-hour the street before the Tower was empty, save for his donkey and collection box. The box was overflowing.

Rolf asked the fat man into the Tower. Insides all aquaver, Saltimbanco followed. He reached Nepanthe's chamber puffing and snorting like a dying dragon. His skin had reddened, his face was wet with perspiration.

Nepanthe's door stood open. Rolf entered without formality. "The man whose presence you requested, Milady."

Turning from the north window, Nepanthe replied, "Thank you, Captain. You may go."

"But…"

"You said he was harmless."

"Yes, but…"

"I shall scream most loudly if I need your help. Begone!" He went.

Nepanthe faced her visitor, said, "Well?" When he didn't respond, she said it again, louder.

Saltimbanco hauled himself out of the wonder the woman had loosed upon him. She was beautiful, with raven hair and ebony eyes, a fine oval face—did he detect a hint of loneliness and fear behind the frown-lines he had more or less expected? He was amazed. The woman wasn't the aging Harpy he had anticipated. Getting on thirtyish, maybe, but not old. His innocent eyes insolently examined her body. He suspected this might be an assignment less unpleasant than expected.

At that point her voice drew him back.

"Yes, woman?" Playing his role to the hilt, he bowed to no nobility, accorded no superiority.

"Teacher, who are you?" she asked, granting him the title of learned honor. "What are you?"

An unexpected sort of question, but practice on the street enabled him to provide an answer that said nothing at all while sounding expansive.

"Self, am Saltimbanco. Am humblest, poverty-stricken disciple of One Great Truth. Am wandering mendicant preaching Holy Word. Am One True Prophet. Also Savior of World. Am weary Purveyor of Cosmic Wisdom. Am Son of King of Occult Knowledge…"

"And the Prince of Liars!" Nepanthe laughed.

"Is one face of thousand-faceted jewel of Great Truth."

"And what's this great truth?"

"Great Truth! Hai! Is wonder of all ages unfolding before sparkle in great and beautiful lady's eyes…"

"Briefly, without the sales chatter."

"So. Great Truth is this: all is lies! All men are liars, all things of matter are lies. Universe, Time, Life, all are great cosmic jokes from which little everyday falsehoods are woven. Even Great Truth is untrustworthy."

Nepanthe hid her amusement behind a hand. "Not original—Ethrian of Ilkazar, five centuries ago—but interesting nevertheless. Do you always follow your creed, tell nothing but lies?"

"Assuredly!" He reacted as though his honor was in question.

"And there's one of them." She laughed again, realized she was laughing. It stopped, was replaced by wonder. How long since she had laughed for no better reason than because she was amused? Could this fat man, who was hardly as foolish as he pretended, also make her cry?

"Why do you preach such strange things?"

Saltimbanco, thoroughly frightened behind his mask of unconcern, thought carefully before replying. A little half-truthful misdirection would be appropriate now. "Numerous be numbers of men who think me no more than big-mouthed nonsense pedlar. Hai! The bigger fools they. They come, enjoy show, eh? Also, after show, many come to poor fat idiot, give him monies to help protect self from self. Great Lady, think! Many people in throng before Tower this day, eh? Maybe three, four, five thousand. Maybe one thousand take pity on moron. Each drops one groschen—one puny groschen, though some give more—into basket watched over by very sad and hungry-looking donkey belonging to cretinic purveyor of preachments. Self counts up swag. Have now ten kronen and more, one month's wages. Goes on thus, every day of year. Self, being frugal, suddenly am as wealthy as wealthiest laugher at imbecilic preacher. Hai! Then self is laugher! But silent, very silent. Men are easily angered to kill."

Saltimbanco chuckled at his fooling those who thought him a fool, then realized he was growing too relaxed. He was revealing his penchant for the accumulation of money. Fear-wolves howled in the back of his mind. He was a professional, yes, but never had learned to banish emotion in tight situations. He did hide it well, though.

"Do you like having people mock you?"

"Hai! Self, am performer, no? Multitudes laugh at fat one, true. No joy. But this one is known to enjoy gold thuswise wrested from unwrestable purses. Crowd and Saltimbanco are even, for fools we have made of one another."

Nepanthe turned back to the north window, studied the storm brewing over the Kratchnodians. Then she whirled back, startling Saltimbanco from a moment of drowsiness.

"Will you take supper with me this evening?" she asked. Then she gasped at the temerity of her action, unsure of what she had done, or why. She only knew she enjoyed the company of this honestly roguish, outwardly jolly, inwardly frightened man. Perhaps there was a feeling of kinship.

While they stood staring at one another, the first snowy tendrils of the storm began whipping around the Tower. She ran to close her windows.

Saltimbanco did dine with the woman that evening, and accepted a further invitation to escape the storm by staying the night. He and she spoke at great length the following day, which eventually led to another dinner invitation, and that to another request that he stay the night. The day following that Nepanthe offered herself as his patron. Apparently prideless, Saltimbanco accepted instantly and quickly moved in—donkey and all. The chambers assigned him were next to Nepanthe's, which caused talk among her servants. Try as they might, however, even the most prying could discover nothing improper resulting from the arrangement.

FOUR: THE YEARS 590-605 AFE
HOW LONELY SITS THE CITY

Loves torn from him, Varth grew bitter. He decided to pursue a course that had long been in his mind. Once the harvest was in, he visited his priestly teacher, engaged the man as agent in the sale of the farm. The money, with that left him by Royal, he buried near the river. Then, carrying a few belongings in an old leather bag, he moved into Ilkazar.

Soon there was another beggar among the city's many, this one brighter, studying, studying—yet unseen, for no one spared an urchin more than a glance. He grew lean and ragged with time, and wiser.

Still he remained silent: and strange. Older persons grew uneasy in his presence—though they never knew why. Perhaps it was his cold stare, perhaps the way the corners of his mouth turned upward in a ghost-grin, revealing his canines, when the future was mentioned. There was something in his gaze which made adults look away. He seemed a hungry thing thinking of devouring them.

However, his strangeness attracted waifs like himself. They treated him with respect and awe their elders reserved for the Master Wizards and King—and a king he soon became, of a shadow empire of beggars and thieves who found his mastery profitable. Looking like a small, skinny idol, he held court in a corner of Farmer's Market, by his directions gifted his followers with unprecedented wealth.

But those followers, no matter their admiration for his leadership, found Varth's nighttime undertakings disquieting. He often wandered the Palace district, studying the castle of the King, or the homes of certain powerful wizards. And he never missed a witch-burning, though his attentions were seldom for the condemned. His eyes were always on the black-hoods, and the wizards who came to see "justice" done.

What justice this? In a city made great by magic, ruled by magic—no matter the King's disclaimers, his policies, and those of the Empire were determined by manipulating sorcerers—why should there be witch-burnings? What power had the witch that so terrified the warlock?

There was an ancient divination—Ilkazar, from King to lowliest beggar, had rock-hard faith in necromancy—which promised city and Empire would fall because of a witch. The Master Wizards reasoned that a dead sorceress could do little to fulfill the prophecy. Therefore, summary execution was ordered for any woman even mildly suspect (or with some bit of property a wizard wanted—for all a witch's property went to her finder).

Varth, with earnings from his beggar empire, went to certain wizards and bought knowledge. In the guise of an eager, voiceless child, he wrested many secrets from many sorcerers. They found him an amusing anomaly among the young, having fallen, like men less wise, into the habit of classing children with other small pets, as sometimes amusing, sometimes bothersome, but never, never interested in matters of weight. They were old men, those wizards, and had forgotten what it was like to be young. Most men did. And so, during his visits, Varth became privy to secrets that would have been kept carefully hidden from older men.

From wizards, and from priests whose interest had been stimulated by the reports of his old tutor, Varth received an unusual education. He nearly laughed the day he learned of the divination that had caused his mother's death. He later learned that she had died to provide a covetous sorcerer with a ready-decorated home, and King Vilis with escape from problems personal, political, and financial.

Someone discovered him weeping one night. Thenceforth he wore a new name: Varth Lokkur, the Silent One Who Walks With Grief. He became an actor, this Varthlokkur. Using pity for his dumbness, he bent strong men to his will. Wizards taught him. Priests took him to their hearts. He made his followers want to aid his secret purpose. They were certain he had one. He became one of Ilkazar's best-known children, and one of its most intriguing mysteries.

One day some priests got together and, hating to see the boy's mind wasted, decided to sponsor his education. But when they went to tell him, he was gone. He had chosen twelve companions and departed the city. Where had he gone? Why? The priests were disturbed for a while, but soon forgot. There had been something unsettling about him, something they preferred not to remember.

Lao-Pa Sing Pass lay two thousand miles east of Ilkazar, the only means of crossing a huge double range of mountains, the Pillars of Ivory and the Pillars of Heaven. To the west lay city-states, small kingdoms, and the sprawling Empire of Ilkazar. To the east was Shinsan, a dread Empire feared for its sorcery and devotion to evil. Butting against the western slopes of those mountains lay the fertile plains of the Forcene Steppe, ideal for grazing. But the nomads shunned it. Too near Shinsan…

From Lao-Pa Sing, on a spring day many months after Varthlokkur had abandoned Ilkazar, a child of twelve came riding. He was no native of Shinsan. His skin was western white sun-browned, not the natural amber of the east. On his face expressions fought: horror of the past and hope for the future. Free of the pass, the boy halted to make certain he still bore his passport to freedom. He drew a scroll from his saddlebag and opened it, stared at words he couldn't read:

> To King and Wizards of Ilkazar:
> My wrath will burn, and I will kill you with the sword, and your wives shall become widows and your children fatherless.

It was signed with a featureless oval sigil.

The message stirred little interest in Ilkazar. There was some grumbling about the audacity of the sender, but no fear. The messenger didn't name the country whence he came.

A year later, another youth, eyes haunted and riding as if fleeing a devil, bore:

> The King and Wizards of Ilkazar, who falsely judged the woman Smyrena:
> They have sown the wind and shall reap the whirlwind.

This was signed with both the null and a stylized mask of death. It caused more thought than had its predecessor, for the messenger admitted he came from Shinsan. The records were examined, the story of Smyrena exhumed. Her son hadn't shared her fate! There was apprehension, and talk about the old prophecy.

But nothing happened and all was soon forgotten—till the year ended and a third messenger came. Then others, year after year, until King and wizards believed. They bought assassins (even the power of the wizards of Ilkazar could not breach the necromantic shield about Shinsan), but the blades went astray. No man was fool enough to enter Shinsan.

> Riches do not profit in the day of wrath.

There were twelve signs beneath the twelfth message, each a promise. King and wizards tried to convince one another that their powers were sufficient to the threat.

In the thirteenth year a young man departed Shinsan, eyes almost as haunted as those of his predecessors. He crossed the Forcene Steppe, paused at Necremnos on the River Roë. He found Ilkazar's legions in the city and on the Steppe to the east. The Empire had grown during his absence. Necremnos was a "protectorate," the protection accepted as an alternative to bloody, futile war. Ilkazar, with its combination of magic and military excellence, was irresistible.

Pthothor the Bald, King of Necremnos, was wiser than his subjects suspected. He knew of the weird of Ilkazar, and had divined that the Fates would strike during his reign.

Varthlokkur spoke with that King concerning the death of empires.

At Shemerkhan he found a ruined city, strongly occupied, starving as its people turned all their effort toward meeting the demands of Ilkazar. Varthlokkur spoke with the King, then rode to Gog-Ahlan.

He found another conquered city, worse than the last. For resisting too long, all honor had been raped away. Her once proud men were permitted no income save what their women could earn serving the lusts of occupying soldiers. Again Varthlokkur spoke with a fallen King, then rode on.

He crossed the passes west of Gog-Ahlan and turned south into Jebal al Alf Dhulquarneni, a black region, subject to no King. Eventually he reached the valley Sebil el Selib, Path of the Cross, where the first King-Emperor of Ilkazar had trapped and crucified a thousand rebellious nobles. There he made camp and his preparations.

A few days later, he entered the city that had given him life, and so much pain. At the gate he was met by wizards awaiting the annual message, which he refused to hand over to anyone but the King. It demanded the death by burning of Vilis and seven times seven of Ilkazar's wizards as atonement for the crime against Smyrena. The demand was refused, as expected. The message ended with promises of famine and pestilence, earthquakes and signs in the sky, the appearance of enemies countless as the stars, and was sealed *13*.

The seal remained cryptic for a time. Once the mystic number was noted, however, the wizards concluded that their enemy had been among them. They searched the city, but he was gone. They searched the Empire and still found nothing. Fear haunted their councils. Yet nothing happened. Or so it seemed for a time.

The fall of Ilkazar, as recorded in *The Wizards of Ilkazar*, a dubious and doubtless exaggerated epic of King Vilis's end, which opens:

> *How lonely sits the city*
> *   that was full of people!*
> *How like a widow she has become*

that was great among the nations!

Barbarians harried the borders of the Empire. Unrest grumbled through the tributary states. The armies were decimated and demoralized by a strange plague. A star exploded and died. From Ilkazar itself a dragon was seen crossing the full moon. An unseasonable storm wrecked shipping in the Sea of Kotsüm. Trolledyngjan pirates raided the western coasts.

And the song says:

> *She weeps bitterly in the night,*
> *tears on her cheeks;*
> *among all her lovers*
> *she has none to comfort her;*
> *******line lost*******
> *they have become her enemies.*

Tributary states rebelled. Entire armies were surprised and overwhelmed. Ilkazar's moneylenders grumbled because loans to the Empire were not being repaid. Those who dealt in booty murmured because there were no new conquests. The people muttered as supplies grew short.

The King, in the traditional manner of politicians, tried to stem gloom's tide with speeches. He promised impossible things that he apparently believed himself…

But he couldn't put the rebels down. They were too numerous, in too many places, and their numbers daily grew—and ill fortune invariably dogged armies sent against them: floods, spoiled rations, disease. And with each rebel victory, more conquered peoples rose.

A whisper, dark, disturbing, ran through Ilkazar. The city would be spared no agony when the foreign soldiers came. The people fled—until the King declared emigration a capital offense. Fool. He should have rid himself of their hunger.

There was no native crop that year. Rust, worms, weevils, and locusts destroyed everything. The only food available was that in storage and a dwindling trickle of tribute.

Though in dread of the wizards of Ilkazar, the rebel Kings, and barbarians after spoil, gathered and united against the Empire.

Says the poet:

> *Happier were the victims of the sword*
> *than the victims of hunger,*
> *who pined away, stricken*
> *by the want of the fruits of the field.*
> *The hands of compassionate women*
> *have boiled their own children;*

they became their food
  in the destruction of her people.

There were armies before Ilkazar, well-fed armies high with the destruction of Imperial legions. They flaunted their fat herds before the watchers on the walls. Within the city, rats found dead sold for a silver shekel each, rats taken alive brought two. People feared the dead ones. They presaged plague.

The dogs and cats were gone, as were the horses of the King's cavalry and the animals of the Royal Zoo. Rumors fogged the air. Children had disappeared. Men in good health were fearful they would be accused of cannibalism. Sometimes those who had fallen to disease were found with flesh torn away, perhaps by rats, perhaps not.

The siege progressed. One day a horseman came from the encircling camps, a grim young man, frightened of the city and the sorceries within—sorceries held at bay solely by the skill of one lone man trained by the mysterious Tervola and Princes Thaumaturge of Shinsan. He delivered a scroll. Someone observed that it came on the date of anniversary for previous messages. It restated Varthlokkur's prior demands, with one significant addition: appended was a list of names of persons to be sent out of the city, and before whom the King was to abase himself.

Vilis had become more amenable. Five days later there was activity on the city walls. The Kings and generals of the rebels, dressed in black, on black horses, with black banners flying, advanced upon the city, stopped just beyond bowshot.

As the sun reached zenith, seven groups of seven tall poles were raised atop the wall. To each was bound, soaked in naphtha, a Master Wizard. The King himself bore the torches that lighted the fires. There was a long period of silence. No cloud marked the sky. All things of earth seemed poised, waiting, uncertain. Then smoke wisped toward the watchers. The stench of burning flesh distressed their horses.

The Silent One betrayed no emotion. His victory was not yet complete.

Once the fires finished their work, the gate opened, and emaciated, wretched people stumbled out. In full view, the King knelt and kissed their dusty feet as they passed. They were few, all who remained of those who once had lent aid to, or had given kindness to, an unhappy orphan. One was a man in tattered executioner's black, another was an aged sergeant. There were priests, a handful of minor sorcerers, and a few withered prostitutes who had once provided a little mothering.

The gates closed. Varthlokkur waited. The sun moved west. He sent a rider. "Where is the third penance?" the rider demanded.

"You've taken all I can give," King Vilis replied. "My power and my Empire are dust. That is cruelty enough!" He seized a bow, shot at the messenger, missed.

"Then all Ilkazar will die!" The rider fled.

Varthlokkur sat silently for a long time, considering. He had made promises he had hoped needn't be kept. He didn't want anyone but Vilis. But there were Kings accompanying him who depended on his word.

Those Kings waited. The city waited. Varthlokkur reached his decision. He raised his right arm, his left, and invoked that which he had kept in waiting, the power no accidental sorcerer ever had mastered. So imperceptibly that only the horses noticed at first, the earth began shaking. The Kings were awed by Varthlokkur's Power. An earth-marid, a King of earth-elementals, reputedly unmanageable save by supreme masters of the eastern sorcery, was answering his summons.

The trembling grew to an earthquake. The city gates collapsed. The poles with wizards toppled from the walls. Spires and minarets shuddered. And the shaking grew. Great buildings fell. The thick wall, Ilkazar's most solid construction, began to crumble. Varthlokkur's arms ached with the effort of holding them upward, motionless, and with the Power flowing through them. Yet he held them high. If they fell prematurely, the earth-marid would abandon work as yet incomplete, and Ilkazar would retain sufficient might to make the assault terribly costly. Fires appeared and spread. Dust from falling buildings joined their smoke, darkened the sky. A great government building slid into the Aeos (which entered Ilkazar through a huge, unbreachable grill), damming it, flooding part of the city.

Varthlokkur eventually was satisfied and allowed the earthquake to die. He loosed his human hounds. The warriors met little opposition. He himself led the Kings to the Palace.

They found Vilis seated amidst the ruins of his citadel, rocking and drooling. He clutched a crown to his chest and sang a childhood song. Soldiers hastily cleared rubble from a corner of Execution Square. They recovered a carven stake, set it up, and bound the King to it. Brands arrived. Varthlokkur stood before Vilis, torch in hand.

His followers expected him to laugh, or brag about this fulfillment of vengeance, but he did not. They expected he would now speak, for the first time in decades, and say something like, "Remember my mother in Hell," but he did not. When at last he broke the long silence, he said only, "You have made me lonely, Royal Ilkazar," and cast the torch aside. Head bowed, he turned and walked from the city slowly, leaving mercy or its lack to his followers.

The poet, hardly impartial, ends with a bitter curse upon Ilkazar, damning her for all eternity. But, before he finishes, he does, briefly, indicate that he understands why Varthlokkur cast the torch aside. No one else then present, and few scholars since, did so. The destruction of Ilkazar and its King meant Varthlokkur had lost his only true companion of fourteen years' purpose. Behind the mask of victory had lain a defeat.

Five: Spring, 996 AFE
By Every Hand Betrayed

Night in Iwa Skolovda, at the end of a savage storm—probably the last of winter. The Kratchnodian Mountains and the valley of the Silverbind were buried by sparkling snow, and temperatures were barely above melting. The Silverbind was high in the flatlands, a foot below flood outside the east wall. Ice jammed the river a few miles down, backing the flow. The wind sang a lonely dirge around the Tower of the Moon. It was a night for earthshaking events, a night for the Wind of Fate.

Nepanthe had slept better since the arrival of the fat man. He hadn't been able to banish the demons of her mind, but he had tamed them a bit. That night, however, she paced, though not from old terror. A premonition rode the wind whispering through the windows and curtains. Apprehension forbid all sleep. Occasionally the future touched her lightly, though seldom clearly. Something was terribly wrong in Iwa Skolovda. She had felt it for hours, yet could not discover what.

Glancing out the window facing north, she finally found a visible wrongness. The sky glowed away toward the north wall. The glow steadily brightened. She knew what it was. Fire. But what flames they must be! To cause such a widespread glow, the fire must be beyond all control. Her apprehension increased. She turned to the clothing set out for the morning.

She had just finished dressing—and was cursing a broken fingernail—when the knocker at her door sounded.

"Enter!" she called, certain she sounded terrified.

Rolf came in, face grim.

"Well?"

"Bad news, Milady."

"I've seen the fires. What's happening?"

"An attack. Hillmen bandits have crossed the wall. There must be a thousand of them, killing, plundering."

Nepanthe frowned. What the devil?

Rolf continued, "The troops are fighting well, under the circumstances."

"Rolf, I don't want to call you a liar, but… well, we both know none of the hill tribes are that big. Hardly any could muster a hundred warriors, counting cripples, old men, and boys. Fighting well under what circumstances?"

"Perhaps I exaggerate, but I'll swear there're more than five hundred. I saw at least a dozen tribal totems. They've got some kind of overall warchief.

"The circumstances are these: your enemies here have joined the bandits. They're attacking us from behind. Our partisans are attacking them. It's absolute chaos. I can't keep civil order and defend the city both."

"When did it start?"

"Three hours ago, Milady."

"Why wasn't I informed?"

"There seemed no need at first. Then I didn't have time."

Faintly, the roars of fighting and fire reached Nepanthe's ears. Furtive shadows raced through the streets below her window, some away from, some toward, the stricken quarter. "The hillman warchief, did you see him? What did he look like?" Unreasonably, she was certain what Rolf's answer would be.

"Tall, thin, dark of skin, face like a hawk's, eyes that look like you can see Hell's fires burning through them. He's not a hillman, northman, or Iwa Skolovdan, nor a westerner. A southerner, I'd guess. From the deserts. I heard his name, but can't remember it. They called him Wizard."

"Varthlokkur!" Nepanthe spat, freighting the name with anger and fear.

"Milady?" Rolf frowned. He had heard the name before. Where? Ah. The old chanson, *The Wizards of Ilkazar.* But that made no sense. That Varthlokkur had lived hundreds of years ago.

"For years I've dreaded that name, Rolf." Her spirits sagged. She became a lost, frightened little girl. "What can I do? Why did Turran leave me alone? He'd know what to do." She wept. It had been a long time since she had. Then she grew hysterical, began raving.

Awed, distressed, and uncertain how he should react, Rolf ran to Saltimbanco's apartment.

The fat man wakened with a long-winded, flowery curse in which Rolf's hopefully illegitimate children were damned for generations.

"Mocker, shut your goddamned mouth and listen!" He drew back, ready to slap the fat man.

Saltimbanco considered the grim face above him, and the name that had been spoken. "What happens?"

"Haroun's here. Early. He's outnumbered, but I've confused things so much he can't help but win."

"Self, assume this is plan."

"Yes. But when I reported the attack and described Haroun, the woman got hysterical, started raving about Varthlokkurs, Fangdreds, El Kabars. You better quiet her down, or she'll blow the whole operation…"

"Self, am acknowledged master of hysterics-soothing. Am also one distressed by naming of secret names. Mocker is dead…"

Moments later, Saltimbanco burst into Nepanthe's apartment, seated himself with her in his ample lap, began comforting. He tried to discover what lay behind her collapse, but failed. She had regained control.

"Self," he declared suddenly, rising abruptly, catching her just before she hit the floor, "will brave barbed shafts of barbarian hordes to speechify rallyment to stouthearted troops!" He vanished before she could protest.

Nepanthe, while seated where Saltimbanco had deposited her, regained her Storm King turn of mind. Coolly, she shouted, "Rolf! Send a man to Ravenkrak with news of what's happened, and the name 'Varthlokkur.' Turran'll know what I mean. Oh, ask for reinforcements. Then muster my guard and horses. Secure a path of retreat. And see if you can catch Saltimbanco before he gets himself killed."

Asking for reinforcements, she knew, was futile. The battle would be lost or won before Turran received her message. But he might bring enough men to retake the city.

Fast, faster than his bulk portended possible, Saltimbanco hurried to the north quarter. Here and there he demoralized the troops with stout patriotic speeches, promises of imminent victory, and exhortations to counterattack mightily. His perfect record for selecting the wrong convinced the men they were already defeated.

The fighting slopped over into the east quarter, which was populated primarily by small merchants and artisans—the bulk of them furriers whose products were internationally renowned—who were Nepanthe's ardent supporters. The attack bogged down as those supporters defended their homes vigorously. It was a pity there were no fresh formations available to take advantage of the situation.

Saltimbanco suddenly appeared near the North Gate, at the command post of the invaders. Shrieking loudly, he alerted his accomplice before hillmen could spit him with spears. The man called Haroun hustled him into a captured house.

Saltimbanco faced the raider across a splintered oak table. "Self, am thinking Great General strikes early—though boldly, with success."

The thin, dark man opposite him remained silent for a long moment before hissing, "I've got a talent. Its buyer paid well. I give value for money."

"Self, am doing same." Saltimbanco was disturbed.

Haroun was cold, remote. Had something gone sour? Then he sighed. The man was always this way at the crisis point in his cameo guerrilla wars. He had to be. Total detachment was necessary. "Is great operation, plan-perfect. Mad-blind, Storm Kings." He chuckled, thinking of the pot of gold at the end of this particular bloody rainbow. "Gold-lined old man, what of him?"

"Nothing. Not a word since last fall. I don't like it. Paid a few people to keep an eye on him. He's recruiting hire-swords in the Lesser Kingdoms."

"Self, am student philosophic of mighty mental thews, yet am unable to reason to end of twisty old man's twisty plan. Am not liking darkness. Am fearful, here, here, here." He smote himself on forehead, heart, purse.

"For the pay, I'll tolerate the mysteriousness. Look, I've got a battle to run. I haven't got time to chat, and nothing to tell. Give Rolf my congratulations. He's learning. Might make a full partner someday. And give my regards to Bragi and Elana. Now go away. We can talk after Ravenkrak falls."

"Hurry-hurry. Always hurry. Self, being keen of eye and keener of keeping head attached, spotted interesting list and copied same. Spies working for

Valther. Same might prove handy."

Irritably, bin Yousif grabbed the list. He gestured at the door.

At sunrise Rolf's patrols found Saltimbanco wandering aimlessly near the South Gate. Vainly, the sun strove to drive its rays through the smoke over the city. The fat man, apparently in shock, was unceremoniously tied into a saddle and drafted into Nepanthe's retreat.

Turran was moving south with the vanguard of his little army, passing through one of those evergreen groves lying in the depths of a canyon of the high range. The wind moaned. Avalanches up the peaks made the canyon roar. Then messages began arriving from the south.

The first was, ostensibly, a report from Nepanthe, but in reality came from one of Valther's spies: Rolf. After reflection, Turran summoned his brother, who appeared quickly. By then a second message had arrived.

"I've got a couple of messages from your man Rolf. One says it looks like Nepanthe's found herself a lover."

"Should we kill him?"

"No. Not yet. Might settle her down."

With a grin, Valther suggested, "Let's help him, then. She's a little overdue, don't you think?"

Turran's laughter drowned the avalanches momentarily. "About fifteen years overdue." His expression soured. "Mother's fault." Valther knew his mother only by hearsay. She had died giving Nepanthe life, only a year after his own birth. The "mother" Turran meant, and to whom all often referred, was their father's second wife, a grimly antisexual woman. "She told Nepanthe about men, and no one's proven her wrong…"

"Wrong. What's wrong?"

"Eh?"

"You didn't call me here to talk about Nepanthe's sex life. Or lack of one."

"No, but that's part of it. This fellow she's falling for. Crackpot of some kind, supposedly harmless, with a knack for beating her moods. No, the problem's what your man tacked on the end of the report. And what he wrote later."

"What?" Valther was growing impatient.

"The night the first message was sent, hill bandits attacked Iwa Skolovda. The city, not outlying hamlets. They came down the Silverbind undetected, crossed the wall, opened the gate—all without being noticed."

"Treachery. Someone was paid."

"Of course. And you haven't heard the worst. Rolf says they were five or six hundred strong."

"No. Impossible. That'd mean someone's united the tribes."

"But they've been feuding for ages."

"Right. I watch these things. There hasn't been a rumor out of that country, except that a wizard took up residence near Gron last fall. I checked him out. An herbalist, a witch-doctor, no real magician."

"Yet somebody organized the tribes if they attacked? Right?"

"Yes."

"So that somebody has to be your witch-doctor if he's the only foreigner around. You accept that?"

"Again, yes. None of the chiefs would take orders from any of the others. But that still doesn't make sense."

"No. No charlatan would have the skill to lead an army. Unless he was something else entirely…"

"I still don't think it's possible…" Valther blanched. "Oh, what a fool! Haroun bin Yousif!"

"What?"

"It was right in front of me all the time. I should've done something six months ago. Gods, I'm blind. That witch-doctor was Haroun bin Yousif."

"What're you gibbering about?"

"Think! If you can't afford the Guild or ordinary mercenaries, want to make war and have a shot at winning, what do you do?"

After a minute, Turran sighed, nodded gloomily. "Hire Haroun bin Yousif, the King Without a Throne. The 'hero' of Libiannin and Hellin Daimiel. I'll buy it. It fits too neat. What's he doing here?"

Valther shook his head. "Last I heard he was supposed to be working with the staff of the Itaskian Army, developing tactics for the Coast Watch militia to use against Trolledyngjan raiders while they're waiting for the regulars to arrive."

"Find out!" Turran's command was as cold and sharp as the winter wind. "I want to know why he left a sinecure to lead savages. I want to know every word he spoke the month before he left, with whom, and why. And every move he made. I want it all, and I want it quick. Flood Itaskia with agents. Because the other message was nasty. Nepanthe couldn't hold Iwa Skolovda. The old King's supporters rebelled in concert with the bandit attack. She claims it was planned. I should've left Redbeard with her. Preshka the pupil isn't Grimnason the master."

"Will we retake the city?"

"No…" A thoughtful gleam entered Turran's eye. "Nepanthe's retreating north with three hundred loyal Iwa Skolovdans. I'll bet the bandits are ahead of her. And we're here…Tell Redbeard to get ready for a forced march."

Chuckling, Valther went after Grimnason.

However, the jaws of the mercenary's trap snapped shut only on bandit rabble. Somehow sensing his peril, bin Yousif abandoned his savage allies and vanished.

SIX: SUMMER, 996 AFE
AT THE HEART OF THE MOUNTAINS OF FEAR

Tall, cold, lonely was Ravenkrak, a vast, brooding fortress built of gray stone set without mortar. It had twelve tall towers, some square, some round, and crenellated battlements like massive lower jaws. Ice rimed the walls in patchlets of white. Glassless windows seemed empty eye sockets when seen from the outer slope. A huge tunnel of an entrance, with portcullis down—like fangs—put the finishing touch on the castle's appearance of a skull.

Cold and drafty the place appeared. Cold and drafty it was.

Nepanthe stood in the parapet of her Bell Tower, braving an arctic wind. Shivering, she took in forbidding visions of bald rock and fields of snow. Yes, the fortress seemed invincible, though she was certainly no expert. It was built triangular on a pointed upthrust. Only one wall, the tallest, could be reached by an enemy. The others blended into the sheer flanking cliffs of the upthrust. But she wasn't happy as she studied Ravenkrak's strength. She thought it was all for nothing, that the enemy they faced couldn't possibly be stopped by weapons and walls. The great dooms brushed defenses aside as a man did spiders' webs while walking through a forest; with scant cognizance, with but an instant's irritation.

The wind's moaning rose to a howl. It slid claws of ice through her garments.

From an open hatchway, a heavy, robed figure climbed into the wind: Saltimbanco. Glancing at him, Nepanthe whispered sadly, "I wish it were over."

The clown was in a rare good humor. "Ah, fair Princess!" he cried (he and her loyal Iwa Skolovdans insisted on the title). "Behold! Steel and silver-encladded knight comes across dangers of half world, scales mighty mountain, impregnates impregnable fortress, comes in knick to rescue fair maiden. 'But what's this?' cries stout knight—in guise of own stout self—'Where hides the bloody dragon?' Self, being warrior of mighty thews, shall smite him hip and thigh, thus… and thus… riposte… left to jaw… got 'im!"

Despite her abysmal mood, Nepanthe laughed at his antics, especially the improbable "left to jaw." Laugh she did, then, realizing that the dragon he meant was her mood, laughed a little louder, forcedly. She remembered a time when she couldn't laugh at all, and anticipated such a time for the future. The near future.

"Alas and alack, Sir Knight," she moaned in feigned despair (which nudged the borders of becoming real), "'tis no dragon which holds me in thralldom bound, but ogres and trolls in number six cavorting through the castle below."

"Hai! Tusse-folk, say you? Woe!" Saltimbanco lamented. "Self, very much fear, maybeso, same left trollsword behind."

"And that's no way to talk about your brothers," said a third voice, good-naturedly.

Saltimbanco and Nepanthe peered at Valther, each with his or her suspicions, each wondering what machinations were behind his appearance. However, Valther was nothing more than he pretended—for the moment.

Seeing her first statement tolerated, Nepanthe spat, "No way to talk about my brothers? You, with the minds of weasels and hearts of vultures? If not ogres and trolls, pray tell what?"

"Careful, Nepanthe. In anger secrets all winged fly. And you're treading close to the drawn line, talking that way." He glanced downward, reminding her of the Deep Dungeons, then changed the subject. "But I didn't come up to argue. Just to view our frigid domain with my baby sister."

All three stared out over the stark, glacier-cleft mountains. The grasping talons of winter never completely released Ravenkrak, merely lightened their grip in summer's season.

"You seem poetically inclined today," Nepanthe observed.

Valther shrugged, pointed outward. "Isn't that a subject fit for a poem?"

"Yes. An ode to a Wind God, or Father Winter. Or maybe an epic concerning the odyssey of a glacier. Certainly nothing human or warm."

"Uhm, truth told," Saltimbanco muttered. Then, assuming Valther wanted to talk to Nepanthe privately, he headed for the hatchway.

"Hold on! Saltimbanco, you don't have to leave." Valther pretended horror at the notion. "There'll be no secrets discussed here. And Nepanthe's mood would fail if you left. If there was ever an elixir of the heart, a potation to buoy the spirit, then it'd be found in you. Proof? Nepanthe. Fair Nepanthe, sweet Nepanthe, once lost in her vapors, a stick of wood for all the heart she showed. And who's to blame for the changes? Even Turran's remarked on it. 'Tis yourself, Knight Ponderous."

Nepanthe stared at Valther, amazed.

And Saltimbanco, who was wont to absorb the most outrageous praise as his due, was embarrassed by Valther's out-of-character speech—though not too embarrassed to remain.

"Harken, sister," Valther continued. "Harken, O wind like a dragon's dying groan. Who salvaged the spirits of a defeated clan? Who brought heart to the heartless? This man who so wisely plays the fool! I think he's no fool at all, but a most clever rogue of an actor and clown!"

Though Saltimbanco wore a slash of a self-conscious grin, his insides were a'boil with fear. Questions threw up sprouts of terror in the guilt-fertile fields of his mind. What did Valther know? Were these allegations? Was he being warned he was suspect?

Nepanthe broke his thought train by asking, "Valt, what's made you so prosy? Did?…" She bit her tongue with mock viciousness, pulled a face, continued, "I was going to say something nasty. I guess I'm pretty poor company. I mean, here're two gentlemen trying to entertain me, and all I do is howl like a Harpy."

Both men protested, but she silenced them with a wave. "Who knows better than me what I've become?" Then she broke out laughing. The mock horror on Saltimbanco's face was that extreme. Evidently, she had just violated some mad philosophical tenet.

When the fat man spoke, however, he had nothing philosophical to say. "Woe!" he cried. "Hear old Ice-Wind howl! Self, am protected by wisely accumulated layers of guardian flesh. Am self-admitted obesity, yet am still to become frozen immobility before tramontane stream. Am pleading, Lord and Lady! May we move party to where great warm fires burn?"

One look at the granite sky, at the snow flurries around them, at the barrenness on every hand, assured the two of Saltimbanco's wisdom.

"Hai!" Valther cried, mimicking Saltimbanco. "The man's right again! Hot mead in the Great Hall, eh? A warm fire, hot wine, a joint of lamb, and friendly conversation. Let's go."

"I'm coming," Nepanthe said, with a little trill of laughter. "But I'll forgo the mutton. Redbeard's wife, Astrid, told me too much meat is bad for the complexion."

Valther and Saltimbanco stared, poised on the borders of laughter—but checked themselves when they realized she was serious. It was laughter at the unexpected, anyway, for when had Nepanthe ever expressed such a feminine concern? Then Valther glanced at Saltimbanco, a new breed of laughter in his eyes.

A dozen huge fireplaces roared merrily around the Great Hall. Every time he entered, Saltimbanco marveled at the hominess of the place. Dogs and small children, without regard to sex or tribe or station, frolicked and fought, snarled, and chewed on discarded bones amidst the deep straw upon the floor, brawlingly thick. Yet seldom did the servants or men-at-arms tread on pup or child…

Turran's soldiers, and Nepanthe's Iwa Skolovdans, were seated at the countless tables, drinking, singing, telling lies, or suffering drunken dreams. Some paid half-hearted attention to their own or others' wives. Turran himself was there, at the head table, locked in a prodigious arm-wrestle with one of Redbeard's brawny sergeants. The nether end of the hall rang metallically as men practiced with dulled and blunted weapons. Banners overhead swayed in an almost imperceptible draft, dancing a quiet, shadowy dance in the flickering light of fires and torches.

In another dance, women (wives and daughters of the soldiers) moved among the tables with wine and pitchers of ale, with huge trenchers heaped with roast lamb, with rare beef, or an occasional lonely fowl.

Nepanthe, Valther, and Saltimbanco wound through this shifting, noisy press, their goal the head table. Nepanthe and Saltimbanco acknowledged greetings from the crowd. Saltimbanco was popular with the troops because he was entertaining. Nepanthe was well-liked simply because, as a woman, she lent glamour to the crusty old castle and its bizarre ruling family. All the Storm Kings were popular, for that matter, being, probably, the best masters these mercenaries had ever known. A man serving their banner had little cause for complaint.

Truly, only an enemy could hate them, and that only because they were the foe. They had already proven themselves merciless toward adversaries, implacable in pursuit of their goals. They cared for their own with the same intensity. Mocker would gladly have thrown in with them, had his loyalties not been bought already.

They reached Turran's table. Turran still grunted in his struggle with Sergeant Blackfang. Glancing up, he smiled. His face was reddened by too much wine and the effort of the contest.

"Ho! Watch me put this bragging rogue down! Oof!" He had lost his concentration. Blackfang took him. He laughed thunderously, smote the sergeant on the shoulder, bellowed for servants.

Valther slipped into the seat beside his brother. Nepanthe and Saltimbanco settled in across the table. Several women appeared with knives and platters and mugs for ale and wine. More came, bearing the liquid refreshments, the mutton, the this and that which made up the staples of Ravenkrak's never-ending meal.

"Hai!" Valther said, pinching a girl at the same time. "Cabbage soup for my sister. No meat in it, mind! She'll ruin her fair skin."

Nepanthe was surprised by the tittering of the women. Why were they?… Because Valther was fondling everything in reach? Her regard fell heavily on the women. Their laughter died. But their silence persisted only till they reached the kitchens, which were soon a'hum.

For there was a secret abroad amongst the women of Ravenkrak, a secret they found delicious, a secret that was no secret at all, save to Nepanthe. It was a secret known to the men as well. How could they avoid knowing it in a place where a man couldn't escape the wagging tongues of wives and daughters? It was known to all men save Saltimbanco himself, and he was getting suspicious. Everyone but Nepanthe *knew* that Nepanthe had fallen in love.

There were those who claimed that Saltimbanco shared the feeling, citing his steady weight loss as evidence. Others argued that that had been caused by the rigors of the retreat to Ravenkrak and the quality of life in the castle. Whatever the truth, though, Saltimbanco was indeed shedding the pounds.

The tittering of the serving girls caused Nepanthe to blush an attractive crimson. She scowled at Valther.

"Ha!" said Turran, after reflection on Valther's statement. "Well!" He burst into laughter.

Nepanthe glowered. She thought of a hundred vicious things to say—but her brothers, the serving girls, Saltimbanco, indeed, the entire hall, suddenly fell silent.

Birdman, the keeper of Ravenkrak's falcons and pigeons, a man so old and infirm he often needed help getting about, had come running into the Great Hall, howling as if his personal banshee was close behind. The silence deepened to that of a mausoleum. Only guttering torch-flames moved. Hundreds held their breaths, anticipating dreadful news. Birdman hadn't left his cotes for months.

The spell broke when a child wailed in fright. The exorcism complete, voices surged and rose like the rush of incoming tides. Birdman staggered the last few steps to the head table.

"Sir!" that ancient stick-figure of a man croaked. "Sir!" and again, "Sir!"

Turran, who had a deep affection for the old fellow, checked his impatience, initiated a friendly inquisition. "Now, then, Birdman," (no one remembered his real name anymore), "what's this? How come so much activity in a man your age?"

Birdman instantly forgot his mission, began arguing his haleness. His greatest fear was forced retirement.

"Your report, Birdman," Turran kept reminding. "The reason for all this excitement?"

The old man banished his fears long enough to say, "Your brother, sir. A message from your brother."

"Which one? Which one?"

"Why, the Lord Ridyeh, of course, sir. To be sure, yes, Ridyeh."

"And what does my brother say?"

"Oh! Why, of course, that's why I'm all the way up here in the Great Hall, isn't it? Uhn… oh? Yes!" He searched his rumpled, unchanged-for-a-week clothing. "Aha! And here he is, here the little devil be." Chortling, he clawed a crumpled, dirty piece of parchment from deep within his greasy tunic.

Turran accepted the ragged bit graciously, bade the old man to sit and sup a mug of wine, then leaned back and read by torchlight.

His face became a battlefield of emotion. His dark eyes radiated displeasure, unhappiness. His long, drooping mustachios seemed alive in the light dancing on his visage. Anger came and went, and something akin to sadness. His nostrils flared, relaxed, flared as he read and reread. At length, having convinced himself of its verity, he crushed the parchment in his fist, rose.

As if unaware of the hundreds of questioning eyes, he turned to his companions. "Valther, Nepanthe, come with me. You, too, fat man." He wheeled on the soldier he had been arm-wrestling. "Blackfang, find my brothers. Send them to the Lower Armories."

He strode toward the main exit like a king, ignoring the humming speculation of the Great Hall. His companions were hard-pressed to match his pace.

The Lower Armories were far beneath the roots of Ravenkrak. They were, with the exception of the Deep Dungeons, the deepest chambers of the fortress.

It was there the Storm Kings practiced their sorceries. There their most potent theurgies lay hidden. There, also, lay the treasures of Ravenkrak, the gems and monies that paid spies, bought traitors, hired assassins, and purchased arms. There too, perfectly protected, lay the Horn of the Star Rider. The Storm Kings had tamed it only to the point where it would provide food, clothing, occasional gold, and firewood. It hadn't become the keystone of power they had hoped.

They were dank places, the Lower Armories, filthy, smelling of old mold, dark and haunted by rats and spiders. Moisture oozed down the ancient walls, slime made the floor treacherous. The ceilings remained lost in shadow. Unlike the homely, lived in atmosphere of the upper fortress, those deep warrens smelled of something Saltimbanco believed vaguely unholy.

This was his first venture into those deep places. Slipping repeatedly in his futile effort to match Turran's pace, he plunged into a dreadful mood wherein he foresaw evil at every turn. He expected a sudden and ignominious end. He did, however, survive the journey, which ultimately led to a dimly lighted room. The cleanliness of the place was to him as water to a thirsty man. He marveled only a moment at the strange blue lighting and the weird thaumaturgical devices ranged about the walls. These Storm Kings had been called sorcerers: here he saw the proof.

They took seats at a round table surrounded by seven chairs, waited silently. No one questioned Turran. He would speak when the time came.

Brock arrived a few minutes later. His eyes widened when he saw Saltimbanco. "What's he doing here?"

"Nepanthe's eating cabbage now: mutton's bad for her complexion," Valther replied, as if that explained everything. It did, except to Saltimbanco and the woman.

"Oh!"

Time passed. Turran grew impatient. His fingers drummed the tabletop. Brock and Valther began fidgeting. Saltimbanco, as he often did in waiting situations, began snoring.

There was a nervous shuffling beyond the door.

"Well?" Turran snapped, irritated. Then, "Oh, it's you," less gruffly. "Come in, Blackfang. Where is he?"

The sergeant entered warily, as if walking on coals. He was awed and frightened and vainly trying to conceal it. "Sir, Jerrad has left the castle. A bear hunt. He may not return this week."

"This month, likely!" Turran grumbled. "I wish he'd tell somebody when he leaves. Thank you, Sergeant. You can go."

Blackfang bowed, took a last awed look at the chamber, made his retreat.

"Nepanthe, will you waken your friend?"

Fingernail in the ribs! Bane of pleasantly dreaming men since the dawn of time. Curses heartfelt and black, also an ancient custom. Saltimbanco erupted into reality.

"Ridyeh sent a message," Turran told them, scowling. "He says our friend bin Yousif turned up in Iwa Skolovda ten days ago. There were several killings afterward. He vanished, reappeared in Prost Kamenets, and there were more murders there. Later, he was seen at the Red Hart Inn in Itaskia, where he passed out gold like it was water. How he managed to come by it so quick is something I'd like to know. Then he disappeared. There were another dozen murders that night. And every victim, in Iwa Skolovda, Prost Kamenets, and Itaskia, was one of Valther's spies."

"What?" Valther jumped up, enraged. "How?..."

"I don't know," Turran growled. "He must've gotten a list. I'll figure it out if I have to put everybody in the castle to the question."

"I do keep records," Valther murmured. "Who's where."

"Oh? That's not very bright, is it? You're supposed to be the spy... What the hell did you think you were doing?"

Valther ignored his brother's ire. "Why would he be desperate to keep us from backtracking him? He's out free."

"Simple," said Nepanthe. "He's *not*. He's covering someone else. Whoever got him the list."

"Ah..."

Saltimbanco began sweating. The wolves were closing in. He had to distract them...

Turran asked, "Valt, who could've gotten to your papers?"

"Anybody. Anytime. I don't lock my door. Never thought there was any need to. Anybody who had the time could've made a duplicate list."

"Well, damn it, start locking your door."

"Famous case of locking barn door after horse is fled," Saltimbanco observed. "Great Lords, Lady, how many people in castle read and write?" He had found his diversion. He would set them to chasing shadows. "Start interviewing them, huh? But we don't mention treachery. Maybe if not scared, traitor makes mistake. Maybe we plant new list. Not knowing everybody watching for him, he maybe does treasonous task again. Pounce! We get him! Hai! Big hanging party! Everybody turns out, much wine, much song, this humble one is hero for thinking of plan, has very good time..."

"Good idea," said Turran. "But no hanging. I'll want to question the man. Brock, tomorrow I want you to ask for men who can read and write. Say we've got some clerical work to do. Offer bonuses so they'll all turn out. We can watch whoever responds. Now, for the bad half of Ridyeh's message."

"You mean there's more, and worse?" Valther asked.

"Yes. Iwa Skolovda and Dvar have formed an alliance. They're raising a mercenary army to attack Ravenkrak. They raised standard two weeks ago, and already they've gathered five thousand men. Remarkable, don't you think? Especially considering that most of these mercenaries are southerners, up from Libiannin, Hellin Daimiel, and the Lesser Kingdoms. And their officers are Guildsmen."

"Sounds like High Crag knew something ahead of time," said Valther. "They'd actually march against Ravenkrak? How'll they find us?"

"Our friend Haroun again. He'll have command. Ridyeh says he visited the Kings when he was in Iwa Skolovda and Dvar."

"But they can't hope to take Ravenkrak…"

"They don't know that. And we're terribly undermanned. But that doesn't worry me much. What does is why all that fuss is being made. Consider. Haroun bin Yousif is a man with a mission and a lot of talent. Between politicking, harassing El Murid, and advising the Itaskian General Staff, he's been living twenty-five-hour days. Though in luxury, to be sure."

"Why," Valther mused, "would a man give up doing exactly what he wants in order to organize hill tribesmen?"

"That's what I'm trying to get at. More, why, after he'd chased Nepanthe out of Iwa Skolovda, did he prematurely scatter them?" Fewer than fifty tribesmen had fallen into the trap Turran had set for bin Yousif.

"He'd finished his job."

"Check. Somebody wanted us out of Iwa Skolovda. Enough to meet the outrageous price bin Yousif would have demanded for the job. And it wasn't the Iwa Skolovdan Royalists. Remember, he was at work in the hills before we took over."

"Foreknowledge," Brock grumbled. "Necromancy." He looked like he had just bitten into a crabapple. "The Star Rider getting even?"

"Possibly. But to the main curiosity. His killing spies while his army fore-recruited gathers. Why?"

"Something big is going on," Valther averred.

"Brilliant. And it's something we didn't anticipate when we went to the flatlands. Something that started earlier and we didn't notice. What?"

Turran spoke in a manner suggesting that his discourse was rhetorical till that final, plaintive "What?" Then it was clear that he was mystified, too.

"We'd better sit back and wait till we find out," Valther said. "We can hold out here as long as we have the Horn." Murmuring, he added, "It must be him. Trying to get it back."

"That's the plan. We're undermanned, but I doubt that they can get to us. If we can hold them off till winter, we'll whip them. They'll be trapped by the weather, at the end of precarious supply lines. I imagine they'll pull out with the first snow and fall apart as soon as they hit the flatlands. Neither Iwa Skolovda nor Dvar can afford to keep them together. They don't have the credit."

"And next summer can see us down in their territory again, against weaker opposition," Valther mused.

"Sounds good, anyway," Brock grumbled. "But I wish we had a better idea of what's going on."

"You," Turran told him, "I'm making siegemaster. Make this stonepile impregnable. Now, let's tell the others. Be cheerful, make it a joke. Laugh because somebody is fool enough to come after us."

Turran and his brothers went to the Great Hall, where they announced the forthcoming siege.

Saltimbanco and Nepanthe wandered through chilly hallways till they reached her quarters in the Bell Tower. Nepanthe settled onto a stool before a large frame and resumed work on her embroideries. Saltimbanco dumped his bulk into the comfort of a large, goosedown-stuffed chair facing the fireplace. Nepanthe's serving girl brought mulled wine, then disappeared.

Nepanthe's sitting room, perhaps the most comfortable in all Ravenkrak, was filled with womanly things. An abandoned summer frock hung in a corner, forgotten; a hastily discarded lace *rebosa* lay across one end of a vanity cluttered with cosmetics she seldom used. The rugs on the floors, the tapestries on the walls, the very scents in the air all bespoke occupation by a woman.

It was a room of sleepy comfort, so peaceful and quiet that Saltimbanco couldn't remain awake. A scant five minutes after arriving, he lapsed into gentle snoring.

Leaving her embroidery to brush her hair, Nepanthe gave her guest a look which would have surprised her had she known she wore it, and wondered about him. He seemed to have sprung into existence fully grown, sometime shortly before having entered Iwa Skolovda.

Past? Did Saltimbanco have one? Indeed, though few men would have taken pride in it, had it been theirs.

His earliest memories were of a picaresque youth spent in company with a blind, alcoholic *sadhu* (source of much of the misinformation integral to his present act—that holy man had been a thorough fraud) wandering between Argon, Necremnos, and Throyes, with occasional forays into Matayanga. That *sadhu* early inspired in him a powerful loathing for honest work, and, from the blind man and others into whose company their travels had led them, he had obtained an intimate knowledge of pickpocketry, sleight-of-hand, ventriloquism, and all the mummery he now used to lend credence to his claims to magical powers.

After evening old scores with the *sadhu*, in finest picaro style (the old man had treated him cruelly, almost as a slave), and having stolen and gambled his way into the enmity of half the middle east, he had fled to the west. In Altea he had joined a carnival, following a gypsy life through the occidental kingdoms. Sometimes he claimed his name, Mocker, came from that of a character he had portrayed in passion plays, though that wasn't true. When not on stage, or in his booth as "Magelin the Magician," he had mixed with the crowds, lifting purses. He had been quite proficient.

But once he had slashed the wrong pursestrings and found his wrists seized in a painful grasp. He had found himself looking at a dusky, aquiline face, into rapacious eyes… He had jerked free, jabbed in a fashion learned in the east. They had scuffled, to no conclusion.

Later Haroun had come to talk, and Mocker had soon found himself in bin Yousif's employ, as an agent to be insinuated into the camp of El Murid, leader of the horde of religious fanatics then besieging Hellin Daimiel.

Acting on inspiration, he had pulled off the coup of the El Murid Wars, successfully kidnapping the Disciple's daughter Yasmid. The confusion in El Murid's camp had allowed Haroun and his partisans the month or so necessary to break the siege of Hellin Daimiel and create a bloated bin Yousif reputation.

In later years he, Haroun, and their mutual "friend," Bragi Ragnarson, had spent several years getting into and out of hare-brained adventures. Then Haroun's conscience had nagged him into resuming his role of King Without a Throne, commander of the Royalists El Murid had driven from Hammad al Nakir when taking over. Then Ragnarson, the fool, had gotten married, and the fat brown man, in his later twenties, had found himself drifting around alone again, tagging along the carnival circuit or undertaking an occasional minor espionage mission. The relationship between the three had faded from others' memories…

Then Haroun had materialized, accompanied by an old man filled with promises of vast wealth.

Mocker, a compulsive gambler, needed money desperately.

It had been a long road into the present, sometimes painful, usually dangerous, seldom happy. Here, in Ravenkrak, he was as at home and as near contentment as ever he had been. He liked these Storm Kings—yet the day would come when he would have to betray them…

SEVEN: THE YEARS 605-808 AFE
EVEN THE SPARROW FINDS A HOME

Fallen, fallen was Ilkazar, like ruin, like death. What more was there when that end had been accomplished?

Varthlokkur wandered away, depressed and lonely. His great work was complete. His goals had been fulfilled.

Already victory tasted of bile. Two decades he had paid for it, and now it seemed without point, possibly even an error. In destroying something he found vile he had also destroyed much that was good. For all its wickedness of heart, the corpus of the Empire had given common folk much for which to be thankful: peace throughout most of the west, a common law and language, relative social and physical security… Like maggots, Varthlokkur foresaw, a thousand petty lords would appear to devour the Imperial cadaver. The west would collapse into chaos.

His responsibility troubled him deeply.

Should he terminate his tale now? Be done with his past, with having to observe and endure the consequences of what he had done?

No, he thought not. There might be something he could do to justify his existence, to redeem the evil he had done, to ease the coming pain.

He looked up. His feet were headed north. As good a direction as any when you have nowhere specific to go. He retreated to his thoughts, harrying something he'd heard from Royal.

There was a time for everything, Royal had told him. A time for birth and death, for love and hatred, for planting and reaping, for mourning and laughter, for war and peace, for construction and destruction. And a time for the love of a woman. Only a man himself could judge when his times had come. As Ilkazar fell farther behind, he realized that, in his country way, Royal had been as wise as the priests and wizards who had taught him later. Loneliness inundated him. He missed Royal and the old woman. Hatred and purpose gone, he had receded to his point of origin, alone in a lonely world.

Loneliness had never been this absolute. Solitude he had known well during his years in Shinsan, but always the intolerable existence of Ilkazar had ameliorated that.

"Fallen, fallen is Ilkazar, that was mighty among the nations…"

The loss of his mother had left him desolate, yet that had been softened by the kindness of the executioner, and of Royal. Now Ilkazar's streets were the dwelling places of jackals. Nothing and no one needed him. His name was already legend, gothic with darkness and dread. It would grow with time and retelling. While he remained Varthlokkur, he would move in a vacuum created by fear that he would again use the Power he had revealed at Ilkazar.

And what of womankind? he asked himself. His ignorance of the other sex was as vast as his knowledge of the Power. Too many years, formative, learning years, had been squandered to purchase vengeance. Could any woman accept the Empire Destroyer? He was sure he'd be ages finding one such. She'd have to be as alienated as he, and as unhappy, as unwise. Where could he find a female mirror of himself?

He took another name. Eldred the Wanderer became a face familiar along the roads connecting the western city-states. He became renowned as a man pursuing a dream, though no one knew its nature—least of all the Wanderer himself. He thought he had found a worthy project when he rediscovered the wretchedness of the poor. His sorcery could alleviate their misery. He raised a poor man to power in Hellin Daimiel, to aid his fellows, but the man proved more cruel and corrupt than any hereditary monarch. In Libiannin, a man raised less high tried torturing him to compel him to give more. Eldred became a man as despised as Varthlokkur had been feared, briefly wresting the title "Old Meddler" from the less obtrusive Star Rider.

Depressed, he fled east, to the steppes behind the Mountains of M'Hand. He found his thoughts trending darkly. Had he any real reason to live? He rehearsed all the old arguments. Then one night, in a gloomy ravine beside a small creek, with the steppe wind moaning through scrawny trees overhead, he took strange instruments from his saddlebags, drew pentagrams, burned incense, sang spells, and performed a powerful divination. Demons added their voices to the mourning of the wind. Familiars of devils came and went, smoke things half-seen. Before dawn, he had had a shadowy look down the river of time.

There were *two* women waiting somewhere, if he could but endure. It would be a wait of centuries, and the divination had been extraordinarily cloudy. One he would use, one he would love. His love waited in a time of flux, when extraordinary powers would be malignly dipping envenomed fingers into the affairs of men. The necromancy couldn't be clarified. Forces Varthlokkur thought of as the Fates and Norns would be squabbling amongst themselves.

Yet he elected to live, to pursue this love-destiny. The Fates, he felt, had commanded him.

Somehow, somewhere (perhaps from the Tervola or Princes Thaumaturge of the Dread Empire), he had acquired an unshakable conviction that the Fates controlled his destiny. A collateral portion of his divination troubled him deeply. Mourning Ilkazar, he had sworn never again to use the Power for destruction. The divination said that he would, during the coming age of confusion. That saddened him. Varthlokkur stared into his fire, lost in contemplation. He had gained command of all sorceries while in Shinsan. Spells had been put upon him. At what cost? He couldn't remember. His selective amnesia disturbed and frightened him. He had become ageless, though not immortal. He would die someday, when the Fates willed, but he need never age. He could reverse his aging when he wanted, to the lower limit of the age he had been when the spells were cast.

He let himself grow old. The old were revered and well-treated. Alone as few men had ever been alone, he cherished even such inconsequential kindnesses as he garnered this way.

He found the proverbs "No man is an island" and "Man lives not by bread alone" uncomfortably true.

Alone. So alone. Could he not find just one friend?

For a time he played shaman to a nomad tribe on the steppe. It was a comedown, but a position for which he was grateful. He couldn't renounce the Power completely. Because he needed to be needed, he deluded himself with the belief that the tribesmen loved him. He still didn't understand human nature. The tribe went to war. Its chieftains became righteously indignant when he refused to use the Power on their behalf. Nor did he employ more than the minimum necessary to insure his survival when they turned upon him.

He wandered again, through the basin of the Roë, amongst the oldest cities of Man. He saw nothing to elevate his opinion of his own species. He wished the time-river would roll faster. *She* waited somewhere downstream.

There was an old road running east from Iwa Skolovda, one that seemed to lead nowhere. Periodically, the Kings of Iwa Skolovda sent colonists along it into East Heatherland and Shara, where they were supposed to supplant the savages through stubbornness and numbers, winning new territories for the Crown. Such movements were invariably devoured by the barbarians.

The road was wide and well-paved near the city, but after a dozen leagues, once it no longer served to bring produce from the countryside, it soon degenerated into a path. One spring day, two hundred years after the fall of Ilkazar, Varthlokkur followed that road, a sad old man who hadn't yet found a thing to make living worthwhile. But recently he'd encountered an interesting legend. It concerned a remote castle of unknown origins, and an immortal of equally nebulous background. Both waited at the end of this road, in that knot of tremendous mountains called the Dragon's Teeth. Both, Varthlokkur had divined, could become an inextricable part of his fate.

He had found a scrap of the legend in one city, a fragment of myth in another, and a piece of speculation in a third. Together, they had hinted of a castle called Fangdred, or the Castle of Wind, as old as The Place of A Thousand Iron Statues, and as feared, and as mysterious as that alleged stronghold of the Star Rider. In Fangdred dwelt an immortal known only as the Old Man of the Mountain, who supposedly had retreated there to escape the jealousy of shorter-lived men.

Maybe, Varthlokkur thought, he and this immortal were two of a kind. Maybe Fangdred could provide what he so desperately needed: a home and a friend.

Varthlokkur feared he was slowly going mad. In the midst of a raging, barbaric world where each man interacted with hundreds of others, living, loving, laughing, weeping, dying, and giving birth, he alone was outside, an observer totally alienated from human involvement. He didn't want to be outside, didn't want to be alone—yet he didn't know how to pass through the doorway of human intercourse. When he helped, he was cursed. When he didn't help, he was hated. Yet there was no way he could abandon the Power that damned him.

And Ilkazar had made him fear human relationships. A romanticized relationship with a mother whose face he couldn't remember had set his feet plodding a narrow, hard, joyless road cruel to the life-paths it had intersected. Relationships never worked the way they did in his dreams; dreams where love dwelt, and peace, without pain, became something real, while harsh, double-edged reality gradually became ghostly.

The sole dam holding the madness at bay was the woman waiting downtime.

He followed that road for weeks, across East Heatherland, into foothills, then up and down the flanks of tremendous, brooding mountains. His path tended ever upward. Each mountain rose taller than the last. Soon he was higher than he had believed possible. The trail hung a half mile above the tops of the trees. Eagles planed below him. But the road continued upward over gray stone and snowy mountains, a barely discernable trail carved from living rock, following ridgetops, sometimes passing through tunnels, climbing, climbing. Finally, in a place so high he could hardly breathe, Varthlokkur paused. The road had taken a sharp turn around a knifelike corner of cliff, and ended.

Weary, cold, he wondered if he had come a thousand miles for nothing. Then, barely discernable through the ice and snow, he noticed steps cut into the flank of the mountain. Tracing their rise, he spied a tower with crenellated battlements peeping over a looming scarp above. With a groan, resigned, determined, he began that last thousand feet of travel.

The stairs ended on a narrow ledge fronting the fortress. The tower, that he had seen from below, perched on the very peak of the mountain, and, like a lighthouse, reached high into the wind. It had no visible doors or windows. The bulk of the stronghold rambled down to this ledge, which overlooked a thousand-foot precipice. So this was Fangdred, and Mount El Kabar. Briefly, before hammering on the sagging gate, Varthlokkur looked out across the Dragon's Teeth.

It was obvious how they had come by their name. Each peak was a giant gray-and-white fang ripping at the underbelly of the sky. Countless hungry fangs huddled deep, narrow, shadowed canyons all the way to a shadowed horizon.

Varthlokkur faced the gate.

An odd current stirred the musty air of the chamber atop Fangdred's Wind Tower. Dust moved nervously, as if suddenly charged with static electricity. Soft sounds, dust-dampened, whispers—a breath of movement. In a seat of ancient carven stone a gaunt figure, so covered with dust and enmeshed in cobwebs that it seemed a mummy, drew a tiny breath. It echoed through the sealed room. Eyes bright with life-pleasure opened in a wizened face. A long white beard tumbled down over a dusty blue smock which itself became dust the moment its wearer stirred.

The eyes, once open, were surprising. Though set in an ancient face, they seemed young and laughter-vibrant. Yet they weren't the eyes of a sane man. He had lived too long to have escaped the kiss of madness.

For a long time the old man remained motionless, his face drawn in concentration. He had been asleep a hundred years, waiting for something interesting to happen. What was it this time? he wondered. His glance halted at a mirror set into the wall. The mirror reflected not the dusty chamber, but a view of the trail to El Kabar. "Ah! A visitor." The sigh so soft barely stirred the dust in his whiskers. It had been ages since anyone had come looking for the Old Man of the Mountain. Life at Fangdred was lonely. He was pleased. A visitor.

That was worth waking for.

He gathered strength for an hour before investing energy in anything more than breathing and moving his eyes. Those eyes aged quickly, the life-joy fading. Too old, too old. His wrinkled hand finally moved a tiny phial in a niche in the arm of his throne. He pushed it with a wrinkled finger. It fell. The sound of its breaking was a cymbal-crash in the empty chamber. Crimson vapor spread, rose. The Old Man inhaled deeply. Each breath of red mist sent a wave of life through his spare frame. Soon there was rosiness in his skin and strength in his long-unused muscles.

At last he rose and stumbled across the chamber, the dust of his smock falling from his otherwise naked body. His bare feet made muted, hollow slaps in the dust. He went to a cabinet of bottles, beakers, and urns, leaned against it while catching his breath. Then he took a small bottle down, unstopped it, swallowed its contents. What was it? Certainly something bitter. He made a frightful face. Also, something of amazing potency. His body visibly livened.

So. This Old Man was a magician, a specialist in the life-magicks, a difficult field indeed. There were other magicks about that chamber, but, with the exception of the far-seeing mirror, none were beyond any sorcerer's apprentice.

Another hour passed. The Old Man grew stronger. When he felt truly ready, he went to a door—invisible till he pulled a lever disguised as ornamentation—which opened on a dark staircase leading downward. Rambling through the castle proper, he observed changes that time had wrought, noting what needed doing to put the place in order.

As he reached a door opening on the courtyard behind the castle gate, there came a sudden *boom! boom! boom!* from the great bronze portal. His visitor had arrived. Hobbling slightly because he had twisted an ankle on the way, he hurried to a huge lever. He shook in the chill wind as he heaved against it. Creaks and groans bespoke a counterweight moving. Turning purple in the cold, he wondered if the gate would yield. Then a line of light appeared at one edge and slowly grew.

They stood a moment, staring at one another, considering. They were much alike, yet different. The Old Man's hair and beard were totally white. There was still a little color in Varthlokkur's. The wizard was taller, but loneliness had engraved similar lines on their faces. They knew one another immediately, not by name, but by their mutual needs. They were friends before words were spoken.

The Old Man indicated his nakedness, motioned Varthlokkur through the gate. The wizard inclined his head slightly, accepting. Still he did not speak.

The Old Man closed the gate, led Varthlokkur into the castle.

The wizard studied the dusty halls as he followed the Old Man, noting the age and gloom, and lack of life-signs in the pools of gray light cast by sunbeams stealing through high windows. Obviously, little happened here.

In a place deep within the fortress, carved from the rock of the mountain itself, the Old Man made passes before a large, dusty cabinet. Varthlokkur nodded, recognizing the counter to a spell of stasis. The cabinet front vanished. Dust cascaded.

The Old Man gestured while he considered the contents. Varthlokkur needed no orders. With a minimal spell of repulsion, he removed the dust from a stone table. The Old Man produced a time-shielded flask of wine. Varthlokkur set out plates, silverware, and pewter mugs. The Old Man brought forth a platter of hot, steaming ham, and another with fresh fruit. He produced new clothing, and hastily dressed. Once he stopped shivering, he joined Varthlokkur.

The wizard found the wine excellent, though it resurrected old sorrows. It was the golden, spiced wine of Ilkazar, as delicate as a virgin's kiss, and nearly unicorn-rare.

"I am Varthlokkur."

The Old Man considered that. Finally, he nodded. "The Silent One Who Walks With Grief. Of Ilkazar."

"And Eldred the Wanderer."

"A sad man. I watched him occasionally. He drank a bitter wine. Dogs can be more humane than men. They don't know the meaning of ingratitude. Nor of treachery."

"True. But I've abandoned anger and disappointment."

"As have I. They'll be what they'll be, and nothing will change them. You came seeking?"

"A place away from all places, and men, and loneliness. Two centuries among men… are enough."

"Any changes these past hundred years? I slept them out, being bored with repetitiveness."

"I thought so. Yes. Cities have fallen. Kingdoms have risen. But Kings and men are the same in their hearts."

"And will always be. Fangdred is a refuge from that. You're welcome. But there's a lot to do to make this place livable. Maybe servants and artisans should be engaged. Why here?"

"As I said, I need a place away, yet not lonely. To wait."

"For?"

"A woman, and destiny. I haven't performed the divination for decades. Would you like to watch? You'd understand better."

"Of course. How soon?"

"She's still two centuries down the river. The Fates hold a veil across the flow, concealing most of her age. Their hands will be in deep then, in a time of strife and true changes. Great powers will contest for empires. Wizards will war as never before. That's what I've divined so far. Seldom have I seen a divination so clouded."

"Ah? What's this about the Fates? Have they ranged themselves against you?" The Old Man's gray eyes flashed as though he were considering challenging the unchallengeable.

"They've taken sides, but I don't know how, nor the nature of my role. They're playing a complex game, apparently against the Norns, with incomprehensible rules and stakes. The players are uncertain, and their allegiances ephemeral."

"You've got a theory?" The Old Man tugged his beard thoughtfully.

"A tenuous one. That possibly the antagonists are systems of manipulation. Magic versus science. Romantic stasis versus clinical progress. The stakes could be the validity of magic and godhead. That puts us on the side of the gods. But I can't understand the Norns fighting us. If they are. They'd have no place in an orderly world either."

The Old Man ran a wrinkled hand through his hair. "I see. Ours is an enchanted world, with magical laws. That system has no room for newness or change. Which's why it hasn't changed much since the advent of the Star Rider." That event antedated even the Old Man's earliest memories—though he knew more than he would ever admit.

"And it'll stay that way unless the Power fails. I don't know if that's right. I have to stay with the magical system. My choices have been made for me, long ago, before I understood enough to choose intelligently.

"Consider a world without magic."

The Old Man closed his eyes, leaned back, imagined. He remained motionless and silent so long it seemed he had fallen asleep. A man less patient than Varthlokkur would have grown irritated. But, then, Varthlokkur had a concept of time unlike that of shorter-lived men.

"It wouldn't be a pleasant world," the Old Man finally replied. "There'd be no room for us. Sorcery would be a bad joke. Dragons and such would be the hardware of children's stories. Gods would be degraded till they had the substance of smoke. An unpleasant world, I'd say. I'd have to support magic, too. Are you tired?"

"In many ways, of many things, and life most of all. But I'm going to wait for her."

"Rest, then. Tomorrow we'll start rejuvenating Fangdred. And then we'll begin getting ready for this future contest."

Actually, Varthlokkur didn't much care about the coming struggle. He thought of it only as the price of finding his woman. "Where should I establish myself?"

"The Wind Tower would suit you best. You'll find the mirror especially useful. I'll show you how to get there."

Even the sparrow finds a home.

EIGHT: SUMMER, 996 AFE
HER STRONGHOLDS UNVANQUISHABLE

The vanguard of the allied army, hurrying ahead of the main force, reached the Candareen days earlier than Turran expected. He had to lock his gate long before he wanted. Luxos and Ridyeh were still away, snuffling along Haroun's backtrail.

As expected, bin Yousif commanded the expedition. And, as Grimnason, Turran's leading mercenary officer, predicted, the man persisted in the unexpected.

Redbeard and Turran crouched in moonlight atop the tall tower over Ravenkrak's gate, watching the camp at the foot of the Candareen. "There!" said the mercenary, indicating a flash of silver on the slope.

"You win." Turran paid out a handful of silver. "I would've bet anything his men would be too tired and his numbers too few."

"That's why he's coming. He knows how people think."

Turran turned to peer over the rear of the parapet into an apparently deserted courtyard. Half the garrison were hidden down there, waiting. He signaled them to be ready.

Bin Yousif's commandos reached the foot of the wall.

"They could've made it," Turran observed. "They're good. Wish I'd hired him first. No offense. You've proven just as able."

Arrows with light lines attached arced over the battlements.

"Metal arrows," said Grimnason. "They'll hook one in the crenellations, then send up their lightest man."

So they did. A climber quickly reached the battlements, pulled up a heavier rope, made it fast, turned to watch the castle.

"Haroun himself!" Turran growled softly. "We've got him this time." He glanced at the camp down the mountain. Its fires burned bright, supporting the appearance of the attackers waiting there for the rest of their army. But here and there on the mountain, moonlight glinted off metal. Those flashes would have remained undetected had it not been for Redbeard's insistent warnings.

One by one, twelve men clambered onto the battlements. They whispered, then spread out. Four followed Haroun down to the courtyard, to the base of the tower, to the tunnel leading through the wall. The others divided equally between the two gatehouses. Haroun's four tried to raise the inner of the two stone blocks sealing the tunnel.

Raiders left the gatehouses.

"We should've left somebody down there," Turran whispered. "They're bound to suspect something."

"But it's too late," Grimnason replied, chuckling. "They're already in the trap." He leaned over the parapet, signaled soldiers hidden among the rocks outside the gate.

A moment later, from below, "Stop! Drop your weapons!"

A bugle sounded two notes. Soldiers rushed into the courtyard and to the wall.

There was an uproar at the gate. Men screamed. Crossbows twangled. Steel rang on steel. Haroun and four of his men broke out, raced downslope. Bin Yousif shouted, "Back! Trap! Get back!"

Torches flared along Ravenkrak's wall. Ready trebuchets hurled their missiles. Arrow engines discharged volleys. Bowmen commenced loosing. Naphtha bombs from the trebuchets scarred the slope with fire. Soldiers with clothing aflame ran like beheaded chickens.

"That was easy," Turran observed. "But more serious assaults worry me. He's too damned crafty."

The others had gone inside. Nepanthe and Saltimbanco, with the wall to themselves, stared down the Candareen. Pools of naphtha still sputtered here and there, painting the broken rocks with eerie lights and shadows. Some of those shadows walked. Haroun's men were collecting their dead.

They stood in silence. Saltimbanco thought about Redbeard—Rendel Grimnason—Bragi Ragnarson. Why on earth had the man warned Turran? Ravenkrak would have fallen, otherwise, and they would have finished the job they had been hired to do. And he would have been in the enviable position of a tool that had never needed to be taken off the shelf.

What the hell was the man up to?

Nepanthe worried, too. She now understood the women's amusement—and didn't like it at all. She had fought herself since her first vague realization. Something deep inside her kept saying it would lead to something wicked.

But that dark corner of her mind relaxed her thralldom while she was with Saltimbanco. The romantic, light part of her soul stole mastery. Saltimbanco's very unconcern with it helped bring it forth.

A wounded man, not far downslope, screamed as his comrades lifted him. Nepanthe shuddered and moved nearer Saltimbanco. Her hand seized his. She was unaware of what she had done. He pretended not to notice.

A while later there was a sound from along the ramparts. Saltimbanco glanced up, expecting another of the sentries who passed regularly. Instead, his eyes met those of Grimnason and his wife. His narrowed. Nepanthe would have been startled by his expression. He showed unwonted hardness and anger. It fled instantly, but wasn't overlooked by the other couple. The man flinched. His wife stared back defiantly.

"Ah," said Nepanthe. "Captain Grimnason. Astrid. Astrid, you look lovely tonight."

"Uhn," Grimnason grunted. "Took a while to talk her into it. What do you think of the dress?" He wouldn't meet Mocker's eye.

"Fantastic. Astrid, really, riding clothes don't become you. You'd be the envy of every woman here if you went to the Great Hall like that. Don't you think so, Saltimbanco?"

"Huh? Oh, verily." His gaze and that of the officer sparked like rapiers meeting. "Madame Grimnason will make very fine Colonel's lady."

Nepanthe's hand tightened on his. "Oh, now you've let the cat out. It was supposed to be a surprise." To the others, she said, "Turran's endorsing you for promotion. He said he'd file with the Guild as soon as we raise siege."

"I'm not with the Guild anymore, Milady."

"They still claim you."

The captain shrugged. "They don't want anybody to get out. But they don't make it worth your trouble to stay in."

"Well, try to look surprised when he announces it. He thinks a lot of you, Captain. How do you always know what Haroun's going to do?"

"Hai!" Saltimbanco cried. "Thank great stars in sky Redbeard knows mind of invidious enemy! Elsewise, where we be now, eh? Maybe all done for, eh? Whole war thing done, and Ravenkrak fallen, maybeso."

The mercenary caught his meaning, but ignored him. "Milady, my people have been soldiers for generations. Tricks get passed down. One is to study the outstanding commanders of our times in case we have a run-in with them. I think I know Haroun fairly well, although I don't think I'd be able to trap him again."

"Is very good general, this Haroun," said Saltimbanco. "Has conquered Iwa Skolovda with bandits, outnumbered. Self, am afraid this obesity will soon be prisoner of same. Great castle is this, but great general is out there. Many men he has, more than we. Is miracle absolute he does not sit in Great Hall tonight. Is miracle absolute all is not done for Ravenkrak." Again, anger edged his voice. Nepanthe mistook it for fright. The Captain understood.

As did his wife. "Lady," she said, "can I talk to you about something? Alone? I'd like to borrow some things, and another dress. But we can't talk about it in front of the men."

Nepanthe nodded. She withdrew her hand from Saltimbanco's, realized for the first time that it had been there. She was startled. She hadn't been hurt. Something tingled inside her. For a second she was flustered, but collected herself and followed Astrid. They strolled into the shadow of the gate tower.

Mocker hardly waited till they were out of earshot. "What is game, Bragi? Mess should be done, but big thickhead opens mouth! Goes tootling off on path of own. Playing treason? Self, am six months unpracticed with rapier, but still can kill fast as lightning…"

The soldier flinched. He didn't doubt that the smaller man could outfence him. Few men alive could match Mocker with a blade. "I'm playing a hunch," he said. "There's something rotten in this setup, but I can't figure what. I stopped Haroun so we'd have time to find out. And I wanted to catch him so I could talk to him. Last time I had a chance at it I had to use all my imagination to keep Turran from laying hands on him."

"Last time?"

"Coming back from Iwa Skolovda. Shhh!"

A sleepy sentry passed, muttering a greeting. He paid them no special heed.

As usual, Saltimbanco was arguing the roundness of the Earth.

The guard gone, Saltimbanco snapped, "Speak on. Am very curious about empty purse that should be full tonight."

"I said there's something wrong. These Storm Kings are just bored people playing chess with live soldiers. Except for Turran, and maybe Valther, they don't give a damn about resurrecting the Empire. There's no real reason anybody should go to so much trouble to destroy them. So why'd the old man hire us? I want to know. I'll keep stalling till I find out…"

"Conscience?" Saltimbanco snorted. "Large friend of self suddenly develops conscience after so many years?"

"No. Self-preservation. If I knew where we stood, and we were safe, I'd cut Turran's throat in a minute—even though I like the guy. No, it's not conscience. We're being used, and I want to know why before my throat gets cut. I'm not changing sides. I'm just getting temporarily uncommitted. You're the one, if any of us does, who's got a reason for selling out."

"Huh?"

"Nepanthe. You two are getting awful thick."

"Is job old man paid for, to divide Storm King family, in case. To be man on inside, in case. Shh! Women come. Is great orb, like ball childrens play with, only big-big."

"What happened to the boat and the giant duck?" Astrid asked, chuckling.

"Hai! Yes. Is great round ball in boat on sea of Escalonian wine, propelled by web-footed duck through starry universe."

Grimnason forced a laugh. His wife slipped under his arm, pulled him away. She slid her arm around his waist.

Nepanthe watched them go, staring at their arms.

Grimnason was a soldier of nebulous origins. Only his wife and a few intimates knew much more than his true name, Bragi Ragnarson, and his country of birth, which was Trolledyngja, north of the Kratchnodian Mountains. But most people he encountered didn't care. They were interested only in his military skills. What employers didn't know—and a couple had suffered for it—was that Ragnarson and bin Yousif were intimates. From opposite sides they engineered conflicts to their own profit, and with such finesse that even losing campaigns contributed to their reputations. Mocker usually played interlocutor.

They hadn't gotten caught yet, though serious analysts at High Crag and on the Itaskian General Staff (each of which had cause to watch both men) were growing suspicious. Their cooperation during the El Murid Wars, and for a few years thereafter, couldn't be concealed. Any serious background check would turn it up.

But they concentrated on minor employers, desperate men who hadn't the time or resources to do much digging.

Unlike the old man who was their ultimate paymaster now, who had approached them with evidence in hand and a solid Grimnason identity for Bragi to assume.

Ragnarson had been born the son of a minor Trolledyngjan under-chieftain, Ragnar of Draukenbring. He had come by war experience, at ten, by sailing with his father through the Tongues of Fire to harry the coasts of Freyland. Then had come a Trolledyngjan war of succession in which Ragnar had followed the losing banner. Bragi and his foster-brother, Haaken Blackfang, had fled across the Kratchnodians and at sixteen had entered the Mercenaries' Guild.

The El Murid Wars had broken immediately. Bragi had found employment aplenty, and opportunities to demonstrate his talent for command. *And* he had met Haroun bin Yousif, the King Without a Throne.

At twenty he had been confirmed Guild Captain. He might have, had he wished, risen high. But he suffered critical character defects: gold fever and an inability to accept peacetime discipline. He had felt he could prosper more outside Guild auspices, as Haroun's accomplice, than as a colonel, or even general. The Guild was a mystery order, spartan, almost monastic, providing little opportunity for personal enrichment.

After a period of consistent failure free-lancing, Ragnarson had assembled a cadre of like-minded former Guildsmen and had returned to hire-swording. He wasn't popular with High Crag, the Guild headquarters, where the old men of the Citadel viewed him as a renegade. They sometimes threatened to accept his resignation.

Nepanthe worked at her embroidery fitfully, thinking. Someone knocked on her door. She was grateful for the interruption, but prayed it wouldn't be Saltimbanco. She didn't want to be alone with him right now. "Enter," she called, ringing for her maid.

Astrid came in timidly, daunted by the luxury of the sitting room. "I came about the clothes. Rendel wants me to wear them tonight."

"I had Anina set them out in the bedroom."

The maid arrived. "Milady?"

"Bring some wine please, then we'll help Astrid with the things we set out this morning."

"Yes, Milady." The maid curtseyed, left. A deep and abiding silence, of brooding women, engulfed the room. Astrid (whose name was Elana), wanted to offer advice and comfort, but fought herself. This woman was the enemy. Yet she couldn't hate Nepanthe. She felt too much compassion for the woman, who had done her no harm. Damn the machinations of men! She would rather be friends than foes.

The silence grew unbounded, frightening, cold. It had to be broken. "I can't thank you enough for loaning the clothes. A soldier's wife doesn't get nice things very often." Her words were just noise to kill the fearful silence.

"Then why stay with Rendel?" Nepanthe asked. Her face revealed a fleeting moment of hope. Astrid sensed that their conversation would slide around to Nepanthe's problem. "You're beautiful and well-bred."

Elana smiled involuntarily. Her mother had been an Itaskian courtesan of considerable notoriety.

"You're mannered and capable of moving in elegant society. You'd have no trouble attracting a Lord of estate."

She had, occasionally, early on, when younger and taking a few tentative steps along the red trail her mother had broken. Another reminiscent smile. "I guess I could have, if I'd wanted one. But Rendel caught my eye." Being able to lower her guard a little and tell a part of the truth was infinitely relaxing. This castle contained no one she could call friend, no one with whom she could just sit and make idle woman-talk. Few of Bragi's staff were married. "I don't miss the luxuries—much—because I don't get time to worry about them." Her smile grew wan. She *did* miss things, things she deeply wanted. A home, children, a few luxuries... But Bragi wasn't ever able to grab enough money... There was always that one more campaign before they could settle down. Maybe this one would really be the last, if that old man paid as well as he had promised, if Bragi decided to go ahead, if they weren't found out... The *if*s, all these terrible *if*s...

Nepanthe wore a shadow-frown of incomprehension.

"You don't understand," said Elana, voicing the obvious. She gathered her wits. Discussing Nepanthe's problems would help submerge her own. "When you meet the right man you'll know what I mean. They don't come in shining armor these days. And when you do find him, the silks and fancies won't mean much anymore. Fisherman, beggar, king, thief, it'll be all the same to you. A tent will be as good as a castle and straw as soft as down as long as you're together. But you've got to accept what comes. Look past the wrappings for the package's contents. Or you might spend the rest of your life wondering why you were such a fool.

"And I'm getting awfully preachy, aren't I?"

"You really love him, don't you?" Nepanthe asked. "Rendel, I mean." She grew flustered, feeling silly for saying the obvious.

Elana had spoken primarily to help Mocker, but, in retrospect, realized she was talking with her heart. "More than I knew, now that you ask. I'm surprised. The gods know it's been no honeymoon—we're both too bullheaded—but I don't think there's anything that could make me run him off. Yes, I love him. Even though I did the proposing myself." She laughed.

"You asked him?"

"I certainly did. He was a real hard case. Took a lot of convincing."

The maid brought wine, served them, told Elana, "If you come to the bedroom, I'll help with the dresses."

Nepanthe's sitting room had been wonderful, but Elana found the woman's bedroom a veritable fairyland. There, riches were thick as fallen leaves in autumn, and as comfortable. "Rendel promised me a room like this when we got married. Till now I never thought I'd even see one."

"Just presents from my brothers," Nepanthe replied, shrugging them off. "Jerrad killed the rugs. They're bearskins, mostly. Ridyeh got the mirror in Escalon. It's supposed to be magic, but none of us can work it. It's awfully old. Luxos made the bed. Carved it by hand, after one he saw in Itaskia, he says."

The maid moved behind Elana, began unlacing her clothing.

Nepanthe continued, "Valther gave me the paintings. Did you ever see anything like them?"

"Only once. In Hellin Daimiel, at a museum."

"That's where he got them—Hellin Daimiel. And I think they were stolen from a museum, but Valther wouldn't do anything like that. I don't think. He never did say how he got them. Brock gave me the little figurines." Tiny little castles and warriors, perfectly shaped, stood on a board no bigger than Elana's hand. "They're hand-carved. The clear ones are diamonds. The red ones are rubies. They're pieces for a game. I think they're stolen, too. Only a king could afford them."

By now, Elana was naked and shivering in Ravenkrak's unheated autumn air. As she joined the maid beside a pile of silken undergarments, she asked, "What did Turran give you?"

"Nothing!" Nepanthe snapped. "Not a thing."

"Milady!" said the maid, as though distressed. "Of course he did. There's the dress, that he said was the easy half of his gift." She giggled. She wasn't more than fourteen, an age when everything is laughter or despair.

Nepanthe bit her lip, frowned, turned away. "Anina, you talk too much."

The maid giggled again, went to a closet.

"Anina!"

Anina brought out a magnificent gown. Elana gasped. There was enough fine silk there to rig sails for a ship. "A wedding dress!" she exclaimed. "Nepanthe, that's the best gift of all."

Nepanthe's bitten lip turned white. Her small hands twisted within one another.

"It's just half the present," said Anina. "The rest's the man to go with it. See, the Lord does the marrying here."

"Enough!" Nepanthe spat. "Anina, get out! I'll help Astrid. Maybe a turn scrubbing floors would teach you to watch your tongue."

The maid tried to look contrite. She failed abysmally, giving way to a fit of giggles.

"Servants!" Nepanthe muttered.

"She meant no harm, Milady."

"I have a name. Call me Nepanthe. Sure, she meant no harm. But she presumes too much."

"I think it's a beautiful present."

Nepanthe jerked the laces with which she was fumbling. Elana gasped. "Which?" Nepanthe demanded.

"The dress, of course. I wore rags when I got married. What a dress! What a wedding would go with it! Like a coronation in old Ilkazar."

"I do not plan to get married, ever," said Nepanthe, each word measured. "I want no man crawling over me and pawing me like… like an animal in a breeding stall!"

Her intensity was frightening. Elana grunted as Nepanthe jerked savagely on another set of laces. She wanted to say something, anything, in rebuttal, comforting, or apologetic, but intuited that silence was best. The subject was closed—unless Nepanthe reopened it.

Silence, interrupted only by the rustle of clothing, hung thick in the bedroom, remaining unbroken till Nepanthe began helping with the shoes.

Elana sat on the edge of the bed. Nepanthe knelt before her, hooking the shoes. Staring at Elana's feet, she stammered, "What's it like, having a man?"

"What?"

Nepanthe's neck colored where her hair had parted and exposed the skin beneath. "You know, like *that.*"

Her answer, Elana knew, would be critical both to her own future and to that of this strange woman. She tried to come up with an instructive answer, couldn't. "What can I say? I can't tell you what it'd be like for you."

"Well, what do you think? Mother never liked it. She said it was wicked… that… well, I don't know."

"But she had seven children."

"I mean my stepmother. My real mother died when I was born."

"That's a face some women put on in company. I don't think very many take it to bed. It's not dirty or evil…"

"But what's it like?" Nepanthe asked plaintively.

Elana shrugged. She began with the basics.

"I know the mechanics…"

"Then what can I tell you? There's only one way to find out. The hard way."

Still looking down, Nepanthe whispered, "Does it hurt, the first time? I've heard…" She let it trail off.

"Some, for some women. You'll forget it quick enough. I hardly remember…"

Nepanthe rose suddenly, walked away. "You're done," she said. "Take a look in the mirror." Then, as Elana admired herself, "Astrid, I'm scared. I can't change! Sometimes, when he's here, I want to, but when I think about it… I don't. I don't want to change! I'm all mixed up. I wish I weren't a woman. Anyway, I wish I were a normal woman."

"Oh, not that abnormal, I think," said Elana, trying to calm her. "We're all afraid—deathly so—before, if we're expecting it to happen. It seems… well…

Oh, hell! I can't explain! It's just different, afterward. The fears go. Slow, for some, but they go. I can't tell you anything except that it's not wrong. Come on, dinner's waiting. Rendel'll be worrying, and Turran'll be holding everything up."

NINE: SUMMER, 996 afe
BEHIND WALLS THAT REACH TO THE SKY

"I wish they'd stop beating those drums!" Turran growled. Leaning on the battlements, he studied the enemy encampment. A dull throbbing echoed upward, like the heartbeat of a world. "They'll drive me mad!"

"That's the idea," said Ragnarson, leaning beside him. "War of nerves. An old bin Yousif trick. He heard they do it in Shinsan."

"It's working." The Storm King turned, glanced along the wall toward where Nepanthe and Saltimbanco strolled together. "Somebody's not bothered. Our windy friend's making headway."

Indeed. They walked hand in hand, and Nepanthe seemed unashamed of being seen.

"Ha!" said Redbeard. "*She's* making headway. He's lost a good four stone. What do you think of the match?"

After considering, Turran replied, "Nepanthe needs a man more than anything else in the world. A one-eyed, one-legged beggar from the blackest slum in Itaskia would suit me if she'd have him. But Saltimbanco pleases me. His origins seem humble, yet his heart's as noble as a king's. I wouldn't prevent a wedding, or even an affair. In fact, if I knew how I'd help him seduce her."

Grimnason nodded, offered, "If there's anything I can do..." Then, "Speaking of Itaskia, have you heard anything about Haroun?"

"No. Gold and knives have sealed a lot of mouths. Ridyeh's having trouble. How long before they reach the wall?"

Ragnarson looked down at bin Yousif's earthworks, long, lazy zigzags advancing up the Candareen. The heavy weapons had been unable to damage them. "Not soon."

"Number three trebuchet!" Turran bellowed. "Fire one at the center approach."

A missile arced through the air, trailing smoke, but fell short. Naphtha spewed and burned amongst broken rocks.

"Not quite," Ragnarson observed. "Another day or two."

"Can we hold till winter?"

Ragnarson was surprised. Turran with doubts about the invincibility of his fortress? Impossible! "They won't be ready to try the wall till autumn. And then they've got to get over it. I don't think they can. Not when they have to bring their gear up that slope under fire."

"Still, I'd like to delay them. Can't we make a sortie? To wreck their siegeworks?"

"I'll put Rolf on it. But it'd be risky. We can't afford casualties. We don't have enough men to defend the whole wall now. Maybe we could use Nepanthe's Iwa Skolovdans. They wouldn't be much loss. Blackfang and Kildragon have drilled them silly, and they're still not much better than recruits."

"What do you think of our chances?"

"Excellent. Standard assault procedure calls for a five-to-one advantage. They've got us by about three. Haroun knows that. But he's got something going, or he would've left. But I can't figure what." He glanced down. Saltimbanco and Nepanthe had left the wall. He saw them enter the Bell Tower. Mocker was certainly taking his time with her. But, from what Elana said, she was a stubborn case. Women. Remarkable creatures.

His thoughts turned to the old man who had hired them. Who was he? Why was the destruction of Ravenkrak so important to him?

Saltimbanco held the door for Nepanthe. She thanked him, walked to her embroidery frame, fidgeted with needles. There were always fires in Ravenkrak, even during the "summer." The chair wasn't as comfortable as when he had been heavier. He closed his eyes halfway and watched the flames through his lashes. They were curious iridescences.

Nepanthe toyed with her embroidery for fifteen minutes, then started pacing. Her gaze refused to leave Saltimbanco. They had been discussing the siege and Turran's plans, but their thoughts tended elsewhere.

Saltimbanco was frightened of himself, of his lusts, and that strange other feeling he had for Nepanthe. The latter he thought he could conquer, but the former... More than once, he had come near rape. And that would destroy everything.

Nepanthe, for her part, had finally admitted to herself that she loved this strangely frightened man. She had admitted that she wanted to... well, that she wanted. But she was terrified. Her talks with Astrid calmed her intellectual fear, but dark emotional currents still surged under the surface of her mind, far too deep to be easily stilled. She was sure she would die a virgin.

She circled the chair where he sat sleepily studying the fire through his lashes, thinking of attacking his ear the way Astrid had described. But no, that was too much. And she was too frightened.

She went to the front of the chair. He looked up with those strange brown eyes. She bit her lip. Her throat became tight and unresponsive. She couldn't say what she wanted. A flicker of emotion crossed his dusky face. What?

Trembling slightly, she took his hand, settled onto the arm of the chair. He squeezed gently, went back to studying the fire. She shifted, leaned toward him. Tightly, hoarsely, she said, "There's something you need..."

When he glanced up, she moved the last six inches and pressed her lips against his. It lasted just a second. Her jaw trembled. She shivered. She felt him quavering as he fought for control. She wanted him to drag her into his lap, but… The enchanted moment died. A door slammed somewhere in her mind. Fear struck. She backed away slowly, fighting herself, not wanting him hurt. She was running again, fleeing herself. She bit her lip painfully, returned to her embroidery.

Moments later, as she cursed a bad stitch and her own ineffectuality, he started snoring. It seemed a pointed sound, a mockery. It cut her to the heart of her being.

Why can't I be a normal woman? Why? Why? Why?

Nepanthe responded to the knock with a glum "Enter." But when Elana came in, she brightened. "Astrid. What do you think about me? Why am I so mixed up?"

Elana paused just inside the door, wondering what had happened. "Company leave already?"

"I kissed him… but he didn't do anything… and I got scared and ruined it."

"So?"

"Well, I wanted…"

"Nepanthe, let it be. You're worrying too much. Don't force it. It won't work. Let it ride. Suddenly, you'll look up and find everything roses." She hoped.

"Maybe. It's just… well… I can't explain."

"Why try? Nepanthe, you're a natural worrier, you know that? You find problems where there aren't any. Do you like being miserable? I mean, sure, it's something to think about, but don't hinge your life on it. You need something to keep you busy, that's what. That's your trouble."

"What? What use am I here? I'm just another mouth, worthless to Ravenkrak."

"You make me mad when you're like this. Something to do? Last night Rendel said Brock hasn't made any hospital arrangements. We'll need a place to doctor the wounded. I hear there's plenty of space in the Deep Dungeons."

"But it's filthy down there. They haven't been used for ages."

"We could clean them up, couldn't we? Look, we've got a castle full of women that're bored silly. This would keep them out of trouble."

"It'd take a lot of time…"

"It'll be a month before they're ready outside. Longer, if Rendel raids them like he's thinking."

"We'd better get started then."

Elana smiled. Her ploy had been effective.

"Let me get my wrap," said Nepanthe. "We'll get the keys, then see what's got to be done."

Elana, with Nepanthe, Saltimbanco, and the male Storm Kings, stood in the parapet of the Black Tower, over Ravenkrak's gate, silent in a strong wind, watching the midnight sortie. Below, besiegers had been working by torchlight till the sortie reached them. Their first warning had been the cries of their fellows. Now flames, fed by naphtha, were devouring lumber and tools. Tents in the workers' camp went up.

The wounded began coming in. The fighting went on. Torches coming up the mountain showed reinforcements on the way. Elana and Nepanthe fled to their makeshift hospital and began the sad, bloody business of putting soldiers together again. Most of the wounded were prisoners. With the enemy advance camp destroyed and two weeks' labor on the earthworks ruined, Ragnarson withdrew. He and Rolf mustered their companies in the courtyard for roll call.

Suddenly, Elana came running, winded from the climb out of the Deep Dungeons. "Bragi," she gasped, almost collapsing. "It's Haaken. He's bad hurt… And he's got… something on the old man."

"Damn!" He turned and bellowed, "Rolf! Kildragon! Elana, stick with him and keep Nepanthe away. Don't let him give us away." Rolf and Kildragon arrived. Ragnarson explained. "Haaken's found what we want. I'll go down as soon as we get muster."

"How is he?" Rolf asked.

"Out cold," Elana replied. "But I can't find anything wrong, even though he looks like he's dying. I'll have to keep him alive before anything." She started off.

"Wait!" said Ragnarson. "There's a room in the Lower Armories no one uses. If we can shuffle him in there, he'd be out of the way. Damn! Damn!" He was scared Haaken would give them away, scared he might lose the only family he had…

High above, Saltimbanco watched the party break up. He glanced at the Storm Kings. They were enthralled by the flames below the walls. He looked back into the courtyard, wondering what the trouble was. Elana had brought the news, so she was the one to see. "Self," he said, "am going down to Deep Dungeons. Will gentle brave troops."

"Ha!" Valther snorted. "Need an excuse to see Nepanthe, eh? Been neglecting you?"

Saltimbanco bowed slightly, took his leave.

TEN: THE YEARS 808-965 AFE
WHAT DOES A MAN PROFIT?

Fangdred changed rapidly, as did its master. The times when he was warm and companionable grew fewer, when he was irritable, more frequent. Which suited Varthlokkur. Two hundred years made aloneness a habit. Too much friendship too fast might set his feet on the wanderer's road again.

Fangdred changed, and in changing caused the Old Man's moodiness.

Servants came, poor people hired in Iwa Skolovda. Though frightened of it, they found service at Fangdred a better hope than any at home. They swept, scrubbed, repaired, replaced. They cooked, sewed, cared for the few horses that appeared in Fangdred's stables. Hogs came to the courtyards, with piglets, ducks, geese, chickens, goats, sheep, and cattle. There was a blacksmith and forge. His anvil rang through the day like a bell. A carpenter. His hammer and saw were busy from dawn till dusk. A miller. A weaver. A mason, a cobbler, a wainwright, a seamstress, a butcher, a baker, a candlestick maker. And their children. Many, laughing, tagging through the castle, plaguing the softhearted cook and baker for something sweet, throwing stones off the wall just to watch them drop out of sight. Varthlokkur often watched them from the Wind Tower. He had never been a child. Oh, and a piper. What a piper! In his own way, he worked a magic as powerful as Varthlokkur's, as immortal as the Old Man's. His twinkling enchantments ran through the castle with the smith's hammering, the carpenter's sawing, and the children's laughter.

As the castle grew homelike and her people settled in, Varthlokkur and the Old Man withdrew from her life.

So. The Old Man enters a courtyard where carpenter and smith are arguing with the mason about the repair of an interior wall. Their argument, and all other sound, ceases. Except the piping: the piper fears nothing. They dread the man who never dies, though he has done nothing to inspire dread.

So. Varthlokkur visits a courtyard where four little girls skip rope to the piper's tune. He watches from a shadow, unseen, amused. But when he steps out to ask about the song, the girls flee. He's hurt. Only the piper remains. He dreads not the Slayer of Ilkazar.

Hurt, the two withdrew from their servants. The Old Man grew irascible, Varthlokkur quiet. But each comforted himself with the knowledge of an advantage over fear: time. Generations would go and come, but they would endure. One day's frightened children were the grandfathers of another. Fear, like salt in the earth, would leech away.

And, a century later, the people no longer held their masters in dread. The Old Man could speak to his carpenter without having to ignore shaking limbs. Varthlokkur could hold one end of the rope for the jumping girls, and they would thank him when done, calling him Uncle Varth.

There was always a piper who was fearless.

The century came and went, slowly, with its attendant changes. One day the wizard, over breakfast, said, "I've not performed a divination in an age. I wonder…"

"If the mists haven't cleared off your lifeline?" The Old Man brightened. A divination promised diversion. "Shall we go to the Wind Tower?"

"Absolutely," Varthlokkur replied, catching his excitement. "Had I a patron god, I'd pray."

"Shall I seal the door?" the Old Man asked as they entered the wizard's workroom.

"Yes. I don't want anybody stumbling in." The Old Man worked a quick, simple spell. The door became part of the wall.

Varthlokkur went to a table where dusty thaumaturgical and necromantic instruments had lain undisturbed since his last divination. He had done little but read and research magic the past century. But neither knowledge nor skill had deserted him. Soon the mirror on the wall was a-flash, giving rapid, still views of the future. He whispered, whispered, narrowed the mirror's attention till he saw only events in which he was interested.

A few clouds veiling the time-river had faded. He stared downtime and saw something of the coming struggle. His theories seemed valid. The Norns and Fates would be at odds. He searched for his woman, caught a glimpse of her face.

"Ah!" the Old Man sighed. "She's beautiful." His eyes sparkled with appreciation. By the time the face faded, each knew it well.

Hair, black as a raven's wing, long, silken. Eyes, ebony and flecked with gold. Lips, full and red with a suggestion at their corners that she would seldom smile. There was also that, around her brows, which suggested she would be quick to anger. Spirited, but sad. A fine oval face with delicate features, marked by loneliness. Both men knew that look. All too often they had seen it in one another.

She was there and gone in an instant, but they recognized and knew her. And Varthlokkur loved her.

"How long?" the Old Man asked.

Varthlokkur shrugged. "Less than a century. A shorter wait than a century ago, but longer now that I've seen her. We'll look again in fifteen or twenty years."

"Was it my imagination?… Did you get the impression that this spat between the Fates and Norns is just plain jealousy? I got the impression that they will make the whole world a bloody chessboard—but out of plain old-fashioned covetousness. Settling whether science or sorcery rules will be a bastard son of the dispute. That the whole battle's over prerogatives."

"Maybe," Varthlokkur said after a minute of thought. "An analogy comes to mind. Something in Itaskia.

"The Itaskian King has two kinds of Royal monies and incomes: One belongs to him as an individual. The other belongs to the King personifying the state. The line of demarcation is vague. The time I mean, there were two fiscal officials, the Royal Treasurer and the Chancellor of the Exchequer, both jealous men with personal animosities. Each one tried to ruin the other with claims of infringement, incompetence, that kind of stuff. What both really wanted was complete control of the money. Fighting over it, in the name of the kingdom, they almost ruined the kingdom."

"I remember. I laughed when the King, when they demanded a judgment, took their heads. And I see the analogy. The Norns would be Treasurers, agents for the Gods. The Fates are Chancellors, responsible to the universe. Both want a hammerlock on dabbling in human affairs."

"About it. Makes you wonder what we're doing, taking sides."

"Uhm. Oh. There was something else. Something about Shinsan. Just a flicker there, that said Dread Empire. Did you catch it?"

After delaying, Varthlokkur replied, "No. I didn't see anything." He turned to a table stacked with magical texts.

The Old Man frowned, asked another question, again received an evasive answer. He decided to drop it. "What're you going to do now?"

"Back to research. I'm on the verge of a breakthrough. A chance to tap a new thaumaturgic Power, almost independent of what we know. Possibly even independent of the Poles."

The Old Man started. "The Poles of Power?"

Two Poles were believed to exist, one rumored to be in the hands of the Star Rider, the other totally lost. They were to the Power somewhat as the poles seen in the chemically generated "electricity" recently demonstrated at the Rebsamen University in Hellin Daimiel.

"Remember when Tennotini proposed his 'Uncertainty Principle'?"

"There was a lot of laughter."

"Looks like he was right. If we accept uncertainty, the sign of Delestin's Constant stops being fixed. That would destroy the concept of directionality." He grew excited. "Look what happens when I put a negative constant into my Winterstorm Functions. I think that, when I take the math to the next level, I'll show that I've opened a new frontier…"

"You lost me way back," said the Old Man. "I'm still wrestling with Yo Hsi's Prime Anchaics."

"Sorry. Before I go on, though, I think I'll take a little trip."

"Ilkazar?" The Old Man didn't look at his guest.

"Yes. A return to the scene of the crime, so to speak. Vengeance was a taste of bitter honey."

"A proverb. I'll add it to the book." Through the ages, the Old Man had been collecting pertinent sayings. "You could see the ruins from here."

"I'm after money. There's a little silver hidden where a tree once stood on a farm, and some gold in a place only I know. That's all wasteland now. Hammad al Nakir. The Desert of Death."

"The treasure?"

"Yes. There's a concealment spell on it."

"The treasure of an empire," the Old Man murmured. "Well, take care."

Varthlokkur returned some months later. He led a train of animals bearing the gold of Ilkazar. After the festivities attending his arrival, Fangdred returned to its customary quietness. That quiet lasted generations.

The Old Man strode Fangdred's windy, ice-rimed wall, caught in the grayest of depressions, considering a return to his long sleep. He and Varthlokkur had been together a century and a half. Nothing had happened. The intrigue was gone. Boredom threatened. His eyes no longer sparkled, no longer retained their reminiscences of youth. Yet he appeared much as he had the day of his awakening: of moderate height, thin, his beard streaming like a banner in the wind. He appeared eighty, had the agility of thirty. But his smiles had fled. Now his face often gathered in a frown. His servants had begun to avoid him. Though generations of closeness had eroded the terror of his name, he was still the Old Man of Fangdred, not to be antagonized when in a darkling mood. Those had been common of late.

Hair and beard whipping wildly, he abandoned the wall for the dubious comfort of the common room. That hall was nearly empty, but he took a seat at the head table without his curiosity being aroused. After a moment of staring into nothingness, he turned to those few servants who had had the courage to brave his mood.

"Steward, go to the Wind Tower. Ask Varthlokkur to come down."

The steward bobbed his head and left.

"Piper, play something."

This piper, like his ancestors, knew no fear. He cocked his eye at his master, assayed his mood, played the song that went:

> Let the day perish wherein I was born,
>   and the night which said,
>   "A man-child is conceived."
> Let that day be darkness!...

The Old Man knew the lament. He surged up. "Piper!" he thundered. "Don't mock me! Your head's not set on a neck of stone." He pounded the table, fist flashing pinkly, and shouted, "I've had it with your games. The wizard has to have you here, you play something for *him*!" He plopped down, face burning.

The piper, mildly intimidated, bowed, played:

> Awake, O North Wind,
>   and come, O South Wind!
> Blow upon my garden,
>   let its fragrance be wafted abroad.
> Let my beloved come to this garden,
>   and eat of its choicest fruits.

A song for a woman calling a lover to her bed, but near enough the wizard's case to mock. He played only the ending, pointedly, as Varthlokkur strode into the hall. Usually the wizard was angered by it, but today he merely laughed and slapped the piper's back in passing.

The Old Man, interpreting Varthlokkur's cheer as evidence he bore good news, shook some of his depression.

"You wanted to see me?" Varthlokkur asked. He was obviously more excited than he had been for a long time.

"Yes. But it might not be important now. You've brought news. What's happening?"

"The Game has finally opened," Varthlokkur replied. "No more empty maneuvers, no more recruitments. Somewhere this fine morning—I don't know where or how, because they kept it damned well hidden—the Norns made their first concrete move."

The Old Man's depression retreated further. He grew excited himself. Battle had been joined. Armies would march. There would be earthquakes, plagues, storms, and mighty works by magicians, as the Director used earthly pawns to cast a tragedy... And he would be in the middle of it for the first time since the Nawami Crusades. He had missed the Director's more recent epics. "Great! And a minute ago I was thinking about going back to sleep..."

The piper tootled a passage. The Old Man sprang up, raging. "Must we endure that fool? I've had too much of him and his ancestors' mockery!" His mood hadn't retreated far. The piper withdrew before anything more could be said. He was fearless, but not without sense.

"We need somebody to remind us we're only human," said Varthlokkur. He was pleased by the Old Man's reaction to the news. Despite the Old Man's rage, he broached a matter that had been bothering him. "There's something I want, if you'll allow it."

"What?" The Old Man continued staring after the dusky little piper.

Varthlokkur leaned, whispered.

The immortal countered, "You think she's willing?"

The wizard shrugged.

"Ask her *after* the ensorcelment, I'd say."

Varthlokkur nodded.

The Old Man clapped his hands. "Mika!" A servant came running. More returned from their hiding places. "Mika, go to the Wind Tower and bring us..." and he named a great many items. Varthlokkur nodded agreement to each. The Old Man knew his life-magicks.

"Marya, help him," Varthlokkur told a plump young woman standing nearby. "And tell your father that I want to talk to him."

She nodded quickly and hustled Mika toward the door.

Marya was Varthlokkur's personal servant, a position she thought the most important in the castle. Very much in awe of her master, she had, from that awe, conceived an emotional attachment. She worshipped him. Not a bright girl, she was, however, dedicated, and even that was more than Varthlokkur asked. She was a dark woman, short, heavy and rounded. She fought her weight with an implacable stubbornness. Her attractiveness came from within: warmth and a capacity for unshakable love. She was an ideal interim woman, the first of the two Varthlokkur's destiny had promised.

The wizard spoke with the girl's father. There was a moment of debate. A certain magic was mentioned. The father gave his assent.

Excitement rippled through the hall. The word spread: a sorcery was to be performed in the common room. The folk gathered for a unique treat. Their masters had never performed their wizardries openly.

Marya, Mika, and the equipment arrived. Varthlokkur and the Old Man set it up, established the preparatory runes, chanted the invocations, were ready. Varthlokkur quaffed a mug of bitter elixir, stepped to the focus of power for the magick. The Old Man, in a good tenor, sang the spell of initiation. Then, silently, he waited, as did the scores in the darkening hall.

Darkening? Yes. Soon all light had been banished save that of the cloud of gray silver forming about Varthlokkur. It grew increasingly dense, till he was totally concealed. Motes in the cloud sparkled, swept about the wizard like a tiny silver whirlwind. Sound came, increasing in pitch to a whine; colors swirled kaleidoscopically, mixed with animate shadow, splashing over floor and ceiling and walls; there were smells of lilac in spring, sour old age, boots wet in the rain, a thousand others quickly come and gone. Then, suddenly, the silver dust winked away, or fell. Light waxed. A murmur ran through the hall. In the power nexus, round which the dust had orbited, a youngster of twenty-five stood where an old man had taken his position.

Yet there was no mistaking his identity. This was Varthlokkur as he had appeared before the walls of Ilkazar, dark with dark hair, thin, hawklike of face, yet a handsome young man. He wore a winning smile as he asked Marya the question.

She fainted.

According to Varthlokkur's wishes, the Old Man, as Lord of Fangdred, married them later that day. Marya went through the ceremony in a daze, unable to grasp her good fortune. Varthlokkur, however, saw it all with a cynic's eye, in schoolmaster's terms. He needed training in dealing with women. Marya would serve.

Yet he treated her perfectly from that day forward. She, not bright, counted herself fortunate—though there were times he unwittingly caused her sadness.

Varthlokkur, a man despite the darkness upon his soul, did conceive an affection for her as time passed (rather as a man for a faithful pet), though never did it rival the feeling he had for she downtime. He permitted Marya no children for a long time, and then only when he saw that the lack was crippling her very soul. She bore him one child, a son.

They would grow old together, and eventually Marya would pass on. But during her lifetime Marya would witness the early moves in the Great Game begun the day of her marriage.

Seven years elapsed after the wedding. Early in the eighth the child was born, brown and round like his mother, with her quietness, and, from the sparkle of his eyes, blessed (or cursed) with his father's intelligence.

One cold winter's day, with a wind howling around the castle and snow blowing down from even higher country, with ice in places a foot thick in Fangdred's courts, Varthlokkur, the Old Man, and Marya took seats in the chill chamber atop the Wind Tower, watching the mirror. The wind rose with time, screaming like souls in torment. An unpleasant day for a birth. Another birth, overwhelmingly important to Varthlokkur.

The mirror presented a peek into a faraway room, deep in the heart of another wind-bound tower. In Ravenkrak, cold and stark as Fangdred, harsh as a weathered skull, home of the Storm Kings. A new member of that family was to arrive. A girl-child.

Marya didn't entirely understand. No one had bothered to explain. She felt distress at her husband's interest in the event. *Why* the interest? she wondered.

A bedridden woman lay centered in the mirror.

"She shouldn't have children," the Old Man observed. "Too slight. Yet this's her seventh, isn't it?"

"Yes," said Marya, to his initial remark. "She's in great pain."

Varthlokkur winced. He read accusation into her words, as though she were asking why she hadn't experienced that particular pain more often. She wanted more children. But the indictment existed only in his mind. She hadn't the guile or subtlety.

"The spasms are closer now," said the Old Man.

"It's time," Marya added, sympathetically.

Indeed. The woman's husband and a midwife moved to her bed. Servants sprang into action, bringing rags, hot and cold water, and spirits to ease the pain. In the background, a man with a falcon riding his shoulder fed wood to a huge fireplace, vainly trying to warm the room.

The woman brought forth a girl-child, as the divinations had promised. She was ugly, shriveled, red, and not the least remarkable. But Varthlokkur and the Old Man remembered another vision of her, as an adult, seen in the mirror earlier. Her father named her Nepanthe, after a magical potion which banished all cares from a man's heart. He placed her at her mother's breast, wrapped both against the angry chill, and resumed managing his castle. Unstaunchable hemorrhaging claimed the mother's life within the hour.

There was great joy in Fangdred when it was over. Varthlokkur and the Old Man declared a holiday and ordered a feast. A bull was slaughtered, wine brought forth, games taken out, contests held, and the piper driven to a frenzy of playing. The people danced, sang, and everyone had a wickedly good time.

Except Marya. She was more than ever confused, and her feelings had taken a battering.

And then the piper.

As day marched into evening and the wine-cask levels sank to the lees, as more than one reveler passed from happiness into drunkenness, more than one mood abjured gaiety. The Old Man grew reticent and testy, till he spoke only in monosyllabic growls and snarls. In his cups, time piled on him, millennia deep in weight. All the evil he had seen and done returned to haunt him. "Nawami," he muttered several times. "My guilt." All the boredom, that only his wickednesses had interrupted, returned to remind him how much more of both awaited his future. He grew increasingly depressed. Death, the specter he had never beheld, became a desirable, lovely, mocking lady, a will-o'-the-wisp forever an inch beyond his reaching fingers.

And Varthlokkur, too, found all his days returning as the lift of the wine began to fail and his temples began to throb. He remembered everything he wanted to drive from his mind: deaths in ancient times; his years in Shinsan and echoes of the bargains he had made there, that he might receive his education; and the hidden evils in his use of those who had become his allies in the destruction of Ilkazar. They were dead now, those people and those days—and many because of him. How many people had died with his name and a curse on their lips? He remembered the screams in dying Ilkazar... Till now they always had remained confined to his worst nightmares. But now, through the throbbing ache left by over-indulgence, they invaded his waking mind...

"Abomination!" the Old Man roared, hurling an empty flagon at the piper. He surged up, smashed a fist against the table. "I told you not to play that!"

The piper, too deep in his cups himself, bowed mockingly, repeated the passage. Silence enveloped the hall. All eyes turned to the Old Man, who had drawn a knife from the wreck of a roast. He began stalking the clown.

The piper, realizing he had gone too far, ran to Varthlokkur. The wizard calmed the Old Man.

Poor fool! No sooner was he safe from one Lord than he antagonized the other with passages from *The Wizards of Ilkazar*. Anything else Varthlokkur could have forgiven. His mood wouldn't permit this.

He gave no warning...

A stumbling, lengthy spell he chanted, often pausing to correct his wine-tied tongue. With a sudden handclap and shout, it was done. The piper drifted upward, weightless. With a growl, Varthlokkur kicked him, spinning him across the room. He shrieked, flailed the air, vomited, and spun into the Old Man's orbit.

It was a pity that Marya and the women had retired. A tempering feminine presence might have averted disaster.

The Old Man seized an arm, spun the piper, then hurled him into a mass of drunken retainers, few of whom had much love for the fool. The little guy habitually told truths nobody wanted to hear.

Pack instincts came to the fore. The piper became a shrieking ball bouncing about the room, with Varthlokkur and the Old Man leading the baiting. They were animals baying after defenseless prey, their cruelty feeding itself. Someone remembered the fool's fear of heights. In a whooping mass, the mob swept from the common room to the outer wall.

Hurled screaming outward, the piper hung over a thousand feet of nothing. He wailed for mercy. They laughed. The wind carried him away from the wall. Varthlokkur, smiling malevolently, drew the piper in until he clawed desperately at the battlements—then released him completely. Down with a wail he hurtled, crying his certainty of death, only to be stopped a dozen feet short of icy, jagged rocks.

The wind drove tendrils through tiny openings in Varthlokkur's clothing. The chill proved sobering. He realized where he was, what he was doing. Shame struck in a sticky gray wave, shattering his insanity. He pulled the piper in, prepared to defend him... And saw there wasn't any need. The cold had had its effect on everyone. Most were leaving, to be alone with their disgrace.

Varthlokkur and the Old Man apologized effusively, offering restitution.

The piper ignored them. He said not a word as he hurried off to nurse his rage and fear. His departing back was the last they saw of him.

A distraught Marya dragged Varthlokkur from dismal dreams. Groaning with hangover, he demanded, "What?"

"He's gone!"

"Uhn?" He sat up, rubbed his temples, found no relief. "Who?"

"The baby! Your son!" Without comprehending, he studied what tears had done to her dusky face. His son? "Aren't you going to do something?" she demanded.

His head began clearing, his mind working. Intuitively, he asked, "Where's the piper?"

Within fifteen minutes they knew. The fool, too, had disappeared, along with a mule, blankets, and food. "Such cruel revenge," Varthlokkur cried. He and the Old Man spent days in the Wind Tower, hunting, hunting— but finally had to concede defeat. Man and child seemed to have vanished from the face of the earth.

"The Fates have used us evilly," said the Old Man. "Cruelly."

Indeed. They had taken a hostage to insure Varthlokkur's participation in the Great Game.

Marya was disconsolate for a time, but eventually made peace with herself. Women of her world often had to accept the loss of children.

ELEVEN: AUTUMN, 996 AFE
THE FIRES THAT BURN...

Again, Saltimbanco sat in the chair before Nepanthe's fireplace—but she was away, Downdeep, tending the wounded. She should be back soon. Her workload had eased as wounds healed. She now had time to spend with her man—for so she sometimes thought him, and so everyone named him. Only Saltimbanco himself was unsure he fit the part. With matters so nebulous between them, she seemed little closer than a friend. Away, as now, she disturbed him not at all. In her presence his soul turned chill. There was something about her, icy and strange, incomprehensible, that made him feel stark emotional nothing-ness when she was near. He went through the motions she permitted, but they somehow seemed directed toward someone else, an imaginary construct, not the genuine woman. An emotional vacuum separated them, one he couldn't fill while her fears persisted. Oh, he had found sex less important than he had earlier thought—but her unreasoning fear! It birthed an unnatural ten-sion devouring the hope of their relationship. Seldom had he been so far at sea—almost as far out as she claimed to be herself.

As he sat thus thinking, examining the relationship, peering at the fire through half-closed eyes, there came a knock at the door. He rose, went, found Elana. "Woman is in Deep Dungeons."

"I know. Look, Haaken is out of his coma. They're going to talk to him. You want to come down?"

"Maybe later. Am needing report, though. Meanwhile, must talk with strange woman." He was silent a moment, then asked, "What is problem for same? Am unable to breach mental walls thicker than ramparts surrounding Ravenkrak."

"She's afraid…"

"Am making no such demands. Woman's body is her own. Am living without that. Is total aloofness and coldness which makes for sadness of this one."

"That's not her only fear. She's afraid she'll hurt you."

"Is stupid! Crazy."

"Foolish, anyway, but real enough for her. If we weren't besieged, she'd run away. She feels trapped. All her fears are closing in. She's uncomfortable. More than she's ever been. There's nowhere to run; she's afraid to accept; so she fights.

"There're cycles in her moods, you know. Sometimes she loves you and wants you—then the fear takes over. Then she can't fight. Or won't."

"What can this one do?"

"Be patient. What else?"

"Self, am being patient for many months. Love grows…" There! He had admitted it at last. "… but patience wears tinsel-thin. Is little finger of frustra-tion-born wrath curling like serpent in back of mind. Is getting very difficult of control. Times are, self is tempted to scream, 'An end!' and go over wall, away, and damned be crazy woman with weird inside-of-head. Many pieces gold is not so tempting as surcease from mental mix-up. Wine and women soon make this one forget, is hoped. Soon, very soon, will do same. Beating head against wall is like for men outside castle. Gets nothing but sore spots. Ravenkrak wall is impossible of scaling: no booty for men outside. Nepanthe wall is impossible of scaling: no treasures for sad fool. Will leave very soon."

Elana started to say something, stopped as a door slammed below.

"Weird woman comes," said Saltimbanco. "Am no longer in mood for seeing. Will slip out back way. Come tell what Blackfang says."

Nepanthe arrived in time to witness his retreat. "What?…"

"He's unhappy."

"We're supposed to lunch together."

"He loves you, and you're not playing fair. He's thinking of going over the wall."

"He wants to desert?"

"Not desert. Escape. He feels trapped."

"Aren't we all? But it'll be over come winter."

"Don't be dense!" Elana snapped, harsher than she intended. "*You*'re the reason he feels trapped. After getting nowhere for so long, he'd rather run and forget. Why should he beat his head against a wall?"

"But you know the trouble I have even been *talking* about that…"

"*That* isn't the problem. It's the other barriers you put up."

"Like what?"

"So many things. Your opinion of yourself, for one thing. You think you're not good enough for him. So you put him off. And then there's the things you talk about doing when the war's over. They aren't very realistic. But you hang on to them to keep the real world from getting to you. Only you keep Saltimbanco out too. And being moody all the time doesn't help."

"You're harsh, Astrid."

"Now the hurt puppy look? What'll move you? Everybody's been patient so long. If a beating would help, I'd tell Rendel to give you one. For your own good. Nepanthe, we're talking about a man whose whole life revolves around *you*. You're killing him and you don't much seem to care. In fact, you're doing everything you can to make him more miserable. Yet you say you love him! Look, you're both twenty-nine. That's a lot of lost years. You can't make those up. And you want to throw the rest away? Grow up, Nepanthe! Wake up! You're wasting something precious."

"But…"

"You always have an excuse, don't you? Think about this. Ten years from now, when you're sitting here in your tower, what will your past be? A wasteland as barren as these mountains?"

"Astrid…"

"I don't want to hear it! I haven't got time. I'm going down to my husband. He's real. You're about to make a nail-biter out of me, too."

"Astrid…"

But Elana left, ignoring her plea. Nepanthe slumped, entered her sitting room, strode to her fireplace. After a moment, she snatched a figurine off the mantel, hurled it across the room.

The crash brought the maid. She found Nepanthe attacking her embroidery with a dagger.

Elana stamped across the courtyard, still fuming.

Valther burst from the tower where old Birdman kept his pigeons. He was pale, stricken.

"Is Nepanthe in the Bell Tower?"

She nodded. As he ran past, he shouted, "Get your husband, and Saltimbanco if you see him, down to the Lower Armories. Fast!" He vanished into the Bell Tower.

Something had happened. What? Then she remembered that Bragi was in the Lower Armories talking to Haaken. The game could be up if they were overheard.

Minutes later she hurtled through a door, gasped, "Something's happened. Valther's running around screaming, collecting everybody for a meeting in the sorcery chamber. Bragi, you're supposed to be there."

Ragnarson froze, thought. "Kildragon." He indicated his brother. "Gag him and hide him. Stick with him. Everybody else, down to the Deep Dungeons. Play 'visit the wounded.' Elana, where's Mocker?"

"I saw him a little while ago, but I don't know where he is now. He's got it bad. Nepanthe isn't helping."

"Sometimes he goes up where the back walls meet and just stares into the canyon," said Kildragon, knotting the gag behind Blackfang's head. "That's where he'll be if he wants to think. It's the loneliest place in Ravenkrak."

"All right, let's get," Ragnarson growled.

Ten minutes later, exhausted, Elana reached the top of one of the short rear walls. A few yards away, staring into the canyon behind the Candareen, were Jerrad and Saltimbanco. They passed a wineskin while grumbling to one another. Silence greeted her approach.

"Something's happened," she said. "Valther wants you in the Lower Armories."

"What is it now?" Jerrad demanded.

Saltimbanco said nothing. After a glance at Elana, he turned back to the canyon... What? What was that? Up the face of that impossible cliff? So! He turned, threw his arm across Jerrad's shoulder. "Come, old friend. We make them happy, eh? But we take this wine, too. Make us happy, too. Hai! We raise some hell at meeting, eh? Good! We go."

The others were waiting when they arrived. Jerrad took his usual seat. Saltimbanco assumed Ridyeh's, saying, "Old plan of fat rascal big failure, eh? New intrigue for finding spy? Maybe still chance for same to be here?"

"Don't sit there!" Valther snapped. "Take a chair off the wall."

Eyebrows rose. Valther hadn't yet divulged his secret. He did so once Saltimbanco settled himself.

"I just picked up a message from Luxos. He used his last pigeon to send it…" He paused. Sorrow and anger fought for control of his face. "Ridyeh's dead!" It was almost a scream.

"What?"

"How?"

"Are you sure?"

Ragnarson and Saltimbanco sat quietly, unsure what to say or do. The operation had just turned nasty. A member of the family had been killed. Their treachery could be pardoned no longer.

"Shut up!" Valther bellowed into the clamor. "All I know is that he was murdered two weeks ago by one of bin Yousif's assassins. Luxos says he was onto something. He went to buy information and never came back. They found him floating in the Silverbind, tied wrist to wrist with the informer. They'd both been knifed. Luxos says he's coming home before he gets the same."

Into the stillness that followed, Turran interjected, "All right, it's no game anymore. We've got a debt to repay now."

"When do we kill Itaskia?" Brock asked. He made it sound like a simple, unarguable balancing of the scales: a city for a brother.

"No, we can't do that," Valther growled. "We can't afford any more enemies. And it's not Itaskia's fault anyway. Bin Yousif did it."

"Bin Yousif is a damned Itaskian War Ministry client," Brock countered. "He's their hole card against El Murid and Lord Greyfells both. Anything he does, you can bet the Ministry is in it up to their necks."

"Damn it!" Nepanthe cried. "Can't we break this siege?"

"No," said Turran. "We don't have the strength. I can't ask Rendel to commit suicide. What's that got to do with it, anyhow?"

Nothing. She was looking for a path of escape from other problems.

One of Ragnarson's mercenaries burst in, put an abrupt end to the meeting. "Captain, they're comin'!"

"Sound the alarm, Uthe."

"Been ringin' a couple minutes. The companies are on station. The cats and ballisters are firin'."

"Well, let's have a look." He rose. "Get moving!" Turran thundered. "The walls!"

When Ragnarson reached the main courtyard he found it a-riot with hurrying men and women. There seemed no apparent purpose to their motion, yet it was without panic, and quickly sorted itself out. The hurry had, in fact, been drilled in during long training, as support for those on the walls. There, men plied bows and served heavy weapons with cool efficiency. The women handed up fresh ammunition. A storm of death fled the battlements.

Ragnarson reached the command post atop the gate tower, quickly surveyed bin Yousif's assault. Haroun had brought up ladders and grapnels, but his attack teams were retreating already. Just a probe. Had Haroun found a weak point? Would he exploit it before Turran finished doing his sums and cleansed his castle? Ragnarson knew he didn't have much time to get Haaken's information. His margin was getting damned narrow. Self-preservation demanded that he plant his feet firmly somewhere, soon.

"Congratulations," said Turran. "Your drills paid off."

"He wasn't serious, just probing. Will you excuse me?" Awaiting no answer, he hurried down to Haaken's hiding place. "The gag!" he snapped on entering. Kildragon removed it. "Well, Haaken, you remembered anything?"

"Yes," Blackfang grumbled. "There was this old codger who looked like he was in charge. I figured to put him in the ground when the odds looked right. So when he wanders off by himself, I go after him. I swear, I never made a sound, but when I'm ten feet away, he jumps around, points a finger, and the next thing I know for sure Elana's waking me up. Bragi, he was some sort of spook-pusher."

"That's it? That's all?" Bragi tried shaking his brother, but Haaken had lost consciousness again.

"Don't get excited," Elana told him. "He already told me most of it. He said the old man kept talking to himself. That he remembers him standing over him, looking sick, and muttering something like, 'Varth, you're doing it again. Should've stayed in Fangdred. Should've never left the Dragon's Teeth. This's all it gets. More blood on your hands.'"

"The Dragon's Teeth, eh? Ah! The Old Man of the Mountain? Sonofabitch!" His last word was a bellow.

"What?"

"I've got it. The Old Man of the Mountain. Gold of Ilkazar, paying us and Haroun. A sorcerer named Varthlokkur. The things Rolf said Nepanthe raved about in Iwa Skolovda. There's a Varthlokkur in *The Wizards of Ilkazar*. Legends are, he lives with the Old Man of the Mountain. Add it up. If this's the same one, we're in it big. He's supposed to be the greatest wizard ever."

"So what?" Kildragon asked, unimpressed. "So we know who he is. We don't know why he dragged us in."

"Power, probably. There're things here he'd want bad. The Horn of the Star Rider. The weather control things." Ragnarson shook his head. The theory seemed inadequate. Yet nothing else came to mind.

Slowly, in a dark mood, Saltimbanco stalked the icy corridors. The question of the old man occupied but a tiny portion of his attention. The remainder went to Nepanthe, to dark arguments and fierce recriminations. A bitter conflict was rehearsing in his head. He felt down, trapped, frustrated, and obliquely angry. He loved, and was continually thwarted. Nepanthe also loved, he knew, but her strange fears and little-girl dreams stood between them like a barrier as impenetrable as time.

It occurred to him that, if he permitted it, the nonsense could go on forever. Elana had described her argument with Nepanthe, which had done little good. Nepanthe remained the same distant, fearful, dreaming woman-child. Well, he had decided, there had to be an end. There *would* be an end. He was done being an emotional handball. Purpose hardened. His stride quickened.

Outside, the first white flecks of winter fell. Time, it seemed, had finally rallied to the Storm King banner. The snow was weeks early.

In the Bell Tower he learned that Nepanthe was in the Lower Armories. Through a window he saw the snow, suddenly realized how near the end had come. He hoped the old man held no grudges, and Nepanthe likewise. When Haroun came, when Ravenkrak fell, he would have to show his true colors—and might then be trapped between parties thinking him traitor. Would the old man pay as promised? He'd have trouble if he didn't. Haroun had an army, and was notoriously short on patience. And Nepanthe. Would she hate him? Would she reject him forever?

These thoughts, and a thousand as grim, stalked his soul as he awaited the woman. Settled in that fireside chair, engrossed in worry, he remained unaware of her entry till she spoke. He glanced up. "Hello."

Her face was colorless. She was suffering her own worries. He almost relented. But the hardness grew within him. It would permit no further vacillation. There must be resolution. A beginning or ending.

"Nepanthe," he said, voice edged with a steeliness previously unshown. "We are going where? Same nowheres? Or would you grow up?"

His hardness and obvious tension so startled Nepanthe that she could stammer only, "I… well…"

His determination hardened further. Through clenched teeth, he growled, "You must make big decision in day. By supper tomorrow. A set wedding day, or no. If no, despairing self is going over wall. Cannot endure off-again, on-again love. Ravenkrak falls before end of month."

"What?"

"Set wedding day, or no. Is ultimatum. No more games. Answer by tomorrow." He strode out, dark and angry.

"Wait! You've got to give me time!"

"Am!" He slammed the door behind him.

Nepanthe stared at it as if it were a dragon astride her road to freedom. Everything was falling apart. She couldn't marry! Couldn't he understand? She loved him, yes, but the truth was, she wasn't ready to accept him as more than someone to lean on when things got rough. She didn't want him to be a someone she owed a responsibility. Biting her lip, she turned toward her bedchamber.

Anina blocked the door. "Tough, ain't it?"

Nepanthe stared, surprised again.

"Ah, well." Anina laughed weakly. "You'll give him the gate now." She returned to the bedroom, came out shortly. She carried a bag.

"Where're you going?" Nepanthe demanded. "I need help dressing for supper."

"Find somebody else. My man doesn't want me around you anymore." That man was Rolf, maneuvering in Mocker's favor. Nepanthe was crushed. Even Rolf, her faithful commander and aide since those first days in Iwa Skolovda…

For the second time in minutes, her door slammed in her face. Another in her mind opened, releasing fears. She threw herself on her bed, wept and thought. She didn't go to supper. Nor did she sleep that night.

As dawn arrived grayly through falling snow, she stood at a window staring toward Haroun's camp, seeing nothing. Her eyes looked inward on rage at the world and people pushing her. What right had they?…

She began pacing. Slowly, as her anger grew, her face reddened. Long-forgotten tears dribbled from the corners of her eyes. "Damn-damn-damn! Why won't they leave me alone? I don't want anybody. I want to be myself!" And a little voice, mocking back in a corner of her mind which seldom allowed its denizens free of shadow, chuckled wickedly, *You're a liar!* "I don't want to be chained!" *Ha! What're your dreams, if not chains that bind? What're the people and things with which you surround yourself, if not walls that keep you in? Run, and all life ahead will be a wasteland as desolate as the past. What'll you do when your bright tomorrows have all become the skeletons of yesterdays? Weep? Why? You won't know what you've missed, only that you were never complete.*

It was a night worse than any from those nightmare-haunted years before Saltimbanco's coming. She wept till tears would come no more, destroyed things, screamed, raged—and could discover no escaping a decision.

Strange, that. She didn't worry the goods and bads of the decision Saltimbanco had thrust upon her, but whether or not it should be made. Decisions were anathema. Each became another brick in the wall of the cell of reality. Each committed her.

Next noon hunger finally drew Saltimbanco to the Great Hall. There he found Turran, Valther, and Brock, directing soldiers who were dismantling the plank-and-trestle tables. He seized a half-loaf and some wine before it could be spirited away, wandered over to the Storm Kings. "Self, am wondering what is happening." All the excitement and anguish of the news of Ridyeh's death seemed banished. He was glad, but wondered why.

"You don't know?" Turran countered. "I guess not. That's her style. Well, I'll never tell."

Brock, usually undemonstrative, gave Saltimbanco a friendly punch on the shoulder, but also refused enlightenment.

Anxious to remain as anonymous as possible these last few days, Saltimbanco left the Great Hall. He intended to stroll to the fortress rear to check the canyon, but found himself straying toward the Bell Tower instead. He surrendered to the impulse.

How haggard Nepanthe appeared when she answered his knock! In silence she let him in. He saw she had been mending her damaged embroidery. Once comfortable in the overstuffed chair, he leaned back, closed his eyes, acted his usual self, waited. Nepanthe had too many woes to worry Ridyeh's death. Here he was safe.

She, biting her lip again (she had developed a sore from doing it so frequently), stared at him a long time. She was pale and more frightened than ever. Her decision troubled her deeply, tormenting the roots of her fear. But she was determined to stand by it.

She slowly moved toward his chair. Shaking. He pretended snores, through cracked eyelids watched anger cross her face. With that to impel her, it seemed she feared less.

He opened his eyes, looked up as she slipped her hand into his. Still biting her swollen lip, she gently tugged. He rose, followed her to her bedroom.

Drums echoed through Ravenkrak's shadowed halls. Trumpets proclaimed the occasion. Bright silk banners flew from every tower. The garrison was out in full dress. The Storm Kings had clothed themselves richly, in contrast to their usual spartan dress. Saltimbanco, no longer of remarkable girth, wore formal clothing borrowed from Brock: a black cape edged with silver, scarlet tunic and hose, and the polished weapons of a Lord. Bathed and combed and dressed, he seemed not at all the clown.

Following Turran's directions—the Storm King was as magnificent as any southern King—Saltimbanco positioned himself beside a dais a-head the Great Hall. The folk of Ravenkrak sat on benches athwart the hall, an ocean of restless white and brown and black faces. Suddenly he was terrified. As it was for Nepanthe, this was no day he had ever desired. Yet he needed her, had to be tied to her.

The drums took a new cadence. The trumpets sounded their final call. The bride had abandoned her tower. She would return alone nevermore.

Turran mounted the dais. His was the task of binding. Orange and gold, scarlet and purple, motionless, he loomed like a fire demon.

From the Bell Tower, proceeding along a dark, cleared aisle between banks of snow, though the continuing blizzard, the bride's party started toward the hall. Six women, clad in dark green embroidered with thread-of-gold, carried Nepanthe's train. Liveried pikemen marched at either hand. All moved with a slow, measured step despite the cold. Ravenkrak's weddings were performed with regal pomp and deliberation.

The bride's party reached the Great Hall. Valther and Jerrad drew their swords and assumed Nepanthe's guardianship. They advanced on the dais slowly.

Saltimbanco experienced eternity during that approach. He stared, marveling anew at Nepanthe's beauty, her dark eyes and hair, her soft skin and delicate features. She seemed beatific this evening, unworldly, under some ecstatic enchantment. Her brothers, too, were under the spell. Briefly, he forgot his fears, hoped this would amply distract them. For the moment they might have thought Ridyeh still living.

Nepanthe reached the dais. The drums fell silent. The ceremony began…

As if bounced through time, Saltimbanco realized it was over, done. Was it true? Yes. The people were leaving for the parties. Where had time gone?

Nepanthe finally looked into his eyes. He took her hand, squeezing gently. At that moment, in that place, she showed neither fear nor doubt.

It was too late for either. She had become committed. She would fight for the commitment as bitterly as she had resisted it.

TWELVE: AUTUMN-WINTER, 996 AFE
THEY DRINK THE WINE OF VIOLENCE

Saltimbanco yawned and stretched, reaching the last leg of a long and lazy approach to wakefulness. He stretched again. He was as relaxed as a cat. His extended left arm came down on something soft and warm and swathed in a mass of silken hair. He yawned again, rolled so he could look into the smiling face of his new wife. He reached slowly, stalking a wisp of dark hair peeping from a fold of coverlet, caught it between thumb and forefinger, curled and twirled it while watching her sleep. Then he drew a fingertip lightly over one soft, rosy cheek, following the line of her jaw, ended by tickling the dimple on her chin. The caress excited something at the corner of her mouth, a something seldom seen before last evening, a happy, demonic something that had spent years in hiding, a something now out and winking merrily. Her smile so lightly grew, drawing with its warmth. Those ruby cushions for his kiss parted slightly, permitting the flight of a sigh. She extended a small, delicate hand to cover his own, pressed it to her cheek. Slowly, so as not to disturb her slumber, he leaned and kissed that taunting quirk at the corner of her mouth.

"Uhm," she sighed, eyes still closed.

"Self, have something to confess."

She opened one sleepy eye.

"Self, am not Saltimbanco. Am not simple, wandering fool…"

"Shhh. I know."

"Hai! How? Am still breathing."

"Deduction. Valther's lists. You were the only one who could've gotten to them and have communicated with bin Yousif. In Iwa Skolovda."

Fear smote deeply. "Ridyeh?" he gasped, unable to articulate his question.

"I hated you then. But it wasn't your fault, really. I… uh… Why talk about it? It's over. Don't make me remember. I don't want to. Kiss me. Touch me.

Love me. Don't talk. Just make me forget."

"No hate? Ravenkrak will die, and self, in one guise, am prime killer."

"Ravenkrak's dead. Only Ravenkrak hasn't heard."

"You change so."

They were interrupted by a knock. Neither moved. It grew insistent. "You'd better go," Nepanthe said. "Probably one of my brothers."

It was. Valther eyed the gown of Nepanthe's Saltimbanco had donned, chuckled, said, "Turran wants Nepanthe in the Lower Armories. Luxos just got home. We got him through the gates three steps ahead of bin Yousif's men."

"Self, am dismayed by lack of respect…"

"My own thought exactly," Valther replied, cutting him short. "But Turran wants her, and what he wants, he gets. Got to run." He chucked Mocker under the chin. "The robe becomes you." Laughing, he ducked a spiritless punch and hurried away.

Mocker found Nepanthe dressing when he returned. Her face clouded. She was still afraid.

"Was Valther. Meeting in Lower Armories. Luxos came back."

"I heard. Will you help me?" She quavered when he touched her. A moment later, in a tremulous whisper, she asked, "What do your friends call you?"

"Many names. Hai! Not good for lady's ears, most. But mostly Mocker."

"Mocker, we have to leave."

"Why?"

"My brothers might find out. We should get out first."

"To where? How to live? Moneys from speechifying in Iwa Skolovda repose in secret place in Tower of Moon—lost forever!" This was a wail.

"I don't care where. And I've got lots of valuable things."

"How to escape?"

"There're ways. But you know bin Yousif, don't you?" There was no accusation in her voice.

"Long time."

"You're friends?"

"When gold is right."

"Anyone else?" She smiled, easing his tension. He understood.

"Redbeard."

"What?" She was startled.

"Rendel Grimnason. True name is Bragi Ragnarson."

"And Astrid?"

"Name is Elana. And Blackfang, Kildragon, Rolf, also. And guess where loyalty of troops lies."

"Oh! Poor Turran. Surrounded by enemies. Even his sister, now. When's it supposed to end?"

Mocker shook his head. "Employer, closed-lip man of first class, tells nothing. Not even name. But we find out. Is magical Machiavelli."

"A magician?"

"Yes. Question still is, why so interested in Ravenkrak?"

"What's his name?"

"Is Varthlokkur…"

"Varthlokkur!" She dropped to the bed. "I *told* Turran, but he wouldn't listen."

Her reaction startled Mocker. "What is trouble?"

"You know what he wants from Ravenkrak? Me! For years he's been after me to marry him. Probably for my power. Not the Werewind, but the power *within.* Storm King blood is strong with it. Our ancestors were nobles of Ilkazar. Matched, little could resist us. Controlling weather would be child's play. Which is why I always turned him down." She flushed. He knew that wasn't her primary reason. "I was afraid Ravenkrak would be first to feel his new strength. I guess he'll destroy us anyway. Sooner or later, destruction overtakes all the children of the Empire. Be ready to leave when I get back. See if your friends will go with us."

She settled her dress more comfortably, gave him a small kiss. "I love you." She struggled with words, but they came. "I'll be back soon."

As Nepanthe left the tower, shawl tightened about her neck and head against the worsening snow, she examined, and marveled at, the changed state of her mind. Though she still feared, her being, like a magnet being drawn, was orienting itself toward one lodestone. Saltimbanco. No, Mocker. But what was the difference? A rose is a rose. Funny. She could almost feel her fears evaporating. She wanted to sing. It was icy cold. A wind had begun driving the already fallen snow (escaping be a grim, miserable undertaking), but she didn't feel it, didn't care. Her sexual fears had already begun to appear foolish—it hadn't been bad at all—yet thoughts of future encounters still disturbed her.

Nepanthe was last to reach the Lower Armories. She found her brothers waiting impatiently. No one criticized her lateness. After offering belated well-wishes for her marriage, Luxos demanded everyone's attention.

"These are Ridyeh's things. What I could recover," he said, indicating a clutter on the table. "A gold coin bin Yousif spent after a meeting with an old man at an Itaskian tavern. Given him by that old man. The mercenaries outside are being paid in the same mintage. Turran?"

Turran examined the coin. "Ilkazar. Scarce these days."

"Thousands are being spent."

"Somebody found the Treasure of Ilkazar?"

"Don't forget, an old man's the source. What old man might know where to find that treasure?"

"Varthlokkur!" Turran snarled.

"Brilliant deduction!" said Nepanthe. "What'd I tell you six months ago?"

"Okay, I apologize. I didn't think he wanted you that bad. That means we've got real trouble. We'll have to fight sorcery and soldiers both."

"I have more," Luxos said. "Concerning who gave that spy list to bin Yousif. I found this paper in Ridyeh's pocket. The river water almost ruined it. But two names are clear: Bragi Ragnarson and Mocker. Meaningless? Rumor has it that bin Yousif operated with men of those names during the El Murid Wars. And one of them was in Itaskia at the time, *and* was seen talking with the same old man. Where are they now? What're they doing? I think they're here. In Ravenkrak."

Nepanthe racked her mind for a diversion.

Offering the paper, Luxos said, "There's another readable line."

Turran frowned over ink badly run, read, "'… short and fat. Ragnarson is blond, tall…' That's all?"

They were at the marches of discovery. Nepanthe knew she had to warn her husband… The thought startled her.

Her declaration to Mocker, a half hour earlier, of a shift of allegiance, had lacked conviction. In the meantime it had matured and grown firm. She rose. To Turran's inquiring glance, she replied, "Bathroom," and left them bent over Ridyeh's effects like ghouls over an open grave.

"Does this *mean* anything?" she heard Turran ask. And, as she drew almost beyond hearing, Valther replied.

"The only fat man here is Saltimbanco…"

Which precipitated a brief silence. Nepanthe started to run—and collided with a breathless soldier. "Milady!" he gasped. "They're striking camp. Looks like they're pulling out."

Turran's strategy had been vindicated. "Thank you. I'll tell my brothers. Return to your station." She pretended to return toward the blue glow of the meeting room. She stopped when the soldier passed out of sight. She had no intention of telling Turran that he had won. Let him stew awhile, arguing, while she and Mocker got away. Anyway, she had a feeling his victory might not be what it seemed.

Diminished by distance, she heard Turran's anguished, "But we couldn't have married our sister to an enemy!"

"We did!" Valther retorted. "I'd swear, now that I think about, nobody else could've gotten to the lists. Not and have gotten them to bin Yousif. Maybe we can hold his merry hanging after all."

"Damn!" Turran roared. Metal rattled as he smote the table. "Well, that's one. What about the other?"

"Grimnason," Valther said sadly.

"What? No! He's been our best man."

"A hunch."

"Ridyeh said blond."

"Hair can be dyed. It doesn't matter anyway. We're inundated by enemies, inside and out. We've been outmaneuvered all the way down the line. Which figures with a fox like Varthlokkur. So, after four hundred years, Ravenkrak falls, unvanquished by arms. Treachery's victim, as we always knew she would be. Hail the Empire."

Nepanthe had heard all she wanted. She ran.

Nepanthe rushed into the courtyard, looked around wildly, through the blinding snow barely discerned Ragnarson atop the wall. In a moment she was at his side, breathless. "Bragi, my brothers…"

"I know." He didn't turn. His gaze was fixed in the direction of bin Yousif's encampment. His expression was one of weariness and sorrow. "Mocker told me you wanted to leave. I don't know if we can, now. By stalling I may have cut all our throats. Haroun won't be happy. He isn't a forgiving man."

"You don't understand," she said. "The game's over. They know. Luxos brought proof. You've got to get out right now."

Ragnarson's shoulders slumped. He sighed. Turning, he replied, "Thank you, Lady. You'd better get your things. Don't bring more than you can carry. Clothes and food. My men are packing already. Can you make it down the mountain in this?"

"I guess so," she replied. "Be careful. They'll do something pretty soon." She left for the Bell Tower.

Ragnarson stood there for a while, staring down the mountain. One by one, as they were ready, his staff came to him. Rolf Preshka, Reskird Kildragon, Haaken on a litter borne by those two, Elana, and a handful of favored soldiers. Finally, he asked, "Where're Mocker and Nepanthe?"

No one knew.

"I don't like leaving the men," Kildragon complained.

In his new, tired voice, Ragnarson replied, "I loathe it. But would you rather be dead?"

Preshka observed, "We're not leaving any of our old people. Lif. Haas. Chotty…" He did the roll of old accomplices.

"Nevertheless," Reskird protested, "there's our reputation …"

"Shut up!"

A figure plunged through the drifts in the court, shouted from the foot of the wall, "Captain, they're coming over the rear wall!"

Stunned, Ragnarson could ask only, "Who?"

"Bin Yousif's men, I think."

"How many?"

"Only a few so far, but more all the time."

"Right. Thank you. Rolf, send everybody back there. That'll distract them till we're out. Hurry."

Preshka departed.

"Elana, what about the costumes?"

"I hid them in the gatehouse."

"Good. Where the hell are Mocker and Nepanthe?"

"This must be them." Two dark shapes staggered from the direction of the Bell Tower. From beyond them came muted sounds of combat.

"May the Gods Above, or the Gods Below, or any Powers here present, cast down, disperse, and render unto destruction the agents of destruction, the Storm Kings of Ravenkrak," Nepanthe said on arriving. "I prayed that at the beginning. Now it's being answered, and I wish I could take it back."

"All right, down to the gatehouse," Ragnarson ordered. Moments later, Kildragon held the guard at sword point while Elana recovered white robes sewn from bedsheets. Preshka returned and claimed his as Ragnarson ordered the gate opened.

A scream, above the growing clamor of battle (from the sound of it, the defense had the upper hand), echoed through the courtyard. Luxos burst from the door to the Lower Armories. "Move out!" Ragnarson growled. Though he had little doubt of the outcome of a duel with Luxos, having practiced with the man, he paused to engage while the others won free.

Ragnarson had learned his fencing in a less than chivalrous school. For him survival meant a lot more than fair play and an honorable death. As Luxos lunged, Bragi swept a hand through the icicles hanging from the tunnel-like gate, hurling them into his assailant's face. He followed up with a groin kick that propelled Luxos back amidst his brothers. Bragi fled only two steps behind his companions.

They took no more than a dozen steps. Then the slope came alive around them. Snowdrifts rose and became white-clad figures rushing the open gate. Ragnarson was hit, buffeted, knocked down, and trampled as bin Yousif's men swept past.

He fell cursing himself for believing that Haroun would go away without one last, cunning attack. He should have foreseen this… The first wave passed, ignoring his people. But the attackers cursing behind the falling snow, down the mountain, wouldn't be preoccupied with seizing a gate. Bragi knelt. He looked around, saw no one. His shout, drowned by the metallic racket behind him, brought no response. Wanting no attention, he kept his mouth shut from then on.

He stood, arranged his camouflage about him, continued down the mountain. Hopefully, the others would reach the place where they had agreed to meet if separated.

With a gasp of relief, Ragnarson dropped his end of the litter before Haroun's tent. His arms and shoulders ached. Beside him, wary, shivering spearmen relaxed only slightly as he dropped to his hams.

He had found Kildragon and Haaken in the lee of a snow-covered earthwork a quarter-mile below the gate. Kildragon had been trying to drag his friend down the mountain unaided, but had not been able to go further. The others had vanished, scattered by the charge… Then Haroun's troops had appeared and, apparently under special orders, had brought them here.

The flap of the tent whipped back. Lean, brown, clad in black, bin Yousif looked like a caricature of Death. "Send them in," he ordered.

Grunting, frowning down the length of spearshafts, Ragnarson lifted his end of the litter. A moment later the tent flap closed behind him. Warmth from a dozen braziers assailed him.

"He all right?"

Bin Yousif bent over Blackfang. Haaken mumbled, "Ready to take my turn carrying Reskird."

A smile, half feral, flashed across bin Yousif's face. "Fine." Turning, "Bragi, you're lucky you've got a good-looking, fast-talking wife. And that my men caught *her* first. I might not have given you a chance to talk." Ragnarson had just noticed Elana crouched in a far corner, being intimate with a brazier. She offered a weary smile.

Bin Yousif continued, "Can't blame you for holding off. My problem is that I don't have a conscience. Well, it came out all right. No hard feelings. The old man's going to pay us off in Itaskia. Ah. Must be some more."

Ragnarson stepped to the flap with Haroun. Another prisoner, Rolf, had indeed arrived—but Bragi's attention wasn't caught by his lieutenant. Beyond and above Preshka, through a slackening snowfall, vermillion flared and fluttered.

"Ravenkrak's burning," Haroun said. "Come in, Rolf."

Ragnarson smote palm with fist. He felt worse each time he betrayed an employer. He was evil, a maggot. A man's oath had meant something once—but he had been a pup then, a fool in the fool's paradise of Trolledyngja.

"If you have to stare, go outside," bin Yousif growled. "Don't leave the flap open."

Ragnarson let the flap fall, masking the outcome of his treason.

From the brazier he had surrounded, Preshka asked, "How'd you know?"

Bin Yousif frowned questioningly, then smiled. "You mean that you'd break out today? I didn't, for sure. But it seemed like a good bet. We spotted Luxos a couple days ago. I thought he might know enough to start you running. So I let him get through."

"What now?" Preshka asked.

"We're supposed to wait at the Red Hart in Itaskia. The old man will pay us off there."

"I don't like it."

"It's the best I could get. He doesn't trust us anymore. Why should he? Blackfang head-bashed him. Bragi stalled forever. And I wouldn't attack."

Someone shouted outside. Haroun went to the flap. "Ah, all here now. Bring him in." Two soldiers, dragging an unconscious and gaudily bandaged Mocker, entered. "Put him on the bed. What happened?"

"Wouldn't surrender," one said. "Wanted to find somebody. His wife, he said."

"Wife? Mocker? Bragi, what's this blather?"

"It's true. Believe it or not. He's married. To Nepanthe. Since last night."

"Oh." A vacant sound, that. Bin Yousif plopped onto a stool, frowned. "That's not good. What's wrong with him? He was supposed to suborn her, that's all. Break up the family. Bad. Bad."

"Why?" Elana asked. "Is there a law says he can't get married?"

"There are a million women… Why'd he pick one the old man wants?"

"Don't you care what *she* wants?"

"No. Hell no! I want to get paid. She's merchandise." He smote his forehead theatrically. "Merchandise. Why? Why not somebody else? And why me? Why am I soft-hearted about that fathead? Should've cut his throat when he stole my purse. Nothing but trouble since. I've got the fool's weakness. Friendship." After a lot of like natter, he ordered Nepanthe found and brought to him. While waiting, he prepared for a hasty departure, to escape Varthlokkur's shadow.

Nepanthe couldn't be found. Haroun and his allies searched three days. During that time they accounted for almost everyone, great and small, involved in the events at Ravenkrak. That fortress was now a smoke-stained ruin. Less than a score were missing, presumably buried in the snow-shrouded rubble. Among the missing, several Storm Kings were prominent.

Then Mocker, following the path he thought Nepanthe had taken after they had become disoriented and separated near the castle gate, happened on a curiosity. It was an area where snow had melted and refrozen. Others had seen it and thought it of no significance, and Mocker likewise—except that Haroun was with him and he had enough background in sorcery to recognize its telltales.

"A spell of concealment was worked here," he said, surprising his companion. "Good deal of heat involved in twisting light around."

"Witchery? What?…"

"I told you the old man wanted Nepanthe. Looks like he found her here, hid her with a spell, took her off down that way when the chance came." He pointed along a track of lesser melting.

"We follow, eh? Catch him quick. Old mans not walk so fast…"

"Fast enough." Knowing it vain, Haroun sent patrols in pursuit. They found neither wizard nor woman. Meanwhile, he disbanded his army, ruining his war chest in the process, and released his prisoners. He was desolate when the last trooper was paid off. Not a farthing remained as profit—because he had had to pay Bragi's men, too.

The old man *had* to show in Itaskia.

Despite Mocker's protests, Haroun led his allies southward in hopes of, if nothing else, salvaging their pay.

THIRTEEN: THE YEARS 981-997 AFE
IN HIS SHADOW SHE SHALL LIVE

Gloom hung like heavy cobwebs beneath the rafters of the room where Varthlokkur and the Old Man sat. Chill dominated the air. Dust scented it dryly. All colors were shades of gray. The only light came from the far-seeing mirror. The scene it examined lay deep in another place of shadow. They were watching sixteen-year-old Nepanthe at her daily business. The mirror presented golden voyeuristic opportunities, but both men meticulously refused to accept them. Nepanthe's routine was a dull one of meals, minor chores, studies, and hours spent over embroideries. When she needed solitude, she withdrew to the castle library and read. Books remained beyond the scope of any brother except Luxos. She learned a lot, and much of it was nonsense.

Varthlokkur and the Old Man watched for hours, the latter patently bored but enduring because something was bothering his friend. Varthlokkur finally articulated it. "Do you think it's time I went to see her?"

"Yes. You may have waited too long already. There's nothing to stop her from finding another lover."

"Not casually. The old dragon, her stepmother, seems determined to turn her into a career virgin." He rose, stalked across the chamber. Over his shoulder, he continued, "She's terrified of men. The woman's been that successful. Watch her when she's around male servants. Still, Nature can't be thwarted forever." He chuckled without feeling.

The Old Man swiveled, watched the wizard pursue some arcane handiwork. Tugging his beard, he asked, "What're you doing?"

"Picking out some gifts to impress Verloya. Her father."

"You're going to go right away?"

"As soon as I can. I'm nervous already, and it's only a couple seconds since I decided to do it."

"Should I ready a transfer spell?"

Varthlokkur grew ghastly pale. "No!" To cover his over-response, he added, "I want to look at the world firsthand. Anyway, the whole transfer business disturbs me. As long ago as Shinsan, when I was helping one of my teachers with transfer research, I noticed some odd perturbations in the transfer stream. I think something lives in there. And it might be something we shouldn't bother. It's a fact that people have transferred and simply vanished forever."

The Old Man had never heard Varthlokkur say a word about what he had done in Shinsan. He wanted to respect the wizard's privacy, yet suffered from curiosity. "You've never said much about Shinsan…"

"The less said, the better."

"What's it like there? I've never been there, at least since Tuan Hoa established the Dread Empire. And the mirror can't see in."

"There's a barrier against far-seeing. Otherwise, it's a country like most. It has the regular natural furniture: hills, rivers, forests. Leaves are green there.

The sky is blue. No matter what you hear, your senses won't see any difference from the rest of the world. Only with your soul can you sense the all-pervading evil… Really, the less you know, the happier you'll be."

Nervously, finding Varthlokkur this expansive, the Old Man hazarded the question that had been bothering him since the beginning. "What did they cost, the skills you used against the Empire?"

Crimson, visible even in that dark chamber, crept into Varthlokkur's neck. His face became grim. The Old Man feared the only result of his prying would be an angry outburst. He directed the conversation back toward safe waters. "You're going the way you are?"

"What's wrong with me?" A tiger with a broken tooth could have snarled no more fiercely.

"I kind of expected you'd make yourself young again, the way you did with Marya."

"And what would Marya think? No. And Nepanthe would be terrified. No, old's best for everyone." The red began draining from his face. "When I've gone, don't tell Marya where. No need to hurt her. She's been a good wife. I may not be able to give her love, or another son, but I can save her pain." Always after his anger fell and his conscience returned, he compensated with concern—though sometimes, as with Ilkazar and the piper (the new piper led the most pampered life of anyone in Fangdred), the concern came too late to prevent a terrible wrong.

"I'll tell her something."

Varthlokkur's journey lasted more than a month. He had to cross some of the most primeval mountains, the Dragon's Teeth and, after Shara and the plains of East Heatherland, the Kratchnodians. The weather was often miserable, with fogs, rains, snows, and winds that were never warm. The dangers of the forest seemed to have a special affinity for him, and bandits more than once dogged his trail. Farmers sometimes met him, a stranger, with weapons bare. The world had gone ragged since his youth. Anarchy had reigned after the fall of the stabilizing Empire of Ilkazar, but then local stability had set in—till the onset of the growing chaos of the present. Mighty forces were in contention, and complete chaos seemed destined to become the ruling order. He despaired, knowing the future only promised worse.

One day, wearily, he passed the end of a long, narrow defile in gray rock and saw Ravenkrak for the first time. As he emerged, the howling mountain gale ripped the clouds from a peak ahead. The mirror did the stronghold no justice. There were twelve tall towers, and decaying walls patched with silver stains of ice. Cold, lonely, and dark it was, like an anciently weathered skull. He also pictured it as a battered pewter crown for the rugged Candareen. He shivered with the loneliness the place inspired. What great madness had inspired the Imperial engineers to build a fortress here?

A man passed the open gate as Varthlokkur approached. He stopped, stared, hurriedly disappeared. He returned before the wizard arrived. "The Master awaits in the Great Hall," he said, and, "Quiet, Demon," to the falcon on his shoulder. "I'll lead the way."

Varthlokkur followed the gateman through starkly empty corridors. Experienced, the fortress was even more forlorn than Fangdred. There were people in Fangdred now, creating illusions of hominess. Ravenkrak lacked the illusions.

The Great Hall proved vast, empty, awaiting events that would fill it. Just a corner of an end was in use. There, before a huge, roaring fireplace, sat Verloya, the Master of Ravenkrak. His children were with him. All seven seemed variations on a common theme. Thin or heavy, short or tall, all were distorted reflections of their father.

"Sit down. Make yourself comfortable," said Verloya. "I imagine it's been a rough trip, there to here." His eyebrows rose questioningly. Varthlokkur ignored the hint. Verloya continued, "I could hardly believe it when Birdman told me there was a stranger on the mountain. Ah!" A servant delivered mulled wine. Despite his determination to be a gentleman, Varthlokkur almost snatched his.

"Pardon me," he said after gulping it. "It was a rough trip."

"No apology necessary. I've been to Iwa Skolovda and back again several times. It's a harrowing journey at its easiest. Ah. The mutton."

Freshly baked trenchers arrived, too. Verloya carved a huge roast while servants brought additional bowls and platters, vegetables and sweetmeats, pitchers of hot wine, and ale. Then they seated themselves, too. All of Ravenkrak's inhabitants fit at that one table before the fire, and left plenty of elbow room for a visiting sorcerer.

During the meal Varthlokkur asked after the Lady of the castle. He was referred to Nepanthe. who stared into her plate at the far end of the table. Later he learned that the second wife had disappeared, while he was traveling, carrying off a fortune, and had become a taboo subject. She had gone chasing impossible dreams of the sort that would one day complicate Nepanthe's life.

Full, Varthlokkur pushed himself away from the table. Now he was ready to answer questions.

Verloya understood. He belched grandly, said, "Now, let's talk—if you don't mind. You'll pardon me if I seem inquisitive. We get visitors so seldomly." Without saying it, he gave the impression that visitors were seldom friendly. Reckless Iwa Skolovdans with a lust for making reputations considered Ravenkrak a prime challenge.

Tamil al Rahman, of the Inner Circle, Proconsul and Viceroy to Cis-Kratchnodia, the province that had included Iwa Skolovda when the Empire had held sway, had fled to Ravenkrak after the Fall. For generations his descendants had striven to give the Empire new life by bringing forth the embryonic life-spark enwombed in Ravenkrak. They had succeeded only in creating an enduring hatred between the stronghold and Iwa Skolovda. That city bore the shock of every mad attempt to revive a body so far gone it no longer had bones.

That barren, bitter castle, Ravenkrak, was all that remained of a dream. Ravenkrak, a handful of people, and an abiding hatred of Iwa Skolovda.

"I understand. Ask away."

"Where are you from?"

Strange, his having asked that before a name. Varthlokkur shrugged. He had decided on complete honesty already. He replied, "Fangdred, in the Dragon's Teeth." His listeners shifted nervously. They knew the name.

"The Old Man of the Mountain?"

"No. A friend of his. You might say a partner."

Another stir. They seemed well aware of the other dark name associated with Fangdred. Nepanthe shook. Varthlokkur was disappointed. He would have a grim struggle winning this one. She was as timid as a unicorn. However, right now, she was just one amongst the frightened. None of her family could conceal their fear.

"Varthlokkur?" Verloya whispered.

Varthlokkur nodded. Nepanthe shook even more. A scratchiness entered Verloya's voice when he said, "You honor us." Varthlokkur involuntarily turned to Nepanthe. He had to tear his eyes away. He had waited so long.

His glance was too much. She uttered a frightened cry, fled with the grace of a gazelle.

"The honor is something best discussed privately... Your daughter... What's the matter?"

Verloya shook his head sadly. "Too much exposure to her stepmother. Excuse her, if you will."

"Of course, of course. I *am* Varthlokkur. There're legends about me. But there's not much fact in them. Consider: What do they say about Storm Kings in Iwa Skolovda? Please, if I've offended the young lady, send my apologies."

Verloya indicated one of his sons. "Tell Nepanthe to come beg pardon."

"No. Please don't. I'm sure it was my fault."

"As you will. Boys, leave us talk." Sons and servants alike moved to a distant table. "Now, sir, what can I do for you?"

"It's ticklish, being whom I am. Are you familiar with the Thelelazar Functional Form of Boroba Thring's Major Term Divination?"

"No. I'm almost totally ignorant of the Eastern systems. A Clinger Trans-Temporal Survey is the best I can manage. We're rather minor wizards here, now, except for our ability with the Werewind."

"Yes, a Clinger would do. What I want you to see is close enough, time-wise."

"A divination brought you here?"

"In a sense. I'd rather demonstrate than explain. Do you mind?" He treated Verloya with all the politeness he could muster. The man was due for a shock.

"The best place would be the Lower Armories, then. Bring your things."

An hour later, having taken it better than Varthlokkur had anticipated, Verloya said, "I can't quite grasp this business of Fates and Norns. The whole mess looked like a chess game where the rules change after every move. It was crazy."

"Quite." Varthlokkur explained his theories once they had resumed seats before the fire in the Great Hall.

The wizard was uneasy and annoyed. There had been some new information this time. The divination had hinted that his old sins would catch him up.

Verloya, too, was troubled. He wasn't pleased by his children's role in the game.

Varthlokkur now suspected whither the thrust of his second great destruction would go. It hurt. And he knew it would change him again, perhaps as radically as had the destruction of Ilkazar.

They sat silently for ten minutes, each nursing his special disappointment. Finally, Varthlokkur remarked, "The divination hasn't changed in two centuries."

"I saw. I understood why you're here. I can't lie. I don't like it. Yet I couldn't change it if I wanted.

"You'll have difficulties with her," he continued. "Today's behavior wasn't untypical. In fact, I guess she must've been damned curious to stick around as long as she did. My fault, I guess. Should've put a lid on my wife's nonsense back when. But I was too busy trying to make men of my sons. I didn't take time to worry about Nepanthe… I'll give you a reluctant blessing for whatever good you might do her. But that's my limit. I just don't like the bigger picture. I'd hoped I could teach the boys better. The Empire is dead."

"Maybe if you used the Power…"

"I won't use magic. I swore never to force anybody to do anything again. This's no exception. It'll be done without, or not at all."

Having come to terms with the girl's father, Varthlokkur began his long and seldom-rewarding effort to light a love-spark in the heart of a unicorn-girl. Occasionally it looked like he was about to break through. More often he appeared destined to inevitable failure. But he had learned patience in his centuries. He had time. Like the eroding waters of a river, he gradually wore the rock of Nepanthe's fear. By the time she was nineteen she looked forward to his increasingly frequent visits, though she saw him more as a kindly philosophy teacher than as a potential lover. There would be no lovers for her, she believed.

He was sure she secretly wanted one. Sadly, she awaited a knight-charming from a jongleur's tale, and in such men her world was painfully lacking.

Which was a pity. A world ought to have a few genuine good guys, and not just a spectrum of people running from bad to worse. Varthlokkur conceived of his world as being populated only by friends and enemies, without absolutes, with good and evil being strictly relative to his own position.

On Nepanthe's twentieth birthday Varthlokkur proposed. At first she thought he was joking. When he declared he was serious, she fled. He hadn't sown his seeds deeply enough. She refused to see him for a year. She hurt him terribly, but he refused to be daunted.

Though she eventually resumed speaking, she remained defensive and flighty, and tried to keep Valther nearby to protect the virtue she fancied threatened.

Verloya's death caused her to relent. It was Varthlokkur who best comforted her at her father's funeral. But the break in her defenses was in appearance only. She wasn't going to let him get too near.

Then Varthlokkur suffered a loss of his own. Marya passed away during one of his increasingly short stays at Fangdred. He began to suspect that she had known what he was doing and had kept her peace. He honestly grieved at her passing. A better wife a man couldn't have asked. Sometimes he wondered why he couldn't be satisfied with the good things that did touch his life. There was no absolute, compelling force, outside himself, making him pursue the destinies he foresaw in his divinations. If he wished, and wanted to employ the will, he could become a simple farmer or sailmaker… He didn't have the will. He believed that it was his duty to fulfill the destinies he had foreseen.

Nepanthe's resistance remained like steel or adamant, wearing but never breaking. Six years later, when her brothers' through-the-halls war games matured into plans for genuine conquests, she still hadn't surrendered. She accepted him as part of her life. Maybe she even expected an eventual pairing. She had learned to be at ease with him again. But she refused to help the relationship to develop an affectionate scope.

Impatience undid Varthlokkur. One evening he proposed. As usual, Nepanthe put him off. The first of their great angry arguments ensued. Afterward, frustrated, he returned to Fangdred determined to pursue a course the Old Man had championed for years.

The Old Man. He might have been a mystery to himself. No man could keep in memory all the ages and events he had seen and heard and experienced. He barely felt he belonged to the realm of humankind. Lusts, loves, hatreds, agonies and joys, passions, what were those in the mill of time? Grist. Just grist for the grinding wheel. What remained of parents dead ten thousand years? Not even a memory, other than unspeakably archaic, alien names. Youth? He had never been young. Or so it seemed now. He had few memories of running joy, of a girl, and wildflowers and clover scents in spring (her name sometimes haunted his lonely dreams, and her face frequently came to him in his odd, brief, happy moments). His past was a corridor infinitely long, passing a million doors with memories shut up inside, all in old man's shades of gray. The color had faded from present and future. The past dwindled back to the dark point where he had first encountered the Director. He missed that most, the brights, the scarlets, the greens, the blues, of mighty loves and aches and passions. He was the oldest man in the world.

Except one, though he thought his friend, the Star Rider, the Director, might well be dead. He had heard nothing from the man since the Nawami Crusades, a thousand years ago, though his handiwork appeared, in hints, in the background of the epic tale of the Fall.

Once the Old Man had wanted to live forever. But then he and the world had been young and he had loathed the thought of missing its future ages. Once when magic had been equally young and unbound, and he still had had the capacity for innovation, he had risked his soul and humanity to seize the immortality he owned. It was an irreversible Star Rider gift that exacted its cruel price in alienation and boredom and a debt he might never completely discharge.

There were times when he thought Death might be his own sweet angel of the morning (with a face like that of his love forgotten), a woman he would gladly embrace when She came. She would give him surcease from this world, where his days were undistinguished marchers in endless columns of sameness. Freedom She would be. Mother Night with a soft black womb wherein he could lie forever at peace…

But Her arms could be achieved easily. Why didn't he jump off Fangdred's wall? Because he also feared the Lady he desired. Nor could he yet tolerate the thought of a world without himself in it. That urge, that overwhelming compulsion, that had driven him to immortality, still burned undampened among the fires of his soul. He might miss something. But what, if he had lived all those ages and had become achingly bored by their historic march? If catastrophes and conquests and the finest artistic products of the human mind weren't enough, what would suffice? To what did he look forward?

When he was in a dark mood, snappish, such were the thoughts he thought. He had no idea what he wanted anymore, nor did he search. He was content to wait till it came to him. Meanwhile, the habits of ages swept him onward. He wished for oblivion, and bent every effort to escape it. Ten thousand years had he lived; perhaps he would see ten thousand more.

And he did have his debts and obligations. There was interest to pay on the long life he had been loaned.

A vast map lay on the table in the gloomy room atop the Wind Tower. On its eastern borders were fangy marks representing the Dragon's Teeth. At the top, more fangs: the Kratchnodians, and among them, the name *Ravenkrak*. Speckled across the middle, and tending south, were the names of cities and kingdoms: Iwa Skolovda, Dvar, Prost Kamenets, Itaskia, Greyfells, Mendalayas, Portsmouth, and a hundred more. Varthlokkur and the Old Man bent over them, considering the possibilities.

"Here," said the Old Man, finger stabbing the Kratchnodians just above Iwa

Skolovda. "The ideal base. The people, bandits all, have a grudge against the city. An able man, unswayed by tribal jealousies, could unite them into an army strong enough to take Iwa Skolovda by surprise, yet not strong enough to hold it. I think that's essentially what you've got in mind. And what you need if they do put Nepanthe on the throne there. We'll get her then, when they lose interest and turn to other conquests."

"Fine, if we can catch her. She's not stupid." Though she tried to hide it, Varthlokkur had discovered in Nepanthe a brilliant intuitive mind. Where she was dullest she had, generally, intentionally blinded herself.

"Settled, then? We hire this bin Yousif and his people, and use them to isolate her at Iwa Skolovda?"

"I guess." A premonition weighed heavily on him. It wouldn't be as simple as the Old Man made it sound.

He ached with the approaching cruelty of his second great destruction. "Somehow, I don't think it'll work. I'll end up fighting her brothers."

The Old Man shrugged. "Blank shields are going begging. You could stomp up an army overnight."

Varthlokkur had no taste for the trend of the Old Man's thoughts. He had had his fill of armies and wars centuries ago.

"Well, they've got the Horn of the Star Rider now," said the Old Man, his amazement barely under control.

Varthlokkur turned to the mirror, drawn more by his companion's tone than the event itself. Somehow, Nepanthe's brothers had managed to locate that elusive ancient, whose origins were more mystery-bound than those of the Old Man. Recently they had been stalking him through the westernmost reaches of the Kratchnodians. Now they had caught him unawares. It was an incredible coup. The Star Rider was far too old to be taken easily.

"They're fools. All fools." Bitterness. "One magical talisman won't make them invincible. Not even the Windmjirnerhorn."

The Horn in question had cornucopian attributes, though it didn't much resemble the mythical horn of plenty. Properly manipulated, the Windmjirnerhorn would provide almost anything asked of it. For ages power-hungry men had tried, and sometimes managed, to steal it. But the Star Rider always stole it back—after greed had destroyed the original thieves.

Turran wanted the Horn as a source of wealth and stores for raising and supplying armies—armies that would never materialize because Turran would never learn to manipulate the Horn correctly. None of the thieves ever had. They always brought their dooms upon them before they did. "They'll find out. Sticking their noses out in the world is just asking to get them bloodied. Ilkazar is still a bogeyman. Like me. And some Iwa Skolovdans still nurse bitter feelings about the Vice-Royalty."

"Which'll be useful to us."

"True. Well, I'd better get on with it. Make my arrangements with bin Yousif.

You'll keep an eye on things?"

The Old Man followed events faithfully. He saw bin Yousif enter the foothills in the guise of a witch-doctor and begin his work. He saw Ragnarson enlist with and assume command of Turran's mercenaries. He saw Mocker begin his slow trek toward Iwa Skolovda in the Saltimbanco avatar. He watched Haroun, insufficiently informed of the aims of his employer, send an agent to make sure Iwa Skolovda's King was aware of Storm King intentions. Varthlokkur's plot survived only because Turran was moving already. Then came the changes of fortune, the worst of which was Haroun's failure to capture Nepanthe at Iwa Skolovda. But Varthlokkur had expected that. He already had an army gathering to move against Ravenkrak.

Then Ravenkrak didn't fall. Ragnarson wouldn't fulfill his contract. And bin Yousif refused to waste lives storming the place. Varthlokkur, impatiently directing the siege himself, angrily responded by taking a battalion around the Candareen to spend a month hacking a stairway up two thousand feet of cliff to attack the castle from behind…

Only to arrive and find that Haroun, by cunning, was getting his job done after all.

But the goal of it all, Nepanthe, was missing when the smoke cleared from the ruins of Varthlokkur's second great destruction. On a snowy morning, after frantically casting spells among the countless dead, the wizard found her halfway down the mountain. He caught her and concealed her, and when the way was clear he set out for Fangdred. A month later, with a still furious Nepanthe in tow, he returned home.

The affair had been a fiasco. Nothing had been gained but death. Varthlokkur's abandoned employees were in an uproar both over not having been paid, and over the abduction of Mocker's wife. Several of Nepanthe's brothers, with the Windmjirnerhorn and their storm-sending equipment, had evaded destruction and were loose, and driven by a bitter thirst for revenge. The wizard had captured his prize, but the matter was far from closed.

And Varthlokkur knew it. He had hardly returned, gotten Nepanthe installed in her new apartment, and had made his presence known when he summoned the Old Man to the Wind Tower. "The goal has been reached," he mumbled. "She's here. But I've left enough loose ends to tie into a rope to hang me."

"'A patch in a shroud to bury me,'" said the Old Man. Varthlokkur didn't recognize the line immediately. It came from *The Wizards of Ilkazar,* from King Vilis's final lament, spoken while he watched the very heart of the Empire dying around him. He had complained of his ruined estate and of how things were hemming him in. Especially Varthlokkur, the patch.

"I have to prepare. Silver and ebony, moonlight and night, these were ever mine. Do we have a craftsman who can make me silver bells? Here, here," he said, digging a small, aged casket from clutter piled in a corner. Bits of dry earth fell to the floor when he opened it. Perhaps two dozen ancient silver coins lay within. "These. Make me bells of these, each marked with my thirteen signs."

The Old Man did not, for a time, respond. He hadn't ever seen Varthlokkur this way. His friend was overflowing with deeds and moods.

"And I'll make the arrow myself." He quickly scrounged a billet of ebony and a kit of small tools from the corner pile. He kept two silver coins from the old casket. "Go! Go! The bells. Get me the bells." Mystified, the Old Man went.

Days later, he returned with the casket of bells. Varthlokkur was fletching an arrow at the time. It had a shaft of ebony. Its head was a coin hammered to a point. Silver from another coin had been inlaid into the shaft finely, in runes and cabalistic signs. "Here. Help me rig this." The wizard had collected a strange pile of odds and ends on the table.

Following Varthlokkur's instructions, the Old Man assembled a mobile of tiny, clapperless bells. They would ring off one another. The arrow turned lazily beneath them.

"My warning device," Varthlokkur told him. "The bells will ring if someone comes after me, starting while he's still fifty leagues away. They'll ring louder when he gets closer. The arrow will point at him. And so it should be easy to find him and stop him." He smiled, proud of his little creation.

It was a pity, the Old Man thought, that Varthlokkur was so single-minded about Nepanthe. Marriage had radicalized her. From a rabbit she had grown into a tigress. She was having no man but the one who had liberated her. That actor. That thief. That professional traitor.

Varthlokkur's face, those days, often expressed his silent agony, over what he had done, over what he seemed to have lost. The Old Man tried to make Nepanthe understand when he wasn't around.

She did, a little, but she was a strong-minded woman. As it had taken her ages to accept a man, so might it cost another decade to swing her affections around.

He shook his head sadly. The Director played a cruel game.

The Old Man abhorred pity in all its forms, yet he was forced to pity his friend Varthlokkur.

FOURTEEN: SPRING, 997 afe
WHILE THEY WERE ENEMIES THEY WERE RECONCILED

A month had passed. Ragnarson, bin Yousif, and their associates had become certain of what they had suspected for some time: Varthlokkur wouldn't appear for the payoff. For at least the hundredth time, Ragnarson asked, "Are you *sure* he said he'd meet us here?"

And bin Yousif, gazing out an open window at the morning sun, replied as always, "I'm sure. He said, 'The Red Hart Inn, Itaskia.' You think it's too early for ale?"

"Ask Yalmar. It's his tavern. Yalmar!"

An aging man limped from the kitchen, without speaking drew and delivered two mugs. As he left, though, he smote his forehead suddenly and said, "Oh. Meant to tell ye. There were a fellow here after ye last night…"

Both jerked to attention. "Dusky old man with a nose like mine?" bin Yousif demanded.

Yalmar considered Haroun's aquiline beak. "Nay, can't say so. Fortyish, black hair, heavy sort."

Bin Yousif frowned. Ragnarson was about to ask something when Elana descended the stair from the rooming floor, her step portentous. "He's gone," she said. "Sometime during the night."

"Mocker?"

"Who else?"

They had been keeping him tied for his own protection, to prevent his charging off after Varthlokkur and Nepanthe—which might also compromise their chances of getting paid.

Bin Yousif sighed. "Well, it's come. I was afraid it would. A mad stab at a hornet's nest, and us without legs to run on."

"What do you mean?" A vacant question. Ragnarson's interest was all in Elana, who had gone to stare out a side window. She seemed terribly distant of late.

"I mean that Mocker's making us help him, like it or not. He knows damned well that to Varthlokkur we're a team. So, whether or not we're involved, he'll take a shot at us when he finds out Mocker's after him. Just in case. Wouldn't you? What's Elana's problem?"

"I don't want anything to do with Fangdred. But, if we're going to get killed anyway, it might as well be facing the enemy. I guess she's worried about Nepanthe. They got pretty close."

Elana wasn't worrying about Nepanthe. Nepanthe's predicament had become secondary. Her problem was her newly discovered pregnancy. How could she tell Bragi and not get herself excluded from his plans? She did feel a little guilty, though, because she was concerned with herself when Nepanthe's problems were so much nastier.

Ragnarson called for more ale, asked the innkeeper, "The man who asked about us. What did he want?"

"Would'na say. Did say ye were friends."

Ragnarson scratched his beard, which had faded to its normal blondness, and asked, "What was his accent?"

"No need to go on about it. He's here."

Haroun glanced up from his drink. Ragnarson turned…

The latter dove to his left, stretched out like a man plunging into water. He rolled, tripped Yalmar intentionally, shouted, "Elana!" Bin Yousif rolled into cover behind a table Bragi was overturning, thundered, "Haaken! Reskird!"

Four men in monkish garb halted in the doorway, startled by the explosive reaction to their appearance. One suddenly fell to his knees, tripped from behind. Before he could rise, a hand was beneath his chin and a blade across his throat. Both were Elana's. In hard tones she told the others, "Turran's dead if anybody even twitches!"

They believed her. They might have been stone for all the life they showed.

Ragnarson, slipping from table to table in a crouch, reached a rack where swords hung, tossed one to bin Yousif, drew another for himself, and moved toward the door. A rapid clumping came from the stairs. Blackfang and Kildragon, half dressed, arrived. They took stations to either side of Elana.

Ragnarson and bin Yousif closed in.

Rolf Preshka appeared behind the Storm Kings, sword in hand. "Damn!" he grumbled. "Jumped out that window for nothing. Ah. Nothing like old friends dropping in." He stared at the four both with frank curiosity and wry amusement.

Elsewhere, the innkeeper made the safety of his serving counter, like a curious owl paused to watch from its cover. He had been schooled well by his long proprietorship. The Red Hart had the most unsavory reputation in all Itaskia.

"You react quickly," said Turran. "Might almost think you had guilty consciences." Though he spoke lightly, there was fear in his eyes. "No need for this. We're unarmed."

"Said the sorcerer, laughing," bin Yousif muttered. "Do you keep your lightning bolts in scabbards now?"

"Sorry," Ragnarson apologized, not meaning it at all. "We're expecting trouble." His eyes flicked over the four, assessing. "But not from you. Let's move to a table." A moment later the four were seated, surrounded by the six, and a pitcher was on its way. "What do you want?" Ragnarson growled.

"To talk to Saltimbanco," said Turran.

"Mocker," Kildragon interjected.

"Saltimbanco, Mocker, that's neither here nor there. He was Saltimbanco to us, but we'll call him Mocker if you want. We want to see him. About Nepanthe."

"She's a big girl. She knew what she was doing," said Elana, falsely sweet. "You won't interfere."

"No, of course not. We didn't plan on it. Even after Ravenkrak, we can't help but be happy for her…Though it hurts that she took sides against her own family." Turran wearily pushed his hair out of his eyes. The slump of his shoulders, the way he held his head, the manner in which he avoided their eyes, all bespoke a tired and defeated man, a man who had seen all his dreams become fuel for merciless flames. "We want her taken away from Varthlokkur, gotten out of Fangdred, so she can't be used in any of his schemes." Even after having known the wizard for years, Turran couldn't picture him as free of evil designs. "Once that's accomplished, she's free to go where she wants, do what she wants, with whomever she wants."

"Uhm!" Ragnarson grunted, his heavy brows pulling together thoughtfully, a small scar on his forehead whitening.

"Look," Turran said with a hint of desperation, "we don't hate you for what you did. Rendel, you were my friend. I think you still are. Astrid…"

"Make it Bragi and Elana," Elana said.

"Whatever, you're the only friend Nepanthe ever had. We'd be fools to hate you just because you were duped by a wizard…"

"Who never paid us," Blackfang growled.

"We'd like to discard the past, make friends, come to terms. With Nepanthe's rescue in mind."

Softly, bin Yousif interjected, "You'd forget real quarrels? Like Ridyeh?"

Four grimaces. Turran visibly struggled with his emotions. "Yes. He's dead now. Hatred won't help him. Nor revenge help the living. And Nepanthe is alive. She *can* be helped. We'll court devils if that's the cost of getting her away from Varthlokkur."

"I almost believe you," Ragnarson told him. "What do you want from us, anyway?"

"Mocker's help. She's his wife. And he has the know-how to pull this sort of thing off…"

"Too bad. The idiot's left already."

"For Fangdred? By himself?"

"Yes. Mad as a hatter, isn't he? Your sister's fault. He's in love. Thinks he should charge around like the fool knights in the stories she used to like. I don't know. I might be wrong. He never showed any symptoms of the disease before. He could be flat crazy. Hey! What happened to Luxos?"

Turran's face darkened again. He replied, "We couldn't get him to leave Ravenkrak. He fought to the end. Even after everybody else surrendered. He was my brother and I'm kind of proud. He was brave, but he was a fool, too. A hundred lunatics like him could've stood off the world. In the end, bowmen shot him down." After a thoughtful moment, "Why do men give their utmost to a lost cause? Look at all the great heroes. None of them were winners in the end."

Ragnarson observed, "Fangdred supposedly would be an even tougher nut than Ravenkrak. We don't have an army anymore. And no money to hire one. How do you figure we can pull this off?"

"Uhn. How?" Turran mumbled dully. He and his brothers, apparently, kept going only because they believed they had to do this one more thing. They were treading water amidst the broken timbers of shipwrecked dreams. "I don't know."

"Magic?"

"We'll do what we can. With swords or the Werewind. Minus Ridyeh, Nepanthe, and Luxos, our control won't be much good. We could manage rain or snow, but nothing like the blizzard we sent to Dvar."

"Even that could be helpful, properly timed," Haroun mused.

"My thought, too," Turran agreed.

"Bragi, I don't like this," Blackfang observed.

"Neither do I, Haaken. But it's not really your fight anymore. You and Rolf and Reskird I'll give what's left of the pay accounts. Elana, find the drafts."

"What's to be done?" bin Yousif asked, posing. Then, "Having a storm in your pocket could be handy, but we'd have to know where and when to send it."

"A suggestion," Valther interjected. "Visigodred and Zindahjira. My agents tell me you have an understanding with them."

Those names silenced the table. They belonged to sorcerers. Powerful sorcerers, though they weren't in a class with Varthlokkur. "You dug deep if you found out about them," bin Yousif observed. "Those things were quietly done."

"Time is a problem," said Ragnarson. "Mocker has a good lead already. Chances are, he'd be dead before we could wrangle a deal with those two. I'm not sure I want to do business with Visigodred anyway. I owe him too much now."

Turran recovered some of his former spirit as he suggested, "We could adjust the time schedule. We could pin Mocker with foul weather till you were ready to help him."

"I suppose," Ragnarson grumbled. To Haroun, "Would Zindahjira work with Visigodred? Aren't they still feuding?"

"We'll give them the Horn of the Star Rider and our storm-sending equipment if they'll help," Turran said. "They can work out who gets what."

Haroun nodded. "Exactly the kind of thing that would convince Zindahjira. He thinks the world-machine only runs when it's oiled with bribes."

"I don't like it," Ragnarson grumped. "But, for lack of any other plan… Well, I'll head for Mendalayas today."

"We'll follow Mocker toward Fangdred," said Turran. "And keep the weather miserable. We don't have the range we used to. We'll set up camp in East Heatherland somewhere, close enough to Fangdred to hit it with our best, if it comes to that."

Yalmar brought a last pitcher of ale. They toasted success, then plunged into their half-baked, precipitous plan.

Ragnarson and his wife reached a hilltop, paused to stare across a valley at gray, gothic Castle Mendalayas. Bragi's thoughts drifted from his wonder at Elana's recently revealed pregnancy to memories of past visits here. Though a sorcerer, Visigodred had proven a perfect host on each occasion. Ragnarson hoped that that state of affairs would persist.

"It's a weird-looking place," Elana said. She brushed a wisp of red hair from her eyes. Her hair color sometimes changed, in secret, piquing Ragnarson's curiosity about the special sorceries of women. Some were better illusionists than master wizards.

"Uhm!" He, too, was having trouble with his hair. A strong, chill wind was blowing down off the Kratchnodians. The mountains lay just north of Mendalayas.

"Why're we waiting?"

"I'm nervous. Are you all right?"

"Don't be silly. Of course I am. It's months before you have to worry." She kicked her mare's flanks.

Soon they were climbing the far side of the valley, through the vineyards surrounding Mendalayas. Those slopes were stark, the vines skeletal brown hands reaching for a leaden sky. They were dismal now, but beauty would return with spring. Next summer fat blue-purple globes would cluster among the browning leaves, wine's parents…

A servant liveried in green awaited them at the castle gate. He bowed. "Good morning, Captain. Lady. Your mounts, if I may?" He led them inside. "I'll see that your things are transferred to your apartment after I stable your animals. His Lordship awaits your pleasure in his study. Alowa, the young lady at the door, will show you there."

Once beyond the servant's hearing, Elana whispered, "This Visigodred is a wizard? He operates like a noble."

"He's that, too. County Mendalayas is his demesne. He holds it in fief from Itaskia, through Duchy Greyfells. Sorcery is just his hobby. At least that's what he says. He's a real hobby nut."

"He knew we were coming."

"One of his affectations. He watches this county like a hawk so he can impress people with his foreknowledge."

The girl at the door, who also wore dark green, said, "My Lord sends greetings and asks if he might receive you in his study."

"By all means. Lead on."

As Ragnarson and Elana followed her through torchlit, richly decorated halls, the girl asked, "What are your dinner preferences? My Lord asked us to make you feel at home."

"Whatever's convenient for the cook," Ragnarson replied.

"Thank you. He'll be pleased to hear that."

They reached Visigodred's study. It was as vast as the common hall of other castles. Its walls were concealed behind glazed cabinets containing collections of knives, swords, bows, crystalware, coins, books, almost everything else collectable. Shelves and shelves of scrolls and bound librums formed semi-partitions dividing the room, and among them stood a dozen tables piled high with as yet unclassified arcana. A carpet collection covered the floor. A hundred rare lamps struggled to overcome the gloom of the windowless hall. A pair of leopards dozed in the circle of warmth before a fireplace at the head of the room.

Something made a sound overhead. Bragi peered upward. A tiny, vaguely human face looked back, chittering. Its owner ran along an oaken beam. Ragnarson shuddered. Not having seen a monkey in years, he forgot the creatures and jumped to the conclusion that it was the wizard's demonic familiar.

The monkey scampered to the end of the beam and dropped into the arms of a tall, thin, gray-bearded gentleman in plain, worn green clothing embroidered with thread-of-silver. He was obviously a man fond of green in its darker shades. His steely eyes radiated strength of character. He smiled and disengaged a hand from the monkey's as Ragnarson approached.

"Welcome back, Bragi." They shook. "It's been a long time. What? Three years? Hush, Billy," he told the monkey. "It's all right." To Ragnarson, "He's frightened. Not many people come calling on a crusty old wizard. Go on, Billy. Go play with Tooth and Claw."

The monkey slipped down Visigodred's leg, carefully kept his master between himself and the strangers, ran toward the leopards. He glanced back to make sure all was well, then grabbed a spotted tail and yanked. The leopard, which had appeared to be sleeping, spun and boxed with a paw. But Billy wasn't there anymore. He scampered away, chittering with monkey laughter.

"Are you collecting animals now?"

"No, not really. They were presents from a friend. A woman called Mist. Dump the books off a couple of those chairs and make yourselves comfortable."

They recovered chairs while Visigodred cleared a small table near the fire. Soon they were comfortably seated, accepting wine from an attentive servant, and were ready to talk. Ragnarson produced a pair of heavy gold coins. Visigodred held them to the lamplight.

"Hmm. Ilkazar. Hammered. Reign of Valis the Red-Hand. Not the Imperial Mint. Mark of the Gog-Ahlan Occupational Mint on this one. I don't recognize the other. Quatrefoil and roses. Shemerkhan, do you think? Extremely rare, the provisional coinage. Ilkazar didn't hold the eastern cities long, and most of the Imperial strikings were remelted after the Fall. Any more where these came from?"

"Enough to ruin the market."

Visigodred's eyebrows rose. "The Treasure of Ilkazar?"

Ragnarson nodded.

"You've found it, then? Congratulations. I knew you'd make it someday. Any big plans?"

"It wasn't me. Somebody else found it. You know the name. Varthlokkur."

The wizard's eyes narrowed. "That's not a good name to throw around. What's the connection?"

"Besides gold, he's got another treasure—of sorts. My friend Mocker's wife. You heard about the fall of the Storm Kings?"

"Who hasn't? News travels fast in this business." Visigodred's eyes sparkled. There was a joke hidden somewhere in that remark.

"No doubt."

"And I know Varthlokkur was involved. It's been a long time since he's stirred any trouble. He's got the Brotherhood into a state you can't imagine. And all because of a woman, eh?"

Elana nodded.

Visigodred lent her a quick, warm smile, and continued, "One Nepanthe, I believe. She catches his fancy, but not vice versa. So he destroys Ravenkrak and carries her off. Traditional sort of thing for people who have the power to make it stick. My colleagues are chasing their tails because of it. A reemergence of the Empire Destroyer...To understate, it's disturbing.

"The thing is, see, he isn't part of the gang." Visigodred chuckled. "The boys in the Prime Circle don't like it when we have these disturbances by somebody who doesn't belong to the club. They can't control him." In a more serious tone, he added, "We don't like having that nasty a potential enemy roaming around out here right now. Too many strange things are happening in the east. We've held several emergency sessions of the Prime Circle. Nothing got decided, of course. Nothing ever will as long as we have to put up with that blowhard Zindahjira.

"But let's get back to the point. What's your connection with all this?"

"Nepanthe married Mocker the night before Ravenkrak fell. And now Mocker is headed for Fangdred. He thinks he's going to rescue her."

"Ah. So. I've overlooked your part in this, haven't I? Rendel Grimnason? You could've picked a more melodic name. So. You're scared the wolf won't bother distinguishing the sheep from the goats, eh?" Visigodred chuckled. "Our fat friend has put you and bin Yousif into a tight spot, eh? He's hung a sword over your heads, so to speak. Let me guess. You want my help."

Elana's head bobbed. Ragnarson nodded once, quickly.

"My Power is useless against his. That's the man who crushed the Empire, Bragi. He defeated the wizards of Ilkazar, whom even the Tervola held in respect. He trained in Shinsan, with Chin, Wu, Feng, and the Princes Thaumaturge themselves. That's something you shouldn't ever forget. The entity we call Varthlokkur was, in a way, created in Shinsan. The Dread Empire will always be part of his story."

"I know."

He didn't. To him the Dread Empire had the substance of a ghost. Shinsan was just a bogeyman supposedly hiding out somewhere in the far east. "We didn't expect you to go it alone. The surviving Storm Kings and..." He let it trail off. Presenting the other name would be tricky.

"And?"

"Zindahjira. Maybe. Haroun's trying to sign him up now."

"That stubborn fool? Bin Yousif will need a week just to get him to admit I'm alive. I have the audacity to survive everything he throws at me."

"There's a potent bribe. Turran is willing to give up the Horn of the Star Rider and his storm-sender if you'll help. One thing for each of you."

"The Windmjirnerhorn, eh? Tempting tidbit, Bragi, but everybody, except the Star Rider, who has anything to do with it gets the dirty end. Still, the proposition has merit. If I could be sure that Zindahjira would get the Horn. He deserves it. What would you want me to do?"

"Nothing that overt, really. Just protect Mocker so he has a chance to get where he's going. And maybe give him a little help when he gets there."

"Hmm. Let's look at the *Register.*" The wizard went to a table, dug deep into a pile of books. He found what he wanted, started back.

Billy the monkey, astride a leopard and wielding a wooden sword, galloped past, close behind a terrified rat. Visigodred dodged nimbly and continued to the table. "Billy's hell on rats. He thinks. Tooth does the real work, though. Watch. She'll bring the rat around to Claw."

She did. Claw, who seemed to be asleep, moved one paw as the rat shot past. End of chase.

"Remarkably intelligent animals," Visigodred noted. "So is Billy. Well, here we are. The *Register.* If Zindahjira and I complement each other, I'll consider the job. Assuming he'll go along. But there'll be a price."

"I thought so. There always is. But it seems to me that you owe me a favor."

"And you owe me several. That more than cancels out, I'd say. I was thinking you could help me make sure the Horn goes where it's best deserved. Ah. Here we are. Zindahjira." He turned a page, peered at it closely. "Hmm. Uh-huh." One thin finger raced across the page as he read. Then he looked up, smiling. "We'd make a good team if the old windbag could keep his temper under control. But we still wouldn't be any match for Varthlokkur. Not in a heads-up fight. Really, the Princes Thaumaturge are the only men alive who could meet him one-on-one and have a chance."

A shriek interrupted Visigodred. He turned. Tooth and Claw had caught a dwarf between them. The fellow wasn't much bigger than Billy. "Tooth! Claw! Behave!" The cats let silent snarls relax into bored yawns, dropped onto their bellies. Their tails lashed slowly. Their eyes tracked the dwarf as he hurried past.

"My apprentice. What is it, Marco?" Visigodred asked. "And I do wish you'd stop teasing the cats."

The dwarf grinned lopsidedly, as if he had a lot to say about keeping leopards in the house but had to keep it to himself because Visigodred had heard it all before. "There's an owl in the parlor. Wants to see a Captain Ragnarson. Says he's fagged and wants to deliver his message so he can get some sleep. Very polite, for an owl. But if you ask me, he's found Gert up in the tower and it ain't sleep he's got on his feeble mind."

Ragnarson's eyebrows rose. It wasn't every day you met a man who talked to owls. Visigodred smiled. "Show him in, Marco. No, go around the other way. I'll let the cats have you one of these days." To Ragnarson, "A message from Zindahjira, no doubt. But routed through you because of his pride."

"Then Haroun must've made good time. It's a bitch of a trip to the Seydar Sea."

The dwarf returned with a huge owl perched on his shoulder. The bird made sounds in his ear. "He don't like being out in the daytime."

The owl fluttered to the table and stalked over to Ragnarson. It lifted a tufted leg. Bragi tried to avoid its wise, darkness-filled eyes as he removed the message. Then the bird took wing and was gone. Ragnarson examined the parchment, passed it on to Visigodred.

The wizard scanned it. "Ah, he's willing. One small hurrah for greed, Bragi. It's just a matter of negotiation now. And here comes dinner. Make yourselves comfortable. You'll be here a while. Marco! Come back here! I've got a job for you." Visigodred smiled again.

Ragnarson groaned silently, understanding. He and Elana were going to be hostages against the chance that they were working another hoax like the one that had destroyed Ravenkrak.

Visigodred began giving instructions to a terribly unhappy dwarf.

Turran and his brothers gave Iwa Skolovda a wide berth in passing. That city's new masters would have liked nothing better than to have had Storm King heads to decorate pikes over its gates. A day and fifty miles east of Iwa Skolovda, riding hard and with a snowstorm running before them, they happened on an abandoned farmhouse.

"What should we send?" Brock asked as they settled in.

"All we can, here to Fangdred, till we find out where he is," Turran replied. "After we get help from those wizards, we can relax."

That night a heavy snow carpeted Shara and the western Dragon's Teeth. Next night there was another fall, and another the night following, and so on till the end of the week. Travel in East Heatherland, Shara, and the Dragon's Teeth became virtually impossible.

The eighth day brought a change in schedule. Toward sundown, with Turran readying the sending gear, taciturn Brock brewing tea, and Jerrad and Valther out collecting firewood, the air over the cottage was split by an echoing scream. Something hit the roof with a resounding thump, rolled off into the snowdrifts against the north wall. Muted, colorful invectives followed, then there was a knock at the door. Turran answered it, found a shivering, grumbling dwarf awaiting his response.

"Damned roc!" the dwarf snarled as he pushed into the cottage. "Sense of humor like you never saw. Likes to watch things fall. Especially when they kick and scream on the way down. Marco's the name. Hey! You! How about some of that tea? I'm freezing my ass off. You Turran?" he asked, of Turran. "Yeah? Like I said, I'm Marco. From Mendalayas. Visigodred sent me, and a pox on the old sumbitch. All the way to the Seydar Sea, a week with that blowhard Zindahjira, and now the devil's own time finding you guys. Ah. Tea. Fit for the gods. I'll bitch about it in the morning, but it's ambrosia tonight. Look, Turran, the boss sent some junk for you. A map." He produced it. "And this thingee'll put you through to Visigodred and Zindahjira when you want. They're on twenty-four-hour watch at Mendalayas. Must be one hell of a broad."

Marco talked and talked. Turran seldom slipped a word in. The dwarf anticipated all his questions. He pointed out the salient features of the land between the farmhouse and Fangdred. He located Mocker, astonishing Turran. The fat man had gotten a lot further than he had expected, having crossed Shara and made it well into the foothills of the Dragon's Teeth.

"This gimmick," said Marco, after taking a last item from his pack, "will give you a permanent view of what your friend is doing. Everything, so have a little respect." It seemed to be a stone, a crystal, a duplicate of the object meant to provide contact with Visigodred and Zindahjira. "The boss would've sent more, but they're all tied up. One for the woman, one for the wizard, one for the Old Man of the Mountain. And another to keep an eye on Zindahjira."

Turran smiled thoughtfully, said, "And one for myself and each of my brothers, no doubt. And still another for you."

The dwarf winked and said, "Let's get on it. It's cold out here, there ain't no girls, and I can't go home where there are till this crap's over. First order of business is a conference. Visigodred and Zindahjira are hanging around waiting for you."

Fifteen: Spring, 997 afe
The Light of Arrows as They Sped, the Flash of a Glittering Spear

Tooth and Claw nervously patrolled the reorganized study, in no mood for loafing by the fire. Billy lay curled in Visigodred's lap, sleeping fitfully, plagued by unhappy monkey dreams. Perhaps the leopards of his mind were closing on the running ghost of his monkey-imagination. Servants came and went, bringing refreshments and carrying away dirty mugs and dishes, or tending the roaring fire. They were as jittery as the pets. At the table where Visigodred and Ragnarson hunched over one of the wizard's seeing-stones, the tension was doubly thick. Mocker had moved to within fifty miles of Fangdred. And Varthlokkur had shown signs, finally, of getting ready to defend himself. An assassin had been sent out from the Castle of Wind. He and Mocker would meet in a matter of hours.

But hours there were, and worrying before the fact was useless. Ragnarson said as much.

"You're right," Visigodred replied softly, with a tremor. "But it's not the encounter that worries me. We'll get him past the ambush. Zindahjira's studying the terrain now, setting it up. The problem is, how do we do it without getting caught?" He paused, chuckled, continued, "That ham-hand Zindahjira wanted to use a smoke-demon. Might as well write our names in fire on a midnight sky."

Ragnarson, from beneath his brows as he watched the crystal ball, studied Visigodred's face. Behind the gray beard and nonchalance, the wizard was pale. Beads of perspiration glittered on his forehead. Was the dread attached to Varthlokkur really that well-founded? Varthlokkur hadn't done anything remarkable that he could see. He considered hints dropped during his conversation with Haroun the previous evening, via the crystals. Zindahjira was scared silly.

He jumped when he felt the touch on his shoulder. The hand slipped down his back. "Anything happening?" Elana whispered.

"No. We're waiting for the guy to pick his ambush. Then we'll decide what to do about it. It'll be hours yet."

She ran slim fingers through his hair, stepped behind him, massaged his neck and shoulders. "You've got to get some sleep," she said.

Bragi turned, smiled weakly, put his hands on her shoulders, gave her a peck on the forehead, said, "You're a regular mother hen. Practicing?"

"Pooh! Typical male reaction. I was just telling you what you're too numb to notice for yourself. Really, you're going to pass out if you don't get some rest."

"Uhm. Guess I am a little groggy. I'll rest after we get Mocker through this."

Visigodred leaned forward, peered into the globe. "I think this's what we're waiting for," he said, his voice more animated than earlier.

Ragnarson and Elana jostled behind him, trying to watch over his shoulder. Tooth and Claw stopped pacing, waited expectantly. Billy stirred in Visigodred's lap, uncurled, sat up, rubbed his eyes with his monkey fists. Visigodred caught him beneath the arms and sat him on the floor.

"Go over by Tooth, Billy. I've got work to do."

The leopards returned to the fire and stretched out, but didn't relax. They remained tense, as if about to spring. Billy sat between them, a hand on a shoulder of each. He remained unnaturally quiet.

A servant came in, asked Visigodred if he needed refreshments.

The wizard said, "Will, call everybody in. We're about to begin."

The servant's eyes widened. He set his pitcher on the nearest table, hurried out.

"Ah, yes, this's the place," the wizard murmured, after returning to the crystal. "Note the cover."

Ragnarson had. The assassin had chosen an ambuscade where the road hung in the side of a steep mountain and was so narrow that a traveler could do little to evade an attacker. The assassin, on the other hand, from the canyon's opposite wall, could operate from rocky cover perfect for his purpose. He had concealment, protective shelter, and a view of a mile of road.

After a time, Visigodred grunted, "Ah!" He had noticed the servants at the door. Waving a thin, blue-veined hand in the direction of another table, he said, "Over there. Each one watch a ball. Tell me if anything happens."

The servants shuffled to seats before balls similar to those before Visigodred. The wizard asked, "Where's Mocker?"

A man described Mocker's surroundings.

Visigodred nodded. "Less than an hour now. Well, what's happening in the Wind Tower?"

"Nothing I can hear, Lord. They're quiet, waiting."

"I don't like not being able to see into that place," Visigodred complained. "They could be doing anything, and I can only listen. Is Zindahjira ready?"

"Yes," a woman replied, fearfully. Zindahjira was no pleasant sight, even shrouded in darkness. Which he always was. He sought shadows as green plants seek the light. "He wants to talk to you."

"Bring the ball."

Ragnarson and Elana moved back, but watched as Visigodred murmured to the crystal. It murmured back, softly, like the susurration of a gentle sea, or of a breeze in pines. Visigodred mumbled some more, then nodded. Turning, he told Ragnarson, "We can do it without getting caught. He had the same idea I did. Just a matter of waiting, and of casting a few spells. One to protect your friend from ordinary weapons. I'll tend to that now."

The couple withdrew to the table displaying the larger battery of crystals. Over a man's shoulder, Ragnarson watched Mocker labor up a steep trail toward his brush with the Dark Lady.

"Oh! Look!" Elana whispered excitedly. "Nepanthe!"

Bragi moved to her side, looked over another shoulder. Yes, there she was, Mocker's wife, seated in her room in Fangdred, perhaps praying. When he asked, the servant observing said she'd just been told about Varthlokkur's intentions. From all appearances, she was steeling herself against the inevitable. Tiny in the crystal, she began pacing her chamber nervously. Her face was both frightened and hopeful.

After what seemed several hours, but was really just one, the wizard called, "Bring me Mocker's crystal, please." Bragi did so. Visigodred studied it, nodded, and whispered the final cantrip of a spell he had been casting. After another eternity of waiting, he said, "We're about to start."

Ragnarson's beard and head cast a strange shadow as he studied the crystals before the wizard. Elsewhere, the low talk of the servants died to a silence broken only by heavy breathing, leopards' claws on naked stone as the cats paced before the hearth, and Visigodred softly murmuring another spell. Tension grew as he finished the incantation. "What're Varthlokkur and the Old Man doing?" he asked of the other table.

"Nothing I can hear, Lord."

Visigodred nodded. Another minute passed. Elana called, "Nepanthe's left her room. Looks like she's headed for the tower."

The wizard nodded again. In one crystal, Mocker strained up that last steep mile to the ambush. In another the assassin moved slightly, getting into position. "It's time," said Visigodred.

The assassin moved again. Visigodred leaned forward, the last cantrip of a powerful spell ready to roll over his lips. Ragnarson gripped the back of the sorcerer's chair so hard his knuckles cracked. Across the room, Elana bit her lower lip white.

There was a little flash of something in sunlight before the assassin's rocks. Ragnarson, eyes on Mocker's globe, saw his friend stagger, fall against the mountainside, slide down to his knees. Then the fat man scrambled for cover with the haste of a rat noticing an approaching terrier. Another flash of crossbow bolt in the assassin's crystal. It hit rock near Mocker's head, scattering bits of stone, stinging him into greater effort.

"Ah," Visigodred sighed. "Here it comes." Ragnarson saw motion on the mountain above and behind the killer. Ice and snow were moving there, drifting down majestically, like a waterfall in low gravity. The whole mountain seemed to be crumbling.

The avalanche swept toward the assassin, a flood of frozen death. It seemed to take forever to reach him. He had plenty of time to notice it and start running. And, once it arrived, it was another forever departing. But once the flow had passed, so had the immediate threat to Mocker. Who, in his crystal, resumed his journey grinning like a boy who knew a secret.

"That should do for a while," said Visigodred, sighing wearily. "You people can go back to work." The servants fled.

"You suppose Varthlokkur'll believe it was accidental?" Ragnarson asked.

"Don't see why not."

"What'll he try next?"

"Who knows? But you needn't worry yet. Why not get some sleep?"

"Hey, Turran," Marco shouted from the cottage door. "The boss wants you. Got work to do. Varthlokkur tried to get your friend." The dwarf was the only one who paid the crystals much mind. As he was willing to do little else, the Storm Kings had left him that as his share of the work.

Turran swung his axe, burying its head deep in the chopping block. He gathered his coat. His dark eyes were piercing as he approached the dwarf. Marco was always as bold as his mouth. Unimpressed by anyone but himself, he returned the stare without flinching.

"Would you call my brothers?" Turran asked, pausing at the door.

"No need. Made a point of hollering loud enough the first time. They heard me. Look there. Running. Looks like Jerrad found us something to eat."

Indeed. Even at a distance, Turran easily recognized the wild goat draped across Jerrad's shoulders. He nodded.

"You talk to the boss," said the dwarf. "I'll start the tea. Damn! It's lousy stuff. Why didn't you bring something fit to drink? Wine. Ale." He turned to the fire, muttering and shaking his head.

Turran grinned, remembering Marco's promise to complain. Then his eyebrows rose. The dwarf was actually doing something. Never, since his arrival, had he done anything more helpful than watch the globes, or lounge around talking in endless streams. Mostly about women. His women. Idly, as he seated himself before a crystal, Turran wondered about Marco's oft-touted, very secret "system." Probably talked till they fell asleep from boredom, then made his move.

He touched the ball in the place Marco had shown him. Visigodred's thin face, like a strange, bearded fish hurtling up from diamond deeps, swam into view.

"Marco says Varthlokkur's made his first move," he said. "We weren't watching. How'd it come out? All right, I suppose, since you're smiling."

The crystal shivered in Turran's fingers, made a soft sound like breezes in a field of ripe wheat. There were words in the whisper, words indistinguishable at more than a yard.

"It went well, with no reaction. They were unhappy at Fangdred, but not suspicious. At least not that I could detect. Just now, Varthlokkur's railing at the Fates and Norns. The Old Man hasn't said anything. He's our real worry. He's not as emotionally involved. Nepanthe's still gloating, of course. Mocker'll be there soon."

"Excellent! Excellent!" said Turran. "My brothers will be pleased. Now then, what did you want?" He listened to the whisper-wind for several minutes, nodding occasionally. When Visigodred finished, he said, "Right away."

"Marco! Visigodred wants you." He placed the crystal before another chair. The dwarf bounded over, said, "Yeah, Chief?"

"You behaving?"

"Don't I always?"

"Not often, but I muddle through. Somebody wants to talk to you." The wizard disappeared, to be replaced by three young women. Turran's eyebrows rose. All three spoke at once. Marco gave Turran a look that said, "This's private." Chuckling, the Storm King joined his brothers, who had just arrived and were ready to clean the goat.

When finished with his conversation, Marco came to supervise. "Poor girls!" he told the room, his demoniac eyes sad. "They're so lonely without me. Poor dear things. What'd the boss want, Turran?"

"A storm around Fangdred, so Varthlokkur can't send out any more ambushers."

Midnight. Everyone was asleep, including Valther, who had the watch. From outside, spaced in a slow cadence, came the sounds of feet breaking crusted snow. The door, not locked, swung slowly inward; limned by moonlight off the snow, a stooped figure paused there, listened. Hearing nothing but heavy snores, the man stepped inside and closed the door.

Picking his way with a staff as though he were blind, this bent old man made a circuit of the room. He examined each sleeper by the glow of the stone on the table. Before leaving each he nodded his satisfaction—till he came to Marco. There he frowned puzzledly, but soon shrugged and moved on.

Across his back he carried a bulky bundle that he quickly, deftly exchanged for a similar bundle Turran had secreted beneath a trap in the cottage floor. Carefully, carefully, like a man with a fragile jar of precious oil, he carried the object out into the Storm Kings' winter's night.

Then, once his footfalls faded, a voice, as old as time, as distant as the first dawn, "Come, my beauty of the sky. We ride home with our treasure again." A peal of laughter echoed over the snowfields. And, after a lightning flash without thunder, hooves crunched snow, then a huge white horse beat vast wings and scaled the night. Dwindling merriment trailed behind.

He always took it back once its damage had been done.

SIXTEEN: SPRING, 997 AFE
FOR LOVE IS STRONG AS DEATH, JEALOUSY IS CRUEL AS THE GRAVE

"I don't understand," Varthlokkur muttered. "He just won't quit." Behind him, like wind chimes, tiny silver bells tinkled endlessly, much louder now than in their first tentative speech of a week ago. The silver-chased arrow pointed unswervingly westward.

The Old Man, seated before the mirror, leaned forward. He felt totally alive as he studied the man crossing a glacier a hundred miles to their west. Off and on, since the first musical intimation of peril, he and Varthlokkur had come to watch the fool fight his way toward them. A strange, unswerving man, he, frightening in his tenacity. Nothing daunted him. Not foul weather, nor mountains, nor any of the small disasters with which Varthlokkur had tried to induce despair. Snowslides, landslides, fallen trees, washed-out roads, he made his way around or over them all with a patience that bespoke an absolute conviction of final victory. And, though he had traveled fewer than fifty miles this past week, he still rose each dawn and gamely challenged the Dragon's Teeth till sundown. He might win the match out of sheer stubbornness.

"He's mad," said the Old Man. "He'll keep on coming till he gets what he wants. Or dies. *You* should understand."

"How so?"

"How many years to ruin Ilkazar?" And, in the back of his mind, the question still. *And at what cost to yourself?*

The wizard flinched, turned away. "Too many, all wasted. And it's been Hell's own hound on my trail ever since. Yes, I guess I understand. But for a woman?"

For what had he claimed vengeance on Ilkazar? A rhinoceros?

"He loves me!"

Both men turned. Nepanthe glared at them from the doorway, her face a mask of poorly controlled anger. Varthlokkur nodded. "Maybe so, though personally I'd bet on wounded pride."

Nepanthe's thoughts were obvious. Of course he was coming for love. Harsh events still hadn't broken the grip romanticism had on her mind, though its hold had begun slipping. "You suppose? You'll learn supposition when he gets here!"

But his remark had dampened her fire, Varthlokkur saw. "Nepanthe, Nepanthe, why can't you be rational? Whether he kills me, or, as is more likely, I..." He let it trail off, saying instead, "Well, we don't have to shout about it."

"You've kidnapped me, separated me from my husband, and you want me to be grateful? You think I should be reasonable about it? Why don't *you* be reasonable? Give me some winter clothes and let me go." She had tried to escape twice already. Twice she had been intercepted and gently returned to her room. "I promise to keep him from killing you."

Varthlokkur turned to hide his amusement. That was his due, wasn't it? The wicked wizards of the romances always ended up spitted on a hero's sword.

The Old Man, far from amused, assumed the argument. "You just won't understand, will you? This man, Varthlokkur, has spent four centuries waiting for you. Four centuries! Why? Because the Fates themselves say you should be his. Yet you'd defy them for so insignificant a thing as this... this actor and thief. What is he? What can he do?"

"He can love me."

"Can he? Does he? How much of that was for Varthlokkur's pay? And Varthlokkur himself, is he incapable of loving you?"

"Can he love at all?" she demanded, though weakly. Her certainties were being undermined. Wicked doubt had begun to insinuate black tentacles through cracks in her bastions of faith. "The whole world knows what he is. The murderer of an entire city."

Angry himself, the Old Man smiled cruelly and snapped, "Dvar!"

Nepanthe's defiance wilted, folding in like a tulip blossom at nightfall. Ilkazar had been a city of antediluvian greed and wickedness. Any sense of justice had to agree that its doom hadn't been undeserved. That wasn't the case with Dvar, a little third-rate spear-carrier of a city, a mutual dependency of Iwa Skolovda and Prost Kamenets. Its single fame was a fierce, always-doomed devotion to the cause of its right to be mistress of its own affairs. Nepanthe, who had been so exhilarated the night that tiny state had been crushed, now shut up and dropped into a chair. She turned her back on the men.

The Old Man stared at her. She was near tears. He had touched an emotional canker. And, once again, he saw why both her husband and Varthlokkur found her attractive. She was beautiful, though loneliness and fear were stains on her loveliness. She had been bravely defiant since her arrival, loudly certain of her impending rescue, never admitting a doubt that her husband would come. But now, he suspected, she had begun to realize that her Mocker was challenging *Varthlokkur*. She had cause to be frightened. Still, he had to admire her. Her fear was for her husband, not for herself. He watched her massage her right temple, caught a glimpse of the crystal tear she wanted hidden.

Varthlokkur left the room. Mocker's endless fight with the mountains had grown tedious.

The Old Man concentrated on the mirror, ignored the woman. Soon he heard the rustle of fabric. She stepped past him and stared into the mirror from close up. "Why're you so harsh?" he asked.

"I should be thankful that he wrecked my home and killed my brothers?"

"And dragged you through the mountains like a common slave," the Old Man interjected. "You made the point earlier. No, I don't expect you to be happy. But I *would* like you to keep an open mind about why. And to contradict you on one score. Your brothers are still alive, except Luxos, who more or less committed suicide."

"What? Why didn't he tell me?"

"Desperation, maybe. He's a great believer in destiny."

"Pardon?"

"Consider: assume you've loved someone for centuries…"

"Love?"

"Love. Let me continue. Suppose you've been waiting for someone you love for three or four *hundred* years. Your husband, for instance. And, when that person, who had been promised you for so long, finally arrives, you get nothing but pain from him. Wouldn't you try just about anything? Even a little cruelty? I'd bet that he hasn't mentioned your brothers because he wants you to feel dependent. Like there's no one else who cares. Why'd you reject him?"

"I'm married. And happy with the husband I have." It wasn't a considered answer. In fact, the Old Man had the feeling that her marriage was a miracle in which she still didn't entirely believe.

"He courted you for twelve years before you ever met this Mocker. I wanted to know why you rejected him then."

She shrugged. "I have to admit that he was a perfectly behaved suitor. And I liked him. As much as I could any man. He really did do a lot for me. He helped me understand myself. More than he'll ever know. I was grateful for that. But he was so *old*. And his name was Varthlokkur. I always thought he wanted to use me, for my Power."

"If he'd come to you young, with another name—what then? And, as to the Power, if he had wanted it, who was to stop him after his demonstration at Ilkazar? Have you no logic at all?"

"I don't know… If he'd come young, maybe. But I had other problems…" She shrugged. Then with a forced laugh, "No one ever accused me of being logical."

"Varthlokkur once had a servant who fell in love with him. For various reasons, he made himself young and married her. The point: he's old by choice, not by necessity. And, despite whatever you've heard, or even have seen, he's a kind, gentle man who abhors force and violence. Maybe it's a reaction against the excesses of his youth. Tell me, has he ever treated you with anything less than kindness and respect?"

"He kidnapped me!"

The Old Man sighed. Full circle and back to that again. "Ignore that. That was my idea, and he did it under protest, for want of any better idea. Otherwise, he'd've gone on for years, mooning over you and getting nowhere."

"You?"

"Yes."

"I guess he treats me all right, but that's a moot point now. I'm married." She indicated the man in the mirror.

"Let's discuss realities. Varthlokkur, for your sake, has held back. He hasn't done anything but block the road. Sooner or later, though, he'll have to do something. This creature you call a husband is going to be dead pretty soon—unless he gives up. Either way, that part of your life is over. I'll take care of it myself, if Varthlokkur doesn't have the will."

"If you kill him, I'll throw myself off the wall," she replied softly. "If he turns back, I'll cry a little before I jump. But he won't give up."

"Don't be melodramatic," the Old Man retorted. But the thing was, he thought her capable of keeping her promise. She was proving to be an incurable romantic.

Varthlokkur was tired. Tired of arguing with Nepanthe, tired of striving to maintain a grasp on Power that seemed to be waning, tired of battling the Fates or whatever malign forces were controlling his destiny. Most frustrating was the recent diminution of his control of the Power. Even his best-conceived experiments were sputtering. There were moments when he considered evading events by cocooning himself in the Old Man's deep sleep. He also considered suicide, but only in that brief and quickly rejected fashion which is a universal experience. Neither death, nor the long sleep, would serve his purpose. Only for Nepanthe had he lived so long; he would have what he wanted.

He often paced the quiet loneliness of the Wind Tower, stretching himself on a rack of thought while searching for ways to reach Nepanthe. And he found ways, but rejected them because they ignored her consent. He wanted her to be aware, understanding, and accepting.

Mocker also troubled him. He could be rid of the pest with a single, smashing magical blow, but, for the sake of peace with Nepanthe, he held back. Still, he had to do something soon. Defend himself he must.

One afternoon he sat before the mirror, chin on fist, watching his enemy climb a mountain. He was sleepy-thoughtful, paying the mirror little heed. He drifted on a cloud of laziness. There was a mood on him, lethargic, and he felt better than he had in a long time. It was as if some off-the-scenes diplomat had arranged a brief truce with the Fates.

A soft sound. The door opened behind him. Still he didn't turn. He would allow nothing to break his mood.

Light footsteps crossed the room, stopped behind him. Still he didn't turn. His eyelids, suddenly unbearably heavy, closed. The footsteps moved to the mirror. He knew that Nepanthe was watching her husband. Here was another opportunity to present his case, but he refused it. He had no desire to sacrifice his mood on an altar of fruitless argument.

He heard the rustle of her dress as she settled into the Old Man's chair, thought he could detect the faint whisper of her breathing. In a moment of euphoric wish-fulfillment, he tried to imagine that breath in his hair, against his shoulder, as he remembered Marya's. Memories stirred. The face of the imagined lover became that of his wife, and he drifted off on a pleasant daydream. Guilt nibbled at the edge of his mind. He should have allowed her another child. But no. What was that saying the Old Man had? "Children are hostages to Fate." Or to anyone able to lay hands on them.

Nepanthe's soft cough brought him back. He cracked an eyelid, looked her way. She stared back nervously. "I don't feel like arguing," he said, closing the eye.

"I don't want to either," she replied, her voice sending chills down his spine. "I just want to know why you can't let me go."

"You see?" Varthlokkur said with a sigh. "Here's one starting. I've told you why a hundred times, but you don't hear me. If I tell you again, you'll say it's not so, and still want a reason. What's the point? Go away and let me snooze, woman. Let me be a tired old man for a day."

Nepanthe shifted in her chair, frowned. Briefly, she remembered what the Old Man had said, wondered about Varthlokkur's looks as a young man. She suspected he would be quite handsome, hawkish, rather like that man bin Yousif. "All right," she said. "For the sake of argument—oh, what a miserable choice of words!—we'll say that you've told me the truth. What're you planning to do?"

He opened both eyes, fixed her with his stare. She stared back as defiantly as ever. "What am I going to do? Do you really care?" A little sharp, that. "Nothing. I'll just react. To you. To him." Pointing to the mirror, "If he keeps coming, I'll have to defend myself. Sometime soon now. As for you, time will decide."

Nepanthe stirred nervously, stared at her husband. Her face paled a little. Varthlokkur assumed she was thinking of his Power.

"I don't want to hurt anybody," he continued. "But you two, by defying the Fates, are forcing me to. For you, the Fates and Norns bend. For me they're inflexible."

"The Fates! The Norns! That's all I ever hear around here. Can't you be honest? Blame things on yourself? You're the one causing all the trouble."

"See? There you go, just like I said. I tell you, I'm following a foreordained course. I *must* do what I do because I'm a pawn of Destiny. The sooner you realize that you're one, too, the sooner we'll finish this unpleasantness."

"There's no argument that can turn me away from *him*," she snapped. "He's my husband. Nothing can change that. I won't let it—and the Fates, or whatever, be damned."

"Not even death?" Varthlokkur asked. "He'll die in a day or two. For your sake I've given him time to think and back down. But pretty soon, if he's still coming, I'll stop him."

"I'll jump off the wall!"

"No you won't. The divinations say you'll live a long time yet."

"Divinations! Mummery!"

Though his skills were in question, Varthlokkur was too tired to fight. Quietly, he responded, "Nepanthe, I've performed divinations for centuries and I haven't yet seen one proven wrong. I've seen errors in interpretation, human errors, but never false predictions. Those old divinations are becoming reality today. You're living at the impact point of an arrow of destiny loosed four hundred years ago. Believe it or not, whichever you want, but be warned. Sometime in the next few days you'll make a decision the Fates have left to you alone. On it will hinge my future, yours, your husband's, and possibly that of empires. Really. I've seen. When you decide, please, and I'll beg on my knees if I have to to get you to do it, be cool and logical. For once, just this precious once, put emotion aside and *think* before you start talking."

Nepanthe shuddered. There was enough strength in his tone to convince her that he believed what he had said. "What decision?"

"On my proposal."

"How could that effect anybody but you and me and Mocker? Don't give me any more of your smooth tongue. You already know my answer."

"Do I? Do you? Maybe. But things change. Moment by moment. You might think it's decided, but there're days yet before it becomes irrevocable. I beg you, when the time comes, consider with your mind, not your heart." That he hadn't as yet shown her his necromantic arguments didn't bother him. He had completely overlooked the fact that she didn't know as much as he.

"I won't be your woman."

"Why not?"

"I'm married."

Varthlokkur sighed. Round full circle and back to that pointless argument yet again. Piqued, he snapped, "You won't be when I get rid of that cretin…" He groaned. The destroying, hurting madness was threatening to claim him again. He was afraid he wouldn't be able to stop it.

"Touch him and I'll kill you!"

He was startled. This was a different Nepanthe. Anger gave way to curiosity.

He studied her face, searching for the truth behind her threat. Ah. She didn't mean it. She was answering his spite with bluster of her own. "I doubt it." And yet, it wasn't impossible. Precautions would have to be taken. A sad business, this.

The Old Man, precariously supporting a silver tray on one hand, eased into the chamber. He frowned as sharp-as-sabers words sliced the air. They had started hurting one another again. "Does this have to go on all the time?" he asked. "The vitriol's beginning to bore me. My father—ah, yes, I did have one, and you needn't look so surprised—had a saying: 'If you can't say something nice, keep your damned mouth shut.'"

"It can stop anytime!" Nepanthe snapped. "Get this bearded lecher to let me go."

"There must be some invisible barrier between you two. No common concepts, or something. Or maybe you just won't listen to each other. I've got an idea." The Old Man's voice became like silk, like honey, like candy-covered daggers. "A way for him to get through to you, Nepanthe. I'll work a spell on your mind. You'll *have* to do what's necessary."

Varthlokkur flashed him a hot, angry look. Unperturbed, he smiled back wickedly, and the more so when he saw that Nepanthe had been shocked into silence. Numbly, she took a cup of wine from the tray. She asked Varthlokkur, "Could he do that?"

"Easily. And your opinion of your husband would become lower than mine. His touch would, literally, make you ill."

She showed every evidence of terror. "What a wicked, horrible thing… Why haven't you done it, then?"

"I wonder, too," the Old Man growled. "It'd save a lot of trouble…"

"And I said that I don't want a slave," Varthlokkur snarled back. "I want a whole woman."

"But you haven't gotten the ghost of that, have you?" the Old Man asked with more false sweetness. "What you're getting is heartaches from a bitch with a brick head… Damn! Now you've got me doing it!"

Varthlokkur and Nepanthe stood open-mouthed, shocked. The Old Man shook his head. He had just shown Nepanthe that their unity was little more than a facade anymore, that there were tensions growing between them. She might make little of that now, but later… Right now his words hurt, he suspected, more than anything Varthlokkur could have said. She gulped her wine, then hurried out. Her shoulders were slumped.

"A beautiful woman," said the Old Man. "Loyal and spirited. I'm sorry. Frustration."

"I understand. How often have I forced myself not to say the same things?" He visibly controlled his own anger. This as yet unbroached dissension between them had to be held in abeyance. The crisis was so close now… He would need even halfhearted allies.

"It might do her some good. Start her thinking. Who knows? There's a proverb in my collection. It's one of the oldest: 'You can't make omelets without breaking eggs.' And speaking of eggs to crack, what're we going to do about her husband? He's getting too close." A change of subject might direct both their frustrations into useful work.

"I don't know. I don't want to hurt her anymore… But I don't have a hope while he's alive, do I? Any ideas?"

"Ideas, yes. You might not like them. Without your problems, I see him with more detachment. I like to think. I've been planning. We've got a fellow here who's magnificent with the crossbow. I talked to him yesterday. He's willing to go down and pick this Mocker off whenever you give the word."

"Well, it's simple and straightforward." Varthlokkur rubbed his forehead, thought for a long time, seeking alternatives. He seemed sadder, older, and wearier than the Old Man could remember. After a time he waved a hand and said, "All right, go ahead. Might as well get it over with."

Varthlokkur and the Old Man watched their assassin take his position among boulders fifty miles to the west. "Does Nepanthe know?" Varthlokkur asked.

"The servants do. They'll carry the tale. There aren't any secrets around here."

The wizard nodded tiredly, tried to concentrate on the mirror. The assassin, in camouflage white and gray, had disappeared amidst snow-speckled granite.

"Ah," said the Old Man. "He's coming."

Far, Mocker rounded a corner of mountain a mile from assassin and ambush…

The door slammed against the wall behind them. Eyes red from weeping, distraught (déjà vu for Varthlokkur: he remembered another weeping woman, of long ago), Nepanthe rushed to the mirror. Her delicate hands folded over her mouth, fencing in a scream.

Varthlokkur turned to her, talons of emotion ripping his soul. She would hate him now. Tangled hair, tears in her eyes… How like the woman Smyrena…

"Now!" said the Old Man.

Varthlokkur's attention jerked back to the mirror. He saw a slight movement where the assassin hid. Mocker staggered, fell. Nepanthe screamed. Then the fat man scuttled for cover. There was more movement in the rocks. A bolt flashed, but Mocker remained unharmed. Nepanthe laughed hysterically.

"I'll be damned!" said the Old Man. "Well, he's dead when he comes out, and he'll have to sometime."

"I doubt it," Varthlokkur replied.

"Why?"

"Look up the mountain."

An avalanche swept toward the arbalester.

Varthlokkur rose, paced. His whole frame slumped in defeat. Nothing was going right anymore. Even the simplest, non-magical projects guttered out as if a dozen pairs of hands were, at cross-purposes, trying to sabotage his every deed. What a hatred the Fates must have for him!

Nepanthe laughed madly, on and on. The Old Man studied her momentarily, then turned to the mirror. He frowned thoughtfully. He grimaced when Mocker scooted out of hiding and resumed walking warily, bow now in hand. The fat man wore a wicked, confident smile.

There was snow that evening, heavy, unseasonal. The road scaling the flank of El Kabar quickly grew too icy for use. Both Nepanthe and Varthlokkur walked Fangdred's walls in the silence and peace of the snowfall, thinking, but didn't meet. The Old Man, when first he heard of the snow, frowned and returned to the Wind Tower.

Much later, Varthlokkur also went to the tower. He was tired, so tired, in heart and mind and body. "Vanity of vanities," he muttered repeatedly. "All is vanity and striving after wind."

"Here," said the Old Man as he entered the tower top chamber, offering a steaming mug exuding the foulest of odors. "This'll perk you up."

"Phew! Or kill me!" Varthlokkur stared at the mug momentarily, then gulped its contents. After several sincere, horrible faces, and a minute, he did indeed feel better. "What was that?"

"You won't believe it, but I'll tell you anyway. Nepanthe. The drink. You know, I wonder just how much foresight her father had, naming her that. She surely is a bitter draught, isn't she?"

Varthlokkur smiled weakly. "What now? We can't send another man out because of this snow. It'll have to be sorcery. But I hate to try anything. My grasp of the Power has gotten so unreliable…"

"Another halfway measure? How about the thing called the Devil's Hawk then? There's a risk, though. The bird's mortal. He could kill it. Want to try something a little more potent?"

"No, no demons. No djinn, no spirits. Once I could manage the nastiest of them, but now I don't think I could handle an ordinary air or fire elemental. Don't ever let Nepanthe know, but the concealment spell I used to get us away from Ravenkrak almost killed us. I don't understand it. I've never had any trouble before. It's just been the past couple of months. Yes, I guess it's going to have to be something like the Devil's Hawk."

Dawn had brightened the eastern horizon before Varthlokkur gained a firm control of that monster (the Power had grown so elusive that he now had trouble managing magicks even as simple as this) and had brought it flapping darkly to roost atop the Wind Tower. Its twenty-foot black wings spread like pinions of night. Its bright golden eyes burned like doors into Hell. Legend said that the creature was the bastard of a hawk and a black ifrit, and thus it had attributes of both the mortal and Outer worlds.

Later, after he had studied the bird, manipulated it, had decided that it would serve his purpose, and he was about to send it off, Nepanthe came to the tower and silently seated herself before the mirror. She was unusually quiet. Perhaps she feared a sharp comment would cause another of the Old Man's crushing outbursts. Varthlokkur took a moment to say, "I'd rather you weren't here when…"

"You won't stop him. I can feel it. I'll see him cut your heart out." Her voice was flinty. She seemed more self-certain, though no less frightened.

Varthlokkur frowned. "We'll see, then." He uttered the word that sent the Hawk along. The tower shuddered as great wings beat the air overhead. The wizard dropped into his usual chair, watched Mocker walk a ridgetop thirty miles from Fangdred.

The bird quickly arrived and began circling. Mocker saw its shadow, sped a futile shaft upward. The Old Man chuckled, then fell silent at a glance from Varthlokkur. The bird dove. Mocker cast his bow aside, readied his sword, stood his ground. Varthlokkur found himself forced to admire the man's courage… The monster broke its plunge just short of the sword, glided away.

The bird dropped into a canyon, caught an updraft, climbed. Varthlokkur and the Old Man cursed softly. Nepanthe laughed like a delighted child.

Again the monster dove, this time from the sun. Mocker was momentarily blinded. Nepanthe's laugh became a whisper when her husband threw forearm across his eyes. But, when the hawk was almost upon him, he crouched, dove aside, hurled his sword.

The huge bird hit the ridgetop, bounced, rolled, flopped fantastically as it went. Mocker was after it in an instant. At first opportunity he darted in and severed the huge head from the neck with his dagger, then jerked his rapier from the dark-as-midnight breast. He cleaned it on wing feathers and grinned.

So it was over almost as soon as it began, and that easily for the man. The Devil's Hawk, with a reputation for murderous cunning almost equaling that of its namesake, had shown no resourcefulness at all. Indeed, it had acted with incredible stupidity, almost as if drugged… "Impossible!" Varthlokkur cried. His fears rose in a sudden flood. He jumped up, paced, muttered.

"Nepanthe, go somewhere else," the Old Man snapped.

She left, silently except for a chuckle as she passed out the door.

The moment she was gone Varthlokkur wheeled, said, "He's going to make it! I won't be able to stop him!" Panic painted his features. He leaned forward, bent with the weight of his cares.

"You're right!" the Old Man growled. "He *will* make it, if you keep on like that. Come on. We haven't got time for defeatism. Let me show you why." He muttered a simple incantation and shifted the attention of the mirror. "Last night, while you walked the wall, I did some snooping. I thought it was just a little bit strange that Mocker had such fantastic luck with our ambush. That first shot was right on the mark, but he wasn't hurt. And that avalanche stretched my credulity for coincidence to the breaking point. And *then* there was the storm that sealed the gates. Just too damned convenient for him if we were going to send out somebody else."

"What're you getting at?"

"Just this: look!" the Old Man snapped, pointing.

Varthlokkur looked. There were five men, one a dwarf, centered in the mirror. Somewhere, in a tumbledown farmhouse, they huddled over a gleaming ball. They seemed terribly excited. Varthlokkur's interest was instantly engaged. "Turran! Jerrad! And Valther and Brock. What?..."

"At a guess, I'd say they're watching Mocker. They're your answer to our remarkable weather."

"I see!"

"While you're at it, notice the little fellow."

"Who? Oh. Who is he?"

The Old Man muttered another minor incantation. The scene vanished, was instantly replaced by another. "His name is Marco. He's the apprentice of this man." A thin, frightened person occupied the mirror. He bent over another crystal ball. Behind him stood a giant of a man. Varthlokkur recognized the latter immediately.

"Ragnarson."

"Yes. I told you to keep an eye on him. The game couldn't be played out with the fat man by himself. Picture their thoughts: point, you owe them money, in their opinions; point, they knew that you know they work with Mocker, and might assume this's a team effort on their part—so, in self-defense, they've made it that. The thin man is Visigodred, a wizard of the Brotherhood's Prime Circle. He caused the avalanche. And he provided the shield that kept the first quarrel from killing Mocker.

"A long time ago I enchanted this room to keep his likes from peeking in, but I couldn't protect myself from eavesdroppers. I expect he's listening right now, and he's scared to death because we've found him out. Right, Visigodred?"

Visigodred nodded. The Old Man laughed, muttered another incantation. "Trapped him that time." The mirror's eye shifted to a dark, gloomy place.

"The other one," said Varthlokkur. "Bin Yousif."

"Uhm. And a sorcerer who lives in a cave beside the Seydar Sea, several hundred miles south of here. Name's Zindahjira."

Varthlokkur shuddered as he thought of the fury of a wizards' war. "How powerful are they?"

"The *Register* lists both as Prime Circle. As good as they come in the west, excepting yourself. I hate to say I told you so..."

"Be my guest. I've earned it. Are they still listening?"

"I expect so. If not, they can when they want. Those crystals..."

"Have a definite weakness. Hand me the Yu Chan book, please." He busied himself with his tools (with a sudden something definite to do, how much better, how much more real he felt), which included an instrument like a large, two-tined fork. He accepted the required book, asked, "Will you get a crystal from the stone cabinet? The amethyst I think." He checked the book. "Yes, the amethyst. I thought I remembered this from my session with Lord Chin. There. All ready." He sang a long, complex incantation from the book, struck the fork, touched a vibrating tine to the gem, said, "That should take care of their eavesdropping. To their devices Fangdred has become a black hole. Now what?"

"Hit back!"

"No. If they're Prime Circle, they'll have powerful defenses."

"Not able to withstand you, though."

"Perhaps not. But for long enough, what with my grip on the Power being so unreliable. While I was crushing them, Mocker would arrive. He'd do his work and save them. Though they might not realize that yet."

"What *do* you plan?"

"Let me think, let me think. Oh, yes. First thing, we'll ready our own defenses. Those two are scared. They'll try hitting first and fast in hopes of catching us off guard. Once we have a solid shield, I'll set up the Winterstorm. The uncertainty version. It's still experimental, but I have a hunch I'll soon find a new source of Power useful."

"What do you want me to do?"

The two men, working in concert where the Old Man had the requisite knowledge, rapidly erected powerful shields around Fangdred. Just in time, too. The first attack came only moments after they finished.

The Old Man listened to the howl and groan and wondered just where he, and all this, fit into the Director's current scheme. He had been awake for centuries now, and had only begun to discern the ragged edges, to sense the master's butterfly touch in such probable preliminaries as the El Murid Wars.

Whatever, it would be bloody. They always were.

SEVENTEEN: SPRING, 997 AFE
AND THOUGHTS FROM VISIONS OF NIGHT

Nepanthe paced her room, brooding about Mocker, Varthlokkur, and the Old Man. A riot of worry galloped through her mind, swept like a tide, crashed against barrier-rocks, chuckled along well-worn channels. She had decided, as she had watched Mocker evade and conquer the hawk that morning, that there was a real chance he would get through. She had begun to suspect it the previous evening, while walking the wall and smelling that strange, familiar smell in the night. Somewhere, somehow, her brothers were stirring. She had recognized the scent of the Werewind.

Where are they? How had they managed an alliance with her husband? What about Ragnarson and bin Yousif? Were they involved too? Was her husband's approach an attention-grabber covering the others as they came from another direction? Hope was a sad thing, she found. When she had had none she had been at peace, though spitting fire around Varthlokkur. But now, with a glimmer of a chance, she was tormented. Like a trapped animal she ran this way and that in search of an unnoticed gap in the bars of her cage. Her heart was a snare drum with a kettledrum's voice, beating fast and loud...

Did Varthlokkur know her brothers had sent weather against him? Frightening thought. They would be defenseless against him. She threw herself onto her featherbed, on her stomach, and, chin on folded hands, stared into infinity. How could she help her rescuers? If she could distract Varthlokkur till Mocker arrived... Thoughts of seduction whirled through her head, were rejected instantly because her attentions would be too transparent, even if desired.

"Mocker, I wish I knew what to do," she whispered. All the loneliness of her stay in Fangdred gathered like a sneering specter. This fortress and its people were all too like the Dragon's Teeth themselves: stark, harsh, and primitive. She rolled over, stared at the ceiling. A tear trickled from her eye. Bad to be alone. She remembered his arms... warm... secure...

Loneliness. Now she understood Varthlokkur a little better. Four centuries made a big loneliness. She thought about his visits to Ravenkrak. His look of loneliness was one reason she had given him the time she had. She saw the same look each time she passed a mirror. If Mocker hadn't come along, and Varthlokkur hadn't lost patience and gone militant, she might be married to him now. She had considered it, truly. He wasn't a bad man, really, though he was too controlled by his unyielding belief in Destiny.

Thoughts of Varthlokkur stirred a notion for distracting him. She wouldn't pretend to do anything else. Though he would know, his nature would force him into predictable paths. She bounced up, hurried to a closet filled with clothing he had given her. He had given her many things since they had come from Ravenkrak.

She hummed as she searched the closet, a delicious pleasure after so long. Ha! Nothing could go wrong now.

Nearby, as if he knew her mind, the current piper played a tune. It was as old as time. Nepanthe laughed when she heard it. So fitting!

> The voice of my beloved!
>   Behold he comes,
> Leaping upon the mountain,
>   Bounding over the hills.

She laughed again, picturing Mocker dancing from mountaintop to mountaintop like the Star Rider in the story about the King of the Under-Mountain. She chose a frock of pale rose, held it to her breast. It looked a perfect fit, though she had seen nothing like it before. So short—just knee-length—and of such fine fabric. She remembered a woman saying that Varthlokkur had conjured the clothing from far empires. She laughed a third time, throatily, and shed the black shapeless thing she had worn since arriving.

She stood before the mirror for a moment, admired her reflected naked-ness, then scented herself with lilac—lightly, lightly, so just the slightest hint hung about her. She had never trained in a woman's devices, but she had her intuitions.

"Beware, Varthlokkur," she chuckled, studying the clothing. She had seen nothing like it before, but functions seemed apparent. Soon she stood before her mirror again, adjusting her hem. She marveled at how nice she looked in the lewd apparel. Probably not lewd where Varthlokkur had obtained it, she thought. What a strange country that must be.

The hem hung at her knees. The skirt was full, but the rest clung close, ac-centuating her curves. Bawdy. She knew the people of Fangdred, though hardly prudish, would be shocked by the bareness of her legs, the obvious outthrust of her breasts. Every woman had a smidgeon of a need to be whorish. Ah! She felt so wonderfully optimistic.

But her optimism died as she left her room. Fangdred suddenly rocked on its foundations. Stone groaned against stone. Wind screamed about the castle like cries from the Pit. No, not wind. No wind, not even the Werewind, made sounds like those. Those were Hell-creatures shrieking, hurling themselves against the fortress. Sorcery! She forgot about vamping Varthlokkur and, terrified, ran for the Wind Tower. Her raven hair streamed behind her, whipped by tongues of air. Frightened people surged through the halls, not a one noticing her dress. Even panicked, she felt disappointment. A woman needs to be noticed when she's behaving naughtily. But everyone else appeared more terrified than she, helter-skelter running nowhere away from the inescapable screaming anger beating at the fortress.

Except that idiot piper. He and she collided where corridors crossed. She could have avoided him had she been paying attention. The fool was playing the dirge from *The Wizards of Ilkazar,* loudly, perhaps mocking Varthlokkur, and she should have heard him. But fear blocked all sensitivity. The piper didn't exist till she bowled him over.

But he noticed her. With a leer, from the floor, he played an old tavern song, "Lady in a Red Dress." Nepanthe blushed and hurried on. The piping pursued her through the windy halls.

The shaking of the walls, and the pandemonium beyond them, was dying when she burst into Varthlokkur's workshop.

The wizard stood at the heart of an elaborate multiple pentagram spangled with scores of swimming magical symbols. In the air, based on the sides of a pentagram on the floor, and each sharing sides with two of the others, out-ward leaning, were five pentagrams traced in blue fire. Above the wizard was a pentagram of red fire, from the sides of which depended five pentagrams in green. These had common sides with the blue below, so that Varthlokkur was completely enclosed by a twelve-faceted jewel of pentagrams. And swimming on the planes of the aerial pentagrams were fiery symbols in silver, gold, violet, and orange. The room was dark except for the light given off by this complex thaumaturgical-topological construct. The symbols in motion blazed when Varthlokkur stroked them with the tip of a short black wand, the room surged and swirled to ebbs and flows of weird color.

Nepanthe stopped a step inside the door. Had she asked her question immediately, all might have come tumbling down. Recovering, she eased the door shut and tiptoed to where the Old Man sat watching, enthralled. She, too, was soon engrossed. This was the first of Varthlokkur's magic she had actually seen. For a moment she felt the Power in her blood yearning toward him, felt the pull of its need for completeness.

The wizard made a magnificent picture there in the heart of his construct, with the varicolored lights teasing over his features. Wand in hand, he seemed a god caressing the stars of his universe.

Unconsciously, wanting to share, Nepanthe touched the Old Man's hand, held it lightly as she had her father's long years past, when frightened or awed.

"It's magnificent, isn't it?"

She nodded dumbly.

"It's a new thing, something he discovered while waiting for you. Never tried it before. A whole new field of magic is opening here. Amazing."

"It's beautiful," she replied.

"Uhm."

"But why? What's happened?"

The Old Man glanced at her with a smirkish smile. "Your husband's cohorts, Ragnarson and bin Yousif, found themselves a couple of wizards crazy enough to attack us. Competent men, Prime Circle, but no match for Varthlokkur. We caught them red-handed after they killed the Devil's Hawk. Now they're trying to get us before we get them. But they haven't hurt us at all, and I doubt that there's any damage they can do."

She nodded while he spoke, too enthralled by light and color to be annoyed by his smugness. Suddenly, Varthlokkur relaxed and sighed. She leaned forward, excited, again feeling that pull. The wizard tucked his wand under his arm, wiped sweat from his brow with his sleeve, and stepped from the heart of his creation. Symbols swirled as his passage disturbed them.

Nepanthe gasped. Varthlokkur heard her. "No need for alarm," he said tiredly. "It's not your usual pentagram. It's not a protection against devils. You might call it a Power matrix. It concentrates the Power so I can project it. The symbols represent the demons outside. When I touch one I sting a soul…" He paused, rubbed his temples. "I'm tired."

The Old Man withdrew his hand from Nepanthe's. "I'll get something to fresh you up. Why don't you sit down for a while?" He left.

Varthlokkur massaged his temples for a full minute, then turned to the thing he had wrought. "I suppose I'd better get rid of that," he mumbled.

"Please don't," said Nepanthe. "Leave it for a while. It's beautiful. Like watching the universe from outside."

Varthlokkur glanced at it, then eased into the Old Man's chair. "Guess it is. Never thought of it as anything but a tool." He looked at her closely, watching the light patterns dancing on her face. He chuckled. "The dress becomes you. But aren't you a bit early? He won't be here till tomorrow."

Silence stretched. She could think of nothing to say. Moreover, she remembered that pull of a moment earlier and was distressed by the temptation.

He rose, said, "Come here," and took her hand, pulled her from her chair. "Go stand in the center of the pentagram."

Uncertainly, she did as she was directed, positioning herself at the heart of a gleaming gold star whose points lay in the angles of the pentagram on the floor. Varthlokkur spoke a few soft words, touched his wand to a silver symbol. It clung. He moved it to her left ear. She started, controlled the impulse, was surprised when she felt nothing. It had looked hot. Varthlokkur spoke again. The symbol attached itself to her.

He repeated the operation, caught her other ear, then filled her hair. And then he brought her out of his construct, to the mirror (which was just a mirror at the moment) and showed her herself with stars in her hair.

She smiled, said softly, "I feel like a goddess. It's fantastic."

"Fitting. You're my goddess. I'll give you the stars of the night."

Her smile became a frown. She shook her head, more to rid herself of the attraction she felt than as a negative. "I've made my choice. That's the end of it."

"Not quite. Let me show you something. The divination I've mentioned so often. That you've always refused to believe." He had finally realized that he had to offer her something more convincing than his word as Varthlokkur, the Empire Destroyer.

Eyes wonder-wide and disturbed, Nepanthe followed him to a table. He selected several items and set them out in an order with meaning known only to himself. He began chanting...

The castle groaned. Screams surrounded it. Dust showered from the shaken ceiling. Varthlokkur slammed a fist into a palm as he looked up. He snapped, "I'd thought them sufficiently warned."

Claws of terror seized Nepanthe's soul. "The magick! You've taken it apart!"

"No, don't worry. We've got other defenses that'll hold till I get it fixed. Come over here, please." Back to the pentagrams they went, Nepanthe cooperating because she knew the attack could be as dangerous for her as for her captors. The Old Man arrived running with ale and sandwiches. He relaxed visibly when he saw the defense already under control.

An hour later, Varthlokkur said, "They were more determined this time." From the heart of his creation he touched symbol after symbol. Each wriggled away from the contact. He told Nepanthe, "This causes a great deal of pain for the demons. It breaks their will to attack. But they can't leave us while Visigodred and Zindahjira bind them. We're balanced just now. I break wills about as fast as they recover. I hope the fact that I'm not bothering to turn the demons around on their masters will scare hell out of those two. I hope they'll get to wondering what I'm cooking up instead."

Still another hour later it had become evident that the attack might not break down at all. Said the Old Man, "They may just try to keep it up till Mocker's at the gate."

"Might be what they're thinking. Let me see. Ah, yes. Get me a pair of tongs, please. Big ones. Thank you. Now, something silver and sharp. A needle—ah! The arrow... What?" He grew even more pallid.

All three stared at the arrow dangling beneath Varthlokkur's mobile of bells. Nepanthe saw nothing unusual. It just hung there, swinging slowly back and forth. The Old Man, wearing a puzzled frown, took it down and handed it to Varthlokkur. They didn't discuss whatever it was that had caused their consternation.

Nepanthe moved closer when the wizard seized a symbol with the tongs. The thing squirmed as if it were alive. It tried to escape. Nepanthe touched her ear fearfully.

Varthlokkur noticed. "No, they're like this only inside the pentagrams, when demons are near." With the care of a master tailor, he pushed the point and shaft of the arrow through the struggling thing in the tongs. It stopped wriggling. Its color quickly faded, and in a moment the tongs grasped nothing but naked air. "Good. This shouldn't take too long." And, within half an hour, he had done the same with all the symbols. "Better leave this up," he said when he finished. "They may try again." He made certain a dully glowing symbol was in place in every plane of his structure. "Now, about that divination." Though he was near collapse, he led Nepanthe to the table where his necromantic materials lay ready. Chants flowed across his tongue with the heavy fluidity of quicksilver. His wand danced over the objects. Time passed. A mist formed over the table. Soon things stirred in the mist, and a soft, fluting voice spoke therefrom. Nepanthe, despite herself, found that she couldn't tear her attention away.

Hours may have passed before it was over. And, when it was, Varthlokkur seemed to be as amazed as she. And the Old Man couldn't close his mouth, so stunned was he. Whole new vistas of perfidy and holocaust had opened to his more ancient, less ignorant mind. Varthlokkur had hardly recognized the tip of the iceberg of what must be going on.

After a long silence, Nepanthe asked, "That wasn't what you expected, was it?" Her throat was almost too tight for speech. She was terribly frightened again.

Varthlokkur shook his head slowly. "No, it wasn't. That I didn't expect at all. And yet you see the choices, yours and mine, and how soon they'll be forced upon us." And Nepanthe, who had lived all her life with magic, could no longer disbelieve. There was simply no defying such absolute revelations.

"And I have a choice of my own," said the Old Man. "But mine's already made." His role in the Director's drama remained fluid, and within his own control. "I'll stand by you, Varthlokkur. You'll do the same, Nepanthe, if you've got any sense at all. Destruction is the only alternative." He turned to Varthlokkur, his expression unreadable.

The wizard inclined his head slightly. "Thank you. It's unnecessary, you know. You can still get out."

"There was a slip. We've seen that your divinations were manipulated. That gives us a chance. You're still Varthlokkur, *the* wizard. *I* won't run just because *you*'ve found the board broader and of a shape different than you thought. You've already decided to fight. I can sense it. Even though you think it's useless. Because you think you owe it to those whom the puppet masters had you destroy. I can do no less. This is my world, too." Pretty speech, he thought. Yet following its tenets would allow him to both pursue his private inclinations and what he saw as his greater purpose.

It hung in the balance now, and Nepanthe didn't like it. Futures rested on her shoulders. She had to decide where to fight: beside her husband, or beside Varthlokkur. And, as the wizard had promised, even love dared not influence her judgment. So many futures could fall with the end of the coming battle, a battle she could help win—if she chose Varthlokkur.

She had just realized that Varthlokkur's need wasn't just the love-sexual thing she had recently come to believe—though that was much of it, of course—but also the Power-need she had suspected in the beginning.

States of maybe. The Power would still be marshalled on the opposing side.

Choosing her husband could bring the world crashing down, and those betrayed would number in hundreds of thousands, or millions. The fates of nations were in her hands, more than ever they had been when she had been but a part of the imperialist dreams of Ravenkrak. That weight settled heavily on her soul. Going to a chair, she dropped in, pulled her feet up under her (the short dress permitted it), and put her chin on her fist as she thought.

Varthlokkur paced. His sins of yesteryear were closing in. He strode like a tiger caged, occasionally glancing at Nepanthe, or the nervous bells, wishing he understood her better, wishing he knew more about why his ward-spell carillon had gone insane. He had to have her help. There was nowhere he could run. The bill-collector was coming, and he was the kind who couldn't be evaded.

The Old Man called Varthlokkur aside, whispered, "There's only one choice we dare let her make—even if we can't force it. You've got to influence her somehow. She's a woman. Youth could be a potent bribe. Make yourself young again.

See how she reacts. Drop a few hints. I've got the tools here and ready."

Varthlokkur studied Nepanthe. Finally, he nodded. "You're right. It couldn't hurt, bad as things are. Get it ready." He turned, gazed at his great work, his contribution to sorcery, his hope. For a moment he saw the art Nepanthe had seen, the beauty. That would all be dust soon, perhaps, or new weapons for his enemies. "For the thing I fear comes upon me, and what I dread befalls me," he whispered. Nepanthe glanced up questioningly, smiled weakly, didn't really see him. He turned back to the Old Man.

"Ready?"

Varthlokkur took a deep breath, shrugged, said, "I suppose."

Her attention attracted by the renewed chanting, Nepanthe turned as silver gray motes enveloped Varthlokkur. Resting her hands on the back of the chair and her chin atop them, enthralled, she listened and watched, and momentarily forgot her dilemma. Then the silver cloud died. And she gasped.

Varthlokkur took a step toward her, hand out, pleading, as young as he had been while calling the earth-marid to Ilkazar. Gone were the wrinkles, gray hair, grizzled beard, and the blue-veined skin which had marred the backs of his hands. As she had expected, he looked a great deal like bin Yousif—though his character wasn't written as plainly on his face. Haroun had the look of a tormented, starving wolf.

She shook her head slowly, afraid to believe. The pull she had felt earlier became stronger than ever. "Can I see him? My husband?"

"In a minute," said the Old Man. "Varthlokkur, get some food inside you." He pointed to the long-forgotten supply of sandwiches and wine, then went to the mirror. After a mumbled incantation, it sprang to life—but showed only psychedelic madness.

"I blinded their eyes. Now they've blinded me," Varthlokkur mumbled through a mouthful. "No, wait. Probably my gimmick there. Yes, I think that's it. Interference."

"He'll be here tomorrow," Nepanthe said.

"Yes," Varthlokkur replied.

"I don't want to hurt him." She was giving ground. She saw by their expressions that they were aware of it. "Damn! I love him."

"Uhn!" the Old Man grunted. He hoped he wouldn't muff his lines. "Varthlokkur! What you've done to yourself... Could you do it to Nepanthe? Could we put the primary spells on her?"

Varthlokkur's new young features expressed strong curiosity. He said, "She'd never be younger than she is now."

"Maybe not, but that's good enough, isn't it?" Nepanthe was hanging on his words already, certain of their importance though she didn't comprehend. "Nepanthe, if you could return to your husband after all, after supporting us in this thing tonight, and could also serve your destiny with Varthlokkur, would you?"

"I don't understand."

"Say yes!" Varthlokkur cried. "I can fix it so you can change back to the age you are now any time you want. You could live with your husband for the rest of his life, then come back to me. I can wait a few more years. Say you will. I know you want to. Your eyes say so. Oh, the Old Man's given me honey and honeycomb when I thought it had to be one or neither at all." He had become tremendously excited. Then a shadow of uncertainty crossed his face. "But you'd have to surrender completely, right now. You know what we have to do. Otherwise there'll be no future at all. For any of us."

"I know," she replied. Her burden had become a devouring dragon. Every argument before her seemed compellingly attractive, yet equally repulsive. Everywhere she turned she saw opportunities to seize things her soul craved, yet in each chance there existed the prospect of terrible pain for others. "And it's the crudest hurt I could do him. If he found out, it would be like I was driving burning knives into him. But if I don't do it, he won't live long enough to find out how much he could've been hurt. That's terribly cruel, to wound to give life, to betray to save."

"Think of yourself as a surgeon, then," said the Old Man. "Letting blood."

His suggestion didn't help. Nepanthe's sorrow-pain ran ocean deep. Would Mocker ever believe, no matter how true it was, that she had betrayed him because of her love? He would hate her... But he would be alive to hate. Damn! This was a cruel game in which to be a pawn. What she had so feared giving even her husband she must now willingly tender Varthlokkur so that her Power could join and feed his in the coming conflict. If she refused... Fangdred rattled to its bones. "Damn fools!" the Old Man spat. "They just won't quit! Let me." He stepped into the Power matrix, which was brightly alive once more. With tongs and arrow he savagely banished the congregation of devils raging round the fortress.

Varthlokkur took Nepanthe aside (she shivered at his touch, for she hadn't permitted it in a long time) and ensorceled her so that she could be returned to her present age. That took a long time.

Afterward, the wizard collapsed into a chair. The Old Man, in little better shape, prepared draughts of the brew nepanthe. The three refreshed themselves. Revived, Varthlokkur asked, "Nepanthe, would you meet me back here in an hour?" In an oblique way, she realized, she was being asked to prepare herself for what had to be done. Shivering, she nodded. Varthlokkur told the Old Man, "I'll be walking the wall if you need me." He took Nepanthe's arm, walked her to the tower stairs. Behind them, the Old Man began preparing the room for her shame. She didn't look back.

In darkness Varthlokkur strolled Fangdred's wall, staring at the Dragon's Teeth. His young hair whipped in a hot southern wind. He saw neither stars nor mountains, nor did he notice the weather. He was lost in time.

In his past. He had fled back to Ilkazar, to his few warm memories of a woman who had died at the stake. She had been a fine woman, as loving as a mother could be… Each memory was a cherished, carefully tended heirloom. The anger, resentment, and cold determination which had guided him, silently and studiously, through his years with Royal, returned.

Royal had been another good person. He and the old woman: dust, dust; ashes, ashes. He hoped they had reached their peasants' heaven. Both deserved more than the cruelties life had offered them. There was no true justice for the living.

He stirred nervously in the hot wind, finally recognizing it as the Werewind of the Storm Kings. Had it become hot to melt the snow?

His thoughts turned to sorcery and dark eastern schools where he had learned the skills that had warped his soul. Evil schools, festers, cesspools of the knowledge of chaos iron-ruled by dread masters. Yo Hsi's wicked face returned to mind, only to be banished instantly by that of his twin brother, Nu Li Hsi. The Princes Thaumaturge of Shinsan. They were lords of evil virtually worshipped as gods in their respective domains in Shinsan, deifically secure in the heart of the Dread Empire. Dread Empire Shinsan. It was as wicked as its reputation. The Tervola were emissaries of Darkness…

Varthlokkur shuddered at his memories, vague as they were. But he couldn't forget completely, even though he had lost the specifics of what had happened there. The Old Man had asked him the price he had paid for his training. Nothing he tried could bring that back to mind. That frightened him. He was sure the cost had been grim. Of one thing he was absolutely convinced. He hadn't finished paying.

He thought of the future, so narrow now, and recoiled into the past again. The past had been bad, but contained no fear anymore. He lingered over his lonely days as Eldred the Wanderer and his early centuries at Fangdred, his studies, and the decades of research which had given him the matchless Power of the Winterstorm equations. And, finally, he thought of Nepanthe.

Nepanthe. His mind, sooner or later, always returned to her. Four centuries was a long love—and there were ages yet before them. There would be a pause, a wait for that man camped out there somewhere nearby, sleeping beneath that gibbous moon…. He *had* to win this battle! Nepanthe had finally surrendered. He couldn't let that victory be devoured by another defeat, couldn't let heart's desire elude him now.

He turned his back to the wind, returned the way he had come. It was almost time. Maybe she was waiting already. His heart stumbled. He glanced toward the Wind Tower. At last…

He had to hurry. Before anything else, to hedge his bets, he had to teach the Old Man to handle the Winterstorm.

Eighteen: Spring, 997 afe
Like a Shadow of All Night Falling

Fear had dissipated Visigodred's intellect. Ragnarson had never seen the man so irritable and unstable, though he had once been present during a battle in Visigodred's interminable feud with Zindahjira. The wizard had remained cool and intelligent then, like a trained soldier maintaining calm in the chaos of battle. "What now, Black Face?" the wizard shouted at the crystal providing communication with Zindahjira. "No, I can't think of anything else! We've already used the best we've got."

Pale, shaking, the old nobleman listened to his equally terrified confederate. Ragnarson, close enough to eavesdrop, heard Zindahjira whiningly repeat his demand that Visigodred think of something. That, too, was strange. Zindahjira was given to bluster and thunder, not this craven whimpering.

The mercenary was badly distressed himself, although he wasn't yet panicky. He had retained the presence of mind to tell Elana to get ready to sneak out.

"Bragi!" He turned to the whisper. Elana had come back. Their gear must be packed, their horses ready. He slowly left the wizard…

The leopard's growl, as it moved to block his path, was murderous, the chatter of the sword-wielding monkey wrathful. He considered clearing his way by blade till Tooth joined her mate.

"Billy's hell on rats," said Visigodred. "Weren't deserting the ship, were you? Only fair that you go down with it. It's yours."

Turran heaved the trap open, seized the bundle beneath. From outside the cottage, his brothers called him to hurry. Their horses pranced nervously, sensing their masters' dread. Marco, contrary to his wont, remained stone silent. Turran hefted the Horn, ran—and tripped as he rushed through the door. His burden fell, bounced, came unwrapped…

The four Storm Kings stared with open mouths, stunned at a block of wood which had been carved and stained to resemble the Windmjirnerhorn….

Haroun bin Yousif was lost in darkness, with Hell on his trail. Zindahjira, having failed to find salvation in Visigodred, bellowed and shrieked behind him, blaming him, cursing him with a fearful wrath. And he had made the mistake of thinking he remembered the way out of the sorcerer's cavern maze. But the cave mouth he could not find—and the vengeful Zindahjira, denied any other outlet for his fear, was drawing ever nearer….

The man was tired. To the roots of his hair and the marrow of his bones, he was tired. He had pushed himself beyond all reasonable endurance. Even his fingernails hurt, or so he would have claimed if asked. A hot wind helped not at all, stealing the moisture of his body as it did.

He shed his battered pack, knelt, leaned on his unstrung bow, stared up the shadowed mountain before him, haloed by the moon behind it. This was it. The last one. El Kabar. Were they waiting up there, knowing he was trying to steal a march by not stopping for the night? Had Bragi and Haroun, almost certainly at work somewhere with magicians (What other explanation for his improbable survival?), as he had planned, managed to shield him from Varthlokkur's eyes? Too late to wonder. His road ran but one direction and he had to accept the destiny waiting at its end. Though it was short now, it had been a long and harrowing road. Itaskia seemed as many centuries as miles behind. He had spent ages with weariness, hunger, and the miseries of rain, snow, and frostbite as his traveling companions, while constantly running at the stirrup of Death. Ravenkrak and the woman he had wed there seemed as remote as the dawn of time.

He was no longer a heavy man. The Dragon's Teeth, hunger, and emotional upheaval, all had gnawed at his flesh like ghouls. Skin hung in folds beneath his chin, about his waist, where fat had all too rapidly vanished…

He shook off the siren call to sleep, ran a hand through his grimy hair, did a few fast jumping jacks to get his blood moving, then knelt and went through his pack, selecting things he might need. The pack he hid among boulders, then strung his bow, set an arrow to its string, made certain his knife and sword were loose in their scabbards. He started the last long league.

He was still an angry man. Months had rattled slowly by, lonely, dry, skeletons of days, since Varthlokkur had taken his wife, yet neither his anger nor his determination had waned. One more hour, he thought, or maybe two, and there would be a reckoning. Curse words and Varthlokkur's name died at his lips in the wind.

He was a stubborn man.

The wind made him nervous and thirsty; nervous because it was unnatural, thirsty because he was sweating profusely. He eyed the stream foaming near the path, water from snow melting in the warmth. Dared he drink? No. Since meeting the assassin he had allowed himself no relaxation. Here at the enemy's gate he couldn't permit himself even this small lapse. Briefly, he wondered if Varthlokkur were toying with him, if he had been allowed to escape assassin and bird to meet a grimmer fate later. Maybe he would be permitted a glimpse of his goal before being cut down. Sorcerers were notorious for their subtle cruelties.

His mood grew darker with time. Once again his weariness, abetted by fear, tempted him to sleep before the final plunge. He fought free, wanting immediate death or victory. He searched the darkness for a hint of trap, then cursed softly as a rock cut through his ragged boot and scored his heel. He felt little pain, but did sense the moist stickiness of oozing blood.

El Kabar loomed as naked as a newborn babe, as silent as death. It revealed traces of silver as the moon eased from behind it. The wind murmured "doom!" while chasing through knifish rocks, carrying with it scents of land long buried by snow. Urged to ever-increasing caution, he picked a shadow upslope, dashed into it, knelt to catch his breath and wish for thicker air. This was nothing a man should breathe. He hoped there would be no prolonged fighting.

His hair fell across his eyes. Bad, if that happened at a critical moment. He tied it back with a strip torn from his ragged coat, stroked his spotty beard, wished he had time to shave. Nepanthe wouldn't be impressed by his appearance.

The roundness and brownness of his face had remained unchanged by hardship, though it had become a bit more leathery. He seemed a shag-encircled henna moon arising as he peeped over a boulder. Bow ready, he ran to another shadow.

He felt terribly foolish by the time he reached the thousand feet of stairs. All his caution had gone for nothing. There he paused to hyperventilate in hopes that he would make the top prepared to fight. In vain. He was still compelled to make frequent stops.

The south wind rose and moaned softly, then died. Its masters had forgotten it hours before, and the Werewind couldn't sustain itself for long. As it faded Mocker first sighted Fangdred, though crenellated ramparts and the turret of the Wind Tower were all he saw. Neither defender nor banner stood limned above the battlements.

Silence. The castle seemed crouched, waiting, a sphinx about to spring.

Of their own accord, it seemed, his feet resumed moving, carrying him toward his fate. Soon he slung his bow, drew his sword. He felt more comfortable with that old friend in hand.

Surely Varthlokkur must be aware of his approach…

His thoughts turned to Nepanthe, to her face, her dark eyes, the way she quivered when he held her. And his anger grew. What cruelties, what indignities had she been forced to endure here?

Collapse seemed inevitable—then he topped the stairs. Sheer willpower took him into the blackness at the foot of the castle wall. There he dropped to his knees, panting, leaning one shoulder against cold stone. Weariness ground his spirit, again tried to tempt him into sleep. He fought it. The fire in his lungs slowly died. He glanced up, southward, across moonlit mountains rolling away like mighty waves… Aptly named, he thought. Fangs hungry for the blood of man. But enough. He was ready. He swatted the string of spittle dangling from his lower lip, reached inside his coat.

Precious as pearl was the brandy flask he brought forth, a treasure he had hoarded since fleeing Itaskia. He spat, teased himself with thought of its fiery taste… Enough! Now. He downed it in a single lengthy draught. A long burning shaft drove toward his stomach. He coughed, gasped, rose.

His heart hammered, his veins burned. He remembered holding a frightened thrush as a child, remembered the light, warm flutter of its heartbeat against his fingers. He had tossed the bird high to its freedom… What a strange thing to remember at an enemy's gate. He crept forward, sword probing the darkness, found the gate open! Trap! cracked across his consciousness. How like the open-doored device that had taken the thrush. At least *he* knew, he thought, what he was walking into. Gripping his weapon so tightly that his hand hurt, he stepped through…

And nothing happened. He looked around in bafflement. He had expected anything but this. Varthlokkur himself waiting, a blast of fire, a demon, anything. But he had encountered absolutely nothing. Fangdred lay silent, to all appearances deserted. Evil thought. What if the wizard had moved on, taking Nepanthe with him, laughing behind his hand? A possibility, it seemed, but first he must explore.

He found light, and people, almost immediately, but again, anything but what he expected. The lights he spied first. They led him to Fangdred's common hall, where… where he found a baffling tableau. Servants stood as if frozen (whatever had happened, it had occurred recently, because the fires still burned high in the fireplaces), not reacting even when, once he found the nerve, he clapped his hands, pinched, and prodded. He felt no heartbeat when he tested a pulse. He heard no breathing even when only inches from a face. Yet, surely, they weren't dead. Their warmth remained, and their color. Fearful strange.

He carefully backed from the hall, blade ready, expecting a momentary return of life and a resounding alarm. But they did nothing, nor did the several living statues he encountered thereafter. The sorcery completely blanketed the castle.

He had almost convinced himself that this was Ragnarson's and bin Yousif's work when he heard soft laughter down a dark corridor. His imagination invested it with depthless evil. Moving closer, he heard a voice talking to itself in a liquid, unfamiliar tongue. He had seen many lands and learned many languages, and was disturbed by this unknown. But he shrugged it off after a moment. The speaker wasn't Varthlokkur, whom he had met once, briefly, on the day the wizard had hired him. He went on, searching.

Chance brought him to the tower stair. He went up with little thought to his line of retreat. (Throughout his approach to Fangdred he had uncharacteristically ignored his avenues of withdrawal, perhaps because subconsciously he *knew* he'd get no chance to run.) A tall tower it was, taller than it had seemed from outside the castle. But finally he came to a landing.

Wan light, in changing pastel shades, slipped round the edges of a door standing slightly ajar. There was a quality, a smell about the place, which evoked memories of the Storm Kings' sorcery chamber beneath Ravenkrak. Here, he sensed immediately, he would find his wizard. Ear to stone, he listened, heard little.

Wait! Was that labored breathing?

How should he enter? In a burst, hoping for surprise? Suppose the door was booby-trapped? Yet if he went in carefully the wizard might have time to defend himself. He decided on full speed and prayed that the wizard felt secure in his own den.

The door swung easily inward. He burst through following mighty figure-eight sword strokes, his gaze sweeping the chamber. There were no defenses.

A young man's face, red and damp, rose from furs piled high beneath a large mirror. His questioning expression quickly changed to one of horror. Pleasure lightninged through Mocker. Though Varthlokkur had changed, he still recognized the man. He altered the direction of his charge, raising his sword for a punishing overhand stroke.

A second face rose from the furs. Dread swept across it.

And the fight deserted Mocker. "Nepanthe!" he screamed. He became a stunned, limp thing moving on impetus alone, his sword arm wilting, his unsteady steps betraying the sudden return of his weariness. He no longer saw, did not want to see, the shame so obvious before him. Wearing the horns already…

Nepanthe and Varthlokkur both babbled explanations, she pleadingly, he in a voice of infuriatingly calm reason. Mocker dropped into a chair, shut them both out. Mad thoughts, and questions… Had he come so far, through so much, for such a bleak reward? He heard, again from afar, the earlier evil laughter. Taunting him? Truly, Varthlokkur had played wickedly. The clincher, now, would have to be an auto-da-fé, death by his own hand, to make the mockery complete.

His hatred flared. Varthlokkur's centuries of madness must end tonight! He leapt from the chair, refreshed by his hatred. He wheeled on the couple as they gathered their clothing. He moved in slowly, the tip of his sword drifting toward Varthlokkur's chest. This should be slow, agonizing, the deserved thrust through the bowels, but he would make it the heart. Not out of consideration, though. Gut wounds, tended by a life-magician of the Old Man's skill, might heal…

The evil laughter came from the doorway as he thrust, as he stared into Varthlokkur's wide, unfearing eyes. The wizard's face was filled with another emotion entirely. Sadness, perhaps?

It was a bad thrust, disturbed as it was by that laughter, but Mocker knew it would be fatal in the long run. Varthlokkur would take a little while dying, that was all—if the Old Man could be kept away. Nepanthe screamed.

Mocker turned to see what new factor had to be considered.

An old man, surely the fabled Old Man of the Mountain, stood just within the door. He seemed stricken. Behind him stood someone else, clad all in black and cowled so deeply that his face remained invisible.

"Yo Hsi," Varthlokkur gasped. "You're a bit earlier than we expected."

The dark one jerked slightly, as if startled. Mocker was startled. That name—like an ill wind, long ago, he had heard it come whispering down from the borderland mountains above Matayanga, wrapped in tales of horror and evil. It was the name of one of the Princes Thaumaturge, one of the two dread lords of Shinsan.

So this was why Varthlokkur had been unconcerned with his own approach. A small fish indeed was he beside this grim destroyer. Could Bragi and Haroun have possibly hired?… But no. Yo Hsi mastered half an empire. He would be no man's hireling. There must be a depth to recent events that he had never suspected. He glanced at Varthlokkur's complex magical construct. Was that elegant device fated to play a part in this drama?

"The curse of the Golmune pollutes even its bastard blood," said Yo Hsi. His laughter filled the room.

The Golmune had been the ruling family of Ilkazar.

"What?" Varthlokkur demanded. He was weakening.

Mocker examined faces quickly. Nepanthe's eyes still sought his own, pleadingly. Varthlokkur stared at Yo Hsi, obviously more distressed by the easterner's presence than by his own approaching death.

The Old Man stood still as stone, expression agonized. But his stillness wasn't the uncanny frozennness of the servants below. His eyes remained in motion. To him Yo Hsi was an enigma, an unfathomable black hole in the fabric of the situation. His would be the direction to strike. Mocker was but a man with a sword.

"Vilis slew his father, Valis, by poison, for the crown, as ever it had been with the Imperial succession. Vilis took a mistress. On her he fathered a son she called Ethrian, after the philosopher. A time came when Imperial political pressures made disavowal of the son necessary. The mistress had become a liability in other affairs. Conveniently, a witchcraft charge was tendered by an intimate of the King."

"No!" Varthlokkur gasped. And yet, from his expression, Mocker saw that he wasn't surprised. There was nothing sudden about the guilt in the wizard's face.

"The woman was burned. Her possessions reverted to the Crown. The son disappeared. Years later he reappeared, to waste Ilkazar, to destroy his father in the family tradition. I was pleased." Yo Hsi laughed that evil laughter.

"Later, there came another Ethrian, born of a serving woman but with the Imperial blood, who was spirited off in revenge by a castle fool, under my protection. In time the child became a wanderer, a thief, an actor."

Mocker's gaze locked with Varthlokkur's. Not possible, he thought. Yet, if the wizard had suspected even a little, some of his strange reluctances would be answered.

"Tonight the father again dies by the hand of the son."

"Why?" The Old Man spoke for the first time.

"The curse of Sebil el Selib. And even now the woman carries in her womb the son that will be the death of this one." Laughter.

Nepanthe whimpered, looked to her husband, nodded slightly. She might indeed. She thought that she had conceived that wedding night on the Candareen.

"Not that," snapped the Old Man, his normal testiness returning. "Why are you here? Why have you, for centuries, fed false divinations to my friend?"

"You know that, do you?" Yo Hsi didn't seem pleased.

"Yes. An answer, if you please. You've offered nothing but nonsense and laughter since appearing." He didn't believe this encounter to be part of the Director's plan. The scripts had never thrust him into such deadly peril.

"A game? An old contest. A war, a struggle." Yo Hsi gestured sweepingly. For a moment the Old Man was puzzled. Then he identified the wrongness. The Prince Thaumaturge, called the Demon Prince in his home domain, was missing a hand. "My brother and I have been using the West as a board on which to play for mastery of Shinsan," said Yo Hsi." Warfare and thaumaturgic dispute have proven pointless on our home grounds. We're too evenly matched. Yet one of us must be master. An empire divided against itself can't grow. The way to shift the balance of power may exist somewhere out here, where there're so many unknowns and unpredictables. Here one of us might find the knowledge or weapon to seize the day. So here we do battle, each to grab first or to deny the other.

"Varthlokkur was once my agent, once my most important tool, for which I made him powerful. My Tervola trained him well. He began his service elegantly, by shattering the single power capable of keeping Nu Li Hsi and myself from using the West—the wizards of Ilkazar. And he demolished the Empire itself, a state with such iron control that nothing could be accomplished here while it endured. But he stopped with that. He ceased returning knowledge to me. Eventually, he hid himself here. I sent divinations meant to get him back in harness, but Nu Li Hsi interfered, subtly twisting them to his own ends. Varthlokkur continued to do nothing. In time I became angry. My Tervola have advised me to come west myself, to punish him for not fulfilling the contract he made with me. I have come, though, too late. Centuries too late. I see that Varthlokkur had forgotten that contract till just now."

"I cheated you," Varthlokkur gasped. "As you would've cheated me. I made that bargain knowing Nu Li Hsi would cleanse from my mind anything that didn't suit him. And now I've cheated you again," he declared, his words scarcely audible. "You destroyed my soul in Shinsan. Your machinations have robbed me of love, cursed me with the hatred of an unknown son, and killed me. But I've done the impossible. I've repaid my debt to Ilkazar. I've defied Yo Hsi, and won. Nu Li Hsi has won, and thus I fulfill one promise made in Shinsan, to the lesser of a pair of evils." He laughed weakly. "His Tervola taught me, too, Yo Hsi."

"You're wrong," the easterner replied, but with little of his earlier certitude. "I win. I've found my victory. In this old man lies knowledge forgotten by all but himself and the Star Rider. Knowledge the like of which you can't even imagine. From him I will milk the weapons of a new, invincible arsenal." To the Old Man, "I've found you out. I know what you are. From now on you have a new master."

With a croaking chuckle, Varthlokkur died. His face seemed beatific. In his own mind, at least, he had redeemed himself.

Still stunned by the revelation of his paternity, Mocker stared down at that man younger than he, whose head lay cradled in Nepanthe's naked lap. Her eyes still pleaded forgiveness. His anger and hatred surged up again, but now they were directed elsewhere. In a fluid, lightning motion he threw himself at Yo Hsi. For an instant he saw startled, cadaverous features within the sorcerer's cowl— then something seized him, hurled him aside, turned him round, round, round. Colors whirled, mixed. He struck confusedly. A scream was his reward. He laughed insanely, was joined by Yo Hsi in his laughter.

Sense returned and, in horror, he stared down at the tiny line of redness where his blade had penetrated Nepanthe's chest inward of her left breast. And still she prayed with her eyes. And Yo Hsi kept on laughing. The madness returned. He flung himself at the easterner again.

Followed a clown's dance, futile as tilting at windmills. Nothing could reach the sorcerer. But the madness wouldn't set him free. Finally, apparently forgetting his earlier oracle (now, with Nepanthe's imminent demise, in doubt), Yo Hsi drew a bronze dagger, plunged it into Mocker's chest.

He fell slowly, his sanity returning, his eyes turning accusingly toward Nepanthe. So long, so far, for this. Briefly, he wondered if Varthlokkur were truly his father, and if he had judged Nepanthe wrongly. Then darkness closed in.

The Old Man, during Mocker's flailing at Yo Hsi, saw the opportunity he had been awaiting. He strode briskly across the chamber, seized Varthlokkur's wand, stepped into the heart of his friend's creation. Before the sham battle reached its inevitable climax, he had completed Varthlokkur's work.

"Come along," said Yo Hsi, when finished. "You have things to tell me. Dawn-time things. Secrets known only to yourself and the Star Rider."

"I have nothing to tell you save this: you're doomed. As he promised."

Laughter. "You're presumptuous. That'll change. My torturers have a way with wills."

"But they'll never see me. You won't leave this room. Varthlokkur told you that he had prepared for you. He was right when he said that you'd lost."

"He had no magic. Great he was, yes, but distracted. My Tervola and I have leeched his power for months. Tonight he couldn't control the weakest ghost. Come."

"Take me."

Irritated, Yo Hsi started toward the Old Man. After three steps, however, he encountered an impassable barrier.

"Varthlokkur may have lost his ability to fight you, but his researches gave him a means to contain you. This thing surrounding me draws on new sources of Power. No agency, no man alive, can free you now. Not even he whom you call my master. You can sustain yourself by your arts, but to the world you're dead. Your powers have been jailed. You'll never leave that cage alive, nor will your magicks. I only wish that Varthlokkur hadn't been distracted by the woman. He might have lived to see his greatest moment, the fall of the evil that made him. That would've finally soothed his torment."

Yo Hsi tried his cage with physical strength and magic. Intolerable fires burned therein. Shadows fought. But nothing yielded. So he tried bargaining.

"You're old, Yo Hsi, and cunning," the Old Man retorted after hearing mighty promises. "But I'm older. Only the Director could sway me now. So let it be. Go gracefully, silently. Or else…" He stroked a symbol in the plane of a pentagram, suspiciously liverish in shape. Yo Hsi groaned, clutched himself. "I have my tortures, too, and *my* magic can pass the cage's walls."

"Go gracefully? No! I'll have something." Yo Hsi's good hand flashed out like the strike of a snake. Taking advantage of the cage's only weakness, that of passing inorganic matter, a dart, poisoned, shot from an apparatus attached to his wrist.

The Old Man dodged, but not quickly enough. He gasped, held his wound, presently staggered, fell slowly to his knees. He smiled once, mockingly, at Yo Hsi, then again, happily, at something invisible. "So long you've waited, Dark Lady." He toppled onto his face, half in, half out of Varthlokkur's magical structure.

Yo Hsi raged from wall to wall of his cage once more, blasting it with the most potent eastern magic, but there were, as he already knew, no exits.

Nineteen: Spring, 997 afe
A March of a Domain of Shadows

"Varthlokkur?" Nepanthe reached for his hand. She peered dazedly about the room. Yo Hsi stood stiffly silent a dozen feet away. The chamber was quiet. Nothing moved but the symbols in Varthlokkur's device. "What happened?"

There was a sound. Yo Hsi turned. In the door stood a shadowy someone who might have been the easterner's twin. "Nu Li Hsi." The shadow *was* his twin. Long ago, they had murdered their father, Tuan Hoa, for his throne, and had brought the Dread Empire to its present schizophrenic state.

The newcomer bowed slightly. "You've slain them all?" Varthlokkur stirred, groggily sat up beside Nepanthe. He didn't say anything.

"As you can see," said Yo Hsi. "We still have a draw."

"Even my Ethrian?" Nu Li Hsi, who was called the Dragon Prince, took a step into the room, peered about warily. "There's something strange here. Something not quite right."

"The Old Man must've closed the cage for me," Varthlokkur grunted.

"You probably sense that." Yo Hsi indicated Varthlokkur's Winterstorm construct. "It's something new."

"Ah. No doubt." Nu Li Hsi regarded the Winterstorm with an obvious professional admiration. He stepped closer.

"He doesn't know." Varthlokkur crowed. "Yo Hsi just might lure him in."

Yo Hsi stiffened momentarily. Varthlokkur could almost read his thoughts. Could something organic pass from outside the cage in? He couldn't let Shinsan go to his brother by default. He struck an exaggeratedly relaxed pose.

And Nu Li Hsi entered the cage, pausing only momentarily to bat the air before his face, as if brushing off a gnat.

"And I prayed that I could trap just one of them," Varthlokkur said. His face became beatific. "Half a world liberated in minutes." He snapped his fingers. "That simply."

The wizard was kidding himself. He knew better. The Princes Thaumaturge would be replaced. The Dread Empire would endure. Impatient heirs already awaited the intercession of Fate.

Mad laughter assaulted the air. "It's the end, brother. You're doomed." Less maniacally, "*We*'re doomed. It agonized me to think that I had to leave the Empire in your filthy hands."

"What the hell are you raving about? I'd heard rumors that you were losing your mind."

"It's a trap. Our pupil has undone his teachers. We can't leave." He laughed crazily again. "He's turned the tables on us, dear brother."

Frowning, Nu Li Hsi tried going to the Winterstorm.

Something barred his way.

Nervously, he retreated toward the door.

Again, something stopped him.

Panicking, Nu Li Hsi made a thunderous trial of the cage's walls. Without effect.

Like animals, the brother-princes hurtled at one another, each shrieking out half a millennium's frustration. They fought with sorcery, blades of bronze, hands, feet, and teeth. All to no conclusion. Each retained his unbreachable defenses, his superb reflexes and combat skills.

They might enjoy one another's company forever.

Varthlokkur rose, approached the trap.

"Don't get too close," Nepanthe warned. "They'd love it if they could get you in there with them."

"Don't worry. I'll look out. Though they couldn't hurt me now. They'd have to be able to see and touch me first. Look there." He pointed.

She looked. And screamed.

"That's us? We're dead?" Nepanthe and Varthlokkur's corpses lay in bloody, tumbled, sweat-wet furs. "I don't want to die!" Hysteria effervesced from the edges of her voice.

Varthlokkur pulled her toward him, tried to comfort her. But he was frightened, too, and she sensed it. She wanted to run, run, run, as badly as she had on that next-to-last night on the Candareen. But from this there was no escape. The swordstroke had fallen already.

How had she come to this? What evil Fate?…She stared at her corpse, morbidly fascinated. Her death-wound was scarcely visible, tricking the tiniest line of scarlet across one breast.

"What happens now?" She wasn't religious, and had never truly believed that death was something that could happen to her.

"We wait. Don't worry. Everything will be all right." But his quavering voice betrayed his lack of confidence.

"You're all right after all?" The Old Man had risen, was coming toward them. He sounded puzzled. His ashen face was frozen in startled ecstasy. That expression quickly transmogrified into confusion.

"All right?" Nepanthe responded to her panic. Feeling foolish, yet unable to stop herself, she snapped, "Wonderful. For a corpse."

The Old Man retreated before her intensity.

"Calm down," Varthlokkur pleaded.

"Varth…" At that moment, when most people would have needed someone to hold and comfort them, all she wanted was to be left alone. She tried to explain. "It's just the way I am. It's the same when I'm sick, or have a headache."

"Nepanthe, we've got to face this together." He couldn't say I need you. "Picture waiting alone."

"Waiting?" the Old Man asked. He was more perplexed than ever. "Waiting for what? What's happening?"

"You don't remember?" The wizard pointed. The Old Man turned. He stared at his corpse. His eyes widened as the truth gradually dawned.

"Son of a bitch. After so long." He went to his clay, carefully avoiding the cage, and stared into his own dead face. Gently, he touched his body's cheek, ran fingertips over its ecstatic smile. "She came lovingly… Those two… Who's the other one? Are they trapped? Alive?"

"Yes. Both of the Dread Empire's tyrants, caged in one fell passage of the shuttle across the loom of the Fates."

The Old Man's expression called the price too dear. But when he spoke, he said, "This may cause more rejoicing than your destruction of Ilkazar. Maybe there'll be a holiday in our memory." That he said sourly. Transitory facial expressions reflected the war going on within him, the struggle which had driven him both to seek immortality and to long for the peace of death.

Nepanthe started crying. Everything had happened too quickly, unexpectedly, shockingly, for her to understand. And she still bore her gigantic burden of guilt. She looked at Mocker, who hadn't yet stirred. There lay the father of her son…The child who, now, would never be born. How could she explain? How could she make him understand that she had tried to buy his life?

How could she obtain his forgiveness? That she had to have, or her shame would be unbearable.

Varthlokkur drew her to him again, offering comfort. This time she entered his arms, drawing support from his embrace.

"So. Even death does not end high treachery."

Nepanthe and Varthlokkur jerked apart. Mocker faced them, hands on hips, lips snarled back over clenched teeth. His dark face had grown darker with rage. He had arisen suddenly, had assessed his situation, and apparently had accepted his own destruction.

Nepanthe forgot her death-terror as shame, and fear of and for her husband engulfed her.

"What is trouble?" Mocker asked. "Would simpleton self, being noted fool, easily manipulated by adulteress wife, harm single hair on head of same? Woe! Am stricken to depth of depthless cretinic soul by very thought."

His remarks only made Nepanthe feel all the more the harlot.

"Who did the killing?" Varthlokkur demanded. "It was a matter of destiny," he tried to explain.

Mocker wouldn't listen. Nepanthe suspected that, though intellectually aware, he hadn't yet made an emotional accommodation to the despair of his situation, that the full, absolute truth hadn't yet dawned on him.

Humming, an elderly man, bent as if by the burden of millennia, entered the room. He skirted the invisible cage deftly, deposited a heavy bundle atop the table.

An absolute silence descended upon the room.

The easterners watched him hungrily, their eyes burning with the passion of wolves when catching sudden sight of unexpected, especially delicious prey. Both quickly babbled pleas for aid.

The elderly visitor squinted, chuckled, glanced at the four corpses, nodded to himself, returned to his bundle.

"The Star Rider," Varthlokkur murmured. He was awed and surprised. "Of all people, why did *he* turn up here?"

His question had occurred to everyone else. The easterners, having recognized the interloper, had fallen into a tense silence.

The Old Man muttered, "There is, after all, someone older and more cunning than I am." There was something in his tone that made Varthlokkur glance his way suspiciously.

The elderly gentleman spoke to his Horn. A flash blinded everyone watching. When sight returned, two tall, steely suits of baroque armor flanked the Star Rider.

"His living statues," Varthlokkur said softly.

There was a place of mystery east of the Mountains of M'Hand, near the Seydar Sea, called The Place of A Thousand Iron Statues. It was believed to have been created by the Star Rider as a place of refuge, a place where his secrets would remain inviolate. No sorcerer yet had been able to fathom the magic animating the living statues guarding The Place's secret heart.

"The bodies," said the Star Rider. "Lay them out here." He indicated the floor immediately before him. Working swiftly, the dark things moved the corpses. Then they moved back against a wall, becoming as motionless as dead metal.

"What's he doing?" Nepanthe asked. The Old Man and Mocker moved closer to her and Varthlokkur. They eyed one another warily.

"I think he's going to try to recall us," the Old Man replied. Hope had exploded into his voice. He eyed them uncertainly. "But why?"

Yo Hsi and Nu Li Hsi reached the same conclusion. "Forget the dead!" they demanded. "Take care of the living."

"Free us," Nu Li Hsi concluded.

The Star Rider murmured to his Horn, setting spells on each of the corpses before paying the slightest heed to the brothers. Finally, squinting, he faced them. "You know who I am? What I am? What you are to me? And you still want my help?" To his Horn, "They're greed and wickedness."

Greed and wickedness. Modern legend said that for twice the age of the Old Man this strange being had walked the earth, appearing randomly. No one knew the why of his name, nor his purpose, but it was certain that each of his appearances omened a startling shift in the course of history. Another of his names was Old Meddler.

Who was he? Where had he sprung from? And why did he tamper?

The theory currently favored by the scholars of Hellin Daimiel was that he was a tool of Right, or Justice. The known historical indicators pointed that way.

He chose that role now, teasing the two dread easterners, whose crimes had been old when Ilkazar was young, into asking for justice. He taunted, questioned, played their fears, maneuvered them into making the plea.

"Justice?" he cackled gleefully. "Then justice I'll give you!"

His hand twitched. The suits of armor stepped forward. He tapped one, pointed. It strode into the trap, seized a startled Yo Hsi. In a workmanlike manner, despite the hideous defenses and sorceries at the Demon Prince's command, the living statue slowly strangled its victim. An unstirring Yo Hsi appeared on the level of reality in which Mocker, Nepanthe, Varthlokkur, and the Old Man already existed. He soon recovered from his death-shock and tried his prison again. Again he had no success.

Meanwhile, the metal thing turned on Nu Li Hsi. The Dragon Prince fled round the trap like a rat caught in a box with a terrier.

No escape did he find. Nor did his command of the Power avail him. The metal monster shrugged off his attacks, caught him, strangled him, contemptuously tossed him aside.

Nepanthe watched unhappily, but wasn't greatly distressed. All emotion paled in this shadowland palatinate to final death.

Flash.

The iron men were no more.

"It left the cage!" said Varthlokkur. "Nothing can do that."

"No? Something can," the Old Man countered. "Things without life. Things immune to sorcery." He eyed the Star Rider, wearing an expression suggesting that he and the interloper shared secrets.

The Star Rider looked back. "I'll have to hurry. There's not much time." He turned to his Horn, murmured.

Mysterious devices appeared. These he quickly attached to the corpses over the vital organs. In a rush, then, he summoned an object resembling a massive, ornate coffin.

"I see what he's up to," the Old Man said excitedly. "Nobody's done it in ages. Full resurrection. A lost art. Only he and I, today, could manage, and I never had the tools. It's the box that's important. Everything else is gimcrackery meant to preserve the vitals." His excitement collapsed into gloom. "But he won't have time to revive all of us. Even he can't do much to slow brain deterioration."

"Quiet!" Mocker rumbled.

Nepanthe whirled. "Don't you talk…" Her rebuke died. The Old Man wasn't his target. He glared at the shades of the easterners. They had begun carping at one another again.

Her gaze traveled on, to her corpse, and she became aware of its nudity. "Cover me, please."

Varthlokkur, chuckling, said, "He can't hear you. Not that it would make any difference." He indicated her ghost-being, and those of the others. Each was mother-naked.

"But he looked at me. Or I could do it myself." She felt foolish, worrying about modesty now.

"A guess, facing our way. He knows we're here, but not where we are. Nor can you move material things. Best get used to being naked."

"Fitting," Mocker grumbled. "Shame of whore-wife made evident to all eyes."

"Be careful," Varthlokkur said angrily.

"Time," the Old Man interjected. "He's working too slow. He can't possibly save us all." A touch of hysteric hope rode his voice as he added, "He'll get me, though. He owes me. I saved *his* life once."

"Smug millenarian!" Mocker snapped. His situation had begun to disturb him at last.

His testiness further upset Nepanthe. "It's silly for us to fight now. So stop."

"Silence, shame of imbecilic believer in anythings!" His self-righteousness was thick enough to cut.

Nepanthe's spirit, the fire her brothers had wanted quenched, flared. She advanced on Mocker like a stalking medusa. He retreated, retreated till, suddenly, he found himself cornered.

Forcing his attention, with a white-hot intensity, she told him everything that had occurred during their separation. "Listen!" she snarled, whenever he tried to interrupt, and, "Look at me!" when his gaze wandered. She finished with, "And that's the absolute truth."

He remained dubious, but found himself inclined to withdraw judgment. "Time will demonstrate verity of same. Or no." Then, startling her with a sudden change of tack, "Is sorcerer truly father of self?"

"He seems convinced."

"Truth told, wife of self is with child? Child of self?"

"Yes. Your baby." She turned to watch the Star Rider, as much to mask her emotions as to watch him struggle to hoist a corpse into his life-giving coffin.

She suffered a surge of panic. What about the baby?

She had to live. So the child could be saved. She rushed round the cage so she could see who had been chosen.

Varthlokkur.

For a moment she hated him with a depth that astounded the rational part of her. She should go first. For the child's sake.

Her own mind mocked her. She wasn't worried about the baby. She just didn't want to die.

Varthlokkur's body flopped into the coffin. The Star Rider slammed its lid, growled at his Horn. As always, he did so in a language nobody understood. The Horn whistled. The coffin began humming.

Nepanthe ran at the Star Rider, shrieked, "Me first, you idiot! Me!" She pounded at him with the heels of her fists. He waved a hand before his face as if to brush away spiderwebs.

Mocker laughed. "More cosmic justice. Wicked woman forgotten. Likewise, self-important old geezer. Am much pleased. Am ecstatical, Star Rider."

"Shut up!" Nepanthe screamed. "Somebody make him shut up. Our son…"

"But is hilarious, Dear Heart, Diamond Eyes. On Candareen, after big wedding, new wife promised to follow fog-headed husband to gates of Hell. Might do same now, maybeso."

Even before he finished he was sorry that vindictiveness had mastered his tongue again. He realized, intellectually, that his fear was taking creeping control of his emotions, his responses.

He couldn't push it back.

Varthlokkur wandered dazedly. His body was calling him back. Struggling to keep control, he paused by Nepanthe long enough to whisper, "Remember your promises once we've been returned to life."

Nepanthe nodded. How much pain would loving two men bring? Boundless, she feared.

It had seemed so elementary before Mocker's arrival.

Varthlokkur rambled toward the coffin, and there mumbled a childhood prayer.

The Star Rider was a slow old man no longer. He knelt among the corpses, swiftly manipulating the devices meant to preserve.

Mocker, yielding to his fear completely, harassed Varthlokkur mercilessly. "Old Devil, Death of Ilkazar, show decency for once. Do right instead of evil…"

The Old Man, too, succumbed to emotion, though he directed his bitterness at the Star Rider. "Ingrate," he said softly. "Have you forgotten Nawami? Who kept you from the tortures of the Odite?"

This Shadowland, Nepanthe reflected, though cooling the gentler emotions, certainly nurtured selfishness. Being dead, with time to anticipate a deeper death ahead, unleashed the black hounds of the soul.

A sudden thought startled Nepanthe. Maybe this was a trial period and one's behavior during the waiting determined a final reward.

She was redeemed from terrifying speculations by a sudden stillness.

Varthlokkur had vanished.

The Star Rider opened the coffin.

The wizard was breathing shallowly. A rosiness had returned to his skin, which twitched and jerked. No blood leaked from his wound.

The Star Rider spoke, using a spell of healing which the Old Man recognized. Then he packed the area of damage with a malodorous unguent and applied bandages.

Nepanthe warily studied her companions-in-shadow from beside the coffin. Identical thoughts haunted their minds.

Who would be next?

The way the Old Man talked, one of them wouldn't make it. Maybe two. The next selected could well be the last to return with a whole mind.

Briefly, Nepanthe hated both men for infringing on her chances. Then she concluded that she would have to be chosen next. Even the Star Rider couldn't be so unchivalrous as to ignore a woman's plight. Could he?

"I saved his life, you know," the Old Man said again. "We were partners. During the Nawami Crusade. The Director slipped up. Nahaman, the Odite, became suspicious…" He shut up, realizing at last that he needed to keep some things behind his teeth even here.

Nepanthe and Mocker exchanged blank glances.

They could be pardoned. Even the wisest of the historians at Hellin Daimiel's Rebsamen University were ignorant of the Nawami Crusades. Those had taken place long ago and far away, and had been so bitter that almost no one had survived to pass along their tale.

"Shut up!" Nepanthe snarled in sudden hatred. She was afraid he was telling the truth, that he did have some extraordinary claim on the Star Rider's mercy. "Do your bragging after he puts me in. I won't have to listen to it then."

Mocker remained unnaturally quiet, his lips forming soundless words. Nepanthe laughed a laugh attared with wormwood. The man who believed in nothing, who mocked everything, who was so soaked in cynicism that he reeked of it, was appealing to false gods.

Where had he learned to pray?

The Star Rider dragged Varthlokkur from the coffin, stretched him out for continued care. Already the wizard appeared healthier.

Nepanthe's potential savior bent over her corpse. She shriek-laughed victoriously.

But he merely moved a leg so he could get to Mocker.

Nepanthe shrieked again, though with less feeling. Resignation began to creep up on her.

The Old Man cursed. "You devil! You ungrateful fiend! I hope *they* roast your black soul…"

The easterners laughed. Having lost interest in bedeviling one another, they had begun baiting their captors.

"Murderer!" Nepanthe snarled, whirling on her husband. "Me. The child. Our blood's on your soul. Unless you make him stop." She started stalking him again, insane in her fear/rage.

The Old Man, stricken by his betrayal, plopped into a chair. He retreated into his memories, which were far clearer now than while he had been alive.

The Director had brought him here, and had used him pitilessly throughout the ages. He was being used mercilessly now. The man would know no remorse at his loss. He was just another tool in the shaper's hands, caught in a situation where a choice of tools to be salvaged had to be made.

What epic of doom was he shaping now, that Varthlokkur and a fat criminal would be more valuable than he?

The Star Rider was an enigma even to he who knew him best, who knew how he had been condemned to this world and why, and with what mission. The man's plans were shadowed mysteries, though of one thing the Old Man was sure. This night's events had been engineered very carefully, perhaps beginning at some point decades in the past.

And the Old Man had a suspicion, growing toward conviction with the ages, that the Star Rider was, subtly, trying to evade the sentence imposed upon him. The desolation of Nawami, of Ilkazar… Neither had been needful. They were irrational excesses—unless they were part of some impenetrable plan.

Nepanthe stalked. Mocker retreated completely round the room before she reached the point where she could no longer sustain her anger. It soon faded into a diluted terror. He then took her into his arms and whispered the same comforting nothings and little jokes that had revived her spirit during bin Yousif's raid on Iwa Skolovda. In the minutes that followed they made their peace, revived their love, forgave one another.

After a misty-voiced, "Doe's Eyes, Dove's Breast, will be better after second birth. Promise," he faded from her company.

The Star Rider worked over the remaining corpses, his hands darting feverishly. Occasionally he made a quick check on Varthlokkur. The Old Man sat in silence, remembering, waiting. The easterners turned on one another again, but with flagging devotion.

Nepanthe's feelings grew ever more pallid. She had little desire to do anything but wait. She seated herself beside the Old Man, took his hand.

The whistle and hum of the coffin stopped. The Old Man's grasp tightened. "He can manage one more. For sure." He said it with little force. He, as did she, wanted to live, but was drifting farther and farther from the shores of life. Before long, Nepanthe suspected, she wouldn't care at all, might not heed the call to resurrection.

Which one? she wondered as the Star Rider tumbled Mocker onto the floor. Hope flared, but couldn't ignite any will to survive. She turned to the Old Man. He had closed his eyes. Maybe it should be better that way, not knowing... Squeezing his hand, she closed her eyes, too.

The waiting went on forever.

A feeling of presence came toward the tower, lightly, as if some dread dark hunter of souls were snuffling an uncertain track.

Time awakened. Its plodding pace rapidly turned into a headlong plunge toward Hell. Faintly, Nepanthe heard the terror of the easterners. Maybe it wasn't imagination. Maybe something *was* coming...

She was fading. She could sense it. Her grasp on the fabric of her existence was weakening, weakening...

A pity that her son would never live...

Blackness.

Happiness, because she was no longer afraid.

TWENTY: SPRING, 997 AFE
AFTERMATH

"A man can work up a powerful thirst climbing El Kabar," Varthlokkur told Mocker. They faced one another over their first evening meal following their resurrection. "I've done it a dozen times."

Mocker peered at this man who might be the father he had never known. He banished a surge of filial feeling, condemning it as unfounded, saccharine. "And in Shadowland," he replied. "Self, having considered, believe same will be leading torture in Hell. Maybe after abstinence."

He avoided the wizard's glance by looking for the wine steward. They were far from comfortable with one another. But the steward wasn't there to rescue him. Like the rest of the staff, the night had left him in wild confusion. None of them could get themselves organized.

"Yes. The Shadowland."

The subject died there, with an unspoken agreement that words spoken then, and deeds done before, were best forgotten.

A child, bolder than his companions in a small party watching and giggling nearby, came over. He stared at Mocker for several seconds, then squealed and fled when the wanderer made an ugly face. "Am forever haunted by couthless, unwashed urchins," Mocker grumbled, recalling Prost Kamenets's Dragon Gate. That he accounted his point of no return, after which it had been too late to escape the strange, grim adventure that had led him to his father.

Surreptitiously, from beneath lowered brows, he studied Varthlokkur. Was some new evil growing in the nest of the wizard's mind? He was who he was, and had done the things he had done. He had his wicked reputation.

Mocker's hand strayed to the hilt of his sword. His gaze lanced about the hall in search of incipient treacheries.

His eyes met hers among unfamiliar faces. He froze. She seemed more beautiful than ever. More desirable, despite the pallor left by her trials. How sound was her mind? How bitter were her memories? Had she suffered any of the brain damage the Old Man had harped upon?

Could he and she abandon past anger and jealousy and salvage something from the wreckage others had made of their lives? Could they recover the happiness that had been theirs, so briefly, before Ravenkrak's fall?

She sat beside him, placed a hand on his. She smiled as if nothing had happened the night before.

Their truce was holding. She remained willing to forget. "What became of the Star Rider?" she asked.

"Gone," said Varthlokkur. "That's the way he is. He never waits around. Probably so he doesn't have to answer questions. He apparently tucked us in, took care of the Old Man, disenchanted the servants, then took off. That's his way. He may not be heard from again for a hundred years."

"Old Man. What of him?" Mocker asked.

"I'm not sure. The tower is sealed. I haven't the skill to bypass the spells warding it. But I suspect that means he's alive. Probably in his deep sleep."

The wizard guessed near the truth. Contrary to his own dire expectations, the Old Man hadn't been allowed to die. But neither had he been permitted to return to life. His body, clad in ceremonial raiment, sat upon the stone throne in the chamber atop the Wind Tower. His eyes, if ever they opened, would gaze into the magical mirror. Beneath his blue-veined, wrinkled hands lay tiny, fragile globular phials. A fresh stock of drugs had gone into his cabinet. One day, if the need arose, the Director might once again cause his eyes to open.

He was completely a tool, unlike the other there. His usefulness was at an end, his edge dulled. But the Star Rider was frugal. He wasted nothing that might, someday, have value again. The chamber atop the Wind Tower became the tool's box, a place of peace and safety. Even Varthlokkur hadn't the power to rifle it. And the fullness of his Power had returned.

The Old Man's Dark Lady had, again, been left standing at the altar.

Sharing the Old Man's chamber, perhaps as memorials or mementos, were the seated cadavers of the Princes Thaumaturge.

The main course arrived. Mocker attacked his portion, willing to let someone else talk for once. He hadn't had a decent meal in months.

"I kind of hate to see the Old Man out of the game," Nepanthe said. Mocker thought he caught a whiff of better-he-than-me. "He was all right, even if he was a grouch."

"He's not gone, just waiting. On the will of the Star Rider. I think there might have been something between them that nobody ever suspected. But, yes, I'll miss him, too. I just wonder how much he knew and never told. We had too many secrets from each other."

Slowly, thoughtfully, the wizard downed several mouthfuls. Then, "For all his crochets and grumbling, he was kind and a good friend. It's too bad he never had a goal. Other than to escape living out his role. Whatever it might be."

"Let's hope he's happier next time around."

"Child?" Mocker grunted around a mouthful of roast pork.

"Fine. And I'm glad you cleaned up and shaved. I never saw a hill bandit as dirty, smelly, and wild as you were." She and Varthlokkur resumed reminiscing and speculating about the Old Man.

Disturbingly, the wizard suggested, "You know, there're scholars who claim the Star Rider is some sort of avatar of Justice. Maybe he judged all of us, not just the Princes."

"You mean?…"

"Yes. The Old Man could've been the only one of us who really got rewarded. The rest of us got dumped right back into the middle of whatever's going on."

Mocker cocked a dubious eye his way, but didn't let up on the chicken he was gnawing.

Nepanthe looked sour. "Sometimes I have premonitions," she said. "And I've gotten one from this. There're hard times coming. A lot of pain and sorrow for my husband and I."

Varthlokkur hadn't yet performed a divination to see what the future looked like unobscured by the interference of the Princes Thaumaturge. He had been putting it off, afraid of what he might foresee.

It would have done him no good. Other Powers were afoot, and had their eyes upon him.

"No doubt," he replied to Nepanthe. "I believe the real reason we're here is that we're expected to be useful again."

Behind the mindless glutton mask Mocker was critically alert, weighing every nuance both of what the wizard said and the way he said it. He was hunting the false note. Father or not, he just didn't trust Varthlokkur's forgiveness.

It was time, he decided, to give the hornets' nest a gentle poke, to see what buzzed, time to cast a stone to see what rose from the turgid deeps of this falsely pacific pond. Hand on sword hilt, he belched grandly, leaned back in his chair.

Eyes closed, conversationally, he observed, "If memory doesn't prevaricate, same being impossible in steel-trap brain of genius like self, time was, man once promised fat trickster and friends vast emoluments for doing small deeds for same. Being possessed of elephantine memory already noted, can say with certainty promissory was: gold double shekel pieces, mintage of Empire, one thousand four hundred. Same gentleman aforementioned advanced mere eighty. Self, considering distance to home of same, touch purse, and cry, 'Woe!' Fingers feel nothing. Not even bent green copper. Foresee great hunger…"

Nepanthe, understanding at last, gasped. "Why not add in what you lost in Iwa Skolovda?" she demanded, amazed by his nerve.

Mocker grinned. His eyes popped open, wide with innocence. "Silver: three hundred twelve kronen. Copper: two hundred thirty-four groschen, of Iwa Skolovda. No gold. Of other realms, various, maybe five silver nobles, of Itaskia, total. Conservative estimate, but self is renowned for generosity, for lack of pinch-penny heart, for interest only in minimal income accommodating subsistence of same. Am, at moment, considering same in new wife, newly impoverished."

He had a point there. The wealth of Ravenkrak had vanished utterly. Someday bits and pieces might begin surfacing when Haroun's soldiers began pawning plunder.

Nepanthe was as destitute as her husband.

Varthlokkur laughed till tears ran down his cheeks. "You've got to be the most brazen footpad since Rainheart, who slew the Kammengarn Dragon."

Mocker grinned again. Nepanthe kicked him beneath the table. He ignored her warning. "In coin of Ilkazar, please. With interest being ten percent from date due on wages, same being morning when soldiers of crafty associate impregnated impregnable fortress Ravenkrak."

"Well, why not?" Varthlokkur mused as he recovered his composure. "I've got buckets full. I do owe you, technically. And there's your friends, who may give me no peace… Nepanthe, you help yourself, too. As a wedding present."

Mocker's eyes narrowed. Something was going on here. After all his trouble, Varthlokkur was backing down this easily? He didn't believe it. There was a catch somewhere. A trick or a trap…

But, "Buckets?" His eyes widened. Avarice banished any other consideration. "Am permitted to pick and choose?"

So greedy, this man. Properly marketed, the right coins, the rare ones, would bring a hundred times intrinsic value from rich collectors. He could parlay a moderate fortune into a huge one. He knew the men who would buy and which coins were in demand. He had once had a go at counterfeiting them—till he had found the necessary research and marketing too much work.

The point passed over Varthlokkur's head. "Of course." To the wizard one coin was like another. Puzzled, he said, "I'll show you the strongroom."

Mocker spent the day there, becoming intimately familiar with every gold piece. Varthlokkur soon lost interest and went about his business. Then Mocker set about filling every pocket he had in addition to putting aside what was "due" himself and his friends. They, Varthlokkur told him, were alive and well, though chastened by close brushes with doom.

After all, as Mocker asked Nepanthe later, what good was gall if he let it go to waste?

Four days ground away. Mocker eventually had to concede that Varthlokkur really meant to let Nepanthe go. He didn't understand why, and remained thoroughly suspicious till long after they made their departure, following friendly farewells.

While traveling, Nepanthe dwelt on her agreement with Varthlokkur. She couldn't quite put it into perspective. Doubts remained. Would the wizard maintain his end? Was it fair to Mocker? Had it placed him in jeopardy? Would he live with the unknown threat of a knife in the dark henceforth?

The gods knew she loved her husband. Shame overwhelmed her whenever she recalled her behavior in the Shadowland. Her heart hammered when she reflected on how close she had come to massacring his feeling for her…

But there was this newly recognized feeling for Varthlokkur to reconcile with that fop Mocker, against the romantic schooling of twenty-nine years… *I did it for you,* she lied to herself, looking at her husband.

But it had all worked out, hadn't it? Everyone had—though compromised—approached his or her desire. The world was rid of several old evils. Maybe the future would bring the fulfillment of a few dreams.

Varthlokkur still hadn't performed a divination. Possibly some subliminal premonition compelled him to avoid looking whither bad news might lie. Whatever, Nepanthe rode westward armed with hope—however forlorn it might be.

"Mocker, I love you."

He flashed her the old Saltimbanco grin. But his mind was far away, haunting the labyrinths of schemes founded on his newly acquired wealth—however foredoomed they might be.

OCTOBER'S BABY

Contents

ONE: THE YEARS 994-995
AFTER THE FOUNDING OF THE EMPIRE OF ILKAZAR
UNTO US A CHILD IS BORN

i) He made the darkness his covering around him

Like a whispering ghost the winged man dropped from the moonless winter night, a shadow on the stars whose wings fluttered with a brief sharp *crack* as he broke his fall and settled onto the sill of a high glassless tower window of Castle Krief. His great wings he folded about him like a dark living cloak, with hardly a sigh of motion. His eyes burned cold scarlet as he studied the blackness within the tower. He turned his terrier-like head from side to side, listening. Neither sight nor sound came to him. He did not want to believe it. It meant he must go on. Cautiously, fearfully—human places inspired dread—he dropped to the cold interior floor.

The darkness within, impenetrable even to his nightseeing eyes, was food for his man-fear. What human evil might wait there, wearing a cloak of night? Yet he mustered courage and went on, one weak hand always touching the crystal dagger at his hip, the other caressing his tiny purse. Inaudible terror whimpered in his throat. He was not a courageous creature, would not be in this fell place but for the dread-love he bore his Master.

Guided by whimper-echoes only he could hear, he found the door he sought. Fear, which had faded as he found all as peaceful as the Master had promised, returned. A warding spell blocked his advance, one that could raise a grand haroo and bring steel-armed humans.

But he was not without resources. His visit was the spearthrust of an operation backed by careful preparation. From his purse he took a crimson jewel, chucked it up the corridor. It clattered. He gasped. The noise seemed thunderous. Came a flash of brilliant red light. The ward-spell twisted away into some plane at right angles to reality. He peeked between the long bony fingers covering his eyes. All right. He went to the door, opened it soundlessly.

A single candle, grown short with time, burned within. Across the room, in a vast four-poster with silken hangings, slept the object of his mission. She was young, fair, delicate, but these traits held no meaning. He was a sexless creature. He suffered no human longings—at least of the carnal sort. He did long for the security of his cavern home, for the companionship of his brothers. To him this creature was an object (of fear, of his quest, of pity), a vessel to be used.

The woman (hardly more than a child was she, just gaining the graceful curves of the woman-to-be) stirred, muttered. The winged man's heart jumped. He knew the power of dreams. Hastily, he dipped into his purse for a skin-wrapped ball of moist cotton. He let her breathe its vapors till she settled into untroubled sleep.

Satisfied, he drew the bedclothes down, eased her nightgarments up. From his pouch he withdrew his final treasure. There were spells on the device, that kept its contents viable, which would guarantee this night's work's success.

He loathed himself for the cold-bloodedness of his deed. Yet he finished, restored the woman and bed to their proper order, and silently fled. He recovered the crimson jewel, ground it to dust so the warding spell would return. Everything had to appear undisturbed. Before he took wing again, he stroked his crystal dagger. He was glad he had not been forced to use it. He detested violence.

ii) He sees with the eyes of an enemy

Nine months and a few days later. October: A fine month for doings dark and strange, with red and gold leaves falling to mask the mind with colorful wonders, with cool piney breezes bringing winter promises from the high Kapenrungs, with swollen orange moons by night, and behind it all breaths and hints of things of fear. The month began still bright with summer's memory, like a not too distant, detached chunk of latter August with feminine, changeable, sandwiched September forgotten. The month gradually gathered speed, rolled downhill until, with a plunge at the end, it dumped all into a black and wicked pit from which the remainder of the year would be but a struggle up a mountain chasing starshine. At its end there was a night consecrated to all that was unholy, a night for unhallowed deeds.

The Krief's city, Vorgreberg, was small, but not unusually so for a capital in the Lesser Kingdoms. Its streets were unclean. The rich hadn't gotten that way squandering income on sweepers, and the poor didn't care. Three quarters was ancient slum, the remainder wealthy residential or given over to the trade houses of merchants handling the silks and spices that came from the east over the Savernake Gap. The residences of the nobles were occupied only when the Thing sat. The rest of the year those grim old skulduggers spent at their castles and estates, whipping more wealth from their serfs. City crime was endemic, taxes were high, people starved to death daily, or any of a hundred diseases got them, corruption in government was ubiquitous, and ethnic groups hated one another to the sullen edge of violence. So, a city like most, surrounded by a small country populated with normally foibled men, special only because a king held court there, and because it was the western terminus for caravans from the orient. From it, going west, flowed eastern riches; to it came the best goods of the coastal states.

But, on a day at the end of October when evil stirred, it also had:

A holiday morning after rain, and an old man in a ragged greatcloak who needed a bath and shave. He turned from a doorway at the rear of a rich man's home. Bacon tastes still trembled on his tongue. A copper sceat weighed lightly in his pocket. He chuckled softly.

Then his humor evaporated. He stopped, stared down the alley, then fled in the opposite direction. From behind him came the sound of steel rims on brick pavement, rattling loudly in the morning stillness. The tramp paused, scratched his crotch, made a sign against the evil eye, then ran. The breakfast taste had gone sour.

A man with a pushcart eased round a turn, slowly pursued the tramp. He was a tiny fellow, old, with a grizzled, ragged beard. His slouch made him appear utterly weary of forcing his cart over the wet pavement. His cataracted eyes squinted as he studied the backs of houses. Repeatedly, after considering one or another, he shook his head.

Mumbling, he left the alley, set course for the public grounds outside the Krief's palace. The leafless, carefully ranked trees there were skeletal and grim in the morning gloom and damp. The castle seemed besieged by the gray, dreary wood.

The cartman paused. "Royal Palace." He sneered. Castle Krief may have stood six centuries inviolate, may have surrendered only to Ilkazar, but it wasn't invincible. It could be destroyed from within. He thought of the comforts, the riches behind those walls, and the hardness of his own life. He cursed the waiting.

There was work to be done. Miserable work. Castles and kingdoms didn't fall at the snap of a finger.

Round the entire castle he went, observing the sleepy guards, the ancient ivy on the southern wall, the big gates facing east and west, and the half-dozen posterns. Though Kavelin had petty noble feuds as numerous as fleas on a hound, they never touched Vorgreberg itself. Those wars were for the barons, fought in their fiefs among themselves, and from them the Crown was relatively safe, remaining a disinterested referee.

Sometimes, though, one of the nearby kingdoms, coveting the eastern trade, tried to move in. Then the house-divided quickly united.

The morning wore on. People gathered near the palace's western gate. The old man opened his cart, got charcoal burning, soon was selling sausages and hot rolls.

Near noon the great gate opened. The crowd fell into a hush. A company of the King's Own marched forth to blaring trumpets. Express riders thundered out bound for the ends of Kavelin, crying, "The King has a son!"

The crowd broke into cheers. They had waited years for that news.

The small old man smiled at his sausages. The King had a son to insure the continuity of his family's tyranny, and the idiots cheered as if this were a day of salvation. Poor foolish souls. They never learned. Their hopes for a better future never paled. Why expect the child to become a king less cruel than his ancestors?

The old man held a poor opinion of his species. In other times and places he had been heard to say that, all things considered, he would rather be a duck.

The King's Own cleared the gate. The crowd surged forward, eager to seize the festive moment. Commoners seldom passed those portals.

The old man went with the mob, made himself one with their greed. But his greed wasn't for the dainties on tables in the courtyard. His greed was for knowledge. The sort a burglar cherished. He went everywhere allowed, saw everything permitted, listened, paid especial attention to the ivied wall and the Queen's tower. Satisfied, he sampled the King's largesse, drew scowls for damning the cheap wine, then returned to his cart, and to the alleyways.

iii) He returns to the place of his iniquity

Once again the winged man slid down a midnight sky, a momentary shadow riding the beams of an October moon. It was Allernmas Night, nine months after his earlier visit. He banked in a whisper of air, swooped past towers, searched his sluggish memory. He found the right one, glided to the window, disappeared into darkness. A red-eyed shadow in a cloak of wings, he stared across the once festive court, waited. This second visit, he feared, was tempting Fate. Something would go wrong.

A black blob momentarily blocked a gap between crenellations on the battlements. It moved along the wall, then down to the courtyard. The winged man unwound a light line from about his waist. One end he secured to a beam above his head. With that his mission was complete. He was supposed to take wing immediately, but he waited for his friend instead.

Burla, a misshapen, dwarfish creature with a bundle on his back, swarmed toward him with the agility of the ape he resembled. The winged man turned sideways so his friend could pass.

"You go now?" Burla asked.

"No. I watch."

He touched his arm lightly, spilled a fangy smile. He was frightened, too. Death could pounce at any moment. "I start." He wriggled, muttered, got the bundle off his back.

They followed the hall the winged man had used before. Burla used devices he had been given to overcome protective spells, then overcame the new lock on the Queen's door…

Came a sleepy question. Burla and the winged man exchanged glances. Their fears had been proven well-founded, though the Master had predicted otherwise. Nevertheless, he had armed Burla against this possibility. The dwarf handed the winged man his bundle, took a fragile vial from his purse, opened the door a crack, tossed it through. Came another question, sharper, louder, frightened. Burla took a heavy, damp cloth from his pouch, resumed care of his bundle while the winged man tied it over his twisted mouth and nose.

Still another question from the room. It was followed by a scream when Burla stepped inside. The cry reverberated down the hall. The winged man drew his dagger.

"Hurry!" he said. Excited, confused voices were moving toward him, accompanied by a clash of metal. Soldiers. He grew more frightened, thought about flying now. But he could not abandon his friend. Indeed, he moved so the window exit would be behind him.

His blade began to glow along its edge. The winged man held it high before him, so it stood out of the darkness, illuminating only his ugly face. Humans had their fears, too.

Three soldiers came upstairs, saw him, paused. The winged man pulled his blade closer, spread his wings. The dagger illuminated those enough to yield the impression that he had swollen to fill the passageway. One soldier squeaked fearfully, then ran downstairs. The others mumbled oaths.

Burla returned with the child. "We go now." He was out the window and down the rope in seconds. The winged man followed, seizing the rope as he went. He rose against the moon, hoping to draw attention from Burla. The uproar was, like pond ripples, now lapping against the most distant palace walls.

iv) He consorts with creatures of darkness

In the Gudbrandsdal Forest, a Royal Preserve just beyond the boundary of the Siege of Vorgreberg, a dozen miles from Castle Krief, a bent old man stared into a sullen campfire and chuckled. "They've done it! They've done it. It's all downhill from here."

The heavily robed, deeply cowled figure opposite him inclined its head slightly.

The old man, the sausage seller, was wicked—in an oddly clean, impersonal, puckish sort of way—but the other was evil. Malefically, cruelly, blackly evil.

The winged man, Burla, and their friends were unaware of the Master's association with him.

v) Bold in the service of his Lord

Eanred Tarlson, a Wesson captain of the King's Own, was a warrior of international repute. His exploits during the El Murid Wars had won renown throughout the bellicose Lesser Kingdoms. A Wesson peasant in an infantry company, Fate had put him near his King when the latter had received a freak, grave wound from a ricocheting arrow. Eanred had donned his Lord's armor and had held off the fanatics for days. His action had won him a friend with a crown.

Had he been Nordmen, he would have been knighted. The best his King could do for a Wesson was grant a commission. The knighthood came years later. He was the first Wesson to achieve chivalric orders since the Resettlement.

Eanred was his King's champion, respected even by the Nordmen. He was well known as an honest, loyal, reasonable man who dealt without treachery, who did not hesitate to press an unpopular opinion upon the King. He stood by his beliefs. Popularly, he was known for his victories in trials-by-combat which had settled disputes with neighboring principalities. The Wesson peasantry believed him a champion of their rights.

Though Eanred had killed for his King, he was neither hard nor cruel. He saw himself only as a soldier, no greater than any other, with no higher ambition than to defend his King. He was of a type gold-rare in the Lesser Kingdoms.

Tarlson, by chance, was in the courtyard when the furor broke. He arrived below the Queen's tower in time to glimpse a winged monster dwindling against the moon, trailing a fine line as if trolling the night for invisible aerial fish. He studied its flight. The thing was bound toward the Gudbrandsdal.

"Gjerdrum!" he thundered at his son and squire, who accompanied him. "A horse!" Within minutes he galloped through the East Gate. He left orders for his company to follow. He might be chasing the wind, he thought, but he *was* taking action. The rest of the palace's denizens were squalling like old ladies caught with their skirts up. Those Nordmen courtiers! Their ancestors may have been tough, but today's crop were dandified cretins.

The Gudbrandsdal wasn't far on a galloping horse. Eanred plunged in afoot after tying his horse where others could find it. He discovered a campfire immediately. Drawing his sword, he stalked the flames. Soon, from shadow, he spied the winged thing talking with an old man bundled in a blanket. He saw no weapon more dangerous than the winged thing's dagger.

That dagger… It seemed to glow faintly. He strode toward the fire, demanded, "Where's the Prince?" His blade slid toward the throat of the old man.

His appearance didn't startle the two, though they shrank away. Neither replied. The winged man drew his blade. Yes, it glowed. Magic! Eanred shifted his sword for defense. This monstrous, reddish creature with the blade of pale fire might be more dangerous than he appeared.

Something moved in the darkness behind Tarlson. A black sleeve reached. He sensed his danger, turned cat-swift while sweeping his blade in a vertical arc. It cut air—then flesh and bone. A hand fell beside the fire, kicking up little sprays of dust, fingers writhing like the legs of a dying spider. A scream of pain and rage echoed through the forest.

But Eanred's stroke came too late. Fingers had brushed his throat. The world grew arctically cold. He leaned slowly like a tree cut through. All sensation abandoned him. As he fell, he turned, saw first the dark outline of the being that had stunned him, the startled faces of the others, then the severed hand. The waxy, monstrous thing was crawling toward its owner… Everything went black. But he tumbled into darkness with a silent chuckle. Fate had given him one small victory. He was able to push his blade through the hand and lever it into the fire.

vi) His heart is heavy, but he perseveres
Burla, with the baby quiet in the bundle on his back, reached the Master's campsite as the last embers were dying. False dawn had begun creeping over

the Kapenrung Mountains. He cursed the light, moved more warily. Horsemen had been galloping about since he had left the city. All his nighttime skills had been required to evade them.

Troops had been to the campsite, he saw. There had been a struggle. Someone had been injured. The Master's blanket lay abandoned, a signal. He was well but had been forced to flee. Burla's unhappiness was exceeded only by his fear that he wasn't competent to fulfill the task now assigned him.

His work, which should have been completed, had just begun. He glanced toward the dawn. So many miles to bear the baby through an aroused country-side. How could he escape the swords of the tall men?

He had to try.

Days he slept a little, and traveled when it was safe. Nights he hurried through, moving as fast as his short legs would carry him, only occasionally pausing at a Wesson farm to steal food or milk for the child. He expected the poor tiny thing to die any time, but it was preternaturally tough.

The tall men failed to catch him. They knew he was about, knew that he had had something to do with the invasion of the Queen's tower. They did turn the country over and shake out a thousand hidden things. The time came when, high in the mountains, he trudged wearily into the cave where the Master had said to meet if they had to split up.

vii) Their heads nod, and from their mouths issue lies

An hour after the kidnapping, someone finally thought to see if Her Majesty was all right. They didn't think much of their Queen, those Nordmen. She was a foreigner, barely of childbearing age, and so unobtrusive that no one spared her a thought. Queen and nurse were found in deep, unnatural sleep. And there was a baby at the woman's breast.

Once again Castle Krief churned with confusion. What had been seen, briefly, as a probable Wesson attempt to interrupt the succession, was obviously either a great deal less, or more, sinister. After a few hints from the King himself, it was announced that the Prince was sleeping well, that the excitement had been caused by a guard's imagination.

Few believed that. There had been a switch. Parties with special interests sought the physician and midwife who had attended the birth, but neither could be found—till much later. Their corpses were discovered, mutilated against easy recognition, in a slum alley. Royal disclaimers continued to flow.

The King's advisers met repeatedly, discussed the possible purpose of the invasion, the stance to be taken, and how to resolve the affair. Time passed. The mystery deepened. It became obvious that there would be no explanations till someone captured the winged man, the dwarf a guard had seen go monkey-ing down the ivied wall, or one of the strangers who had been camped in the Gudbrandsdal. The dwarf was working his way east toward the mountains. No trace of the others turned up. The army concentrated on the dwarf. So did those for whom possession of the Crown Prince meant leverage.

The fugitive slipped away. Nothing further came of the strange events. The King made certain the child with his Queen, at least in pretense, remained his heir. The barons stopped plaguing odd strangers and resumed their squabbles. Wessons returned to their scheming, merchants to their counting houses. Within a year the mystery seemed forgotten, though countless eyes kept tabs on the King's health.

Two: Year 1002 afe
The Hearth and the Heart

i) Bragi Ragnarson and Elana Michone

Suffering in silence, brushing her coppery hair, Elana Ragnarson endured the grumbling of her husband.

"Bills of lading, bills of sale, accounts payable, accounts receivable, torts and taxes! What kind of life is this? I'm a soldier, not a bloody merchant. I wasn't meant to be a coin counter…"

"You could hire an accountant." The woman knew better than to add that a professional would keep better books. His grumbling was of no moment anyway. It came with spring, the annual disease of a man who had forgotten the hardships of the adventurer's life. A week or so, time enough to remember sword-strokes dangerously close, unshared beds in icy mud, hunger, and the physical grind of forced marches, would settle him down. But he would never completely overcome the habits of a Trolledyngjan boyhood. North of the Kratchnodian Mountains all able males went to war as soon as the ice broke up in the harbors.

"Where has my youth gone?" he complained as he began dressing. "When I was fresh down from Trolledyngja, still in my teens, I was leading troops against El Murid… Hire? Did you say hire, woman?" A heavy, hard face encompassed by shaggy blond hair and beard momentarily joined hers in her mirror. She touched his cheek. "Bring in some thief who'll rob me blind with numbers on paper?

"When me and Mocker and Haroun were stealing the fat off Itaskian merchants, I never dreamed I'd get fat in the arse and pocket myself. Those were the days. I still ain't too old. What's thirty-one? My father's father fought at Ringerike when he was eighty…"

"And got himself killed."

"Yeah, well." He rambled on about the deeds of other relatives. But each, as Elana pointed out, had died far from home, and not a one of old age.

"It's Haroun's fault. Where's he been the last three years? If he turned up, we could get a good adventure started."

Elana dropped her brush. Cold-footed mice of fear danced along her spine. This was bad. When he began missing that ruffian bin Yousif the fever had reached a critical pitch. If by whim of fate the man turned up, Bragi could be lured into another insane, byzantine scheme.

"Forget that cutthroat. What's he ever done for you? Just gotten you in trouble since the day you met." She turned. Bragi stood with one leg in a pair of baggy work trousers, the other partially raised from the floor. She had said the wrong thing. Damn Haroun! How had he gotten a hold on a man as bullheadedly independent as Bragi?

She suspected it was because bin Yousif had a cause, a decades-deep vendetta with El Murid which infected his every thought and action. His dedication to vengeance awed a man like Bragi.

Finally, grunting, Ragnarson finished dressing. "Think I'll ride over to Mocker's today. Visit a spell."

She sighed. The worst was past. A day in the forest would take the edge off his wanderlust. Maybe she should stay home next time he went to Itaskia. A night on his own, in Wharf Street South, might be the specific for his disease.

"Papa? Are you ready?" their eldest son, Ragnar, called through the bedroom door.

"Yeah. What you want?"

"There's a man here."

"This early? Tramp, huh, looking for a handout? Tell him there's a soft touch next house north." He chuckled. The next place north was that of his friend Mocker, twenty miles on.

"Bragi!" A look was enough. The last man he had sent north had been a timber buyer with a fat navy contract.

"Yes, dear. Ragnar? Tell him I'll be down in a minute." He kissed his wife, left her in troubled thought.

Adventures. She had enjoyed them herself. But no more. She had traded the mercenary days for a home and children. Only a fool would dump what they had to cross swords with young men and warlocks. Then she smiled. She missed the old days a little, too.

ii) A curious visitor

Ragnarson clumped downstairs into the dining hall and peered into its gloomy corners. It was vast. This place was both home and fortress. It housed nearly a hundred people in troubled times. He shivered. No one had kindled the morning fires. "Ragnar! Where's he at?"

His son popped from the narrow, easily defended hallway to the front door. "Outside. He won't come in."

"Eh? Why?"

The boy shrugged.

"Well, if he won't, he won't." As he strode to the door, Ragnarson snatched an iron-capped club from a weapons rack.

Outside, in the pale misty light of a morning hardly begun, an old, old man waited. He leaned on a staff, stared at the ground thoughtfully. His bearing was not that of a beggar. Ragnarson looked for a horse, saw none.

The ancient had neither pack nor pack animal, either. "Well, what can I do for you?"

A smile flashed across a face that seemed as old as the world. "Listen."

"Eh?" Bragi grew uneasy. There was something about this fellow, a *presence...*

"Listen. Hear, and act accordingly. Fear the child with the ways of a woman. Beware the bells of a woman's fingers. All magicks aren't in the hands of sorcerers." Ragnarson started to interrupt, found that he could not. "Covet not the gemless crown. It rides the head precariously. It leads to the place where swords are of no avail." Having said his cryptic piece, the old man turned to the track leading toward the North Road, the highway linking Itaskia and Iwa Skolovda.

Ragnarson frowned. He was not a slow-witted man. But he was unaccustomed to dealing with mystery-mouthed old men in the sluggish hours of the morning. "Who the hell are you?" he thundered.

Faintly, from the woods:

"Old as a mountain,

Lives on a star,

Deep as the ocean flows."

Ragnarson pursued fleas through his beard. A riddle. Well. A madman, that's what. He shrugged it off. There was breakfast to eat and the ride to Mocker's to be made. No time for crazies.

iii) Things she loves and fears

Elana, who had overheard, could not shrug it off. She feared its portent, that Bragi was about to hie off on some harebrained venture.

From a high window she stared at the land and forest they had conquered together. She remembered. They had come late in the year to a landgrant so remote that they had had to cut a path in. That first winter had been cold and hard. The winds and snows pouring over the Kratchnodians had seemed bent on revenge for the disasters wrought there the winter previous, in Bragi's last campaign. The blood of children and wolves had christened the new land.

The next year there had been a flareup of the ancient boundary dispute between Prost Kamenets and Itaskia. Bandits, briefly legitimatized by letters of marque from Prost Kamenets, had come over the Silverbind. Many hadn't gone home, but the land had also drunk the blood of its own.

The third had been the halcyon year. Their friends Nepanthe and Mocker had been able to break loose and take a grant of their own.

Things had turned bad again late in the fourth year, when drought east of the Silverbind had driven men from Prost Kamenets into a brigandry their government ignored as long as its thrust lay across the river. Near the rear of the house, the granary stood in charred ruins. A half-mile away the men were rebuilding the sawmill. There were contracts for timber to be delivered to the naval yards at Itaskia. Those had to be met first.

Counting wives and children, there had been twenty-two pioneers. Most were dead now, buried in places of honor beside the greathouse. She and Bragi had been lucky, their only loss a daughter born dead.

Too many graves in the graveyard. Fifty-one in all. Over the years old followers of Bragi's and friends of hers had drifted in, some to stay a day or two out of a journey in search of a war, some to settle and die.

The grain was sprouting, the children were growing, the cattle were getting fat. There was an orchard that might produce in her lifetime. She had a home almost as large and comfortable as the one Bragi had promised her during all those years under arms. And it was all endangered. She knew it in her bones. Something was afoot, something grim.

Her gaze went to the graveyard. Old Tor Jack lay in the corner, beside Randy Will who had gotten his skull crushed pulling Ragnar from between a stallion and a mare in heat. What would they think if Bragi threw it up now?

Jorgen Miklassen, killed by a wild boar. Gudrun Ormsdatter, died in child-birth. Red Lars, brought down by wolves. Jan and Mihr Krushka. Rafnir Shagboots, Walleyed Marjo, Tandy the Gimp.

Blood and tears, blood and tears. Nothing would bring them back. Why so morbidly thoughtful? Break yourself out, woman. Time goes on, work has to be done. What man hath wrought, woman must maintain.

Maxims did nothing to cheer her. She spent the day working hard, seeking an exhaustion that would extinguish her apprehensions.

In the evening, as twilight's pastels were fading into indigo, a huge owl came out of the east, flew thrice round the house widdershins, dipping and dancing with owls from beneath the greathouse eaves. It soon fled toward Mocker's.

"Another omen." She sighed.

iv) Mocker and Nepanthe of Ravenkrak

Mocker's holding lay hip by thigh with Ragnarson's. Both were held under Itaskian Crown Charter. On his own territory each had the power and responsibility of a baron—without the privileges. Though neighbors, both found distance between homes a convenience. They had been friends since the tail-end years of the El Murid Wars, but each found the other's extended company insufferable. The disparity in their values kept them constantly on the simmering edge. A day's visit, a night's drinking and remembering when, that was their limit. Neither was known for patience, nor for an open mind.

Ragnarson covered the distance before dinner, pretending that once again he was racing El Murid from Hellin Daimiel to Libiannin.

Mocker wasn't surprised to see him. Little astonished that fat old reprobate.

Ragnarson reined in beside a short, swarthy fellow on his knees in mud.

Laugh lines permanently marked his moon-round brown face. "Hai!" he cried. "Great man-bears! Help!" Tenants came running, grabbing weapons. The fat man rose and whirled madly, dark eyes dancing.

A boy the age of Bragi's Ragnar ran from a nearby smokehouse, toy bow ready. "Oh. It's only Uncle Bear."

"Only?" Bragi growled as he dismounted. "Only? Maybe, Ethrian, but mean enough to box the ears of a cub." He seized the boy, threw him squealing into the air.

Wiping her hands on her apron, a woman came from the nearby house. Nepanthe always seemed to be wiping her hands. Mocker left a mountain of woman's work wherever he passed. "Bragi. Just in time for dinner. You came alone? I haven't seen Elana since…" Her smile faded. Since the bandit passage last fall, when Mocker's dependents had holed up in Ragnarson's stronger greathouse.

"Pretty as ever, I see," said Ragnarson. He handed his reins to Ethrian, who scowled, knowing he was being gotten rid of. Nepanthe blushed. She was indeed attractive, but hardly pretty as ever. The forest years had devoured her aristocratic delicacy. Still, she looked younger than thirty-four. "No, couldn't bring the family."

"Business?" She did most of Mocker's talking. Mocker had never mastered the Itaskian tongue. His vanity was such that he avoided speaking whenever he could. Ragnarson was not sure that inability was genuine. It varied according to some formula known only to Mocker himself.

"No. Just riding. Spring fever." Shifting to Necremnen, an eastern language in which Mocker was more at home, he continued, "Strange thing happened this morning. Old man appeared out of nowhere, mumbled some nonsense about girls who act like women. Wouldn't answer a question straight out, only in riddles. Weirdest thing is, I couldn't find a trace of him on the road. You'd think there'd be fresh droppings, coming or going."

Nepanthe frowned. She didn't understand the language. "Are you going to eat?" Pettishly, she brushed long raven hair out of her eyes. A warm breeze had begun blowing from the south.

"Of course. That's why I came." He tried charming her with a smile.

"Same man," Mocker replied, proving he could mangle even a language learned in childhood, "beriddled self. Portly pursuer of predawn pissery, self, rising early to dispose of excess beer drunk night before, found same on doorstep before sunrise."

"Impossible. It was barely sunup when he turned up at my place…"

"For him, is possible. Self, having encountered same before, know. Can do anything."

"The Old Man of the Mountain?"

"No."

"Varthlokkur?"

They were at Mocker's door. When Ragnarson said the latter, Nepanthe gave him a hard stare. "You're not mixed up with him again, are you? Mocker…"

"Doe's Breast. Diamond Eyes. Light of life of noted sluggard renown for pusillanimity, would same, being contender for title World's Laziest Man, being famous from south beyond edge of farthest map to north in Trolledyngja, from west in Freyland, east to Matayanga, for permanent state of cowardice and lassitude…"

"Yes, you would. How'd you get known in all those places?"

Mocker continued, in Necremnen, "Was famous Star Rider."

"Why?" Ragnarson asked.

"Why what?"

"Oh, never mind. That's why you weren't surprised to see me?"

The fat man shrugged. "When Star Riders come calling on fat old fool sequestered in boundless forest, am surprised by nothings. Next, Haroun will appear out of south with new world-conquering scheme in hand, madder than ever." This he said sourly, as if he believed it a distinct possibility.

"If you two can quit chicken-clucking for a minute, we can eat," said Nepanthe.

"Sorry, Nepanthe," Ragnarson apologized. "Some things…"

She sighed. "As long as it's not another woman."

"No, not that. Just a minor mystery."

v) Another strange visitor

The mystery soon deepened. Ethrian returned from the stables and, after having been scolded for being as slow as small boys will, said, "There's a man coming. A funny man on a little horse. I don't think I like him." Having so declaimed, he set about devouring his dinner.

Mocker rose, went to a front window, came back wearing a puzzled frown. "Marco."

It took Ragnarson a moment to recall anyone by that name. "Visigodred's apprentice?" Visigodred was a wizard, an old acquaintance.

"Same." Mocker looked worried. Ragnarson was disturbed himself.

A clatter and rattle at the front door. "He's here."

"Uhn." Both men looked at Nepanthe. For a moment she stared back, a little pale, then went.

"About goddamn time," came from the other room, then, "Oh, beg your pardon, my dear lovely lady. Husband home? I hope not. Seems a shame to let a beautiful chance meeting go to waste."

"Back here."

Marco, a dwarf with the ego of a giant, came strutting into the kitchen, not a bit abashed about having been overheard. "Timing was right, I see." He pulled up a chair, snagged a huge hunk of bread, smeared it with butter. He ignored inquiring looks till he had gorged himself. "Suppose you're wondering what

I'm doing here. Besides stuffing my face. So am I. Well same as always, doing the old man's legwork. Got a message for you."

"Humph!" Mocker snorted. "No time. Am occupied with profound compunctions—Computations? Constructions?—philosophic. How to get lentils in earth without straining back of and mud-bespattering self of, portly peasant, self. Am no wise interested in problems and peculations of old busybody who would interfere with ponderations on same." He looked at Nepanthe as if for approval.

Ragnarson was irritated. Did Nepanthe control Mocker that much? Once he had been a wild-eyed heller, game for any insane scheme Haroun concocted. Bragi met Nepanthe's eyes across the table. Why the laughter there? He thought, she knows what I'm thinking.

"What the boss wanted me to tell you was this: 'In a land of many kings trust no hand but your own, nor allow you the right far from sight of the left. Men there change loyalties more often than underwear. Stand wary of all women, and tamper not with the place, and name, and cloak, of Mist.' What the hell that means I don't know. He's not usually that hard to pin down. But he's got a stake in it somehow. I guess his girlfriend is in. Well, got to go. Thank you for a delightful meal, my lady."

"Hold on," Ragnarson growled. "What the hell, hey? What's going on?"

"You got me, Hairy. I just work for the man, I don't read his mind. You want to know more, you check with himself. Only he won't see you. Told me to tell you that. I forgot. He said there's no way he can help you this time. Did all he could by sending me. Now, if you don't mind, I'll be getting along. There's two, three little birds at home might pine away if I don't get back to them soon." Refusing to answer further questions, he returned to his pony. The last they saw of him, he was entering the forest at a brisk trot, a bawdy song trailing behind him.

"You'd think a man like Visigodred could find an apprentice with a little more couth," Ragnarson said. "Well, what do you think?"

"Self, am bamboozled. Befuddled by dearth of sense." Mocker's eyes flicked toward Nepanthe. One chubby brown hand made the deaf-mute's sign for "Be careful."

Ragnarson smiled, glad to see the spark of rebellion.

It did not occur to him that, were Mocker visiting him, he would have seemed as henpecked. Ragnarson was not an empathetic person.

"Heard from informant Andy the Bum," said Mocker, returning to Necremnen. "News of Itaskia. Andy was pestilential mendicant always beside entrance of Red Hart, intelligent behind ubiquitous flies and filth. Sometimes remembers old contributor, self, with missives relating Wharf Street South street talk."

Mocker was talking as plainly as he could. Must be important. "Month past, maybe more counting time for letter to make tortuous way from correspondent to recipient, Haroun visited Itaskia."

Nepanthe caught the name. "Haroun? Haroun bin Yousif? Mocker, you stay away from that cutthroat…"

Ragnarson wrestled with his temper. "That's not charitable, Nepanthe. You owe the man."

"I don't want Mocker involved with him. He'd end up using us in one of his schemes."

"It was one of those that got you together."

"Elana…"

"I know what Elana thinks. She has her reasons." Elana was the first real friend Nepanthe had ever had. In a sort of pathetic, desperate way, she tried to secure that friendship by making herself a mirror of Elana. Even Mocker had less influence than Ragnarson's wife.

His curtness upset Nepanthe. Usually he was gentle beyond the reasonable. He was secretly afraid of women.

Nepanthe sulked.

"What about him?"

"Was putting finger in nasty place, coming out dirty. Was talking to scurriliousest of scurrils of Wharf Street South. Brad Red Hand. Kerth the Dagger. Derran One Eye. Boroba Thring. Breed known for stab-in-back work. Very secretive. Went off without visiting friends. Accident Andy discovered same. Whore friend, also friend of Kerth, relayed story."

"Curious. Men he's used before. When he wanted murder done. Think he's up to something?"

"Hai! Always. When was Haroun, master intriguer, not intriguing? Is question like Trolledyngjan, 'Does bear defecate in wilderness?'"

"Yeah, the bear shits in the woods. The question is, does he have plans for us? He can't manage on his own. I wonder why? He's always so self-sufficient." Faced with a real possibility of becoming involved, Ragnarson's lust for adventure perished quickly. "Andy have anything else to say?"

"Men named vanished, no word to friends or paramours. Seen crossing Great Bridge. Nervous, in hurry. Self, expect communication from old sand devil soon. Why? Haroun is one-man nation, yes, but must justify villainous activities of self to self. Must have associates, men of respected morals. Kingship thing. Must have mandate of, license from, men with values, with judgments of respect. He respects? You see? Itaskian knife swingers are tools, not-men, dust beneath feet, of morals to spit on. Hairy Trolledyngjan and fat old rascal from east, self, not much better, but honorable in mind of Haroun. Men of respect, us. Comprehend?"

"Makes sense in a left-handed way. An insight, I think. I always wondered why he never put the knife work on us. Yes."

Mocker did a most un-Mockerlike thing. He pushed his chair back while food remained on the table. Ragnarson started to follow him to the front of the house.

"Don't get involved with Haroun," said Nepanthe. "Please?"

He searched her face. She was frightened. "What can I do? When he decides to do something, he gets irresistible as a glacier."

"I know." She bit her lip.

"We're not planning anything, really. Haroun would have to do some tall talking to involve us. We're not as hungry as we used to be."

"Maybe. Maybe not." She began clearing the table. "Mocker doesn't complain, but he wasn't made for this." With a gesture she indicated the landgrant. "He stays, and tries for my sake, but he'd be happier penniless, sitting in the rain somewhere, trying to convince old ladies he's a soothsayer. That way he's like Haroun. Security doesn't mean anything. The battle of wits is everything."

Ragnarson shrugged. He couldn't tell her what she wanted to hear. Her assessment matched his own.

"I've made him miserable, Bragi. How long since you've seen him clown like he used to? How long since he's gone off on some wild tangent and claimed the world is round, or a duck-paddled boat on a sea of wine, or any of those crackpot notions he used to take up. Bragi, I'm killing him. I love him, but, Gods help me, I'm smothering him. And I can't help it."

"We are what we are, will be what we must. If he goes back to the old ways, be patient. One thing's sure. You're his goddess. He'll be back. To stay. Things get romanticized when they slide into the past. A dose of reality might be the cure."

"I suppose. Well, go talk. Let me clean up." She obviously wanted to have a good cry.

vi) An owl from Zindahjira

Ragnarson and Mocker were still on the front step when darkness fell. They were deep into a keg of beer. Neither man spoke much. The mood was not one suited to reminiscing. Bragi kept considering Mocker's homestead. The man had worked hard, but everything had been done sloppily. The patience and perfection of the builder who cared was absent. Mocker's home might last his lifetime, but not centuries like Ragnarson's.

Bragi glanced sideways. His friend was haggard, aging. The strain of trying to be something he was not was killing him. And Nepanthe was tearing herself apart, too. How bad had their relationship suffered already?

Nepanthe was the more adaptable. She had been a man-terrified, twenty-eight-year-old adolescent when first their paths had crossed. She was no introverted romantic now. She reminded Bragi of the earthy, pragmatic, time-beaten peasant women of the treacherous floodplains of the Silverbind. Escape from this life might do her good, too.

Mocker had always been a chimera, apparently at home in any milieu. The man within was the rock to which he anchored himself. What was visible was protective coloration. In an environment where he needed only be himself, he must feel terribly vulnerable. The lack of any immediate danger, after a lifetime of adjustment to its continual presence, could push some men to the edge.

Ragnarson was not accustomed to probing facades. It made him uncomfortable. He snorted, downed a pint of warm beer. Hell with it. What was, was. What would be, would be.

A sudden loud, piercing shriek made him choke and spray beer. When he finished wiping tears from his eyes, he saw a huge owl pacing before him.

He had seen that owl before. It served as messenger for Zindahjira the Silent, a much less pleasant sorcerer than the Visigodred who employed Marco.

"Desolation and despair," Mocker groaned. "Felicitations from Pit. Self, think great feathered interlocutor maybe should become owl stew, and tidings bound to leg tinder for starting fire for making same."

"That dwarf would be handy now," said Ragnarson. Both ignored the message.

"So?"

"He talks to owls. In their own language."

"Toadfeathers."

"Shilling?"

"Self, being penurious unto miserhood, indigent unto poverty, should take wager when friend Bear is infamous as bettor only on sure things? Get message."

"Why don't you?"

"Self, being gentleman farmer, confirmed anti-literate, and retired from adventure game, am not interested."

"I ain't neither."

"Then butcher owl."

"I don't think so. Zindahjira would stew us. Without benefit of prior butchery."

"When inevitable is inevitable… Charge!" Mocker shouted the last word. The owl jumped, but refused to retreat.

"Give him a beer," said Ragnarson.

"Eh?"

"Be the hospitable thing to do, wouldn't it?" He had drunk too much. In that condition he developed a childish sense of humor. There was an old saw, "Drunk as a hoot owl," about which he had developed a sudden curiosity.

Mocker set his mug before the bird. It drank.

"Well, we'd better see what old Black Face wants." Bragi recovered the message. "Hunh! Can you believe this? It says he'll forgive all debts and transgressions—as if any existed—if we'll just catch him the woman called Mist. That old bastard never gives up. How long has he been laying for Visigodred? 'Tain't right, hurting a man through his woman."

Mocker scowled. "Threats?"

"The usual. Nothing serious. Some hints about something he's afraid to mix in, same as Visigodred."

Mocker snorted. "Pusillanimous skulker in subterranean tombs, troglodytic denizen of darkness, enough! Let poor old fat fool wither in peace." He had begun to grow sad, to feel sorry for himself. A tear trickled from one large, dark eye. He reached up and put a hand on Ragnarson's shoulder. "Mother of self, longtime passing, sang beautiful song of butterflies and gossamer. Will sing for you." He began humming, searching for a tune.

Ragnarson frowned. Mocker was an orphan who had known neither father nor mother, only an old vagabond with whom he had traveled till he had been able to escape. Bragi had heard the story a hundred times. But in his cups, Mocker lied more than usual, about more personal things. One had to humor him or risk a fight.

The owl, a critic, screeched hideously, hurled himself into the air, fluttered drunkenly eastward. Mocker sent a weak curse after him.

A little later Nepanthe came out and led them to their beds, two morose gentlemen with scant taste for their futures.

THREE: YEAR 1002 AFE
THE LONG, MAILED REACH OF THE DISCIPLE

i) A secret device, a secret admirer

Elana rose wondering if Bragi had reached Mocker's safely. How soon would he be home? The forest was a refuge for Itaskia's fugitives. Several bands roamed the North Road. Some had grievances with Bragi. He took his charter seriously, suppressed banditry with a heavy hand. Some would gladly take revenge.

She went to a clothing chest and took out an ebony casket the size of a loaf of bread. Some meticulous craftsman had spent months carving its intricate exterior. The work was so fine it would have eluded the eye but for the silver inlay. She did not know what the carving represented. Nothing within her experience, just whorls and swirls of black and silver which, if studied overlong, dazed the mind.

Her names, personal and family, were inset in the lid in cursive ivory letters. They were of no alphabet she knew. Mocker had guessed it to be Escalonian, the language of a land so far to the east it was just a rumor.

She didn't know its source, only that, a year ago, the Royal Courier, who carried diplomatic mail between Itaskia and Iwa Skolovda, had brought it up from the capital. He had gotten it from a friend who rode diplomatic post to Libiannin, and that man had received it from a merchant from Vorgreberg in the Lesser Kingdoms. The parcel had come thither with a caravan from the east. Included had been an unsigned letter explaining its purpose. She didn't know the hand. Nepanthe thought it was her brother Turran's.

Turran had tried Elana's virtue once. She had never told Bragi.

With a forefinger she traced the ivory letters. The top popped open. Within, on a pillow of cerulean silk, lay a huge ruby raindrop. Sometimes the jewel grew milky and light glowed within the cloudiness.

This happened when one of her family was in danger. The intensity of light indicated the peril's gravity. She checked the jewel often, especially when Bragi was away.

There was always a mote at the heart of the teardrop. Danger could not be eliminated from life. But today the cloudiness was growing.

"Bragi!" She grabbed clothes. Bandits? She would have to send someone to Mocker's. But wait. She had best post a guard all round. There had been no rumors, but trouble could come over the Silverbind as swiftly as a spring tornado. Or from Driscol Fens, or the west. Or it could be the tornado that had entered her thoughts. It was that time of year, and the jewel did not just indicate human dangers.

"Ragnar!" she shouted. "Come here!" He would be up and into something. He was always the first one stirring.

"What, Ma?"

"Come here!" She dressed hurriedly.

"What?"

"Run down to the mill and tell Bevold I want him. And I mean run."

"Ah..."

"Do it!" He vanished. That tone brooked no defiance.

Bevold Lif was a Freylander. He was the Ragnarsons' foreman. He slept at the mill so he would waste no time trekking about the pastures. He was a fastidious, fussy little man, addicted to work. Though he had been one for years, he wasn't suited to be a soldier. He was a craftsman, a builder, a doer, and a master at it. What Bragi imagined, Bevold made reality. The tremendous development of the landgrant was as much his doing as Ragnarson's.

Elana didn't like Bevold. He presumed too much. But she acknowledged his usefulness. And appreciated his down-to-earth solidity.

Lif arrived just as she stepped from the house.

"Ma'am?"

"A minute, Bevold. Ragnar, start your chores."

"Aw, Ma, I..."

"Go."

He went. She permitted no disobedience. Bragi indulged the children to a fault.

"Bevold, there's trouble coming. Have the men arm themselves. Post the sentries. Send someone to Mocker's. The rest can work, but stay close to the house. Get the women and children here right away."

"Ma'am? You're sure?" Lif had pale thin lips that writhed like worms. "I planned to set the mill wheel this morning and open the flume after dinner."

"I'm sure, Bevold. Get ready. But don't start a panic."

"As you will." His tone implied that no emergency justified abandoning the work schedule. He wheeled his mount, cantered toward the mill.

As she watched him go, Elana listened. The birds were singing. She had heard that they fell silent when a tornado was coming. The cloud cover, just a few ragged galleons sweeping ponderously north, suggested no bad weather. Tornados came with grim black cumulo-nimbus dreadnoughts that flailed about with sweeps of lightning.

She shook her head. Bevold was a good man, and loyal. Why couldn't she like him?

As she turned to the door, she glimpsed Ragnar's shaggy little head above a bush. Eavesdropping! He would get a paddling after he brought the eggs in.

ii) Homecoming of a friend

Elana sequestered herself with her teardrop the rest of the morning. She held several through-the-door conversations with Bevold, the last of which, after she had ordered field rations for dinner, became heated. She won the argument, but knew he would complain to Bragi about the wasted workday.

The jewel grew milkier by the hour. And the men more lax.

In a choice between explaining or relying on authority, she felt compelled to choose the latter. Was that part of the jewel's magic? Or her own reluctance to tell Bragi about Turran's interest?

By midafternoon the milkiness had consumed the jewel's clarity. The light from within was intense. She checked the sky. Still only a scatter of clouds. She returned the casket to the clothing chest, went downstairs. Bevold clumped round the front yard, checking weapons for the twentieth time, growling.

"Bevold, it's almost time. Get ready."

Disbelief filled his expression, stance, and tone. "Yes, Ma'am."

"They'll come from the south." The glow of her jewel intensified when she turned the pointed end toward Itaskia.

"Send your main party that way. Down by the barrow."

"Really…"

What Lif meant to say she never learned. A warning wolfs howl came from the southern woods. Bevold's mouth opened and closed. He turned, mounted, shouted. "Let's go."

"Dahl Haas," Elana snapped at a fifteen-year-old who had insinuated himself into the ranks. "Get off that horse! You want to play soldier, take Ragnar and a bow up in the watchtower."

"But…"

"You want me to call your mother?"

"Oh, all right." Gerda Haas was a dragon.

Elana herded Dahl inside, stopped at the weapons rack while he selected a bow. The strongest he could draw was her own.

"Take it," she said. She took a rapier and dagger, weapons that had served her well. She had had a bit of success as an adventuress and hire-sword, herself.

She added a light crossbow, returned to the horse left by Dahl.

She overtook the men at a barrow mound near the edge of the forest, not far from the head of a logging road which ran to the North Road.

In military matters Bevold was unimaginative. He and the others milled about, in the open, completely unready for action.

"Bevold!" she snapped, "Can't you take me seriously? What'll you do if fifty men come out of the woods?"

"Uh…"

"Get run over, that's what. Put a half-dozen bowmen on the barrow. Where's Uthe Haas? You're in charge. The rest of you get behind the barrow, out of sight."

"Uh…" Bevold was getting red.

"Shut up!" She listened. From afar came the sound of hoofbeats. "Hear that? Let's move. Uthe. You. You. Up. And nobody shoots till I say. We don't know who's coming." She scrambled up the mound after Haas.

Lying in the grass, watching the road, she wondered what prehistoric people had built the barrows. They were scattered all along the Silverbind.

The hoofbeats drew closer. Why wasn't she back at the house? She wasn't young and stupid anymore. She should leave the killing and dying to those who thought it their birthright.

Too late to change her mind now. She rolled onto her back, readied the crossbow. She studied the clouds. She had not looked for castles and dragons in years. Childhood memories came, only to be interrupted when a rider burst from the forest.

She rolled to her stomach and studied him over the crossbow. He was wounded. A broken arrow protruded from his back. He clung weakly to a badly lathered horse. Neither appeared likely to survive the day. Both wore a thick coat of road dust. They had been running hard for a long time. The man's scabbard was empty. He was otherwise unarmed.

She glimpsed his face as he thundered past. "Rolf!" she gasped. "Rolf Preshka!" Then, "Uthe, get ready." While the bowmen thrust arrows in the mound for quick use, she waved at Bevold. A lot of horses were coming. She had no idea who their riders might be, but Preshka's enemies were her own.

Rolf had been her man before Bragi, though Ragnarson didn't know the relationship's depth. She still felt guilty when she remembered how she had hurt him. But his love, rare for the time, and especially for an Iwa Skolovdan, was the unjealous kind. The kind that, when at last she had set her heart, had caused him to help her snare Ragnarson.

Preshka, like Bragi, was a mercenary. After Elana's marriage he had joined Ragnarson as second in command. When Bragi had gotten out, Preshka had joined the party that had beat its way in to the landgrant. But he had been unable to put down roots. Two years later, Bragi's foster brother, Haaken Blackfang, and Reskird Kildragon had come by. Rolf had gone off with them, leaving a wife and child mystified and hurt.

In her own way, Elana cared for Preshka as much as her husband. Though their relationship had remained proper since her marriage, she missed him. He had been around so long that he had become a pillar of her universe.

Now he was home. And someone was trying to kill him.

iii) Sons of the Disciple

A flash-flood of burnoosed horsemen roared from the wood. Elana had a moment to be startled by their appearance so far from Hammad al Nakir, another to wonder at their numbers—there were forty or fifty, then it was time to fight. "Go!" she shrieked.

Her bowmen leapt up, loosed a flight that sent the leaders tumbling over their horses' tails, caused tripping, screams, and confusion behind.

Bevold's group swept round the mound, loosed a flight, abandoned their bows for swords. They crashed the head of the line while confusion yet gripped their foes. In the first minute they looked likely to overwhelm the lot.

"The riders!" bellowed Uthe Haas. "Aim at the riders."

"Don't count your chickens, Uthe," Elana replied from the grass. There was little she could do with her crossbow. "Take what you can get." Haas, smelling a victory still far from certain, wanted the mounts as prizes.

They almost pulled it off. Half the enemy saddles were clear before they recovered.

The wild riders of Hammad al Nakir had never learned to handle the Itaskian arrow-storm. The appearance of Itaskian bow regiments had ordained their defeat during the wars. In a dozen major battles through Libiannin, Hellin Daimiel, Cardine, and the Lesser Kingdoms, countless fanatics had ridden into those cloth-yard swarms, through six hundred yards of death, and few had survived to hurl themselves upon the masking shieldmen.

But the commander here wasn't awed. He seized the ground between Lif's men and the barrow, eliminating the screen Bevold could have provided, then sent everyone unhorsed to get the bows.

"Those are soldiers, not bandits," Elana muttered. "El Murid's men." Royalist refugees from Hammad al Nakir were scattered throughout the western kingdoms, but they were adherents of Haroun's. They would not be after Preshka. Assuming Rolf was still a friend of bin Yousif.

She got her chance to fight. Two quick shots with the crossbow, then the attackers arrived. Her first had deep, dark eyes and a scimitar nose. His eyes widened when he recognized her sex. He hesitated. Her rapier slipped through his guard. She had a moment before she engaged again.

The man had been middle-aged, certainly a survivor of the wars. If these were all veterans, they were El Murid's best. Why such an investment to take one man, nearly a thousand miles from home?

Her next opponent was no gentleman. Neither was he a dainty fencer. He knew the limitations and liabilities of a rapier, tried to use the weight and strength of his saber to smash through. As he forced her back, she met his eyes over crashing blades. He could have been the twin of the man she had killed. The fires of fanaticism burned in his eyes, but, having endured the wars, were dampened. He no longer believed El Murid's salvation could be delivered to the infidel with hammer blows. The Chosen, even in the grace and might of God, had to spread the faith with cunning and finesse. The idolaters were too numerous and bellicose.

The man wasn't so much interested in killing her as in forcing her out of position. Without a shield, rapier-armed, and physically less powerful, she was the weak point in the defense box they had formed. Her chance lay in taking advantage of his effort.

She parried a feint, thrust short and low at his groin, backed a step *before* he unleashed the edge-blow meant to force her to do just that. She made no effort to parry. His blade slid past a fraction of an inch from her breast. Being a half-second ahead gave her time to thrust at his groin again before he returned to low guard. She scored.

His blocking stroke smashed into her blade near the hilt, bent it dangerously, forced it from the wound. Her own momentum took her to her knees. She used her impetus to prick the thigh of the attacker on her opponent's left. Then she had to get the rapier up to block her antagonist's weak followup.

Instead of raining blows upon her while she was down, he used his greater strength to force his weapon down while he tried to knee her in the face. Again she let him have his way. With her left hand, beneath their locked blades, she used her dagger, going first for the big vein inside his left thigh, then the ligaments behind his knee. Neither blow was successful, but she hurt him. He backed off to let another man take his place.

The man she had pricked went down. Uthe grabbed the opportunity to force her inside the box. No gentlemanly gesture, she realized. She was becoming more a liability than an asset.

Between and over the heads of the fighters, she tried to see how Bevold was doing.

Not well. He was trying to reach the mound, but his men had become hopelessly disorganized and it seemed unlikely any could push through. Half his saddles were empty anyway. As she watched, Bevold himself succumbed to a blow on the helmet.

And desert men by ones and twos continued to straggle from the forest. Soon they would send a detachment after Rolf.

She looked homeward to check Preshka's progress. There was no sign of him, but she did see something that buoyed her spirits. Riders in the distance, only specks now, but coming fast, straight through the grainfields.

"Bragi!" she shrieked. "Bragi's coming!"

Uthe and the others took it up as a war chant, vented a moment of wild ferocity on their enemies.

Elana felt something underfoot. She looked down. Her crossbow. She still had quarrels. She snatched it up, cocked and loaded it, looked for a target.

Just then the man on Uthe's left, growing too enthusiastic, broke the shield wall. An enemy took instant advantage. He paid the price of his foolishness. The man to his left fell as well.

That two-man hole, for the seconds it existed, loomed ominous. Elana put a bolt into a man trying to open it wider, clubbed a second with the crossbow, bought time for the gap to close.

A square then, with Elana cramped inside, too crowded to do anything but jab with her dagger.

Why was Bragi taking so long?

Only a minute had passed since she had spotted the riders, but it seemed an age. What good help that arrived too late?

iv) To ride against time

This time there was no lack of motivation in Ragnarson's ride. He didn't have to pretend he was racing El Murid. When Elana's messenger met him on the road, he took only a moment to order the man on to Mocker's for reinforcements. He began galloping.

The horse was fresh but incapable of carrying such a heavy rider so hard so long. It collapsed a mile north of his northernmost sentry post. There was no flogging the animal on. Carrying only his weapons, he ran. That was difficult. His legs were stiff and his thighs were chafed from two hard days in the saddle.

It never occurred to him that Elana might have sent her message before danger was actually upon her. He expected to be too late to do anything but count the dead. But he ran.

By the time he reached the lookout post he was almost as winded as the abandoned horse. Out of shape, he thought, as he staggered the last hundred yards, lungs afire.

The sentry remained on duty. He ran to meet Ragnarson. "Bragi, what happened?"

"Horse foundered," he gasped. "What's going on, Chotty?"

"Your wife got up excited. Put out sentries. Sent Flay to get you. But nothing happened till a minute ago."

"What?" His guts were about to come up. All this action after last night's beer.

"South call. The wolf."

"Uhn. Any others?" They reached the man's hiding place. He had only one horse.

"No."

"No ideas?"

"No."

He had a vague notion of his own, inferences drawn on yesterday's mysteries. "Got your horn? Get up behind me here. She can carry us to the house."

As they rode, Ragnarson sounded the horn, alternating his personal blast with those for the greathouse. Anyone not already in a fight would meet him there.

He found a few men there ahead of him, saw a half-dozen more coming. Good. Now, where was Elana?

Gerda Haas came from the house.

"Where's Elana?"

"Crazy fool you married, Ragnarson. Like I told Uthe when you did, you'll get nothing but trouble from that one."

"Gerda."

"Ah, then, she rode off with Uthe and Bevold and the others. South. Took my Dahl's horse, she did, just like…"

"How many?"

"Counting her ladyship and the sentries already down there, nineteen I'd guess."

Then all the help he could hope for was already in sight.

Ragnar came running round Gerda, but the old dragon was quick. She caught his collar before he got out of reach. "You stay inside when you're told."

"Papa?"

"Inside, Ragnar. If he gives you any trouble, whack him. And I'll whack him again when I get back. Where's Dahl?"

"In the tower." She scooped Ragnar up and brushed the tears from his eyes. The boy was unaccustomed to shortness from his father.

"Toke," Ragnarson ordered, "get some horses for me and Chotty. Dahl! Dahl Haas!" He bellowed to the watchtower, "What you see?"

"Eh?"

"Come on, boy. Can you see anything?"

"Lot of dust down by the barrow. Maybe a big fight. Can't tell. Too far."

The barrow lay near the tip of a long finger of cleared land pointing south, with the millstream and lumbering road meandering down it. He had been clearing that direction because the logs could be floated to the mill. It was two miles from the house to the barrow.

"Horsemen?" Bragi called.

"Maybe. Like I said, a lot of dust."

"How long?"

"Only a couple minutes."

"Uhn." Bad. Must be something besides, a gang of bandits. His people could take care of that with a flight of arrows.

Toke came round the house with the horses. The women had started saddling them when he and Chotty had come in sight. "All right, everybody that can use one, get a lance. Gerda, get some shields." He was wearing a mail shirt already—a habit when he traveled—so needed waste no time donning that. "And for god's sake, something to drink."

While he waited he looked around. Elana had done well. All the livestock had been herded into the cellars, the heavy slitted shutters were over the windows, the building had been soaked with water against fire, and no one was outside who had no need to be.

A girl Dahl's age brought him a quart of milk. Ugh. But this was no time for ale or beer. Beer made him sweat, especially across his brow, and he needed no perspiration in his eyes during a fight.

"Lock up after us," he told Gerda as he swung into the saddle and accepted shield, ax, and lance from another of the women. "Helmet? Where's my damned helmet?" He had left it with the foundered horse. "Somebody find me a helmet." To Gerda again, "If we're not back, don't give up. Mocker's on his way."

The girl who had brought him the milk returned with a helmet. Ragnarson groaned. It was gold- and silver-chased with high, spread silver wings at the sides, a noble's dress helmet that he had plundered years ago. But she was right. It was the only thing around that would fit his head. If he weren't so cheap, he'd have a spare. He disappeared into the thing, glared around, daring someone to laugh.

No one did. The situation was too grim.

"Dahl, what's happening?"

"Same as before."

Everyone was mounted, armed, ready. "Let's go."

He wasted no time. He rode straight for the barrow, over sprouting wheat.

v) Sometimes you bite the bear, and sometimes the bear bites you

Even while still a long way away, Ragnarson saw that the situation was grim. There were four or five men on the barrow, afoot, surrounded. As many more were below, on horseback, hard-pressed. Men from both sides, unhorsed, were fighting on the ground. There were more attackers than defenders, and those professionals by their look. He couldn't see Elana. Fear snapped at his heart like the sudden bite of a bear trap.

He was not afraid of the fighting—much; a truly fearless man was a fool and certain to die young—but of losing Elana. They had an odd, open marriage. Outsiders sometimes thought there was no love between them, but their interdependence went beyond love. Without one another, neither would have been a complete person.

He slowed the pace briefly, signaled his lancers into line abreast. Those who couldn't handle a lance stayed back with their bows.

Some cavalry charge, Ragnarson thought. Six lances. In Libiannin Greyfells had commanded fourteen thousand horses and ten thousand bows, plus spearmen and mercenaries.

But every battle was the big one to the men involved. Scope and scale had no meaning when your life was on the line. It came down to you and the man you had to kill before he could kill you.

The foreigners weren't expecting more company. Indeed, a freehold this size should have had fewer men about, but Ragnarson's land wasn't a freehold (in the sense that he had been enfiefed and owed the Crown a military obligation), and many of his hangers-on weren't married.

The attackers noticed his approach only after he was less than a quarter-mile distant. They had hardly begun to sort themselves out when he struck.

Ragnarson presented his lance, swung his shield across his body, gripped his reins in his lance hand. His shield was a round one, in the Trolledyngjan style, and not fit for a horseman. He paid the price almost immediately.

As his lancehead entered the breast of his first opponent, a glancing saber stroke slashed his unshielded left thigh. The sudden pain distracted him. He lost his lance as the man he had slain went over his horse's tail.

Then his mount smashed into two others, momentarily trapping him. He couldn't drag out his sword. He clawed at the Trolledyngjan ax slung across his back while warding off swordstrokes with his shield, began chopping kindling from the nearest unfamiliar target.

A progression of dark faces appeared before him, men his own age with deep-set, dark eyes and heavy aquiline noses, like a parade of bin Yousif's. Desert men. But not Haroun's Royalists. What were they doing this far from Hammad al Nakir?

Three opponents he demolished with his berserk, overpowering attack, then, with a sinking in his stomach, felt his mount going down. Someone had slashed her hamstrings. He had to hurl ax and shield away as he leapt to avoid being pinned beneath. The jump threw him face-first into someone's boot and stirrup. A swordstroke proved the small battle-worth of his fancy helmet. A wing came off. A dent so deep that the metal bruised his scalp left him half-unconscious. On hands and knees, with hooves stamping all around, he lifted his visor to heave the milk he had drunk.

With bile in his mouth, thinking the pukes and a dented helmet were cheaper than a shaved ear, he rose in the melee like a bear beset by hounds, sprang bare-handed at the nearest enemy not looking his way. With his forearm across the man's throat, using him as a shield, he struggled out of the thickest press.

While strangling his victim, he looked around. The remaining horsemen were drifting toward the forest. Only a handful from either side were still in their saddles. His own people, on the ground, were having the best of a more numerous foe. They were in their element, being infantrymen by trade. Here and there they were linking up in twos and threes. In a bit they would have a shield wall.

Things weren't going that well atop the mound. He saw Elana now. She, Uthe Haas, and another man were trying to hold off three times their number and managing well enough that their attackers had not noticed their comrades withdrawing.

There was no one to send to the mound. Except himself. And he would be no use charging into that mess. Just fodder for the Reaper. But a bowman could help.

There must be a bow somewhere. His people all used them. He trotted over the litter of dead and wounded, and broken, abandoned, and lost weapons. He found a crossbow of the type El Murid's men preferred, but it was useless without a string. He had never gotten the hang of the things anyway. Then he found a short bow of the desert variety, a weak thing easily used from a horse's back, but that had suffered the ungentle caress of a horse's hoof. Finally, as he was about to snatch up a sword and go screaming up the barrow anyway, he found his hamstrung mare with his bow and arrows still slung behind her saddle.

He went to work.

This was the kind of fighting he preferred. Stand off and let them have it. He was good with a bow. Target plinking, he thought.

His fourth victim went down. Yes, much better than getting up toe to toe and smelling your opponent's rotten breath and sweat and fear. And you didn't have to look them in the eyes when they realized they were going to die.

For Ragnarson that was the worst part. Killing was damned discomfiting when he was nose to nose with the fact that he was ending a human life.

His sixth score broke the siege. The survivors followed their comrades toward the forest. Trotting, Ragnarson lofted a few desultory shafts to keep them moving, at the same time shouted, "Let them go!" to Elana and Uthe. "They've had enough. Let's not get anybody killed after we've won."

Elana sent a look toward the forest, then threw herself at her husband. "Am I glad to see you!"

"What the hell do you think you're doing, woman? Out here without even a helmet. Why the hell aren't you at the house? I've a mind to… Damn! I will." He dropped to one knee, bent her across the other, reared back to smack her bottom. Then he noticed his men gathering. Grinning, those who had the strength left.

"Well," he growled, "you know what to do. Pick up the mess." He rose, set a subdued Elana back on her feet. "Woman, you pull something like this again, I'll break your butt and not care who's watching."

Then he hugged her so hard she squealed.

As often happened in a wild mixup, there were fewer dead than seemed likely in the heat of action. But virtually all his people were wounded. The enemy had taken some of their injured with them. The worst hurt had been left behind. Bevold Lif, still dazed, stumbled up to report four of their people killed. The count on the enemy wasn't final. His men were still making corpses out of casualties.

"Damn!" Elana said suddenly. "How's Rolf?"

"Rolf who?"

"Rolf Preshka. Didn't you see him? They were chasing him. He was bad hurt."

"No. Preshka? What the hell? Where'd he come from? Bevold! Take over here. I'll be back in a little while." To Elana, "Let's catch a couple horses."

Of those there was no shortage. The raiders had left most of theirs behind. The animals, once safe from the fighting, had begun cropping wheat sprouts. They would have to be rounded up or the damage they would do would cut into the plunder-profit from their capture. Good desert horses sold high.

"Which way was he headed?"

"Toward the house."

"He didn't make it."

"You think they caught him?"

"Didn't see any of them on the way down. No telling what happened."

They had ridden a mile when Elana said, "Over there." A riderless horse grazed beside the millstream.

They found Preshka not far away. He was alive, but barely. The arrow had penetrated a lung. It would take a miracle to save him. Or perhaps Nepanthe, if they could get her down from Mocker's. She had studied medicine during her lonely youth, with the wizard Varthlokkur as tutor, and she had the magic of her family.

"Here," Ragnarson said, "we'd better make a litter." He drew his sword and set to work on some saplings left to shade the creek. "Might be good fishing this summer," he observed, spotting a lazy carp. "Maybe we can put some up for winter."

Elana, slitting Preshka's jerkin so she could look at his wound, frowned. "Why not just catch them when you get the taste? The rest will be there when you want them."

"Uhn. You're right." He had two long poles cut, was lopping branches. "Thing like today put me in mind of times when there wasn't no coming back. Talking about fish, what do you think of us putting a dam across the creek up where those high banks are?"

"Why?" She was too worried about Rolf to care.

"Well, like I told Bevold the other day, so we'd have water in a dry spell."

"There was water last summer. The springs kept running."

"Yeah, well." He dragged the poles over. "What I was thinking about was stocking some fish. How the hell are we going to finish this thing?"

"Go catch his horse, stupid!" His poking about was frustrating. "He must've had blankets. And hurry."

He ran off. And she was immediately sorry she had snapped at him. It was obvious his leg was giving him a lot of pain. He had claimed the wound was just a scratch. He didn't like to cause concern.

"I've decided," he said when he returned.

"What? Decided what?"

"I'm going to raise some hell about this. I mean, when we took the grant we said we'd do some fighting. In defense of law and order." He sneered his opinion of the phrase. "But not to fight wars on our own. We kept up our end. I didn't even cry about not getting any help the last time raiders came over from Prost Kamenets, even if the army should've been here. But by damn, having to fight El Murid's regulars in my wheat field, a hundred miles *north* of Itaskia, is too much. I got to go down about the timber contract anyway, and pick up some things, so I'll just go early and burn some ears. If them asses at the War Ministry can't keep this from happening, they're going to tell me why. In fact, I'm going to the Minister himself. He owes me. Maybe he can shake some people awake."

"Now, dear, don't do something you'll be sorry for." His friendship with the War Minister was pretty insubstantial, based as it was on a few secret, illegal favors done the man years ago. Men in such positions were notoriously short of memory.

"I don't care. If a citizen can't be safe at home, then why the hell pay taxes?"

"If you don't, you'll get troops up here quick, all right," she replied. They rigged the litter between their horses, hoisted Preshka in.

"Well, I'm going down. Tomorrow."

FOUR: YEAR 1002 afe
THE NARROWING WAY

i) Return of the Disciple

Ragnarson did not leave for Itaskia next morning.

He woke to find the household in an uproar.

All his people had spent the night at the greathouse, vainly awaiting Mocker. He assumed Nepanthe, unwilling to let her husband out of sight, would come along and could be put to doctoring.

He went to see what was the matter.

Luck rode with him in a small, left-handed way. Bevold Lif, despite his bashed head, had risen early to go to the mill. He had started out afoot and had quickly returned. El Murid's men were back, waiting for dawn.

Ragnarson quietly tried to get the animals back into the cellars, the building doused down, and weapons readied. If they had the confidence to return, the raiders had picked up reinforcements.

As false dawn lightened the land, he counted their horses. There were nearly thirty surrounding the house, at a distance demonstrating their respect for the Itaskian bow.

"You think they'll attack?" Bevold asked.

"I wouldn't," Ragnarson replied. "But there's no figuring those people. They're crazy. That's why they did so well in the wars. That and being able to field every grown man. Iwa Skolovda and Prost Kamenets have the same problem on their Shara borders. Nomads don't have to stay home to get the crops in. And they don't use much equipment a man can't make himself, so their cavalry doesn't need a broad peasant base…"

"That'll reassure everybody," Elana said sarcastically. Bragi, as he aged, had developed a tendency to lecture. "Uthe and Dahl are in the tower. Uthe said to tell you they have a 'shaghûn.'"

"Uhn," he grunted. "That's not good."

"Why not?"

"A shaghûn's a sort of priest-knight. They're a fighting order like the Guild's Knights Protectors. One with a group this small is unusual."

"So?"

"They're sorcerers, too. Not big-time, but they've got some magic."

"But I thought El Murid killed all the magicians…"

"Sure!" Ragnarson interrupted, sneering. "All that didn't get religion. You ever hear of a priest who wouldn't make a deal with his devil to get what he wanted? El Murid's no different. He's a politician first, same as all of them. He just started out with ideals. After reality kicked his ass a few times, he started compromising. The shaghûn system worked for the Royalists—Haroun is supposed to be one, but he didn't get much training before he had to run—so why not for him?"

Bragi was a cynic who disapproved of any organization structured for purposes other than warfare. His opinions of governments were as severe as those regarding priesthoods.

"What can we do?" Elana asked.

"About what?"

"About this hedge-wizard, you lummox!" Mornings they both could be bears.

"Oh. I'll have to kill him. Or give up and see what he wants. How's Rolf?"

"Still in a coma. I don't think he'll come out."

"Grim. Where's Mocker? And where's that shaghûn? If I'm going to get him, I got to know where." He sent someone to get Uthe from the tower.

Elana started to ask why *he* had to do it. She knew. It was his way. The more dangerous the task, the less likely he was to delegate it.

"Let's go to the study," Bragi said. He had a room of his own off the main hall where, supposedly, he attended to business. It was more a museum filled with mementos, and a library. "I hope he stays alive long enough to tell me why I've got El Murid's horses trampling my wheat."

"I'd like to see him live a little longer than that." She revealed too much emotion. Bragi frowned puzzledly, was about to ask something when Uthe arrived.

The men went to four maps hung on a wall. One was of the west, political; another of the Itaskian Kingdom; a third of the landgrant with inked notations about resources and special features. The last was of the area around the house, with large blank borders where the forest still stood. It was to this that Bragi and Uthe went. Haas pointed out the location of the shaghûn, then of nearby horsemen. Bragi traced an approach route with one heavy forefinger.

"Did you see his colors?" Ragnarson asked. "Did you recognize them?"

"Yes. No."

"Guess we couldn't tell much anyway. Bound to have been a big turnover. Most of them died before El Murid gave up and went home. Well, I don't know what else I can do. Wish I'd known he was out there when it was still dark."

He grabbed Elana, kissed her swift and hard. "Uthe, if it don't work, you take over. Wait for Mocker. He's bound to come—though how much good he'll be I don't know." He kissed Elana again.

ii) His regiment arrives

The ground was cold. His leg ached. The dew on the grass had soaked through his trousers and jerkin. A breeze from the south did nothing to make him more comfortable. His hands were chilled, shaking. He hoped they wouldn't ruin his aim. There was little chance he would get a second shot. The shaghûn would have a protective spell ready for instant use.

A hundred yards more, at least, before he dared a shot. And they the hardest since he had slipped out the tunnel from the cellars. There was no cover but a fencerow.

Where was Mocker? he wondered.

The yards slowly passed under his belly. He expected an alarm at any moment, or the cry of the shaghûn ordering an attack.

It was light enough to storm the house. Why were they waiting?

From the end of the fence he would have to trust luck to cross five yards of naked pasture to a ditch.

They would get him there for sure.

A sudden outcry and stirring of horses startled him. He almost let fly before realizing the horses were moving away. He raised his head.

Mocker had come.

And how he had come. The column emerging from the forest, both horse and foot, was the biggest Ragnarson had seen since the flareup with Prost Kamenets. At their head, fat and robed in brown and astride his pathetically bony little donkey, rode Mocker.

They were not Royal troops, though they were disciplined and well-equipped. Their banners were of the Mercenaries' Guild. But Ragnarson knew few of their names could be found on Guild rosters. They were Trolledyngjans.

The desert horsemen, after first rushing toward the newcomers, retreated. Even a shaghûn was no advantage against such numbers.

Their flight passed near Ragnarson. The shaghûn, in a burnoose as dark as night, was an easy target.

One shaft, from a bow few men could pull, flew so swift its passage was nearly invisible. It burst through the shaghûn's skull.

For a long minute Bragi watched the riders gallop off.

In an hour they would have disappeared without a trace. They came and went like the sandstorms of their native land, unpredictable and devastating.

"Hai!" Mocker cried as Bragi trotted up. "As always, one believed old fat windy fool, self, arrives in nick, to salvage bacon of friend of huge militant repute but, as customary, leaguered up by nearest congregation quadriplegic. Self, am thinking same should admit same before assembled host..."

"Speaking of which," Ragnarson interrupted, "where'd you turn this crowd up?"

"Conjuration." The fat man grinned. "Self, being mighty sorcerer, wizard of worldwide dread, made passes in night, danced widdershins round yew tree, nude, burned unholy incense, called up demon legion..."

"Never changes, does he? Blows hard as a winter wind."

The speaker was a man even more massive than Ragnarson, mounted on a giant gray. He had the shaggy black hair of a wild man, and behind his beard a mass of dark teeth.

"Haaken! How the hell are you? What you doing here?" Haaken Blackfang was his foster brother.

"Been recruiting. Headed south now." Without alcohol in him Blackfang was as reticent as Mocker was loquacious.

"Thought that was where you were. With Reskird and Rolf. Speaking of Rolf, he turned up yesterday, three-quarters dead, with that gang after him."

"Uhn," Blackfang grunted. "Not good. Didn't expect them to get excited this soon. Figured another year."

"What're you talking about?"

"Rolf's job to explain."

"He can't. Might never explain anything. Mocker, did you bring Nepanthe? We need medical help."

Before the fat man could reply, Blackfang interjected, "He didn't. I'll loan you my surgeon."

Ragnarson frowned.

"He's good. Youngster with a case of wanderlust. Now then, where to settle this lot? Looks like your fields have been hurt enough."

"Uhn. East pasture, by the mill. I want my animals near the house till this blows over." He wondered if there would be room, though. Blackfang's baggage continued rolling from the forest, wagon after wagon. This looked like a *volkswanderung.* "What you got here, Haaken, a whole army?"

"Four hundred horse, the same afoot."

"But women and children..."

"Maybe word hasn't filtered down. There's trouble in Trolledyngja. Looks like civil war. The Pretender's grip is slipping. Fair-weather supporters are deserting him. Night raiders haunt the outlands. Lot of people like these, whether they favor him or the Old House, don't want to get involved."

A similar desire, after their family had been decimated in the civil war that had given the Pretender the Trolledyngjan throne, had driven Ragnarson and Blackfang over the Kratchnodians years ago.

"Had a letter from the War Minister a while back," said Ragnarson. "Wanted to know why there hadn't been any raids this spring. He thought something like Ringerike might be shaping up. Now I understand. Everybody stayed home to keep an eye on the neighbors."

"About it. Some decided to try their luck with us."

"What about the Guild? They won't like you showing their colors. And Itaskia won't want Trolledyngjans roving round the countryside."

"All taken care of. Fees paid, passes bought. Every man's a Guild member. At least honorarily. Doing everything by the book. We can't leave any enemies behind us."

"Will you explain?"

"Later, if Rolf can't. Shouldn't we put the doctor to work?"

"Right. Mocker, take him to the house. I'll help Haaken get his mob camped. You travel all night?"

"Had to to get here in time. Thought about sending the horse ahead, but they couldn't've gotten here before dark last night, and I didn't figure anything would happen till morning."

"True. True. You're a welcome sight."

iii) Missive from a friend

Rolf came round briefly while the surgeon, who doubted there was much hope, was removing the arrow. He had ridden too far and hard with the shafthead tearing his insides.

Preshka saw the anxious faces. A weak smile crossed his lips. "Shouldn't have... left," he gasped. "Stupid... Couldn't resist... one more try..."

"Be quiet!" Elana ordered while fidgeting, trying to make him more comfortable.

"Bragi... In kit... Letter... Haroun..." He passed out again.

"Figures," Ragnarson grumbled. "This much going on, couldn't be anyone else. Haaken, you feel like explaining?"

"Read the letter first."

"All right. Damn!" He didn't like this mystery piling on mystery, and nobody leaking any light. "I'll hunt the thing up. Meet me in the study."

The country, Haroun's letter began, *is Kavelin in the Lesser Kingdoms, among the easternmost of these, against the Kapenrung Mountains where they swing southwest out of the Mountains of M'Hand, and therein borders on Hammad al*

Nakir. In the southwest Kavelin is bounded by Tamerice, in the west by Altea, and in the northwest and west by Anstokin and Volstokin. (I am assembling a portfolio of military maps and will get them to you when I can.) El Murid is an enemy, of course, though there has been no action since the wars, which Kavelin survived virtually unscathed. Altea is traditionally an ally, Anstokin mostly neutral. There are occasional incidents with Tamerice and Volstokin. The most recent war was with Volstokin.

Governmentally, this is a parliamentary feudality, power balanced between the Crown and barons. In force of arms the latter outweigh the Crown, but internecine intrigues dissipate the advantage. Under the current, mediocre King, the Crown is little more than an arbiter of baronial disputes. Although, unlike Itaskia, Kavelin has no tradition of intrigue for the throne, a struggle for succession is taking shape. There is a Crown Prince, but he is not the King's son. By listening at the proper doors one learns that the genuine prince was kidnapped on the day of his birth and a changeling substituted.

Historically and ethnically Kavelin is even more muddled than the usual Lesser Kingdom. The original inhabitants, the Marena Dimura, are a people related to those of the south coastal kingdoms of Libiannin, Cardine, Hellin Daimiel, and Dunno Scuttari. They form the lowest class, the pariahs. Only the most lucky (relatively) are so well off as to be slaves, bond-servants, or serfs. The majority run wild in the forests, living in a poverty and squalor that would shame a pig.

When, between 510 and 520 in the Imperial dating Ilkazar occupied the region, Imperial colonists moved in.

Their descendants, the Siluro, today form that class which manages the daily work of government and business. They are educated, officious, self-important, and schemers of the first water, and through their hands flows most of the wealth of the kingdom. A lot, in the form of bribes, sticks.

In the last decade of the Imperial era, about 608, when Ilkazar crossed the Silverbind in the north and Roë in the east, whole villages of Itaskians were transported to Kavelin in what has been called the Resettlement. These people, the Wessons (most came from West Wapentake), still speak a recognizable Itaskian and constitute both the bulk of the population and of the peasant, soldier, and artisan merchant classes. As with Itaskians, they are stolid, unimaginative, slow to anger, and slower to forgive a wrong. Their leaders still resent the Resettlement and Conquest and scheme to set those right.

The final group are the Nordmen, the ruling, enfiefed class. Their ancestors were proto-Trolledyngjans who came south with Jan Iron Hand for the final assault on Ilkazar. They decided life as nobles in a southern clime was better than going home to become commoners again in the icy North Waste. Can you blame them?

Everyone does. It has been centuries since the Conquest and still all three lower groups plot to topple the Nordmen. Add to actions forwarding these schemes the almost constant state of warfare among the barons, and the problem of the succession (for which several candidates have begun to vie), and you see we have an *interesting political situation.*

Native industries include mining (gold, silver, copper, iron, emeralds), dairying (Kavelin cheese is famous south of the Porthune), and a modest fur trade. Economically, Kavelin's major importance is its position astride the east-west trade route. The fall of Ilkazar and subsequent drastic climatic changes in Hammad al Nakir forced the movement of trade northward. Kavelin became its benefactor by virtue of controlling the Savernake Gap, only pass through the Kapenrung Mountains connecting with the old Imperial road to Gog-Ahlan, which is the only developed way through the Mountains of M'Hand south of the Seydar Sea. Mocker is familiar with the eastern trade; he can explain more fully than I. He was in both Kavelin and the east before the wars.

Do you see the potentialities? Here is a kingdom, rich, yet small and relatively weak, beset by enemies, ripe for internal strife. If the King died today, as many as twenty armed forces with different loyalties might take the field. Most would be pretenders, but the Queen would attempt to defend her regency, and independent Siluro, Wesson, and even Marena Dimura units, under various chieftains, might align themselves with men they felt likely to improve their lot. Moreover, nobody would dare go all out because of greedy neighbors. Volstokin, especially, might loan troops and arms to a favorite.

Inject into all this a Haroun bin Yousif with my backing. (El Murid, much as he may want to, will not dare interfere directly in Kavelin's internal affairs. He is not yet ready to resume the wars, which would be the inevitable result of his interference with a Western state.) Add a Bragi Ragnarson with a substantial mercenary force.

There would be battles, shifts of loyalties, a winnowing of pretenders. By proper exploitation we should not only become wealthy men, but find a kingdom in our pockets. In fact, I genuinely believe a kingship to be within your reach.

Ragnarson looked up and leaned back, fingers probing his beard. What Haroun really thought and planned was not in the letter. He didn't explain *why* he offered kingship, or reveal what he himself hoped to gain. But it would have to do with El Murid. Bragi rose and went to the map of the west, looking for Kavelin.

"Ah, yes." He chuckled. The mere location of Kavelin cast light on bin Yousif's plan. It was ideally sited for launching guerrilla incursions into Hammad al Nakir. From the border to El Murid's capital at Al Rhemish was less than a hundred miles. Swift horsemen could reach the city long before defensive units could be withdrawn from more distant frontiers.

That country, rugged, waterless badlands in which small bands of horsemen would be difficult to find, was suited to Haroun's style. It was the same country in which the last Royalists had held out after El Murid's ascension to power.

Haroun's goal was obvious. He wanted a springboard for a Royalist Restoration. Which explained the presence of El Murid's raiders here. They wanted to spoil the scheme. The western states, long plagued by El Murid and weary of supporting rowdy colonies of Royalist refugees, would, if Haroun could manage it, gleefully support a fiat.

Haroun's letter continued. Bragi read it out of a sense of debt to Rolf, but he had made up his mind. Haroun would not drag him in this time. Yesterday's action, and his wounded leg, were all the adventure he wanted. Haroun could find another catspaw.

Haroun always talked fine and promised the moon, but seldom came near delivering.

The only crown Bragi felt likely to win, if he went to Kavelin, was the kind delivered with a mace.

iv) Knives in passing

Another dawn. Behind them the Trolledyngjan women were striking camp. Bragi, Mocker, Haaken, and Blackfang's staff were already under way. Uthe Haas, and Dahl, rode with Bragi, ostensibly to help with his business in Itaskia, but, he suspected, more as Elana's watchers. He had not had the strength to argue. His wound and another evening of drinking had washed the vinegar out of him.

"Why don't you just ride along till we meet up with Reskird?" Blackfang asked. "He'll want to swap a few lies, too. Been years since we've all been together."

Reskird Kildragon was in the hills somewhere south of the Silverbind, near Octylya, training bowmen for service in Kavelin. These were prosperous times in Itaskia. Kildragon had been able to recruit few veterans. The youngsters he had assembled were all raw, with the customary, bullheaded Itaskian predilection for using their weapons their own ways. Bragi didn't envy Reskird his job.

"I'll think about it." He wanted to say, "No," but he would hear about that all the way to Itaskia. And if he indulged his emotions and agreed, he would hear about it from Uthe. "Ought to ride ready. Might be ambushed."

The ambush didn't come till after he had wearied of staying alert. The least likely place, he thought, was Itaskia itself. El Murid's men would be too obvious there.

He overlooked the national prosperity that had eased suspicions. He was telling Dahl an exaggerated tale as they, Uthe, Mocker, Haaken, and two others entered Itaskia's North Gate. The city watch had insisted that the main party remain outside, Trolledyngjans and alcohol having a reputation for not mixing.

"It was here that business with the rats started," said Ragnarson. "When Greyfalls tried to take over. I was over there, Mocker was up Wall that way, and Haroun was on that roof over there…"

Someone was watching from the same spot Haroun had occupied then, a dark-skinned man who vanished the instant Bragi spotted him. "Watch it," said Ragnarson. "We've got friends here."

"We'll be all right on King's," Haaken replied.

"Damned rules. Laws," Ragnarson growled. "Don't know if I want to see the Minister this bad." He slapped his thigh where, till the gate guards had compelled him to check it, his sword had hung. The only personal weapons allowed were blades shorter than eight inches. "Wasn't this way in the old days."

"There was more killing then, too," Uthe observed.

"Fallacy," Mocker interjected. "Same number cadavers in gutter mornings, now as then. Holes just smaller. Self, if decide man wants murdered, will dispose of same. Can exterminate with hands, ropes, rocks, bludgeons…"

"Maybe," Uthe replied, "but it's inconvenient, not being able just to grab a sword and stick him."

They crossed Wall Street and entered King's, a busy artery sweeping grandly to the heart of the city and kingdom with identical names. Bragi had convinced his companions that they should take rooms near the Royal Palace, where he had business.

In New Haymarket Square in New Town, only a few hundred yards from North Gate, the blow fell.

Two men, dusky and hawk-nosed, exploded from a throng watching a puppet show, hurled themselves at Ragnarson and Mocker with daggers and screams.

The dagger thrust at Ragnarson slid over the mail beneath his sleeve as he threw up an arm, then slashed up his chest and along his jaw. His beard kept the gash from being nasty. He brought his right hand across to strike back. His horse, spooked, reared and neighed wildly, dumping him. As he went down he saw Mocker doing the same, heard the screams and squeals of panicky onlookers. Then his head hit cobblestones.

Mocker had a moment more to react. He threw himself, robes flying, off his donkey. His attacker plunged his dagger into an empty saddle. As the assassin bounced back, Dahl Haas kicked him in the temple.

Mocker came up off the pavement shrieking, "Murder! Watch! Help! Help!" He plumped his considerable weight atop the man Dahl had kicked, began strangling him. "Murder! Dastardest dastard attacks poor old mendicant in middle of street in middle of day… What kind city this where even poor traveler is prey for assassin? Help!" Which only spurred bystanders to flee before they themselves were butchered or nabbed as material witnesses.

Several city watchmen turned up with amazing alacrity—as everywhere, they were wont to appear only after the dust settled and there was little danger to themselves—but were unable to get through the dispersing crowd.

Haaken, Uthe, and Blackfang's bodyguards piled onto the man who had attacked Ragnarson. Dahl tried to control the horses while complaining that his foot hurt.

The police finally sorted things out. A half-dozen bolder onlookers, who had hung on for the denouement, supported Blackfang's story. Despite an obvious desire to arrest everyone, the officers settled for two battered would-be assassins and Haaken's promise to file a complaint.

Mocker and Dahl then brought Ragnarson around. "Damn!" Bragi growled. "I'm going to start sleeping in a helmet, way my head's getting smacked anymore." He struggled to his feet, cursing the pain. Dahl and Mocker hoisted him into his saddle. "One thing. I'm going to see the Minister while I'm still hurting. That'll keep me ornery enough to growl him down."

"Or get yourself thrown out," Haaken observed. "But it won't hurt to stop off. I'll get my excuses in ahead of time. Moving that gang of mine is touchy. Can't let them get our passes revoked. The Guild wouldn't help."

"Good thinking. Mocker, you need to take care of anything there?"

The fat man shrugged. "Self, always have business at Ministry of War. Ministry has evil habit. Late payment on contracts. No interest, no penalty. Owes guineas six hundred twelve, four and six, on salt pork supplied for winter maneuvers on Iwa Skolovdan border. But let poor old pig farmer be hour late delivering same. Hai! Sky falling, maybe, self thinks when agent shows up threatening repossession of soul." He laughed. "Can have same. Is already in hock to six devils. Take to Debtor's Court, scoundrelest scoundrels of state collectors! See who wins case." He flashed an obscene gesture at the Royal Palace.

v) Secret master, silent partner

The War Minister was a small man, wizened, who had been ancient when Bragi had met him years earlier. Now, within the plush vastness of his private office, he seemed so small and old as to be inhuman.

"So," said Ragnarson. "The heart of the web. Comfortable. Good to see my taxes well-spent." Times past, because of their nature, their conferences had been held in less opulent surroundings.

"Rank and privilege, as they say." The old man extended his hand.

Ragnarson frowned suspiciously. This was going too smoothly. He hadn't been kept cooling his heels. "You'd think I had an appointment."

"In a sense. Make yourself comfortable. Brandy?"

"Uhn." Ragnarson sank into a chair that threatened to devour him. He was not a poor man, but brandy was beyond his means. "Looks like you got something on your mind, too."

"Yes. But your business first. And pardon me for skipping the amenities. Time presses."

Ragnarson sketched recent events.

"Oh, my," said the Minister, shaking his head. "Worse than I thought. Worse. And sure to get worse still. Dear me, dear me. But they wouldn't listen. Told me to forgive and forget, not to hold grudges."

"What're you talking about?"

"Greyfells. They brought him back. Inland Ministry. Wouldn't listen to me. Even moved Customs to his control."

"What? No! I don't believe it." The Duke of Greyfells, as near an arch-traitor as was boasted by Itaskian history, back in favor? Astounding.

But Greyfells was a bouncer. During the wars, while commander of Itaskian expeditionary forces and prime candidate for supreme commander of the allied armies, he had been in touch with El Murid, plotting treason. Only astonishing victories by Haroun's Royalist guerrillas, with the aid of Trolledyngjan mercenaries and native auxiliaries, in Libiannin and Hellin Daimiel, had forced Greyfells to maintain his loyalty.

Later, there had been plots to seize the Itaskian Crown. Greyfells, once, had been in the succession. Haroun, Mocker, and Ragnarson had ruined his schemes. One of the favors done the War Minister. Greyfells had renounced his place in the succession to evade the embarrassment of a treason trial.

"Politicians!" Bragi snorted into his snifter. The Duke kept complicating his life, and Itaskia's, and he was getting tired of it. How many times would the man reach for the throne?

"My Lord the Duke has bounced back," said the Minister. "My people at Interior think he's in touch with his old accomplice. They've struck a devil's bargain. El Murid to support Greyfells's next power grab. And Greyfells to keep Itaskia out of the next war, and refuse passage to troops from our northern neighbors. You know what that means. Hellin Daimiel, Cardine, and Libiannin still haven't recovered. Dunno Scuttari and the Lesser Kingdoms never were powerful. Sacuescu couldn't keep a gang of old ladies from plundering the Auszura Littoral. El Murid would be at the Porthune and gates of Octylya in a month. There'll be a catastrophe if Greyfells has his way. And he probably will. He grows more golden-tongued with the years. The King no longer hears his critics."

"Then my days are numbered," said Ragnarson. His dreams were smoke if Greyfells was back. Inland oversaw the management of Royal Grants even when their original issuance was under the purview of War. Greyfells would find an excuse to revoke his charter.

"True," said the Minister. "He's working on it. The raid demonstrates it. That, which came to my attention only yesterday, was meant to rid Greyfells of a pain in the neck, and El Murid's side of a potential thorn."

"Politics don't interest me," said Ragnarson. "That's a well-known fact. All I ever wanted from politicians was for them to leave me alone."

"But there's your friend, the Royalist, and your talent for warfare. Your friend's a threat to El Murid. That makes you a threat."

"I'm just one man…"

"And not that important from where I sit. But important in some minds. And in the mind is reality. It's no objective thing. You pose a threat if only because they think you do. You aren't the sort who won't fight back."

"No. Where do you stand?"

"I always stand opposite Greyfells. And this time, behind your friend. This isn't to leave this room. The Ministry has been making available certain aid. Funds for which we aren't accountable, and weapons. This may have to stop. But I'll remain behind your friend. His success would delay war, maybe prevent it…"

The Minister's secretary appeared. "Your Lordship, there's a gentleman who insists on seeing this gentleman." His nose wrinkled. Ragnarson glanced down to see if he had forgotten to shake the horse manure off his boots.

Blackfang rolled in. "Bragi, one of my lads says they raided your place again. My people caught them. Got most of them. What you want to do?"

For a long time Ragnarson said nothing. Guards came to drag Blackfang away, but the Minister shooed them off. Finally, Bragi said, "I'll let you know in a minute. Wait outside." After Blackfang and the secretary departed, he asked, "What would happen if Greyfells were assassinated?"

The Minister frowned thoughtfully behind steepled fingers. "They'd want heads. Yours if they connected you. His son would take his place."

"If both were to go?"

"He has four sons. Peas from a pod. Chips from the block. But it'd buy a few months. And get the kingdom turned upside down. How many people at your place? Better think about them."

"I am."

"Something could be arranged… If I could get them to safety?…"

"You'd have a corpse. I hate to lose the place, but it looks like I'm damned no matter what."

"Keeping it could be fixed. Your grant runs to the river. That puts it in a military zone. I could take it over till this blows away. I'll have to put troops in anyway, if you and your eastern friend leave a forty-mile gap unpatrolled. If I don't, I'll have the north woods thick with bandits from Prost Kamenets, and trade with Iwa Skolovda cut off. But getting you, and your eastern friend, off the hook would take some doing. You might have to stay away for years."

"I think," said Ragnarson, "I'll have to do that anyway. To get help reaching Greyfells." He was on the edge of decision. He knew where to buy the knife, but the price would be playing Haroun's game in Kavelin.

"We'll meet tomorrow, then. Where're you staying?"

"King's Cross, but I may move. We had some trouble in New Haymarket. Greyfells might try to have us arrested."

"Uhm. Charge would only have to stick till something regrettable happened in the dungeons. He's foxy. All right. Wansettle Newkirk, ten in the morning. You know it?"

"I can find it."

"Good luck then."

Ragnarson rose, shook the Minister's hand, joined Blackfang. He remained uncommunicative the rest of the day.

FIVE: THE YEARS 995-1001 AFE
THEIR WICKEDNESS SPANS THE EARTH

i) But the evil know no joy

At last. The end of a long and tiring journey. Burla glanced back to see if he had been overtaken at the penultimate moment, sighed, slipped into the cave. His friend Shoptaw, the winged man, greeted him with anxious questions. "Fine, now," Burla replied with a wide, fangy grin. "But tired. Master?"

"Come," the winged man said.

The old man was solicitous and apologetic. "I'm sorry you had to go through this. But Burla, you did me proud. Proud. How's the child?"

Swelling in the Master's praise, Burla replied, "Good, Master. But hungry. Sad."

"Yes, so. You weren't prepared to bring him so far. I feared…"

Burla laid the baby before the Master. The old man opened its wrappings. "What's this? A girl?" Thunderheads rumbled across his brow. "Burla…"

"Master?" Had he done wrong without knowing?

The old man held his temper. Whatever had happened, it had not been Burla's fault. The dwarf didn't have the brains. "But how?…" he asked aloud, wondering how a counterswitch had been made. Then he looked closer. The hereditary mark was there.

The King had lied. To support his shaky throne he had announced the birth of a son when a daughter had been born. The fool! There was no way he could have pulled it off…

Realization. His own schemes had been dealt a savage blow. A wildcat was growling in his embrace. Willy-nilly, he had inherited the Krief's plot. "Oh, damn, damn…"

Two days passed before he trusted his temper enough to confront his shadowy ally. The failure was the easterner's fault. He should have used spells to assure the sex of the child. The old man would have done it himself had he suspected the other's sloppiness.

But no one accused the Demon Prince of incompetence. No sorcerer was more powerful or touchy than Yo Hsi, nor had any had more time to perfect his wickedness. He was an evil spanning unknown centuries. Only one man dared openly challenge the Demon Prince, his co-ruler and arch-enemy in Shinsan, the Dragon Prince, Nu Li Hsi. And, perhaps, the Star Rider, the old man thought, but he was irrelevant to the equation.

The old man, who had taken great pains to remain anonymous, was a noble of Kavelin, the Captal of Savernake, hereditary guardian of the Savernake Gap. His castle, Maisak, in the highest and narrowest part of the pass, had seen countless battles fought beneath its walls. Only once had it been threatened, when El Murid's hordes, by sheer numbers, had almost swamped it. The Wesson, Eanred Tarlson, had prevented that. That near-defeat had led the Captal to reinforce his defenses with sorcery.

A greater sorcery was in the Savernake Gap now. That of Shinsan. The Demon Prince's interlocutors had come to the Captal and found a bitter, ambitious man, Kavelin's only non-Nordmen noble gone sour over the treatment he received in Vorgreberg. The emissaries had tempted him with the Crown of Kavelin in exchange for service to Yo Hsi and eventual passage west for Shinsan's legions. Yo Hsi was ready to settle his ancient struggle with the Dragon Prince. A united Shinsan would move swiftly to fulfill its age-old goal of world dominion.

The Captal, from his lonely aerie, had seen little of the world but that contained in the caravans flowing past Maisak. Since the fall of Ilkazar, the west had been weak and divided. The major powers, Itaskia and El Murid's religious state, were deadly enemies evenly matched. Neither showed much interest in using sorcery for military purposes.

Shinsan hinged its strategies on sorcery. Physical combat was a followup, to occupy, to achieve tactical goals. Rumor whispered dreadful things of the powers pent there, awaiting unity to release them.

The Captal had chosen what he thought would be the winning side. Western sorcery and soldiery had no hope against the Dread Empire.

Yo Hsi had established a transfer link between Maisak and a border castle in his sector of Shinsan. The old man now used it. He bore the child in his arms.

The place he went was dark and misty. There were hints of evils out of sight, evils more grim than any he had created in the caverns in the cliffs against which Maisak stood.

A squad of soldiers, statue-like in black armor, surrounded his entry point. He could see nothing beyond them. He, and they, might have been the entire universe.

Was Yo Hsi expecting trouble? He had never been greeted this way before. "I want to see the Demon Prince. I'm the Captal of Savernake…"

Not a weapon wavered, not a man moved. Their discipline was frightening.

From the darkness, a darker darkness still, Yo Hsi materialized. Fear cramped the Captal's guts. The man hadn't been the same since losing his hand—though, perhaps, the change had begun earlier, with the failure in the child's sex. Consistency of oversight suggested that Yo Hsi was developing a godlike self-image that underestimated everyone around him.

"What do you want? You've dragged me away from sorceries of the highest and most difficult sort."

His face came visible in the sourceless light. It was drawn and haggard. The eyes were surrounded by marks of strain. The Captal felt a new touch of fear. Had he made an ally of a man incapable of fulfilling the scheme?

"We've got a problem."

"I don't have time for guessing games, old man."

"Eh?" The Captal controlled himself. He had just learned his status in the easterner's thoughts. "The child. Your Prince changeling. It's a girl."

The Captal had been enthusiastic when Yo Hsi had first proposed the switch. Couldn't miss, what with both Princes their creatures...

The Demon Prince flew into a screaming rage.

It was all the Captal's fault, of course. Or his minions had betrayed him, or...

After several minutes of abuse, the old man could tolerate no more. The Demon Prince had slipped over the borders of reason. The ship of alliance was no longer sound. Time to abandon it and cut his losses.

With a slight bow the Captal interrupted, said, "I see I'll find no comfort in the source of our embarrassment. You may consider our alliance dissolved." He spoke the word that would return him to his own dungeons.

As he flickered away, he grinned. The expression on Yo Hsi's face!

The moment he materialized in Maisak he initiated dissociative spells to close the transfer stream. To pursue the discussion Yo Hsi would have to walk from the hold of his nearest secret ally.

ii) He bears the burden of loyalty

Eanred Tarlson was one man who never ceased worrying the mysterious exchange.

Following his encounter in the Gudbrandsdal there was a long period for which he had no memories. His wife, Handte, said he had lain on the border-land of death for a month. Then, gradually, he had recovered. Six months had passed before he could get around under his own power. Kavelin spent that time under intense pressure from its neighbors.

At home, in the taverns with his men, or maneuvering in the field, Tarlson never stopped puzzling. Something kept ragging the corners of his mind. A clue that only he held. Some memory of having encountered the old man before, long ago. But his bout with death had left his mind unreliable.

"Maybe it's a memory from a previous life," his wife observed one evening, a year after the swap. She was the only one he had told. "I was reading one of Gjerdrum's books. There's a man at the Rebsamen, Godat Kothe, who says the half-memories we get sometimes are from other lives."

Gjerdrum had just finished a year in Hellin Daimiel, courtesy of the Krief. Handte Tarlson, with a thirst for knowledge and little opportunity to indulge it, had instantly begun devouring his books.

Eanred frowned. That reminded him of a problem he had to face soon. The Nordmen were upset that a common Wesson, on state funds, was being sent to a university considered a noble preserve.

It had begun without Tarlson's knowledge, during his unconsciousness. There had been strong opposition, which was stronger now. Gjerdrum had outperformed his classmates. Though Tarlson felt immensely honored, he feared he would have to ask the boy to withdraw.

He felt a quirk of irritation. It startled him. It wasn't like him to feel antagonism over accidents of birth. Still, they couldn't accuse him of ambition. He had never asked honors or titles, only the opportunity to serve.

"Maybe. But I'm sure it's a memory from this life. I'll find the handle someday." After a long pause, "I have to. I'm the only one who saw them all."

"Eanred, tell the King. Don't take everything on yourself."

"Maybe." He considered it.

Weeks passed before he spoke with the Krief. The occasion was his induction into the Order of the Royal Star, the Crown's household knights. The endowment was hereditary and carried a small living.

The Nordmen were bitter. But their opposition remained muted. The ceremony took place in Vorgreberg, where Tarlson was immensely popular.

He could be put in his place when the mad King died.

Afterward, in his private-audience chamber, the Krief asked, "Eanred, how are you? I've heard the pressure's bothering you."

"Fine, Sire. Never better."

"I don't believe it. You showed nerves today."

"Sire?"

"Eanred, you're the only loyal subject I've got. You're invaluable as champion, but worth immeasurably more as a symbol. Why do you think the barons hate you? Your very existence makes their treasons more obvious. They resist honoring you because it makes you more prominent, makes your loyalty a greater example to the lower classes. And that's why I refuse to let you take Gjerdrum out of the Rebsamen."

Tarlson was startled.

The King chuckled. "Thought you had that in mind. In character. Bring me a brandy, will you?"

While Tarlson poured, the Krief continued, "Eanred, I don't have much time left. Three or four years. If I do things that seem strange, don't be surprised. I'm chasing a grand plan. So the scramble for succession won't destroy Kavelin. Thank you. Pour one for yourself." For several minutes he sipped quietly while Tarlson waited.

"Eanred, when I'm gone, will you support the Queen?"

"Need you ask, Sire?"

"No, but I don't envy you the task. My remotest cousins will be after the Crown. You'll have no support."

"Nevertheless..." He remembered his wife's suggestion. "Maybe if we found the true Prince..."

"Ah. You know. I guess everyone does. But it's not that easy. There're facts known only to myself and the Queen. And the kidnappers. Eanred, the Prince was a girl. Fool that I was, I thought we could pretend otherwise..."

Tarlson dropped into a chair. "Sire, I'm a simple man. This's a bit complicated... But there's something I've got to tell you. It may help." He described what he had seen the night of the abduction.

"The Captal," the Krief said when Eanred finished. "I suspected it. The creatures in the tower, you know. But I kept asking myself, what did he have to gain? Now I wonder if he was a willing accomplice, or under duress? I've no ideas about your attacker. He must've been a Power..."

"You haven't investigated?" The puzzle had been answered. The old man *had* been the Captal of Savernake. Eanred had seen him briefly during the wars.

"I had my reasons. For now I have a son, though he'll never be King. Meanwhile, I keep hoping there'll be an acceptable heir..." For a moment his face expressed intense anguish. "The girl's no more my blood than the changeling."

"Sire?"

"Don't know how it was managed. But I didn't father the child. Haven't had the capacity since the wars. No need to be shocked, Eanred. I've managed to live with it. As has the Queen, though she wasn't told till recently... I'd run out of excuses. And it was time she knew. She might find a way to give me an heir before it's too late." He smiled a tight, agonized smile.

"I doubt it, Sire. The Queen..."

"I know. She's young and idealistic... But a man has to live by his forlorn, twisted hopes."

Tarlson shook his head slowly. More than the knighthood, the Krief's confessions were honors that showed the high esteem in which he was held. He wished there was something he could do...

He returned home in a dour, bitter mood, silently cursing Fate, yet with a renewed respect for the man who was his lord and friend. Let the Nordmen call him weakling. The man had a strength they would never understand.

iii) She walks in darkness

Three times emissaries of the Demon Prince came to Maisak. Each time the Captal sent them home with polite but firm refusals. Then he heard nothing for a long time.

He considered going to the Krief. But temptation called. He might stumble into something yet...

News came, whispering on demon wings, of a great thaumaturgic disaster. It stirred awe and fear among sorcerers throughout the west.

Yo Hsi *and* the Dragon Prince had been destroyed. In his hidden fortress deep in the Dragon's Teeth, the sorcerer Varthlokkur, the murderer of Ilkazar, had stirred and twitched and lashed out with unsuspected power.

The Captal, like sorcerers everywhere, retired to his most secure fastness to cast divinations and lay a wary inner eye on the Power in the north. The possibilities were unimaginable. The Empire Destroyer loose again. What would he do now?

And what of Shinsan? Nu Li Hsi's heir-apparent was a crippled child, incapable of holding the Dragon Throne. Yo Hsi's daughter was a postulant of a hermitic order, uninterested in her father's position and power... Would Varthlokkur seize Shinsan before the Tervola could select an Emperor?

Across the west, sorcerers gathered their strength, saw to their defenses.

And nothing happened. The Power in the Dragon's Teeth quietly faded away. The Captal's probes sensed only patient waiting, not ambition, not gathering sorcery.

Nor were there thaumaturgic hostings in Shinsan. Both successions proceeded smoothly.

He returned to his experiments.

She came at night, under a full moon, three years to the day after the baby change. In her train were imps and cockatrices, griffins, and a sky-patrolling dragon. She rode a milk-white unicorn.

She was the most beautiful woman he had ever seen. He loved her from the beginning.

Shoptaw roused him from slumber with the news.

"Has the alarm been given?" he asked.

"Yes, Master."

"What's the matter?"

"Great magic. Terrible power. Many strange beasts. Men without souls."

"You've been to see them?"

"I flew with five..."

"And?" A pang of distress. "Someone was hurt?" He loved his creations as a man loved his children.

"No. Very frightened, though. Not get close. Great winged beast, eyes and tongue of fire, large as many horses..."

"A dragon?"

Shoptaw nodded.

Dragons were incredibly rare, and sorcerers who had learned dragon mastery rarer still. "They didn't act hostile?"

"No." But the winged man drew his crystal dagger.

The Captal's gaze wandered its edges and planes. There was a glow almost indiscernible.

"No inimical intentions," he translated. "Well, let's have a look at them."

She was a half-mile away when first he spied her, a glowing point below the circling dragon. He recognized the unicorn, was awed. Unicorns, he had on high authority, were extinct.

"Mist," he whispered once she had drawn closer. "Yo Hsi's daughter."

She stopped before the gate, showed the palms of both hands. The Captal smiled. He knew the gesture was empty if she intended evil.

Yet it *was* a gesture. No sense antagonizing her when she had Shinsan's best at her back. A fight would be hopeless. He would last barely long enough to send a message to Vorgreberg.

He delayed the message pending outcome of the parlay.

She understood his position. She did not ask that he admit anyone to his fortress. "I've come to discuss a matter of mutual interest." Her bell-like voice turned his spine to water.

"Eh?" Her beauty was totally distracting.

"You had an arrangement with my father. I want to renew it."

He gawked.

She descended from her exotic mount, said something to one of her captains. The soldiers of Shinsan began pitching camp with the same precision shown in everything they did. Among the imps there was an increase in erratic, chaotic behavior.

The Captal found his tongue. "I'd heard you weren't interested in the Demon Throne." He glanced at the unicorn. "But I've heard other tales that, obviously, were unfounded."

She rewarded him with a melting smile. "One must create images to survive a heartbeat from a throne. Had my father believed me interested, he'd've had me killed. The greater the power, the greater the fear of its loss."

"The bargain with your father," the Captal said, after he and the woman had made themselves comfortable inside, "became untenable when he lost touch with reality. He made grave errors and blamed them on others."

"I know. And I apologize. He was a brilliant man once. I think you'd find me a more compatible partner."

Oh, the suggestiveness she put into her words!

"Show me the profit. You have the Demon Throne, but do you have its power? Dare you look beyond your borders? The Dragon Prince, too, had an heir."

"O Shing? I haven't run him to ground yet, but it's only a matter of time."

"Tervola have declared." The Tervola were the sorcerer-generals who commanded Shinsan's armies. Traditionally, they gave no loyalties to anything but Shinsan itself. "Not many yet. Lords Feng and Wu support O Shing. Lord Chin has declared for me. You see that I've captured his token."

"The dragon?"

"Yes."

"Uhm. And the unicorn? I'd thought the beast pure fable."

"They're rare. Rarer than dragons. But there'll always be unicorns while there're virgins—though we're rarer than dragons, too."

The Captal stirred nervously. "You're not one of those… those whose power depends on…"

Her perfect lips formed the tiniest pout. "Sir!" Then she laughed. "Of course not. I'm no fool to hinge my strength on something so easily lost. I'm as human as any woman."

The old man felt a twinge of envy for the man who would first reach Mist's bed.

"What's your offer?" he asked.

"The same as my father's. But I won't cheat you."

He was hooked, but he continued to wriggle. "What're your plans?"

"I mean to test my power. On Shinsan's borders there're a few small kingdoms that have been troublesome. And I'll finish O Shing."

"And then?"

"Then the great eastern powers. Escalon and Matayanga."

"Ah?" She was ambitious indeed, though only to fulfill what Shinsan considered its destiny. And he saw an opportunity to hedge his bets. "I might be interested. But you haven't convinced me. If you succeed in Escalon, then I'll commit myself." Escalon commanded sorceries as powerful as those of Shinsan.

Mist wanted to reopen the transfer link. She had a friend in the west, an Itaskian named Visigodred. His residence was far from the focus of events and he was completely apolitical. She would leave control of the link in his hands.

iv) Mistress of the night

She looked seventeen. An enemy might have suggested nineteen. But she was old beyond the suspicions of all but the Tervola. She had been an apparent seventeen when Yo Hsi had engineered Varthlokkur into destroying Ilkazar. She herself was unsure of her age. She had spent centuries cloistered from the temptations of life and power...

Yo Hsi had never forgotten that he and Nu Li Hsi had usurped their father, Tuan Hoa. He had always anticipated his own usurpation by descendants... Males he had had murdered at birth. Mist had been allowed life on her mother's promise that she would spend her existence confined to a nunnery.

Survival had been the obsession of her early existence. She had done everything to assure her father that she had rejected ambition.

She succeeded. And cozened him into placing upon her the sorceries yielding eternal youth.

Those victories won, she turned to sorcerous self-education.

With the centuries never ending there was time to learn cautiously, by nibbles, without being obvious. By the time she was exposed she had become as powerful as any Tervola. The Power was in her blood. Still she showed no ambition beyond the scholarly. Her father chose not to destroy her.

But she had ambitions. And patience. Varthlokkur and the destruction of the Empire had shown her that Yo Hsi contained the seeds of his own destruction. She needed but wait.

Varthlokkur had come to Shinsan as a child, a fugitive full of hatred. The master magicians of Ilkazar, trying to evade a prophecy that from a witch would spring the Empire's doom, had burned his mother. Yo Hsi had undertaken his education, forging a weapon with which to demolish the one power capable of challenging Shinsan. But he had not supervised the boy's education himself. He had left that to the Tervola. They had seen no reason to keep him from meeting Nu Li Hsi as well.

Each Prince had thought to use him against the other. He had shaken their mastery, after crushing Ilkazar, and had hidden in the Dragon's Teeth. When, after centuries, they had striven to regain control, he had trapped them both...

Mist had ascended the Demon Throne without risk or effort. Only a little muddying of the thaumaturgic visions of her father and Nu Li Hsi. Just enough to hasten them to their fates.

The conquest of Escalon appeared easy. She needed but overwhelm the magic of the Monitor and Tear of Mimizan. O Shing was on the run. Her back was clear.

Appearances were deceiving. Escalon controlled more Power than she expected, and O Shing's weakness was the pretense of the broken-winged pheasant.

He struck while she was committed in Escalon, during the height of a battle. Only the greater threat of an Escalonian offensive saved her by forcing him to assume control of the armies.

Mimicking O Shing's game, she struck back while he was involved in a gargantuan operation against the Monitor. She forced another change of command, resumed control of the adventure she had initiated.

In Escalon she captured some western mercenaries. Among them were interesting brothers named Turran and Valther, minor wizards who had been involved in the affair that had led to her father's doom. They seemed to have no particular allegiance to Escalon, and no love for Varthlokkur, whom she would have to face someday. She took them into her growing coterie of foreign followers.

The Tervola issued dire warnings about foreigners. She ignored them.

The younger brother, Valther, caught her fancy. He was a pleasant, witty man, sharp of mind, always ready with a quip or tall tale. And he was impressed by her looks. Most men were terrified of what she was.

It developed so subtly that neither recognized more than a surface involvement. They hawked together in lands far from the war, danced on mountaintops deep in Shinsan, skipped through transfer links to cities and fortresses unknown outside the Dread Empire. She showed him the fains and shrines of her father and grandfather, and let him join the hunt for O Shing.

But there was the war, her war, that had to come before all else, that would mean loss of the Demon Throne if she failed.

The bond developed, deepened. The Tervola saw, understood, and disapproved.

There came a night of rites and celebration before the final assault on Tatarian. Spirits were high. O Shing seemed broken. Escalon had little Power left...

Over the objections of her generals, she invited Turran and Valther.

Her pavilion, huge and rich, had been erected within sight of Tatarian's defensive magicks, and everything in it had been plundered from Escalon. Mist meant to accept the Monitor's surrender there, in humiliating circumstances. He had caused her untold unhappiness.

"Valther," she said, when he and Turran arrived, "come sit with me."

The man flashed a broad smile. The demon-faced visors of sullen Tervola tracked him like weapons. His brother sent a dark look after him. Valther sat, leaned close, whispered, "My Lady looks radiant tonight. And ravishing. Good news?"

She flushed slightly.

The entertainment began. Musicians sounded their instruments. Escalonian dancing girls came in. Valther clapped to the music, ogled them unabashedly.

The Tervola remained stern. One departed.

Mist watched with angry eyes. She foresaw difficulties, a possible power struggle. She held the Demon Throne only by grace of these dark, grim men hiding behind obscene masks.

Did they think she would be a puppet?

She found her hand in Valther's, begging support.

Another of the Tervola departed.

She had to improve her position. How? Only something swift and savage would impress these cold old men.

The evening progressed lugubriously, fatefully, tension building with each new entertainment. Tervola continually departed.

They were sending a message she refused to heed.

Experimentally, clumsily, she responded to Valther.

More Tervola left. Piqued, she allowed Valther more liberties.

Who were they to approve or disapprove? She was the Demon Princess...

She drank a lot.

She forgot the war and her responsibilities, relaxed, devoted herself to enjoyment.

In Shinsan hedonism was forbidden. From bottom to top in that chill culture each person had a position and purpose to which unswerving duty was obligated.

But she behaved like a romantic teenager, caring about nothing.

Finally, just one grim, pale-faced man remained. Valther's brother. And Turran obviously wished he were elsewhere.

The Escalonian captives, entertainers, and servants, also wore expressions of desperation.

"Out!" she screamed. "All of you, out of my sight. You cringing lice!"

As Turran left, he sent his brother a look of mute appeal. But Valther was busy tickling a toe.

Damned Tervola! Let them frown behind their devil masks! She was her own woman.

Never a word was said, but, next morning, she realized everyone knew, from the mighty to the spearmen.

When the Escalonian dawn painted her pavilion with bloody rays, her unicorn was gone.

Before she could be challenged, she unleashed the assault on Tatarian, following a suggestion a helpful Valther had whispered deep in the night.

The city that had held so long collapsed in hours.

The Tervola were impressed.

v) Their heads meet, and they spark wickedness

The defense of Escalon had collapsed. Tatarian lay in ruins. Mist, though still unable to claim victory over O Shing, eyed Matayanga.

It was time, the Captal decided.

Mist had come to visit often. His infatuation had grown to the proportions of the great romances. Yet he prided himself on being a hard-nosed realist. He considered facts and acted accordingly, no matter the pain.

But he had a blind spot. The child from Vorgreberg.

They had given her the name Carolan, but the nickname Kiki had attached itself. Shoptaw and Burla, her constant companions, preferred the latter. She was a bright-eyed, golden-haired imp, all giggles and bounce. She was happy, carefree, yet capable of seriousness when discussing her destiny, which the Captal had never hidden.

The old man could not have loved her more. Everyone loved her… And spoiled her. Even Mist.

The winged man brought Kiki. The Captal smiled. He no longer worried about himself, he worried about Kiki. Should he subject a child not yet six to the torments of a play for Kavelin's throne?

"It's about Aunt Mist, isn't it, Papa Drake?" she asked, eyes disconcertingly big.

"Yes. The thing in Escalon's done. We've got to decide about Kavelin."

She placed her hands on his.

"We've got to figure what's best for you."

"I thought you wanted …"

"What I want isn't important. I've got Maisak. I've got Shoptaw and Burla. And you." The winged man stirred embarrassedly. The Captal reddened. He had begun to understand the costs of Vorgreberg. "But you… got to do what's best."

"Why don't you talk to Aunt Mist?"

"I know what she wants."

"Talk to her anyway. She's a nice lady." Carolan had her determined face on. "But sometimes she's spooky."

The Captal laughed. "She's that. I'll see if she's got time to visit."

She was there in hours.

The Captal generally greeted her with some small flattery. This time she looked terrible.

"What's happened?" he asked.

She collapsed into a chair. "I was a fool."

"You won, though."

"And came out too weak to go on. Drake, O Shing's pet Tervola, Wu, is a demon. A genius. They almost overthrew me..."

"I'd heard. But you came back."

"Drake, legions are fighting legions. Tervola are fighting Tervola. That's never happened before. And Escalon... The Monitor was stronger than I thought, All I won was a desert. He even got the Tear of Mimizan out before the collapse. And a quarter of Shinsan is as lifeless as Escalon. I'm losing my grip. The Tervola are having second thoughts. They would've abandoned me already, except I managed a coup in the attack on Tatarian."

Once again, it seemed, he had joined a loser.

"So you want the Gap as bride-price for their support?"

She smiled weakly. "I don't blame you. No more than the Tervola. We respect strength and ability. In your place, I'd wonder about me, too."

The Captal chuckled nervously. She had read his mind.

"Can I sweeten the partnership?"

So she was weak. Desperately so. "No Escalon. No conquest outright. Hegemony and disarmament. Suzerainty without occupation..."

"A return to Empire?" she asked. "With Shinsan replacing Ilkazar?"

"Any rational man could see we need unity. The problem is questions of local sovereignty."

"And how would you enforce *my* sovereignty?"

The old man shrugged. "I'm not worried about the mules, just about loading the wagon. Agree in principle?"

"All right. We'll manage something. What about Kavelin?"

"The King's sick. He'll go soon. The scramble's about to begin. The barons are forming parties. Breitbarth looks strong. El Murid and Volstokin are interested. Which means Itaskia and Altea and Anstokin... Well, you see the possibilities. I'm sending my winged men to watch my neighbors. I should send them farther afield, to where the real plotting will take place."

"And Carolan?"

"I don't know. I want to protect her."

"So do I. But you'll need support. She's the tool you'll have to use."

"I know. I know. A quandary. That's why I asked you here. She insisted I talk to you."

"Why not ask her what she wants? She's got her feet on the ground. She's thought about it."

Carolan wanted to be Queen.

So the Captal chose to betray his homeland for the sakes of a six-year-old and a woman who should have been his enemy.

SIX: YEAR 1002 AFE
THE MERCENARIES

i) A matter of discipline

"Looks just like army," said Mocker, as he and Ragnarson descended the slope of the valley where Blackfang and Kildragon had established their training camp. The River Porthune was near, and beyond it, Kendel, northernmost of the Lesser Kingdoms.

They were a week behind Blackfang. It had taken Bragi that long to conclude his business and convince Uthe that he and Dahl dared return to Elana unaccompanied. He had finally explained the situation fully, trusting Uthe's discretion. Even then Bragi had been forced to compose a long explanatory letter admonishing Elana and Bevold to cooperate with the Minister's agents.

"Uhn." Ragnarson grunted. "A baby one. Or an overgrown street gang." He had been sour for days. First, Mocker had insisted on coming south. Bragi would rather he were in charge at home. Elana was unpredictable. Bevold had no imagination. And the two were sure to feud.

His last hope of evading the Kavelin commitment had evaporated when Royalist rowdies, at the gate of Itaskia's citadel, had murdered Duke Greyfells.

The shock waves were still rattling windows and walls. A quiet little war between Haroun's partisans and those of El Murid, in the ghetto, was no cause for excitement. But an assassination…

Half of Itaskia had gone into shock. The other half had gone on a witch-hunt.

"Look what Reskird's recruited. Children." Ragnarson indicated a line of young swordsmen being drilled by a grizzled veteran.

"Self," Mocker observed with a chuckle, "remember boy from icy northland, big as a horse, bald-chinned…"

"That was different. My father raised me right."

"Hai!" Mocker cried. "'Raised right,' says he. As reever, arsonist, lier in ambush…"

Bragi was in no mood for banter. He didn't argue. He continued surveying the encampment. The area occupied by Kildragon's trainees pleased him. They had even put up a log stockade behind a good deep ditch.

But the Trolledyngjan camp was a despair. He had seen better among savages. This had come on recently, too. There had been no sloppiness when they had camped at his place.

"The families. We'll have to do something, or there'll be trouble. First time some girl gets caught in the puckerbushes with an Itaskian…"

"Self, am no expert… Hai! Such strange expression. Am, admittedly, expert in most things, being genius equal to girth, but even for genius of such breadth, self, all things not known. But don't tell. Public thinks fat old reprobate infallible, omniscient, near divine in wisdom."

"How about turning your omniscience to the point?"

Mocker did so, but Ragnarson paid little attention.

They entered the Trolledyngjan encampment. Ragnarson's nose rose. Trolledyngjans were notoriously undisciplined and unfastidious, but this much filth meant deep trouble and a lack of leadership.

He heard angry voices. "May get to try your suggestion."

"Uhn," the fat man grunted. He, too, had been surveying the surly faces watching from tents and wagons. "Self, will keep hand to hilt."

The voices proved to be those of Blackfang and a large, brutish young man, arguing amidst a mass of grumbling Trolledyngjans. With Mocker's donkey in his wake, Bragi forced his mount into the press.

The onlookers moved reluctantly, with hard glares. How could Haaken have let it go this far?

Ragnarson thundered. "What the hell is this, Blackfang? A pigsty?" He studied the man facing his foster brother.

A brute. A young swine. But that was more in mind and manner than appearance. Not too bright, greedy, and a catspaw, Ragnarson guessed.

Blackfang saluted, replied, "A bit of difficulty explaining something, sir. Some folks think we ought to be raiding, not running off to some bird-in-the-bush Lesser Kingdom."

"Eh? What kind of fool are you? You recruit suicides? Settle it. Thrash the lout, get this camp cleaned up, and report to my quarters."

Blackfang's antagonist could contain himself no longer. "Who's this old swineherd muck-mouth, and where's she get off giving orders to men?" Ragnarson wore Itaskian dress. "Are we slaves to every eunuch who rides in?…"

Ragnarson's boot found his mouth. He looked up from the ground puzzledly, a finger feeling loosened teeth.

"Ten lashes," Bragi said. "Special consideration so it won't be said I spite the children of old enemies. But I'll hang him next time."

The man was about to spring. Discretion bit him. He frowned questioningly.

"Up, you," Ragnarson ordered. "Which of Bjorn Thorfinson's whelps are you?"

"Eh? Ragnar…"

"Ragnar? The gall of the man. But no matter. It's an honorable name. Wear it with honor. There's a saying, 'Like father, like son.' I hope it's not true in your case. Blackfang, somewhere there's a man with a purse full of gold. Someone who was poor when he left the north. Bring him when you report."

He nudged his mount forward. Mocker followed, grinning hugely.

ii) Child with the ways of a woman

Ragnarson had met the Trolledyngjans and Itaskians who were to be his staff. Though Kildragon had nominal control of the latter, a question of loyalties might arise. Most of the Itaskians were raw youths, but their officers and sergeants were obvious veterans, and almost as obviously the Minister's hand-picked men, detached from regular service.

But the Trolledyngjans were the pressing problem. Their leaders were solid, experienced men who knew the lay of things. The young men had never seen a real war. They wanted to plunder the countryside, called wiser heads cowards for demurring. Their exposure to Itaskian military procedures had been sketchy. Wolf-strikes by coast-reevers gave the raiders no true picture of the capacity of the attacked.

"Reskird," said Ragnarson, after a lot of useless talk, "clear your drill ground. Dig a trench down the middle, as wide and deep as you can in two hours. Arm your best men with shields and pikes. Scare up blunt arrows for the rest, and pad the tips. Blackfang will attack you in the Trolledyngjan fashion. We'll give your youngsters some confidence and knock the cockiness out of Haaken's."

Kildragon, a dour man, replied, "Two birds, eh? Show them Itaskian firepower, they'll lose interest in plunder. And we'll build some mutual respect."

"Right." To the Trolledyngjan officers, Ragnarson said, "Push the Itaskians hard. Try to break them. Straight frontal attack, no tricks. See how they stand up…"

A racket approached. Blackfang stalked in, pushing a scared Trolledyngjan. "Here's our gold man," he growled. "Caught him trying to sneak into the hills."

Ragnarson considered the youth, who had been one of Haaken's bodyguards in Itaskia. "Took you long enough, and then you didn't get the right one."

"Eh? He had it when we caught him."

"When did he get it? He was with us in Itaskia. Mocker?" The fat man nodded. "He ever give you any trouble before?"

"No."

"Where'd you get it, Wulf?"

The soldier wouldn't answer.

Blackfang drew back a fist.

"Self," said Mocker, "being accustomed to use of brain instead of fist, would suggest is time for brainwork. Who does boy have for friends? Is friend rabble-rouser? Is friend?…"

"Don't have no friends," Blackfang interjected. "Just that girl Astrid he's always sniffing round…"

"Ah?" said Mocker. "Girl? Is said, 'Look for woman.' Might same be sister of mouth-man in camp in morning? Saw same with boy on trek to Itaskia."

"Bjorn had a daughter?" Ragnarson asked. Vague recollection of a face.

Young. What was it the Star Rider had said? Beware of the girl who acts like a woman? "Get her."

"Never thought about a woman," Blackfang said, leaving.

He soon returned with a howling, kicking adolescent in tow and a group of sullen youths trailing. "Where's her brother?" Ragnarson asked. "I want him here, too." Ragnar appeared almost instantly. "Wulf, you and Ragnar stand back, out of the way." To Reskird, "If they move, cut them down. Girl, shut up."

The girl had been alternating threats, pleas, and calls for help.

"Blackfang, watch the door. Kill anybody who sticks his head in."

His officers stirred nervously. He was daring mutiny.

"Sit down, girl," said Ragnarson, offering his chair. "Mocker?"

The fat man grunted, began playing with an Itaskian gold piece taken from Wulf. The girl watched fearfully. Sometimes the coin seemed to vanish, but reappeared in his other hand. Over and over it turned. Droning, Bragi told his officers the tale of how her father, while young, had betrayed his father to the Pretender's followers.

The coin turned over, vanished, appeared. Ragnarson spoke of their mission in Kavelin. He talked till everyone was thoroughly bored.

Then Mocker took over whispering. He reminded the girl that she was weary, weary...

She had no chance. At last Mocker was satisfied. "Has been long time," he said, "but is ready. Ask questions gently."

"What's your name?" Ragnarson asked.

"Astrid Bjornesdatter."

"Are you rich, Astrid?"

"Yes."

"Very rich?"

"Yes."

"Have you been rich long?"

"No."

"Did you get rich in Itaskia?"

"Yes."

"A man gave you gold to do something?"

"Yes."

"An old man? A thin man?"

"Yes. Yes."

Ragnarson and Mocker exchanged glances. "Greyfells."

"Sorcery!" Wulf hissed. "It's sorcery..." Kildragon's blade touched his throat.

"Did the man want you to cause trouble? To keep your people from going to Kavelin?"

"Yes. Yes."

"Satisfies me," said Ragnarson. "You. Ragnar. Want to ask her anything?"

The boy did, and showed unexpected intelligence. He followed Bragi's lead and kept his questions simple. It took but a few to convince him that he had been used.

Wulf refused his opportunity. Ragnarson didn't push. Let him keep his illusions.

"Well, gentlemen," Bragi said, "you see a problem partially resolved. My friend will make the girl forget. But what about the men? This can happen again as long as we've got camp followers. I want them left here."

After the gathering dispersed, Bragi told Kildragon, Blackfang, and the fat man, "Keep an eye on Ragnar and Wulf. I tried to plant a seed. If it takes root, they'll handle our problem with the Trolledyngjans."

iii) News from Kavelin

The sham battle had been on an hour. The Trolledyngjans were getting trounced.

"My point's been made," said Ragnarson to a runner. "The Itaskians look good. Tell Blackfang to withdraw." As the messenger departed, a dust-covered rider approached from the direction of the Porthune. He was a tall, lean man, weathered, grim, who rode spear-straight. A soldier, Ragnarson thought. A man too proud to show weariness.

"Colonel Ragnarson?" the rider asked as he came up.

"Right."

"Eanred Tarlson, Colonel, commanding the Queen's Own Guard, Kavelin. I have a letter from Haroun bin Yousif."

Ragnarson took the letter, sent a runner to prepare quarters. "Queen's Own?"

"The King was dying when I left Vorgreberg."

Ragnarson finished Haroun's brief missive, which urged that he waste no time moving south. "You came alone? With trouble brewing?"

"No. I had a squadron when I left."

"Uhm," Ragnarson grunted. "Well, you're here. Relax. Rest."

"How soon can you move?" Tarlson demanded. "You're desperately needed. The Queen had little but my regiment, and that likely to disappear if someone spreads the rumor that I'm dead."

"The problem of succession, eh? The changeling and the foreign queen."

Tarlson gave him an odd look. "Yes. How soon?"

"Not today. Tomorrow if it's desperate. If I had my druthers, not for weeks. The men are green, not used to working together."

"Tomorrow, then," said Tarlson, as if yielding a major point.

Ragnarson recognized a strong-willed man who might cause problems unless things were made clear immediately. "Colonel, I'm my own man. These men march to my drum. I take orders only from my paymaster. Or mistress. I appreciate the need for haste. You wouldn't have come otherwise. But I won't be pushed."

Tarlson flashed a brief, weary smile. "Understood. I've been there. I'd rather you took the extra days and arrived able to fight, anyway." He glanced at the Trolledyngjan encampment. "You're bringing families?"

"No. They're staying. Shouldn't you get some rest? We'll start early."

"Yes, I suppose."

Ragnarson turned to greet Kildragon and Blackfang, who were arguing as they rode up, Haaken claiming Reskird had cheated. "Looked good. They might do if we can get them an easy first fight. Any injuries?"

Headshakes. "Just bruises, mostly egos," said Blackfang.

"Good. We move out tomorrow. Haroun says the arrow's in the air."

Both men claimed they needed more time.

"You can have all the time you want. On the march. Haaken, get the families settled in the stockade."

The leading elements moved out at first light. By noon the rearguard was over the Porthune.

An officer from Kendel's army, as if by magic, appeared to lead them through back country, by obscure ways, out of the sight of most eyes, to the Ruderin border, where they were passed on to a Ruderiner for the march down the Anstokin border to the River Scarlotti, over which they would ferry to Altea.

Days went by. Miles and clouds of dust passed. Ragnarson did not push the pace, but kept moving from dawn till dusk, with only brief pauses to eat and rest the animals, for whom the march was punishing. Cavalry mounts were expensive. He had as yet received no advance from Kavelin's Queen.

Ten days into the march, in Ruderin, near the northernmost finger of Anstokin, he decided it was time for a rest.

Tarlson protested. "We've got to keep moving! Every minute wasted ..." Each day he grew more pessimistic, more dour. Ragnarson had tried to get to know him, but the man's anxieties got in the way. He grew ever more worried as no news came north to meet them.

Ragnarson, while his troops were involved in maintenance and training, asked Tarlson if he would care to go boar hunting. Their guide said a small but vicious wild pig inhabited the region. Tarlson accepted, apparently more to keep occupied than because he was interested. Mocker tagged along, for once deigning to mount a beast other than his donkey.

They had no luck, but Ragnarson was glad just to escape the cares of command. He had always loved the solitude of forests. These, so much like those around his grant, infected him with homesickness. For the most part they rode quietly, though Mocker couldn't stifle himself completely. He mentioned homesickness, too.

Toward midafternoon Tarlson loosened up. In the course of conversation, Ragnarson found the opportunity to ask a question that intrigued him.

"Suppose we find the Queen deposed?"

"We restore her."

"Even if the usurper is supported by the Thing?"

Tarlson took a long time answering, as if he hadn't considered the possibility. "My loyalty is to the Throne, not to man or woman. But no one could manage a majority."

"Uhm." Ragnarson remained thoughtful. He hoped Haroun's scheme wouldn't put them on opposite sides. Tarlson was the only Kaveliner with any military reputation, and he clearly had the will to manage armies.

Ragnarson wrestled serious self-doubts. He had never commanded such a large force, nor one so green and ethnically mixed. He feared that, in the crunch, control would slip away.

It was nearly dark before they abandoned the hunt, never having heard a grunt.

On the way back they struck the remnants of a road.

"Probably an Imperial highway," Tarlson mused. "The legions were active here in the last years."

iv) A castle in the darkness

Darkness had fallen. There was a quarter-moon, points up, that reminded Ragnarson of artists' renderings of Trolledyngjan warships. "What warriors," he mused aloud, "go reeving in yonder nightship?"

"The souls of the damned," Tarlson replied. "They pursue the rich lands eternally, their captain's eyes fiery with greed, but the shores of the earth retreat as fast as they approach, no matter how hard they row, or how much sail they put on."

Ragnarson started. This was another side of Eanred. He had begun to fear the man was a small-minded, undereducated boor.

"Varvares Codice," said Mocker, "same being attributed to Shurnas Brankel, legend collector of pre-Imperial Ilkazar. Hai! They send fire arrows."

A half-dozen meteors streaked down the night.

"Ho! What's this?" asked Ragnarson. They had topped a rise. Something huge and dark lay in the vale below.

"Castle," said Mocker.

"Odd," said Tarlson. "The guide didn't mention any strongholds around here."

"Maybe ruin left over from Imperial times," Mocker suggested. There was hardly a place in the west not within a few hours' ride of some Imperial remnant.

They drew close enough to make out generalities. "I don't think so," said Ragnarson. "The Empire built low, blockish walls with regularly spaced square towers for enfilading fire. This's got high walls with rounded towers. And the crenellated battlement didn't become common till the last century."

Tarlson reacted much as Ragnarson had minutes before. Mocker laughed.

The road ran right into the fortress, which made no sense. There were no lights, no watchfires, no sounds or smells of life.

"Must be a ruin," Ragnarson opined.

Curiosity had always been a weakness of Mocker's. "We see what's what, eh? Hai! Maybe find chest of jewels forgotten by fleeing tenants. Pot of gold buried during siege, waiting to jump into hands of portly investigator. Secret passage with skeletons of discarded paramours of castle lord, rings still on finger bones. Maybe dungeon mausoleum full of ancestors buried with riches ripe for plucking by intrepid grave robbers…"

"Ghoul!" Tarlson snapped.

"Pay him no mind," said Ragnarson. "Weird sense of humor. Just wants to poke around."

"We should get back."

He was right, but Ragnarson, too, was intrigued. "Like the old days, eh, Lard Bottom?"

Mocker exploded gleefully, "Hai! Truth told. Getting old, we. Calcification of brainpan setting in. We go, pretending twentieth birthday coming still, and no sense, not care if dawn comes. Immortals, we. Nothing can harm."

That was the way they had been, Ragnarson reflected.

"We explore, hey, Hulk?" Mocker stopped his mount beneath the teeth of a rusty portcullis.

"Go ahead," said Tarlson. "I'm going to get some sleep."

"Right. See you in the morning, then." Ragnarson followed Mocker into a small courtyard.

He got the feeling he had made a mistake. There was something wrong with the place. It seemed to be *waiting…* And a little surreal, as if he could turn suddenly and find nothing behind him.

Overactive imagination, he told himself. Came of remembering what they had gotten into in the old days.

Mocker dismounted and entered a door. Ragnarson hurried to catch him.

It was dark as a crypt inside. He pursued Mocker's shuffling footsteps, cursing himself for not having brought a light. He bumped into something large and yielding. Mocker squawked like a kicked hen.

"Do something," Bragi growled, "but don't block the road."

"Self, am listening. And trying not to be trampled by lead-footed stumbler about without sense to bring light. Am wondering about sound heard over stampede rumble of feet of same."

"Let's go back, then. We can come by tomorrow."

Logic had no weight with Mocker. He moved ahead.

So gradually that they did not immediately realize it, light entered their ken. Before they had advanced a hundred feet, they could see dimly, as through heavy fog at false dawn.

"Something's wrong here," said Ragnarson. "I smell sorcery. We'd better get out before we stir something up."

"Pusillanimous dullard," Mocker retorted. "In old days friend Hulk would have led charge."

"In the old days I didn't have any sense. Thought you'd grown up some, too."

Mocker shrugged. He no longer was anxious to go on. "Just to end of passage," he said. "Then we follow example of Tarlson."

The corridor ended in a blank wall. What was the sense of a passage that went nowhere, that had no doors opening off it?

"We'd better go," said Ragnarson. The sourceless light was bright now. He turned. "Huh?" His sword jumped into his hand.

Blocking their withdrawal was a curtain of darkness, as if someone had taken a pane of starless night and stretched it from wall to wall.

Mocker slid round him and probed the darkness with his blade. A deep thrust got results. Laughter like the cackling of a mad god.

"Woe!" Mocker cried. "Such petty end for great mind of age, caught like stupidest mouse in trap…" He charged the darkness, sword preceding him.

"You idiot!" Ragnarson bellowed. He muttered, "What the hell?" when his companion seemed to slide out of existence as he hit the blackness.

"Might as well." He hit the darkness seconds behind the fat man.

He felt like he was tumbling down the entire well of eternity, rolling aimlessly through a storm of color and sound underlain by the whispering of wicked things. It went on and on and on and… Without breaking stride he entered a vast, poorly lighted chamber.

That room, or hall, was an assault on rationality. The air was overpoweringly foul. From all-surrounding, shadowed mists came rustlings, and for a moment he thought he saw a manlike, winged thing with the head of a dog, then a small, apelike dwarf with prodigious fangs. Everything seemed unstable, shifting, except the floor, which was of jet, and a huge black throne carved with exceptionally hideous designs. They reminded him of reliefs he had seen in the temples of Arundeputh and Merthregul at Gundgatchcatil. Yet these were worse, as if carved by hands washed more deeply in evil.

Mocker, sword in hand, prowled round that throne. "What is it?" Ragnarson asked, seldom having seen the fat man so upset.

"Shinsan."

They were trapped fools indeed.

The mists stirred. An old man stepped forth. "Good evening," he said. "I trust you speak Necremnen? Good."

The old man turned to the throne, knelt, touched forehead to floor, muttered something Ragnarson couldn't understand. For an instant new mists gathered there. An incredibly beautiful woman wavered in their depths. She nodded and disappeared. The old man rose and turned.

"My Lady honors me. But to business. You're going where My Lady wishes you wouldn't. Kavelin is already too complex. Go home."

Ragnarson retorted, "Simple as that, eh? Might interfere with your plans, so we should turn back?"

"Yes."

"I can't do that." His fingers, in deaf-mute signs, flashed a message to Mocker. "I've given my word."

"I've tried to be reasonable. My Lady won't tolerate disobedience."

"Terrible. Hate to disappoint her."

Mocker suddenly lunged, sword reaching.

A silvery filament lightninged from the old man's hand, brushed Mocker's cheek. The fat man collapsed. By then Ragnarson was moving in. The thread darted out again. Bragi tangled it on his blade, ripped it from the old man's grasp, continued to bore in.

The sorcerer sprang straight up and disappeared in the mists overhead. Bragi, mystified, tried a few desultory sword swipes that got no result, then knelt to check Mocker's pulse.

A shimmering, sparkling dust drifted down upon him. When the first scintillating flakelet touched his skin, he tumbled across his friend.

Seven: Year 1002 afe
Into Kavelin

i) High sorcery

Ragnarson woke with a headache like that memorializing a week-long drunk. The demoniac whispering of his dream-haunts resolved themselves into the mutterings of Mocker.

Their cell was a classic, even to slimy stone walls. Beyond the rusty-barred door stood the winged thing, dog-teeth bared, a glowing dagger in hand. Other creatures stirred behind it, squat things heavily clothed, with faces like owls. The winged man opened the door.

Six owl-faces pounced on Mocker, bound him before Bragi reacted. Bellowing like a thwarted bull in rut, ignoring the agony in his head, he grabbed two, smashed them together, then used his fists on their faces. A neck went *snap!* He lifted the second overhead, hurled it skull-first against the floor.

A tide of weird creatures washed in. He went down. In moments he was trussed and being carried away. He tried counting turns and steps, but it was hopeless. Not only did his head hurt too much, his captors kept jabbing him in retribution for his attack.

They reached a vast room. It might have been the one where he and Mocker had been received, with the mists removed. It was huge. Every fixture was black. The monsters dumped him onto a stone table. He heard voices. Forcing his head around, he saw the old man arguing with the woman in the mists. The old man suddenly slumped in defeat.

The mist-woman faded. The man turned, selected a bronze dagger from a collection on a table, faced Ragnarson, raised his arms, began to chant.

Ragnarson noticed a pentagram chalked on the floor. A conjuration! He and Mocker were to be delivered to some Thing from Outside. He struggled against his bonds. The porters ignored him, nervously concentrated on their master.

A darkness animate became pregnant and gave birth to itself in the pentagram. The sorcerer stopped singing. Sighs escaped the creatures around Ragnarson.

Bragi shouted, hoping to disturb the wizard. It did no good. Furious with frustration, because his bonds would not yield, he performed the only act of defiance left him. He spit in the eye of one of the owl-faces.

It jumped as if hornet-stung, staggered, flailed its arms.

One crossed the barrier of the pentagram.

It withered swiftly, blackened. The creature screamed in soul-deep terror. The sorcerer tried to pull it out, then to chant the demon down. Too late. The owl-face was lost. The darkness in the pentagram gradually sucked it in.

The remainder of the old man's servants fled, shrieking. Their rush washed against and overturned the table where Bragi lay. He hit the floor hard, groaned, found one hand had been wrenched free. And not five feet away lay the sorcerer's dagger, that he had dropped when he had tried to save his servant. Bragi slithered to the blade, cut his bonds, then did likewise for a Mocker whose eyes were wide with terror.

A finger of blackness began to leak from the pentagram where the owl-face had broken its barrier.

The old man had disappeared again.

Staggering weak, Bragi and Mocker prepared to pursue his example. Mocker's gaze fell on a table where their weapons lay. He moved to get them. His fat man's run would have been amusing in other circumstances. He passed perilously near the pentagram, but the darkness within remained preoccupied with its victim.

It finished with the owl-face as Bragi and Mocker considered how best to escape, began slithering from the pentagram, writhing like a cat getting through a small hole.

"Self," said Mocker, "am of opinion any place elsewhere is better than here."

"Where's here?" Ragnarson asked. "Maybe I could figure where I'm going if I knew where I'm starting."

"Friend Bear doesn't want to know," Mocker replied.

"Bullfeathers. If you know, tell me."

Mocker shrugged. "Are in small quill of Shinsan poked through cloth of universe into Ruderin. Are in two places at same time, Ruderin valley and small frontier castle in Pillars of Ivory on Shinsan border with Sendelin Steppe. Could be long walk home if luck turns bad."

"Turns bad?" Ragnarson snorted. "Can't be worse than it is." The darkness still confined had grown visibly smaller. "I vote we walk while we talk."

The darkness chose that moment to strike. They managed to evade it and flee.

The flight was an eon of fear, of oxygen-starved lungs and already punished muscles refusing to be tortured more but going on all the same. Always close behind was a snakelike black tendril.

Something came hurtling at them. Ragnarson grabbed it, Mocker stabbed it, and together they sacrificed it to the tendril. Only after the darkness began surrounding it did they see that it was another of the old sorcerer's servants.

Chance eventually brought them back to the point where their flight had begun. The demon had evacuated the chamber completely. The uproar it had caused echoed from corridors opening on the room.

Feeling momentarily secure, Ragnarson prowled round the throne. "Hey," he said suddenly, "I think I've found a way out." He had noticed that, from a certain angle, he could vaguely discern a rectangle of darkness that obscured the black pillars and walls behind it. It seemed the same size as the curtain they had plunged into getting here.

"Self, would be grateful for same," said Mocker. "Magic binding two localities together is unraveling."

For some time there had been a gentle trembling in the floor. Ragnarson hadn't paid it any heed, thinking it the demon rumbling around. "What if?…"

"If fool-headed venturers don't find exit, then long walk home from Shinsan for same," Mocker replied.

"Here, then. Looks like the way we came in." He ran at the rectangle. The whirling, kaleidoscopic sensations returned. After a stench-filled eternity he stepped into the corridor where they had originally been entrapped. Mocker appeared an instant behind him.

They were still trapped.

"Make yourself comfortable," said Ragnarson, sitting with his back to a wall and his sword across his lap. "I'm not going back through that."

"Self, would prefer dying in west, too," said Mocker. "Though in Ruderin back country of own stupidity? Not even battle to end heroic life with heroic death, lots of witnesses to final bravery? Woe!"

Stone grumbled around them. Dust fell from the ceiling.

"Sounds bad," said Ragnarson.

"Crushed to death. Ignominious end for great mind. Am fool. Friend should have pointed out same, dragged fat idiot to camp kicking and screaming if needful."

"Is the light getting weaker?"

"Verity. Magicks devolving. Portal to Shinsan weakening also."

Indeed it was, getting fluttery around the edges and occasionally showing a swift-running shot of color.

"Maybe we can get out. If the place don't fall down first."

"Maybe so."

The curtain winked out of existence. They found themselves staring into the startled faces of several mercenaries. "Ghosts!" one cried.

"Boo!" said Mocker, then cackled madly. "Out of way. Everybody's out of way before very important head, head of self, gets mashed by falling castle."

Fifteen minutes later they were astride their mounts, atop a hill, watching the castle collapse. Fogs of darkness engulfed its base, darkness untouched by the morning sun. A plume of that blackness, like smoke, rose against the dawn and bent its head eastward. The destruction proceeded in unnatural silence.

"Going home," said Mocker.

"We'll hear from them again," Ragnarson replied.

Tarlson and Blackfang, who had been working round the rim of the valley, arrived. "You're lucky I mentioned the castle to the guide," said Eanred. "He said there wasn't any such place, so I scared up a rescue party."

"I'm grateful," said Ragnarson.

They talked at some length. When Ragnarson mentioned the winged man, Tarlson grew silent and withdrawn.

ii) Passage to Kavelin

The march to the Altean ferry was disconcerting. A regiment of Anstokin infantry paced them along the Ruderin border, making no overt moves but slowing their progress by forcing them to remain battle-ready. Crossing the River Scarlotti while Anstokin's force maneuvered nearby was a laborious business that took two days.

Tarlson grew jumpy as a cat. Still there were no messages from Kavelin, just rumors relayed by Altean officers. Those were not good. Skirmishing had broken out all over the kingdom. The Queen still held Vorgreberg, but the populace were being whipped up by a dozen propagandists. Lord Breitbarth, a cousin of the dead King and the strongest pretender, was assembling a major force at Damhorst, near the Kavelin-Altean border, where Ragnarson was expected to cross. Damhorst lay on the great eastern trade route, which linked Vorgreberg with the Altean capital and the coastal city-kingdoms.

Ragnarson, too, grew concerned at the paucity of news. He had expected to hear from Haroun by now. All he knew was what he had coaxed from the Alteans. One went so far as to loan him a map of the border country, a violation of his orders. Though Kendel, Ruderin, and Altea covertly supported bin Yousif's scheme, openly none could do more than grant passage to mercenaries.

There was a point, Ragnarson saw while studying the map, where the borders of Anstokin, Volstokin, Kavelin and Altea all came together. It was hilly country, almost without roads.

"What I'm thinking about," said Ragnarson, meeting with Blackfang,

Kildragon, and Tarlson, "is following the highway to this town, Staake, so it looks like I'm committed to it. Then I'll abandon the wagons, make a night march north, and enter Kavelin through the hills above this Lake Berberich. I'll swing around and take Breitbarth in the flank. Assuming he's surprised. Mocker'll let us know."

Mocker had vanished at the ferry.

Tarlson paced, mumbled, shook his head. "Your men are green. They won't stand up to it."

"Maybe not. Now's a good time to find out. I've never had much use for positional warfare."

"Bin Yousif's influence."

Bragi studied Tarlson thoughtfully. How much did he know? Or suspect?

"'Possibly. I've followed his career."

"As you said when we met, it's your command. I'll help any way I can."

"What I want is guides. Scouts. Woodsmen for outrunners."

"That's Marena Dimura country. They're touchy people. They could go either way."

"How do they stand on Breitbarth?"

"They'd like his head. He hunts them like animals."

"Lesser of two evils, then. Ride over and sign them up. Promise them Breitbarth if we catch him."

"A noble? You'd buy those savages with the life of a noble?"

"Just another man to me." He was puzzled by Tarlson's incredulity. Eanred didn't hold the Nordmen in high esteem. "I'm not one of your Kaveliner chevaliers. War's serious business. I fight to win."

"But you'll unite the Nordmen against you."

"They're unanimous already: the Queen, my employer, has to go. They're all against me anyway." He felt like saying more, but held his tongue. They might be enemies some day.

"All right. I'll go."

Reliable news awaited them at Staake, little of it good. None had come before because Baron Breitbarth had intercepted all the messengers. But one of Tarlson's men finally reached Ragnarson.

Breitbarth had convinced several barons that disposing of Ragnarson was the chief business at hand. He had gathered twenty-two hundred men at Damhorst. Further, his claim to Kavelin's crown had been recognized by Volstokin, which threatened intercession. There were rumors of a pact between Breitbarth and Volstokin's King. And, grimmest news of all, Breitbarth had seized the money meant for Ragnarson's mercenaries.

From Vorgreberg the news was better. The Queen's Own had remained loyal, and the Queen herself had managed to still unrest by going to the people in the streets. But bands of partisans had begun raiding in the country.

And there was a letter from Haroun, that came to him he knew not how. It appeared in his tent while he was out.

It covered the same information, in greater detail, and said more about Volstokin.

Not only had King Vodicka made an agreement with Breitbarth, he had made another with El Murid. After the dust had settled and Breitbarth had been crowned, Volstokin, with aid from El Murid, would occupy Kavelin...

After reflection, Bragi called Blackfang. "Make sure there's plenty of wood for the watchfires. I want them kept burning all night." The Kavelin border was just two miles away, and Damhorst only ten beyond. If his ruse was detected, Breitbarth would soon know. He needed every minute.

Moonrise came early, just after nightfall, but it was little help, being a barely visible slice.

"Has Tarlson shown yet?" he asked. He had Alteans to lead him to the border, but after that he would be on his own. Unless Tarlson turned up.

He didn't. They had to start. It took four hours to reach the border, every minute of which Ragnarson grew more worried. The men performed well enough, moving excitedly but quietly. For them it was still an adventure.

Tarlson met them at the border. "They'll help," he said, sounding surprised. "Didn't have to promise anything. Said our victory would be reward enough."

"Uhm." Bragi thought he sensed the touch of Haroun. What had bin Yousif promised?

"But we've got a problem. Two thousand Volstokiners are camped just north of here, right over their border. Rumor is they'll move to support Breitbarth if he needs it."

Ragnarson wondered if he were entering a trap.

As the night waned, his patrols reached Lake Berberich. Going slowed because of heavy fog. He didn't know whether to curse or praise it. It slowed him, but concealed him.

A Marena Dimura runner, badly winded, came sprinting up the column. Tarlson translated.

"Volstokin's moving. Their vanguard's only a mile behind us..."

iii) Saltimbanco

Could an oddly dressed, short fat man on a donkey, remarkable for his inability to handle any language properly, slide unnoticed through a hundred miles of Altean farmlands, cross a heavily patrolled border, penetrate forty miles of soldier-dense Kavelin, then appear as if by magic on the caravan route from Vorgreberg to the west? Mocker had his doubts. But also his years of experience. He dropped out of sight at the Scarlotti ferries and reappeared days later at the hamlet of Norr, well behind the Kavelin-Altean border.

Mocker arrived after the men had already gone to the fields. The women were gathering at the well. Even the youngest was a tangle-haired mess, but they were Wessons and clean.

"Hai!" the fat man cried, trying to look pathetic and harmless. "Such visions eyes of poor old wanderer have not seen in age. Hand of Queen of Beauty fell heavily on town." Suspicious eyes turned his way. "Where are menfolk? In land of humble traveler, self, husbands never stray from sprites like these." He tried not to wrinkle his nose as a crone smiled and shifted a babe from breast to wrinkled breast.

"But wait. Must observe proprieties. Must introduce self lest same be suspect for wickedry. Am called Saltimbanco. Am student philosophic of Grand Master Istwan of Senske in Matayanga. Am sent west on quest for knowledge, to seek same at academies in Hellin Daimiel." Children too small to work gathered around him. He did a ventriloquism trick and made the donkey ask for a drink. That frightened some women and disarmed others. Then he asked a meal for himself, for which he offered what he claimed was his last copper, and while he ate told several outrageous lies about the shape of the Earth. He then traveled on.

He repeated the performance in every hamlet till he reached Damhorst, thus building himself a small reputation. It was a hurry-up specter of his usual meticulous preparation. He hoped that in the disruption no one would have time to check his back trail.

Damhorst was a large town with a substantial castle atop a tall hill. As happened where armies gathered, leeches were common. One more wouldn't be noticed. A common ground at town's center was crowded by the tents of whores, ale sellers, a tattoo artist, fortune-tellers, amulet sellers, and the like. Saltimbanco would fit like a fish in water.

He arrived early. Few of his colleagues were stirring, but he quickly learned that Bragi was approaching Staake. Mumbling, he spread a rug where he would be out of traffic, yet could watch everything.

"Identical spot." He chuckled. A long time ago, when he really had been coming west, he had paused here to bilk a few Damhorsters. "And same props. Should have thrown away, Nepanthe said. Might need someday, self replied. Hai! Here is husband of same, in business at old stand." Around him he spread a collection of arcana that included bleached apes' skulls and bones from little-known eastern animals, moldy books, and glass vials filled with nasty concoctions. "So many years. Am getting old. But bilking widows hard work even for youngest, virilest man." He chuckled again. He had made his first fortune in Damhorst, by making promises to a lusty young widow named Kersten Heerboth, and had gambled it away in Altea.

He settled against a wall, nodded sleepily. Occasionally, when a rider or lady in a litter passed, he would lift his head to call desultorily, "Hai! Great Lady," or Lord, "before you sits mighty thaumaturge out of mysterious, easternmost east, with secrets of life as unlocked by mightiest of mighty eastern necromancers. Have gold-rare vials of water of fountain of youth, to supplement beauty of already most beautiful damsels of glorious Damhorst. Have potation guaranteed to banish wrinkles forever. Have cream to end eternally ghost of whiskers on great ladies' lips. Husband getting shiny on top? Have secretest dust, made at midnight full moon by Matayangan magicians, heretofore unseen west of Necremnos, guaranteed to restore hair on statue. Just mix same with blood of Escalonian snow snake, only furry snake in world, and will correct same. Snake blood also available here, prepared by adepts of bearded turtle cult deep in darkest heart of Escalon." And so forth.

It was river water, mud, and the like, but there had been a time when he had made a living selling it to ladies on the downhill side of thirty.

Near noon a shadow fell on his lap, into which he stared sleepily. He looked up into one of the nastiest faces he had ever seen. It was scarred, one-eyed, neither clean-shaven nor bearded, and wore a grin with several teeth missing and the rest rotten. Before he could say a word, the man left.

"Derran One-Eye," he muttered. "Hired blade of friend Haroun." He looked around quickly, thought he saw a familiar back vanish round a corner a block distant. Haroun? Here? He was tempted to follow. But Haroun would contact him if necessary.

Later, he decided Derran's appearance was an ill omen he should have heeded. He should have gathered his props and fled, and damn finding out what Breitbarth was up to.

Things soured that afternoon. A lady came by, a lady getting a bit paunchy and looking more than a bit wealthy. She appeared a certain victim. Did he still have the true touch? He accepted the challenge.

"Hai! Great Lady, shadow of Goddess of Love and Beauty on Mundane plane, glow of desire, harken to words of acolyte of greatest mage of east, self. Am in possession of one only packet rarest of rare herbs of Escalon, well-known but impossible of finding amantea, famous to corners of world for efficacy of treatment of teeny, tiny bit less than perfect waistlines…"

"It's him!" the woman shrieked. "And he hasn't changed a word. Harlin, Flotron, seize him."

The armed men who had been walking before and behind her sedan, puzzled, started toward the fat man.

"Woe!" Mocker cried, stumbling to his feet. "Of all ill fortunes," he shouted at the sky, "of all potential evils…" He shook a fist, gathered the skirts of his robe, and ran.

He had been seated in one position too long. Kersten's bravos overhauled him. "Self, should have stayed home," he moaned as they dragged him back. "Should have listened to Nepanthe. Should have stayed pig farmer and mud grubber. But evil gods, maybe wicked sorcerer, lured poor foolish self to fateful appointment…"

"You've been a long time delivering those emeralds," the woman said.

"O Light of Life, Doe Eyes, Dove's Breast, humblest of humble cowards encravens self. In past time, still remembered with great joy as happiest hour of otherwise miserable life, while returning from goldsmith, self was set upon by rogues. Fought like lion, armed with love, breaking bones, maiming, leaving five, six crippled for life. But dagger thrust ended resistance. Still have gruesome scar on fundament, result of same…"

"Thrash him, boys, before he breaks my heart by telling me how he couldn't possibly face me after losing all my money."

Harlin and Flotron tried to follow orders, but Mocker never accepted thrashings meekly. He got the best of it, briefly, with tricks that would have embarrassed Derran One-Eye. But he got no chance to escape. Kersten carried more weight than avoirdupois. Damhorsters by the dozen piled on. Soon he found himself being hustled to the castle and its dungeon.

There he learned things he feared he would never pass on to Bragi—because the grimmest news was that Kersten had married Baron Breitbarth.

Hour after hour, day after day, he sat on the straw-covered floor and mumbled to himself about his stupidity. When self-pity grew boring, he wondered how Bragi was doing. Well, he trusted. His companions in durance assured him that their turnkeys wouldn't be so tight-lipped and sour were things going the Baron's way.

iv) First blood

"Haaken! Reskird! Close it up! Don't worry about noise. They know we're here. Move it! They're on our ass. Eanred, ask him what's ahead."

"He came from behind."

"He knows the country, doesn't he?"

Tarlson talked with the scout.

"The lake, he says. A talus beach on the right, narrow, along the lakeside. Hills and some bluffs on the left. Very rugged, bushy country, full of ravines, but not high."

"What about this fog? Is it common? How long will it last?"

Questions and answers, questions and answers. It went so slow. "Haaken. Reskird." He gave orders.

The Trolledyngjan infantry, which had been marching at the rear, began double-timing forward. The Itaskians crowded the edge of the road till they were thoroughly mixed.

"Reskird!" Ragnarson bellowed, "get those horses back. I want contact within the hour." He galloped to the head of the column where Blackfang was replacing the vanguard with heavily armed horsemen. "Hurry it up, damn it. If the Volstokiners knew we were coming, so did Breitbarth. He'll be moving north."

Back down the line he galloped, shouting, "Move it! Move it!" at every officer he saw. Dozens of pale, tense young faces ghosted past in the mist. He saw no smiles now, heard no laughter. It had stopped being an adventure. "Tarlson! Where are you? Stick close. And keep your scout. I want to know when we get to the steepest hillsides." By the time he reached the column's rear, Kildragon and the light horse, with a platoon of bowmen, had faded back.

Soon he had done all he could, and was considering prayer. He had fifteen hundred men sandwiched between two superior, better rested, better trained forces—though as yet he had no idea where Breitbarth was. This was not the easy battle he had wanted for blooding.

Trumpets sounded in the distance. Kildragon had made contact.

On the column's right, only yards away but invisible in the mist, the lake waters lapped gently against the shore.

"Here," Tarlson said at last.

"To your left!" Ragnarson shouted. "Upslope. Move it!"

The soldiers began climbing.

The hills, barely tall enough to be called such, rose above the mist. In the dawnlight Ragnarson arranged his troops in strong clumps on their lakeward faces.

He hoped the mist would not burn off too soon.

Reskird's party soon passed below, invisible, raising a clatter, and moments later were followed by a strong force of cavalry. Ragnarson signaled his officers to hold fire.

The mist had begun to thin by the time the enemy main force moved to where Ragnarson wanted them. He could discern the vague dark shapes of mounted officers hurrying their infantry companies… He gave the signal.

Arrows sleeted into the mist. Cries of surprise and pain answered them. Ragnarson counted a minute, during which thousands of arrows fled his bows, then signaled a charge. The Trolledyngjans led, shaking the hills with their warcries.

Ragnarson leaned forward in his saddle, wearily, and awaited results.

The Volstokiners had been in good spirits, confident of victory. The sudden rain of death had stunned them. They could see no enemies. And while trying to form up over the dead and wounded, the Trolledyngjans hit them like an avalanche of wolves.

The fog cleared within the hour. Little but carnage remained. The surviving Volstokiners had run into the water. Some, trying to swim away, had drowned. Ragnarson's archers were using heads for targets. Trolledyngjans on captured horses were splashing about, chopping heads. The water was scarlet.

"Won't you take prisoners?" Tarlson asked. He spoke not a word of praise.

"Not yet. They'd just go home, re-arm, and come back. I hope this'll put Volstokin out of the picture."

A messenger from Blackfang arrived. The commander of the Volstokin vanguard, some four hundred men, stunned, had asked terms after only a brief skirmish.

"All right," said Ragnarson, "they can have their lives and shoes. The enlisted men. Strip them and send them packing."

Below, his men, tired of slaughter, were allowing surrender. "Let's see what we've caught." He wanted to get down there before there were disputes over loot. The Volstokiners had even brought a bevy of carts and wagons full of camp followers.

He dismounted and walked slowly through the carnage. His own casualties were few. In places the Volstokiners were heaped. Luck had ridden with him again. He paused a moment beside Ragnar Bjornson—no older than he had been in his first battle—who grinned through the pain of a wound. "Some folks will do anything to get out of walking," Bragi said, resting a hand on the youth's shoulder. Someone had said the same to him long ago.

It was terribly quiet. It always seemed that way afterward, as if the only sound left in the world was the cawling of the ravens.

A dead man caught his eye. Something odd about him. He paused. Too dark for Volstokin. An aquiline nose. Haroun had been right. El Murid had advisers in Volstokin.

He shook his head sadly. This little backwater kingdom was becoming the focus of a lot of intrigue.

Haaken came in with thirty prisoners and hundreds of heavily laden horses. "Got some odd ones here, Bragi," he said, indicating several dusky men.

"I know. El Murid's. Kill them. One by one. See if the weakest will tell you anything." The remainder he had herded together with officers already captured.

Volstokin had lost nearly fifteen hundred men while Bragi had had sixty-one killed. Had his people been more experienced, he thought, even fewer would have been lost. It had been a perfect ambush.

"What now?" Tarlson asked.

"We bury our dead and divide the spoils."

"And then? There's still Lord Breitbarth."

"We disappear. Got to let the men digest what they've done. Right now they think they're invincible. They've got to realize they haven't faced a disciplined enemy. And we'll need time to let the news spread. May swing some support to the Queen."

"And to Lord Breitbarth. Hangers-back would join him to make sure of you. They've got to keep the Crown up for grabs."

"I know. But I want to avoid action for a few weeks. The men need rest and training. Haaken! See the Marena Dimura get shares." He had noticed the scouts, as ragged and bloody as any of his troops, lurking about the fringes, eyeing plunder uncertainly. One, who was supposed to be a man of importance, seemed enthralled by a brightly painted wagon filled with equally painted but terrified women. "Give the old man the whore wagon."

That proved a providential act. It brought him warning, next day, of a party of Breitbarth's horses ranging far ahead of the Baron. In a brisk skirmish he took two hundred prisoners, killed another hundred, and sent the remainder to their commander in a panic. Tarlson said Breitbarth relied heavily on his knights and was a cautious sort likely to withdraw after the setback.

He did so. And more barons rallied to Damhorst. Breitbarth's force swelled to three thousand.

The westward movement of baronial forces left partisans from the underclasses free to slaughter one another elsewhere. More and more Marena Dimura gravitated toward Ragnarson, who remained in the hill country near the Volstokin border, moving camp every few days. The natives kept him informed of Breitbarth's actions.

Those amounted to patrols in force and a weekly sally north a day's march, followed by a day's bivouac, then a withdrawal into Damhorst.

Ragnarson began to worry about Mocker. He should have heard from the fat man by now.

Eanred left him, declaring it was time to resume his command. The Queen was under little pressure, but rumor had marauders riding to the suburbs of Vorgreberg. That had to stop.

It was now an open secret that Breitbarth held the money intended for Bragi's men, but they, fat on loot and self-confidence, weren't grumbling. Everyone told everyone else that the Colonel would take them down to Damhorst and get it back.

EIGHT: YEAR 1002 AFE
CAMPAIGN AGAINST REBELLION

i) In flight

The news the Marena Dimura brought caused Ragnarson to grow increasingly unsettled. Breitbarth grew stronger by the day. His numbers reached four thousand, many heavily armed knights. The Baron's sallies became more daring. Ragnarson's patrols came under increasing pressure. He had added four hundred men to his force, but they were Marena Dimura and Wessons without training. He used them as guides and raiders.

He began to fear Breitbarth would split his force and move against Vorgreberg.

During his examination of the country toward Damhorst he had found the place where he wanted to do battle. It was on the north side of a dense forest belonging to Breitbarth himself. It began near the Ebeler a dozen miles northeast of Damhorst. Roads ran round both sides, from Damhorst to the town and castle of Bodenstead, but the western route was the shortest and likeliest way Breitbarth would come to relieve Bodenstead.

This was gently rolling country. A lightly wooded ridge ran from Bodenstead northwest a mile to the hamlet of Ratdke, overlooking plains on either side. From Bodenstead through the forest ran a hunting trail, unsuitable for Breitbarth's knights, along which Ragnarson could flee if the worst happened.

North of the western route were thick apple orchards on ground too soft for heavy cavalry. The Baron would have to come at him through a narrow place, under his bows.

But even the best-laid plans, and so forth.

To taunt Breitbarth, Ragnarson brought his main force south, moving swift as the news of his coming, laying a trail of destruction from one Nordmen castle to the next. He met surprisingly little resistance. The knights and lesser nobility who remained in their fiefs showed a preference for surrender to siege. The fires of burning castles and towns bearded the horizons as Ragnarson's forces spread out to glean the richest loot.

At first he thought Breitbarth was practicing Fabian tactics, but each prisoner he interviewed, and each report he received, further convinced him that the Baron was paralyzed by indecision.

His train and troops became so burdened with plunder that he made a serious miscalculation. Hitherto he had kept the Ebeler, a deep, sluggish tributary of the Scarlotti, between himself and Breitbarth. But at the insistence of his followers, who wanted to get their loot to safekeeping with the men he had left at Staake, he crossed the river at Armstead, a mile from Altea and just twelve from Damhorst. It took two days to clear the narrow ford. Breitbarth missed a great opportunity.

But the Baron didn't remain quiescent long. When Bragi marched east into the wine-growing country on which the Baron's wealth was based, Breitbarth came out of Damhorst in a fury.

Whether Breitbarth had planned this Ragnarson wasn't sure, but he did know that he had gotten himself into a trap. This was relatively flat country, clear, ideal for Breitbarth's knights. He had nothing with which to face those. Even the fury of his Itaskian bows wouldn't break a concerted charge across an open plain.

He found the eastern Ebeler fords closed and had no time to force them. Breitbarth was close behind, his troops raising dust on all the east-running roads. There was nothing to do but run ahead of him.

Breitbarth gained ground. His forces were unburdened by loot, of which Bragi's men had already re-amassed tons, and his men were fresh. In a few days his patrols were within eyeshot of Ragnarson's rearguard.

He was in the richest wine country now, and the vineyards, with the hedgerows around them, reduced the speed he could make by compelling him to stay on the road.

"Haaken," he said as they rose on their fourth morning of flight and saw dust already rising in the west, "we don't run after today."

"But they've got us three to one..."

"I know. But the more we run, the worse the odds. Find me a place to make a stand. Maybe they'll offer terms." He had grown pessimistic, blamed himself for their straits.

Just before noon Blackfang returned and reported a good place not far ahead, a hillside vineyard where Breitbarth's knights would have rough going. There was a town called Lieneke in the way, but it was undefended and the inhabitants were scattering.

Haaken had chosen well. The hill was the steepest Ragnarson had seen in days, hairy with large grapevines that could conceal his men, and the only clear access for horsemen was the road itself, which climbed in switchbacks and was flanked by tall, thick shrubberies. Moreover, the plain facing the hill was nearly filled by Lieneke, which would make getting troops in formation difficult. Ragnarson raised his banners at the hillcrest.

The position had disadvantages. Though he anchored his flanks on a wood at his right and a ravine on his left, neither could more than slow a determined attack. He worried.

He stationed every man who could handle a bow in the vineyards and behind the hedges. The rest he kept at the crest of the hill, in view from below, including the recruits gathered in Kavelin. He feared those, if committed, would flee under pressure and panic the bowmen. Haaken he gave command of the left, Reskird the right. He retained control of the men on the crest.

Breitbarth appeared before Ragnarson completed his dispositions, but remained on the outskirts of Lieneke. Troops began piling up in the town.

Late in the afternoon a rider came up under a flag of truce, said, "My Lord, Baron Breitbarth wishes terms."

So, Ragnarson thought, the man isn't a complete fool. "I want the surrender of himself and one hundred of his knights, and his oath that no vassal of his will again stand in rebellion against the Queen. Ransoms can be arranged later."

The messenger was taken aback. At last he blurted, "Terms for your surrender."

Ragnarson chuckled. "Oh. I thought he'd come to turn himself in. Well, no point you wasting your trip. Let's hear them."

Bragi was to return all plunder, surrender himself and his officers to the mercy of Breitbarth, and his men were to accept service in Breitbarth's forces for the duration of the unrest in Kavelin.

They weren't the sort of terms usually offered mercenaries. They meant death for Bragi and his officers. No one ransomed mercenaries. He had to fight. But he kept up negotiations till dark, buying time while his men dug trenches and raised ramparts along their flanks. Breitbarth showed no inclination to surround the position. Perhaps he expected a diplomatic victory. More likely, he just did not see.

Night brought drizzling rain. It made the men miserable, but Bragi cheerful. The hill would be treacherous for horsemen.

Dawn came, a bright, clear, hot summer's morning. Breitbarth ordered his forces. Ragnarson did the same.

The Baron sent a final messenger. As the white flag came up the hill, Bragi told Haaken, "I'd better get this going before somebody down there suffers a stroke of smarts." Breitbarth, confident in his numbers and knights, had made no effort to surround him or get on his flanks.

The terms offered were no better. Bragi listened patiently, then replied, "Tell the Baron that if he won't come surrender, I'll come down and make him." The negotiations had given him enough insight into Breitbarth to anticipate that the challenge, from a ragtag hire-sword, would throw him into a rage. These Kaveliners, even his Marena Dimura, were bemused by chivalry and nobility. It was a blind spot he meant to exploit mercilessly.

ii) Second blood

The baronial forces stirred. At the crest of the hill, Bragi and a handful of messengers, behind the ranks of Trolledyngjans and Marena Dimura, waited and observed. Ragnarson directed his brief comments to an Itaskian sergeant named Altenkirk, whose service went back to the wars, and who had spent years in the Lesser Kingdoms advising the native armies.

"Now we see if they learned anything from the wars and Lake Berberich," he said.

"He'll send the knights," Altenkirk promised. "We're only commoners and infantry. We can't beat our betters. It's a chance to blood their swords cheaply." His sarcasm was strong.

Ragnarson chuckled. "We'll see. We'll see. Ah. You're right. Here they come, straight up the road."

With pennons and banners flying, trumpets blaring, and drums beating in Lieneke. The townsfolk turned out as if this were the tournament Breitbarth seemed to think. All night knights and men-at-arms had been swelling the Baron's forces in hopes of a share of glory.

As it began, Ragnarson received a messenger from Vorgreberg. The situation there had become grim because news of his entrapment below the Ebeler had reached the local nobility. Several had marched on the capital, hoping to seize it before Breitbarth. Eanred was playing one against another, but his job had been complicated by a Siluro uprising in Vorgreberg itself. A mob had tried to take Castle Krief by surprise, and had failed. Hundreds had been slaughtered. House to house fighting continued. Would Ragnarson be so kind as to come help?

"Tell him I'll get there when I can." He returned to the matter at hand.

Breitbarth's knights started up the road four abreast, apparently unaware that it narrowed on the hillside. At the first turn they became clogged, and the sky darkened with arrows.

Breitbarth broadened his attack, sending more knights to root out Ragnarson's archers. As they blundered about on the soft earth of the vineyards, becoming entangled in the vines, arrows sleeted down upon them.

Turning to Altenkirk, Ragnarson said, "Send a Trolledyngjan company down each side to finish the unhorsed."

It went on. And on. And on. Attacking in three divisions, Breitbarth's best seldom got close enough to strike a blow.

On the left they began to waver. Ragnarson saw Blackfang appearing and disappearing among the vines as he prepared a counterattack.

"I think," said Altenkirk, after having returned and surveyed the situation, "that you've done it again. They'll break."

"Maybe. I'll help them along. Take charge of the Marena Dimura. Hold them back till it's sure." He led the mounted Trolledyngjans down the far left side of the vineyard, outflanking Blackfang, then wheeled and charged a mass of already panicky knights.

Breitbarth's right collapsed. Pressured by Bragi's horsemen, under a terrible arrowstorm, they fled into their center, which broke in its turn and fell back on Breitbarth's left. In a confusion of tripping horses and raining arrows, the slaughter grew grim.

Resistance collapsed. Hundreds threw down their arms. Hundreds more fled in unknightly panic, with Reskird's arrows pursuing.

Ragnarson hastily solidified his line and wheeled to face Lieneke, where the indecisive Baron retained a strong reserve. Such of the enemy as remained on the hill he left to the Marena Dimura.

In brisk order the Trolledyngjans formed a shield wall. The Itaskians, sure they could bring the world to its knees, fell in behind and began arcing long shots at Breitbarth.

"I could still lose," Ragnarson told himself, staring at the massed Kaveliners. The Baron's reserves were mostly spearmen, but there were enough knights to make him uncomfortable.

He need not have feared. Those knights broke at the first flight. Only Breitbarth's infantry stood fast, and they seemed as dazed as the Baron, who did little to defend himself. The arrowstorm, applied from beyond the range of Breitbarth's arbalesters, broke up the infantry formations.

Ragnarson suffered his heaviest casualties in the final mixup. His Trolledyngjans broke formation to wolf in and catch someone who would bring a good ransom.

His men had performed near optimum, yet the battle left him unsatisfied. "Haaken," he said after they had occupied Breitbarth's pavilion, "we didn't win a thing."

"What? It's a great victory. They'll be bragging for years."

"Yes. A great slaughter. A dramatic show. But not decisive. That's the key, Haaken. Decisive. All we've gained is loot and prisoners. There're more Volstokiners —the Marena Dimura say they're levying heavily up there —and more Nordmen. They can lose indefinitely, as long as they win the last battle."

Reskird came in. "What's up?"

"Depressed. Like always, after," Blackfang replied. "What's the score?"

Kildragon dropped onto a couch. "Breitbarth had taste," he said, looking around. "We've counted two thousand bodies and a thousand prisoners already. What I came about was, one of Breitbarth's people said they've got a fat brown man in the dungeon at Damhorst. Could be Mocker. Also, Volstokin himself has marched with five thousand men."

"Going to be a hard winter up there, then," said Blackfang, "pulling so many men off the farms."

"Expect they figure they'll live off the spoils," Kildragon replied. "Bragi, what next?"

Ragnarson shook his preoccupations. "You been thinking about replacing the Itaskian officers with loyal people? Haaken, what about your officers? Will they stick?"

"As long as we're winning."

Kildragon, after consideration, replied, "The same. I don't think they've had specific instructions. Yet."

"Good. I've been thinking some things that won't win us any points with Haroun or the Queen."

"Such as?"

"First, putting everyone on a horse, prisoners too, and roaring off to spring Mocker. After that, I don't know. We'll keep out of Volstokin's way, unless we can nab Vodicka himself. He'll take casualties because his people are green…"

"That's what they thought about us," Reskird reminded.

"Uhm. Maybe. We'll see. Maybe we'll go to work on him if he splits his forces. Meanwhile, we stay out of the way till the pieces fall."

"Tarlson won't like that."

"Too bad. He worries too much. Vorgreberg hasn't been taken since Imperial times."

iii) Speaking for the Queen

Getting Mocker out proved easier said than done. Bragi marched swiftly westward, but the Baroness had sealed her gates the moment news of her husband's defeat had arrived. Ragnarson had no stomach for a siege, what with Volstokin just a few days north of the Ebeler. He tried negotiation.

The Baroness knew about Volstokin, too. She tried to hold him till Vodicka arrived.

"Looks like Lard Bottom's going to languish a while," Ragnarson told Kildragon. "I'll pull out tonight. All the loot over the border?"

"Last train left this morning. You know, if we quit now we'd be rich."

"We've got a contract."

"You want to try something tonight?"

"No. She'll expect it. Might've worked when we first showed."

"What about Vodicka?"

"He's headed for Armstead?"

"So I'm told. I'm never sure I can trust the Marena Dimura."

"Take two hundred bowmen. Make him pay to cross. But pull out once they get a bridgehead. I'll head south, wipe out a few barons. Catch up when you can."

"Right. You want I should play cat and mouse?"

"No. You might get caught. I can't afford to lose two hundred bows."

Bragi slipped away in the night, leaving Kildragon to keep the campfires burning. He returned to Lieneke, then turned south and plundered the provinces of Froesel and Delhagen, destroying nearly forty Nordmen castles and fortresses, till he came to Sedlmayr, one of Kavelin's major cities and, like Damhorst, a focal point of Nordmen rebellion. This was mountainous country where goat herding, sheep herding, dairying, cheese making, and wool production were important. The snow-topped mountains reminded him of Trolledyngja.

He besieged Sedlmayr a week, but had no heart for it, so was about to move on again when a deputation of Wesson merchants, deep in the night, spirited themselves into his camp. Their spokesman, one Cham Mundwiller, was a forthright, lean, elderly gentleman whose style reminded Bragi of the Minister.

"We've come to offer you Sedlmayr," Mundwiller said. "On conditions."

"Of course. What?"

"That you minimize the fighting and looting."

"Reasonable, but hard to guarantee. Wine? It's Baron Breitbarth's best." The Baron had taken hard the fact that the Baroness refused to go his ransom. "Master Mundwiller, I'm interested. But I don't understand your motives."

"Having you camped here is bad for business. And production. It's almost shearing time, and we can't get the cheese in to the presses, or out to the caves for aging. Second, we've no love for Baron Kartye or his brother vultures in Delhagen. Their taxes devour our profits. We're Wessons, sir. That makes us the beasts of burden whose backs support the Nordmen. We hear you're correcting that with a sword."

"Ah. I thought so. And your plans for Sedlmayr's future?"

They were evasive. Slippery as merchants, Ragnarson thought, smiling wryly.

"Might they involve Colonel Phiambolis? Or Tuchol Kiriakos? You'd have a hard time convincing me they're tourists accidentally caught by my siege. Too big a coincidence, them being siege specialists. And Baron Kartye, being Nordmen, would be too proud to hire mercenaries." The presence of Kiriakos and Phiambolis, two of the masterminds behind Hellin Daimiel's years-long stand against El Murid, had been one of his reasons for wishing to move on.

"How did you know?…" one merchant gasped.

"My ears are covered with hair, but they're sharp." The presence of the mercenaries had been reported by a Sir Andvbur Kimberlin of Karadja, a Nordmen loyalist he had recently freed.

Enough former prisoners, and recruits picked up here and there, had stuck for Ragnarson to replace all losses as well as to form a native battalion under Sergeant Altenkirk, who spoke Marena Dimura well. He was now considering splitting that battalion and giving Sir Andvbur command of the Wessons.

"You might even be thinking of declaring Sedlmayr a free city—after I've killed your Nordmen for you."

Expressions said he had struck close. He chuckled.

Mundwiller put a bold face on it. "You're right." To the others, who protested, "He might as well know. He'd act on his suspicions." To Ragnarson, "One gold solidi for each soldier, five for sergeants, twenty for officers, and a hundred for yourself."

"Interesting," said Ragnarson. "A fortune for a night's work. But not that much compared to the loot we've already taken. And there's my contract with the Queen. The more I learn about the woman, the more I want to keep it. Were she not saddled with a nation of opportunists, she might be one of the better rulers Kavelin's had." Quote from Sir Andvbur, an idealistic youth who placed the good of the kingdom first, who believed nobles should be curators and conservators, not divinely appointed exploiters.

But even the Queen's enemies had little evil to say of her. There was nothing personal in the Nordmen rebellion. It was generated by power-lust alone.

Ragnarson's admiration for the woman, in large part, stemmed from the fact that she did not interfere. In other times and places he had suffered snowstorms of directives from employers.

Tarlson was another matter. He sent out blizzards of messages.

"What can we offer?" Mundwiller finally asked.

"Your allegiance to Her Majesty."

They did a lot of foot-shuffling and floor-staring.

"Suppose a direct charter could be arranged, with Sedlmayr and Delhagen as Royal fiefs in keeping of a Council of Aldermen? Direct responsibility to the Crown."

That wasn't what the majority wanted, but Mundwiller saw they would get nothing better. "Can you speak for the Queen?"

"No. Only to her. But if Sedlmayr swears allegiance, supports the throne, and faithfully resists the rebels, I'll press your cause powerfully. She should be amenable, coming from the Auszura Littoral. She'll be familiar with the Bedelian League and what those cities have done to hasten recovery from the wars."

"We'll have to consider what might happen if we announce fealty. An army of two, Phiambolis and Kiriakos, isn't much defense against outraged Nordmen."

"I don't think they'll bother you till they rid themselves of the Queen."

"It's your chances we'll be studying."

"You'll get no better offer. Or opportunity," said Ragnarson.

Once the deputation left, Bragi told Blackfang, "Start packing in the morning. Make it look like we're planning to slip away in the night. I don't want to wait while they play games."

Next night Cham Mundwiller was back, upset, wanting to know why Ragnarson was leaving.

"What's your decision?" Bragi asked.

"For. Reluctantly on some parts. Our more timid souls don't think your luck will hold. Personally, I'm satisfied. It's what I've been arguing for all along."

"Tonight?"

"Everything's ready."

"Then so are we."

"One little matter. Some articles for you to sign. That was the hard part, getting them to accept a position from which they couldn't back down."

Ragnarson chuckled as he examined the parchment. "An exchange, then. My own guarantees." He handed the man a document he had had prepared. "And my word, which's worth more. Unless your fealty becomes suspect."

"As an act of good faith, some information which, I believe, only I outside the Nordmen councils possess."

Ragnarson's eyebrows rose questioningly.

"The Captal of Savernake has been making the rounds of the barons. He slipped out of Sedlmayr just before you arrived."

"So?"

"He claims the true child of the old King is in his custody. You've heard the stories about a changeling? He's trying to find backers for his 'real' heir."

"The Captal," Bragi interjected. "He's old?" He described the sorcerer he and Mocker had encountered in Ruderin.

"You've met?"

"In passing. You've told me more than you realize, friend. I'll return the favor, but don't spread it around. The power behind the Captal is Shinsan."

Mundwiller went pale. "What interest could they have in Kavelin?"

"A passage to the west. A quietly attained bridgehead against the day when they move to attain world dominion. All spur-of-the-moment speculation, of course. Who knows the motives of Shinsan?"

"True. We move at the second hour. I'm to lead you to the postern we hold."

iv) Savernake Gap

Bragi occupied Sedlmayr without disturbing its citizens' sleep, capturing the Nordmen and disarming their troops. Baron Kartye had assumed he would decamp in the night.

Sedlmayr taken, Ragnarson secured Delhagen, then decamped in earnest.

Ragnarson departed with twenty-five hundred men, over half of them Kaveliners. None were men he had given Reskird to dispute the Armstead ford. If forced to fight, he would miss those bows.

Kildragon, he learned, had held the ford so successfully that he had almost turned Vodicka back—till the Baroness Breitbarth had surprised him from behind. He had barely gotten out. Fleeing east, he had encountered Volstokiners who had crossed the river above him. He had abandoned everything but his weapons, swum the Ebeler, and was now hiding in the Bodenstead forest.

Vodicka had shown his gratitude to the Baroness by making her prisoner and sacking Damhorst. That gentleman had abandoned all pretense, was destroying everyone and everything as he advanced toward Vorgreberg.

The barons harrying the capital now eyed him as the greater danger.

In Volstokin itself there was trouble, bands of horsemen cutting, in the guerrilla style, at the roots of royal power. Ragnarson suspected Haroun.

Good. Nothing prevented him from doing what he wanted. He marched eastward, passed within twenty miles of Vorgreberg, struck the caravan route east of the city and, spreading panic among the Nordmen, swept on till he entered Savernake, at the juncture of the Kapenrungs and Mountains of M'Hand, where the Savernake Gap debouched into Kavelin. He considered the Captal the most dire threat to the Queen.

His arrow-straight drive didn't slow till he had entered the Gap itself and had climbed above the timberline. Then he stopped cold. He summoned Blackfang, Altenkirk, Jarl Ahring, subbing for Kildragon, and Sir Andvbur Kimberlin of Karadja, in command of the new Wesson battalion.

The five considered the Gap above. Behind them, men seized the opportunity to rest.

"I don't like it," Ragnarson said. "Too quiet." The pass did seem as still as a desert.

"Almost as if time had stopped," said Blackfang. "You'd expect an eagle or something."

Altenkirk spoke to one of the Marena Dimura. The man examined the road ahead.

Ragnarson, blue eyes frosty, studied the sky. He had scouts out. They were to send up smoke in case of trouble.

"I've been this way before," said Sir Andvbur, "and have heard tell it gets like this when the Captal's expecting a fight."

The Marena Dimura said something to Altenkirk, who translated, "The scouts are still ahead of us."

"Uhm. The Captal knows we're coming. In Trolledyngja they defend passes by rolling rocks down on people. Altenkirk, put a company on each face. Have them root out anything bigger than a mouse. It'll be slow, but caution's more important than speed now."

"It's only four or five miles to Maisak," said Sir Andvbur. "Around that bluff that looks like a man's face. It's built against the mountain where the pass narrows. The Imperial engineers used natural caverns for barracks, laying the least possible masonry."

Bragi had gone through the Gap to Necremnos once, a few years after the wars, but his memories were vague. He had been in a hurry to see a woman.

Marena Dimura filtered up the rugged slopes. The troops below perked up, saw to their weapons. The day-after-day, week-after-week grind of the march, without a pause to loot or fight or carouse, had eroded morale. Prospective action lifted that.

"What's that?" asked Ragnarson, indicating a wisp of blackness over the formation Sir Andvbur had pointed out. "Not smoke?"

"The Captal's sorcery, I'd guess," said the knight.

"Send your people for more firewood. We'll make our own light. Have some men stand by with what we've got. Ahring, bring your best bowmen up to support the Marena Dimura."

Once they had left, Ragnarson told Blackfang, "Maybe it's mother's witch-blood, Haaken. I've got a bad feeling."

"You're sure this's the sorcerer from Ruderin?"

"Reasonably."

"Think I'll have a bad feeling myself." He chuckled. "Here we sit without even Mocker's phony magic, getting ready to storm a vassal of Shinsan."

"That's my worry, Haaken. The Captal's just supposed to be a dabbler. But what's Shinsan put in?"

"Imagine we'll find out."

"Haaken, I don't know what I'd do without you." He laughed weakly. "Don't know what to do with you, either, but that's another problem."

"Don't start your death dance yet."

"Eh?"

"We've been through the campaigns. You're going to tell me how to run things after you've found the spear with your name."

"Damn. Next time I'm using new people." He laughed.

Marena Dimura shouted on the slopes. Something broke cover, ran a few yards toward them, then fled the other way. A bowstring twanged. The creature jumped, screamed, fell. Ragnarson and Blackfang moved up, a dozen bowmen at their backs.

"What is it?" Blackfang asked. The body was the size of that of a six-year-old. It had the head of a squirrel.

"Colonel!"

Bragi glanced up. A Marena Dimura tossed something. He caught it. A child-sized crossbow.

Haaken caught a quiver of bolts, pulled one out, examined its head. "Poisoned."

Ragnarson had the word passed, saw shields start to be carried less sloppily.

"Poor fellow," said Blackfang, turning the corpse with a foot. "Didn't want to fight. Could've gotten off a shot."

"Maybe the light was too bright." Ragnarson studied the black cloud growing over the bluff with the face of a man.

During the next hour, as the sky darkened, the Marena Dimura flushed two score creatures of almost as many shapes. Several of Ragnarson's people learned the hard way about the poisoned bolts. The little people weren't aggressive, but they got ferocious when cornered.

"Wait'll you see the owl-faced ones," Ragnarson said as they reached the natural obelisk he had marked as their goal for the hour. "Some as big as you, and even uglier."

"Speaking of ugly," Haaken replied with sudden grimness.

They had found the missing scouts.

The men hung on a gallows-like rack, from curved spikes piercing the bases of their skulls. The flesh was gone from their faces, fingers, and toes. Their bellies had been ripped open. Their bowels hung to the ground. Their hearts had been cut out. Painted in blood on a pale boulder were the Itaskian words, "Leave Kavelin."

"That's Shinsan work, sure," Blackfang growled.

"Must be," Sir Andvbur agreed. "The Captal's dramatics were never this grisly."

"Get that writing cleaned up," said Ragnarson. "Then let the men see this. Ought to get them vengeance-mad."

The sight did stir a new, grim determination, especially among the Marena Dimura. Hitherto they had done no more than flush the Captal's timorous creatures. Now they hunted for blood.

Intensity of resistance rose sharply. Bragi moved more archers up to support the Marena Dimura, and Trolledyngjans to shield the bowmen from any sudden charge. He had fires and torches lighted and slowed the advance to an even more cautious pace.

A little later, while they waited for the Trolledyngjans to clear the road of a band of armored owl-faces behind a boulder barricade, he asked Sir Andvbur, "How long before the snows come? Soon?"

"Within the month, this high up."

"Bad. We've got to take Maisak or they'll have all winter to strengthen it."

"True. We couldn't maintain a siege once winter came."

"Not with what we've got. Haaken, get those boulders cleared. We don't want bottlenecks behind us."

Against continually increasing resistance, Ragnarson's men had the best of the casualty ratio.

It became completely dark. The men grew concerned about sorcery. There was little Bragi could do to reassure them.

As they neared the bluff, resistance ceased. Ragnarson ordered a halt.

"I'd trade my share of the plunder for a staff wizard," he muttered. "What do we do now? Even during the wars nobody rooted the Captal out. And then he was using more normal defenses. Why should he fear an attack from this direction?"

"It's the caverns," said Sir Andvbur. "Maisak's built over their easternmost mouths. There're lots of openings here on the west slope. During the wars, once he'd pushed some scouts past, El Murid almost took Maisak by sending men back underground. Most vanished in the maze, but some did reach the fortress."

"He didn't seal them?"

"Those he could find. But what's been sealed can be unsealed."

"Uhm. Altenkirk, pass the word to look for caves. But not to go in."

The next phase of the Captal's defense exploded on leathery wings. Flying things, from man-sized like the one Ragnarson had seen in Ruderin to creatures little bigger than the bats they resembled, suddenly swarmed overhead. Bragi's staff were the focal point, but escaped injury. The winged things' only weapon was a poisoned dart impelled by gravity.

"This can't be his last defense," Ragnarson declared.

"There's an open, flat place the other side of Stone Face," said Sir Andvbur. "Suitable for battle."

"Uhm. Could we see it from up top?" Ragnarson indicated the highest point of the formation. No one answered. "That's what we'll do. Haaken, take over. Don't go past the bluff. Altenkirk, give me three of your best men. One should speak a language I do. Sir Andvbur, come with me."

v) Woman of the mists

The peak provided a god's eye view of the pass and Maisak. From it Ragnarson saw things he hadn't cared to view. In the open area Sir Andvbur had described, drawn up in line of battle, statue-still among hundreds of illuminating fires, were the most fearsome warriors he had ever seen, each clad in black, chitinous armor.

"Shinsan," he whispered. "Four, five hundred. We'll never cut our way through."

"We've beaten armies three times our number."

"Armed rabbles," said Ragnarson. "The Dread Empire trains its soldiers from childhood. They don't question, they don't disobey, they don't panic. They stand, they fight, they die, and they retreat only when they've got orders. And they're the best soldiers, fighting, you'll find. Or so I'm told by people who're supposed to know. This's my first encounter."

"We could bring bowmen up."

"Right. Having come this far, I can't pull out without trying." He turned to send a Marena Dimura to Blackfang and Ahring. "Sir Andvbur. What do you make of that?" He indicated the far distance, where countless fires burned.

"Looks like the eastern barons have gotten together."

"Uhm. How far?"

"They're still in high pastureland. Near Baxendala. Three days. Two if they hurry. I don't think they will, considering the showing you've made. They'll piddle around till it's too late to back out."

"Think they'll come after us? Or wait there, hoping we get the worst of the Captal?"

Sir Andvbur shrugged. "You never know what a Nordmen will do. What's unreasonable to a logical mind. Tell you what. If you want to go ahead here, I'll take my Wessons down and set an ambush. We won't be much help against Shinsan."

"This requires a staff meeting," said Ragnarson. "Those Shinsaners will wait. Let's slide back down."

To his surprise, he found his officers unanimous. They should try taking Maisak. They found the presence of Shinsan unsettling, but an argument for immediate attack. The advance base must be denied the Dread Empire. The baronial forces they would worry about later.

They were getting a little blasé about the barons, Bragi feared.

He detailed Sir Andvbur, the Wessons, Altenkirk, and half the Marena Dimura to prepare a reception for the barons twelve miles west, in the pines around the tiny lake and marshy meadow where the Ebeler had its headwaters. As always, he chose ground difficult for horsemen.

He prepared meticulously for his engagement with Shinsan, bringing up tons of firewood, having his men erect a series of rock barricades across the floor of the pass, preparing boulders for rolling down on those positions as they were lost, and locating dozens of snipers on the slopes to support the Trolledyngjans, who would do the close fighting. He had several thousand arrows taken to the bluff top. And he sent Marena Dimura to hunt ways to bring small forces against Maisak itself, and to locate every possible cave mouth. He invested a day and a half preparing.

From the bluff it looked as though the enemy hadn't moved, though Bragi knew they rotated for rest. "Well," he muttered, looking down at all that armor, "no point putting it off." Blackfang was awaiting the first onslaught. "Loose!"

Twenty shafts began their drop. In the gloom and shifting light, downhill shooting was tricky. Ragnarson didn't expect much, though his bowmen were his best.

But figures toppled, a few with each flight. Their armor wasn't impervious.

"Gods, are they mute?" one archer muttered. Never a cry echoed up. But Shinsan's soldiers fought and died in utter silence. It disconcerted the most fearless enemies.

The enemy commander had to make a decision. From his Marena Dimura Ragnarson knew a force couldn't be sent up the bluff from the Maisak side. Shinsan would have to withdraw into the fortress, or advance, to break through and secure the bluff from behind. Standing fast meant slow but certain slaughter. The peak was high enough that arrows from bows below were spent on arrival.

Shinsan did three things: sent a company against Ragnarson's walls of stone, withdrew forces that couldn't be brought to bear, and rolled out a pair of heavy, wheeled ballistae with which they fired back.

"Take care!" Ragnarson snapped after a shaft the size of a knight's lance growled a foot over his head. "Duck when you see them trigger. You won't see the shaft coming. You, you, you. Put some fire arrows on them."

He had a sudden premonition, pulled five men back and had them watch for an aerial attack.

"Colonel, they're moving a platoon to the canyon."

"Hurt those you can. Mind the ballistae. You men, look sharp. Now's the time they'll come."

And they did, a swarm of leather-winged hellspawn who, though anticipated, exploded upon them in a sudden shower of poisoned darts. The bigger ones tried to force his archers off the bluff. One man plunged to his death. Then they were gone.

Ragnarson searched the rim for grapnels with depending lines, found two, smiled grimly. He would have tried that himself. Those gone, he threw the enemy casualties after them. He expected Shinsan would send the winged things each time reinforcements went in below, and wasn't disappointed. His men soon slaughtered most of them. He lost two more people. The arrow fire scarcely slackened. He plied a dead man's bow himself.

A messenger came from Blackfang. The first barricade had fallen. The spirits of the men remained good, though they were awed by the prowess and determination of their enemies. They knew they were in a real fight this time.

Ragnarson had had seven barricades erected, manning the first four with a hundred men apiece. The rest of his forces were building an eighth and ninth. To beat him Shinsan would have to seize old walls faster than he could build new ones.

The first four hours of fighting were uneventful, Haaken's Trolledyngjans hacked it out toe to toe with Shinsan while the Itaskians showered the enemy with arrows. Casualties were heavy on both sides, but the ratio favored Ragnarson because of his superior bows. Even fighting from barricades the Trolledyngjans got the worst of the close combat.

When Haaken sent word that the fifth wall was weakening, he began withdrawing from the bluff. Otherwise he would be cut off. It would have been nice to have denied it to the enemy, but he thought the battle would be decided before Shinsan could take advantage of it. He left two Marena Dimura to keep an eye on Maisak.

Before he departed, he examined the western slopes. It should be true night down there. He saw no campfires, but did spot the beacon Sir Andvbur was supposed to light when the barons neared his position. Assuming he beat Shinsan, which wasn't likely, could he handle the barons? His men would be weary and weak.

"Colonel."

He turned.

A new dimension had been given Shinsan's attack. He wondered if it were because of his withdrawal.

From Maisak's gate came the woman he and Mocker had seen in mists in Ruderin. She rode a dark-as-midnight stallion trapped in Shinsan armor. Both moved in intensely bright light. Even at that distance Bragi was awed by the woman's beauty. Such perfection was unnatural.

Beside her, on a white charger, rode a child equally bright, perhaps six, in golden breastplate and greaves, with a small sword in hand and a child-sized crown on his head. This was a simple thing, iron, like a helmet with the top removed.

"Must be the Captal's Pretender," Bragi muttered. A stream of Kaveliners followed the woman and child. The Captal had, apparently, found support for his royal candidate.

The battle was lost, he thought. Shinsan had softened him up for these men to break and give the child-king an imaginary victory. Time to worry about keeping it from becoming a rout.

Which, unhorsed, would dishearten those troops most? He drew a shaft to his ear, released, put a second in the air while the first yet sped.

He let fly at the two stallions, assuming the sorceress would have shielded herself and her puppet with spells.

The first shaft found the heart of the white, the second the flank of the black. The white screamed and threw the child. The black, like the soldiers of Shinsan, made no sound, but it staggered and slowly went down, hindquarters first. Two more shafts whistled in, one missing, the last turning to smoke in the invisible protection around the woman.

She shrieked, a sound of rage so loud it should never have come from mortal lips. She swung a glittering spear round to point at the peak. Mists of darkness enveloped her.

Ragnarson ran. The bluff behind him exploded. He put on more speed as he heard stone grinding and groaning. The bluff was falling apart, sliding away into the pass. Two hundred yards downslope he glanced back. The peak looked as though some antediluvian monster had taken a bite—and was still nibbling.

"What the hell happened?" Blackfang demanded when he reached the canyon floor.

"Witch got mad at me."

"Cut off her nose to spite her face, then."

"Eh?"

"Must've been three hundred Shinsaners where the mountain fell."

Ragnarson's men were finishing the survivors. Some were about to go haring over the rockfall toward Maisak. "She'll really be mad now. Call them back. We're pulling out."

"Why? We've won."

"Uhn-uh. There's still one hell of a mob over there. Kaveliners. But she's the problem…"

"As you say."

"Now the barons," Ragnarson mumbled, as he settled on a rock, exhausted.

After a while he had men collect enough Shinsan armor and weapons to convince any doubters in Kavelin.

NINE: YEAR 1002 AFE
FAMILY LIFE

i) Ill wind from Itaskia

Elana didn't worry till Bragi had been gone a week. By the end of the second week she was frantic.

The third raid had left her all raw nerves, and Bevold, who had fallen days behind schedule, had become insufferable.

She spent much of her time watching her teardrop, till Gerda chided her for neglecting Ragnar and Gundar. She realized she was being foolish. Why did the women always have to wait?

One bright spot was Rolf. His chances looked better daily.

Came an afternoon when Ragnar, playing in the watchtower, shouted, "Ma, there's some men coming."

They were near enough to count. Six men. She recognized Uthe's and Dahl's mounts.

Despair seized her. "That bastard. That lying, craven son-of-a-bitch with a brain like sheep shit in shallow water trying to make it to dry land. He's let Haroun talk him into it. I'll kill him. I'll break every bone in his body and kill him!"

"Ma!"

Ragnar had never seen her like this.

"All right." She scooped him up and settled him on her hip. He laughed. "Let's go watch Uthe weasel."

She moved a chair to the porch and, with Ragnar and Gundar squirming in her lap, waited.

One glimpse of Uthe's face was enough. Bragi had gone chasing Haroun's dreams. She was so angry she just glared and waited.

Uthe approached reluctantly, shrugged and showed his palms in a gesture of defeat.

"Goodwife Ragnarson?" one of Haas's companions asked. She nodded.

"Captain Wilhusen, Staff, War Ministry. His Excellency offers his apologies and heartfelt condolences for any inconvenience caused by his calling your husband to active service."

Active service? They couldn't do that. Could they?

"Elana?"

She turned slightly, allowed another face to focus. "Turran! And Valther. What?…"

"We work for the army now. Kind of slid into it sideways."

"And Brock?" Her anger she ignored for the moment.

"Poisoned arrow in Escalon."

"Oh. I'm sorry."

"Don't be. We've been dead for years. Just won't lie down."

"You'll see Nepanthe, won't you? She's been so worried."

"There'll be time to catch up. We'll be seeing a lot of each other."

"I don't understand. But come in. You must be tired and hungry."

"You've done well," said Turran, following her in.

"Bragi's worked hard. Too hard, sometimes. And we've had good people helping. It hasn't been easy."

"No doubt. I know what this country was like."

"Well, make yourselves comfortable. Captain. Valther. You. I didn't catch your name. I'm sorry."

"Sergeant Hunsicker, ma'am, with the Captain, and don't go to no bother on my account."

"No bother. Gerda, we've guests. Hungry guests." A moment later, "Some explanations, please," she demanded, unable to control her anger. "Where's my husband?"

"Captain, may I?" Turran asked. He received a nod.

While he talked, Elana considered the changes four years had wrought. He was handsome as ever, but gray had crept into his raven hair, and he had lost a lot of weight. He was pale, looked weak, and at times shook as if suddenly chilly. When she asked about his health, he replied cryptically that, once again, this time in Escalon, they had chosen the losing side.

A shadow ghosted across Valther's face. He looked older than Turran, who had a decade on him. He had been a lively daredevil four years ago; now he seemed almost retarded. When, with a sort of childlike curiosity, he wandered over to stare into the fireplace, Elana whispered, "What happened to Valther?"

"It comes and goes," Turran replied. "He never talks anymore. Escalon was hard for him. But the bad periods get shorter. Sometimes he seems almost ready to speak, then his mind wanders… I haven't given up hope." He went on explaining why Bragi hadn't come home.

She didn't understand why she had to turn her home over to Captain Wilhusen, but it was clear she had little choice.

"Where can we go?" she asked. "We can't stay in the kingdom. We can't go north to Bragi's people. We've all got enemies in Iwa Skolovda, Dvar, and Prost Kamenets. And we can't go south if Greyfells's partisans want us."

"Enemies all around us, yes," said Turran. "The Minister has offered to let you use his estate on the Auszura Littoral."

"We can't get there from here."

"We can, but it'll be hard."

"How?"

"One way is through Driscol Fens, over the Silverbind, through Shara, south to the Lesser Kingdoms, then down the River Scarlotti to the coast."

"Which means sneaking past Prost Kamenets, then hoping we can get out of Shara without being murdered or enslaved. I trust the alternative's more palatable."

"You go west through the forests to the Minister's manor at Sieveking, then catch a naval transport going south. It looks easier, but there're problems. First, this vessel's too small to let you take any personal effects. Second, it's lightly armed and has a small crew. It wouldn't stand off a determined pirate. There are still some around in the Red Islands."

"A dilemma with more horns than a nine-headed stag. I'll talk it over with my people. And Nepanthe. Her lot will have to go too, I suppose."

"Of course."

ii) Walk to the coast

With one exception, the people chose to abandon everything to Captain Wilhusen. The exception was Bevold Lif. The Freylander refused to budge. They had survived bandits, wolves, weather, and war, he declared, and he would survive Greyfells's political successors. He was staying. Somebody had to keep the soldiers from stealing the silverware.

They left the grant with little but food and clothing. Preshka was the only adult not walking. He rode a donkey. The forest paths were impassable for wagons and horses.

The way led within forty miles of Itaskia, and for two days they had to travel open farmlands above the capital, hurrying to cross a strait of civilization which ran north to Duchy Greyfells and West Wapentake, a strait that separated two great islands of forest in the midlands. Unfriendly eyes found them there. As they reached the western forest, they spied the dust of many riders.

"You think they'll wait for us on the other side?" Elana asked.

Turran shrugged. "They don't know where we'll come out."

"How much figuring would it take? They know where the Minister's place is…"

"But we've got the jewel. We can slip past them in the dark."

"You hope. You said you'd tell me about it."

"Later."

"It's later. Talk."

"All right. After I make sure they don't come in after us. Go on a few miles. We'll catch up."

She took the trail-breaker's position, following a path tramped by generations of deer. Valther followed her, hand on sword hilt but eyes faraway, as if he were remembering another retreat. Turran had promised to tell that tale, too.

After posting sentries she sat with Rolf, who was pale with discomfort. Valther remained near her, as he always did when Turran was absent.

"How're you feeling?" she asked, laying one hand on Rolf's.

"Miserable." He coughed softly. "Lung's never going to be right."

"Think we'll make it?"

"Don't worry. It's out of our hands. We will or we won't. Depends on how much manpower they want to waste. They're not stupid. Catching us won't change the big picture."

"Tell me about Kavelin. I've never been there."

"I've told what's to tell. Except that it'd be a nice country if someone skimmed off about fifty thousand Nordmen and ambitious commoners. I liked it. Might settle there if Bragi straightens them out."

"You think he can? I mean, sixteen hundred men against a whole country, and maybe El Murid?"

"Sixteen hundred plus Bragi, Mocker, and Haroun."

"Who're only men. Rolf, I'm scared. It's been so long since I was on my own."

"I'm here. I'll always be here… I'm sorry."

"No, don't be. I understand. Ah, here's Turran."

The man came over, squatted by his brother, said, "Well, no worse. I was afraid being chased would hurt… Oh, they've posted watchers, but the rest went south again. Guess they'll wait on the other side. How're you making it, Rolf? Pushing too hard?"

"I'll survive. Iwa Skolovdans are feisty."

Turran smiled wanly. "Won't lay down and die, that's sure." Once, briefly, he had been master of that city. "Might as well make camp. We could do a few more miles, but we'll be better off for the rest. Especially the children."

Elana snorted. "Not Ragnar. Nor Ethrian. They've put in more miles than any of us. But maybe you'll find time to tell the story you've been promising."

Turran's dark eye went to Valther. "All right. After supper."

"I'll tell Nepanthe."

iii) War in the east

"I suppose the story begins," Turran told an audience of Elana, Nepanthe, Preshka, and Uthe and Dahl Haas, "when Valther talked Brock and me into going to Hellin Daimiel. Jerrad wouldn't go. He went back to the mountains. I guess he's probably hunting and trying to rebuild Ravenkrak. Fool. Anyway, in Hellin Daimiel we were approached by a representative of the Monitor of Escalon. He was recruiting westerners to help in a war.

"We became part of a devil's catch of hedge wizards, assassins, mercenaries, and marginal types that might be useful in a wizard's war.

"It was a long journey east. By the time we reached Tatarian, Escalon's capital, there were a thousand of us.

"We found out that the country was at war with Shinsan. Escalon was strong, but no match for the Dread Empire.

"Escalon was losing. The whole kingdom lay under a siege of night. Demonic, poisonous hordes of hell-things fought for both sides.

"We foreigners were thrown in right away. And we stalled Shinsan for a while. But then they started advancing again.

"The Monitor decided to chance everything on one vast thaumaturgic battle. It defies description. It lasted nine days. When it was over an area as big as Itaskia had been wasted. Millions died. In Escalon only Tatarian and the major cities survived. In Shinsan, we don't know. We hadn't lost, but we hadn't won, and that, in the long run, meant our defeat.

"It was during that battle that we lost Brock. We got too involved to look out for ourselves. An arrow got through and wounded him.

"That it had been loosed a thousand miles away in Shinsan was no excuse. We'd been provided with ways of sensing the attack. We just didn't pay attention.

"The wound was minor, but the shaft bore soul-devouring spells. In the end he begged us to give him a clean death."

Turran paused for a moment, locked in his memories.

"Afterward, the Monitor decided Escalon was lost. He summoned Valther and me. He told us that Shinsan would turn on Matayanga next. He believed the world's hope, ultimately, lay in the west because Yo Hsi and Nu Li Hsi had been destroyed here. What he was trying to do, he told me, was to buy time. He hoped somebody like Varthlokkur or the Star Rider would see what was happening and do something about the west's political choas.

"That's when he gave me the jewel, Elana. The one I sent you. You've been using it for a warden, its least important power.

"The Monitor believed it was one of the Poles of Power. How he came by it I don't know, and I don't think it really is a Pole, but one thing's sure. It's important. I saw him use it. He could move mountains... He wanted me to get it to the Star Rider. But I don't think so. I don't know why. When this's over, I'm going to try to take it to Varthlokkur. He knows the Dread Empire. I think he'd have the best shot at stopping them."

Silence closed in, drawing a tight circle round the campfire. For several minutes Turran's audience digested what he had had to say. Then his sister, glancing at a fitfully dozing Valther, asked, "Why didn't you come home? You lost Brock, and the war was over..."

"It wasn't over. Just lost. There was time to buy. We thought we could help. After the great wizards' battle both sides had to rely on ordinary soldiers for a while. It's generally conceded that I'm a pretty good general. Impetuous and over-optimistic, they tell me, but less so when I'm working for somebody else. I managed to take the battle to Shinsan for several months."

"I'm confused. You've mentioned Nu Li Hsi's heirs, and Yo Hsi's. Who were you fighting?"

"Both. Sometimes one, sometimes the other. They were feuding. Shinsan's army wasn't. It took the orders of whoever gave them. When we first got to

Escalon, we fought Yo Hsi's daughter. After the great battle, it was O Shing. I don't know when they made the changeover. The transition couldn't be detected. A few months later we were fighting Mist again.

"I saw the woman… Unbelievable. So much evil in such a beautiful package."

"But what about Valther?" Nepanthe demanded.

"You never did have any patience, did you? Well, it's a complicated story. Try not to interrupt." Nepanthe and Turran had been bickering for years.

"By some snare of the Power he still had, the Monitor caught one of the Tervola. He managed to keep the man alive long enough to find out that Mist herself would take charge of the final assault on Tatarian.

"The Monitor planned one last cast of the dice. Its only objective was Mist's death.

"Valther and I were heart and soul of the plan. And we blew it.

"Our job was to get captured." Turran talked in little gusts, like an indecisive breeze. During his pauses he poked the fire with a stick, threw acorns at tree trunks, used the fingernails on one hand to clean those on the other. He didn't want to relive these memories. "Because we'd been involved in her father's death. The Monitor thought she'd want to question us. If she did, we were supposed to change sides, then kill her when we got the chance.

"It worked too good.

"The woman has a weakness. Vanity. Make it two. Insecurity, too. We played to them. And she started keeping us around like pets. She had a million questions about the west.

"Things started going wrong when Valt started believing what he was saying…"

Sighs escaped his listeners. They became more attentive. Turran stirred the fire again.

"It was my fault… I should've… In Shinsan they use herbs to increase their grasp of the Power. It stops you from getting older, too. But once you use them, you have to keep on…"

"You?…" Nepanthe interjected.

"In the service of the Dread Empire, one must. After he had betrayed Escalon, Valt tried to make it up by killing Mist. It didn't work.

"I don't know. Maybe her wickedness was polluted by mercy. Maybe an accidental thread of love got woven into her tapestry of evil. Whatever, of all the possible punishments, she chose the simplest. She took away our supply of herbs."

"That's why he's this way?" This time it was Elana who couldn't restrain herself. "How come you recovered?"

"I'm not an expert on the human mind. Yes, I recovered. That was six months ago, in an asylum in Hellin Daimiel. For a while I didn't know if what I remembered was true or just a nightmare. Nobody knew anything about us. The

Watch had found us in the street and committed us for our own protection. The scholars who studied us told me Valther is using drug withdrawal as an excuse not to come back and face his guilt."

"If only Mocker were here," Nepanthe mused. Her eyes were sad as she gazed at Valther. "He might be able to reach Valt."

"Time is the cure," Turran told her. "It worked for me. So I keep hoping."

iv) Auszura Littoral

With Elana's jewel guiding them, they slipped through their enemies to Sieveking. But the transport wasn't yet there. When *Dingolfing* did arrive it was in no condition to sail to the Auszura Littoral. The ship had encountered heavy weather shortly after leaving Portsmouth, then had met a Trolledyngjan reever off Cape Blood. Her captain, Miles Norwine, said rigging repairs might take a week. Heavy damage, where the Trolledyngjan had rammed, would have to wait for the yards at Itaskia.

"It seems," said Elana, standing on the quay with Turran and Nepanthe, "that somewhere in the house of the gods, probably in the jakes, there's a little pervert who gets his pleasure making me miserable."

Turran chuckled. "Know what? I'll bet the head man over there's been thinking the same thing." He indicated tents crowning a hill overlooking the estate.

Later, a messenger brought the news that Bragi had crossed the Porthune.

"The renegades," said Turran, "might try their luck when they find out. I'd better get something ready."

That night he and the men laid an ambush at the edge of the estate. Elana, with Dahl Haas under her wing, went to observe.

Sure enough, near midnight, men came sneaking through the brush. Turran sprang his trap. The surprise was complete. In minutes a dozen had been slaughtered and the rest sent whooping up the hillside.

Dahl, half-wild, used his dagger to finish a casualty who came staggering toward Elana, then, realizing what he had done, heaved his supper and began crying. Elana was trying to calm him when his father appeared.

"What happened?" Uthe asked.

Elana explained.

Uthe put his arm around his son. "You did well," he said. "It's always hardest the first time. Lot of men do their conscience-racking first, get themselves killed hesitating."

Dahl nodded, but reassurances did little good. The experience was too intensely personal.

Captain Norwine got his rigging repaired and a patch on his hull. He was willing to risk the trip. Elana put it to a vote. It went in favor.

Dingolfing put out and beat round Cape Blood, sailed south past the Silverbind Estuary, Portsmouth, and the Octylyan Protectorate without mishap. Norwine hugged the coast like a babe his mother. He was prepared to go aground if trouble developed. They weathered a minor storm off the Porthune, spending two nervous days at the pumps and buckets, but came through with no damage other than to landlubbers' stomachs.

"Sail ho!" a lookout cried just north of Sacuescu. Norwine put his helm over and ran for shallow water. Turran and the shipboard Marines prepared for a fight. But the vessel proved to be the *Rifkin*, out of Portsmouth. The fat caravel dipped her merchant's colors to *Dingolfing*'s naval ensign.

Norwine kept everyone at stations once they passed Sacuescu. They were near the Red Isles where, despite regular patrols by the Itaskian Navy, pirates lurked. But their luck held. They made the fishing port of Tineo, midway between Sacuescu and Dunno Scuttari, without incident.

From Tineo it was a twelve-mile walk to the Minister's villa, which occupied a headland with a spectacular view of the sea. The staff expected them. They seemed accustomed to hiding friends of the Minister.

The Auszura Littoral was all Turran had promised, and utterly peaceful. So peaceful that, after a few months, it began to grate. There was nothing to do but wait for rumors from Kavelin, which were unreliable by the time they filtered through to Tineo.

Rolf began wandering, sometimes accompanied by Uthe, to Sacuescu and Dunno Scuttari. Elana didn't weather his absences well. He was her last touchstone, almost her conscience. His absences grew more frequent and extended. She found herself thrown more and more into the company of Nepanthe, Turran, and Valther.

Nepanthe, after Rolf, had been her best friend for years, but her constant company was wearing. Nepanthe was a worrier.

Turran remained a perfect gentleman, ever attentive and willing to entertain. She began to fear what might happen. She tried to stay near Gerda, whose basilisk eye could still the passion of a cat in heat.

Then Rolf and Uthe disappeared. She thought it another of their jaunts till she discovered their weapons missing.

"Gerda, where've they gone?" she demanded. Like certain gods, the woman saw the sparrows fall.

"Where do you think? Kavelin, of course. With help for himself. Who'll be coming home someday, I'll remind you, and be expecting everything as he left it."

Why couldn't Rolf stay put? Was he sublimating his love? Or just searching for the spear with his name?

Autumn leaves were falling on the Littoral. Would it be getting on winter in Kavelin?

The night Rolf left she sat up late with the Tear of Mimizan. Troubled, she used the thing more as a focus for her attention than as a means of checking Bragi's well-being.

The jewel suddenly seized her attention. The light within was strong and growing stronger. Bragi was in trouble.

The light flashed suddenly, so brightly she was momentarily blinded. At the same instant there was a scream from another room.

"The children!" she gasped. She rushed toward the sound. It went on and on. Behind her, the ruby painted her bedroom shades of blood.

The screamer was Valther.

"She's here!" the man kept saying. "She's here. She's loosed her magic…"

"Who?" Nepanthe asked repeatedly.

"Must be Mist," Turran guessed. "Nothing else could've done this."

"But why?"

"Who knows the ways of Shinsan?"

"The jewel," Elana interjected. "Before he screamed, it flashed so bright it almost blinded me."

Nepanthe's eyes met hers. Neither woman voiced her fear.

"She's in Kavelin, then," said Turran. He remained thoughtful while Nepanthe and Elana calmed Valther, who began asking, "What happened?" and "Where am I?"

"It grows too complex," Turran mused aloud. "A three-sided war… Nepanthe, get a couple of horses ready. And weapons. I'll look after Valther."

"But…"

"Looks like we're getting a second chance. Elana, the Tear is the most valuable thing in the west right now. Guard it well. If Kavelin goes, get it to Varthlokkur."

Things went so fast Elana had no time to protest. Before she exploded in frustration, the brothers had gone. Valther remained puzzled, but seemed determined to rectify his treason.

She and Nepanthe stood on a balcony and watched them ride toward the coast road. Turran hoped to overtake Rolf and Uthe.

A stir in the gardens caught her eye. She said nothing to Nepanthe, merely peered intently till she could make out a small old man nodding to himself. He had spoken to Bragi at the landgrant. Quick as a bolting rabbit, he scooted out a small side gate.

A moment later she gasped. The old man, astride a winged horse, rose toward the moon and sped eastward.

TEN: YEAR 1002 AFE
THE CLOSING CIRCLES

i) From the jaws of despair

Ragnarson collapsed onto a rock. He could scarcely remain awake. The Nordmen gave up their weapons meekly, though puzzledly. They couldn't believe that they had been beaten by lesser men.

For Bragi, too, it seemed a dream. It had taken two man-breaking weeks, but he had slipped out of the destroying vise.

He had fled Maisak certain he would never escape the Gap. Enemies had lain before and behind him, and there had been no way to turn aside.

He had outrun the Captal, almost flying into the arms of the eastern barons, who were pursuing Sir Andvbur Kimberlin, then had *made* a way to the side, out of the inescapable trap of a box canyon. At least, his enemies had thought it inescapable.

While they had taken the measure of one another and he had goaded them into fighting, his men had cut stairs up the canyon wall. Abandoning everything but weapons, they had climbed out one by one. Meanwhile, with a few Trolledyngjans and Itaskians, Ragnarson had harassed the Captal's surviving Shinsaners so they wouldn't get the best of the barons.

The desultory, constricted, unimaginative combat between pretenders had taken four days to resolve itself. The barons had had numbers, the Captal sorcery and men fanatically devoted to his child-pretender.

Ragnarson felt that, this time, he had won a decisive victory. He had won time. The Captal couldn't muster new forces before winter sealed the Gap. The succession might be determined by spring. And the eastern Nordmen had been crushed. For the moment he and Volstokin commanded the only major forces in Kavelin. If he moved swiftly, while winter prevented external interests from aiding favorites, he could fulfill his commission.

And he could return to Elana.

If Haroun would let him. What Haroun's plans were, he didn't know.

He had sent his men up the stone stairs, over mountains, and into the Gap behind the barons. The animals and equipment he had abandoned had become bait. They had rushed to the plunder.

Ragnarson's captains, led by Blackfang, had struck savagely. In bitter fighting they had closed the canyon behind the Nordmen. Bragi and a small group had held the stairs against a repeat of his own escape.

There was no water in that canyon. Ragnarson's animals had already devoured the sparse forage. The arrowstorm, once the mouth narrows had been secured, had been impenetrable. The Nordmen had had no choice.

There had been more to it, as there was to all stories: heroism of men pushing themselves beyond believed limits; inspired leadership by Blackfang, Ahring, Altenkirk, and Sir Andvbur; and unsuspected bits of character surfacing.

Ragnarson studied Sir Andvbur. His judgment of the young knight's coolness and competence had proven out during Kimberlin's operation around the headwaters of the Ebeler. Under him, the Wessons had shown well against the barons, particularly during disengagement and withdrawal.

But the first thing he had done, after getting his troops safely into the box canyon, had been to throw a tantrum.

"Both leaders think they can handle us later," he had said.

"You sound bitter."

"I am. Colonel, you haven't lived with their arrogance. Kavelin is the richest country in the Lesser Kingdoms, and that's not just in wealth and resources. There're fortunes in human potential here. But you find Wesson, Siluro, and Marena Dimura geniuses plowing, emptying chamberpots, and eating grubs in the forests. They're not allowed anything else. Meantime, Nordmen morons are pushing Kavelin toward disaster. You think it's historical pressure that has the lower classes rebelling? No. It's because of the blind excesses of my class... Men like Eanred Tarlson could help make this kingdom decent for everybody. But they never get anywhere. Unless, like Tarlson, they obtain Royal favor. It's frustrating. Infuriating."

Ragnarson had made no comment at the time.

He hadn't realized that Sir Andvbur had a Cause. He decided he had best keep an eye on the man.

Blackfang and Ahring took seats beside him. "We should get the hell out before Shinsan tries for a rematch," said Haaken. "But there ain't nobody here who could walk a mile."

"Not much choice, then, is there? Why worry?"

Blackfang shrugged.

"What about the prisoners?" Ahring asked.

"Won't have them long. We're going to Vorgreberg." He glanced up. The sky was nasty again. There had been cold rain off and on since his withdrawal from Maisak. It was getting on time to worry about wintering the army.

Two days later, as he returned to the march, the Marena Dimura brought him a young messenger.

"Wouldn't be related to Eanred Tarlson, would you?" Bragi asked, as he broke Royal seals.

"My father, sir."

"You're Gjerdrum, eh? Your father said you were at university."

"I came home when the trouble started. I knew he'd need help. Especially if anything happened to him."

"Eh?" But he had begun reading.

His orders were to hasten to Vorgreberg and assume the capital's defense. Tarlson had been gravely wounded in a battle with Volstokin. The foreigners were within thirty miles of the city.

"Tell her I'm on my way," he said.

The boy rode off, never having dismounted. Ragnarson wondered if he could get there in time. The rain would complicate river crossings in the lowlands. And Tarlson's injuries might cost the Queen the support he brought her by force of personality. He might lead his men to an enemy city. "Haaken! Ahring! Altenkirk! Sir Andvbur!"

ii) Travels with the enemy

"Woe! Am foolest of fools," Mocker mumbled over and over.

The dungeon days had stretched into weeks, a parade of identical bores.

Kirsten had forgotten him due to other pressures. Those he could judge only by his guards. Always sullen and vicious, they became worse whenever the Breitbarth fortunes waned. News arrived only when another subversive was imprisoned.

One day the turnkeys vanished. Every available man had been drafted to resist Volstokin's perfidy.

After crushing resistance, Vodicka visited the dungeons. Mocker tried to appear small in his corner. The Volstokiners were hunting someone. And he had had a premonition.

"This one," he heard.

He looked up. A tall, lean, angular man with a wide scar down one cheek considered him with eyes of cold jade. Vodicka. Beside him was another lean man, shorter, dusky, with high, prominent cheekbones and a huge, hawklike nose. He wore black. His eyes were like those of a snake.

Inwardly, Mocker groaned. A shaghûn.

"Hai!" He bounced up with a broad grin. "Great King arrives in nick to rescue faithful servant from mouldering death in dungeon of perfidious ally. Breitbarth is treacher, great lord. Was plotting treason from beginning…"

They ignored him.

Mocker sputtered, fumed, and told some of his tallest lies. Vodicka's men put him in chains and led him away. No one explained why.

But he could guess. They knew him. He had done El Murid many small embarrassments. There was the time he had sweet-talked/kidnapped the man's daughter. There was the time he had convinced an important general that he could reveal a shortcut through the Kapenrungs, and had led the man into an army-devouring ambush.

Still, daylight seen from chains was sweeter than dungeon darkness. And at least an illusion of a chance to escape existed.

He could have gotten away. Escape tricks were among his talents. But he saw a chance to lurk on the fringe of the enemy's councils.

He got to see a lot of daylight—and moonlight, starlight, and weather—the next few months, while Volstokin's drunken giant of an army lumbered about Kavelin's western provinces. Vodicka wanted his prizes near him always, but never comfortable.

Mocker didn't get along with his fellow prisoners. They were Nordmen, gentlemen who had barely paid their ransoms to Bragi's agents when taken by Vodicka.

Ragnarson had won himself a low, black place in Vodicka's heart. He had already plundered the best from Ahsens, Dolusich, Gaehle, Holtschlaw, and Heiderscheid provinces. Bragi's leavings were not satisfying the levies, who had been called from their homes for a campaign that would last past harvest time.

Vodicka kept escalating his promises to keep his army from evaporating.

Mocker wished he could get out among the troops. The damage he could talk… But his guards, now, were men of Hammad al Nakir. They were deaf to words not approved by their shaghûn. His chance to escape had passed him by.

The looting improved in Echtenache and Rubbelke, though there a price in blood had to be paid. In Rubbelke, sixty miles west of Vorgreberg and fifteen north of the caravan route, a thousand Nordmen met Volstokin on the plains before Woerheide.

Vodicka insisted that his prisoners watch. His pride still stung from the difficulty he had had forcing the Armstead ford.

Vodicka was more talented at diplomacy and intrigue than at war, but refused to admit his shortcomings.

Tons of flesh and steel surged together in long, thunderous waves amidst storms of dust and swirling autumn leaves. Swords like lightning flashed in the thunderheads of war; the earth received a rain of blood and broken blades and bodies.

Volstokin's knights began to flee. Enraged, Vodicka prepared to sacrifice his infantry.

Mocker watched with delight and game-fan commentary. The Nordmen had no infantry of their own. Unhorsed, without the protection of footmen, they would be easy prey for Volstokin's more mobile men-at-arms.

The shaghûn asked Vodicka to hold the infantry. He would turn the tide.

Mocker had encountered many wizards. This one was no mountain-mover, but was superior for a survivor of El Murid's early anti-sorcery program. If he were an example of what the Disciple had been developing behind the Sahel, the west was in for some wicked surprises.

He conjured bears from smoke, unnaturally huge monsters misty about the edges but fanged and clawed like creatures bred only to kill. The Nordmen recognized them harmless, but their mounts were impressed beyond control. They broke, many throwing their riders in their panic.

"Now your infantry," said the shaghûn.

"Woe," Mocker mumbled, "am doomed. Am condemned to hopelessest of hopeless plights. Will never see home of self again." His fellow prisoners watched him curiously. They had never understood his presence. He had done nothing to enlighten them. But he had learned from them.

He knew who planned to betray whom, and when and how, and the most secret of their changing alliances. But Mocker suspected their scheming no longer mattered. Vodicka's and Bragi's armies were the real powers in Kavelin now.

Vodicka's leadership remained indecisive. Twenty miles from Vorgreberg he went into camp. He seemed to be waiting for something.

What came was not what he wanted. From his seat outside Vodicka's pavilion, Mocker listened to the King's curses when he discovered that the Queen's Own, though inferior in numbers, were upon him. While the surprise attack developed, Vodicka and the shaghûn argued about why Tarlson was so confident.

Mocker learned why they had been waiting.

They were expecting another Siluro uprising.

But Tarlson should have anticipated that possibility. Had he rounded up the ringleaders?

Mocker supposed that Tarlson, aware of his position, had elected to rely on boldness and speed.

He brought his horsemen in hard and fast, with little armor to slow them. From the beginning it was obvious he was only mounting a raid in force.

Yet it nearly became a victory. Tarlson's men raged through the camp, trailing slaughter and fire. One detachment made off with cattle and horses, another drove for the Royal pavilion.

Mocker saw Tarlson at their head, shouted them on. But Vodicka's house troops and the shaghûn's bodyguards were hardened veterans.

The shaghûn crouched in the pavilion entryway, chanting over colored smokes. If there had ever been a time for a Mocker trick, this was it. He had begun to despair of ever winning free. He wracked his brain. It had to be something that wouldn't get him killed if he failed.

A not-too-kind fate saved him the trouble.

A wild thrust by a dying spearman slipped past Tarlson's shield and found a gap behind his breastplate. The Wesson plunged from his saddle. With the broken spear still protruding, he surged to his feet.

A youth on a big gray, hardly more than a boy, came on like a steel-edged storm, drove the Volstokiners back, dragged Eanred up behind him. Tarlson's troops screened his withdrawal.

In minutes it was over, the raiders come and gone like a bitter breath of winter wind. Mocker wasn't sure who had won. Vodicka's forces had suffered heavily, but the Queen's men might have lost their unifying symbol…

Mocker reassumed his muddy throne. His future didn't seem bright. He would probably die of pneumonia in a few weeks.

"Ignominious end for a great hero of former times," he told his companions. He cast a promising, speculative glance the shaghûn's way.

iii) Reinforcements for Ragnarson

Two hundred men sat horses shagged with winter's approach, forming a column of gray ragged veterans remaining death-still. The chill wind whipped their travel cloaks and pelted them with flurries of dead leaves while promising sleet for the afternoon. There were no young men among them. From beneath battered helmets trailed strands predicting life's winter. Scars on faces and armor whispered of ancient battles won in wars now barely remembered. Not one of that hard-eyed catch of survivors wore a name unknown.

From distant lands they had come in their youth to march with the Free

Companies during El Murid's wars, and now they were men without homes or homelands, wanderers damned to eternal travel in search of wars. Before them, a hundred yards away, beyond the Kavelin-Altean border, stood fifty men-at-arms in the livery of Baron Breitbarth. They were Wessons, levies still scratching where their new mail chafed, warriors only by designation.

Rolf Preshka coughed into his hand. Blood flecked the phlegm. Paroxysms racked him till tears came to his eyes.

From his right, Turran asked, "You okay?"

Preshka spat. "I'll be all right."

On Preshka's left, Valther resumed sharpening his sword. Each time they halted, sword and whetstone made soft, deadly music. Valther's eyes sought something beyond the eastern horizon.

Preshka waved a hand overhead.

The column took on metallic life. The mercenaries spread out. Shields and weapons came battle-ready.

The boys beyond the border saw their scars and battered arms, and the dark hollows where the shadows of the wings of death had passed across their eyes. They could cipher the numbers. They shook. But they didn't back down.

"Be a shame to kill them," said Turran.

"Murder," Preshka agreed.

"Where're their officers? Nordmen might be less stubborn."

The *scrape scrape* of Valther's whetstone carried during a lull in the wind. The Kaveliners shuddered.

Rolf turned. Several places to his right were three old Itaskians still carrying the shields of Sir Tury Hawkwind's White Company. "Lother. Nothomb. Wittekind. Put a few shafts yonder. Don't hurt anybody." Qualifications for the White Company had included an ability to split a willow wand at two hundred paces.

The three dismounted. From well-oiled leather cases they drew the bows that were their most valued possessions, weapons from the hand of Mintert Rensing, the acknowledged master of the bowmaker's trade. They grumbled together, picking targets, judging the breeze.

As one three shafts sped invisibly swift, feathered the heads of leopards in the coats of arms on three tall shields.

The Kaveliners understood. Reluctantly, they laid down their arms.

Preshka coughed, sighed, signaled the advance.

East of Damhorst he encountered a band of Kildragon's foragers. They were lean men with a few scrawny chickens. The larders of twice-plundered Nordmen were growing empty; Kildragon wouldn't permit looting the underclasses. Since Armstead, Reskird had been fighting a guerrilla campaign from the Bodenstead forest, hanging on even after his enemies had given up trying to hunt him down. He had lost a third of his Itaskians, but had replaced them several times over with Wessons and Marena Dimura. He and Preshka joined forces, continued along the caravan route toward Vorgreberg. Other than Volstokin's army there was no force strong enough to resist them. The Nordmen had collapsed.

Preshka wondered where Bragi was. Somewhere deep in the east at last rumor. After Lake Berberich, Lieneke, and Sedlmayr, he had disappeared.

Rolf moved fast, avoiding conflict. There was little resistance. The faces he saw in the ruined towns and castles had had all the fight washed out. He always explained that he was bringing the Queen's peace. His force grew, as angry, defeated, directionless soldiers abandoned the Nordmen for the Queen.

He passed south of Woerheide, heard the peasants mumbling about sorcery. It was chilling. What did this shaghûn have in his bag of tricks?

And where was Haroun? As much as anyone, bin Yousif was responsible for events in Kavelin. His dark ways were needed now. But there was hardly a rumor of the man.

Then came news of Tarlson's action near Vorgreberg, and of the Queen's forces wavering while mobs bloodied the streets of the capital.

And still no news of Bragi beyond a rumored baronial force having pursued him into the Savernake Gap.

When Preshka's scouts first reported contact with Volstokin's foragers, Rolf told Turran, "We can't handle Vodicka by ourselves." He considered his mercenaries. They had come on speculation, on the basis of his reputation. Would they fight?

"We can distract him," Turran said. "Eat up small forces."

Valther sharpened his sword and stared eastward. Hints of mountain peaks could be seen when weather permitted.

"He's been dallying for months," Reskird observed. "Should've driven straight to Vorgreberg."

"Was it his idea?"

"Eh?"

"El Murid's people might've conned him. So he'll be too unpopular to rule once he's done their catspawing. Want to bet there's a Siluro candidate in the wings, waiting till Bragi's been disposed of?"

"Might take some disposing," Kildragon observed. "He's beaten Volstokin before."

"This mob's got a shaghûn. A first-rater, you can bet."

"We haven't reached a decision," Turran interjected.

Preshka glanced his way, frowned. The man still hadn't explained his sudden urge to join this venture.

"They can't know much about us yet," said Kildragon. "So we sneak up on them, hide out—that's hilly country—and give them a swift kick once in a while. Keep them tottering till Vorgreberg gets organized. Way Vodicka's been vacillating, he won't attack with us behind him."

They sneaked, following a corridor of devastation so thorough Volstokin's foragers no longer wandered there. On a gray, icy morning at winter's head, in a drizzle that threatened to become snow, Preshka hurled his force at Vodicka's. He held no one in reserve.

Vodicka's troops were not surprised. Their trouble with Tarlson had taught them to be alert. They reacted well.

Preshka's lung was so bad his fighting capacity was nil. Though he retained overall control, he assigned Kildragon tactical command. Because of his stubborn insistence on joining the assault, Turran, Valther, and Uthe Haas stayed near to guard him.

Cursing the rain because of the damage it might do their weapons, the Itaskian bowmen generated a shower of their own from behind Preshka's veterans. The recruits held the flanks, to prevent encirclement of the thrust toward Vodicka's gaudy pavilion.

A spasm racked Preshka. He thought about Elana, the landgrant, and the heartaches he had suffered there. Was this better?

The Volstokiners fought doggedly, if with little inspiration. But Preshka's force penetrated to the defenses of the Royal pavilion.

If he could capture Vodicka, Rolf thought…

"Sorcery!" Turran suddenly growled. He sniffed the wind like a dog. Valther did the same, his head swaying like a cobra's about to strike.

"Hoist me up," Preshka ordered. A moment later, as his feet returned to the bloody mud, "The shaghûn. And Mocker, in chains."

"Mocker?"

"Uthe, can you see?"

"No."

"We've got to get that shaghûn. Otherwise, we're dead. Kildragon! Put your arrows around the tent door." But his words were swept away by the crash. "I think," he told Turran, "that I just brought you here to die. The attack was a mistake."

Colored smokes began boiling up before the pavilion.

iv) Vorgreberg

It was raining hard. Bits of sleet stung Ragnarson's face and hands. The rising waters of the Spehe, that formed the boundary between the Gudbrandsal Forest and the Siege of Vorgreberg, rushed against his mount, threatened to carry them both away. The far bank looked too soggy to climb.

"Where's the damned ford?" he thundered at the Marena Dimura scout there.

The man, though shivering blue, grinned. "Is it, Colonel? Not so good, eh?

"Not so good, Adamec."

They had been pushing themselves to the limit for a week, a thousand men strung out along remote, twisty ways, trying to come to the capital unannounced.

His mount fought the current bravely, stubbornly, squished up the far bank.

As Ragnarson rose in his stirrups to survey the land beyond, the beast slipped, began sliding, reared.

Rather than risk being dragged under and drowned, Bragi threw himself into the flood. He came up sputtering and cursing, seized the lance a passing soldier offered, slithered up the bank behind him. Across his mind flashed images of the main hall of his home, warm and *dry,* then Haroun's eagle's face. He staggered to his feet cursing louder than ever.

"Move it there!" he thundered. "It's open country up here. You men, get that safety line across. I'll have your balls on a platter if somebody drowns."

He glanced northeast, wondered how Haaken was coming along. Blackfang, with the bulk of the force and the prisoners, was hiking the caravan route, his function for the moment that of diversion.

Bragi's horsemen, exhausted, on staggering mounts, came out of the river by ones and twos, ragged as bandits. Their banners were tattered and limp. The one thing impressive was that they had done the things they had. He wished he could promise them that the hard days would be over when they reached the city. But no, the business in Kavelin was far from done.

The final rush to Vorgreberg reminded Ragnarson more of a retreat than of a dash to action. He waved to startled Wessons peeping from hovel doors, sometimes gave a greeting in the Queen's name. He had the surviving Trolledyngjans with him, as well as the best of the Itaskians and Wessons. Of the Marena Dimura he had brought only a handful of scouts. They would be of no value in street fighting.

A few columns of smoke rose on the horizon, fires still smoldering in the rain. As they drew nearer Vorgreberg, they encountered bands of refugees camped in the muddy fields. From these he learned that the Queen still ruled, but that her situation was precarious. The rumor was circulating that she was considering abdication to avoid further bloodshed.

That would be in character, Ragnarson thought. All he had heard suggested that the woman was too good for the ingrates she had inherited.

And what of Volstokin?

The refugees knew little. Vodicka had been camped west of the Siege, doing nothing, for a long time. He was waiting. For what?

Ragnarson kept pushing. The rain and sleet kept falling. One thing about the weather, he thought. It would keep the mobs small.

He reached the suburbs unannounced, unexpected, and laughed aloud at the panic he inspired at the guardpost. While his Wesson sergeants answered their challenge, he swept on toward the city wall.

At the gate he again surprised soldiers, men hiding from the weather while the gate stood open. Sloppy, he thought, driving through. In a time so tense, why were they not alert?

Morale problems, he imagined. Despair caused by Tarlson's injury. A growing suspicion that it no longer mattered what they did.

That would change.

The alarm gongs didn't sound till he had reached the parklands around Castle Krief. As the panicky carillon ran through the city, he ordered, "Break the banners."

The men bearing the old, tattered standards dropped back. Others removed sheaths from fresh banners representing the peoples forming Ragnarson's command, as well as standards he had captured in his battles. He made sure Sedlmayr's banner was up near his own. The Royal standard he took in his own hand.

The castle's defenders reached the ramparts in time to observe this bit of drama. After a puzzled minute they broke into ragged cheers.

His eyes met hers the instant he entered the vast courtyard. She stood on a tower balcony. She was a tall woman, fairy slim, small-boned, with long golden hair stringing in the downpour. Her eyes were of a blue deeper than a summer sky at zenith. She wore simple, unadorned white that the rain had pasted to her slight curves...

He learned a lot about her in that moment, before turning to survey the mud-spattered, weary, ragged cutthroats behind him. What would she think?

He dipped his banner in salute. The others did the same.

His eyes locked with hers again. She acknowledged the salute with a nod and smile that almost made the ride worthwhile. He turned to shout orders to keep traffic moving. When he looked back, she was gone.

The political picture could be judged by the fewness of the servants who helped with the animals. Nowhere did he see a dusky Siluro face. Among the soldiery, Nordmen were scarce. Virtually all were flaxen-haired Wessons.

One, a youth trying to keep his head dry with his shirttail, came running. "Gods, Colonel, you made good time."

"Ah, Gjerdrum." He smiled weakly. "You said to hurry."

"I only got back last night myself. Come. Father wants to see you."

"Like this?" He had had time to become awed. This was a Royal Palace. In the field, at war, a King was just another man to him. In their own dens, though, the mighty made him feel the disreputable brigand he currently appeared to be.

"No formalities around here anymore, sir. The Queen... She's a lady who'll understand. If you see what I mean. The war, you know."

"Lead on, then." He left billeting, mess, and stabling to his sergeants and the Queen's.

Tarlson was dying. Propped up in a huge bed, he looked like a man in the final stage of consumption. Like a man who should have died long ago, but who was too stubborn to go. He was too heavily bandaged to move.

She was there too, in her rain-soaked garments, but she stayed in a shadowed corner. Ragnarson nodded, went to Tarlson's side. He tried to avoid dripping and dropping mud on the carpeting.

"I'd heard you'd picked up another scar," he said.

Eanred smiled thinly, replied, "I think this one had my name. Sit. You look exhausted."

Ragnarson shuffled.

From behind him, "Sit down, Colonel. No need preserving furniture for Vodicka's plunderers." She had a melodious voice even when bitter.

"So you finally came," said Tarlson.

"I was summoned."

"Frequently." Tarlson smiled. "But you were right. We couldn't've won defending one city. If I hadn't been rash, you might still be chastising barons."

"I think they've had enough—though I'm out of touch. About the west and south you know. And the east has surrendered."

"Ah? Gjerdrum suggested as much, but wasn't clear."

"He didn't waste any time asking questions."

"He's got a lot to learn. You came swiftly. Alone?"

"With a thousand. The rest are afoot, with prisoners. As I've said before, I believe in movement."

"Yes, per Haroun bin Yousif. I want to talk about him. When the pressure is off. Maybe your arrival will help."

Ragnarson frowned.

"We intercepted messages from Vodicka to the Siluro community. They're supposed to revolt this week. I hope they'll reconsider now."

Ragnarson remembered the laxity of the Queen's troops. "My men won't be much help if it breaks tonight. And yours don't look good for anything."

"What do you suggest?" Tarlson asked.

His wounds had taken the vinegar out of him, Ragnarson thought. "Lock the gates. Use the Palace Guard to flood the Siluro quarter. Post a curfew. Enforce it. They can't do anything if you grab them as they leave their houses."

"And leave the palace undefended?"

"In my hands, you mean? Yes. Eanred, you've got your suspicions. I'm not sure why. Let's just say our goals are similar."

Tarlson didn't apologize. "Kavelin makes one suspicious. No matter. Be your intentions good or evil, we're in your hands. There's no one else to stop Vodicka."

Ragnarson didn't like it. He was becoming too much a principal in Kavelin's affairs.

"I know my contract," he said stiffly. "I'll try to keep it. But the loyalties of my men lie differently."

"Meaning?"

"They've been in Kavelin for months, fighting, and dying, for a cause not their own. They're full of spirit. They haven't let loose for a long time. What happens when they go for a drink and realize they haven't been paid a farthing?…"

"Ah." Tarlson glanced past Ragnarson.

"Sums have been held in the Treasury, Colonel," said the Queen. "Though you should be rich with the booty you've taken."

Ragnarson shrugged.

"And what's happened to your fat friend?" Tarlson asked. "As I recall, he disappeared at the Scarlotti ferries."

"That's a ghost that's haunted me since. I don't know. I sent him to Damhorst. All I've heard is that he might be in Breitbarth's hands."

"He may be with Vodicka now," said Tarlson. "I saw a chain of prisoners during the attack…"

"Was he all right?"

"Not sure it was him. I just caught a glimpse of a fat man hopping around screaming. Then I got spear bit."

"That's him. I wonder what Vodicka's doing with him?"

"What're your plans?"

"Don't have any. I was called to defend Vorgreberg. I didn't extend my imagination beyond getting here."

"There're two considerations. The Siluro. Vodicka. The Siluro we can handle now. If we can send Vodicka packing before spring, we might have an edge on the barons next summer."

"Next summer you'll have real problems."

"Eh?"

"The Captal of Savernake."

"What about him?" Tarlson's face darkened. He stole a glance past Ragnarson.

"He's got his own army and Pretender up there. A child about six. I tried to get him, but…" He stopped because of the emotions parading across Tarlson's face.

"But what?"

"His allies. It was pure luck that we got out. Those people… The grimmest soldiers in the world."

"There were suspicions… The King told me… Who? El Murid?"

"Shinsan."

His sibilant whisper fostered a dreadful silence broken only by a gasp from behind him. Tarlson's face became so pale and immobile that Ragnarson feared he had suffered a stroke.

"Shinsan? You're sure?"

"Blackfang's bringing the proof. Armor from their dead. And the child… He's training with Mist herself. She was at Maisak."

"The child… Did she seem well?" The Queen's voice held such excited interest that Ragnarson half-turned. Then it added up. The child was hers… Then, stunningly, the "she" reached his consciousness.

"Shinsan!" Tarlson gasped.

Ragnarson turned back. Despite his condition, Eanred was trying to rise.

He almost made it. Then he collapsed, fighting for breath. Bloody foam rose to his lips.

"Maighen!" the Queen shouted. "Find Doctor Wachtel! Gjerdrum! Come help your father."

As the boy rushed in, Ragnarson went to the Queen. She seemed ready to faint. He helped her retain her feet.

"Eanred, don't die," she begged softly. "Not now. What'll I do without you?"

When aloofness and dignity abandoned her, Ragnarson caught a glimpse of the frightened woman behind the facade. So young, so defenseless.

Ignoring his filth, she clung to him, head over his heart. "Help me!" she begged.

What else could he do?

v) Hour of reprisal

Mocker thought the crash and clash and screaming meant that the Queen's Own had come back for a sudden rematch. He was so sick that he didn't look up. Why bother?

The clangor moved closer. For a long time he did nothing more ambitious than blow his nose on his sleeve. He was sorry immediately. The stench of the corpse five places to his right reached him despite the downpour. The fellow had died four days earlier. No one had bothered to remove him. As the Siluro uprising continued to be delayed, the Volstokiners became increasingly lax, increasingly defeatist. Vodicka and the shaghûn had had bitter arguments about it. Vodicka himself had become dull-witted and unconcerned.

Mocker's stomach turned. The little he had had to eat had been moldy, spoiled. Staggering to his feet, he dragged his nearer chainmates along in his rush to the cathole latrine five paces away.

While he squatted with the skirts of his robe around his waist, a spent arrow plopped into the mud nearby. He reached, slipped, fell, came up cursing. The other prisoners cursed him back. A quarter of their number had died already, and disease soon would have them all—and Vodicka's army as well. Dysentery was endemic. In the chain, now, there were no friends, just animals who growled at one another.

The arrow was Itaskian. No native weapon would have used one so long.

He wanted to shout for joy, but didn't have the energy.

He had long despaired of having this opportunity, yet he had prepared. It had taken slow, careful work. He had wanted no one, especially his favor-seeking companions, to discover what he was doing.

First there had been the chains. Each man's right hand was linked to the left ankle of the man on his right. He had, for days, been grinding away at a link with bits of sandstone. That done to his satisfaction, he had gone on to provide himself with weapons.

When the shaghûn and his gaudy smokes appeared at the pavilion entrance, Mocker broke the weakened link and took the best of his weapons from within his robe.

Making the sling had been more difficult than cutting the chain. Everyone was always toying with the latter…

He had three stones, though he expected to get but one shot before being brought down himself. And it had been years…

The sling, twisted of fabric strips from his robe, hummed as he wound up. A few apathetic eyes turned his way.

He let fly.

"Woe!" he moaned. He shook his left fist at the sky, got a faceful of rain. He had missed by such a wide margin that the shaghûn hadn't noticed that he was being attacked.

But no one gave Mocker away. No dusky guards came to pound him back to the mud. The attack was ferocious. Must be some bad fighters out there, he thought.

He turned, glared through the downpour, almost immediately spied Reskird Kildragon. His hopes surged. The best fighters in this end of the world.

His second stone scored. Not with the eye-smashing accuracy he had had as a boy, but close enough to shatter the shaghûn's jaw. The soldier-wizard staggered from his smokes, one hand reaching as if for help. He came toward the prisoners.

Mocker checked the haggard Nordmen. Some were beginning to show interest.

Wobbling on legs weak with sickness, he went to the shaghûn. He swung his length of chain, beat the man to the mud.

Still no interference. But dusky faces were beginning to glance back from the fighting. He used the shaghûn's dagger to finish it quickly.

"Vodicka now," he said, rising with the bloody blade. But through the uproar he heard Kildragon bellowing for his men to close up and withdraw.

And there was no way he could reach them.

"Am doomed," he muttered. "Will roast slow on spit, no skald to sing last brave feat." His hands, deft as those of the pickpocket he had been when Haroun had picked him up early in the wars, ran through the shaghûn's garments, snatched everything loose. He then scooted round the pavilion's rear, hoping to vanish before anyone noticed what had happened.

The Nordmen watched with eyes now jealous and angry. From within the pavilion came Vodicka's querulous voice. He sounded drunk or ill.

Then came shouts as the murder was discovered.

ELEVEN: YEAR 1002 AFE
CLOSING TIGHTER

i) Dying

Death just did not belong in the day. It had dawned bright, warm, and almost cloudless. By noon the streets had dried.

"It isn't right," Gjerdrum said, staring out a window near his father's bed. "In stories it always comes during a stormy night, or on a morning heavy with mist."

The Queen sat beside the bed, holding Tarlson's hand. He had been in a coma since the previous afternoon. "My father calls Death the ultimate democrat," she said. Deep shadows lurked beneath her eyes. "Also the indisputable autocrat and the great leveler. She's not impressed by anything or anyone. Nor by what's fitting and proper."

"Mother wouldn't come. She's locked herself in their bedroom… Says she won't come out till he comes home. Because he always did. He'd take wounds that'd kill a bear, but he always came home. But she knows he won't make it this time. She's trying to bring him back with her memories."

"Gjerdrum, if there was anything… You know I'd…"

"I was conceived in that room. When he was just another Wesson footman. The night before the Queen's Own and the Guard went to meet El Murid in the Gap. Why didn't he ever move? He took over some of the other rooms, but he never moved…"

"Gjerdrum!"

He turned.

"His eyes. They moved."

Tarlson's eyes opened. He seemed to be grasping for his bearings. Then, in a hoarse whisper, "Gjerdrum, come here."

"Don't push yourself, Father."

"There're some things to say. She came, but I couldn't go. Be quiet. Let me hurry. She's waiting. What's Ragnarson doing?"

"Cleaning up the Siluro. He slept a couple hours, then took the regiment and Guard into the quarter. All we've had from him since is prisoners and wagons full of weapons. Doing a house-to-house. They're screaming. But anyone who argues gets arrested. Or killed."

"Gjerdrum, I don't trust that man. I'm not sure why. It may be bin Yousif. There's a connection. They've fought each other, and while their employers got destroyed, they got rich. He knows too much about what's going on. And he may be working for Itaskia. Some of his 'mercenaries' are Itaskian regulars."

He lay quietly for several minutes, regaining strength. "It's a game of empires," he said at last, "and Kavelin's the board.

"Gjerdrum, I made a promise to the King. I've tried to keep it. I pass it to you, if you will… Though the gods know how you'll manage. Any way you can… Tell your mother… I'm sorry… My duty… This time she'll have to come to me. Where the west wind blows… She'll understand… I'll… I'll…"

His eyes slowly closed. For a moment Gjerdrum thought he had fallen asleep. At last, of the Queen, "Is he?… Did he?…"

"Yes."

They spent few tears. Waiting for the inevitable had dulled its painful edge.

"Gjerdrum, find Colonel Ragnarson. Tell him to come to my chambers. And inform the Ministers that there'll be a meeting at eight. Don't tell *anyone* what's happened."

"Ma'am." He snapped a weak salute. In duty there was surcease from pain.

ii) Interview

Ragnarson sat stiffly erect as his horse *clop-clopped* through empty streets. He had to keep an iron grip. He was so tired he had begun seeing things.

A Trolledyngjan rode at either hand, ready for trouble. But they didn't expect anything. The populace had been cowed. They appeared only in brief flashes, in cracks between curtains.

Today Vorgreberg, tomorrow the Siege. Next, Vodicka. And Kavelin before spring. Get the kingdom united in time to meet the Captal and Shinsan.

The palace was as deserted as the city. With the Queen's go-ahead, he had sent out every man able to bear arms. They had met little resistance once it was clear they would not tolerate it.

She was pacing when he reached her, pale, wringing her hands. Her eyes were shadowed.

"Eanred died."

She nodded. "Colonel, it's falling apart. My world. I'm not a strong person. I tend to run rather than face things. Eanred was my strength, as he was my husband's. I don't know what to do now. I just want to get away…"

"Why'd you call me?" He had known from the moment their eyes met that she would appreciate strength and directness more than flourishes and formalities. "I'm a sword-for-hire. An outsider. An untrustworthy one, so Eanred thought."

"Eanred trusted no one but the Krief. Sit down. You've been up long enough."

She was a startling woman. No Royal person he had ever encountered would have treated a blankshield as an equal. And no queen or princess would have had him to her private chambers unchaperoned…

"You're smiling. Why?"

"Uh? Thinking of Royalty. Princesses. A long time ago, in Itaskia… Well, no matter. An unsavory episode, seen from here."

"Brandy?"

She had startled him again. A Queen serving a commoner…

"They're stuffy in Itaskia? Your Royalty?"

"Usually. Why'd you want to see me?"

"I'm not sure. Some questions. And maybe because I need someone to listen." She walked slowly to a window.

Watching her move, Ragnarson's thoughts slipped into channels far from respectful.

"I've called a conference of Ministers. I'll either abdicate and return to my father…"

"My Lady!"

"… or appoint you Marshal and put it all on you." She turned, her gaze locking with his.

He was flabbergasted. "But… Marshal?… I never commanded more than a battalion before this spring. No. You'd get too much resistance. Better pick a Kaveliner…"

"Who could I trust? Who's commanded who hasn't been in touch with the rebels? Eanred. But he's dead. Even my Ministers have hedged their bets."

"But…"

"And though I hate to speak ill of the dead, Eanred couldn't've handled it. He was at his best as Champion. As a field commander he was mediocre. The King understood this."

She retrieved the decanter, poured more brandy.

"He wasn't strong, the King. Couldn't force his will. But he knew men. He could talk to someone fifteen minutes and tell all about them. He knew who could be trusted and who couldn't, and who would be happiest and do best in which post. I wish he were here."

"You need to trust me, but don't know if you can. Ask your questions."

She moved a chair to face him. "What's your connection with the Itaskian Crown?"

"Appointive landgrave. Nonhereditary sort of half-title with a reserve commission. Army. Brevet-Captain of Infantry. I get the use of, and title to, formerly nonproductive border territory in return for playing sheriff and defending the frontier. For political reasons I'm currently active on the War Ministry rolls. My assignment is to prevent El Murid from gaining control of the Savernake Gap and flanking the Tamerice-Hellin Daimiel Line. I'm also a genuine Guild Colonel, though on the Citadel's bad side. My Itaskian assignment doesn't conflict with my contract to yourself."

"At the moment. Your orders might change. Anything else?"

He shrugged. "What?"

"Men the King trusted he sent on trade missions. With other assignments. He knew Kavelin's importance. Those men have continued reporting. For instance: Tamerice was in touch with the Wessons in Sedlmayr and Delhagen. Altea has considered annexing Dolusich, Vidusich, and Gaehle. Anstokin plans the same for the lower tier of provinces in Volstokin, all the way to the Galmiches—assuming we best Vodicka."

"One King always tries to profit from another's distress. The Sedlmayr matter is settled. Altea, I'm sure, prefers friendship and cooperation to war over wastelands. And Anstokin has a historical claim to most of those provinces."

"I was leading up to the fact that we have people in Itaskia. Our best. When your King stomps, the ground rocks throughout the west."

Ragnarson's immediate reaction was *so what?* Then he asked, "In whose party?"

"Excuse me?"

"You suspect Itaskian intentions. I want to point out that we're split. Each party controls part of the government. The Greyfells party is pro-El Murid. The other, intensely anti-El Murid. I wondered if your spies took that into account."

"Which line do you follow?"

"Greyfells and El Murid have been my enemies since the wars."

"I believe you, Colonel. But there's still Haroun bin Yousif. What does he want?"

"We're as close as men can be. But his mind is like one of those puzzle boxes where, when you finally get it open, all you've got is another box."

"But you've got an idea?"

"A guess. Based on geography. He's ready to go back to Hammad al Nakir. There's no better base than Kavelin. Al Rhemish is just over the Kapenrungs. If he could seize the holy places, he might manage a restoration. We only see the fanatics outside. Behind the Sahel, El Murid's support is far from unanimous."

"I see. A problem. But one that can be dealt with when the time comes. He won't have calculated Shinsan into his plans." She rose, returned to the window. "The city? Can it be pacified? The Siege?"

"Those are battles already in hand. I'm looking beyond, to Vodicka."

"Good. There's more to be said and asked, but later. I want you to rest now. That's an order. I want you fresh after the council. If I stay on…" She came to him, took his hands in hers, turned them palms up, studied them, then looked him in the eye. "I'd be in these hands. Be gentle."

iii) Confrontations

Ragnarson had the feeling that a long time had passed. He lay drifting on the edge of sleep, his conscience telling him he should be up and busy, but instead he continued wondering how much meaning he dared attach to the Queen's final words.

Came a knock. "Enter," he grumbled, rising to a sitting position. A lone candle illuminated his room.

Gjerdrum stuck his head in. "Sorry to wake you, Colonel. We've caught a vagrant. Hard to understand him, but I think he says he knows you."

"Eh? Fat man? Dark?"

"Looks like he used to be fat. But he's sick now. I'd say he's had a rough time for a couple months."

"Where is he? Let me get my pants on. How's the chances of me getting something new to wear?"

Gjerdrum glanced at the near-rags he was donning. "I'll try to find something."

"The Queen. How'd her council go?"

"Still on."

"Lead away. Where's he at?"

"Dungeon. We thought that'd be safest."

It was Mocker. Mocker in pathetic shape. He snoozed on a straw-strewn floor.

"Open up," he told the turnkey. "Quietly. Don't wake him."

There had to be a trick. He could not welcome Mocker without one. He hunkered down and tickled the fat man's ear. He had grown an ugly, scraggly beard. This Ragnarson tweaked gently. "Wake up, darling," he said in a squeaky falsetto.

Mocker smiled, placed one hand over Ragnarson's. He frowned in consternation—then bounced up ready for a fight.

Bragi roared, rocked back on his heels. "Got you!"

"Hai!" Mocker groaned in a weak imitation of his former self. "Greatest of great spies risks life and limb of very self-important self, endures months of incarceration, debilitation, and torture at behest of friend, weary unto death and on edge of pneumonia, with Volstokiners hordes pursuing, treks thirty miles godforsaken country after redoubtedly—redoubtably?—singlehandedly slaying arch-shaghûn of Volstokin advisers, shaghûn-general direct from councils at Al Rhemish, thereby saving bacon of ingrate associates Preshka and Kildragon, and am welcomed to saved city by dungeon-chucking natives too ignorant to recognize renowned self, there to be set upon by hairy Trolledyngjan of dubious masculinity and questionable morals. Woe! In whole universe is no justice. Very demons of despair pursue self through vale of tears called life…"

Ragnarson got lost in the twists and turns. "Rolf's here? In Kavelin?" If Rolf had joined Reskird, Elana might have, too.

"Said same, no? Preshka, Rolf. Iwa Skolovdan. Former Guild Captain. Age thirty-six. Nineteen years service. Began with Lauder's Company…"

"All right. All right. Give me the part about the shaghûn again."

Mocker regained his verve while he detailed his escape.

"Come on," said Ragnarson. "We'll clean you up and have the Royal physician look you over." On the way, Ragnarson bombarded his friend with questions. Each answer pleased him more than the last.

"Gjerdrum," he said, as they neared his room, "scare up the physician. Then have all officers assemble in the officers' mess. Have them bring maps of the area where Vodicka's camped. And I want my Marena Dimura there. Then meet me at the council chamber. How do I get there?"

"But you can't…"

"Watch me. I could care less about being respectful to a gang of lard-assed Nordmen hypocrites. Tell me."

Reluctantly, the youth gave directions.

"Carry out your orders. Wait. What the hell time is it, anyway?"

"Around midnight."

Ragnarson groaned. He had wasted eight hours sleeping.

Two Palace Guards blocked the council chamber door. "Announce me," he told the senior.

"Sorry, sir. Lord Lindwedel left instructions that they weren't to be disturbed for any reason."

"Eh? Why? What if something happened?"

The soldier shrugged. "I got the idea they were going to have it out with Her Majesty."

"Ah." The old snake had found out about Eanred.

"You'd better get out of the way." His cold determination made the younger guard gulp.

"No, sir," the senior said. "Not till my orders change." His knuckles whitened on the haft of his short ceremonial pike.

Bragi hit him with a left jab. His helmet clanged off the wall. Ragnarson snatched his pike, knocked the second soldier's feet from beneath him, rattled the first's brains again, then hit the door. It was neither locked nor barred. He crashed through.

Just in time.

Seven old Nordmen surrounded the Queen like lean gray wolves a terrified fawn. She had been weeping, was about to sign a document. The triumph on the Ministers' faces, before they turned, told Ragnarson he had guessed right. They had bullied her into abdicating.

He took three swift steps, smashed the pike head down on the document. Hurling Ministers aside, Bragi seized the document, flung it into a nearby fireplace.

Lindwedel shouted, "Guards!"

"Keep your mouth shut, you old vulture!" Ragnarson growled, drawing his sword. "Or I'll cut you a new one about four inches lower." He backed to the door, locked and barred it.

He wished he had a few Trolledyngjans along. He would have to hurry instead…

"You men get over against that wall." He moved to the Queen's side. She appeared uncertain whether to be grateful or angry. He scowled at a Minister edging toward the door.

"If I were younger, I'd…"

"You'd get your ass killed. Haven't met a Nordmen yet who could butcher a chicken without help. Let's get this settled civilly. We'll let the Lady make up her mind on her own."

Their glares promised trouble. There would soon be plots to eliminate the foreigner who defended the foreign Queen.

"Why'd you bust in?" the Queen whispered.

"Friend of mine just arrived," he replied softly. "From Vodicka's camp. Wanted you to know what he said. When I got trouble outside, I figured these old buzzards were up to something."

"What was so important?"

"Vodicka's shaghûn is dead, Vodicka has gone insane, and his army has been decimated by sickness. His men are deserting. My associate Kildragon has placed a force west of them as an anvil against which I can hammer them. I'll begin tightening the noose in the morning."

"You're pushing too hard. Killing yourself. You've got to rest sometime."

"You rest between wars," he muttered. Then, "We can't ease off. There're still too many variables. And Shinsan's vultures are perched on the crags of the Kapenrungs."

"You won't wait for your man Blackfang?"

"No. But he'll be here soon. I don't intend getting in a fight anyway, just to maneuver Vodicka into a bad position."

"The numbers don't look good."

"Numbers aren't important. Still want to run away? To quit when we've got a glimmer of hope?"

"I don't know. I wasn't made for this. Intrigue. War."

"I promise you, if it's within my power, that I won't go till I can leave you with the quietest country in the Lesser Kingdoms. If I have to leave rebels hanging like apples from every tree."

"But you're a mercenary. And have a family and home, I hear."

Did she sound just the least disappointed? "I have no home while the Greyfells party retains any power. The appointment?"

"They'll never agree."

"Bet?" He turned to the Ministers. "Her Majesty wishes your confirmation of my appointment as Marshal of Kavelin."

Some turned red and sputtered. Lord Lindwedel croaked, "Never! No base-born foreigner…"

"Then we'll hang you and appoint some new Ministers."

The door rattled as someone tried it. The Ministers perked up.

Ragnarson could force his will here, he knew, but how would he keep them from reneging?

Haroun's would be the simplest solution. *He* would have them murdered.

"You wouldn't dare!"

Men smashed against the door.

"Try me. The charge is treason. I believe Her Majesty will support it."

Axes began splintering the door.

The Queen touched his arm. "Appearances will decide this. Back into the corner like you're defending me."

She had chosen. He smiled, did as she suggested. She attached herself to his left arm in the classic pose of damsel hanging on protector.

Lord Lindwedel surrendered. "All right, damn it. Have the documents prepared."

Bragi held his pose long enough for Gjerdrum and the Queen's troops to catch a glimpse. Thus it was that, dishonestly, he won their loyalty.

iv) The challenge

There was snow on the ground, a sprinkling scarcely thicker than frost, tainted ruby in the dawnlight. A harsh cold wind stirred skeletal trees. Bragi, astride a shivering horse at wood's edge, glanced up the road that snaked over the hill masking Vodicka's camp. With him were the irrepressible Mocker and a dozen of his own and the Queen's men. Mocker blew into shaking hands and bemoaned the impulse that had brought him into the field.

For a week Ragnarson had maneuvered his forces into position, hoping for a fiat that would spare lives. He would need every man in the spring.

To the north, blocking the route to Volstokin, were Blackfang and Ahring with the Trolledyngjans and Itaskians. Sir Andvbur, for the moment commanding the Queen's Own and Palace Guard, held the routes eastward. In the south lay Altenkirk with eleven hundred Wessons and Marena Dimura. The woods behind Vodicka were held by Kildragon and Preshka.

Everyone had been in position since the day before. The men had been given a night's rest and plenty to eat… This one he wouldn't hurry. It would be his most crucial battle, one that, in its handling more than its winning, could make him as Marshal of Kavelin.

"You'd better get going," he told Mocker.

The fat man kicked his new donkey into a walk. He had volunteered to find Haroun. He would skirt the battle zone and, hopefully, would know the outcome before passing Kildragon's last outpost. He also bore messages to Vodicka's family.

Ragnarson turned to another of his companions. "Bring her out."

Against his advice and over the protests of her supporters, the Queen had insisted on joining him.

In minutes she was at his side, bundled in furs that concealed ill-fitting chain mail. She bubbled.

Ragnarson nodded. "We begin." He urged his mount forward. She kept pace. His party trailed by twos.

Ragnarson's heart hammered. His stomach flipped and knotted. Doubts plagued him. Had he chosen the best course? Sure, it was the way to slay the rumors about him not leading from the front, but… What if Vodicka refused his challenge?

He leaned toward the Queen, said, "If you bring as much excitement and stubbornness to ruling as you do to getting in a fight, you'll…"

Her thigh brushed his. He wasn't sure, but it seemed she'd guided her mount the slightest bit closer to his. He remembered riding thigh by thigh with Elana, with mortal dangers waiting to strike.

"You're a beautiful woman," he croaked, forcing the compliment. Then he ameliorated his boldness with, "You shouldn't risk yourself like this. If we're taken…"

There was red in her face when she looked his way. Had he angered her?

"Marshal," she said, "I'm a woman. Noble by birth, Queen in marriage to a man *long* dead, and leader by circumstance. But a woman."

He thought he understood. And that was more frightening than anything that might be waiting beyond the hill.

They crested that hill. "You're sure the messages went out?" He had asked her to send commands to every Nordmen to post public pledges of fealty or face banishment or death. News of today's events would pursue the messengers, would convince or condemn.

"Yes." Slight exasperation.

He studied the encampment. Vodicka had restructured it along Imperial lines, throwing up ramparts and cutting trenches. Towers for archers were under construction. It had taken two attacks for Vodicka to learn that he wasn't on bivouac.

"Banners," Ragnarson growled over his shoulder. They had been noticed.

The Krief family ensign broke beside a white parlay flag. Ragnarson advanced till they were just beyond the range of a good Itaskian bow. This would be the point for one of Greyfells's rogues to materialize.

They waited. And waited. The nearest gate finally opened. Horsemen came forth.

"Here," Ragnarson told the Queen, "is where, if I were Haroun, you'd learn the difference in our thinking. He'd make some innocuous signal and our bowmen could cut them down. Haroun goes for the throat."

Vodicka wasn't with the party.

"They look like they've spent a year besieged already," the Queen remarked. She was old enough to remember the bitter sieges in her homeland.

Ragnarson signaled an interpreter. The common speech of Volstokin was akin to Marena Dimura. The upper classes used a different dialect.

The party was a mixed bag including several senior officers of Volstokin's army, a few of El Murid's advisors, Kaveliner turncoats, and a man with a bow who looked Itaskian.

A Kaveliner recognized the Queen, babbled excitedly to his companions.

"Tell them our business is with Vodicka," Ragnarson told his interpreter. The lingua franca of the upper classes was the speech of Hellin Daimiel.

An officer replied, "I speak for King Vodicka. No need for the interpreter." He spoke flawless upper-class Itaskian. "I'm Commander of the Household, Seneschal Sir Farace Scarna of Liolios."

"Guild Colonel Bragi Ragnarson, Marshal of Kavelin, with and speaking for Her Supreme Highness Fiana Melicar Sardyga ip Krief, Queen of Kavelin, daughter and ally of His Highness Dusan Lorimier Sardygo, Lord Protector of Sacuescu, the Bedelian League, and the Auszura Littoral, and Prince Viceregal to Their Majesties the Kings of Dunno Scuttari and Octylya." Which didn't mean much, Sacuescu being powerless, Dunno Scuttari still recovering from the wars, and Octylya an Itaskian Protectorate as subject to pressure from the Queen's enemies as friends.

"What do you want?"

Ragnarson was pleased by Sir Farace's businesslike manner. A fighting man all his life, Bragi judged.

"I challenge Vodicka to individual combat. And demand the surrender of himself and his forces. The former as Champion, the latter as Marshal."

"Champion?"

"Your King has had that much success, Sir Farace," the Queen interjected.

Sir Farace said something in his own tongue. Reluctantly, all but he withdrew a hundred yards.

"Pull back the same distance, Dehner," Bragi ordered.

"The lady, too, and it please you."

Ragnarson turned. She was putting her stubborn face on. "My Lady."

"Must I?"

"I think so."

Once they were alone, scant swordswings apart, Sir Farace asked, "Man to man? Not as Seneschal and Marshal?"

"All right."

"Can you beat us?"

"Easily. But I'll starve you out instead. I've talked to deserters. I know what's going on inside."

"Damned foreigners… Intrigues and magic. And greed. Destroyed an army and a King." He paused, spat. "I'd surrender. Save what I could. But I'm not His Majesty. The weaker he gets, the more he grows sure we can finish Kavelin if we'll just hold on till we get another sorcerer from Al Remish." He spat again. "He won't surrender. He might fight."

"You could sally, come over the hill, and surrender."

"No."

"I didn't think so. How bad is he?"

"Very. Healthy, he'd give you a battle. He fought Tarlson to a draw once. Years ago. He wears the scar proudly."

"What happens if I kill him? In Volstokin?"

"You wouldn't notice the change. His brother, whom you defeated at Lake Berberich, succeeds. The war goes on."

"How, with Volstokin in ruins and threatened by famine?"

"The rumors are true?"

"I know bin Yousif."

"Why this confrontation?"

"This army's a nuisance. I've got more dangerous enemies to worry about. Suppose I grabbed Vodicka and threw him in a cell somewhere? Kept him in style, but didn't ransom him?"

"A regency. Probably the Queen Mother. His Majesty's brother, Jostrand, isn't that popular."

"And this infamous alliance with El Murid?"

"Dead. Dead as the Emperors in their graves."

"Then imprisonment might best serve both Volstokin and Kavelin."

"Perhaps."

"A gift to show my feeling that there should be peace between us. Anstokin moves with spring. They intend to take the provinces above Lake Berberich, all the way to the Galmiches."

Sir Farace grew pale. He started to say something, nodded. Then, "Of course. We should've anticipated it."

"Our sources are unimpeachable."

"I believe you. I'll talk to His Majesty, but I guarantee nothing. Good fortune."

"The same." He said it to Sir Farace's dwindling back.

v) Personal combat

"Well, what'd he say?" the Queen demanded.

"We might work something out."

"You won't attack?"

"Not if I can help it."

"But…"

"I didn't get this old fighting for fun. Let's get back to the woods. This wind's killing me."

While the others piled brush into a windbreak and got a fire going, and saw to the horses and weapons, Bragi and the Queen sat on a log and stared at Vodicka's encampment. Bragi was looking for weaknesses, the gods knew what.

"Beckring," Ragnarson said presently. "Find Sir Andvbur. Tell him I need a crossbow, a pony or his runtiest horse, and a Cerny." The Cerny, a breed developed near that small city in Vorhangs, was a gigantic horse meant to bear the most heavily armored knights.

"Now what?" the Queen asked.

"Hedging my bets. That's another way you stay alive in this business."

"I don't understand."

"I just remembered. Haroun isn't the only guy who thinks his way. His whole race … Can you kill a man? If he's trying to kill you?"

"I don't know."

"Better think about it. Better be ready when the time comes." He began fiddling with his boots.

Beckring brought the animals and weapons just as a party left Vodicka's camp. Ragnarson explained as he hurried his people to the meeting point. He rode the Cerny, she the pony. The men crowded close so they could hear.

When the Volstokiners arrived, without Vodicka or Sir Farace, Ragnarson had the Cerny sideways to them with the Queen masked behind him. He presented his shield side.

Sir Farace had been replaced by an idiot, a terrified, drooling victim of some disease that had crippled both brain and body.

Ragnarson had anticipated the action. Vodicka had done the same in other wars. He ignored the man, concentrated on the "advisers."

They were too studiedly disinterested. He locked gazes with a hawk-nosed veteran who wore a mouth-corner scar that drew his lips into a permanent smirk.

Smirk-mouth's eyes flicked, for the scantest instant, to the man who was to provide his diversion…

Ragnarson spurred the Cerny. His right hand, already low, yanked the throwing knife from his boot, snapped it at Scar-mouth's throat. The Queen, no longer masked, discharged the crossbow into the chest of a second rider while all eyes remained on Bragi. His party produced their weapons and surrounded her. Before the startled Volstokiners, unprepared for their allies' treachery, recovered, Bragi had gotten round their flank. There he met a third adviser in a flurry of swordplay, unhorsed him, and faced the Volstokiners as they turned to run.

The mixup was brief. Bragi lost one man. The other party lost five before they surrendered.

Ragnarson dismounted, removed his ax from his wargear, separated Scar-mouth's head from his body. He handed it to the idiot. "Tell Vodicka this's the game I play with treachers. Tell him I say he's a coward, a baseborn whoreson who sends assassins after people he's too craven to face himself."

"We better get out of here," said one of Bragi's men.

"Yeah." He scrambled onto the Cerny.

While they watched Sir Andvbur's men skirmish with Volstokiners who had come out to aid their fellows, Bragi told the Queen, "You look ill. He would've killed you."

"It's not that. I've seen men die… The head…"

"Didn't give me any joy either. But gruesome doings sometimes save lives."

"I know. I understand. But that doesn't make me like it."

His own stomach was in poor shape.

The skirmishing died away. After transferring his gear to a fresh horse, Ragnarson mounted, said, "Time for the next phase." He took a Royal standard from a bearer, spurred downhill.

He went at a trot, carefully studying the ground and distant ramparts. He went to a canter, then, at bowshot, to a gallop. Volstokiners watched in surprise as he spurred past their earthworks, shouting insults at Vodicka. A few desultory arrows reached for him.

One whirred past his nose. He laughed like one of the battle-crazy berserker heroes of his boyhood homeland. His hair and beard whipped with the speed of the horse's passage. He hadn't felt such exhilaration in years.

He stopped beyond bowshot and waited. Then his high spirits got the better of him. He made a second passage, this time planting the Queen's standard on a mound near Vodicka's gate.

"You're mad!" the Queen cried, when he returned for a fresh mount. "Completely insane!" But she was laughing. And there was a new, more promising sparkle in her eyes.

"He's got to come out now. Or admit he's a coward to his whole army."

"He'll come in full knight's regalia," said Sir Andvbur, who had grabbed an opportunity to put himself near the Queen. "You won't be able to handle him…"

His spirits still soared. "Watch me!" Despite the cold, he shed garments till he was down to basic Trolledyngjan war gear. He hung helmet, shield, and sword on his horse, then ran into the woods where a Guard's infantry company lay hidden. He returned with a long pike.

"What you got to do," he explained, "is outgut them. When they *know* you're easy meat, but you stand your ground and grin, they get nervous. And make mistakes."

He realized he was showing off, but what he saw in the Queen's eyes made rational behavior impossible.

He rode to the meeting point, dismounted, planted a fresh standard, walked twenty paces downslope, leaned on the pike.

Trumpets winded. The encampment gate opened. A knight came forth.

This time Ragnarson faced Vodicka. He continued leaning on the pike, motionless. The horseman trotted back and forth, getting the feel of the earth, then rode uphill and stopped a hundred yards away.

As Ragnarson examined that mass of blood and steel, weighing nearly a ton and a half, he began to doubt. The horse was as protected as its rider.

Bragi continued leaning as if bored. He was committed.

Vodicka wasted no time talking. He couched his lance and charged.

The King's horse began to loom castle-huge. Bragi dropped to one knee, set his pike, lifted his shield. Could he hold each solidly enough?

He had made a major miscalculation. Vodicka's lance outreached his pike.

He shifted slightly, was unable to finish before impact.

Vodicka came in with his lancehead aimed at Ragnarson's chest, intending to blast him off the pike and finish him with his sword.

Bragi twisted his shield and pushed, to deflect the lance.

It ripped through his shield, down the underside of his forearm. Its impetus bore him over backward. But his right arm and hand remained oak-firm for the instant needed to bring Vodicka to grief. The pike head met the horse at the juncture of shoulder and breastplate. The screaming beast's momentum levered it into the air.

Ragnarson's sprawl forced Vodicka's lancehead into the earth.

Rearing horse and levering lance separated Vodicka from his saddle. As Ragnarson scrambled away, Volstokin's King landed with a horrendous clangor. Bragi was on him instantly, swordtip at the slot in the man's visor.

"Yield!"

"Kill me," muffled, weak.

Ragnarson glanced toward Vodicka's encampment. No rescue mission yet. He wrestled the helmet free. Yes, he had caught the genuine fish. He punched the King's jaw.

"Ouch!" He kissed his knuckles, with a knife cut the straps and laces holding Vodicka's armor. He finished barely in time to get uphill ahead of a band of would-be rescuers.

"He's in bad shape," Ragnarson told the Queen as he rode up. "Better get him to a doctor. To the palace. Won't be worth a farthing dead. Somebody find me some bandages."

While men dragged Vodicka away, the Queen took Ragnarson's hand. "For a minute I thought…"

"So did I. I'll grow up one of these days." Examining his arm, he found no major veins severed. A surgeon put a field dressing on, told him to avoid exertion for a few days.

"Sir Andvbur," he said, "begin the next phase."

The knight's men began pushing earthworks forward.

TWELVE: THE YEARS 1002-1003 AFE
COMPLICATIONS AND NEW DIRECTIONS

i) Recovery and preparation

Volstokin's army fell apart. Man by man, then by companies, Vodicka's soldiers surrendered their weapons, and began the walk home. Within a week the encampment was deserted—except for El Murid's advisers and a few high officers. Ragnarson withdrew to the capital. Blackfang and the Trolledyngjans finished the job.

Pledges of fealty flooded in, especially from the provinces wasted. From Walsoken, Trautwein, Orthwein, and Uhlmansiek the response was spotty. From Loncaric and the Galmiches there was a forbidding silence. From Savernake they expected nothing, and nothing was what they got.

Rumors from the east had winged men soaring the cold winter nights, flitting from castle to castle.

Kavelin had two small industrial regions, the Sieges of Breidenbach and Fahrig. Breidenbach served the mines of the Galmiches, Loncaric, and Savernake. The Royal Mint was located there. To secure this, and as an experiment, Ragnarson sent Sir Andvbur Kimberlin north—across Low Galmiche.

Militarily, Fahrig was more important. It lay at the heart of iron-rich Forbeck, and received ores from Uhlmansiek and Savernake as well. It was there Kavelin's iron and steel were made, and weapons and armor forged.

Both Sieges were heavily Wesson. The Queen would find support there.

Forbeck and Fahrig became Ragnarson's pet winter project. Securing them would not only insure his weapons supply, it would split the still rebellious provinces into two groups. The southern tier were comparatively weak.

They had gotten numerous declarations of fealty out of Forbeck, mostly from lesser nobles whose fortunes depended on open trade routes. The great landholders favored the Captal's pretender.

While Ragnarson studied, pondered, maneuvered his troops through the Siege of Vorgreberg, made requests and recommendations, and wished he controlled some means of communication as swift as the Captal's, the Queen put in eighteen-hour days trying to rebuild a shattered hierarchy. There were banishments and outlawries, and instruments of social import, each bitterly resisted in council.

Most resisted was confirmation of Ragnarson's bargain with the aldermen of Sedlmayr. On confirmation, Sedlmayr sent Colonels Kiriakos and Phiambolos and six hundred skilled arbalesters to Vorgreberg, and raised levies to pacify Walsoken.

Another edict guaranteed certain rights of free men, especially Wessons.

Even for serfs there was a new right. One son in each family would be permitted to leave the land for service with the Crown. For Kavelin, with its traditional class rigidities, this was a revolutionary device for social mobility.

Though they moaned, the Nordmen yielded little there. The chaos in the west had separated countless serfs from their masters. Many had become robbers and brigands. The device would bring them out of outlawry.

Men began filtering into the Siege.

Responsibilities went with rights. Ragnarson, slyly, injected into the decrees the concept of every man a soldier in defense of his own. Each adult male was ordered to obtain and learn to use a sword.

He was surprised how easily that slipped past the Ministers. Men with swords stood a little taller, stopped being unquestioning instruments of their lords' wills.

Two months passed. Warnecke came into the fold. Vodicka became the dour, grimly silent tenant of a tower shared with a manservant sent him by Sir Farace. The Wessons of Fahrig hinted interest in a charter like Sedlmayr's. Rolf Preshka's health deteriorated till he spent most of his time in bed. Turran and Valther disappeared. But their hands could be seen. The winter in the lowlands was unusually mild. In the high country it was bitter beyond memory. Sir Andvbur occupied Breidenbach. And Bragi spent more and more time in the field, drilling his forces in the southeastern portion of the Siege.

One blustery morning his engineers threw a pontoon across the Spehe to the Gudbrandsdal. He invaded Forbeck.

ii) Ghost hunting

Mocker huddled between buildings in Timpe, a minor city in Volstokin, cursing the weather and his own ill fortune. He had been in the kingdom two months and had yet to uncover a hint of Haroun's whereabouts. The warmest trail hadn't been hot since autumn. A few guerrillas remained, but the big man had vanished.

A ragged party of soldiers appeared, returning from Kavelin. They exchanged bitter words with people in the streets. Mocker retreated to deeper shadows. No point giving foul tempers a scapegoat.

"Well," said a voice from the darkness, softly, "see what the hounds have flushed."

One hand darting beneath his robes for a dagger, Mocker looked around. He saw no one. "Haroun?"

"Could be."

"Self, have been traipsing over half arse-end of world…"

"So I've heard. What's your problem?"

Mocker tried to explain while hunting. He saw nothing but unnaturally deep shadow.

"So what's Bragi want?" the sourceless voice demanded. "He's doing all right. He could make himself king."

"Hai! Enemies thus far ground in mill of great grinder northern friend like ants in path of anteater. But now anteater comes to narrow in road where lion waits…"

"What're you babbling about? El Murid? He won't attack. He's got trouble at home."

"Woe! Know-it-all son of sand witch, spawn of mating of scorpion with open-mouthed jackass, or maybe camel, plotting like little old lady Fates, mouth always open and eyes always closed…"

"I missed something. And I'm being told to shut up long enough to hear what."

"Hai! Is not stupid after all. O stars of night, witness. Is able to add up twos." Carefully, wasting fewer words than usual, he told what Bragi had encountered in the Savernake Gap.

"I should've expected something. Always there're complications. The gods themselves contend against me." Angrily, "I defy them. The Fates, the gods, the thrones in Shinsan. Though the world be laid in ruin and the legions of Hell march forth from the seas, I'll return."

It was the oath Haroun had sworn while fleeing from Hammad al Nakir long ago.

Of all the Royal House, descendants of the Kings and Emperors of Ilkazar, only Haroun had survived to pursue a restoration. He alone had been nimble, swift, and hard enough to evade the arrows, blades, and poisons of El Murid's assassins, to become, in exile, the guerrilla chieftain known as the King Without a Throne.

Mocker decided it was time an old, nagging question got asked. "Haroun, in case Fates serve up wicked chance with left hands, ending life of old marching companion, what of Cause? Are no successors, hey? Leaders of Royalists, yes. Grim old men in dark places, lying poisoned blades in hand for enemies of Haroun. But no sons of same to pick up swords and go on pursuing elusive crown."

Bin Yousif laughed bitterly. "Perhaps. Perhaps not. I've taken roads walked alone, have secrets unshared. Still, if I'm gone, what do I care?"

"Well, I've hoarded a trick or two, like a miser. Guess it's time to spend them."

Mocker, still trying to detect something in the darkness, was startled by a sudden wail from a few feet away. "Haroun?"

The answer was a moan of fear. The darkness faded.

Haroun was gone. Always, in recent years, it had been that way. There was no more closeness, no shared truth between them. Yet Haroun continued presuming on friendships formed in younger days.

The sounds of distress continued. Mocker pushed into the dying darkness.

He found an old beggar barely this side of death. "Demons," the man mumbled. "Possessed by demons."

Mocker shuddered, frowned. Haroun had found him, but he hadn't found Haroun. From somewhere else, anywhere, by sorcery, bin Yousif had spoken through the old man. So. His old friend *had* been studying the dark arts.

With the best of intentions, no doubt. But Haroun's character…

The appearance of several soldiers at the street exit, drawn by the beggar's wails, made Mocker take to his heels.

Very dissatisfactory, he thought, his robes flying. The trip had been a waste. He should abandon everything and return to Nepanthe.

iii) The night visitors

Operating armies in winter, even on Kavelin's small scales, presented almost insuperable problems. Bragi crossed the Spehe with rations for ten days. That he entered the Gudbrandsdal was more to take advantage of game than to come at Forbeck unexpected.

He passed through the forest slowly, pursuing routes previously marked by the Marena Dimura, his men scattering to hunt. Two days passed before he allowed his patrols beyond the forest's eastern verge.

The loyalties of the Forbeck nobility seemed proportional to distance from Vorgreberg. They encountered resistance only beyond Fahrig. The Nordmen there supported the Captal's pretender.

Blackfang's Trolledyngjans, who found the winter mild, whooped from town to castle.

After three weeks, Ragnarson passed command to Blackfang and returned to Vorgreberg.

Little had happened in his absence. An assassin, of the Harish Cult of Hammad al Nakir, had been caught climbing the castle wall. He had committed suicide before he could be questioned. Three Ministers had been thrown in the dungeon. Her Majesty had coped.

He saw her briefly before retiring. She was haggard.

Deep in the night a daydream came true, something he had both wanted and feared.

At a touch he suddenly sat upright in darkness. His candle was out. He grabbed for the dagger beside it.

A hand pushed against his chest. A woman's hand. "What?..." he rumbled.

A barely audible, "Shh!" He lay back. Fabric rustled as clothing fell. Long, slim nakedness slid in beside him. Arms surrounded him. Small, firm breasts pressed against his chest. Hungry lips found his...

Next morning he was still unsure it hadn't been a dream. There was no evidence save his own satiation. And the Queen seemed unchanged.

Had it been someone else? Her maidservant, Maighen, whose flirting eyes had long made her willingness evident? But Maighen was a plumpish Wesson with breasts like pillows.

Each night the mystery compounded itself, though she came earlier and earlier and stayed longer and longer.

The day Haaken sent word of the surrender of the last rebels in Forbeck, Gjerdrum asked, "What're you doing nights, anyway?"

Ragnarson flashed a guilty look. "A lot of worrying. How do you beat sorcery without sorcery?"

Gjerdrum shrugged.

All questions had their answers. Sometimes they weren't pleasant; sometimes the circumstances of resolution were distressing.

The latter was the case the night Bragi unraveled the mystery of his lover's identity.

The first scream barely penetrated his passion. The second, cut off, grabbed like the hand of a clawed demon.

It had come from the Queen's chambers.

He grabbed his weapons and, naked, charged up the corridor.

The guards before the Queen's door lay in a heap. Blood trickled over the edge of the balcony to the floor below.

Ragnarson hit the door, broke the lock, charged through. He roared into the Royal bedchamber in time to seize a man trying to force himself through a window. He clapped the man's temple, knocked him out.

Ragnarson turned to the Queen's bed. Maighen. And over her now, clenched fist at her mouth, the Queen herself, naked. A dagger protruded from Maighen's throat.

Despite the situation, his eyes roamed a body he had known only by touch. She reddened.

"Get something on," he ordered. He grabbed a blanket, tied it around his waist, returned to Maighen.

There was no hope.

Gjerdrum and three guardsmen entered.

"Get those doors closed," Ragnarson ordered. "Don't let anyone in. Or out. You men. Watch that fellow over there. Gjerdrum, get the city gates closed. No one in or out till I give the word."

It looked, he thought, as if Maighen had been sleeping in the Queen's bed and the assassin had tried to smother her. She had fought free, screamed, and had taken a panicky dagger.

Turning again, he found Gjerdrum still there. "I thought I told you… Wait! Gjerdrum, don't let it out who died. Let them think it was Her Highness. Let's see who tries to profit. But do mention that we've caught the killer."

Gjerdrum frowned, nodded, departed.

"You men," Ragnarson told the guardsmen, "are going to be out of circulation a while. I don't want you talking to anyone. Understand?" Nods. "All right. You, watch the door. No one gets in. No one." Turning to the Queen, softly, "Slip back to my quarters. Stay out of sight."

"What do you mean?"

"You know perfectly well. There's a passage you use, else those two in the corridor would've spread tales. Be a good girl and scoot."

The assassin came round. He was a Wesson barely old enough to sport a beard. An amateur who had panicked, and who was now eager to cooperate.

But he didn't know who had hired him, though he provided a weak description of the interlocutor.

Bragi promised him that, if he helped trap his principal, he would be allowed to go into exile.

The youth knew but one thing for certain. He had been hired by Nordmen.

Ragnarson jumped to a conclusion. "If they know we've got you, they'll try to kill you…"

"Bait?"

"Exactly."

"But…"

"Your alternative is a date with the headsman."

iv) The worms within

There were four men in the cell with the assassin. Two were genuine prisoners. One was a spy who had been set to watch them. The last was Rolf Preshka.

Rumors of the Queen's murder had run like hares before hounds, threatening to undo all that had been won. Heads leaned together, plotting…

Virtually no one would accept the succession of Crown Prince Gaia-Lange, who had been removed to safety with his grandfather in Sacuescu.

Ragnarson expected the assassin's employers to move swiftly. He wasn't disappointed. Just before dawn three men stole to the cell where Rolf and the youth lay. One was the night turnkey. A soldier and a Nordmen accompanied him.

Rolf controlled a cough as a key squeaked in the lock. He didn't think they could be handled. They were healthy, armed, and Bragi wanted them alive.

But Bragi was nearby. Using information he had bullied from the Queen, he had brought the guardsmen from her chambers to the turnkey's office by secret ways. He had watched the soldier and Nordmen come to the turnkey, had seen gold change hands. Now, hearing the distance-muted rattle of keys, he led the guardsmen through a hidden door.

Weapons clashed in the gloom below. Bragi signed two men thither, left the third to hold the dungeon door.

Reaching the cell, he thundered, "Give it up, you."

Preshka and the boy had backed into a corner. The spy and prisoners had been slain.

The Nordmen attacked Rolf ferociously. The turnkey threw up his hands. The soldier, for a second, seemed torn. Then he too dropped his weapon. Bragi hurled him and the turnkey outside.

He, Rolf, and the youth subdued the Nordmen, though the man tried to get himself killed.

"To the stairs," Ragnarson growled. Sounds of fighting came from the turnkey's office. The would-be killers had left a rearguard of their own, beyond the dungeon door.

The guardsmen returned with another soldier. Both captives, Ragnarson noted, were from companies recently recruited.

He dumped the soldiers and turnkey in with the corpses. The Nordmen and assassin, blindfolded and with hands bound, he took up the secret ways to his apartment.

"Ah, Sir Hendren of Sokolic," the Queen said with false sweetness, as Bragi removed his blindfold. "So you wanted me dead. And I thought you a loyal knight." She slapped him viciously. "I never saw so many stab-in-the-back cowards. Kavelin's infested."

The man went pale. He saw his death before him, but still stood tall and silent.

"Yes, I'm alive. But you might not be long. Unless you tell me who had you hire the boy."

Sir Hendren said nothing.

"Then we'll do it the hard way." Bragi shoved the Nordmen into a chair, began binding his legs.

"What?..." the Queen began.

"Castrate him."

"But..."

"If you don't want to stay…"

"I was going to say he's Lord Lindwedel's man."

"You're sure?"

"As stoutly as Eanred was the Krief's."

"Is that true?" he asked Sir Hendren.

The knight glowered.

"Be back in a few minutes." Bragi gave the Queen a dagger. "Use it if you have to."

He went to Lindwedel's apartment. Circumstantially, he found the Queen's allegations confirmed.

Lindwedel, who rose before noon only in the gravest times, was awake, dressed, and in conference.

After amenities, Lindwedel asked, "What can I do for you, Marshal?"

It took some tall lying, worthy of Mocker at his most imaginative, but he convinced the plotters that they should come to his apartment. He hinted that there were secrets he had uncovered during his tenure, and that he wanted to discuss bringing his troops round to their cause.

The Queen, he discovered, had anticipated him. She and the assassin had gone into hiding. Sir Hendren had been gagged, moved against the wall, and covered with a sheet like a piece of useless furniture. "Ah," Bragi said, pleased. The Ministers glanced at him, puzzled. He stood beside the door while they filed in.

The Queen stepped from hiding. Ragnarson chuckled as sudden pallor hit Nordmen faces.

"Greetings, my lords," she said. "We're pleased you could attend us." She made a sign. The assassin crossed to Sir Hendren, removed the sheet.

Lindwedel plunged toward the door. "Got you again," said Bragi.

"Lindy, Lindy," said the Queen. "Why'd you have to have it all?"

Drawing himself up stiffly, trying to maintain his dignity, Lindwedel refused to reply.

Not so some of his co-conspirators. They babbled the tiniest details of the plot.

They were still babbling when they were hauled before a tribunal. They named more and more names, exposing a vast conspiracy.

The conspirators, silent or talkative, next noon, wore puzzled expressions as the headsman's ax fell. They didn't understand.

Ragnarson, for symbolism, had chosen a Wesson who abjured the black hood. The lesson wasn't wasted.

There was a new order. The masks were off and the despised Wessons were the real power supporting the Crown.

He expected the nocturnal visits to cease. And for three nights they did. But on the fourth she returned. She woke him, and this time didn't extinguish the candle.

THIRTEEN: THE YEARS 1001-1003 AFE
IN THEIR WICKEDNESS THEY ARE BLIND, IN THEIR FOLLY THEY PERSIST

i) He watches from darkness

Once again the winged man came to Castle Krief, this time gliding noiselessly through a moonless, overcast night. He deeply feared that the men would be waiting for him, their cold steel ready to free his soul, but the only soldier he saw was asleep at his post on the wall. He drifted into an open window unnoticed.

Heart hammering, crystal dagger half-drawn, he stole through darkened corridors. His mission was more daring and dangerous than either previous. This time he truly tempted the Fates.

Twice he had to use the tiny wand the Master's lady had given him. He need only point it and squeeze and a fine violet line would touch his target. The sentry would fall asleep.

The first time he almost fainted. When he stepped in front of the man, he found the soldier's eyes still open. But unseeing. Shaking and sighing, Shoptaw made his way to his goal.

It was tricky, finding the room where the Krief held his secret audiences. The Master had visited Castle Krief but once, and that the day before Shoptaw's last visit. Their knowledge of the castle's interior came from men the Master had recruited to help Kiki claim her inheritance. None had been intimates of the King. They knew of the room's existence, but not its location.

So Shoptaw had to trust his own judgment. He was pleased that the Master had such faith in him, but feared that faith might be misplaced. He knew he wasn't as intelligent as the real men... As always, he persevered, for his friend Kiki, for the Master. He found a plain small room down a narrow passage from an ornate large one. It felt right.

He searched the room carefully, preternaturally sensitive fingertips probing for the mechanisms hidden in the walls. It took three hours to find the hidden doorway. With a half-prayer that no one would use it soon, he slipped through.

The passage behind had been designed to his purpose. It ran round three sides of the chamber, had tiny holes for hearing and seeing. Long-undisturbed dust lay deep within, a promising sign. He shed the small pack he had been able to bring, prepared for a long stay.

He had chosen correctly. But for a long time he learned nothing that would be of interest to the Master.

Then came the break he had been awaiting. He knew it the moment the chamber door opened, alerting him, and he reached a peephole in time to see the lean dark man follow the King in. He didn't recognize the man. He was new, a foreigner.

The dark man spoke directly. "Her Majesty will need supporters without a political stake."

"A point you made in your letter."

"None of your Nordmen fit."

"I have the King's Own and the Guard. Their loyalties are beyond question."

"Perhaps. But we're speaking of a time when you won't be here to guide those loyalties."

The King, thought Shoptaw, was a tired old man. The wasting sickness was devouring him. He didn't have long to live. His face often revealed some internal pain.

"Don't overstep good taste, sir."

"You've had time to investigate. You've been stalling for it. You know tact isn't my strong point."

"No. Yet the reports were, in the balance, favorable."

The dark man smiled a thin smile that made Shoptaw think of hungry foxes.

"Granted, I need someone. Granted, your proposal sounds good. Still, I wonder. Your specialty's guerrilla warfare. How would Fiana use you? You couldn't prevent the barons from taking Vorgreberg. Then you'd be unemployed... There is, too, the question of what you hope to gain personally."

"Good. You did your homework. I don't mean to conduct the Queen's defense myself. For that I have in mind a talented gentleman in retirement in Itaskia. He'd conduct the conventional campaign. Most of the arrangements have been made. When we conclude a contract, a regiment will begin gathering."

"Yes, no doubt. You've been ducking in and out of Kavelin for years. Spent a lot of time with the Marena Dimura, I hear. Which leads back to your interest in the matter."

"I could lie to you. I could say it's profit. But you'd know I was lying.

"No matter what you do, no matter how well you prepare, there's going to be a period of adjustment after you pass on. Neither Gaia-Lange nor Fiana is acceptable to your nobility. And you have greedy neighbors. They're watching your health now. They'll complicate and prolong it. Itaskia and El Murid will be watching them, to guard their own interests..."

"My intention is to hit my old enemy while he's distracted."

The Krief chuckled. "Ah. You're devious."

The dark man shrugged. "One sharpens the weapon at hand."

"Indeed. Indeed. Your friend. Do I know him?"

"Unlikely. He's not one of your glory chasers. He's preferred to keep his operations small. But he's as competent as Sir Tury Hawkwind. *And* has a good relationship with such as Count Visigodred and Zindahjira, of whom, I'm sure, you *have* heard."

"Ah? Any man might find such friends useful. His name?"

"Ragnarson, Bragi Ragnarson. Guild Colonel. Though he operates independent of High Crag."

"Not the Ragnarson who was in Altea during the wars?"

"The same. He knocked the point off the spear El Murid ran up the north slope of the Kapenrungs."

"I remember. A lucky victory. It allowed Raithel time to block the thrust. Yes. This might be what I need…"

The winged man had heard enough. For the first time in his vigil he became impatient. He had to fly, to warn the Master.

For he had heard the name Bragi Ragnarson before. Ragnarson was one of the men who had destroyed the father of the Master's lady. He must be terrible indeed.

ii) The wicked persist in their wickedness, and know no joy

"Papa Drake," said Carolan, whispering, "why's Aunt Mist always so sad?"

The old man glanced across his library. Mist stood staring out a westward-facing window, deep in her own thoughts. "She lost something, darling."

"Here? Is that why she's here so much now?"

"You might say. Someone she loved very much… Well…" He dithered, then decided he might as well tell her the whole story.

When he finished, Carolan went over, took Mist's hand. "I'm sorry. Maybe someday…"

Mist frowned, glanced at the Captal, then flashed a bright smile. She hugged the child. "You're priceless."

Through the window, over Mist's shoulder, Carolan saw something hurtling across the sky. "Shoptaw! Papa Drake, Shoptaw's coming. Can I go?…"

"You just wait, young lady. Business first. But you can tell Burla."

As she ran out, Mist said, "He's in an awful hurry. Must be bad news."

Within the half-hour they had heard it all.

"Not to deprecate the man's ability," said Mist, as the Captal began fussing, "but he can be neutralized. I can ask Visigodred not to get involved, and bully Zindahjira into minding his own business. And if we slip the word to El Murid, he'll take care of this Ragnarson for us."

"And if that fails?" The Captal remembered that this Ragnarson had been associated with Varthlokkur. He was more frightened of that man than he had been of Mist's father.

"We'll handle it ourselves. But why worry? Unless the economic picture changes and the politics of High Crag shift, he won't gather much of an army. And if he does, he'll find himself facing my troops, assuming he survives the rebels."

"So many difficulties already…"

"We won't win any victories sitting here."

To the Captal it seemed but moments till their first failure. Nothing they did prevented Ragnarson from leaving Itaskia. Try as he might, he couldn't shake his pessimism.

"I feel Death's hot breath on the back of my neck," he once confided to Burla.

One day Mist announced, "He's in Ruderin. He knows the King's dead. I'll need your help setting a trap."

The Captal, with his creatures, transferred to a small fortress in Shinsan, which, with the help of the Tervola, was projected into Ruderin.

There were complications. Always there were complications.

The whole thing collapsed. And the Captal lost dozens of his oldest friends.

He also suffered a crisis of conscience.

Back in his own library, to Mist, he said, "Don't ever ask me to do anything like that again. If I can't kill more cleanly than that…"

Mist ignored him. She had her own problems. The Tervola were growing cooler and cooler. Her followers still hadn't taken care of O Shing. And Valther… He had disappeared. He had been gone from Hellin Daimiel for months.

But that worry she kept secret. Neither the Tervola nor the Captal would understand…

She spent more and more time at Maisak, delegating more and more authority to her retainers.

iii) The spears of dread pursue them…

Months passed. The excitement of the succession reached a feverish pitch. The Captal did some quiet campaigning. At first he was received coolly, even with mockery, but the swift parade of rebel disasters scrubbed the disdainful smiles from Nordmen faces. A few began mustering at Maisak.

"There're so few of them," said Carolan.

"They don't know you yet," the Captal replied. "Besides, a lot of them want to be King, too."

"The man that's coming… He scares you, doesn't he?" There was no longer any doubt that Ragnarson's swift march was aimed at Maisak. "Is he a bad man?"

"I suppose not. No more than the rest of us. Maybe less. He's on the law's side. We're the bad ones from the Crown's viewpoint."

"Aunt Mist's scared, too. She says he's too smart. And knows too many people." Shifting subject suddenly, "What's she like?"

"Who?"

"My mother. The Queen."

The Captal had supposed she knew. Burla and Shoptaw could deny her nothing. But this was the first time she had brought it up.

"I don't know. I've never met her. Never even seen her. You probably know more than I do."

"Nobody knows very much." She shook her head, tossing golden curls, almost lost the small iron diadem she wore, symbolic of Kavelin's Iron Crown, a legend-haunted treasure that never left the Royal vaults in Vorgreberg. "She's shy, I guess. They say nobody sees her much. She must be lonely."

The Captal hadn't thought of that. Hadn't thought of Fiana as a person at all. "Yes. Probably. Makes you wonder why she stays on. Practically no one wants her…"

Shoptaw appeared. "Master, hairy men very close. In Baxendala now. Traveling fast. Here soon. Maybe two, three day." Though the Trolledyngjans were in the minority in Ragnarson's forces, they had so impressed the winged man that he thought of all enemies as hairy men.

"How many?"

"Many, many. Twice times us, maybe."

"Not good. Shoptaw, that's not good." He thought of the caves, whose mouths he had for years been trying to locate and seal. Ragnarson had a knack for discovering his enemies' weak points. He would know about the caves.

"Shoptaw, old friend, you know what this means?"

"War here." The winged man shuddered. "We fight. Win again. As always."

Carolan hadn't missed their uncertainty. "You'd better tell Aunt Mist."

"Uhn." The Captal didn't like it, though. She would want to bring in her own people. There were more Shinsaners in Maisak now than he liked, a half-dozen grimly silent veterans who were training his troops and keeping their eyes on him.

iv) …And the thing they fear comes upon them

The first troops came through next day, immediately behind Mist and several masked Tervola. She had said she was bringing six hundred. The stream seemed endless to a man who had often heard what terrible soldiers they were. Yet she was honest. He counted exactly six hundred, most of whom left the fortress immediately. Mist was considerate of his sensibilities.

And before long Ragnarson encountered the Captal's little ambushers.

The Captal followed the reports in quiet sorrow, standing rod-stiff in the darkness atop Maisak's wall. It was murder, pure and simple. The little people couldn't cope with the hairy men. He could console himself only with the knowledge that none of them had been conscripted. They had asked for weapons.

There was a fierce, bloodthirsty determination in the enemy's approach that startled and frightened him. It didn't seem characteristic of the Ragnarson who had swept the lowlands. Then he learned what had been done to Ragnarson's scouts.

He was enraged. His first impulse was to confront Mist and her generals… But no, with their power they would simply push him aside and take over. He did order his small friends to cease disputing the pass. In a small way, in lessened readiness and increased casualties, Shinsan would pay for its barbarity.

Ragnarson didn't come whooping in as expected, as past performance suggested he would.

Many of the Captal's friends, and a startling number of Mist's troops, died before the Tervola felt ready to commit Carolan's men.

Mist visited his station on the wall, from which he watched Shinsaners being harassed by bowmen. "We're ready." She had sensed his new coldness and was curious. He had already told her he wouldn't discuss it till the fighting ended.

"You're positive she'll be safe?"

"Drake, Drake, I love her, too. I wouldn't let her go if there was a ghost of a chance she'd get hurt."

"I know. I worry like a grandmother. But I can't help feeling this man's more dangerous than you think. He *knew* what he was up against when he came here. Why'd he keep coming?"

"I don't know, Drake. Maybe he's *not* as smart as you think."

"Maybe. If Carolan gets hurt…"

Mist wheeled and went below. Soon she and Carolan, leading Kaveliner recruits, departed Maisak's narrow gate.

When the swift-sped arrows dropped from the darkness, he said only, "I knew it. I knew it," and plunged down steps to ground level.

In moments he was beside Carolan. "Baby, baby, are you all right?"

Subsequent events seemed anti-climactic. He bickered with Mist, dispiritedly.

"Sometimes, Drake," she once murmured, "I wish I could give it all up."

iv) What does a man profit?

Winter came early, and with a vengeance. The Captal had never seen its like. In normal times it would have been cause for distress. But there were no late caravans to be shepherded through the Gap. Hardly a traveler had crossed all summer.

The Captal welcomed the weather. He would have no trouble with Ragnarson before spring.

Mist damned it. She foresaw them facing a united Kavelin next summer.

The Captal kept his winged creatures watching the lowlands. Ragnarson seemed unable to avoid success— yet each redounded to the Captal's benefit. Ever more Nordmen turned to his standard. Because of his power, he thought. Because he was the one enemy Ragnarson hadn't been able to reduce.

He realized these new allies would abandon him the instant the loyalists collapsed, but that was a problem he could solve in its time. For the present he had to concentrate on old enemies.

Though his couriers brought news consisting entirely of lists of towns and castles and provinces lost, he began to hope. In the free provinces several hitherto uncommitted Nordmen were turning rebel for each turning loyalist.

The edicts flowing from Vorgreberg had changed the root nature of the struggle. The issue, now, was a power struggle between Crown and nobility, one which would preserve or sweep away many ancient prerogatives. And it had become a class war. The underclasses, bought by Crown perfidy, strove to wrest privilege from their betters.

The Captal contacted Baron Thake Berlich in Loncaric, a recidivist who had been captured by Ragnarson in the Gap and paroled by Fiana. The man's response had been to raise stronger forces for the rematch. He had been one of the Krief's commanders during the wars. He was the logical man to bring Ragnarson to heel. But he was a conservative of a stripe judged bizarre even by his own class.

Through Berlich, using the Baron's interlocutors— whom he kept in careful ignorance of the messages they bore—he reached Sir Andvbur Kimberlin of Karadja, in Breidenbach. Kimberlin had publicly voiced displeasure with the Queen's tepid social reforms. The Captal invited the knight to help him build a new society, hinting that while he controlled Carolan, he wasn't long for this world and was looking for someone who understood, who could carry on after he was gone.

As winter lugubriously progressed toward a spring that was no spring at all in the Gap, the Captal grew less and less pessimistic. The rebel coalition, spanning the extremes of political dissatisfaction and opportunism, waxed strong, reaching into Vorgreberg itself.

That fell apart.

"Stupid, greedy pigs!" the old man grumbled for days. "We had it in our hands. But they had to try cutting us out." Even Carolan stayed out of his way.

He decided there was no choice but to bring in eastern troops, to give the rebels backbone. And, to use a little wizardry.

News of the sudden shift at High Crag (where the ruling junta had for a decade discouraged mercenary involvement in actual warmaking), that had led to an offer of three veteran regiments to the Crown, again pushed the Captal toward despair. It was contagious. Mist became a sad, resigned woman. She returned to Shinsan to prepare a legion for transfer to Maisak when the snows melted.

The Captal, self-involved, overlooked her mood. Burla, Shoptaw, and Carolan understood Mist's unhappiness. The man she had lost, and his brother, had reappeared. In Kavelin. Working the other side again.

v) Glitter of an enemy spear

Three men crouched beneath an ice overhang and, when not cursing the temperature, considered the fortress west of them.

"It'll work," promised the one with a single eye. "They can't sense us."

"The spells. The spells," another grumbled. "If that Shinsaner bitch wasn't in there, I'd believe in them."

"Just think about the gold, Brad," said the third. "More than… More than you've ever dreamed."

"I believe in that less than Haroun's spells. Maybe this's his way of getting rid of us. We know too much."

"A possibility," Derran admitted. "And I haven't overlooked it."

"If there's trouble, it'll come at payoff time," Kerth said.

"Uhm."

"It's dark enough," said Brad.

"Give it a few more minutes," said Derran. "Let 'em start thinking about bedtime. Some of those things can see like cats." For the hundredth time he patted his purse. Inside, carefully protected, lay a small bundle of plans of Maisak's interior, obtained by bin Yousif from a winged man taken several months earlier.

"You're sure there'll be no sentries?" Brad asked.

Derran concealed his exasperation. "No. Why the hell would they be watching for someone in this?" He gestured at deep snow now invisible in darkness. "Probably someone at the gate, but that's all that's logical." He checked the night, the few lights visible in the fortress. "Hell, you're right, Brad. Let's go."

It took a half-hour to slog the short distance to the castle wall, then just minutes to set a grapnel and climb up. Five minutes later they had finished the two owl-faced creatures at the gate and prepared it for their retreat. If all went right, they would be well on their way before their visit caused an alarm.

Maisak was thick with smells and smokes, but in the outer works, in the winter chill, they encountered no other evidence of occupation.

"Lot of men here," Kerth observed. "Wonder how they keep them fed?"

"Probably with transfers from Shinsan," Derran replied. "That door there, with the brass hinges. That look like the one we want?"

"Fits the description."

"Okay. Brad, you open. Kerth, cover." He went in low and fast so Kerth could throw over him, but the precaution proved unnecessary. The corridor was empty.

"All right," said Derran, "let's see. Commissary down that way. Third room this way."

In that room they found a half-dozen odd little people sleeping. "Look like rabbits," Brad said, after they had been dispatched.

"Place's supposed to be full of weirds," Derran replied. "Kerth, find the panel. We'll clean up." Soon they were climbing a dusty circular stair in complete darkness.

The stair ended in a landing. There was a wall with peepholes. Beyond the wall lay an empty, poorly lighted corridor.

"Brad, you watch." Derran felt for the mechanism that would allow access to the corridor. A small panel scraped aside. They awaited a reaction. Brad hastily assembled a crossbow.

"Go." Derran tapped Kerth's shoulder.

Daggers in hand, the man rushed the one door opening off the corridor. He paused beside it. Closed, he signaled. Derran joined him, pointed to the regular stair. Kerth checked it, signaled it was clear. Derran dropped to his stomach and peered beneath the door with his good eye. From his bundle of plans he took one of the Captal's library, indicated the position of each person in the room.

A final problem. Was the door locked? Barred? Haroun's captive had claimed there were no locked doors in Maisak, only hidden ones.

Derran stood, placed his back to the door, took its handle in his left hand, held his sword vertically in his right. Kerth readied his daggers, nodded.

Explosion. Derran slammed the door open. As his momentum carried him out of the way, one of Kerth's weapons took wing. Its pommel smacked the Shinsaner woman between the eyes.

Derran didn't pause to appreciate the throw. It was what he had expected. Kerth had spent countless hours practicing.

The woman was the key. If she wasn't silenced, all was lost.

In passing he crossed blades with the old man, pushed through his guard, left him clutching his wound in amazement. He grabbed the woman, shoved a hand into her mouth, with his free hand tossed Kerth his dagger. Kerth took it on the fly and turned to two weird creatures who had thrown themselves in front of the little girl…

A wall opened up and men with swords stepped in. Ragnarson's men.

FOURTEEN: YEAR 1003 AFE
THE ROADS TO BAXENDALA

i) In by the back door

Though April was near, the snow remained deep and moist. The two men fought it gamely, but were compelled to take frequent rests.

"Must be getting old," Turran grumbled, glancing up the long, steep slope yet to be climbed.

Valther said nothing, just made sure moisture hadn't reached his sword. He seldom spoke even now.

"Almost there," Turran said. "That bluff up there… That's the one that looked like a man's face." The last time they had been in the Gap it had been summer and they had been hurrying to their fates in Escalon. Nothing looked familiar now.

Valther stared uphill, remaining statue-still till a bitter gust reached him. "Better camp," he muttered.

"Uhm." Turran had spotted a likely overhang. It would yield relief from the wind while they hunted a usable cave. Though those were reportedly numerous, they had become harder to find near Maisak.

"Think they've spotted us yet?" Turran asked after they made the overhang.

Valther shrugged. He didn't care. He would feel nothing till they had come face to face with Mist.

"That looks like one," said Turran, indicating a spot of darkness up the north slope. "Let's go."

Valther hoisted his pack and started off.

They had little firewood left. Turran used the minimum to heat their supper, then extinguished the blaze. They would wrap in their blankets and crowd one another for warmth. The mouth of the cave was small and inconveniently located anyway. The smoke didn't want to leave.

During the night Turran shivered so hard that when he rose he had cramps.

Valther didn't notice the chill.

For breakfast they had jerky warmed by their body heats, washed down with snow melted the same way.

Afterward, Valther said, "Time to begin."

"Is she here?" Turran asked.

Valther's eyes glazed. For a moment he stared into distances unseen, then shrugged. "I don't know. The aura's there, but not strong."

Turran was surprised his brother showed that much spirit. He seemed genuinely eager for the coming confrontation.

Turran was not. He saw no way they could best the mistress of Shinsan. Surprise was a tool that could be used against anyone, but how did one surprise a power so perceptive it could detect an enemy's heartbeat a hundred miles away?

But the attempt had to be made. Even in full expectation of death. It was a matter of conscience. They had betrayed those who had trusted them. Just trying would help even the balance.

"Ready?"

Valther nodded.

From his purse Turran took a small jewel the Monitor had given him. He set it on the cave floor. They joined hands, stared into the talisman. Turran chanted in liturgical Escalonian, of which he understood not a word.

In a moment he felt little monkey-tugs at the fringes of his soul. There was a sudden, painless wrench, as of roots pulling away, then his awareness floated free.

The sensing was nothing like that of the body. He did not "see" objects, yet knew the location and shape and function of everything about him.

Valther hadn't shed his clay. He was too distracted by obsessions that Turran could now trace. Valther lay trapped in a sort of in-between, and would remain there till Turran freed him or pulled him back to the mundane plane.

Just as well, Turran reflected. Valther might have gone haring direct to Maisak, to see Mist, and so have given them away.

There was no sense of time on that level. Turran had to concentrate to make events follow one another in temporal parade. He saw why the Monitor had told him not to use the stone unless he had to. He could get lost on this side, and forget his body, which would perish of neglect.

This was how most ghosts had come into being, the Monitor had told him.

While Turran had had no training in this sorcery, the wizardries of his family had taught him discipline. He began his task.

He floated the slopes between their hiding place and the bluff which masked Maisak. He felt no cold, nor any pressure from the wind.

He discovered he could sense not only the realities obvious to corporeal senses, he could look around, beneath, and within things, and it was with this faculty that he searched for entrances to the caverns honeycombing the mountains. Many came clear. Most had been sealed. Those that had not, he probed deeply. He found the one he was hunting.

Just in time. His attachment to his body was attenuating. His will and concentration were suffering moments of vagary.

As he reentered his body, he learned another danger of the magic.

Feeling returned. All the aches and pains of a hard march, more intense for having gone unfelt for a time. And his senses suddenly seemed severely limited. What a temptation there was to withdraw…

He reached out and brought his brother back.

Turran's eyes opened. Their hands parted.

Valther had less trouble recovering. "Did you find it?" he asked.

Turran nodded. "I don't want to try that again."

"Bad?"

"Just the coming back."

"Let's go." Valther was ebullient.

Turran rose stiffly, got his gear together. "We'll need the torches. It's long…"

Valther shrugged, drew his sword, ran his thumb along its edge. He didn't care about the in-betweens, just the destination.

"What I wouldn't give for a bath," Turran grumbled as he hoisted his pack. "I'll lead."

It was snowing again. That was their fault. The past several months they had used their weather magic to confine winter's worst to the high country.

The cave mouth was a half-mile from their hiding place, naturally but cunningly hidden. He had a hard time locating it. It had to be dug out. It was barely large enough to accept a man's body. He sent Valther in, pushed their packs through, slithered in himself.

"I've got a feeling," he told Valther as they prepared the torches, "that we'd better hurry. My memory's getting hazy."

But speed was impossible. The subterranean journey was long and tortuous and in places they had to dig to enlarge passages for crawling. Once they climbed twenty feet up a vertical face. Another time they had to cross a pit whose Stygian deeps concealed a bottom unguessably far below. At a point where several caverns intersected they found skeletons still arrayed in war gear of Hammad al Nakir. Though they pushed hard, they couldn't make the journey in one day. They paused for sleep, then continued.

They knew they were close when they reached caverns where the walls had been regularized by tools. Those would be passages worked during the wars, when the Captal's fortress had had to have space for thousands of soldiers.

Then they came on a large chamber occupied by Kaveliners who supported the Captal's pretender. Those who were awake were bored. Their conversation orbited round women and a desire to be elsewhere. Nobody challenged the brothers as they passed through.

"That was the worst," Turran said afterward. "Now we take a side tunnel to the Captal's laboratories and get into his private ways."

Valther nodded, caressed the hilt of his sword.

It was strange, Turran thought, that their coming hadn't been sensed or foreseen. But, then, their weak plan had been predicated on inattention by the enemy.

In the laboratories, in a dark and misty chamber they recognized as one where transfers were made, they encountered trouble.

It came in the form of an owl-faced creature guarding the transfer pentagrams. He was asleep when they spotted him, but wakened as they tried slipping past. They had to silence him.

"Have to hurry now," Turran said. The thing's disappearance would raise an alarm.

Because they followed secret stairs, they reached the Captal's chambers before they encountered second trouble. And this came as a total surprise.

They pushed through a secret panel into a room full of murder. It had been a library or study, but now it resembled a paper-maker's dump. Against one wall an evil-faced, one-eyed man, unarmed, struggled with a woman. He had the heel of one hand jammed firmly into her mouth.

An old man lay unconscious and bleeding on the floor. Now, with a pair of long daggers, a second killer stalked two weird creatures guarding a child. One creature was a frail winged thing defending himself with a blazing crystal dagger, the other an apelike dwarf wielding a short, weighted club.

All eyes turned to the brothers. The failure of hope in the winged man and ape-thing spurred Kerth. One of his blades shattered the crystal dagger while the other turned the dwarf's club. Then the first arced over into the dwarf's throat. He went down with a squeal.

"Burla!" the child screeched, falling on him. "No. Don't die."

Workmanlike, Kerth wheeled and dispatched the winged man.

When Kerth wheeled on the child, Valther said, "No." He said it flatly, without the least apparent emotion. The assassin froze.

Kerth and Derran exchanged glances. Kerth shrugged, stepped away from the girl.

Sudden as lightning, a dagger was in the air, hurtling toward Valther. The man got his sword up in time to deflect it. It had been a gut-throw.

And a feint. The second dagger followed by two yards, bit deep into Valther's right shoulder. Turran jabbed with his own blade, missed the block.

There was a *crack* from Derran's direction. Mist sagged in semiconsciousness. The One-Eye blew on his knuckles.

Turran charged Kerth, who had already armed himself with the Captal's weapon…

The universe turned red.

Mist forced herself up on her hands, stared through an open window. In the starkest terror Turran had ever witnessed, she croaked, "O Shing. He's raised the Gosik of Aubochon!"

None knew the name, but each knew Mist. Their conflict ceased. In moments all crowded the window, staring up at a pillar of red horror.

"The portal!" Mist cried. "He'll try the portal while we're distracted. We've got to destroy it."

Too late. The clack of armor echoed up the same stair Turran and Valther had used.

ii) Approaching storm

March sagged toward April. Spring came to the lowlands. The days of reckoning drew rapidly closer. Ragnarson grew ever more dour and pessimistic. Things were going too well. The censuses were in. Crops had suffered less than anticipated. In areas where there had been little fighting there had been surpluses. Only the Nordmen, it seemed, were suffering.

Volstokin hadn't been as lucky. Ambassadors from the Queen Mother were pleading credit and grain in both Kavelin and Altea.

Favorable weather permitted early plowing. This, to Ragnarson's delight, meant more men for summer service. Hedging against the chance they would be in the field at harvest, the Queen was buying grain futures in Altea, a traditional exporter.

The winter had caused changes at every level. Kavelin had shaken her lice out. As the kingdom settled down and vast properties changed hands, the citizens looked forward to a prosperous future. Because good fortune attended the Queen's supporters, her strength waxed. Feelers drifted in from provinces still in rebellion.

With the exception of Ragnarson and his aides, no one seemed worried about the summer.

Bragi never eased the pressure on the rebels. After Forbeck and Fahrig, he launched expeditions into Orthwein and Uhlmansiek, using the campaigns to temper his growing army. He suffered few setbacks. Each victory made the next easier.

Anticipating fat looting in the Galmiches and Loncaric, squads, companies, and battalions poured into the capital. From the Guild-Masters in their fortress-aerie, High Crag, on the seacoast north of Dunno Scuttari, came congratulations, word that Ragnarson had received nominatory votes for promotion to Guild General, and an offer of three regiments on partial advance against a percentage of booty...

On Royal instructions Ragnarson accepted the mercenary regiments. He dreaded leading so many men. What would happen when they learned the real nature of the enemy?

Tents dotted the roadsides and woods of the Siege. Long wagon trains bearing supplies rumbled toward the city. Dust raised by moving soldiery hung like a vaporous river over the caravan route. Ragnarson was awed by their numbers, almost as many as Kavelin had raised during the El Murid Wars. His original mercenary command now seemed an amusingly small force. But it still formed the core of his army.

The more he thought about controlling so many men, the more nervous he became.

Nights the worries slid away in the magic of the Queen's arms. No one yet seemed suspicious.

In late March Sir Andvbur went over to the Captal.

What negotiations had passed between the two Ragnarson never learned, but he suspected Sir Andvbur's idealism had motivated his treachery.

The knight's coup failed. Having foreseen trouble, and having gotten the man away from the center of power, Ragnarson then had surrounded him with trustworthy staffers. Few men joined Sir Andvbur when, after brief skirmishing, he fled across Low Galmiche toward Savernake.

Loncaric and Savernake remained in the grip of unnatural winter. Ragnarson took the opportunity to pinch off the depending finger of Low Galmiche and eliminate the last rebel bastions near the Siege.

When he could find nothing else, he wondered what had become of Mocker, Haroun, Turran, and Valther. And worried about Rolf. Though Preshka hadn't been injured in the dungeon confrontation, the exertion had exacerbated his lung troubles.

Yet everything went so well that he received the bad news from Itaskia with relief.

Greyfells partisans had driven the Trolledyngjan families over the Porthune into Kendel. Kendel's military ran hand in glove with Itaskia's. A light horse company had swum the river and slaughtered the raiders. Kendel had decided to send the families on to Kavelin.

What, Ragnarson sometimes wondered, was Elana doing? She wasn't the sort to sit and wait.

On the last evening of March, Ragnarson gathered his commanders to discuss the summer campaign. Meticulously prepared maps were examined. Where to meet the enemy became the point of contention. Ragnarson listened, remembering an area he had seen the previous fall.

"Here, at Baxendala," he said suddenly, jabbing a map with a forefinger. "We'll meet them with every man we have. Talk to the Marena Dimura. Learn everything you can."

Before the inevitable arguments began, he strode from the room.

The die had been cast. All time was an arrow hurtling toward the decision at the caravan town of Baxendala.

He went walking the castle's outer wall, to bask in the peace of what would soon be a chill April Fool's morning.

Soon, in the white gown she had worn the morning they had first locked eyes, the Queen joined him. Moonlight like trickles of silver ran through her hair, gaily. But her eyes were sad. Ignoring the sentries, she held his hand.

"This is the last night," she whispered, after a long silence. She stopped, pushed her arm around his waist, stared at the moon over the Kapenrungs. "The last time. You'll leave tomorrow. Win or lose, you won't come back." Her voice quavered.

Ragnarson scanned the black teeth of the enemy mountains. Was it really still winter there? He wanted to tell her he would return, but could not. That would be a blemish on his memory.

She had sensed that he would always go back to Elana. Their relationship, though as intense and fiery as a volcanic eruption, was pure romance. Romance demanded a special breed of shared deception, of reality suspended by mutual consent...

So he said nothing, just pulled her against his side.

"Just one thing I ask," she said, softly, sadly. "In the dark tonight, in bed, say my name. Whisper it to me."

He frowned her way, puzzled.

"You don't realize, do you? In all the time you've been here you've used it only once. When you announced me to Sir Farace. Her Majesty. Her Majesty. Her Highness. The Queen. Sometimes, in the night, Darling. But never Fiana. I'm real... Make me real."

Yes, he thought. Even when she had been no more than a conception spawned by Tarlson's characterizations, he had felt an attraction that he had pushed off with formalities.

"Gods!" a nearby sentry muttered. "What's that?"

Ragnarson's gaze returned to the mountains.

Beneath the moon, over a notch marking the approximate location of Maisak, stood a pillar of reddish coruscation. It coalesced into a scarlet tower.

The world grew silent, as if momentarily becalmed in the eye of a storm.

The pillar intensified till all the east was aflame. A flower formed at its top. The trunk bifurcated, took on a horrible anthropomorphism. The flower became a head. Where eyes should have been there were two vast Stygian pools. The head was far too large for the malformed body that bore it up. Its horns seemed to scrape the moon as it turned slowly, glaring malevolently into the west.

The thing's brilliance intensified till all the world seemed painted in harsh strokes of red and black. A great dark gulf of a mouth opened in silent, evil laughter. Then the thing faded as it had come, dying into a coruscation that reminded Bragi of the auroras of his childhood homeland.

"Come," he said to the Queen when he could speak again. "You may be right. It may be the last time either of us gives ourself freely."

Deep in the night he spoke her name. And she, shaking as much as he, whispered from beneath him, "Bragi, I love you."

iii) Elana and Nepanthe
On the Auszura Littoral, Elana and Nepanthe, up late after a day of increasing, undirected tension, released sharp cries when the Tear of Mimizan took on a sudden, fiery life that was reflected in crimson on the eastern horizon.

iv) King Shanight
From the Mericic Hills, at Skmon on the Anstokin-Volstokin border, Shanight of Anstokin, restless before the dawn of attack, watched the scarlet rise in the east, a head with its chin on the horizon. After meeting those midnight eyes he returned to his pavilion, called off the war.

v) Mocker
In Rohrhaste, near the site of Vodicka's defeat, Mocker suddenly erupted from an uneasy sleep, saw scarlet beneath the moon. For one of the few times in his life he was stricken dumb. In lieu he loaded his donkey and hurried toward Vorgreberg.

vi) Sir Andvbur Kimberlin of Karadja
Sir Andvbur and two hundred supporters, traveling by night to evade loyalist patrols, paused to watch the demon coalesce over the Gap. Before it faded, half turned back, preferring the Royal mercy. Kimberlin continued, not out of conviction, but for fear of appearing weak before his companions.

vii) The Disciple
In the acres-vast tent-Temple of the Disciple at Al Rhemish, a sleepy fat man moaned, staggered to the Portal of the North. This gross, jeweled El Murid bore no resemblance to the pale, bony, ascetic fanatic whose angry sword had

scourged the temples and reddened the sands in earlier decades. Nor was his insanity as limited. The red sorcery stirred a mad rage. He collapsed, thrashing and foaming at the mouth.

viii) Visigodred

At Castle Mendalayas in north Itaskia a tall, lean insomniac paced a vast and incredibly cluttered library. Before a fireplace a pair of leopards also paced. From a ceiling beam a monkey watched and muttered. Between the pacer and leopards, on a luxurious divan, a dwarf and a young beauty cuddled.

The lean old man, sporting a long gray beard, suddenly faced south-southeast, his nose thrusting like that of a dog on point. His face became a mask of stone. "Marco!" he snapped. "Wake up. Call the bird."

ix) Zindahjira

In the Mountains of M'Hand, above the shores of the Seydar Sea, lay a cave in which dwelt the being called Zindahjira the Silent. Zindahjira was anything but silent now. The mountains shook with his rage. He did not appreciate being involved in intrigues not his own. But by his own twisted logic he had a responsibility to right matters in the south. When his rage settled, he called for his messenger owls.

x) Varthlokkur

Fangdred was an ancient fortress poised precariously atop Mount El Kabar in the Dragon's Teeth. There, in a windowless room, tiny silver bells tinkled. A black arrow inlaid with silver runes turned southward. In moments a tall young man, frowning, hurried in. His haunted eyes momentarily fixed on arrow and bells.

He was Varthlokkur, the Silent One Who Walks With Grief, sometimes called the Empire Destroyer or the Death of Ilkazar. He was the man who had ended the reign of the Princes Thaumaturge of Shinsan. Those Princes remained like trophies in an impenetrable chamber atop Fangdred's Wind Tower. Kings trembled at the mention of Varthlokkur's name.

He was old, this apparent young man. Centuries old, and burdened heavily with the knowledge of the Power, with his guilt over what he had wrought with the Empire.

He spoke a Word. A quicksilver pool in a shallow, wide basin ground into the top of a table of granite shivered. Iridescences fluttered across its face. A portrait appeared.

Varthlokkur stared at a gargantuan, megacephalic demon whose ravenlike feet clutched the feet of mountains.

This manifestation couldn't be ignored.

He began his preparations.

xi) Haroun bin Yousif

The long, cautious cavalry column was less than thirty miles from Al Rhemish when the northern sky went scarlet. Filtering four thousand Royalists through the Lesser Kingdoms and the Kapenrungs undetected had been a military feat which, meeting success, had astonished even its planner.

The demon head loomed. Haroun gave the order to turn back.

xii) The Star Rider

On the flank of a snow-deep peak high in the Kapenrungs, on a glacier that creaked and groaned day and night, one surprised and angry old man stood between gigantic pillars of legs and stared miles upward at scarlet horror. He spat, cursed, turned to his winged horse. From its back he unlashed the thing known as Windmjirnerhorn, or the Horn of the Star Rider. He caressed it, spoke to it, glanced, nodded. The demon began to fade.

He then sat and pondered what to do about these dangerous ad libs. O Shing was getting out of hand.

xiii) King Vodicka

Half an hour after the night had regained its natural darkness Volstokin's King concluded that he had been used by greater, darker powers to play attention-grabber while Evil slithered in to gnaw at the underbelly of the West.

After writing brief letters to Kavelin's Queen, his mother, and his brother, he threw himself from the parapet of his prison tower.

FIFTEEN: YEAR 1003 AFE
BAXENDALA

i) The site

Baxendala was a prosperous town of two thousand, twenty-five miles west of Maisak. Its prosperity was due to its being the last or first chance for commercial vices for the caravans. The mountain passage was long and trying.

Ragnarson had chosen to fight there because of topography.

The townsite had once marked the western limit of the huge glacier that had cut the pass. The valley, that became the Gap, there narrowed to a two-mile-wide, steep-sided canyon, the floor of which, near the town, was piled with glacial leavings.

Baxendala itself was built against the north flank of a sugarloaf hill half a mile wide, two long, and two hundred feet high, astride a low ridge that ran to the flank of Seidentop, a steep, brush-wooly mountain constricting the north wall of the canyon. The River Ebeler ran around the south side of the loaf where the valley, in a long, lazy curve, had been dug a bit deeper, and, because of barriers a dozen miles farther west, had formed a shallow marsh three-quarters of a mile wide. The marsh lay hard against both the sugarloaf and the steep southern wall of the valley. A narrow strip of brushy, firm ground ran below the southern face. It could be easily held by a small force.

Atop the sugarloaf, commanding a good eastern view, stood a small fortress, Karak Strabger. From it Ragnarson could follow every detail of battle. By anchoring his flanks on Seidentop and Baxendala, along the ridge, he could defend a space little more than half a mile wide. There was no more defensible site to the west, and but one equaling it farther east. And Sir Andvbur, having fought there last autumn, knew that ground better than he.

Ragnarson descended on the town two weeks after the night of the demon. The Strabger family fled so hurriedly they left breakfast half-cooked in the castle kitchen. The rebel forces were training farther east, near the snow line. Three days after Bragi's arrival an attempt was made to dislodge him. Baron Berlich led the rebel knights into another Lieneke. His attack collapsed under a shower of Itaskian arrows. Berlich himself was slain.

The survivors, to Ragnarson's dismay, suffered an attack of rationality. When they selected a new commander they chose the man he believed most dangerous, Sir Andvbur Kimberlin.

Kimberlin opted for Fabian tactics. He took up a defensive position at the site of his previous year's battle. His patrols tried to lure Ragnarson into attack. Bragi ignored them.

Though Kimberlin's force, at eight thousand, was the largest Ragnarson had yet faced, he was more concerned with the sorcery-rich army the Captal would bring out of Maisak.

Bragi waited, skirmished, fortified, scouted, husbanded his resources. He constantly reminded his officers of the need to stand firm here. To, if necessary, endure the heaviest casualties. The enemy would be stopped at Baxendala, or not at all. The west depended on them. There would be no stopping Shinsan if this stand failed.

ii) The waiting

Ragnarson stood on the parapet of Karak Strabger's lone tower and surveyed the power that was, for the moment, his. He had twenty-five thousand Kaveliners, plus the men he had brought south. In the west, on the horizons and beyond, great clouds of dust hung in the spring haze. Surprising allies were hurrying to join him.

One cloud, on the caravan route, marked Shanight of Anstokin with the regiments raised to invade Volstokin. North of him came Jostrand of Volstokin and three thousand puzzled veterans of Lake Berberich and Vodicka's defeat. In Heiderschied, rushing in forty-mile marches, was Prince Raithel of Altea, a hard-driving old warrior who had won glory and honor during the wars. Ragnarson hoped Raithel would arrive in time. His ten thousand were the best soldiers in the Lesser Kingdoms.

He had heard there were troops on the move in Tamerice and Ruderin and kingdoms farther away.

This curdling of the Lesser Kingdoms into a one-faced force with chin thrust belligerently eastward had begun the night of the red demon.

The sudden power and responsibility awed Ragnarson. Princes and kings were coming to be commanded by a man who had been but a farmer a year ago...

There were others who awed him more than Shanight, Jostrand, or Raithel.

Beside the sugarloaf, above Baxendala, stood a dozen tents set off by ropes. One housed his old friend Count Visigodred of Mendalayas, another Haroun's dread acquaintance, Zindahjira. The denizens of the others he knew only by repute: Keirle the Ancient; Barco Crecelius of Hellin Daimiel; Stojan Dusan from Prost Kamenets; Gromachi, the Egg of God; The Hermit of Ormrebotn; Boershig Abresch from Songer in Ringerike; Klages Dunivin; Serkes Holdgraver of the Fortress of Frozen Fire; and the Thing With Many Eyes, from the shadowed deeps of the Temple of Jiankoplos in Simballawein.

One tent stood alone, as if the others had crowded away. Before it stood a battered Imperial standard. Within lurked the man whose capital-hopping had started so many armies toward Baxendala, whose name frightened children into good behavior and made grown men glance over their shoulders.

Varthlokkur.

His appearance guaranteed the gravity of the conflict. The high and the mighty, from Simballawein to Iwa Skolovda, would hold all else in abeyance till they knew what was afoot.

Even the Greyfells party, Ragnarson had heard, had joined the truce.

Ragnarson had mixed feelings about Varthlokkur's presence. The man could, without a doubt, be an asset. But what about old grudges? Varthlokkur owed himself and Mocker.

But Mocker, who had most to fear, was in and out of the wizard's tent constantly, when not hiding from soldiers he had bilked with crooked dice.

Ragnarson smiled weakly. Mocker was incorrigible. A middle-aged adolescent.

He spied signal smoke up the Gap. Heliograph operators bustled about him. He returned to the War Room he had set up in the castle's Great Hall.

While awaiting the report, he asked Kildragon, "How's Rolf?" Preshka had insisted on coming east.

"The same. He'll never heal if he won't take time out."

"And the evacuation?" He had been trying to get civilians to leave the area.

"About hit the limit. The rest mean to stay no matter what."

"Guess we've done what we could. Can't force people... Colonel Kiriakos?"

He had surveyed the man's work from the parapet. He and Phiambolos were working hard to complicate Shinsan's attack.

Kiriakos was the sort who, finding a pot of gold, would worry about getting a hernia hauling it away. "Too slow. I won't get done if you don't give me more men." His projects were straining the army already. Trenches, traps, fortifications, chevaux-de-frise, a pontoon across the marsh a few miles west, and finding raw materials were devouring hundreds of thousands of man-hours each day. But Kiriakos was a bureaucrat born. There was no project that couldn't be done bigger and better if only he were given more money and men…

Am I getting old? Ragnarson wondered. What happened to my penchant for motion? His cavalry commanders had been asking, too. Shinsan's was an army mainly infantry in orientation, with little missile weaponry. But Sir Andvbur was out there… All he could say was that he felt right fighting positionally.

A Sedlmayrese sergeant came from the tower, drew Bragi aside. "Captain Altenkirk," he whispered, "says he's taken prisoners. The men called Turran and Valther, and a woman. The Captain thinks she's the one you saw at Maisak."

Ragnarson frowned. A windy message for heliograph, susceptible of error. But justified if true. They had captured Mist? How?

"Thank you. Send 'Well done.' And keep it quiet." He retreated to a corner to think. So many possibilities… But he would know the truth when Altenkirk came in.

He would have to take precautions. He headed for the wizards' compound.

iii) Prisoners

Altenkirk had taken no chances. He brought his prisoners in gagged, bound, and blindfolded, unable to twitch, inside the large wicker baskets farmers filled with grain and hung from their rafters to beat the rats and mice. Each was litter-borne by prisoners from Kimberlin's army and surrounded by Marena Dimura ready to destroy baskets and bearers in an instant. Each litter was piled with oil-soaked faggots. Horsemen with torches rode nearby.

In other circumstances Ragnarson would have been amused. "Think you took enough precautions?" he asked.

"I should've killed them," Altenkirk replied. "It's got to be a trick…"

"Maybe. Let's let the witchmen have them."

The baskets were grounded before the sorcerers. Soldiers who could do so absented themselves. Zindahjira, the Egg of God, and the Thing With Many Eyes failed customary standards of what was human.

"What's the smell?" Ragnarson asked Visigodred, near whom he had positioned himself for his nerve's sake.

"The Thing's project. You'll see."

"Uhn." They had to make everything a mystery. He nodded to Altenkirk. "Turran first."

Altenkirk cautiously pried the lid off a basket. Sorcerers tensed like foxes waiting at a rabbit hole.

But Turran had been confined so long that he needed help getting out. Ragnarson went to the man, removed his gag. He beckoned Visigodred.

To Turran, "I'm sorry. Altenkirk's a cautious man."

"Understand."

"Water," Visigodred said, offering a cup. Turran drained it. While Bragi and a soldier supported Turran, Visigodred rubbed his legs. To Altenkirk the wizard said, "Let the others out. They'll cause no trouble."

There was a stir just before Mist came forth. Ragnarson turned. His eyes met the Queen's. So. She had ignored his advice again, had come to join the final battle. With perfect timing, he thought. Her eyes, on Mist, were hard and jealous.

"All I need," he mumbled, "is for Elana to turn up now."

A long draught of wine gave Turran a little life. He asked for a physician, to examine his brother, then admonished, "I thought we were on the same side." And, after a pause, "She's come over."

Hum and buzz. Sorcerers' heads nodded together. Visigodred, who had a relationship with Mist that seemed almost fatherly, fussed round the woman like a hen.

"Did you ever see such a mantrap?" Ragnarson mumbled to Preshka, who, despite continued ill health, had come to investigate the commotion.

"It's obscene. No woman ought to look like that."

Turran gained more life. "They'll be here soon. They started bringing troops through last week."

"Uhn?" Ragnarson's suspicions hadn't died completely. "Let's hear about it."

"We couldn't use the back stairs," he said, after recounting the confrontation in the Captal's library, "so we picked up Brad Red Hand and tried the hallways…"

"You joined forces?"

"No choice. O Shing's people would've killed us all. Enemy of my enemy, you know. We picked up Brad and went through the halls to the stairs Derran had used to reach the old man's floor. But it opened in a hall already occupied by O Shing's men. We had to fight through. Valther picked up his wound there. Derran was killed. Kerth, the Captal, and the little girl were captured. Brad tore a muscle in his left arm. We got through, but we couldn't save anybody but ourselves."

"And Mist? She couldn't use a spell or two?"

"Colonel, there were six men in that room. Three were Tervola. You know what that means? We tried. We killed the soldiers. She barely handled the sorcerers. But when it settled out, we couldn't carry the wounded. I was lucky to get Valther out. And the child wouldn't leave the old man. If there was anything that could've been done…"

"I wasn't criticizing." He had had to leave people behind, too. He knew the spear thrusts of guilt that drove to the heart of one's being.

"We hoped to reach the main gate or the Captal's creatures, but the fight gave

O Shing's men time to cut us off. The only escape was the caverns. It may've been my memory or their sorcery, but for a long time we couldn't find a way out. Every passage we took led back to Maisak. Each time we returned something more grim had happened. They tortured Kerth till he told all he knew about Haroun. They enchanted the Captal and girl into being cooperative. They've done the same to the rebel captains. We kept stealing food and trying to find a way out. When they started bringing troops through, I knew I couldn't put off leaving my body anymore. It'd become imperative that I get Mist to you."

"And Brad?"

"They detected the sorcery. Came hunting. His bad shoulder betrayed him. They got him before Mist could drive them off."

"And Mist? Is she a refugee? Does she want help to regain her throne? I won't help her. There's no way I'll do anything to benefit the Dread Empire. I *will* help destroy it. It's like a poisonous snake. Any good it does is incidental to its deadliness."

"I think," Turran said softly, "that she's run out of ambition. O Shing's successes have crushed her." He nodded her way. She was fussing over Valther. "There's her subliminatory device."

"Ah?"

"I don't know how long it'll last. Long enough for us to benefit, though."

"I can't ask much more." With great reluctance, Ragnarson took his eyes off Mist, studied the assembled sorcerers. Each indicated he believed Turran. Only Varthlokkur expressed reservations, and those weren't related to Mist's turn of coat.

"Power won't affect this battle's outcome," he said. "The divinations are shadowy, but they suggest its result will depend on the courage and stamina of soldiers, not on any efforts of my ilk." He seemed mildly puzzled.

Varthlokkur knew his business. He was probably right. But Ragnarson was puzzled, too. He could not see how, with so much thaumaturgic might moving toward collision, massive destruction could be avoided. "See if you can get this straightened out," he told Preshka, then went to welcome the Queen to Baxendala.

iv) The enemy arrives

Sir Andvbur's rebels came down the canyon like leaves driven by an autumn wind, without organization, whipping this way and that, mixing units inseparably. Before and among them fled bands of Ragnarson's horsemen and Marena Dimura. Signal smokes rose rapidly nearer, climbing toward a cloud of darkness driving down from Maisak like the grasping hand of doom. Sir Andvbur's people pelted against Ragnarson's defenses in such disorder that his own men became mildly infected. He had a brisk afternoon's work keeping order.

Night fell without the true enemy appearing. But his campfires, as they sprang into being, were disturbing in their numbers. Ragnarson got little sleep. He stayed up studying a blizzard of conflicting reports.

By morning it had sorted itself out. The Captal and his Kaveliners had moved to Ragnarson's extreme right, beyond the marsh, where Blackfang and Kildragon held the narrows. Sir Andvbur's thousands had taken positions against the flank of Seidentop, facing the mercenary regiments from High Crag. Shinsan held the center, facing Prince Raithel's Altean veterans.

A quarter-mile behind the front line, which was sixteen thousand strong, Ragnarson had drawn up a more numerous but potentially weaker second line. Volstokin he had anchored against Seidentop, in touch with the fortifications and heavy weapons Colonel Phiambolos had installed there. In the center were the Kaveliners, his handpicked veterans scattered among them as cadre. On the right, their backs against Baxendala, lay Anstokin's army. They maintained close contact with the ramparts and trenches Tuchol Kiriakos had constructed between level ground and Karak Strabger's wall. The main engagement Ragnarson meant to be infantry against infantry, the lines holding while heavy engines on the flanks and bowmen behind the lines decimated the enemy. Only two thousand horsemen, the best, did he allow to retain their animals. These he stationed west of Baxendala, out of view behind the slope running to Seidentop.

Dawn was a creeping thing, a dark tortoise dragging in from the east and never quite seeming to arrive. But gradual visibility came to the valley.

Ragnarson, the Queen, Turran, Mist, Varthlokkur, Colonels Phiambolos and Kiriakos, runners and heliograph men crowded the top of Karak Strabger's lonely tower. When O Shing's camp became visible, Ragnarson's heart fell. He beckoned Mist.

Shinsan was in formation already. Mist peered into the morning haze. A small, sharp intake of breath. "Four legions," she said throatily. "He's brought four legions. The Eighth. On the right. His left. The Third. The Sixth. Oh. And I thought Chin mine, body and soul." The remaining legion stood in reserve behind Shinsan's center. "The First. The Imperial Standard. The best of the best."

Her knuckles whitened as she squeezed the stone of the battlements.

"The best," she repeated. "And all four at full strength. He's made a fool of me."

Bragi wasn't disappointed. He hadn't expected good news. But he had hoped O Shing would make a smaller showing. "He's here himself?"

She nodded, pointed. "There. Behind the First. You can see the tower. He wants to watch our destruction from a high place."

Ragnarson turned. "Colonel Phiambolos, relay the word to Altenkirk." The engineer departed for Seidentop. "Varthlokkur? You've seen enough?"

The wizard nodded. "We'll begin. But I doubt we'll do any good." He departed.

"Colonel Kiriakos?"

The Colonel clicked his heels and half bowed. "Gods be with you, sir." He left to assume command of the castle and sugarloaf.

"Turran?"

The man shrugged. "You've done all you could. It's up to the Fates."

"Your Majesty, everything's ready."

She nodded coolly, regally. There was the slightest strain between them because, after her journey from Vorgreberg, he had spent the night in battle preparations.

"Now we wait." He glanced at O Shing's tower, willing it to begin.

Though he concealed it, he didn't think he had a chance. Not against four legions, nearly twenty-five thousand easterners. With so many O Shing might not commit his auxiliaries…

But he did. At some unseen signal Sir Andvbur threw his full weight against the mercenary regiments, all his people fighting afoot.

"That man," said Turran, "needs hanging. He learns too fast."

The mercenaries, though better fighters, were hard-pressed till Phiambolos's engines found the range.

After an hour, Ragnarson asked Turran, "What's he doing? It's obvious that he can't break through."

"Maybe trying to weaken them for the legions. Or draw them out of line."

Ragnarson glanced toward the mountains. The dark cloud from Maisak was fading. "They'll let us have the sun in our eyes." He had hoped they would overlook that.

Mist interjected, "He's buying time to ready a sorcery."

And Turran, "There goes a wagonload of the Thing's poison." In time Visigodred had admitted that the foul stench from the sorcerers' enclave was caused by their distillation of a drink to be served weary troops on the fighting line. There was little if any magic involved, but the liquor would combine the encouraging effects of alcohol with a drug that staved off exhaustion. Little sorceries like that, Ragnarson thought, might be more important than the ground-shakers.

"Marshal," said the Queen, "you have smoke across the marsh."

Bragi turned. It was Haaken's signal. He allowed himself a small grin. "Good. Runner." A man presented himself. "Tell Sir Farace to cross the pontoon."

A key adjunct to his plans, hastily developed during the night, after the enemy's dispositions had become clear, was developing perfectly. Blackfang and Kildragon had laid a trap. The Captal had been lured in.

"The witchery begins," said Mist. Arm spear-straight, she indicated a mote of pinkish light at the foot of O Shing's tower. "The Gosik of Aubochon again." Awe and horror filled her voice. "In the flesh. The man's mad! There's no way to control it…"

"Kimberlin's breaking off," said Turran.

Ragnarson had noticed. "This's the critical point," he said, looking down at the still untested Alteans. "Will they hold when they realize what's happening?"

"Back!" Mist snapped. "I need room!"

The pink became scarlet flame; from it rose dense red smoke. In moments, within the smoke, an immense horned head with Stygian eyes formed. This thing was no moonscraping monster such as had loomed over the Kapenrungs, but Bragi guessed it would stand a hundred yards tall. It seemed to grow from the earth itself.

Mist stood with arms outstretched and head thrown back, screaming in a tongue so liquid that Ragnarson wasn't sure she was using words. A strong chill wind began to blow, whipping her hair and garments.

He checked his tame sorcerers.

As the Gosik took on awesome solidity, the twelve hurled their counter-weapons. Bolts of lightning. Spears of light. Balls of fire in weird and changing colors. Stenches that enveloped the tower. A misty thing the size of several elephants that coalesced between the armies and trailed bloody slaughter through immobile legions before attaching its hundred tentacles and dozen beaked mouths to one of the Gosik's legs...

Mist brought her hands together sharply. Down the canyon, echoing from wall to wall, ran a deafening, endless peal of thunder. Over the Gosik a diadem of lights appeared, sparks in rainbowed rings racing angrily. The diadem began to fall.

Ragnarson wasn't sure, but from its enclosing circle, it seemed, a nebulous face as ugly as the Gosik's glared down, swelled till all the interior was a gap through which a hungry mouth prepared to feed.

A touch of shadow crossed the parapet. A few hundred feet up, a lonely eagle patrolled, above Mist's unnatural wind, apparently unconcerned with the human follies below. For an instant Bragi envied the bird its freedom and unconcern. Then...

He released a small, sharp gasp. For an instant the eagle flickered and was an eagle no longer. It became a man and winged horse far higher than he had thought, almost above visual discrimination. He turned to ask Turran's opinion.

Turran had missed it. Everyone had. All attention was on the Gosik.

Every magick in the valley had perished.

The Gosik itself came apart like a crumbling brick building, chunks and dusts falling in a rain that masked O Shing's tower. It bellowed louder than Mist's thunder had done.

Turran groaned, clawed at his chest, staggered. Ragnarson stared, thinking it was his heart.

Mist screamed, a cry of pain and deprivation. She fell to her knees, beat her forehead against parapet stone.

"It's gone," Turran groaned. "The Power. It's gone."

The Queen tried to stop Mist. "Help me!" she snapped at the messengers.

Ragnarson leaned over the parapet. His wizards appeared to have gone insane.

Several had collapsed. Most were flopping about like men in the throes of the falling sickness. The Thing sped round and round in a tight circle, chasing its own forked tail. Only Varthlokkur seemed unaffected, though he might have been a statue, so still was he as he stared at the Gosik of Aubochon.

Ragnarson looked up again. The eagle slid toward Maisak, to all appearances a raptor going about its business. He frowned. That old man again. Who was he? What? Not a god, but certainly a Power above any other the world knew.

Ragnarson's companions remained unaware of anything but the sudden vacuum of sorcery. For Turran and Mist it was a loss beyond description, almost a theft of the soul.

v) Opening round

O Shing wasted no time. The legions moved. High on the Thing's brew and Bragi's quickly spread tale that western sorcery had conquered the eastern, the troops waited with renewed confidence.

Shinsan advanced behind a screen of Sir Andvbur's infantry, the rebels more driven than leading the assault. Theirs was the task of neutralizing the traps. Their casualties were heavy. Ragnarson's bowmen had a tremendous stock of arrows, and easy targets.

Before the lines met, Ragnarson's troops sprang one of their surprises. He had had the Alteans armed with javelins, a tactic unseen since Imperial times. Their shower reassured his troops of the foe's mortality.

"Runner!" Ragnarson snapped. He sent orders to ready the second line.

"So much for being Shinsan's ally," Bragi muttered. Several thousand rebels, between his own and Shinsan's lines, were being cut down by friend and foe.

Bragi's first line held better than he had expected. He blessed the Thing.

The Alteans held the Third. The flanking legions, under merciless bombardment from Phiambolos and Kiriakos's engines, had increasing difficulty maintaining formation.

The enemy commander sent Sir Andvbur to clear Seidentop. Karak Strabger he would not be able to reach unless the Alteans broke. Kimberlin's men got entangled in nasty little battles in brushy ravines and around Phiambolos's fortifications.

Ragnarson had his heliographers send a message.

Altenkirk and a thousand Marena Dimura were hidden on the slopes east of Seidentop. They were to take the rebels and Sixth Legion in the rear. Ragnarson didn't expect them to do more than keep the enemy off balance.

What Ragnarson wanted most was to compel O Shing to commit his reserve. The First Legion, waiting patiently before their emperor's tower, would be the key.

The first line wouldn't compel its commitment. The Altean left had begun to waver. He ordered his archers withdrawn behind the second line. He didn't want them lost in a sudden collapse. He then sent messages reminding his second-line commanders that under no circumstances were they to leave their positions to aid the first line.

The Alteans yielded slowly. The enemy wedged open their junction with the mercenaries. Altenkirk attacked. The fighting round Seidentop grew bloody. The Marena Dimura, high on the Thing's brew, refused to be driven off till they had taken terrible casualties. They, too, did better than Ragnarson had expected. They forced Sir Andvbur to abandon his assault. And they gave better than they got. Kimberlin's troops were unable to pursue them. But in the meantime the Alteans had gotten split off the mercenaries. The commander of the Third Legion was ready to roll up both halves of the line.

Ragnarson expected the reserve legion to drive through the gap, against his second line. But no. O Shing held it.

"They're burning the bridge," Turran said from behind him. The man had recovered, though now he seemed a little insubstantial.

Bragi turned. Yes. Smoke rose from the pontoon. Haaken had either lost or won his part of the battle. There would be no knowing which for a long time yet. He wished he had arranged some signal. But he hadn't wanted any false hopes raised or despair set loose.

The mercenary regiments began to crumble. Crowding Seidentop for its supporting fire, they withdrew. Prince Raithel tried to do the same, but had more difficulty. The fighting washed up the foot of the sugarloaf. Kiriakos couldn't give him much support.

Ragnarson glanced at the sun. Only four hours of light left. If Shinsan took too long, the battle would stretch into a second day. For that he wasn't prepared.

Clearly victorious, the legions disengaged, puzzling Ragnarson. Then he understood. O Shing would send the fresh legion against the center of the second line while the Third backed off to the reserve position.

For a time the battlefield was clear. Bragi was awed by the carnage. It would be long remembered. There must have been twenty thousand bodies on the field, about evenly distributed. The majority of the enemy fallen were rebels.

Sickening. Ragnarson loathed the toe-to-toe slugfest. But there was no choice. A war of maneuver meant enemy victory.

O Shing allowed the legions an hour's rest. Ragnarson didn't interfere.

Before, the numbers had been slightly in the enemy's favor. This time they would be strongly in his. But his men would be greener, more likely to break.

Two and a half hours till sunset. If they held, but Haaken couldn't carry out his mission, could he put anything together for the morrow?

It began anew. The First Legion drove its silent fury against Kaveliners who outnumbered it three to one. The flanking legions held Anstokin and Volstokin while strong elements of each turned on Seidentop and Karak Strabger.

The Thing's false courage continued to work. The Kaveliners stood and continued believing their commander was invincible.

Ragnarson turned away after an hour. Even with the support of the most intense arrow storm Ahring could generate, Shinsan was getting the best of it.

And, redoubt by redoubt, Kiriakos and Phiambolos were being forced to yield their fortifications. By nightfall Karak Strabger would be cut off. Seidentop would be lost. Captured engines would be turned on the castle come morning.

Then he caught moving glitter at the eastern end of the marsh. It was Sir Farace and the horse, come round the marsh through the narrow strip where Haaken and Reskird had pulled a near repeat of Lake Berberich.

At first O Shing was unconcerned, perhaps thinking the column was the Captal's returning. How long would it last?

A while. Long enough for Sir Farace and Blackfang to ford the Ebeler. O Shing and his Tervola were intent on the slaughter before them. Anstokin was being driven into the streets of Baxendala. The Kaveliners were being decimated, though the arrow storm was wreaking its havoc, too. Volstokin was desperately trying to retain contact with Phiambolos, who had begun evacuating Seidentop. A hundred pillars of smoke rose from pyres marking abandoned engines. The main battle was lost.

"Turran." Bragi glanced at the sun. "Can we hold till dark? Would they keep on afterward? Or wait till dawn to finish it?"

"We can hold. But you may have to send the mercenaries and Alteans back in."

"Right." He sent orders to Prince Raithel to stand by.

Peering toward Sir Farace, he saw that Haaken and Reskird had brought their infantry. Blackfang had had good reason for burning the pontoon. If Sir Farace failed, there would be no one to hold the right bank. Trolledyngjans. Proud men. Fools eager, even facing incredible odds, to balance their earlier defeat at Maisak.

The knights formed hurriedly, in two long ranks. O Shing's generals finally awakened, began to form the reserve legion facing them.

Shrieking trumpets carried over the uproar around Karak Strabger; the best knights of four kingdoms trotted toward the best infantry in the world. Haaken, Reskird, and their infantry ran at the stirrups of the second wave.

Had he known there would be no magic, Ragnarson reflected, he would have chosen a knights' battle. It wasn't a form of warfare with which the easterners could easily cope.

The first wave went to a canter, then a full charge, hit before the Third Legion had finished reforming.

What followed was a classic demonstration of why heavy cavalry had become the preferred shock weapon of western armies. The horsemen plowed through the enemy like heavy ships through waves, their lances shattering the front ranks, then their swords and maces smashing down from the height advantage.

Had the Shinsaners been anyone else they would have been routed. But these men stood and silently died. Like automatons they killed horses to bring knights down where their heavier armor would be a disadvantage.

The second wave hit, then the infantry. Without that second wave, Ragnarson reflected, the first might have been lost simply because the enemy didn't have the sense to run. They would have stood, been slaughtered, and have slowly turned the thing around...

If the legionnaires would not panic, O Shing would. With trumpets and flags he began screaming for help.

Altenkirk and his Marena Dimura, now completely cut off, launched a suicide attack on Kimberlin, made sure the rebels did nothing to save the eastern emperor.

"We'll survive the day," Ragnarson said, spirits soaring. He drew his sword, gathered his shield. "Time to counter-attack." The Tervola were trying to disengage forces to aid their emperor, who was in grave danger.

As he and his staff howled out the castle gate to join Kiriakos, Ragnarson saw that Sir Farace had shifted his attack. While the stricken Third Legion ordered itself around O Shing, Volstokin's seneschal had wheeled his lines and charged the First from behind.

Ragnarson's immediate reaction was anger. The man should have gone for checkmate... But he calmed himself. The knight had seen more clearly than he. O Shing was only a man. This battle was no individual's whim, it was a playout of a nation's aspirations. The Tervola could and would replace O Shing if necessary, and could win without him. With few exceptions their loyalties were to ideas, not men.

The sun had reached the peaks of the Kapenrungs. The slaughter continued shifting in favor of the west. The Sixth and Eighth tried to close a trap but were too weary and heavily engaged to act quickly enough. Sir Farace withdrew before the jaws closed and formed for yet another charge. Before dark all four legions had suffered the fury of the western knighthood, the sort of attack Breitbarth had meant to hurl against Ragnarson at Lieneke. The assault on Baxendala had been broken.

Shinsan disengaged in good order. Ragnarson sent riders to Haaken and Reskird, ordering them to recross the Ebeler before they were trapped. Altenkirk he ordered off Kimberlin. Sir Farace he had stand off from the withdrawal. The mercenaries and Alteans, who had had a respite, he kept in contact. With the remnants of one mercenary regiment he launched a night assault on the rebels.

He had judged their temper correctly. Most of the common soldiers yielded without fighting. Sir Andvbur accepted the inevitable.

Though it meant straining men already near collapse, Ragnarson kept the pressure on Shinsan throughout the night, allowing only his horsemen to rest. All of them, even those who had fought afoot. With the rebel knights out he could afford to launch cavalry attacks.

O Shing resumed operations at dawn, withdrawing toward Maisak with the First Legion in rearguard, masking his main force with trenches dug during the night. The situation left Ragnarson in a quandary. As soon as he sent his horse in pursuit, the First, evidently rested, came out to challenge his exhausted infantry. He didn't want to settle for the single legion the enemy seemed willing to sacrifice. There was no predicting when the Power would return. If it did do so soon, Shinsan could still turn it around.

Both sides had been drained. Nearly ten thousand Shinsaners had fallen. Virtually all the rebels were dead or captured. Haaken had sent word that the Captal and his pretender were in hand. And Ragnarson feared his own losses, not yet determined, would include more than half his force.

His allies from Altea, Anstokin, and Volstokin refused to join the pursuit. The Kaveliners and mercenaries grumbled when he made the suggestion, but had less choice. He compromised. They would advance slowly, maintaining light contact, till O Shing had evacuated Kavelin. His allies undertook the destruction of the Imperial Legion.

vi) Campaign's end

Approaching stealthily, cautiously, unexpectedly, the Royalist forces of Haroun bin Yousif came to a Maisak virtually undefended. In a swift, surprise night attack they carried the gate and swept the defenders into eternity. In the deep dungeons they found the portals through which Shinsan's soldiers had come. Bin Yousif led a force through, surprised and destroyed a small fortress near Liaontung, in the Dread Empire.

Returning, he destroyed the portals, then prepared surprises for O Shing's return. If he returned.

He did, skirmishing with Ragnarson's troops all the way. The would-be emperor, trying to salvage control of the Gap, threw his beaten legions at Maisak's walls.

Soldiers of Shinsan did not question, did not retreat. For three bloody days they attacked and died. Without their masters' magicks they were only men. As many died there as had at Baxendala.

When O Shing broke off, Ragnarson, with Haroun, harried him to the ruins of Gog-Ahlan.

There Turran told Bragi, "There's no percentage in pushing him any more. The Power's returning."

Reluctantly, Ragnarson turned back toward Kavelin.

SIXTEEN: THE YEARS 1003-1004 AFE
SHADOWS OF DEATH

i) New directions and vanishing allies

When Bragi went looking for Haroun, his old friend was gone. Side by side they had harried O Shing, moving too swiftly to visit, then the Royalists had evaporated.

When Bragi returned, autumn was settling on Vorgreberg. For the first time in years there was no foreboding lying over the capital. The rebellion was dead. All but a few of its leaders had been caught. But recognition of Gaia-Lange and/or Carolan remained unsettled.

In Ragnarson's absence the Queen had restructured the Thing along lines proposed by the scholars of Hellin Daimiel, adding commons drawn from among Wessons, Marena Dimura, and Siluro. Final judgmental authority had been vested in three consuls, one elected by the commons, another by the nobility. The third was the Queen herself. Before he reached Baxendala returning, Bragi learned that he had a painful decision to make.

Representatives of the commons met him in the Gap and begged him to become publican consul.

He was still worrying it when he reached Vorgreberg.

The crowds had turned out. He accepted the accolades glumly. Haaken and Reskird grinned, shouted back, clowned. His soldiers wasted no time getting themselves lost in taverns and willing arms.

Sourly, he entered Castle Krief.

And there she was again, in the same place, wearing the same clothing…

And Elana was with her. Elana, Nepanthe, and Mocker.

Haaken leaned close. "Remember the tale of Soren Olag Bjornson's wife." It was a Trolledyngjan folk story about the vicissitudes of an unfaithful husband.

Bragi started. If Haaken knew, the liaison might be common knowledge.

Maybe a consulship would keep him too busy to get in trouble with either woman.

ii) The new life

Ragnarson accepted the consulship, retained the title Marshal, and received a vote of generalship from High Crag. His most difficult task was integrating his arrogant, overbearing Trolledyngjan refugees into Kaveliner society, and, with the Queen, making compensation to the mercenary regiments. Kavelin's finances were a shambles.

There came a time when final action *had* to be taken in the matters of Sir Andvbur and the Captal of Savernake. To Ragnarson's regret, Kimberlin had to be hanged. The Captal was more cooperative. After a long conversation with the Queen, concerning Carolan, he was allowed pen, parchment, and poison.

The best physician in Hellin Daimiel was brought in to attend Rolf Preshka. But the man neither improved nor worsened. The physician believed it was a matter of mind, not disease.

Time eased Bragi's longing for the Itaskian grant. The War Minister wrote that it would be a long time before he could come back. The Greyfells party had grown no weaker. Meantime, Bevold Lif continued his improvements. Ragnarson began looking forward to playing big fish in his new small pool.

There would be a respite before bin Yousif again maneuvered him into the role of stalking horse.

iii) One pretender

Crown Prince Gaia-Lange was playing in his grandfather's garden when the hawkfaced man appeared. The boy was puzzled, but felt no fear. He wondered how the dark man had gotten past the guards. "Who're you?"

"Like you, my prince, a king without a throne." The lean man knelt, kissed the boy on both cheeks. "I'm sorry. There're things more important than princes." He rose, vanished as silently as he had come. The boy's hands touched where lips had touched. His expression remained puzzled.

Hands and expression were still there when his heart beat its last.

It was another Allernmas evening.

iv) Party kill

Shadow from shadow, a lean dark man momentarily appeared in the room where the wine for the leaders of the Greyfells party, meeting before seizing Itaskia's throne, had been decanted. He dribbled golden droplets into each decanter.

Itaskia's morticians were busy for a week.

v) Autumn's child

Like a black ghost that had come on the wings of the blizzard moaning about Castle Krief, the dark man passed the chambers of the Marshal and his wife, the chambers of the Queen, and entered the door of the Princess's room. Drowsy guards never knew he had passed. The child slept in candlelight, golden hair sprayed over cerulean pillows. One small hand protruded from beneath the covers. Into it he emptied a tiny box. The spider was no larger than a pea.

The dark man pricked her palm with a pin. She made a fist.

Death came gently, silently. She never wakened.

He murmured, "October's baby, autumn's child, child of the Dread Empire. Fare you better in the Shadowland." For an instant, before he snuffed the candle and departed, a deep sadness ghosted across his face. One tear rolled down a dark, leathery cheek, betraying the man inside.

ALL DARKNESS MET

Contents

ONE: THE YEARS 980-989
AFTER THE FOUNDING OF THE EMPIRE OF ILKAZAR
O SHING, EHELEBE

The woman screamed with every contraction. The demon outside howled and clawed at the walls. It roared like a wounded elephant, smashed against the door. The timbers groaned.

The physician, soaked with perspiration, shook like a trapped rabbit. His skin was the hue of death.

"Get on with it!" snarled the baby's father.

"Lord!…"

"Do it!" Nu Li Hsi appeared undisturbed by the siege. He refused even to acknowledge the *possibility* of fear, in himself or those who served him. Would-be Lord of All Shinsan, he dared reveal nothing the Tervola could call weakness.

Still the physician delayed. He was hopelessly trapped. He couldn't win. A demon was trying to shatter the sorceries shielding his surgery. Inside, his master was in a rage because the mother couldn't deliver normally. The child was just too huge. The woman was a friend, and the surgeon doubted she could survive the operation. The only assistant permitted him was his daughter. No fourteen-year-old was ready to face this.

Worse, there were witnesses. Two Tervola leaned against one wall. These sorcerer-generals, who managed Shinsan's armies and made up her nobility, were waiting to see the product of the Dragon Prince's experiments.

The goal was a child who could develop into a superstrong, supercompetent soldier, thinking, yet with little ability to become a personality in his own right, and immune to the magicks by which foes seized control of enemy soldiers.

"Start cutting," Nu Li Hsi said softly, with the "or else" transmitted by intonation, "before my brother's attacks become more imaginative."

For a millennium Nu Li Hsi and his twin, Yo Hsi, had battled for mastery of Shinsan, virtually from the moment they had murdered Tuan Hoa, their father, who had been Shinsan's founder.

"Scalpel," said the surgeon. He could scarcely be heard. He glanced around the cramped surgery. The Tervola, with their masks and robes, could have been statues. Nu Li Hsi himself moved nothing but his eyes. His face, though, was naked. The Princes Thaumaturge felt no need to hide behind masks. The surgeon could read the continuing anger there.

The Dragon Prince, he realized, expected failure.

This was the Prince's eleventh try using his own seed. Ten failures had preceded it. They had become reflections on his virility….

The surgeon opened the woman's belly.

A half hour later he held up the child. This one, at least, was a son, and alive.

Nu Li Hsi stepped closer. "The arm. It didn't develop. And the foot…" A quieter, more dangerous anger possessed him now, an anger brought on by repeated failure. What use was a superhuman soldier with a clubfoot and no shield arm?

That wounded elephant roar sounded again. Masonry shifted. Dust fell. Torches and candles wavered. The walls threatened to burst inward. The door groaned again and again. Splinters flew.

Nu Li Hsi showed concern for the first time. "He *is* persistent, isn't he?" He asked the Tervola, "Feed it?"

They nodded.

The Tervola, second only to the Princes Thaumaturge themselves, seldom became involved in the skirmishes of Shinsan's co-rulers. If the *thing* broke the barriers contiguous with the room's boundaries, though, it would respect neither allegiances, nor their lack. Yo Hsi would make restitution to the surviving Tervola, expressing regrets that their fellows had been caught in the cross fire.

The Dragon Prince produced a golden dagger. Jet enamel characters ran its length. The Tervola seized the woman's hands and feet. Nu Li Hsi drove the blade into her breast, slashing, sawing, ripping. He plunged a hand into the wound, grabbed, pulled with the skill of long practice. In a moment he held up the still throbbing heart. Blood ran up his arm and spattered his clothing.

The screams of the doctor's daughter replaced those of the sacrifice.

From outside, suddenly, absolute silence. The thing, for the moment, was mollified.

No one who hadn't been in the room would know that it had been there. The spells shielding the walls weren't barriers against things of this world, but of worlds beyond, Outside.

Nu Li Hsi sighed resignedly. "So… I have to try again. I know I can do it. It works on paper." He started to leave.

"Lord!" the surgeon cried.

"What?"

The doctor indicated woman and child. "What should I do?" The child lived. It was the first of the experimental infants to survive birth.

"Dispose of them."

"He's your son…" His words tapered into inaudibility before his master's rage. Nu Li Hsi had serpent eyes. There was no mercy in them. "I'll take care of it, Lord."

"See that you do."

As soon as the Dragon Prince vanished, the surgeon's daughter whispered, "Father, you can't."

"I must. You heard him."

"But…."

"You know the alternative."

She knew. She was a child of the Dread Empire.

But she was barely fourteen, with the folly of youth everywhere. In fact, she was doubly foolish.

She had already made the worst mistake girls her age could make. She had become pregnant.

That night she made a second mistake. It would be more dire. It would echo through generations.

She fled with the newborn infant.

One by one, over an hour, six men drifted into the room hidden beneath The Yellow-Eyed Dragon restaurant. No one upstairs knew who they were, for they had arrived in ordinary dress, faces bare, and had donned black robes and jeweled beast masks only after being out of sight in a room at the head of the basement stair.

Even Lin Feng, The Dragon's manager, didn't know who was meeting. He *did* know that he had been paid well. In response he made sure each guest had his full ten minutes alone, to dress, before the next was admitted to the intervening room. Feng supposed them conspirators of some sort. Had he known they were Tervola he would have fainted. Barring the Princes Thaumaturge themselves, the Tervola were the most powerful, most cruel men in all Shinsan, with Hell's mightiest devils running at their heels...

Waking, following his faint, Feng probably would have taken his own life. These Tervola could be conspiring against no one but the Princes Thaumaturge themselves. Which made him a rat in the jaws of the cruelest fate of all.

But Feng suspected nothing. He performed his part without trepidation.

The first to arrive was a man who wore a golden mask resembling both cat and gargoyle, chased with fine black lines, with rubies for eyes and fangs. He went over the chamber carefully, making sure there would be no unauthorized witnesses. While the others arrived and waited in silence, he worked a thaumaturgy that would protect the meeting from the most skilled sorcerous eavesdroppers. When he finished, the room was invisible even to the all-seeing eyes of the Princes Thaumaturge themselves.

The sixth arrived. The man in the gargoyle mask said, "The others won't be with us tonight."

His fellows didn't respond. They simply waited to learn why they had been summoned.

The Nine seldom met. The eyes and spies of the Princes and uninitiated Tervola were everywhere.

"We have to make a decision." The speaker called himself Chin, though his listeners weren't sure he was the Chin they knew outside. Only he knew their identities. They overlooked no precaution in their efforts to protect themselves.

Again the five did not respond. If they didn't speak they couldn't recognize one another by voice.

It was a dangerous game they played, for Imperial stakes.

"I have located the woman. The child's still with her. The question: Do we proceed as planned? I know the minds of those who can't be with us. Two were for, one was against. Show hands if you still agree."

Four hands rose.

"Seven for. We proceed, then." Behind ruby eyepieces Chin's eyes sparkled like ice under an angry sun. They fixed on the sole dissenter present.

A link in the circle was weakening. Chin had misjudged the man behind the boar mask. The absentee negative vote he understood, accepted, and dismissed. Fear hadn't motivated it. But the Boar…The man was terrified. He might break.

The stakes were too high to take unnecessary chances.

Chin made a tiny sign. It would be recognized by only one man.

He had convened the Nine not for the vote but to test the Boar. He had learned enough. His decision was made.

"Disperse. The usual rules."

They didn't question, though meeting for so little seemed tempting Fate too much. They departed one by one, reversing the process of entry, till only Chin and the man who had been signaled remained.

"Ko Feng, our friend the Boar grows dangerous," Chin said. "His nerve is failing. He'll run to one of the Princes soon."

Ko Feng, behind a bear mask, had presented the argument before. "The cure?" he asked.

"Go ahead. What must be, must be."

Behind the metal bear, cruel lips stretched in a thin smile.

"He's Shan, of the Twelfth Legion. Go now. Do it quickly. He could spill his terror any time."

The Bear bowed slightly, almost mockingly, and departed.

Chin paused thoughtfully, staring after him. The Bear, too, was dangerous. He was another mistake. Ko Feng was too narrow, too hasty. He might need removing, too. He was the most ambitious, most deadly, most coldhearted and cruel, not just of the Nine, but of the Tervola. He was a long-run liability, though useful now.

Chin began to consider possible replacements for the Boar.

The Nine were old in their conspiracy. Long had they awaited their moment. For centuries each had been selecting eight subordinates carefully, choosing only men who could remain loyal to the ultimate extremity and who would, themselves, build their own Nines with equal care.

Chin's First Nine had existed for three hundred years. In all that time the organization had grown downward only to the fourth level.

Which was, in truth, a fifth level. There was a higher Nine than Chin's, though only he knew. Similar ignorance persisted in each subsidiary Nine.

Soon after the Bear's departure Chin faced another door. It was so well concealed that it had evaded the notice of the others.

It opened. A man stepped through. He was small and old and bent, but his eyes were young, mischievous, and merry. He was in his element here, conspiring in the grand manner. "Perfect, my friend. Absolutely perfect. It proceeds. It won't be long now. A few decades. But be careful with Nu Li Hsi. He should be given information that will help us, yet not so much that he suspects he's being used. It's not yet time for the Nines to become visible."

Chin knew this man only as the master of his own Nine, the world-spanning Master Nine, the Pracchia. Chin, perhaps, should have paid more attention to the old man and less to his problems with his own Nine. Evidence of the man's true identity was available, had he but looked for it.

"And the child?" Chin asked.

"It's not yet his time. He'll be protected by The Hidden Kingdom."

That name was a mystery of the Circle of which Chin was junior member. Ehelebe. The Hidden Kingdom. The Power behind all Powers. Already the Pracchia secretly ruled a tenth of the world. Someday, once the might of Shinsan became its tool, Ehelebe would control the entire world.

"He'll be prepared for the day."

"It is well."

Chin kept his eyes downcast, though the ruby eyepieces of his mask concealed them. Like the Bear, he had his reservations and ambitions. He hoped he hid them better than did Ko Feng.

"Farewell, then." The bent old man returned to his hiding place wearing an amused smile.

Moments later a winged horse took flight from behind The Yellow-Eyed Dragon, coursed across the moon into the mysteries of the night.

"Lang! Tam!" she called. "Come eat." The boys glanced from their clay marbles to the crude hut, crossed gazes. Lang bent to shoot again. "Lang! Tam! You come here right now!" The boys sighed, shrugged, gathered their marbles. It was a conundrum. Mothers, from the dawn of time, never had understood the importance of finishing the game.

There in the Yan-lin Kuo Forest, astride Shinsan's nebulous eastern border, they called her The Hag of The Wood even though she hadn't yet reached her twentieth birthday. With woodcutters and charcoal-burners she plied the ancient trade, and for their wives and daughters she crafted petty charms and wove weak spells. She was sufficiently tainted by the Power to perform simple magicks. Those and her sex were all she had.

Her sons entered the hut, Tam limping on his club foot.

The meal wasn't much. Boiled cabbage. No meat. But it was as good as the best forest people had. In Yan-lin Kuo the well-to-do looked at poverty from the belly side.

"Anybody home?"

"Tran!" Happiness illuminated the woman's face.

A youth of seventeen pushed inside, a rabbit dangling from his left hand. A tall man, he swept her into the bow of his right arm, planted a kiss on her cheek. "And how are you boys?"

Lang and Tam grinned.

Tran wasn't of the majority race of Shinsan. The forest people, who had been under Dread Empire suzerainty for a historically brief time, had a more mahogany cast of skin, yet racially were akin to the whites of the west. Culturally they were ages behind either, having entered the Iron Age solely by virtue of trade. In their crude way they were as cruel as their rulers.

Of his people Tran was the sole person for whom the woman felt anything. And her feelings were reciprocated. There was an unspoken understanding: they would eventually marry.

Tran was a woodsman and trapper. He always provided for The Hag, asking nothing in return. And consequently received more than any who paid.

The boys were young, but they knew about men and women. They gobbled cabbage, then abandoned the hut.

They resumed their game. Neither gained much advantage.

A shadow fell across the circle. Tam looked up.

A creature of nightmare loomed over Lang. It wore the shape of a man, and a man might have lurked within that chitinous black armor. Or a devil. There was no visible evidence either way.

He was huge, six inches taller than Tran, the tallest man Tam knew. He was heavier of build.

He stared at Tam for several seconds, then gestured.

"Lang," Tam said softly.

Four more giants entered the clearing, silently as death by night. Were they human? Even their faces were concealed behind masks showing crystal squares where eyeholes should be.

Lang stared.

These four bore naked, long black swords with razor edges and tips that glowed red hot.

"Ma!" Lang shrieked, scampering toward the hut.

Tam shrieked, "Monsters!" and pursued Lang.

With club foot and half an arm he wasn't much of a runner. The first giant caught him easily.

The Hag and Tran burst from the hut. Lang scooted round and clung to Tran's leg, head leaning against his mother's thigh.

Tam squirmed and squealed. The giant restrained him, and otherwise ignored him.

"Oh, Gods," the woman moaned. "They've found me." Tran seemed to know what she meant.

He selected a heavy stick from her woodpile.

Tam's captor passed him to one of his cohorts, drew his blade. Indigo-purple oil seemed to run its length. It swayed like a cobra about to strike.

"Tran, no. You can't stop them. Save yourself."

Tran moved toward the giant.

"Tran, please. Look at their badges. They're from the Imperial Standard. The Dragon sent them."

Sense gradually penetrated Tran's brain. He stood no chance against the least of Shinsan's soldiers. No one alive had much chance against men of the Imperial Standard Legion. That was no legion brag. These men had trained since their third birthdays. Fighting was their way of life, their religion. They had been chosen from Shinsan's healthiest, stoutest children. They were smart, and utterly without fear. Their confidence in their invincibility was absolute.

Tran could only get himself killed.

"Please, Tran. It's over. There's nothing you can do. I'm dead."

The hunter reflected. His thoughts were shaped by forest life. He decided.

Some might have called him coward. But Tran's people were realists. He would be useless to anyone hanging from a spike which had been driven into the base of his skull, while his entrails hung out and his hands and feet lay on the ground before him.

He grabbed Lang and ran.

No one pursued him.

He stopped running once he reached cover.

He watched.

The soldiers shed their armor.

They had to be following orders. They didn't rape and plunder like foreign barbarians. They did what they were told, and only what they were told, and their service was reward enough.

The woman's screams ripped the afternoon air.

They didn't kill Tam, just made him watch.

In all things there are imponderables, intangibles, and unpredicatables. The most careful plan cannot account for every minuscule factor. The greatest necromancer cannot divine precisely enough to define the future till it becomes predestined. In every human enterprise the planners and seers deal with and interpret only the things they know. Then they usually interpret incorrectly.

But, then, even the gods are fallible. For who created Man?

Some men call the finagle factor Fate.

The five who had gone to The Hag's hut became victims of the unpredictable.

Tam whimpered in their grasp, remembering the security of his mother's arms when wolf calls tormented the night and chill north winds whipped their little fire's flames. He remembered and wept. And he remembered the name Nu Li Hsi.

The forest straddled Shinsan's frontier with Han Chin, which was more a tribal territory than established state. The Han Chin generally tried not to attract attention, but sometimes lacked restraint.

There were a hundred raiders in the party which attacked the five. Forty-three didn't live to see home again. *That* was why the world so feared the soldiers of Shinsan.

The survivors took Tam with them believing anyone important to the legionnaires must be worth a ransom.

Nobody made an offer.

The Han Chin taught the boy fear. They made of him a slave and toy, and when it was their mood to amuse themselves with howls, they tortured him.

They didn't know who he was, but he was of Shinsan and helpless. That was enough.

There was a new man among those who met, though only he, Chin, and Ko Feng knew. It was ever thus with the Nines. Some came, some went. Few recognized the changes.

The conspiracy was immortal.

"There's a problem," Chin told his audience. "The Han Chin have captured our candidate. The western situation being tense, this places a question before the Nine."

Chin had had his instructions. "The Princes Thaumaturge have chivvied Varthlokkur till his only escape can be to set the west aflame. I suggest we suborn the scheme and assume it for our own, nudging at the right moment, till *it* can rid us of the Princes. Come. Gather round. I want to repeat a divination."

He worked with the deftness of centuries of experience, nursing clouds from a tiny brazier. They boiled up and turned in upon themselves, not a wisp escaping. Tiny lightning bolts ripped through…

"Trela stri! Sen me stri!" Chin commanded. "Azzari an walla in walli stri!"

The cloud whispered in the same tongue. Chin gave instructions in his own language. "The fate, again, of the boy…"

That which lived beyond the cloud muttered something impatient.

It flicked over the past, showing them the familiar tale of Varthlokkur, and showed them that wizard's future, and the future of the boy who dwelt with the Han Chin. Nebulously. The thing behind the cloud could not, or would not, define the parameters.

There were those imponderables, intangibles, and unpredictables.

As one, Chin's associates sighed.

"The proposal before us is this: Do we concentrate on shaping these destinies to our advantage? For a time the west would demand our complete attention. The yield? Our goals achieved at a tenth the price anticipated."

The vote was unanimous.

Chin made a sign before the Nine departed.

The one who remained was different. Chin said, "Lord Wu, you're our brother in the east. The boy will be your concern. Prepare him to assume his father's throne."

Wu bowed.

Once Wu departed, that secret door opened. "Excellent," said the bent old man. "Everything is going perfectly. I congratulate you. You're invaluable to the Pracchia. We'll call you to meet the others soon."

Chin's hidden eyes narrowed. His Nine-mask, arrogantly, merely reversed his Tervola mask. The others wore masks meant to conceal identities. Chin was mocking everyone…

Again the old man departed wearing a small, secretive smile.

Tam was nine when Shinsan invaded Han Chin. It was a brief little war, though bloody. A handful of sorcerer's apprentices guided legionnaires to the hiding places of the natives, who quickly died.

The man in the woods didn't understand.

For four years Tran had watched and waited. Now he moved. He seized Tam and fled to the cave where he lived with Lang.

The soldiers came next morning.

Tran wept. "It isn't fair," he whispered. "It just isn't fair." He prepared to die fighting.

A thin man in black, wearing a golden locust mask, entered the circle of soldiers. "This one?" He indicated Tam.

"Yes, Lord Wu."

Wu faced Tam, knelt. "Greetings, Lord." He used words meaning Lord of Lords. O Shing. It would become a title. "My Prince."

Tran, Lang, Tam stared. What insanity was this?

"Who are the others?" Wu asked, rising.

"The child of the woman, Lord. They believe themselves brothers. The other calls himself Tran. One of the forest people. The woman's lover. He protected the boy the best he could the past four years. A good and faithful man."

"Do him honor, then. Place him at O Shing's side." Again that Lord of Lords, so sudden and confusing.

Tran didn't relax.

Wu asked him, "You know me?"

"No."

"I am Wu, of the Tervola. Lord of Liaontung and Yan-lin Kuo, and now of Han Chin. My legion is the Seventeenth. The Council has directed me to recover the son of the Dragon Prince."

Tran remained silent. He didn't trust himself. Tam looked from one man to the other.

"The boy with the handicaps. He's the child of Nu Li Hsi. The woman kidnapped him the day of his birth. Those who came before... They were emissaries of his father."

Tran said nothing, though he knew the woman's tale.

Wu was impatient with resistance. "Disarm him," he ordered. "Bring him along."

The soldiers did it in an instant, then took the three to Wu's citadel at Liaontung.

Two: SPRING, 1010 AFE
MOCKER

These things sometimes begin subtly. For Mocker it started when a dream came true.

Dream would become nightmare before week's end.

He had an invitation to Castle Krief. He. Mocker. The fat little brown man whose family lived in abject poverty in a Vorgreberg slum, who, himself, scrabbled for pennies on the fringes of the law. The invitation had so delighted him that he actually had swallowed his pride and allowed his friend the Marshall to loan him money.

He arrived at the Palace gate grinning from one plump brown ear to the other, his invitation clutched in one hand, his wife in the other.

"Self, am convinced old friend Bear gone soft behind eyes, absolute," he told Nepanthe. "Inviting worst of worse, self. Not so, wife of same, certitude. Hai! Maybeso, high places lonely. Pacificity like cancer, eating silent, sapping manhood. Calls in old friend of former time, hoping rejuvenation of spirit."

He had been all mouth since the invitation had come, though, briefly, he had been suicidally down. The Marshall of all Kavelin inviting somebody like him to the Victory Day celebrations? A mockery. It was some cruel joke...

"Quit bubbling and bouncing," his wife murmured. "Want them to think you're some drunken street rowdy?"

"Heart's Desire. Doe's Eyes. Is truth, absolute. Am same. Have wounds to prove same. Scars. Count them..."

She laughed. And thought, I'll give Bragi a hug that'll break his ribs.

It seemed ages since they had been this happy, an eon since laughter had tickled her tonsils and burst past her lips against any ability to control.

Fate hadn't been kind to them. Nothing Mocker tried worked. Or, if it did, he would suffer paroxysms of optimism, begin gambling, *sure* he'd make a killing, and would lose everything.

Yet they had their love. They never lost that, even when luck turned its worst. Inside the tiny, triangular cosmos described by them and their son, an approach to perfection remained.

Physically, the years had treated Nepanthe well. Though forty-one, she still looked to be in her early thirties. The terrible cruelty of her poverty had ravaged her spirit more than her flesh.

Mocker was another tale. Most of his scars had been laid on by the fists and knives of enemies. He was indomitable, forever certain of his high destiny.

The guard at the Palace gate was a soldier of the new national army. The Marshall had been building it since his victory at Baxendala. The sentry was a polite young man of Wesson ancestry who needed convincing that at least one of them wasn't a party crasher.

"Where's your carriage?" he asked. "Everyone comes in a carriage."

"Not all of us can afford them. But my husband was one of the heroes of the war." Nepanthe did Mocker's talking when clarity was essential. "Isn't the invitation valid?"

"Yes. All right. He can go in. But who are you?" The woman before him was tall and pale and cool. Almost regal.

Nepanthe had, for this evening, summoned all the aristocratic bearing that had been hers before she had been stricken by love for the madman she had married... Oh, it seemed ages ago, now.

"His wife. I said he was my husband."

The soldier had all a Kaveliner's ethnic consciousness. His surprise showed.

"Should we produce marriage papers? Or would you rather he went and brought the Marshall to vouch for me?" Her voice was edged with sarcasm that cut like razors. She could make of words lethal weapons.

Mocker just stood there grinning, shuffling restlessly.

The Marshall did have strange friends. The soldier had been with the Guard long enough to have seen several stranger than these. He capitulated. He was only a trooper. He didn't get paid to think. Somebody would throw them out if they didn't belong.

And, in the opinion locked behind his teeth, they pleased him more than some of the carriage riders he had admitted earlier. Some of those were men whose throats he would have cut gladly.

Those two from Hammad al Nakir... They were ambassadors of a nation which cheerfully would have devoured his little homeland.

They had more trouble at the citadel door, but the Marshall had foreseen it. His aide appeared, vouchsafed their entry.

It grated a little, but Nepanthe held her tongue.

Once, if briefly, she had been mistress of a kingdom where Kavelin would have made but a modest province.

Mocker didn't notice. "Dove's Breast. Behold. Inside of Royal Palace. And am invited. Self. Asked in. In time past, have been to several, dragged in be-chained, or breaked—broked— whatever word is for self-instigated entry for purpose of burgurgalry, or even invited round to back-alley door to discuss deed of dastardness desired done by denizen of same. Invited? As honored guest? Never."

The Marshall's aide, Gjerdrum Eanredson, laughed, slapped the fat man's shoulder. "You just don't change, do you? Six, seven years it's been. You've got a little gray there, and maybe more tummy, but I don't see a whit's difference in the man inside." He eyed Nepanthe. There was, briefly, that in his eye which said he appreciated what he saw.

"But you've changed, Gjerdrum," she said, and the lilt of her voice told him his thoughts had been divined. "What happened to that shy boy of eighteen?"

Gjerdrum's gaze flicked to Mocker, who was bemused by the opulence of his surroundings, to the deep plunge of her bodice, to her eyes. Without thinking he wet his lips with his tongue and, red-faced, stammered, "I guess he growed up…"

She couldn't resist teasing him, flirting. As he guided them to the Great Hall she asked leading questions about his marital status and which of the court ladies were his mistresses. She had him thoroughly flustered when they arrived.

Nepanthe held this moment in deep dread. She had even tried to beg off. But now a thrill coursed through her. She was glad she had come. She pulled a handful of long straight black hair forward so it tumbled down her bare skin, drawing the eye and accenting her cleavage.

For a while she felt nineteen again.

The next person she recognized was the Marshall's wife, Elana, who was waiting near the door. For an instant Nepanthe was afraid. This woman, who once had been her best friend, might not be pleased to see her.

But, "Nepanthe!" The red-haired woman engulfed her in an embrace that banished all misgivings.

Elana loosed her and repeated the display with Mocker. "God, Nepanthe, you look good. How do you do it? You haven't aged a second."

"Skilled artificer, self, magician of renown, having at hand secret of beauty of women of fallen Escalon, most beautiful of all time before fall, retaining light of teenage years into fifth decade, provide potations supreme against ravishes—ravages?—of Time," Mocker announced solemnly—then burst into laughter. He hugged Elana back, cunningly grasping a handful of derriere, then skipped round her in a mad, whirling little dance.

"It's him," Elana remarked. "For a minute I didn't recognize him. He had his mouth shut. Come on. Come on. Bragi will be so glad to see you again."

Time hadn't used Elana cruelly either. Only a few gray wisps threaded her coppery hair, and, despite having borne many children, her figure remained reasonably trim. Nepanthe remarked on it.

"True artifice, that," Elana confessed. "None of your hedge-wizard mumbo jumbo. These clothes—they come all the way from Sacuescu. The Queen's father sends them with hers. He has hopes for his next visit." She winked. "They push me up here, flatten me here, firm me up back there. I'm a mess undressed." Though she tried valiantly to conceal it, Elana's words expressed a faint bitterness.

"Time is great enemy of all," Mocker observed. "Greatest evil of all. Devours all beauty. Destroys all hope." In his words, too, there was attar of wormwood. "Is Eater, Beast That Lies Waiting. Ultimate Destroyer." He told the famous riddle.

There were people all around them now, nobles of Kavelin, Colonels of the Army and Mercenaries' Guild, and representatives from the diplomatic community. Merriment infested the hall. Men who were deadly enemies the rest of the year shared in the celebration as though they were dear friends—because they had shared hardship under the shadow of the wings of Death that day long ago when they had set aside their contentiousness and presented a common front to the Dread Empire—and had defeated the invincible.

There were beautiful women there, too, women the like of which Mocker knew only in dreams. Of all the evidences of wealth and power they impressed him most.

"Scandalous," he declared. "Absolute. Desolution overtakes. Decadence descends. Sybariticism succeeds. O Sin, thy Name is Woman... Self, will strive bravely, but fear containment of opinion will be impossible of provision. May rise to speechify same, castrating—no, castigating—assembly for wicked life. Shame!" He leered at a sleek, long-haired blonde who, simply by existing, turned his spine to jelly. Then he faced his wife, grinning. "Remember passage in *Wizards of Ilkazar,* in list of sins of same? Be great fundament for speech, eh? No?"

Nepanthe smiled and shook her head. "I don't think this's the place. Or the time. They might think you're serious."

"Money here. Look. Self, being talker of first water, spins web of words. In this assemblage famous law of averages declares must exist one case of foolheadedness. Probably twenty-three. Hai! More. Why not? Think big. Self, being student primus of way of spider, pounce. Ensnare very gently, unlike spider, and, also unlike same, drain very slow."

Elana, too, shook her head. "Hasn't changed a bit. Not at all. Nepanthe, you've got to tell me all about it. What have you been doing? How's Ethrian? Do you know how much trouble it was to find you? Valther used half his spies. Had them looking everywhere. And there you were in the Siluro quarter all the time. Why didn't you keep in touch?"

At that moment the Marshall, Bragi Ragnarson, spied them. He spared Nepanthe an answer.

"Mocker!" he thundered, startling half the hall into silence. He abandoned the lords he had been attending. "Yah! Lard Bottom!" He threw a haymaker. The fat man ducked and responded with a blur of a kick that swept the big man's feet from beneath him.

Absolute silence gripped the hall. Nearly three hundred men, plus servants and women, stared.

Mocker extended a hand. And shook his head as he helped the Marshall rise. "Self, must confess to one puzzlement. One only, and small. But is persistent as buzzing of mosquito."

"What's that?" Ragnarson, standing six-five, towered over the fat man.

"This one tiny quandary. Friend Bear, ever clumsy, unable to defend self from one-armed child of three, is ever chosen by great ones to defend same from foes of mighty competence. Is poser. Sorcery? Emboggles mind of self."

"Could be. But you've got to admit I'm lucky."

"Truth told." He said it sourly, and didn't expand. Luck, Mocker believed, was his nemesis. The spiteful hag had taken a dislike to him the moment of his birth... But his day was coming. The good fortune was piling up. When it broke loose...

In truth, luck had less to do with his misfortunes than did compulsive gambling and an iron-hard refusal to make his way up by any socially acceptable means.

This crude little brown man, from the worst slum of the Siluro ghetto, had had more fortunes rush through his fingers than most of the lords present. Once he had actually laid hands on the fabled treasure of Ilkazar.

He wouldn't invest. He refused. Someday, he knew, the dice would fall his way.

The fat man's old friend, with whom, in younger days, he had enjoyed adventures that would've frightened their present companions bald, guided him onto the raised platform from which his approach had been spotted. Mocker began shaking. A moment's clowning, down there, was embarrassing enough. But to be dragged before the multitudes...

He barely noticed the half-dozen men who shared the dais with the Marshall. One eyed him as would a man who spotted someone he thinks he recognizes after decades.

"Quiet!" Ragnarson called. "A little quiet here!"

While the amused-to-disgusted chatter died, Mocker considered his friend's apparel. So rich. Fur-edged cape. Blouse of silk. Hose that must cost more than *he* scrounged in a month... He remembered when this man had worn bearskins.

Once silence gained a hold, Ragnarson announced, "Ladies and gentlemen, I want to introduce somebody. A man I tracked down at considerable inconvenience and expense because he's the critical element that has been missing from our Victory Day celebrations. He was one of the unspoken heroes who guided us up the road to Baxendala, one of the men whose quiet pain and sacrifice made victory possible." Ragnarson held Mocker's hand high. "Ladies and gentlemen, I give you the world's foremost authority."

Puzzled, the ambassador from Altea asked, "Authority on what?"

Ragnarson grinned, punched Mocker's arm. "Everything."

Mocker had never been one to remain embarrassed long. Especially by public acclaim. He had forever been his own greatest booster. But here, because he had a predisposition to expect it, he suspected he was being mocked. He flashed his friend a look of appeal.

Which, despite years of separation, Ragnarson read. Softly, he replied, "No. I didn't bring you here for that. This's a homecoming. A debut. Here's an audience. Take them."

The wicked old grin seared the fat man's face. He turned to the crowd, fearing them no more. They would be his toys. Boldly, insolently, he examined the people nearest the dais. The merry mayhem in his eyes sparkled so that each of them recognized it. Most perked to a higher level of gaiety ere he spoke a word.

He founded the speech on the passage from the epic, and spoke with such joy, such laughter edging his voice, that hardly anyone resented being roasted.

The years had taught him something. He was no longer indiscreet. Though his tongue rolled inspiredly, in a high, mad babble that made the chandeliers rattle with the responding laughter, he retained sufficient command of his inspiration that, while he accused men of every dark deed under the sun, he never indicted anyone for something whispered to be true.

In the Siluro quarter, where dwelt the quiet little men who performed the drudgework of civil service and the mercantile establishments, there were few secrets about the mighty.

He finished with a prophecy not unlike that of the poet. Punctuation, hellfire and brimstone.

And envoi, "Choice is clear. Recant. Renounce high living. Shed sybaritic ways. Place all burden of sin on one able to bear up under curse of same." He paused to meet eyes, including those of the sleek blonde twice. Then, softly, seriously, "Self, would volunteer for job."

Bragi slapped his back. People who remembered Mocker now, from the war, came to greet him and, if possible, swap a few lies about the old days. Others, including that svelte blonde, came to praise his performance.

Mocker was disappointed by the blonde. There was a message in her eyes, and nothing he could do.

"Oh, my," he muttered. "That this obesity should live to see day…" But he wasn't distraught. This was his happiest evening in a decade. He wallowed in it, savoring every instant.

But he didn't stop observing. He soon concluded that there were skunks in paradise. The millennium hadn't arrived.

Three hard men in fighting leathers stood in the shadows behind the dais. He knew them as well as he knew Ragnarson. Haaken Blackfang, Bragi's foster brother, a bear of a man, a deadly fighter, bigger than his brother. Reskird Kildragon, another relic of the old days, and another grim fighter, who sprang like a wolf when Bragi commanded. And Rolf Preshka, that steel-eyed Iwa Skolovdan whose enmity meant certain death, whose devotion to Bragi's wife bordered on the morbid, and should have been a danger to her husband—except that Preshka was almost as devoted to him.

And, yes, there were more of the old comrades, in the out-of-the-ways, the shadows and alcoves of balconies and doors. Turran of Ravenkrak, Nepanthe's brother, white of hair now but none the less deadly. And their brother Valther, impetuous with blade and heart, possessed of a mind as convolute as that of a god. Jarl Ahring. Dahl Haas. Thorn Altenkirk. They were all there, the old, cold ones who had survived, who had been the real heroes of the civil war. And among them were a few new faces, men he knew would be as devoted to their commander—otherwise they would be on the dance floor with the peacocks.

All was not well.

He had known that since climbing to the dais. Two of the occupants of seats of honor were envoys from Hammad al Nakir. From their oldest enemy, El Murid. From that hungry giant of a nation directly south of Kavelin, behind the Kapenrung Mountains. It had taken the combined might of a dozen kingdoms to contain that fanatic religious state in the two-decades-gone, half-forgotten dust-up remembered as the El Murid Wars.

These two had survived that harrowing passage-at-arms, as had Mocker and Bragi and most of those iron-eyed men in the shadows. They remembered. And knew that that argument wasn't settled.

One, in fact, remembered more than any other guest. More, especially, than this happily self-intoxicated little brown man.

He remembered a distant day when they had last met.

He remembered whom it was who had come out of the north into the Desert of Death, using cheap mummer's tricks to establish a reputation as a wizard, to strike to the heart the hope of his master, El Murid, the Disciple. The envoy had been a young trooper then, wild, untameable, in the rear echelon of Lord Nassef's Invincibles. But he remembered.

A fat, young brown man had come to entertain the guardians of El Murid's family with tales and tricks—and then, one night, had slain a half-dozen sentries and fled with the Disciple's treasure, his Priceless, the one thing he valued more than the mission given by God.

The fat man had kidnapped El Murid's virgin daughter.

And she had never been seen again.

It had broken El Murid—at least for the time the infidels needed to turn the tide of desert horsemen sweeping the works of the Evil One from their lands.

And he, Habibullah, who slew like a devil when his enemies came to him face to face—he had lain there, belly opened by a blow struck in darkness, and he had wept. Not for his pain, or for the death he expected, and demanded when the Disciple questioned him, but for the agony and shame he would cause his master.

Now he sat in the palace of the infidel, and was silent, watching with hooded eyes. When no one was listening, he told his companion, "Achmed, God is merciful. God is just. God delivers his enemies into the hands of the Faithful."

Achmed didn't know how, but recognized that this embassy to the heathen had borne fruit at last. Unexpected fruit, sweet and juicy, to judge by Habibullah's reaction.

"This charlatan, this talker," Habibullah whispered. "We'll see him again."

Their exchange passed unnoticed.

All eyes had turned to the shadows behind the dais. Mocker whirled in time for the advent of the Queen, Fiana Melicar Sardyga ip Krief. He hadn't seen her for years, despite her inexplicable habit of wandering the streets to poll Vorgreberg's commons. Time hadn't treated her kindly. Though still in her twenties, she looked old enough to be the blonde's mother.

It wasn't that beauty had deserted her. She retained that, though it was a more mature, promising beauty than Mocker remembered. But she looked exhausted. Utterly weary, and buoyed only by wholehearted devotion to her mission as mistress of the nation.

She seemed unexpected.

She came directly to Bragi, and there was that in her eyes, momentarily, which clarified Elana's bitter remark.

It was a rumor he had heard in the Siluro quarter.

Hardly anyone cared as long as her affairs of the heart didn't collide with affairs of state.

Mocker studied Rolf Preshka. The man's pained expression confirmed his surmise.

"Your Majesty," said Bragi, with such perfected courtliness that Mocker giggled, remembering the man's manners of old. "An unexpected honor."

The assembly knelt or bowed according to custom. Even the ambassadors from Hammad al Nakir accorded the lady deep nods. Only Mocker remained straight-necked, meeting her eyes across Bragi's back.

Amusement drained five years from her face. "So. Now I understand the hubbub. Where did they exhume you?"

"Your Majesty, we found him in the last place anybody would look," Ragnarson told her. "I should've remembered. That's the first place to go when you're hunting him. He was here in the city all the time."

"Welcome back, old friend." Fiana did one of those things which baffled and awed her nobles and endeared her to her commons. She grabbed Mocker in a big hug, then spun him round to face the gathering. She stood beside him, an arm thrown familiarly across his shoulders.

He glowed. He met Nepanthe's eyes and she glowed back. Behind the glow he felt her thinking *I told you.* Oh, his stubborn pride, his fear of appearing a beggar before more successful comrades…

He grinned, laid a finger alongside his nose, did to the Queen what he had done to so many of his audience, roasting her good.

The lady laughed as hard as anyone.

Once, when she controlled herself long enough, she rose on tiptoes and whispered to Ragnarson. Bragi nodded. When Mocker finished, Fiana took her place in the seat that, hitherto, had been only symbolic of her presence. She bade the merriment continue.

Winded, Mocker sat cross-legged at Fiana's feet, joining her and the others there in observing the festivities. Once she whispered, "This's the best Victory Day we've had," and another time, "I'm considering appointing you my spokesman to the Thing. They could use loosening up."

Mocker nodded as if the proposition were serious, then amused her by alternately demanding outrageous terms of employment and describing the way he would bully the parliament.

Meanwhile, Bragi abandoned them to dance with his wife and visit with Nepanthe, whom he soon guided to the lurking place of her brothers. She hadn't seen them in years.

Mocker had a fine sense of the ridiculous. There was funny-ridiculous and pathetic-ridiculous. He, dancing with a wife inches taller, was the latter.

He had an image to maintain.

THREE: SPRING, 1010 AFE
OLD FRIENDS

It was the day after, and Mocker had remained in Castle Krief. Merriment had abandoned everyone but himself. Business had resumed. Bragi took him to a meeting, he explained, so he would get an idea of what was happening nowadays, of why old friends lay back in shadows wearing fighting leather instead of enjoying a celebration of victories won.

"Self," Mocker said as they walked to the meeting, "am confessing overwhelming bambazoolment. Have known large friend, lo, many years. More than can count." He held up his fingers. On those rare occasions when he wasn't proclaiming himself the world's foremost authority, he pretended to be its most ignorant child.

Ragnarson hadn't brought him because he was ignorant or foolish. And Mocker had begun to suspect, after the Queen's entrance last night, that he hadn't been "exhumed" just because he was one of the old fighters and deserved his moment of glory. Nor even because Bragi wanted to give him a little roundabout charity by introducing him to potential suckers.

Bragi trusted his intuitions, his wisdom. Bragi wanted advice—if not his active participation in some fool scheme.

It was both.

Those the Marshall had gathered in the War Room were the same men Mocker had discovered in last night's shadows, plus Fiana and the ambassadors of Altea and Tamerice. Their countries were old allies, and the ambassadors Bragi's friends.

"Mocker," Ragnarson told him after the doors were locked and guards posted, "I wanted you here because you're the only other available expert on a matter of critical importance. An expert, that is, whose answers I trust."

"Then answer damned question."

"Huh? What question?"

"Started to ask same in hall. Bimbazolment? Fingers?"

"All right. Go ahead."

"Self, am knowing friend Bear long ages. Have, till last night, never seen same shaven. Explain."

The non sequitur took Ragnarson off stride. Then he grinned. Of that device Mocker was past master.

"Exactly what you're thinking. These effete southerners have turned me into a ball-less woman."

"Okay. On to question about Haroun."

Ragnarson's jaw dropped. His aide, Gjerdrum, demanded, "How did you…?"

"Am mighty sorcerer…"

The Queen interrupted, "He gave enough clues, Gjerdrum. Is there anybody else who calls both bin Yousif and the Marshall friend?"

Mocker grinned, winked. Fiana startled him by winking back.

"Too damned smart, this woman," he mock-whispered to Bragi.

"Damned right. She's spooky. But let's stick to the point."

"Delineate dilemma. Define horns of same." Mocker's ears were big. He lived in a neighborhood frequented by exiles who followed El Murid's nemesis, Haroun bin Yousif, the King Without a Throne. He knew as much of the man's doings as anyone not privy to his councils. And he knew the man himself, of old. For several years following the El Murid Wars, before he had grown obsessed with restoring Royalist rule to Hammad al Nakir, bin Yousif had adventured with Mocker and Ragnarson. "Old sand rat friend up to no goods again, eh? Is in nature of beast. Catch up little chipmunk. Does same growl and stalk gazelle like lion? Catch up lion. Does same lie down with lamb? With lamb in belly, maybeso. Mutton chops. Mutton chops! Hai! Has been age of earth since same have passed starved lips of impoverished ponderosity, self."

Bragi prodded Mocker's belly with a sheathed dagger. "If you'll spare us the gourmet commentary, I'll explain."

"Peace! Am tender of belly, same being…"

Bragi poked him again. "This's it in a nutshell. For years Haroun raided Hammad al Nakir from camps in the Kapenrungs. From Kavelin and Tamerice, using money and arms from Altea and Itaskia. I've always looked the other way when he smuggled recruits down from the northern refugee centers."

"Uhm. So?"

"Well, he became an embarrassment. Then, suddenly, he seemed to get slow and soft. Stopped pushing. Now he just sits in the hills with his feet up. He throws in a few guys now and then so's El Murid stays pissed, but don't do him no real harm.

"And El Murid just gets older and crankier. You saw his ambassadors?"

"Just so. Snakes in grass, or maybe sand, lying in wait with viper fangs ready…"

"They're out in plain sight this time. They've delivered a dozen ultimatums. Either we close Haroun down or they'll do it for us. They haven't so far. But they're on safe ground. Attacking Haroun's camps would cause a stink, but nobody would go to war to save them. Not if El Murid doesn't try converting us to the one true faith again. It might even solve a few problems for cities with a lot of refugees. Without Haroun keeping them stirred up, they'd settle down and blend in. Distracting the troublemakers is the main reason Haroun gets help from Raithel."

Altea's ambassador nodded. Prince Raithel had died recently, but his policies continued.

"So. Old friend, in newfound, secure circumstance, is asking, should same be safeguarded by selling other old friend down river?"

"No. No. I want to know what he's up to. Why he hasn't done anything the past few years. Part I know. He's studying sorcery. Finishing what he started as a kid. If that's all, okay. But it's not his style to lay back in the weeds.

"El Murid is a sword hanging over Kavelin by a thread. Is Haroun going to cut the thread? You know him. What's he planning?"

Mocker's gaze drifted to his wife's brother Valther. Valther was the shadow man of Vorgreberg, rumored to manage Bragi's cloak and dagger people.

Valther shrugged, said, "That's all we know. We don't have anybody in there."

"Oho! Truth exposes bare naked, ugly fundament before eyes of virginal, foolish self. O Pervert, Truth! Begone!" And to Bragi, perhaps the simplest statement he had ever made: "No."

"I didn't make my proposition."

"Am greatest living necromancer. Am reader of minds. Am knowing blackest secret at heart of hearts of one called friend. Am not one to be used."

Gjerdrum countered, "But Kavelin needs you!"

An appeal to patriotism? No bolt could have flown wider of its mark. The fat man laughed in Gjerdrum's face. "What is Kavelin to me? Fool. Look. See self. Am clear blue-eyed Nordmen? Am Wesson?" He glanced at Bragi, shook his head, jerked a thumb at Eanredson.

Bragi knew Mocker. Mocker was terribly upset when he spoke this plainly. Ragnarson also knew how to penetrate the fat man's distress.

He produced a large gold coin, pretended to examine it in a shaft of light piercing one of the narrow windows. "How's Ethrian?" he asked. "How's my godson?" He spun the coin on the polished tabletop inches beyond Mocker's reach. He produced another, made a similar examination.

The fat man began sweating. He stared at the money the way alcoholics stare at liquor after an enforced abstinence. They were Kaveliner double nobles specially struck for the eastern trade, beautiful pieces with the twin-headed eagle and Fiana's profile in high, frosted relief. They weren't intended for normal commerce, but for transfers between commercial accounts in the big mercantile banks in Vorgreberg. The gold in one piece represented more than a laborer could earn in a year.

Mocker had seen hard times. He did mental sums, calculating temptation's value in silver. The things he could do for Ethrian and Nepanthe…

Ragnarson deposited the second coin atop the first, dropping his eye to table level while aligning their rims. He produced another.

Mocker changed subtly. Bragi sensed it. He stacked the third coin, folded his arms.

"Woe!" Mocker cried suddenly, startling the group. "Am poor old fat cretin of pusillaminity world-renowned, weak of head and muscle. Self, ask nothings. Only to be left alone, to live out few remaining years with devoted wife, in peace, raising son."

"I saw the place where you're keeping my sister," Turran observed, perhaps more harshly than intended.

Bragi waved a hand admonishingly.

"Hai! Self, am not…"

"Like the old joke," said Bragi. "We know what you are. We're dickering price."

Mocker stared at the three gold coins. He looked round the room. Heads pointed his way like those of hounds eager to be loosed.

He didn't like it. Not one whit. But gold! So much gold. What he could do for his wife and son…

He had aged, he had mellowed, he had grown concerned with security. Having to care for others can do that to a man.

He raised his left hand, jerkily, started to speak. He looked round again. So many narrowed eyes. Some he didn't know. He had things to say to Bragi, but not here, not now, not before an audience.

"Define task," he ordered. "Not that poor old fat mendicant, on brink of old age, near crippled, agrees to undertake same. Only purpose being to listen to same, same being reasonable request to allow before telling man to put same where moon don't glow."

"Simple. Just visit Haroun. Find out what he's up to. Bring me the news."

Mocker laughed his most sarcastic laugh. "Self, am famous dullard, admitted. Of brightness next to which cheapest tallow candle is like sun to dark of moon. Forget to come in from rain sometimes, maybeso. But am alive. See? Wound here, here, everywhere, from listening to friends in time past. But am favored of Gods. Was born under lucky star. Haven't passed yet. Also, am aware of ways men speak. Simple, says old friend? Then task is bloody perilous…"

"Not so!" Ragnarson protested. "In fact, if I knew where Haroun was, I'd go myself. But you know him. He's here, he's there, and the rumors are always wrong. He might be at the other end of the world. I can't take the time."

"Crippled. Excuse limps like sixty-year-old arthritic."

Actually, it was unvarnished truth. And Mocker knew it. He rose. "Has been enjoyable matching wits with old half-wit friend. Father of self, longtime passing, said, 'Never fight unarmed man.' Must go. Peace." He did an amusing imitation of a priest giving a blessing.

The inner door guard might have been deaf and blind. Or a path-blocking statue.

"So! Now am prisoner. Woe! Heart of heart of fool, self, told same stay away from palaces, same being dens of iniquitous…"

"Mocker, Mocker," said Bragi. "Come. Sit. I'm not as young as I used to be. I don't have the patience anymore. You think we could dispense with this bullshit and get down to cases?"

Mocker came and sat, but his expression said he was being pushed, that he was about to get stubborn. No force in Heaven or Hell could nudge a stubborn Mocker.

Ragnarson understood his reluctance. Nepanthe was absolutely dead set against allowing her husband to get involved in anything resembling an adventure. Hers was an extremely dependent personality. She couldn't endure separations.

"Turran, could you convince Nepanthe?"

"I'll do it," Valther said. He and Nepanthe had always been close. "She'll listen to me. But she won't like it."

Mocker grew agitated. His domestic problems were being aired…

Bragi began massaging his own face. He wasn't getting enough sleep. The demands of his several posts were getting to him. He considered resigning as publican consul. The position made limited demands, yet did consume time he could use being Marshall and virtual king-surrogate.

"Why don't you list your objections—take them down, Derel—and we'll deal with them in an orderly fashion."

Mocker was appalled. "Is end. Is perished. Is dead, absolute, friend of youth, wrapping self in cocoon of time, coming forth from chrysalis as perfect bureaucrat, all impatient and indifferent. Or is imposter, taking place of true gentleman of former time? Rising from Sea of Perdition, snakes of rules and regulations for hair—not my department, go down hall to hear same—Bastard Beast-Child of order… Enough. Self, am beloved get of Chaos. Am having business of own. Otherwheres. Open door."

He was irked. And Ragnarson *was* tempted to apologize, except he wasn't sure what to apologize for. "Let him go, Luther. Tell Malven to take him to his room." One by one, he palmed the double nobles.

Part of his failure came from inside, he reflected. He *had* changed. But as much blame lay with Mocker. Never had he been so touchy.

Michael Trebilcock, one of the faces Mocker didn't know, asked, "What now?"

Ragnarson gestured for silence.

Mocker didn't make it past Luther. As the guard stepped aside, the fat man turned and asked musingly, "Double nobles five?" He grinned. "Hai! Might soothe conscience, same being sufficient to keep wife and son for year or two in eventuation of certain death of cretinic chaser-after-dreams of old friends." He then railed against the Fates for several minutes, damning them for driving him into a corner from which he had no exit but suicide.

It was all for show. The mission Bragi had shouldn't be dangerous.

They settled it then, with Mocker to leave Vorgreberg the following morning. The group gradually dissolved, till only Bragi and Fiana remained.

They stared at one another across a short space that, sometimes, seemed miles.

Finally, she asked, "Am I getting boring?"

He shook his head.

"What is it, then?"

He massaged his face again. "The pressure. More and more, I have trouble giving a damn. About anything."

"And Elana, a little? You think she knows?"

"She knows. Probably since the beginning."

Fiana nodded thoughtfully. "That would explain a lot."

Bragi frowned. "What?"

"Never mind. You have trouble with your conscience?"

"Maybe. Maybe."

She locked the door, eased into his lap. He didn't resist, but neither did he encourage her. She nuzzled his ear, whispered, "I've always had this fantasy about doing it here. On the table. Where all the important laws and treaties get signed."

There were some things Ragnarson just couldn't say, and first among them was "no" to a willing lady.

Later, he met with Colonel Balfour, who commanded the Guild regiment being maintained in Kavelin till the country produced competent soldiers of its own. High Crag was growing a little arrogant, a little testy, as the inevitable withdrawal of the regiment drew closer. Each year the Guild grew less subtle in its insistence that the regiment's commission be extended.

There were mercenaries and Mercenaries. The latter belonged to the Guild, headquartered at High Crag on the western coast just north of Dunno Scuttari. The Guild was a brotherhood of free soldiers, almost a monastic order, consisting of approximately ten thousand members scattered from Ipopotam to Iwa Skolovda, from the Mountains of M'Hand to Freyland. Ragnarson and many of his intimates had begun their adulthood in its ranks and, nominally, remained attached to the order. But the connection was tenuous, despite High Crag's having awarded regular promotions over the years. Because the Citadel recognized no divorce, it still claimed a right to demand obedience.

The soldiers of the Guild owned no other allegiance, to men, nations, or faith. And they were the best-schooled soldiers in the west. High Crag's decision to accept or reject a commission often made or broke the would-be employer's cause without blows being struck.

There were suspicions, among princes, that the Citadel—High Crag's heart, whence the retired generals ruled—was shaping destiny to its own dream.

Ragnarson entertained those suspicions himself—especially when he received pressure to extend the regiment posted to Kavelin.

Ragnarson had, on several occasions, tried to convince the Guild factors that his little state just couldn't afford the protection. Kavelin remained heavily indebted from the civil war. He argued that only low-interest loans and outright grants from Itaskia were keeping the kingdom above water. If El Murid died or were overthrown, that aid would end. Itaskia would lose its need for a buffer on the borders of Hammad al Nakir.

Following the inevitable bitter argument with Balfour, Bragi spoke to the Thing, doing his best to shuffle his three hats without favoring any one. Still, as chief of the armed forces, he concentrated on an appropriations measure.

The bill was for the maintenance of the Mercenary regiment. The parliament supported its hire even less enthusiastically than Ragnarson.

Such matters, and personal problems, distracted him so much during subsequent months that he took little notice of the enduring absence of his fat friend, whom he had instructed to disappear, so to speak, anyway.

His immediate goal, Mocker decided, had to be Sedlmayr. Kavelin's second largest city nestled between the breasts of the Kapenrungs within days of Haroun's primary camps. He would make inquiries there, alerting Haroun's agents to his presence. Their response would dictate his latter activities.

There were a dozen moving camps within fifty miles. He might end up wandering from one to another till he located Haroun.

The rooftops of Vorgreberg had just dipped behind the horizon when he heard the clop-clop of a faster horse coming up behind him. He glanced back. Another lone rider.

He slowed, allowing the rider to catch up. "Hail, friend met upon trail."

The man smiled, replied in kind, and thereafter they rode together, chance-met companions sharing a day's conversation to ease the rigors of the journey. The traveler said he was Sir Keren of Sincic, a Nordmen knight southbound on personal business.

Mocker missed the signs. He had taken Bragi at his word. No danger in the mission. He didn't catch a whiff of peril.

Until the four ambushers sprang from the forest a half day further south.

The knight downed him with a blow from behind as he slew a second bush-whacker with a sword almost too swift to follow. Half-conscious, he mumbled as they bound him, "Woe! Am getting old. Feeble in head. Trusting stranger. What kind fool you, idiot Mocker? Deserve whatever happens, absolute."

The survivors taunted him, and beat him mercilessly. Mocker marked the little one with the eye-patch. He would undergo the most exquisite tortures after the tables turned.

Mocker didn't doubt that they would. His past justified that optimism.

After dark, following back-ways and forest trails, his captors took him south-eastward, into the province of Uhlmansiek. So confident were they that they didn't bother concealing anything from him.

"A friend of mine," said the knight, "Habibullah the ambassador, sent us."

"Is a puzzlement. Self, profess bambizoolment. Met same two nights pass-ing, speaking once to same, maybeso. Self, am wondering why same wants inconsequential—though ponderous, admit—self snapped up like slave by second-class thugs pretending to entitlement?"

Sir Keren laughed. "But you've met before. A long time ago. You gutted him and left him for dead the night you kidnapped El Murid's daughter."

That put a nasty complexion on the matter. Mocker felt a new, deeper fear. Now he knew his destination.

They would have a very special, very painful welcome for him at Al Rhem-ish.

But Fate was to deprive him of his visit to the Most Holy Mrazkim Shrines. They were somewhere in the Uhlmansiek Kapenrungs when it happened.

They rounded a bend. Two horsemen blocked their path. One was Guild Colonel Balfour, the second an equally hard and scarred Mercenary battalion chieftain. Mocker remembered both from the Victory Day celebration.

"Hai!" he cried, for, if Sir Keren had made any mistake at all, it had been leaving him ungagged. "Rescue on hand. Poor old fat fool not forgotten…" The little fellow with an eye missing belted him in the mouth.

Sir Keren's rogues were old hands. Despite his circumstances, Mocker found himself admiring their professionalism. They spread out, three against two. There was no question of a parley.

The currents of intrigue ran deep.

The one-eyed man moved suddenly, a split second after Sir Keren and his comrade launched their attack. His blade found a narrow gap below the rim of Sir Keren's helmet.

Balfour's companion died at the same moment, struck down by Sir Keren's companion. Balfour himself barely managed to survive till the one-eye skewered the remaining man from behind.

Mocker's glee soon became tempered by a suspicion that his rescue wasn't what it seemed. It might, in fact, be no rescue at all. He seized the best chance he saw.

Having long ago slipped his bonds, he wheeled his mount and took off.

They must be ignorant of his past, he reflected as forest flew past. Otherwise they would've taken precautions. Escape tricks were one way he had of making his meager living.

He managed two hundred yards before the survivors noticed. The chase was on.

It was brief.

Mocker rounded a turn. His mount stopped violently, reared, screamed.

A tall, slim man in black blocked the trail. He wore a golden cat-gargoyle mask finely chased in black, with jeweled eyes and fangs. And while words could describe that mask, they couldn't convey the dread and revulsion it inspired.

Mocker kicked his mount's flanks, intending to ride the man down.

The horse screamed and reared again. Mocker tumbled off. Stunned, he rolled in the deep pine needles, muttered, "Woe! Is story of life. Always one more evil, waiting round next bend." He lay there twitching, pretending injury, fingers probing the pine needles for something useful as a weapon.

Balfour and the one-eyed man arrived. The latter swung down and booted Mocker, then tied him again.

"You nearly failed," the stranger accused.

Balfour revealed neither fear nor contrition. "They were good. And you've got him. That's what matters. Pay Rico. He's served us well. He deserves well of us. I've got to get back to Vorgreberg."

"No."

Balfour slapped his hilt. "My weapon is faster than yours." He drew the blade a foot from its scabbard. "If we can't deal honorably amongst ourselves, then our failure is inevitable."

The man in black bowed slightly. "Well said. I simply meant that it wouldn't be wise for you to return. We've made too much commotion here. Eyes have seen. The men of the woods, the Marena Dimura, are watching. It would be impossible to track all the witnesses. It'll be simpler for you to disappear."

Balfour drew his blade another foot. Rico, unsure what was happening, moved to where he could attack from the side.

The thin man carefully raised his hands. "No. No. As you say, there must be trust. There must be a mutual concern. Else how can we convert others to our cause?"

Balfour nodded, but didn't relax.

Mocker listened, and through hooded eyes observed. His heart pounded. What dread had befallen him? And why?

"Rico," the stranger said, "Take this. It's gold." He offered a bag.

The one-eyed man glanced at Balfour, took the sack, looked inside. "He's right. Maybe thirty pieces. Itaskian. Iwa Skolovdan."

"That should suffice till the moves have begun and it's safe for you to return," said the masked man.

Balfour sheathed his weapon. "All right. I know a place where no one could find us. Where they wouldn't think of looking. You need help with him?" He nudged Mocker with a toe.

The fat man could feel the wicked grin behind that hideous mask. "That one? That little toad? No. Go on, before his friends hear the news."

"Rico, come on."

After Balfour and Rico had departed, the tall man stood over Mocker, considering.

Mocker, being Mocker, had to try, even knowing it futile.

He kicked.

The tall man hopped his leg with disdainful ease, reached, touched...

Mocker's universe shrank to a point of light which, after a momentary brightness, died. After that he was lost, and time ceased to have meaning.

FOUR: SPRING, 1011 AFE
INTIMATIONS

Ragnarson dismounted, dropped his reins over a low branch. "Why don't you guys join me?" he asked as he seated himself against an oak. A cool breeze whispered through the Gudbrandsdal Forest, a Royal Preserve just over the western boundary of the Siege of Vorgreberg. "It's restful here."

He narrowed his eyes to slits, peered at the sun, which broke through momentary gaps in the foliage.

Turran, Valther, Blackfang, Kildragon, and Ragnarson's secretary, a scholar from Hellin Daimiel named Derel Prataxis, dismounted. Valther lay down on his belly in new grass, a strand of green trailing from between his teeth. Ragnarson's foster brother, Blackfang, began snoring in seconds.

This had begun as a boar hunt. Beaters were out trying to kick up game. Other parties were on either flank, several hundred yards away. But Bragi had left the capital only to escape its pressures. The others understood.

"Sometimes," Ragnarson mused, minutes later, "I think we were better off back when our only problem was our next meal."

Kildragon, a lean, hard brunet, nodded. "It had its good points. We didn't have to worry about anybody else."

Ragnarson waved a hand in an uncertain gesture, reflecting his inner turmoil. "It's peaceful out here. No distractions."

Kildragon stretched a leg, prodded Blackfang.

"Uhn? What's happening?"

"That's it," said Bragi. "Something." Peace had reigned so long that the first ripples, subtle though they were, had brought him worriedly alert. His companions, too, sensed it.

Valther grumbled, "I can't put my finger on it."

Everyday life in Vorgreberg had begun showing little stutters, little stumbles. A general uneasiness haunted everyone, from the Palace to the slums.

There was just one identifiable cause. The Queen's indisposition. But Bragi wasn't telling anyone anything about that. Not even his brother.

"Something's happening," Ragnarson insisted. Prataxis glanced his way, shook his head gently, resumed scribbling.

The scholars of Hellin Daimiel took subservient posts as a means of obtaining primary source material for their great theses. Prataxis was a historian of the Lesser Kingdoms. He kept intimate accounts of the events surrounding the man he served. Someday, when he returned to the Rebsamen, he would write the definitive history of Kavelin during Ragnarson's tenure.

"Something is piling up," Bragi continued. "Quietly, out of sight. Wait!"

He gestured for silence. One by one, the others saw why. A bold chipmunk had come to look them over. As time passed and the little rascal saw no threat, he sneaked closer. Then closer still.

Those five hard men, those battered swords, veterans of some of the grimmest bloodlettings that world had ever seen, watched the animal bemusedly. And Prataxis watched them. His pen moved quietly as he noted that they could take pleasure in simple things, in the natural beauties of creation. It wasn't a facet of their characters they displayed in the theater of the Palace. The Palace was a cruel stage, never allowing its actors to shed their roles.

The chipmunk finally grew bored, scampered away.

"If there was anything to reincarnation, I wouldn't mind being a chipmunk next time around," Turran observed. "Except for owls, foxes, hawks, and like that."

"There's always predators," Blackfang replied. "Me, I'm satisfied here on top of the pile. Us two-leggers, we're Number One. Don't nothing chomp on us. Except us."

"Haaken, when did you take up philosophizing?" Bragi asked. His foster brother was a taciturn, stolid man whose outstanding characteristic was his absolute dependability.

"Philosophizing? Don't take no genius to tell that you're in the top spot being people. You can always yell and get a bunch of guys to gang up on any critter that's giving you trouble. How come there's no wolves or lions in these parts anymore? They all went to Ipopotam for the season?"

"My friend," said Prataxis, "you strip it to its bones, but it remains a philosophical point."

Blackfang regarded the scholar narrowly, not sure he hadn't been mocked. His old soldier's anti-intellectual stance was a point of pride.

"We can't get away from it," said Ragnarson. "But the quiet may help us think. The subject at hand, my friends. What's happening?"

Valther spat his blade of grass. While searching for another, he replied, "People are getting nervous. The only thing I know, that's concrete, is that they're worried because Fiana has locked herself up at Karak Strabger. If she dies…"

"I know. Another civil war."

"Can't you get her to come back?"

"Not till she's recovered." Bragi examined each face. Did they suspect?

He wished the damned baby would hurry up and the whole damned mess would get done with.

His thoughts slipped away to the night she had told him.

They had been lying on the couch in his office, on one of those rare occasions when they had the chance to be together. As he had let his hand drift lightly down her sleek stomach, he had asked, "You been eating too much of that baklava? You're putting on a little…"

He had never been a smooth talker, so he wasn't surprised by her tears. Then she whispered, "It's not fat. Darling… I'm pregnant."

"Oh, shit." A swarm of panic-mice raged round inside him. What the hell would he do? What would Elana say? She was suspicious enough already…

"I thought… Doctor Wachtel said you couldn't have any more. After Carolan you were supposed to be sterile."

"Wachtel was wrong. I'm sorry." She'd pulled herself against him as if trying to crawl inside.

"But… Well… Why didn't you tell me?" She had been well along. Only skilled dress had concealed it.

"At first, I didn't believe it. I thought it was something else. Then I didn't want you to worry."

Well, yes, she had saved him that, till then. Since, he'd done nothing *but* worry.

Too many people could get hurt: Elana, himself, his children, Fiana, and Kavelin—if the scandal became a cause célèbre. He spent a lot of time cursing himself for his own stupidity. And a little admitting that his major objection was having gotten caught. He'd probably go right on bedding her if he got through this on the cheap.

Before it showed enough to cause talk, Fiana had taken trusted servants and Gjerdrum and had moved to Karak Strabger, at Baxendala, where Ragnarson had won the battle Kavelin celebrated on Victory Day. Her plea of mental exhaustion wasn't that difficult to believe. Her reign had been hard, with seldom a moment's relief.

Horns alerted him to the present.

"Game's afoot," Kildragon observed, rising.

"Go ahead," Bragi said. "Think I'll just lay around here and loaf."

Haaken, Reskird, Turran, and Valther were habituated to action. They went. They would get more relaxation from the hunt.

"And you, Derel?"

"Are you joking? Fat, old, and lazy as I am? Besides, I never did see any point to hounding some animal through the woods, and maybe breaking my neck."

"Gives you a feeling of omnipotence. You're a god for a minute. 'Course, sometimes you get taken down a peg if the game gives you the slip or runs you up a tree." He chuckled. "Damned hard to be dignified when you're hanging on a branch with a mad boar trying to grab a bite of your ass. Makes you reflect. And you figure out that what Haaken said about us being top critter isn't always right."

"Can you manage this charade another two months?"

"Eh?"

"My calculations say the child will arrive next month. She'll need another month to make herself presentable…"

Ragnarson's eyes became hard and cold.

"Too," said Prataxis, who hadn't the sense to be intimidated, because in Hellin Daimiel scholars could make outrageous, libelous remarks without suffering reprisals, "there's the chance, however remote, that she'll die in childbirth. Have you considered possible political ramifications? Have you taken steps? Kavelin could lose everything you two have built."

"Derel, you walk a thin line. Take care."

"I know. But I know you, too. And I'm speaking now only because the matter needs to be addressed and every eventuality considered. The Lesser Kingdoms have been stricken by deaths lately. Prince Raithel last year. He was old. Everybody expected it. But King Shanight, in Anstokin, went during the winter, in circumstances still questionable. And now King Jostrand of Volstokin has gone, leaving no one but a doddering Queen Mother to pick up the reins."

"You saying there's something behind their deaths? That Fiana might be next? My God! Jostrand was dead drunk when he fell off his horse."

"Just trying to make a point. The Dark Lady stalks amongst the ruling houses of the Lesser Kingdoms. And Fiana will be vulnerable. This pregnancy shouldn't have happened. Bearing the Shinsan child ruined her insides. She's having trouble, isn't she?"

It took a special breed not to be offended by the forthrightness of the scholars of Hellin Daimiel. Ragnarson prided himself on his tolerance, his resilience. Yet he had trouble dealing with Prataxis now. The man was speaking of things never discussed openly.

"Yes. She is. We're worried." *We* meant himself, Gjerdrum, and Dr. Wachtel, the Royal Physician. Fiana was scared half out of her mind. She was convinced she was going to die.

But Bragi ignored that. Elana had had nine children now, two of whom hadn't lived, and she had gone through identical histrionics every time.

"To change the subject, have you thought about Colonel Oryon?"

"That arrogant little reptile? I'm half tempted to whip him. To send him home with his head under his arm."

He found Balfour's replacement insufferably abrasive. High Crag's recent threat to call in Kavelin's war debts had done nothing to make the man more palatable. And Bragi thought he was kicking up too much dust about Balfour's disappearance.

Ragnarson wondered if that was related to High Crag's threats. Though ranked General on its rosters, he had had little to do with the Mercenaries' Guild the past two decades. High Crag kept promoting him, he suspected, so a tenuous link would exist should the Citadel want to exploit it. He wasn't privy to the thinking there.

"Actually," he said, "you've conjured enough into the Treasury to pay them off. They don't know yet. My notion is, they want to do to us what they've done to some of the little states on the coast. To nail us for some property. Maybe a few titles with livings for their old men. That's their pattern."

"Possibly. They've been developing an economic base for a century."

"What?"

"A friend of mine did a study of Guild policies and practices. *Very* interesting when you trace their monies and patterns of commission acceptance. Trouble is, the pattern isn't complete enough to show their goals."

"What do you think? Would it be better to give them a barony or two? One of the nonhereditary titles we created after the war?"

"You could always nationalize later—when you think you can whip them heads up."

"If we pay there won't be much left for emergencies."

"Commission renewal is almost here. There won't be much favorable sentiment in the Thing."

"Ain't much in my heart, either." Ragnarson watched the sun play peekaboo through the leaves. "Hard to convince myself we need them when we haven't had any trouble for seven years. But the army isn't up to anything rough yet."

The real cost of the war had been the near-obliteration of Kavelin's traditional military leadership, the Nordmen nobility. Hundreds had fallen in the rebellion against Fiana. Hundreds had been exiled. Hundreds more had fled the kingdom. There was no lack of will in the men Bragi had recruited since, simply an absence of command tradition. He had made up somewhat by using veterans he had brought to Kavelin back then, forming several sound infantry regiments, but the diplomatically viable military strength of the state still hinged on the Guild presence. Their one regiment commanded more respect than his native seven.

Kavelin had greedy neighbors, and their intentions, what with three national leaderships having changed within the year, remained uncertain.

"If I could just get the Armaments Act through..."

Soon after war's end Fiana had decreed that every free man should provide himself with a sword. Ragnarson's idea. But he had overlooked the cost. Even simple weapons were expensive. Few peasants had the money. Distributing captured arms had helped only a little.

So, for years, he had been pushing legislation which would enable his War Ministry to provide weapons.

He wanted the act so he could dispense with the Mercenaries. The Thing wanted rid of the Mercenaries first. An impasse.

Bragi was finding politics a pain in the behind.

Reskird and Haaken returned, then Turran and Valther. Empty-handed. "That kid Trebilcock, and Rolf, got there first," Reskird explained. "Tough old sow anyway."

"Sour grapes?" Bragi chuckled. "Valther, you heard anything from Mocker yet? Or about him?"

Most of a year had passed since he had sent the fat man south. He hadn't heard a word since.

"It's got me worried," Valther admitted. "I made it top priority two months ago, when I heard that Haroun had left his camps. He's gone north. Nobody knows where or why."

"And Mocker?"

"Practically nothing. I've scoured the country clear to Sedlmayr. He never made it there. But one of my men picked up a rumor that he was seen in Uhlmansiek."

"That's a long way from Sedlmayr…"

"I know. And he wasn't alone."

"Who was he with?"

"We don't know. Nearest thing to a description I have is that one of them was a one-eyed man."

"That bothers you?"

"There's a one-eyed man named Willis Northen, alias Rico, who's been on my list for years. We think he works for El Murid."

"And?"

"Northen disappeared about the right time."

"Oh-oh. You think El Murid's got him? What're the chances?"

"I don't know. It's more hunch than anything."

"So. Let's see. Mocker goes to see Haroun. El Murid's agents intercept him. Question. How did they know?"

"You've got me. That bothers me more than where Mocker is. It could cost us all. I've tried every angle I can think of. I can't find a leak. I put tagged information through everybody who was there when we conned Mocker into going. Result? Nothing."

Ragnarson shook his head. He knew those men. He had bet his life on their loyalties before.

But the word had leaked somehow.

Had Mocker told anybody?

Thus the spy mind works. There had to be a plot, a connection. Coincidence couldn't be accepted.

Habibullah hadn't had the slightest idea of Mocker's mission. He had simply set his agents to kidnap a man, acting on news, which was common talk in the Siluro quarter, that he was traveling to Sedlmayr. Mocker had spread that story himself. The man in black had other resources.

"Keep after it. In fact, get in touch with Haroun's people."

"Excuse me?"

"Haroun has people here. I know a little about your work. I've done some in my time. Admit it. You know them and they know you. Ask them to find out. Or you could go through our friends from Altea. They're in direct contact. Even if you find out they don't know anything, we're ahead. We'd know Mocker didn't reach the camps. Oh. Ask the Marena Dimura. They know what's happening in the hills."

"That's where I got my Uhlmansiek rumor."

The Marena Dimura were the original inhabitants of Kavelin, dwelling there before Ilkazar initiated the wave of migrations which had brought in the other three ethnic groups: the Siluro, Wessons, and Nordmen. The semi-nomadic Marena Dimura tribes kept to the forests and mountains. A fiercely independent people—though they had supported her during the civil war—they refused to recognize Fiana as legitimate monarch of Kavelin. Centuries after the Conquest they still viewed the others as occupying peoples… They put little effort into altering the situation, though. They took their revenge by stealing chickens and sheep.

It was early spring. The sun rolled west. The afternoon breeze rose. The air grew cooler. Shivering, Bragi announced, "I'm heading back to town. Be damned cold by dark." It would take that long to get home.

Prataxis and Valther joined him. They had work to do.

"You ought to go see your wife sometime," Ragnarson told Valther. "I had a wife who looked like that, I wouldn't go out for groceries."

Valther gave him an odd look. "Elana isn't bad. And you leave her alone all the time."

Guilt ragged Ragnarson's conscience. It was true. His position was opening a gulf between him and Elana. And he hadn't only neglected her. The children, too, were growing up as strangers. He stopped chiding Valther. The man's marriage was even more successful than Mocker's.

"Yeah. Yeah. You're right. I'll take a couple days off soon as I get the new armaments thing lined up. Maybe dump the kids on Nepanthe and take Elana somewhere. There's some pretty country around Lake Turntine."

"Sounds perfect. And Nepanthe would love having them. She's going crazy, bottled up with Ethrian."

Nepanthe was staying at the Palace. There were no children her son's age at Castle Krief.

"Maybe she should move out to my place?" Ragnarson's family occupied the home of a former rebel, Lord Lindwedel, who had been beheaded during the war. It was so huge that his mob of kids, and servants, and Haaken when he stayed over, couldn't fill it.

"Maybe," Valther murmured. "My place would be better." His wasn't far from Ragnarson's.

The head of an intelligence service doesn't always tell his employer all he knows.

FIVE: SPRING, 1011 AFE
A TRAVELER IN BLACK

North of the Kratchnodians, at the Trolledyngjan mouth of the Middle Pass, stood the inn run by Frita Tolvarson. It had been in his family since the time of Jan Iron Hand. The main trade road from Tonderhofn and the Trolledyngjan interior passed nearby, spanned the mountains, formed a tenuous link with the south. For travelers it was either the first or last bit of comfort following or preceding a harrowing passage. There was no other hospice for days around.

Frita was an old man, and a kindly soul, with a child for almost every year of his marriage. He didn't demand much more of his customers than reasonable payment, moderate behavior, and news of the rest of the world.

There was a custom at the inn dating back centuries. Every guest was asked to contribute a story to the evening's entertainment.

Winding down from the high range, a path had been beaten in the previous night's snow. The first spring venturers were assaulting the pass from the south. The path made a meandering ribbon of shadow once it reached the drifted moor, its depths unplumbed by the light of a low-hanging, full Wolf Moon. A chill arctic wind moaned through the branches of a few skeletal trees. Those gnarled old oaks looked like squatting giants praising the sky with attenuated fingers and claws.

The wind had banked snow against the north wall of Frita's establishment. The place looked like a snowbound barrow from that direction. But on the south side a traveler could find a welcoming door.

One such was crossing the lonely moor, a shivering black silhouette against the moonlit Kratchnodians. He wore a dark great cloak wrapped tightly about him, its hood pulled far forward to protect his face. He stared down dully, eyes watery. His cheeks burned in the cold. He despaired of reaching the inn, though he saw and smelled the smoke ahead. His passage through the mountains had been terrible. He wasn't accustomed to wintery climes.

Frita looked up expectantly as a cold blast roared into the inn. He put on a smile of welcome.

"Hey!" a customer grumbled. "Close the goddamned door! We aren't frost giants."

The newcomer surveyed the common room: there were just three guests.

Frita's wife bade him quit gawking and offer the man something to drink. He nodded to his oldest daughter. Alowa slipped off her stool, quickly visited the kitchen for mulled wine. "No!" she told a customer as she passed him on her way to the newcomer. Frita chuckled. He knew a "yes" when he heard it.

The newcomer accepted the wine, went to crouch before the fire. "There'll be meat soon," Alowa told him. "Won't you let me take your cloak?" Her blonde hair danced alluringly as she shook it out of her face.

"No." He gave her a coin. She examined it, frowned, tossed it to her father. Frita studied it. It was strange. He seldom saw its like. It bore a crown instead of a bust, and intricate characters. But it was real silver.

Alowa again asked the stranger for his cloak.

"No." He moved to the table, leaned forward as if to sleep on his forearms.

There'll be trouble now, Frita thought. She won't rest till she unveils the mystery. He followed her to the kitchen. "Alowa, behave yourself. A man deserves his privacy."

"Could he be the one?"

"The one what?"

"The one the Watcher is waiting for?"

Frita shrugged. "I doubt it. Mark me, girl. Let him be. That's a hard man." He had caught a glimpse of the man's face as he had turned from the fire. Fortyish, weathered, thin, dark-eyed, dusky, with a cruel nose and crueler lines around his mouth. There was a metallic sound when he moved. The worn hilt of a sword protruded through the part in his cloak. "That's no merchant trying to be first to the prime furs."

Frita returned to the common room. It lay silent. The handful of customers were waiting for the newcomer to reveal something of himself and his business. Frita's curiosity grew. The man wouldn't push back his hood. Was his face so terrible?

Time passed, mostly in silence. The newcomer had dampened the mood that had prevailed earlier, when there had been singing, joking, and good-natured competition for Alowa's favors. The stranger ate in silence, hidden in his hood. Alowa, gradually, moved from mystification to hurt. Never had she encountered a man so oblivious to her charms.

Frita decided the time for tales had come. His guests had begun drinking to fill the time. The mood was growing sour. Something was needed to lighten it before drink led to unpleasantness. "Brigetta, get the children." Nodding, his wife rose from her needlework, stirred the younger children from their evening naps and the older from the kitchen. Frita frowned at the youngsters when they began playing with one of the traveler's dogs.

"Time for tales," he announced. There were just seven people at the table, including himself. Two of the others were his wife and Alowa. "A rule of the house. Not required. But he who tells the best pays no keep." His eyes lingered on the one they called the Watcher, a small, nervous, one-eyed rogue. He had arrived nearly a year ago, in company with a gentleman of means, who had behaved like a fugitive. The gentleman had left the Watcher and had hurried northward as if his doom pursued him. Yet nothing had ever come of it.

Frita didn't like the Watcher. He was a sour, evil, small-minded little man. His only redeeming feature was a fat purse. Alowa made him pay for what she gave everyone else freely, and hinted that his tastes were cruel.

One guest said, "I'm from Itaskia, where I was once a merchant sailor." And he told of grim sea battles with corsairs out of the Isles, with no quarter given nor taken. Frita listened with half an ear. The feud of Itaskia's shipping magnates with the Red Brotherhood was a fixture of modern history.

The second visitor began his tale, "I once joined an expedition to the Black Forest, and there I heard this tale." And he spun an amusing yarn about a toothless dragon who had terrible problems finding sufficiently delicate meals. The smaller children loved it.

Frita had heard it before. He hated to declare an old story the winner.

But, to his surprise, the Watcher volunteered a tale. He hadn't bothered for months.

He stood, the better to fix his audience's attention, and used his hands freely while speaking. He had trouble moving his left arm. Frita had seen it bare. He had taken a deep wound in the past.

"Long ago and far away," the Watcher began, in the storyteller's fashion, "in a time when elves still walked the earth, there was a great elf-king. Mical-gilad was his name, and his passion, conquest. He was a mighty warrior, undefeated in battle or joust. He and his twelve paladins were champions of the world till the events whereof I speak."

Frita frowned, leaned back. A story new to him. A pity its teller had little feel for the art.

"One day a knight appeared at the gates of the elf-king's castle. His shield bore an unknown coat of arms. His horse was twice as big as life and black as coal. The gate guards refused him passage. He laughed at them. The gates collapsed."

Yes, Frita thought, it would make a tale in the mouth of a competent teller. The Watcher described the elf-king's encounter with He Who Laughs, after the stranger had slain his twelve champions. He then fought the king himself, who overcame him by trickery, but couldn't kill him because of the unbreachable spells on his armor.

Frita thought he saw where it was going. He had heard so many tales that even the best had become predictable. It was a moral tale about the futility of trying to evade the inevitable.

The elf-king had his opponent thrown on a dung heap outside his castle, whereupon He Who Laughs promised another, more terrible meeting. And, sure enough, the next time the elf-king went a-conquering, he found the knight in black and gold riding with his enemies.

As he talked, the Watcher nervously played with a small gold coin. It was a tic Frita no longer noticed. But the newcomer seemed mesmerized by the constant tumble of the gold piece.

In the end, He Who Laughs ran the elf-king down and slew him.

The ex-sailor from Itaskia said, "I don't understand. Why was the king afraid of him if he wasn't afraid of anybody else?"

For the first time the newcomer uttered more than a monosyllable. "The knight is a metaphor, my friend. He Who Laughs is one of the names of the male avatar, the hunter aspect, of Death. She sets that part of herself to stalk those who would evade her. The elves were supposed to have been immortal. The point of the story was that the king had grown so arrogant in his immortality that he dared challenge the Dark Lady, the Inevitable. Which is the grossest form of stupidity. Yet even today men persist in the folly of believing they can escape the inevitable."

"Oh."

All eyes were on the newcomer now. Especially that of the Watcher. The remark about the inevitable seemed to have touched his secret fears.

"Well then," said the innkeeper. "Which wins? The pirate? The dragon? Or the lesson of the elf-king?"

Half a dozen little ones clamored for the dragon.

"Wait," said the newcomer. His tone enforced instant silence. "I would like a turn."

"By all means," Frita nodded, eager to please. This man had begun to frighten him. Yet he was surprised. He hadn't expected this dour, spooky stranger to contribute.

"This is a true story. The most interesting usually are. It began just a year ago, and hasn't yet ended.

"There was a man, of no great stature or means, completely unimportant in the usual ways, who had the misfortune to be a friend of several powerful men. Now, it seems the enemies of those men thought they could attack them through him.

"They waylaid him one day as he was riding through the countryside..."

From beneath his hood the newcomer peered at the Watcher steadily. The one-eyed man tumbled his coin in a virtual blur.

"Just south of Vorgreberg..." the stranger said, almost too softly for any but the one-eyed man's ears.

The Watcher surged up, a whimper in his throat as he dragged out a dagger. He hurled himself at the stranger.

One finger protruded from the newcomer's sleeve. He said one word.

Smoke exploded from the Watcher's chest. He flew backward, slammed against a wall. Women and children screamed. Men ducked under the table.

The stranger rose calmly, bundled himself tightly, and vanished into the frigid night.

Frita peeked from beneath the table. "He's gone now." He joined his surviving guests beside the body.

"He was a sorcerer," the sailor muttered.

"Was that the man he was watching for?" Alowa asked. Her excitement was pure thrill.

"I think so. Yes. I think so." Frita opened the Watcher's shirt.

"Who was he?" the sailor asked.

"This here fellow's version of He Who Laughs, I reckon, the way he went on."

"Look at this," said the other man. He had recovered the coin the dead man had dropped when going for his knife. "You don't see many of these. From Hammad al Nakir."

"Uhm," Frita grunted. The silver coin the stranger had given him had been of the same source, but of an earlier mintage.

Bared, the dead man's chest appeared virtually uninjured. The only mark was a small crown branded over his heart.

"Hey," said the ex-sailor. "I've seen that mark before. It's got something to do with the refugees from Hammad al Nakir, doesn't it?"

"Yes," Frita replied. "We shared our meal with a celebrity. With a king."

"Really?" Alowa's eyes were large. "I touched him…"

The sailor shuddered. "I hope I never see him again. Not that one. If he's who I think you mean. He's accursed. Death and war follow him wherever he goes…"

"Yes," Frita agreed. "I wonder what evil brought him to Trolledyngja?"

SIX: SPRING, 1011 AFE
THE ATTACK

Three men lurked in the shadows of the park. They appeared to be devotees of the Harish Cult of Hammad al Nakir. Dusky, hawk-nosed men, they watched with merciless eyes. They had been there for hours, studying the mansion across the lane. Occasionally, one had gone to make a careful circuit of the house. They were old hunters. They had patience.

"It's time," the leader finally murmured. He tapped a man's shoulder, stabbed a finger at the house. The man crossed the lane with no more noise than the approach of midnight. A dog woofed questioningly behind the hedges.

The man returned five minutes later. He nodded.

All three crossed the lane.

They had been studying and rehearsing for days. No one was out this time of night. There was little chance anyone would interfere.

Four mastiffs lay rigid on the mansion's lawn. The three dragged them out of sight. Poisoned darts had silenced them.

The leader spent several minutes examining the door for protective spells. Then he tried the latch.

The door opened.

It was too easy. They feared a trap. A Marshall should have guards, enchantments, locks and bolts protecting him.

These men didn't know Kavelin. They couldn't have comprehended the little kingdom's politics had they been interested. Here political difficulties were no longer settled with blades in darkness.

They searched the first floor carefully, smothering a maid, butler, and their child. They had orders to leave no one alive.

The first bedroom on the second floor belonged to Inger, Ragnarson's four-year-old daughter. They paused there, again using a pillow.

The leader considered the still little form without remorse. His fingers caressed a dagger within his blouse, itching to strike with it. But that blade dared be wielded against but one man.

To the Harish Cult the assassin's dagger was sacred. It was consecrated to the soul of the man chosen to die. To pollute the weapon with another's blood was abomination. Deaths incidental to a consecrated assassination had to be managed by other means. Preferably bloodless, by smothering, drowning, garroting, poisoning, or defenestration.

The three slew a boy child, then came to a door with light showing beneath it. A murmur came through. Adult voices. This should be the master bedroom. The three decided to save that room for last. They would make sure of the sleeper on the third floor, Ragnarson's brother, before taking the Marshall himself, three to one.

The plans of mice and men generally are laid without considering the foibles of fourteen-year-old boys who have been feuding with their brothers.

Every night Ragnar booby-trapped his door certain that some morning Gundar would again sneak in to steal his magic kit…

Water fell. A bucket crashed and rattled over an oaken floor. From the master bedroom a woman's frightened voice called, "Ragnar, what the hell are you up to?" Low, urgent discussion accompanied the rustle of hasty movement.

A sleepy, "What?" came from behind the booby-trapped door, then a frightened, "Ma!"

Ragnar didn't recognize the man in his doorway.

The intruder pawed the water from his eyes. His followers threw themselves toward the master bedroom. The door was locked, but flimsy. They broke through.

Inside, a man desperately tried to get into his pants. A woman clutched furs to her nakedness.

"Who the hell…?" the man demanded.

An assassin flicked a bit of silken handkerchief. It wrapped the man's throat. A second later his neck broke. The other intruder rushed the woman.

They were skilled, these men. Professionals. Murder, swift and silent, was their art.

Their teachers had for years tried to school them to react to the unexpected. But some things were beyond their teachers.

Like a woman fighting back.

Elana hurled herself toward the bodkin laying on a nearby wardrobe, swung it as the assassin rounded the bed.

He stopped, taken aback.

She moved deftly, distracting with her nakedness. Seeing him armed with nothing more dangerous than a scarf, she attacked.

He flicked that scarf. It encircled her throat. She drove the dagger in an upward thrust. He took it along his ribs.

Gagging, Elana stabbed again, opened his bowels.

Ragnar suddenly realized that death was upon him. He scrambled to the shadowed corner where he had hidden the weapons Haaken had been training him to use. They were there by sheer chance. He had been too lazy to return them to the family armory after practice, and Haaken had forgotten to check on him.

He went after the assassin in the wild-swinging northman fashion before the man recovered from the drenching. His blows were fierce but poorly struck. He was too frightened to fight with forethought or calculation.

The assassin wasn't armed for this. He retreated, skipping and weaving and picking up slash wounds. He watched the boy's mad eyes, called for help. But there would be none. Through the door of the master bedroom he saw one of his comrades down.

The other wrestled with a woman... And someone was stirring upstairs.

The man, though, was dead. He lay halfway between bed and door, silk knotted round his throat.

The night was almost a success. The primary mission had been accomplished.

The leader fled.

Ragnar chased him to the front door before he realized that his mother was fighting for her life. He charged back upstairs. "Ma! Ma!"

The house was all a-scream now. The little ones wailed in the hall. Haaken thundered from the third floor, "What's going on down there?"

Ragnar met the last assassin coming from the bedroom. His mouth and eyes were agape in incredulity.

Ragnar cut him down. For an instant he stared at the bodkin in the man's back. Then he whipped into his parents' bedroom. "Ma! Papa! Are you all right?"

No.

He saw the dead man first, his pants still around his knees.

It wasn't his father.

Then he saw his mother and the disemboweled assassin.

"Ma!"

It was the howl of a maddened wolf, all pain and rage…

Haaken found the boy hacking at the assassin Elana had gutted. The corpse was chopped meat. He took in the scene, understood, despite his own anger and agony did what he had to do.

First he closed the door to shield the other children from their mother's shame. Then he disarmed Ragnar.

It wasn't easy. The boy was ready to attack anything moving. But Haaken was Ragnar's swordmaster. He knew the boy's weaknesses. He struck Ragnar's blade aside, planted a fist.

The blow didn't faze Ragnar. "Like your grandfather, eh, Red?" He threw another punch. Then another and another. The boy finally collapsed. Ragnar's grandfather had, at will, been capable of killing rages. Berserk, he had been invincible.

Shaking his head dolefully, Haaken covered Elana. "Poor Bragi," he muttered. "He don't need this on top of everything else."

He poked his head into the hall. The surviving children and servants were in a panic. "Gundar!" he roared. "Come here. Pay attention." The ten-year-old couldn't stop staring at the assassin lying in the hall. "*Run* to the Queen's barracks. Tell Colonel Ahring to get your father. Right now."

Haaken closed the door, stalked round the bedroom. "How will I tell him?" he mumbled. He toyed with disposing of the dead man. "No. Have to do it in one dose. He'll need all the evidence.

"Somebody's gonna pay for this." He inspected the chopped corpse carefully. "El Murid has got himself one big debt."

The hand of the Harish had reached into Vorgreberg before.

There was nothing he could do there. He slipped out, sat down with his back against the door. He laid his sword across his lap and waited for his brother.

One oil lamp flickered on Ragnarson's desk. He bent close to read the latest protest from El Murid's embassy. They sure could bitch about petty shit.

What the hell was Haroun up to?

Haroun was what he was, doing what he thought necessary. Even when he made life difficult, Bragi bore him no ill will. But when bin Yousif stopped conforming to his own nature…

There hadn't been a serious protest in a year. And Valther said there had been no terrorist incursions for several. Nor had many bands of Royalist partisans passed through Kavelin bound for the camps. Nor had Customs reported the capture of any guerrilla contraband.

It was spooky.

Ragnarson wasn't pleased when people changed character inexplicably.

"Derel. Any word from Karak Strabger?"

"None, sir."

"Something's wrong up there. I'd better…"

"Gjerdrum can handle it, sir."

Ragnarson's right hand fluttered about nervously. "I suppose. I wish he'd write more often."

"I used to hear the same from his mother when he was at the university."

"It'd risk letters falling into unfriendly hands anyway." The Queen's condition had to remain secret. For the good of the state, for his own good—if he didn't want his wife planning to cut his throat.

Bragi didn't know how to manage it, but the news absolutely had to be kept from Elana.

Rumors striking alarmingly near the truth ran the streets already.

He massaged his forehead, crushed his eyelids with the heels of his hands. "This last contribution from Breidenbach. You done the figures yet?"

"It looks good. There's enough, but it'll be risky."

"Damned. There's got to be an honest, legal way to increase revenues."

In the past, when he had been on the other end, Bragi's favorite gripes had been government and taxes. Taxes especially. He had seen them as a gigantic protection racket. Pay off or have soldiers on your front porch. "By increasing the flow of trade."

Economics weren't his forte, but Ragnarson asked anyway. "How do we manage that?"

"Lower the transit tax." Prataxis grinned.

"Oh, go to hell. The more you talk, the more I get confused. If I had the men I'd do it the Trolledyngjan way. Go steal it from the nearest foreigner who couldn't defend himself."

Prataxis's reply was forestalled by a knock.

"Enter," Ragnarson growled.

Jarl Ahring stepped in. His face was drawn.

Premonition gripped Ragnarson. "What is it? What's happened, Jarl?"

Ahring gulped several false starts before babbling, "At your house. Somebody… Assassins."

"But… What…?" He didn't understand. Assassins? Why would…? Maybe robbers? There was no reason for anyone to attack his home.

"Your son… Gundar… He came to the barracks. He was hysterical. He said everybody was dead. Then he said Haaken told him to have me find you. I sent twenty men over, then came here."

"You checked it out?"

"No. I came straight here."

"Let's go."

"I brought you a horse."

"Good." Ragnarson strapped on the sword that was never out of reach, followed Ahring at a run. And then at a wild gallop through deserted streets.

A quarter mile short of home Ragnarson shouted, "Hold up!" A patch of white in the park had caught his eye.

The man was on the verge of dying, but he recognized Ragnarson. Surprise shone through agony. He tried to use a dagger.

Bragi took it away, studied him. Soon he was dead. "Loss of blood," Ragnarson observed. "Somebody cut him bad." He handed the knife to Ahring.

"Harish kill-dagger."

"Yeah. Come on."

The news was spreading. Lean, sallow Michael Trebilcock had arrived already, and Valther and his wife, Mist, showed up as Bragi did. Their house stood just up the lane. Neighbors clogged the yard. Ahring's troops were keeping them out of the house.

Bragi took the dagger from Ahring, passed it to Valther's wife. "It is consecrated?"

That tall, incredibly beautiful woman closed her oval eyes. She moaned suddenly, hurled the blade away. A soldier recovered it.

Mist took two deep breaths, said, "Yes. To your name. But not in Al Rhemish."

"Ah?" Ragnarson wasn't surprised. "Where, then?"

"It's genuine. A Harish knife. Under your name is another, without blood."

"Stolen blade. I thought so."

"What? How?" Ahring asked.

"There still some here?" Bragi asked. Harish assassins usually worked in teams. And they didn't leave their wounded behind.

"Yes sir," a soldier replied. "Upstairs."

"Come," Ragnarson told Ahring, Valther, and Mist. "You, too, Michael."

Trebilcock was a strange young man. He had come from the Rebsamen with Gjerdrum when Ragnarson's aide had graduated from that university. His father, Wallice Trebilcock of the House of Braden in Czeschin of the Bedelian League, had died shortly before, leaving him an immense fortune.

He didn't care about money, or anything but getting near the makers and shakers of history.

Ragnarson had felt a paternal attraction from their first meeting, so the youth had slipped into his circle through the side door.

Ragnarson, though unaware of the extent of his losses, was already in a form of shock. It was a protective reaction against emotion, a response learned the hard way, at fifteen. It had been then that disaster and despair had first overtaken him, then that he had learned that swords don't exclusively bite the men on the other side.

He had learned the night he had watched his father die, belly opened by an axe...

Others had died since, good friends and brothers-in-arms. He had learned, and learned, and learned—to stifle emotions till the smoke had cleared, till the dust had settled, till the enemy had been put away.

He knelt by the dead man in the hallway, opening his clothing. "Here." He tapped the man over his heart.

"What?" Valther asked. "He has the tattoo. They always do."

"Look closer," Ragnarson growled.

Valther peered intently at a tricolor tattoo, three cursive letters intertwined. They meant "Beloved of God." Their bearer was guaranteed entry into Paradise. "What?"

"You see it?"

"Of course."

"Why?"

Valther didn't reply.

"He's dead, Valther. They fade with the spirit."

"Oh. Yes."

So they did, with a genuine Harish assassin, supposedly to indicate that the soul had ascended. Some cynics, though, claimed they vanished to avoid an admission that a Cultist had failed.

"Somebody went to a lot of trouble here," Bragi observed. "But for that, the frame would've worked." It should have. Not many men outside the Harish knew that secret. Most of those were associates of Haroun bin Yousif.

Ragnarson's mysterious friend had researched the Cult thoroughly. He'd had to. He had been its top target for a generation.

And he was still alive.

"There's a trap here," said Bragi.

"What now?" Valther demanded.

"You've got the mind for this. Suppose these are part of the plan? If they failed, and we didn't jump to the conclusion that El Murid was responsible? Who would you suspect then?"

"Considering their apparent origins…"

"Haroun. Of course. There're other folks like them, but who else would be interested?"

"A double frame?"

"Levels. Always there're these levels. Direct attack is too unsubtle…"

"Is something beginning?"

"Something has begun. We've been into it for a long time. Too many impossible things have happened already."

Bragi rose, kicked the corpse, growled, "Get this out of my house." Then he dropped to a knee beside Haaken. He slid an arm around his brother's shoulders, crushed him to his chest. "Haaken, Haaken, it was an evil day when we came south."

Tears still rolled down into the wild dark tangle of Haaken's beard.

He sniffed. "We should've stood and died." He sniffed again, wrapped both arms around Bragi. "Bragi, let me get the kids and we just go home. Now, and the hell with everything. Forget it all. Just you and me and Reskird and the kids, and leave these damned southrons to their own mercies."

"Haaken…"

"Bragi, it's bad. It's cruel. Please. Let's just go. They can have everything I've got. Just take me home. I can't take it anymore."

"Haaken…" He rose.

"Don't go in. Bragi, please."

"Haaken, I have to." There were tears in his own eyes. He knew part of it now. Elana. She was a loss more dire than his father. Mad Ragnar had chosen his death. Elana… She was a victim of his profession.

Blackfang wouldn't move. And now the younger children, Ainjar and Helga, clung to his legs, bawling, asking for Mama, and what was wrong with Inger and Soren?

Ragnarson asked a question with his eyes. Haaken nodded.

"My babies? No. Not them, too?"

Haaken nodded again.

The tears faded. Ragnarson turned slowly, surveying the faces in the hall. Every eye turned from the flame raging in his. Hatred was too mild a word.

Blood would flow. Souls would spill shrieking into the outer darkness. And he wouldn't be gentle. He would be cruel.

"Move aside, Haaken."

"Bragi…"

"Move."

Haaken moved. "You lead, Bragi," he said. "I'll follow anywhere."

Ragnarson briefly rested a hand on his shoulder. "We're probably dead men, Haaken. But somebody will carry the torches to light our path into Hell." For an instant he was startled by his own words. Their father had said the same thing just before his death. "Valther! Find out who did this."

"Bragi…"

"Do it." He shoved into the bedroom.

Valther started to follow him. Mist seized his arm.

She had the Power. Once she had been a Princess of the Dread Empire. She knew what lay behind that door.

Ragnarson had his emotions under control again. He kept hand on sword hilt to remind himself. This was a battlefield. These had fallen in a war…

"Oh."

Haaken tried to pull him out.

"No. Valther. Come here."

The man with his pants half on was Valther's brother Turran.

Their eyes met over the corpse, and much went unsaid—words which couldn't be spoken lest blood be their price.

"Take care of him." Ragnarson moved round the bed to his wife. First he dropped to one knee, then he sat. He held her hand and remembered. Twenty years. Sixteen of them married. Hard times and good, fighting and loving.

That was a long time. Nearly half his life. There were a lot of memories.

Behind him, Valther shed tears on his brother's chest.

An hour passed before Bragi looked up.

Rolf Preshka, Captain of the Palace Guards, sat on the edge of the bed. His grief mirrored Ragnarson's.

Bragi had never known for sure, but he had suspected. Rolf had joined him when Elana had. They had been partners before... But there hadn't been a moment's dishonor since. He knew Preshka that well.

There was that, beneath the grief, which said that Rolf, too, meant to extract payment in blood and pain.

But Preshka was in no shape for it. He had lost a lung in the war. He refused to die, but he was never healthy either. That was why he held the unstrenuous Palace command.

Later still, Nepanthe came. She cried some. Then she and Mist calmed the children and moved them to Valther's house.

"You are my hand that reaches beyond the grave," Bragi told Ragnar before he left, and went on to explain what he knew and felt. Things Ragnar should know in case the next band of assassins succeeded.

The boy had to grow up fast.

Throughout the night Michael Trebilcock observed in silence. Trebilcock remained an enigma. He was a sponge, soaking up others' pain and joy and never revealing any emotion himself.

Once, though, he came and rested a comforting hand on Bragi's shoulder. For Trebilcock that was a lot.

Before sunrise all Bragi's old comrades had come, except Reskird, whose regiment was on exercise around Lake Turntine.

Shortly before dawn, thunder rolled over the mountains. Lightning walked the cloudless night.

It was an omen.

SEVEN: SPRING, 1011 AFE
THE OLD DREAD RETURNS

The wind never ceased its howl and moan through the wild, angry mountains called the Dragon's Teeth. It tore at Castle Fangdred with talons of ice and teeth of winter. The stronghold was the only evidence that Man had ever braved these savage mountains. The furious wind seemed bent on eradication.

It was a lonely castle, far from any human habitation. Only two men dwelt there now, and but one of those could be called alive.

He was old, that man, yet young. Four centuries had he lived, yet he looked not a tenth of that. He stalked Fangdred's empty, dusty halls, alone and lonely, waiting.

Varthlokkur.

His name. The west's dread.

Varthlokkur. The Silent One Who Walks With Grief. Also called the Empire Destroyer.

This man, this wizard, could erase kingdoms as a student wipes a slate.

Or such was his reputation. He was powerful, and *had* engineered the downfall of Ilkazar, yet he was a man. He had his limitations.

He was tall and thin, with earth-toned skin and haunted mahogany eyes.

He was waiting. For a woman.

He wanted nothing to do with the world.

But sometimes the world assailed him and he had to react, to protect his place in it, to secure his own tomorrows.

The other man sat on a stone throne, before a mirror, in a chamber high atop a tower. Its only door was sealed by spells which even Varthlokkur couldn't fathom. He wasn't dead, but neither was he alive. He, too, waited.

A malaise had descended on Varthlokkur. Evil stalked abroad again. Not the usual evil, everyday evil, but the Evil that abided, awaiting its moment to engulf.

This evil had struck before, and had been driven home.

It waxed again, and its burning eyes sought a target for its wrath.

Varthlokkur performed his divinations. He conjured his familiar demons and sped them over the earth on wings of nightmare. He sang the dark songs of necromancy, calling up the dead. He wheedled from them secrets of tomorrow.

It was what they wouldn't, or couldn't, tell him that inspired dread.

Something was happening.

It had its foundation in Shinsan. Once again the Dread Empire was preparing to make its will its destiny. But there was more.

For a while Varthlokkur concentrated on the west and unearthed more evidence of sprouting evil. Down south, at Baxendala, where the Dread Empire had been turned before…

If one word could describe Varthlokkur, it might be *doleful*. His mother had been burned by the Wizards of Ilkazar. His foster parents had passed away before he was ten. Obsessed with vengeance for his mother, he had made devil's bargains in Shinsan—and had rued his decision a thousand times. The Princes Thaumaturge had taught him, then used him to shatter forever the political cohesion of the Empire.

And then? Four centuries of loneliness in a world terrified of him, yet constantly conspiring to use him. Four centuries of misery, awaiting the one pleasant shadow falling across his destiny, the woman who could share his life and love.

And there had been pain and sadness in that, too. She had taken another husband—his own son, from a marriage of convenience, ignorant of his paternity, by then known under the name Mocker...

Those blind hags, the Norns, snickered and wove the threads of destiny in an astounding, treacherous warp and woof.

But he had beaten them. He and Nepanthe had come to an understanding. He had the sorcery to enable it.

Upon her he had placed the same wizardries that had made him virtually immortal. In time Mocker would perish. Then she would share Varthlokkur's destiny.

So he waited, in his hidden stronghold, and was sad and lonely, till the undertides of old evil washed against his consciousness and excited him.

He performed his divinations, and they were clouded, irresolute, shifting, revolving on but one absolute axis. Something wicked was afoot.

The first nibble of the beast would be at the underbelly of that little kingdom at the juncture of the Kapenrungs and Mountains of M'Hand. At Kavelin.

His final necromancy indicated that he had to get there quickly.

He prepared transfer spells that would shift him in seconds.

Thunder stalked the morning over the knife-edged ridges of the Kapenrungs. Lightning sabered the skies. A hard north wind gnawed at the people and houses of Vorgreberg.

In the house on Lieneke Lane, sad and angry men paused to glance outside and, shivering, ask one another what was happening.

Suddenly, in the bedroom where the lips of Death had sipped, a mote of darkness appeared. Preshka spied it first. "Bragi." He pointed.

It hung in the air heart high, halfway between bed and door.

Ragnarson eyed it. It began growing, a little black cloud taking birth, becoming more misted and tenuous as it expanded. Within, a left-handed mandala revolved slowly, remaining two-dimensional and face-on no matter from what angle Ragnarson studied it.

"Ahring! Get some men in here."

In seconds twenty men surrounded the growing shadow, shaking but ready. Their faces were pale, but they had faced sorcery before, at Baxendala.

The mandala spun faster. The cloud grew larger, forming a pillar. That pillar assumed the shape of a man. The mandala pulsed like a beating heart. For an instant, vaguely, Bragi thought he saw a tired face at the column's capital.

"Be ready," he snarled. "It's coming through."

A voice, like one come down a long, twisted, cold cavern, murmured, "Beware. Shield your eyes."

It was powerfully commanding. Ragnarson responded automatically.

Thunder shook the house. Lightning clawed the air. Blue sparks crackled over the walls, ceilings, and carpets. Ozone stench filled the air.

"Varthlokkur!" Ragnarson gasped when he removed his palms from his eyes.

A mewl of fear ran through the room. Soldiers became rigid with terror. Two succumbed to the ultimate ignominy, fainting.

Ragnarson wasn't comfortable. They were old acquaintances, he and Varthlokkur, and they hadn't always been allies.

Michael Trebilcock showed less fright and more mental presence than anyone else. He calmly secured a crossbow, leveled it at the sorcerer.

The idea hadn't occurred to Bragi. He appraised the pale youth. Trebilcock seemed immune to fear, unaware of its meaning. That could be a liability, especially when dealing with wizards. One had to watch the subtleties, what the left hand was doing when the sorcerer was waving his right. To not fear him, to be overconfident, was to fall into the enemy's grasp.

Varthlokkur carefully raised his hands. "Peace," he pleaded. "Marshall, something is happening in Kavelin. Something wicked. I only came to see what, and stop it if I can."

Ragnarson relaxed. Varthlokkur, usually, was straightforward. He lied by omission, not commission. "You're too late. It's struck already." The rage that had been driven down by fear returned. "They killed my wife. They murdered my children."

"And Turran, too," Valther said from the doorway. "Bragi, have you been downstairs yet?"

"No. It's bad enough here. I don't want to see Dill and Molly and Tamra. Just take them out quietly. It's my fault they died."

"Not that. I meant they didn't just kill everybody. They searched every room. Lightly, like they'd come back again if they didn't find what they wanted the first time."

"That don't make sense. We know they weren't robbers."

"It wasn't for show. They weren't just here to kill. They were looking for something."

Varthlokkur's expression grew strained. He said nothing.

"There wasn't anything here. Not even much money."

"There was," Varthlokkur interjected. "Or should have been. Looks like the secret was kept better than I expected."

"Uhn? Going to start the mystery-mouthing already?" Bragi had always thought that wizards spoke in riddles so they couldn't be accused of error later.

"No. This is the story. Turran, Valther, and their brother Brock served the Monitor of Escalon during his war with Shinsan. In the final extremity the Monitor, using Turran, smuggled a powerful token, the Tear of Mimizan, to the west. Turran sent it to Elana by trade post. She had it for almost fifteen years. I thought you knew."

Ragnarson sat on the edge of his bed. He was confused. "She kept a lot of secrets."

"Maybe one of the living can tell us something," Varthlokkur observed, searching faces with dreadful eyes.

"I saw it once," Preshka volunteered. "When we were on the Auszura Littoral, when I was wounded and we were hiding. It was like a ruby teardrop, so by so, that she kept in a little teak casket."

"Teak?" Bragi asked. "She didn't have any teak casket, Rolf. Wait. She had one made out of ebony. Runed with silver. It just laid around for years. I never looked inside. I don't even know if it was locked. It was always around, but I never paid any attention. I thought she kept jewelry in it."

"That's it," Preshka said. "Ebony is what I meant. The jewel, though… It was spooky. Alive. Burning inside."

"That's it," said Varthlokkur. "One of its most interesting properties is its ability to escape notice. And memory. It's incredibly elusive."

"Hell, it ought to be around somewhere," Ragnarson said. "Seems like I saw it the other day. Either in that wardrobe there, or in the clothes chest. She never acted like it was anything important."

"A good method of concealment," Varthlokkur observed. "I don't think it's here. I don't feel it."

Ragnarson grumbled, "Michael, Jarl, look for it." He buried his head in his hands. Too much was happening. He was being hit from every direction, with worries enough for three men.

He had a premonition. He wasn't going to get time to lie back and absorb his grief, to settle his thoughts and redefine his goals.

The search revealed nothing. Yet the assassin in the park had carried nothing. And Ragnar had said the man hadn't gotten into the master bedroom. "Jarl, where's Ragnar?"

"Mist took him to her place."

"Send somebody. It's time he saw what grown-up life can be like." He might not be alive much longer. There would be more assassins. Ragnar would have to be his sword from beyond the grave.

"Jarl," he said when Ahring returned, "bring some more men over here tomorrow. Find this amulet or talisman or whatever. Valther. Do you think Mist would mind taking care of my kids for a while? I'll be damned busy till this blows away."

"With Nepanthe's help she can handle it."

Ragnarson eyed him. The strain remained. Valther must have known… But that was spilled ale.

What would he have had Valther do? Rat on Turran? Who else had known? Who had cooperated? Haaken?

Haaken had been in the house… No. He knew his brother. Haaken would have cut throats had he known.

He was starting to dwell on the event. He had to get involved in the mystery.

Varthlokkur beckoned him to an empty corner. "I appeared at an emotional moment," the sorcerer whispered. "But this wasn't what brought me. That hasn't yet happened. And it might, if we're swift, be averted."

"Eh? What else can happen? What else can they do to me?"

"Not to you. To Kavelin. These things aren't personal. Though you could suffer from this, too."

"I don't understand."

"Your other woman."

Ragnarson's stomach tightened. "Fiana? Uh, the Queen?"

"The child is what caught my attention."

"But it's not due…"

"It's coming. In two or three days. The divinations, though obscure, are clear on one point. This child, touched by the old evil in Fiana's womb, can shake the roots of the earth—if it lives. It may not. There're forces at work…"

"Forces. I'd rid the world of your kind if I could…"

"That would leave you a dull world, sir. But the matter at hand is your Queen. And child."

"Gods, I'm tired. Tired of everything. Ten years ago, when we had the land grant in Itaskia, I griped about life getting dull. I'd give anything to be back there now. My wife would be alive. So would my kids…"

"You're wrong. I know."

Ragnarson met his gaze. And yes, Varthlokkur knew. He had lived with the same despair for an age.

"Karak Strabger… Baxendala. That's almost fifty miles. Can we make it?"

"I don't know. Fast horses…"

"We'll rob the post riders." One of Ragnarson's innovations, which Derel had proposed, was a fast postal system which permitted rapid warning in case of trouble. Its way stations were the major inns of the countryside. Each was given a subsidy to maintain post riders' horses.

The system was more expensive than the traditional, which amounted to giving mail to a traveler bound in the right direction, to pass hand to hand to others till it reached its destination. The new system was more reliable. Ragnarson hoped, someday, to convince the mercantile class to rely on it exclusively, making his system a money-earner for the Crown.

"Jarl. Have some horses saddled and brought round front. Make it… three. Myself, the wizard, and Ragnar. Haaken's in charge till I get back. His word to be law. Understand?"

Ahring nodded.

"Valther?"

"I've got it." He eyed Bragi, expression unreadable.

Bragi realized that his going to the Queen would support the rumors. But he didn't comment. His associates could decide for themselves if they should keep their mouths shut.

He studied faces. His gaze settled on Michael Trebilcock. The pallid youth still held his aim on Varthlokkur. A machine, that man.

"Excuse me," Ragnarson told the wizard. "Michael, come with me a minute."

He took Michael downstairs, outside, round to the garden. Dawn had begun painting the horizon toward the Kapenrungs. Somewhere there Fiana lay in pain, this child of theirs struggling to rip itself from her womb before its time.

"Michael."

"Sir?"

"I don't know you very well yet. You're still a stranger, even after several years."

"Sir?"

"I've got a feeling about you. I like you. I trust you. But am I right?"

The garden was peaceful. From the rear Ragnarson's house looked as innocent of terror as were its neighbors.

"I'm not sure I follow you, sir."

"I don't know who you are, Michael. I don't know *what*. You stay locked up inside. I only know what Gjerdrum says. You don't give away a thing about yourself. You're an enigma. Which is your right. But you've become part of the gang. I hardly noticed you doing it. You're unobtrusive.

"You hear things. You see things. You know everybody. I've got a feeling you've got the kind of mind that leaps to conclusions past missing data, and you're usually right. Am I wrong?"

Trebilcock shook his head. In the dawnlight he appeared spectral, like a mummy returned to life.

"The question, again. Can you be trusted?" Bragi waited half a minute. Trebilcock didn't respond. "Are you really with me? Or will I have to kill you someday?"

Trebilcock didn't react in the slightest. Again Ragnarson had the feeling that fear, to this young man, was meaningless.

"You won't need to kill me," Michael finally replied. "I've been here since graduation. This's my country now. You're my people. I am what I am. I'm sorry you don't see it. And you can't help thinking whatever you do. But I'm home, sir."

Ragnarson peered into Trebilcock's pale, pale eyes and believed. "Good. Then I've got a job for you."

"Sir?" For the first time since he had met Michael, Bragi saw emotion. And thought he understood. Michael was a rich man's son. What had he ever been able to do for himself or others?

"It's simple. Do what you do. Eyes and ears. Hanging around. Only more of it. Gjerdrum says you're always prowling anyway." Ragnarson stared toward the sunrise. "Michael, I can't trust anybody anymore. I hate it…"

Ahring came out. "The horses are ready. I had some things thrown together for you."

"Thank you, Jarl. Michael?"

"Sir?"

"Good luck."

Ragnarson left the pale young man in deep thought. "Jarl, I've changed my mind. You know what's happening with me and the Queen?"

"I've heard enough."

"Yeah. Well. There's not much point my hiding it now. But don't quote me. Understand?"

"Of course."

"Does it suggest any problems?"

"A thousand. What scares me is what might happen if she doesn't make it. Your witch-man friend sounded... They say she had trouble with the first one."

"Yeah. Here's what I want. All capital troops but the Vorgrebergers and Queen's Own confined to barracks starting tomorrow, before what's happening leaks. And right now have Colonel Oryon report to me ready to travel. I'll keep one serpent in my pocket by taking him along. Oh. Put the provinces on alert. Militia on standby. Border guards to maximum readiness. Valther can drop hints about an intelligence coup. It'll distract questions about the confinement to barracks. Got it?"

"It's done."

It was well past dawn before three men and a boy rode eastward.

EIGHT: WINTER-SPRING, 1011 AFE
THE PRISONER

The pain never ended.

The whispers, the gentle evils in his ears, went on and on and on.

He was stubborn. So damned stubborn that yielding in order to gain surcease never occurred to him.

He didn't know where he was. He didn't know who had captured him. He didn't know why. Pain was the extent of his knowledge. The man in black, the man in the mask, was his only clue. They wouldn't tell him a thing. They just asked. If they spoke at all.

At first they had questioned him about Bragi and Haroun. He had told them nothing. He couldn't have. He didn't know anything. They had been separated too long.

He wakened. Sounds...

The Man in the Mask had returned.

"Woe!" Mocker muttered, slumping lower against floor and wall. It would be rough this time. They hadn't visited for weeks.

But there were just four of them this round. He was thankful for little favors.

Each bore a torch. Mocker watched with hooded eyes as the assistants placed theirs in sconces beyond his reach, one on each wall. The Man in the Mask fixed his above the door.

Mask closed the door. Of course. Not because Mocker might escape. He didn't order it locked from without. He simply closed it so his prisoner wouldn't get the idea there was a world beyond that slab of iron.

Mocker's world was twelve by twelve by twelve, black stone, without windows. Furniture? Chains.

There were no sanitary facilities.

Having to endure his own wastes was good—for his captors' designs.

The most distressing thing was the Mask's silence. Invariably he just stood before the door, statuelike, while his assistants demonstrated their pain-mastery.

This time they had given him too long to recover, and hadn't brought enough muscle.

He exploded.

He tripped the nearest, drove stiffened fingers into the man's throat. He screamed, "Hai!" in bloodthirsty exultation. Cartilage gave way. He made a claw, yanked with all his remaining strength.

One was dead. But three were left.

He hoped they would get mad enough to kill him.

Death was all he had to live for.

He scrambled away, bounced up, threw a foot at the crotch of the Man in the Mask.

The others stopped him. They were no off-the-street amateurs. They put him down and took him apart.

There had been so much pain, so often, that he didn't care. It had gone on so long that he no longer feared it. Only two things mattered anymore. Hurting back, and getting them to kill him.

They didn't get mad. They never did, though this was the worst he had done them. They remained pure business.

Once they had beaten him, they rolled him onto his belly and bound his wrists behind him. Then they pulled his elbows together. He groaned, writhed, sank his teeth into a bare ankle.

The blood taste was pure pleasure.

He tasted his own when a boot smashed into his mouth. He wouldn't learn. Resistance just meant more pain.

They attached a rope at his elbows and hoisted him.

It was an old torture, primitive and passive. When first Mocker had arrived he had been fifty pounds overweight. His weight had yanked his shoulder bones from their sockets.

After he had screamed awhile, and had lost consciousness, someone would doctor him so they could hoist him up again.

Back then there had been no night whispers, just the pain, and the unending effort to break him.

Why?

For whose benefit?

What would the program be this time? Five or ten days on the hook? Or straight to the point for once?

One thing was certain. There would be nothing to eat for a while. Food was strictly for convalescents.

When he was fed at all he got pumpkin soup. Two bowls a day.

One week they had given him cabbage soup. But that petty change had been enough to revive his morale. So it was pumpkin soup or nothing.

The remnants of his most recent meal splashed the floor. Bile befilthed his mouth. He spat.

"Day will come," he promised in a whisper. "Is in balance of eternity, on great mandala. Reverse of fortunes will come."

His torturers spun him. Around and around and around, till he was drunk with dizziness and pain. Then they hoisted him to the ceiling, brought him down in a series of jerks. He heaved again, but there was nothing left in his stomach.

One of them washed his mouth.

This time was different, he realized. Radically different. This was new.

He paid attention.

The Man in the Mask moved.

He peered into Mocker's eyes, pulling each lid back as would a physician. Mocker saw eyes as dark as his own behind slits from which the jewels had been removed. No. Wait. This mask wasn't the one he usually saw. Instead of traceries of black on gold, this bore traceries of gold on black. A different man? He didn't think so. The feeling was the same.

There was no emotion, no mercy in those eyes. They were the eyes of a technician, the bored eyes of a peasant halfway through a day's hoeing midway through planting season.

That mask, though… The changes were slight, yet, somehow, the alienness was gone. He began searching the burning attic of his mind.

The mask, the black robes, and the hands forever encased in the most finely wrought gauntlets he had ever seen, those were things he knew…

Tervola. Shinsan. He remembered them so well he was sure this wasn't a genuine Tervola.

Trickery was the way *he* would have programmed this had their roles been reversed.

That mask… He remembered it now. He had seen it at Baxendala. It had lain abandoned on the battlefield after O Shing had begun his retreat. Gold lines on black, ruby fangs, the cat-gargoyle. That one, Mist had said, belonged to a man called Chin, one of the chieftains of the Tervola.

They had assumed, then, that Chin had perished.

Maybe he hadn't, though the eye-crystals had been removed from the mask...

"Chin. Old friend to rescue," Mocker gasped, straining for a sarcastic smile.

The man's only response was a slight hesitation before he said, "There will be more pain, fat one. Forever, if need be. I can wait. Or you can listen. And learn."

"Self, am all ears. Head to toe, two big ears."

"Yes. You will be. The time of crudeness has ended. Now you begin listening and answering." He straightened, faced the door.

Two men pushed a wheeled cart through. Mocker ground his teeth though he didn't understand what he saw on the cart.

The Man in the Mask made him understand those sorcerer's tools.

The pain was worse than any he had known before. This agony was scientifically applied, to one purpose. To drive him mad.

Mocker never had been very stable. It took just two days to crack him completely.

They let him rave in darkness for a week. Something happened then. More pain. Smoke smells, of flesh burning. Screams that weren't his own. Men struggling. A scream that was his own when he hit the floor of the cell... Darkness. Peaceful, restful darkness.

The night whispers returned. They changed, becoming gentle, delicate whispers, happy, cheerful whispers, like those of a nymph beneath a waterfall. They calmed him. They shaped him.

Then there were gentle, feminine hands, and the distant murmur of grave-voiced men. But for a long time he was bound, his eyes blindfolded. His memories remained vague, confused. A man in a mask. El Murid's men... he thought. And Mercenary officers.

They kept him drugged and he knew that, but occasionally he came round long enough to catch snatches of conversation.

Once, evidently, a new nurse: "Oh, dear! What happened?" Horror filled her voice.

"He was tortured," a man replied. "Burned. I don't entirely understand it. From what he says, he was set up by men he thought were his friends. Nobody knows why yet. Lord Chin rescued him."

What? Mocker thought. His brains must be scrambled. Wasn't Chin the torturer?

"It was a complicated plot. One of his friends apparently tipped El Murid's agents, who kidnapped him. Then he sent mercenaries who staged a rescue—then turned him over to this Haroun, who wore the mask the Lord lost when the Dragon tried invading the west."

"You said..."

"There's a link between man and mask. The Lord lost his, but he still knows everything that happens if someone wears it… Hold it. I think he's coming around. Better give him another sniff. He needs a lot more healing before we let him wake up."

It may have been a day or week later. It was another man and another woman. This time the man seemed to be the newcomer.

"… says Lord Chin transferred right into the dungeon. For some reason bin Yousif wore the captured mask that day instead of the one he'd had made to look like it. Lord Chin knew the minute he put it on. He'd broken the eye crystals, apparently thinking that was enough to end the connection."

"Bet the Lord caused an uproar."

The woman laughed musically. "They're still petrified, thinking Shinsan's coming again. They're chasing their tails. They don't know there's a new order here, that Ehelebe has come."

"What happened?"

"The one called Haroun got away. Lord Chin punished the others."

"Bin Yousif would. He's slippery."

"He can't run forever. Ehelebe has come. None shall escape the justice of the Pracchia."

Even in his dazed state Mocker thought that a little preachy. Perhaps the woman was a fanatic or recent convert.

"What were they trying to do?"

"Lord Chin thinks they were preparing him as a weapon against Shinsan. The man called Ragnarson is paranoid about it… Get that cotton and the bottle. He's waking up."

People stirred. Mocker smelled something sweet.

"How much longer?"

"A month, maybe. The Lord…"

There were more, shorter episodes, quickly ended by sharp-eyed physicians and nurses.

Then came the day when they didn't put him back under.

"Can you hear me?"

"Yes," he whispered. His throat was dry and raw, as if his screams had never stopped.

"Keep your eyes closed. We're going to remove the bandages. Ming, get the curtain. He hasn't used his eyes for months."

Hands ran over his face. The cold back edge of a scalpel dented his cheek. "Don't move. I have to cut this."

The cloth slipped away. "Now. Open your eyes slowly."

For a while he saw nothing but bright and dim. Then shapes formed and, finally, vaguely discernible faces developed. Three men and five women surrounded him. They seemed anxious. One man's mouth became a hole. Mocker heard, "Can you see anything?"

"Yes."

A hand appeared. "How many fingers?"

"Three."

The women tittered.

"Good. Inform Lord Chin. We've succeeded."

They ran more simple tests, and freed him from the restraints. The speaker told him, "You've been laid up a long time. Don't try getting up without help. We'll start exercising you later."

The group fell silent when the Tervola entered. A man in black, wearing a mask. Black on gold, rubies, the cat-gargoyle.

Mocker shrank away.

A soft laugh escaped the mask. The Tervola sat on his bed, folding the sheet back. "Good. The burns healed perfectly. There won't be much scarring."

Mocker stared at the mask. This one had jewels where the other had been open.

"How...?"

"My fault. I apologize. I miscalculated. Your enemy controlled more power than I expected. He proved difficult. You were burned in the process. For that I offer my deepest apologies. You had suffered enough. A year of torture. Amazing. You're a strong man. Few of my colleagues could have endured."

"Self, being short of memories of interval incarcelated, am wondering, question being, where is same? Self."

"Ehelebe." The man examined Mocker's eyes. Mocker noted that he used his left hand. The Man in the Mask had been right-handed. Haroun was right-handed.

"Same being? Have never heard of same. Is where?"

"Ehelebe isn't a 'where.' It's a state of mind. I'm not being intentionally obscure. It's a nation without a homeland, its citizens scattered everywhere. We call ourselves The Hidden Kingdom. Wherever there are enough of us, we maintain a secret place to gather, to take refuge, to be at peace. This's such a place."

"Being same system known for cult of Methregul."

Methregul was a demon-god of the jungle kingdom of Gundgatchcatil. He had a small, secret, vicious following. The cult was outlawed throughout the western kingdoms. Its bloody altars were well hidden. Today it was a dying creed. It had been more widespread in Mocker's youth.

"The structures are similar. But the ends are as different as day and night. Our goal is to expunge such darknesses from the world."

Mocker was regaining his wits quickly. "Self, self says to self, what is? Tervola saying same has mission to combat evil?" He laughed. "High madness."

"Perhaps. But who better to alter the direction of Shinsan? You'd be surprised who some of us are. I often am myself, when my work brings me into contact with brothers previously unknown to me."

Mocker wanted to ask why he had never heard of the organization. Old habit stifled the question. He would wait and watch. He needed data, and data not volunteered, on which to base conclusions.

"You've recovered remarkably. With a little wizardry and a lot of care from these good people." He indicated those watching. "You'll see when you get to the mirror. They repaired most of the damage. The bones and the flesh are fine now. You'll have a few scars, but they'll be hidden by your clothing. The only worry left is how you are up here." He tapped Mocker's head.

"Why?"

"Excuse me?"

"Have been told self was saved from wickedry. Am not ungrateful. But many persons labor many hours to repair ravishes—ravages?—of mad cruelty of captor who never says why self was imprisoned. Am wondering."

"Ah. Yes. *My* motives. No, they aren't entirely altruistic. I hope I can convince you to commit your talents to our cause."

Mocker sniffed. "Talent? Self? Lurker in dusty streets unable to support wife and child? Of morals only wafer thickness better than Tervola class? Of gambler habit capable of possessing self to point of self-destruction?"

"Exactly. You're a man. Men are weak. Ehelebe takes our weaknesses and makes them strengths serving Mankind."

Mocker wished he could see the man's face. His voice and apparent honesty were too disarming. He began reviewing everything that had happened from the moment he had received Bragi's invitation to the Victory Day celebration.

His mind froze on Nepanthe. What was she doing? Had she given up on him? What would become of her if Bragi and Haroun really were in cahoots against him?

"No. Self, have had gutsful of politics in time past. Year in dungeon with torturer for lover is final convincer."

"Sleep on it. We'll start your therapy when you wake up." Chin led everyone out.

Mocker tried to sleep, and did doze off and on. A few hours later, a slight sound brought him to the alert.

He cracked one eyelid.

His visitor was a bent old man.

Is Old Meddler himself, Mocker thought. Is infamous Star Rider.

The Star Rider's legends were as old as the world, older, even, than those of the Old Man of the Mountain, whom Mocker suspected was but the Star Rider's catspaw. Nobody seemed to know who this man was, or what motivated him. He moved in his own ways, keeping his own counsel. He was more powerful than the masters of Shinsan, or Varthlokkur. Bragi claimed he had made it impossible for sorcery to influence the course of battle at Baxendala. He meddled in human affairs, from behind the scenes, for no discernible reason. He was the subject of an entire speculative library at Hellin Daimiel's great Rebsamen university. He had become a mystery second only to the mystery of life itself.

So what the hell was he doing here?

Once is accident, twice coincidence. Three times means something is going on. This was Mocker's third encounter with the man.

He continued pretending sleep.

The bent old man stayed only seconds, considering him, then departed.

Was the Star Rider a sneak visitor? Or was he involved in this Ehelebe business? In times past, insofar as Mocker knew, the man had always meddled on behalf of the people Mocker considered the "good guys"...

Twice before the Star Rider had entered his life. Twice he had benefited. It was an argument favoring Lord Chin—assuming the old man wasn't here screwing up the clockwork.

A few weeks later, once he was able to get around and do some spying. Mocker overheard someone informing Chin that Bragi had just dumped Nepanthe and Ethrian into the old dungeons beneath Castle Krief.

He returned to his quarters and thought. The Star Rider had saved his life years ago. Varthlokkur had told him the man wouldn't have bothered if he hadn't had use for him in some later scheme. Was this the payoff?

Of one thing there was no doubt. Bragi and Haroun weren't going to get away with a thing.

NINE: SPRING, 1011 AFE
A SHORT JOURNEY

"Damned saddles get hard," Oryon grumbled. He, Bragi, Ragnar, and the wizard had just ridden up to the Bell and Bow Inn.

"Change of horses," Ragnarson told the innkeeper. "On the Crown Post." He showed an authority he had written himself. "We're over halfway there, Colonel. Twenty more miles. We won't make it till after dark, though... In time?" he asked Varthlokkur.

"You ready to tell me what this's about?" Oryon demanded. Ragnarson had told him nothing.

"Trust me, Colonel."

Oryon was a short, wide bull of a man Bragi had first met during the El Murid Wars. He hadn't liked the man then, and felt no better disposed toward him now. But Oryon was a stubborn, competent soldier known for his brutal directness in combat. He led his troops from the front, straight ahead, and had never been known to back down without orders. He made a wicked enemy.

Oryon neither looked it, nor acted it, but he wasn't unsubtle. Dullards didn't become Guild Colonels. He realized that a crisis was afoot, that Ragnarson felt compelled to separate him from his command.

Why?

"Something to eat, landlord. No. No ale. Not with my kidneys. Still got to make Baxendala tonight."

"Papa, do we have to?" Ragnar asked. "I'm dead."

"You'll get a lot tireder, Ragnar."

"Uhn," Varthlokkur grunted. "You know how long it's been since I've ridden?"

The innkeeper mumbled, "Five minutes, sirs."

Only Oryon seated himself immediately. Despite his complaint, he was more accustomed to saddles than the others. Oryon was, as he liked to remind Ragnarson, a field soldier.

Varthlokkur took up a tiny salt cellar. "A trusting man, our host." Salt was precious in eastern Kavelin.

Varthlokkur twitched his fingers. The cellar disappeared.

It was a trick of the sort Mocker might have used. Pure prestidigitation. But even the High Sorcery was half lie.

Ragnarson suspected the wizard was making a point. He missed it himself. And Ragnar merely remarked, "Hey, that was neat, Mr. Eldred. Would you teach me?"

Varthlokkur smiled thinly. "All right, Red." His fingers danced in false signs. He said a few false words. The salt reappeared. "It's not as simple as it looks." The salt disappeared. "You need supple fingers."

"He doesn't have the patience," Bragi remarked. "Unless he can learn it in one lesson. I gave him a magic kit before."

"I'll do it slowly once, Red. Watch closely." He did it. "All right, what did I do? Where is it?"

Ragnar made a face, scratched his forehead. "I still missed it."

"In your other hand," Oryon grumbled.

"Oh?" Varthlokkur opened the hand. "But there's nothing here either—except an old gold piece. Now where did that come from?"

Oryon stared at the likeness on that coin, then met Varthlokkur's eye. He had grown very pale.

"Actually, if you'll check behind the boy's ear, and dig through the dirt…" He reached. "What? That's not it." He dropped an agate onto the table. Then a length of string, a rusty horseshoe nail, several copper coins, and, finally, the salt. "What a mess. Don't you ever wash there?"

Ragnar frantically checked the purse he wore on his belt. "How'd you do that?"

"Conjuring. It's all conjuring. Ah, our host is prompt. Sir, I'll recommend you to my friends."

"And thank you, sir. We try to please."

Ragnarson guffawed. Somber Oryon smiled.

"Sirs?" asked the innkeeper.

"You don't know his friends," Oryon replied. Bragi read concern, even dread, in the taut lines the Colonel strove to banish from his face.

The innkeeper set out a good meal. It was their first since leaving Vorgreberg.

"Colonel," Ragnarson said, after the edge was off his hunger and he was down to stoking the fires against the future. "Any chance we can speak honestly? I'd like to open up if you will, too."

"I don't understand, Marshall."

"Neither do I. That's why I'm asking."

"What's this about, then? Why'd you drag me out here? To Baxendala? To see the Queen?"

"I brought you because I want you away from your command if she dies while I'm there. I don't know what you'd do if it happened and you heard before I could get back to Vorgreberg. The Guild hasn't given me much cause to trust it lately."

"You think I'd stage a coup?"

"Maybe. There's got to be a reason why High Crag keeps pressuring me to keep your regiment. They know we can't afford it. So maybe the old boys in the Citadel want a gang on hand next time the Crown goes up for grabs. I know you have your standing orders. And I'll bet they cover what to do if the Queen dies."

"That's true." Oryon gave nothing away there. It took no genius to reason it out.

"You going to tell me what they are?"

"No. You know better. You're a Guildsman. Or were."

"Once. I'm Marshall of Kavelin now. A contract. I respect mine. The Guild generally honors its. That's why I wonder— One word. Wasn't going to tell you for a while. But this is a good enough time. Your contract won't be renewed. You'll have to evacuate after Victory Day."

"This'll cause trouble with High Crag. They feel they have an investment."

"It'll bring them into the open, then. Every king and prince in the west will jump on them, too. High Crag has stepped on a lot of toes lately."

"Why would they? The legalities are clear. Failure to fulfill a contract."

"How so?"

"Kavelin owes High Crag almost fifteen thousand nobles. The Citadel doesn't forgive debts."

"So you've said during our negotiations. They want payment now? They'll have it." He laughed a bellybreaker of a laugh. "About four years ago Prataxis started applying a little creative bookkeeping at Inland Revenue, and some more in Breidenbach, at the Mint. We've been squirreling away the nobles, and now we'll pay you off. Every damned farthing you've imagined up." His smile suddenly disappeared. "You're going to take your money, sign for it, and get the hell out of my country. The day after Victory Day."

"Marshall… Marshall, I think you're overreacting." Oryon's wide, heavy mouth tightened into a little knot. "We shouldn't be at cross-purposes. Kavelin needs my men."

"Maybe. Especially now. But we can't afford you, and we can't trust you."

"You keep harping on that. What do you want me to admit?"

"The truth."

"You were a Guild Colonel. How much did they tell you?"

"Nothing."

"And you think I'm told more? Once in a while I get a letter. Usually directions for the negotiations. Sometimes maybe a question about what's happening. Marshall, I'm just a soldier. I just do what I'm told."

"Well, I'm telling you. To march. Kavelin's in for rough times. The signs are there. And I don't need to be watching you and everybody else, too."

"You're wrong. But I understand."

Varthlokkur continued demonstrating his trick to Ragnar while they argued. The wizard occasionally glanced at Oryon. The soldier shivered each time he did.

"You may not need a regiment after all," Oryon muttered at one point, nodding toward Varthlokkur.

"Him? I don't trust him either. We're just on the same road right now. Innkeeper. What's the tally here?"

"For you, Marshall? It's our pleasure."

"Found me out, eh?"

"I marched with you, sir. In the war. All the way from Lake Berberich to the last battle. I was in the front line at Baxendala, I was. Look." He bared his chest. "One of them black devils done that, sir. But I'm alive and he's roasting in Hell. And that's the way it should be."

"Indeed." Ragnarson didn't remember the man. But a lot of Wesson peasants had joined his marching columns back then. They had been stout fighters, though unskilled. "And now you prosper. I'm pleased whenever I see my old mates doing well."

He often found himself in this situation. He had never learned to be comfortable with it.

"The whole country, sir. Ten years of peace. Ten years of free trade. Ten years of the Nordmen minding their own business, not whooping round the country tearing up crops and property with their feuds. Marshall, there's them here that would make you king."

"Sir! For whom did we fight?"

"Oh, aye. That was no sedition, sir. The only complaint could be raised 'gainst Her Highness is she's never wed and give us an heir. And now these strange comings and goings of a night, and rumors… It worries a man, Marshall, not knowing."

"Excuse me," Ragnarson told his table mates. "Sir, I've just had a thought. Something in the kitchen…" He placed his arm round the innkeeper's shoulders and guided him thither.

"You whip up something. A dessert treat. Meanwhile, tell me what you don't know. Tell me the rumors. And about these comings and goings."

"Them others?"

"Not to be trusted. The boy's all right though. My son. Too bullheaded and big-mouthed, maybe. Gets it from his grandfather. But go on. Rumors."

"Tain't nothing you can rightly finger, see? Not even really a rumor. Just the feeling going round that there's something wrong. I thought you might ease my mind. Or say what it is so's I got the chance to be ready."

"Makes two of us. I don't know either. And I can't nail anything down any better than you. Comings and goings. What have you got there?"

"Tain't much, really. They don't stop in here."

"Who doesn't?"

"The men what travels by night. That's what I calls them. From over the Gap. Or going over. Not many, now. One, two groups a month. As many coming as going, two, three men each."

"You seen them in the daytime?"

"No. But I never thought they was up to no good. Not when they skulks around in the night and skips the only good inn ten miles either way."

"Do they come by on the same nights every month?" Ragnarson's brain was a-hum. Thinking he might be on the enemy's track raised his spirits immensely.

"No. Just when they gets the feeling, seems like."

"How long has it been going on?"

"Good two years. And that's all I can tell you, excepting that some went past this morning. After the sun was up, too, come to think. Riding like Hell itself was after them. Less they steals horses up the line, they's going to be walking by now."

"You said…"

"I never seen them by light? Yes, and it's so. These ones just showed me their backsides going away. Three of them, they was, and I knew it was the same kind 'cause of the way they just went on by."

"What's that got to do with it?"

"Everybody stops here, Marshall. I picked this spot the day we dragged ourselves back through here after we chased that O Shing halfway to them heathen lands in the east. It's right in the middle of everywhere. Gots water and good hayfields… Well, never mind the what do you call it? Economics? People just stops. It's a place to take a break. You stopped yourself, and it's plain you're in as big a hurry as them fellows this morning. Even people what has no business stopping do. Soldiers. A platoon going up to Maisak? They stops, and you don't hear the sergeants saying nay. Just everybody stops. Except them as rides by night."

"Thanks. You've helped. I'll remember. You can do something else for me."

"Anything, Marshall. It was you made it possible for a man like me to have a place like this for himself…"

"All right. All right. You're embarrassing me. Actually, it's two things. We go back out, you put on a show of what a good choice of dessert I made."

"That's it?"

"No. It starts when we leave. You never saw us and you don't know who we were."

"True enough, excepting yourself, sir."

"Forget me, too."

"Secret mission, eh?"

"Exactly."

"It's as good as forgotten now, sir. And the other thing?"

"Don't argue with me when I pay for my meal. Or I'll box your damned ears."

The innkeeper grinned. "You know, sir, you're a damned good man. A real man. Down here with the rest of us."

Ragnarson suffered a twinge of guilt-pain. What would the old veteran think if he found out about Elana and the Queen?

"That's why we followed you back then. Ain't why we joined, I grants you. Them reasons you can figure easy enough. Loot and a chance to break our tenancy. But it's why we stuck. And there's plenty of us as remembers. The hill people, too. Some of them comes in here of a time, and they says the same. You go up on the wall over there in Vorgreberg City sometime if'n you got trouble, and you stomp good and hard and you yell 'I needs good men' and you'll have ten thousand before the next sun shows."

He only wished it were true, dire as tomorrow smelled.

"You marks me, sir. There's men what never marched in the long march, and men what even missed Baxendala, but they'd come, too. They maybe wouldn't have the sword you said they should have, because swords is dear, and everybody wanting one, and they wouldn't have no shields, except as some makes they own out of oak in the old way, or maybe green hide, and they wouldn't have no mail, but they'd come. They'd bring they rakes and hoes and butchering knives, they forge hammers and chopping axes…"

Ragnarson sniffed, brushed a tear. He was deeply moved. He didn't believe half of it, but just having one man show this much faith reached down to the heart of him.

"The hill people, too, sir. 'Cause you done one thing in this here country, something not even the old Krief himself could do, and, bless him, we loved him. Something not even Eanred Tarlson could do, and him a Wesson himself and at the Krief's ear.

"Sir, you gave us our manhood. You gave us hope. You gave us a chance to *be* men, not just animals working the lands and mines and forges for drunken Nordmen. Maybe you didn't mean it that way. I don't know. We likes to think you did. You being down in Vorgreberg City, we judges only by what we seen in the long march. Coo-ee, we gave them Nordmen jolly whatfor, didn't we sir? Lieneke. I was right there on the hill, not fifty feet from you, sir."

"Enough. Enough."

"Sir? I've offended?"

"No. No." He turned away because the tears had betrayed him. "That's what I wanted. What Her Majesty wanted. What you say you've got. Down there in Vorgreberg, it's hard to see. Sometimes I forget that's only a little bit of Kavelin, even if it's the heart. Come on now. Let's go. And remember what I said."

"Right you are, sir. Don't know you from the man in the moon, and I'll gouge you for every penny."

"Good." Ragnarson put an arm around the man's shoulders again. "And keep your eyes open. There's trouble in those riders."

"An eye and an ear, sir. We've got our swords in this house, me and my sons. Over the door, just like it says in the law. We'll be listening, and you call."

"Damn!" Ragnarson muttered, fighting tears again.

"Sir?" But the Marshall had fled to the common room.

"What do you think?" Ragnarson asked, referring to the creamed fruit he had helped the innkeeper prepare. "Mixed. A trick my mother used to pull when I was a kid." And then, to Oryon, "Colonel, I don't think I'm as frightened of High Crag as I was."

"I don't understand."

"I thought of something when we were mixing the fruit. You know my old friend? Haroun?"

"Bin Yousif? Not personally."

"Five, six years ago he published a book through one of the colleges at Hellin Daimiel. You might read it sometime. Your answer is there."

"I've read it already. Called *On Irregular Warfare,* isn't it? Subtitled something like *The Use Of The Partisan In Achieving Strategic As Well As Tactical Objectives.* Excellent treatise. But his own performance discredits his thesis."

"Only assuming he *has* failed to do what he wants. We don't know that. Only Haroun knows what Haroun is doing. But that's not the answer. Now, innkeeper, the tally. We have to get going."

Somehow, now, the future looked a lot brighter.

TEN: THE YEARS 989-1004 AFE
LORD OF LORDS

"It's a whole new world, Tam," said Tran. The forester couldn't stifle his awe of Liaontung.

"What's that?" Tam asked their escort, an old centurion named Lo. Tam and Lang were as overwhelmed as Tran.

"Ting Yu. The Temple of the Brotherhood. It was there before Shinsan came."

Lo was their keeper and guide. Their month in his care hadn't been onerous. An intimate of Lord Wu and a senior noncom of the Seventeenth Legion, Lo had been a pleasant surprise. He was quite human when outside his armor.

"Where do you live, Lo?" Tam asked. "You said you had your own house that time we visited the barracks."

The boy's curiosity invariably amazed the centurion. He had never married, and had had no childhood himself. He knew only those children in legionary training. "It's not far, Lord." With a hint of embarrassment, "Would it please you to visit, Lord?" Behind his embarrassment lay a gentle, almost defiant pride.

Tran sipped tea and shook his head as Lo showed them his tiny garden.

"What's this one?" Lang asked, fingertip a whisker off the water.

Lo leaned over the pool. "Golden swallowtail." Sadly, "Not a prime specimen, though. See the black scales on this fin?"

"Oh!" Tam ejaculated as another goldfish, curious, drifted from beneath the lily pads. "Look at this one, Lang."

"That's the lord of the pool. That's Wu the Compassionate," Lo said proudly. "He *is* purebred. Here, Lord." He took crumbs from a small metal box, dribbled a few onto Tam's fingertips. "Put your fingers into the water—gently!"

Tam giggled as the goldfish sampled his fingerprints.

Tran studied the exotic plants surrounding the pool. There was a lot of love here, a lot of time and money. Yet Lo was a thirty-year veteran of the Seventeenth. Legionnaires quailed before him. But for an intense loyalty to Lord Wu, he could have become a centurion of the Imperial Standard Legion, Shinsan's elite, praetorian legion.

What was Lo doing breeding goldfish and gardening? Obviously, Shinsan's soldiers had facets outsiders seldom saw.

Tran wasn't happy. The revelation made it difficult to define his feelings. Soldiers shouldn't stop being sword-swinging automatons and start being human…

Liaontung was a nest of paradoxes and contrasts. Once it had been the capital of a small kingdom. A century ago Lord Wu and the Seventeenth had come. Liaontung had become an outpost, a sentinel watching the edge of empire, its economy militarily dependent. Reduction in enemy activity had drawn colonists, then merchants. Yet the military presence persisted.

The Tervola, with their vastly extended lives, under the Princes, were patient conquerors. Take it a week or a century, they pursued operations till they won. They knew they would outlive their enemies. And no foe had their command of the Power.

Wu's latest foes, the Han Chin, were gone. The frontiers of his domains had drifted so far eastward that the Seventeenth soon would have to relocate. Liaontung would change, becoming less a border stronghold.

Lord Wu himself was an enigma. He could slaughter an entire race without reluctance or mercy, yet his subjects called him Wu the Compassionate.

Tran asked why.

"To tell the truth," Lo replied, "it's because he cares for them like a peasant cares for his oxen. And for the same reasons. Consider the peasant."

Now Tran grasped it. The poor man's ox was his most valued possession. It tilled his earth and bore his burdens.

"No," Lo said later, when Lang wandered too near a city gate. He gently guided them toward Liaontung's heart, Wu's citadel atop a sheer basaltic upthrust. It had been a monastery before Shinsan's advent.

Lo was the perfect jailor. He kept the cage invisible. Soon Tam had few opportunities to stray. Lord Wu directed him into intensive preparation for Tervola-hood and laying claim to the Dragon Throne. Lo remained nearby, but seldom invoked his real authority.

Tam's principal tutors were Select Kwang and Candidate Chiang, Tervola Aspirants destined to join Shinsan's sorcerer-nobility. Both were older than Lo, and powerful wizards. Kwang had but a few years to wait to become full Tervola. His destiny was guaranteed. Chiang's future would remain nebulous till the Tervola granted him Select status.

His chances were excellent. Lord Wu was a powerful patron.

The Tervola of the eastern legions, including Wu, also contributed to Tam's education. He was the child of their secret ambitions.

Aspirants, usually the sons of Tervola, were selected for their raw grasp of the Power, and advanced by attaining ever more refined control.

Tam stunned his tutors.

He learned in weeks, intuitively, what most Aspirants needed years to comprehend.

His first few tricks, like conjuring balls of light, amazed Lang and Tran.

"His father is a Prince Thaumaturge," Lo observed, unimpressed.

Time marched. Tam's magicks ceased being games and tricks. And, despite the swiftness of his progress, his instructors grew impatient, as if racing some dread deadline.

"Of course they want to use you," Tran responded to an unexpectedly naive question. "They've never hidden that. Just don't let them make you a puppet."

"I can't stand up to them." Kwang and Chiang had shown him his limitations.

He could best neither, though his raw talent dwarfed theirs.

"True. And don't forget. Be subtle. Or suffer the fate they plan for your father."

Blood began to tell in a growing need to dominate.

"Lord Wu," Tam once protested, when the Tervola was his instructor, "can't I go out sometimes? I haven't left the citadel for months."

"Being O Shing is a lonely fate, Lord," Wu replied. He set his locust mask aside, took Tam's hands. "It's for your safety. You'd soon be dead if the agents of the Princes discovered you."

Nevertheless, Tam remained antsy.

The roots of his malaise lay in his treatment by minor functionaries. They granted honors mockingly, treated him as O Shing only when Wu was present. Otherwise, they bullied him as if he were a street orphan. Till Tran cracked a few skulls. The persecutions, then, became more subtle.

When Tam was promoted to Candidate-nominee the bureaucrats tried separating him from his brother and Tran. He threw a fit, set his familiar on his chief tormentor, one Teng, and refused to study.

Wu finally intervened. He permitted Tam to retain his contacts and interviewed everyone who came in daily contact with Tam. Many left with gray faces. Then he summoned Tam.

"I won't interfere again," he said angrily. "You have to learn to deal with the Tengs. They're part of life. Remember: even the Princes Thaumaturge are inundated by Tengs. Only men of his choler, apparently, become civil servants."

There was something about Wu that Tam had, hitherto, seen in no one else. Maturity? Inner peace? Self-confidence? It was all that, and more. He awed Tam as did no other man.

The bitter years began when Tam was fourteen.

Treacheries took wing. Double and triple betrayals. A wizard named Varthlokkur destroyed Tam's father and uncle, Yo Hsi.

Lo brought the news. "Pack your things," he concluded.

"Why?" Lang demanded.

"The Demon Prince had a daughter. She's seized his Throne. It means civil war."

"I don't understand," said Tam, gathering his few belongings.

"You, you, get packing," Lo snapped at Lang and Tran. "The Throne, of all Shinsan, is up for grabs, Lord. Between yourself and Mist. And she's stronger than we are. The western Tervola support her." More softly, "I wouldn't give a glass diamond for our chances."

"She's that terrible?"

"No. She's that beautiful. I saw her once. Men would do anything for her. No woman like her has ever lived. But she's that terrible, too, if you look past her beauty. Lord Wu believes she conspired in the doom of the Princes."

"Why involve me?" Silly. This was the deadline Kwang and Chiang had been racing.

"You're Nu Li Hsi's son. Come on. Hurry. We have to hide you. She knows about you."

It was all too sudden and confusing. Willy-nilly, tossed by the whims of others, he fled a woman he didn't know.

O Shing was, Wu believed, the strongest Power channel ever born. But he hadn't the will to back it, nor the training to employ it. He had to be kept safe while he grew and learned.

"Oh, lord," Tam sighed. They were three miles from Liaontung. The band included Lo, Chiang, Kwang, and a Tervola named Ko Feng.

A black smoke tower had formed over Liaontung. Lightnings carved its heart. Here, there, hideous faces glared out.

"She's fast," Ko Feng snarled. "Come on! Move it!" He ran. The others kept up effortlessly. Being physically tireless was an axiom in Shinsan. But Tam…

"Damned cripple!" Feng muttered. He caught the boy's arm. Lo took the other.

The black tower howled.

"Lord Wu will show her something," Kwang prophesied.

"Maybe," Feng grumbled. "He was waiting."

Tam found most of the Tervola tolerable. He liked Lord Wu. But sour old Feng he loathed. Feng made no pretense of being servant or friend. He plainly meant to use Tam, and expected Tam to reciprocate. Feng called it an alliance without illusion.

Their flight took them to a monastery in the Shantung. Feng left to rejoin his legion. Elsewhere, the Demon Princess routed the Dragon Prince's adherents.

Her thoughts seldom strayed far from O Shing. She traced him within the month.

Tam sensed the threat first. Pressed, his feeling of the Power had developed swiftly.

"Tran, it's time to leave. I feel it. Tell Lo."

"Where to, Lord?" the centurion asked. He didn't question the decision. One of his darker looks silenced Select Kwang's protest. That made clear whom Wu had put in charge.

O Shing knew little about the nation being claimed in his name.

"Lo, you decide. But quickly. *She* is coming."

Kwang and Chiang wanted to contact Wu or Feng. "No contact," O Shing insisted. "Nothing thaumaturgic. It might help them locate us."

They didn't argue. Was Wu using this hejira to further his education?

Again they were just miles away when the blow fell. This time it was mundane, soldiers directed by a Tervola Chiang identified as Lord Chin, a westerner as mighty as Lord Wu.

"Tran," said Tam, as they watched the soldiers surround the monastery, "take charge. You're the woodsman. Get us out. Everyone, this man is to be obeyed without question."

There were complaints. Tran wasn't even a Citizen… Lo's baleful eye silenced the protests.

Chin stalked them for six weeks. The party declined to six as the hunters caught a man here, a man there. Chiang went, victim of a brief, foredoomed exchange with Lord Chin. He didn't choose to go. Surprised, in despair, he fought the only way he knew.

His passing allowed the others to escape.

In the end there were Tam, Lang, Tran, Kwang, Lo, and another old veteran from the Seventeenth. They hid in caves in the Upper Mahai. Their stay lasted a year.

Men drifted to the Mahai, to O Shing. The first were regular soldiers from legions torn by the conflicting loyalties of their officers. Later, there were Citizens and peasants, fleeing homes and cities ruined by the Demon Princess's attacks.

Lord Wu, though far from Mist's match in the Power, won a reputation as a devil. Her chief Tervola, Chin, could defeat but never destroy him.

O Shing gave the recruits to Tran to command.

Tran played guerrilla games with them. His tactics were unorthodox and effective. Much enemy blood stained the rocky Mahai.

Tam learned to keep moving, to be where his foes least expected him. He learned to command. He learned to stand by his own judgment and will. He learned to trust his intuitions, Tran's military judgments, and Lang's assessments of character.

In the crucible of that nightstalk he learned to control and wield his awesome grasp of the Power.

He learned to survive in an inimical world.

He *became* O Shing.

Mist's attempts to hunt him down became half-hearted, though. Overconfident of her grip on Shinsan, sure time would bring the collapse of the eastern faction, she and her Tervola became embroiled in foreign adventures. Greedily, her Tervola devoured small states all round Shinsan's borders.

It was a different Shinsan without the balance and guidance of the Princes Thaumaturge. Everything speeded up. Patience and perseverance gave way to haste and greed. Old ways of doing, thinking, believing, collapsed.

In one year six men became thirty thousand. More than the barren Mahai could support. Peasants and Citizens received war-training in their Prince's struggle to stay alive.

"It's time to move," Tam told his staff one morning. He seemed almost comical, commanding captains ages older than he. "We'll go to the forest of Mienming. It's more suited to Tran's war style."

Lord Chin was adapting. He was using a semisentient bat to locate and track Tran's raiders. Food could be stolen but concealment could not.

The old sorcerers returned to their commands and prepared for the thousand-mile march. No one questioned O Shing's wisdom.

Mist's troops met them at the edge of the Mahai. Skirmishing continued throughout the long march. A third of O Shing's army perished forcing a crossing of the Taofu at Yaan Chi, in the Tsuyung Hills. For three days the battle raged. Sorceries murdered the hills, and it seemed, toward the end, that O Shing would become one with the past, that his gamble had failed.

Tam redoubled his stakes, raising hell creatures few Tervola dared summon.

Mist's army collapsed.

Eyebrows rose behind a hundred hideous masks as the news spread. Chin defeated? By a child and a woodsman untrained in the arts of war? Six legions overwhelmed by half-trained peasants scantily backboned by the leavings of shattered legions?

The Tervola weren't bemused by Yo Hsi's daughter. They didn't enjoy being ruled by a woman. Quiet little missions penetrated the Mienming. This Tervola or that offered to slip the moorings of a hasty alliance if O Shing dealt her another outstanding defeat.

Seizing power wasn't the lodestone of Tam's life. Survival was the stake he had on the table. Chin was a tireless hunter.

O Shing was still in hunted-beast mind-set when Wu reentered his life.

Mist's Tervola had coaxed her into invading Escalon. Escalon was no impotent buffer state. The neutralist Tervola, constituting most of their class, joined the venture. Expansion was ancient national policy.

They weren't pleased with the war's conduct. Escalon was strong and stubborn. Mist had no feel for imaginative strategy. Her angry hammer blows consumed legions.

In Shinsan soldiers weren't, as elsewhere, considered fodder for the Reaper. Tervola loved spending men like a miser loved squandering his fortune. Two decades went into preparing a soldier. Quality replacements couldn't be conjured from beyond the barrier of time.

Divining future trouble, they had begun training enlarged drafts years ago, but those wouldn't be ready for a decade.

Their wealth and strength were being squandered.

They simmered with rebellious potential.

Wu and Feng wanted to take advantage.

"No!" Tam protested. "I'm not ready."

"*We* aren't ready," Tran growled. "You'll waste what little we've husbanded."

"It's now or never," Feng snarled.

Lord Wu tried persuasion. And O Shing acquiesced, overawed by Wu's age and ancient wisdom.

Tran got to choose the time.

Most of Escalon and a tenth of Shinsan lay under the shadow, terror, and destruction of Mist's assault on the Monitor and Tatarian, Escalon's capital. Lo led Tran's best fighters through the transfer…

O Shing followed minutes later. Mist had fled. Want it or not, he had inherited a war. The legions were in disarray. Tervola were demanding orders. He had no time to think. With Tran's help he battled the Monitor to a draw.

Afterward, Tran muttered, "We haven't gained anything. We're on the bull's-eye now, Tam." He indicated Wu and Feng, who were celebrating with small cups of Escalonian wine.

"Drink," Feng urged, offering Tam a cup. The professional grouch was radiant. "They say it's the world's finest wine."

"Sorry," Tam mumbled. This was the first time he had seen Feng without his mask. He was as ugly in fact as spirit. At one time fire had ravaged half his face. He hadn't fixed it. Tam feared that said something about the man within.

"Celebration's premature," Tran grumbled. "Somebody better stay sober."

O Shing's reign lasted a month.

Mist did as she had been done. Her shock troops transferred through during the height of a battle.

In the Mienming, Tam sat in the mud cradling Lo's head. The centurion was almost gone.

"This is the price of our lives," Tam hissed. Wu, maskless, moist of eye, knelt beside the man who, possibly, had been his one true friend. "Was a month worth it?"

Wu just held Lo's hand.

The centurion had fought like a trapped tiger. His ferocity had allowed O Shing, Wu, Feng, and the others to escape.

"No more, Wu," said Tam. He spoke in a tone suited to his title. "I've seen children more responsible. Amongst the forest people you despise." He indicated Tran, sitting alone, head between his knees. He and Lo had grown close.

"What'll satisfy you? All our deaths? This time Lo and Kwang. Next time? Tran? My brother? If you persist, I promise I'll be the last. After you, My Lord."

Wu met his gaze, recoiled.

Neither he nor Chin seemed able to learn. They bushwhacked one another repeatedly. Chin finally got the upper hand.

O Shing remained in Mienming nursing his grudge against Tervola.

Mist completed her Escalonian adventure. Success stabilized her position, though not solidly. Her sex, the casualties, and her failure to capture the Tear of Mimizan remained liabilities.

O Shing first heard of the Tear from Wu. Wu wasn't sure what it was, just that it was important. It was the talisman which had made possible the Monitor's prolonged defense of Tatarian.

"It's one of the Poles of Power," Feng opined.

"Bah!" Wu replied. "Monitor's propaganda. There's no proof."

The Poles were legendary amongst the thaumaturgic cognoscenti. One, supposedly, was possessed by the Star Rider. The second had been missing for ages. Even the highest wizards had nearly forgotten it. During the recent conflict the Monitor had hinted that the Tear was the lost Pole.

Every sorcerer living would have bartered his soul to possess a Pole. The man who mastered one could rule the world.

In time, sensing the restlessness of the Tervola, Mist looked for another foe to divert them. She took up a program inherited from her father, which she had quietly nurtured since her ascension.

O Shing spent ever more time alone, or with Tran and Lang. Only those two still treated him as Tam. Only they considered him as more than a means to an end.

Lo's death cost Wu O Shing's love and respect.

Wu was changing. No one called him "the Compassionate" now. A poisonous greed, a demanding haste, had crept into his soul.

And O Shing was changing too, becoming cynical and disenchanted.

The man in the cat-gargoyle mask made his first presentation to the Pracchia. Nervously, he said, "Mist plans to invade the west now. She's suborned the Captal of Savernake. Maisak, the fortress controlling the Savernake Gap, will be Shinsan's. Ehelebe-in-Shinsan can assume control of the invasion whenever the Pracchia directs. We have moved with care, into leading positions in both political factions. I have become Mist's chief Tervola. Members of my Nine are close to the Dragon Prince. We still recommend that nominal rule be invested in the latter. He remains the more manageable personality." He detailed plans for eliminating Mist and making O Shing the Pracchia's puppet.

"Absolutely perfect," said he who was first in the Pracchia. "By all means encourage Mist's plans. She'll take care of herself for us."

O Shing, Lang, and Tran watched the commandos disappear. O Shing still shivered with the strain of a recently completed sorcery. Mist and the Captal certainly would be diverted.

"Why're we here, Tran?" he whispered.

"Destiny, Tam. There's no escape. We must be what we must be. How many of us like it? Even forest hunters ask the same question."

O Shing met Wu's eye. Lord Wu was in disguise. He wore no mask. His expression was taut, pallid, frightened.

Lang whispered, "Friend Wu is spooked." Lang took tremendous pleasure in seeing the mighty discomfited, perhaps because it brought them nearer his own insignificance. "That thing you called up... He wasn't looking for that."

"The Gosik of Aubochon? I was just showing off."

"You scared the skirts off him," Tran said. "He's having second thoughts about us."

Wu was frightened. Not even the Princes Thaumaturge, at the height of their Power, had dared call that devil from its hell. And, though O Shing hadn't gone quite that far himself, he *had* opened a portal through which the monster could cast a shadow of itself, a doorway through which it might burst if O Shing's Power weren't sufficient to confine it.

Wu wasn't certain whether O Shing had overestimated himself or was genuinely able to control the devil. Either way, he had trouble. If the Gosik broke loose, the world would become its plaything. If O Shing truly commanded it, the Dragon Prince was more powerful than anyone had suspected, and had trained himself quietly and well. Those who intended using him might find the tables turning.

Worse, the youth was winning allegiances outside the Tervola. He was popular with the Aspirants. This sudden Power might tempt him to replace Tervola with Aspirants he trusted.

But it was too late to change plans. Rectifications had to wait till Mist had been destroyed.

Wu felt like a man who bent to catch a king snake and discovered that he had hold of a cobra.

News filtered back. Mist had been completely surprised. Only a handful of supporters, all westerners, were with her. Tran's commandos were occupying Maisak. The woman would be theirs soon.

The same promises were still coming through two days later. The lives of Tervola had been lost, and the survivors kept saying, "Soon."

"This'll never end," Tam told Lang while awaiting their turn to transfer. "She'll get away. Just like we always did. There must be a reason."

Tran had been sitting silently, lost in thought. "May I hazard a guess?"

"Go ahead."

"I think there're other plots afoot. One catches things here and there if one listens."

"They'd *let* her get away?"

"Maybe. I'm not sure. She's smart and strong. Whatever, there's something happening. We'd best guard our backs."

O Shing would remember that later, when Wu brought Lord Chin to swear fealty.

Tam remembered escaping Mist's hunter almost miraculously. He graciously accepted Chin's oath, then became thoughtful. Tran was right.

He told Tran and Lang to be observant. No conspiracy could operate without leaving *some* tracks.

The battle at Baxendala upset everyone.

The preliminaries proceeded favorably enough. Chin assumed tactical command, quickly drove the westerners into their defense works. Then he had no choice but frontal attack. Nobody worried. The westerners were a mixed lot, from a half-dozen states, politically enmired, commanded by a man with little large-scale experience, and already had shown poorly against the legions. They would punch through.

The battle, as Shinsan's did, opened with a wizards' skirmish. O Shing, emboldened by Wu's reaction earlier, conjured the Gosik himself...

A bent old man, high above the battlefield, became enraged. This wasn't in his plan. He took steps, knowing the result might delay his ends.

But O Shing was becoming dangerous. He was outside the control of Ehelebe-in-Shinsan...

He ended the efficacy of the Power, using his Pole of Power, which had the form of a gold medallion.

The cessation of the Power rattled O Shing. His Tervola were dismayed. Never had they known the Power to fail.

"We retain our advantages," Chin argued. "They're still weak and disunited. We'll slaughter them." His confidence was absolute.

Chin's prediction seemed valid initially. The westerners were stubborn, but no match for the legions. Their lines crumbled...

Yet Tam couldn't shake a premonition of disaster.

Tran felt it, too. And acted. He ordered O Shing's bodyguard to be ready.

Then it happened. Western knights exploded from a flank long thought secured by local allies. They hit the reserve legion before anyone realized they weren't friendly.

The soldiers of Shinsan had never encountered knights. They stood and fought, and died, as they had been taught—to little real purpose.

Chin panicked. It communicated itself to O Shing.

"Stand fast!" Tran begged. "It'll cost, but we'll hold. They won't break."

Nobody listened. Not even the youth who had vowed to respect Tran's advice above all others'.

The horsemen turned on the legions clearing Ragnarson's defense works. Chin and Wu cried disaster.

Tran cajoled and bullied enough to prevent a rout.

That night O Shing ordered a withdrawal.

"What?" Tran demanded. "Where to?"

"Maisak. We'll retain control of the pass, transfer more men through, resume the offensive." He parroted Chin. "The Imperial Standard will remain here." His lips were taut. He hated that sacrifice. The legion would be lost if reinforcements didn't arrive in time.

"Stand here," Tran urged again.

"We're beaten."

Tran gave up. When O Shing's ear went deaf there was no point in talking on.

Maisak greeted them with arrows instead of paeans for its overlord.

The King Without a Throne had gotten there first.

Chin blew up. Never had soldiers of Shinsan been so humiliated.

"Attack!" he shrieked. "Kill them all!"

O Shing ignored Tran again.

The assault cost so many lives, uselessly, that Chin's standing with the Tervola plummeted. They wouldn't listen to him for years.

Tervola also questioned O Shing's acceding to Chin's folly when the barbarian, Tran, had foreseen the outcome...

After that secondary defeat O Shing put his trust in Tran again. The hunter guided the survivors across the wilderness, through terrible hardships. Two thousand men reached Shinsan. Of twenty-five thousand.

The western adventure, so optimistically begun, traumatized O Shing. The bitter trek across the steppes renewed his acquaintance with fear. Three times he had endured the fleeing terror: with the Han Chin, ducking Mist, and now escaping the west.

He wanted no more of it.

The terrors would shape all his policies as master of Shinsan.

That much he had gained. Mist had been beaten. She resided with the enemy now, lending her knowledge to theirs.

He became a dedicated isolationist. Unfortunately, the Tervola didn't see it his way.

ELEVEN: SPRING, 1011 AFE
MARSHALL AND QUEEN

Ragnarson's party reached Karak Strabger at midnight. Bragi grumbled about the castle's disrepair. It hadn't seen maintenance since the civil war. Something needed doing. Baxendala was crucial to Kavelin's defense.

Fortifications were like women past thirty. They required constant attention or quickly fell apart.

He gave his mount to one of the tiny garrison, glanced at Varthlokkur.

"Not time yet. She's resting. We have a day."

"I'll go see her. For a minute. Ragnar, stay with Mr. Eldred. The duty corporal will find you someplace to sleep."

"I need it," Ragnar replied. A shadow crossed his brow.

"I'll be down in a minute." He hugged his son. They had lost a lot, and had had too much time to remember while riding.

Ragnarson wasn't a demonstrative man. His hug startled Ragnar, but clearly pleased him. "Go on. And behave. Everybody in the army has permission to wax your ass if you act up."

It was a long climb. Gjerdrum and Dr. Wachtel had wanted Fiana inaccessible.

She was alone except for a maid asleep in a chair. Only a candle beside her bed illuminated the room.

He stood over Fiana awhile, staring at beauty wasted by pain. She slept peacefully now, though. He wouldn't disturb her after what Varthlokkur suggested she had been through.

Gone was the elfin quality that had stunned him when first they met. But she had been barely twenty then, and tormented only by the cares of office.

The maid wakened. "Oh. Sir!"

"Shh!"

She joined him.

"How is she?"

"Better tonight. Last night… We thought… It's good you're here. It'll help. That you couldn't be…. That made it hard. Can you stay?"

"Yes. There's no reason not to anymore."

The maid's blue eyes widened.

"Do I sound bitter?" His attention returned to the pain lines on Fiana's face. "Poor thing."

"Wake her. I'll go."

"I shouldn't. She needs the rest."

"She needs you more. Goodnight, sir."

He settled on the edge of the bed, stared, thought. A good man, that innkeeper had said. And he had brought Fiana to this.

He liked to believe he was one of the good guys. Wanted—even needed—to think so. By the standards of his age, he was. So why was it that every woman who entered his life got nothing but pain for her trouble? How happy had he made Fiana? Or Elana? He never should have married. Pleasure he should have taken in chance encounters and houses of joy. Elana would have been better off with Preshka. The Iwa Skolovdan would have done right by her…

He was holding Fiana's hand. Too tightly. Her eyelids fluttered. He stared into pale blue eyes pleasantly surprised.

"You came," she murmured.

He thought of Elana. A tear escaped.

"What's wrong?"

"Nothing. Nothing to worry your pretty head about. Go back to sleep."

"What? Why? Oh! You look terrible."

"I didn't clean up."

"I don't care. You're here."

He smoothed her hair on her cerulean pillow. The blue framed her blondness prettily. The maid had taken good care of her hair. Good girl. She knew how to buoy sinking spirits.

"You're exhausted. What've you been doing?"

"Not much. Haven't slept for a couple days."

"Trouble? Is that why you came?"

"No. Don't worry about it. Come on. Go back to sleep. We'll talk in the morning."

She eased over. The mound of her belly was incredibly huge. Elana had never been that big. "Here. Lay down with me."

"I can't."

"Please? You've never stayed with me all night. Do it now."

"I brought my son. I told him I'd be back down."

"Please?"

He bit his lip.

"It might be the last time we can." Fear crossed her face. "I'm scared. I won't live through it. It's so bad…"

"Now wait a minute. There's nothing to worry about. You'll be all right. Funny. Women always get so scared. They go through it all the time. Elana…"

She wasn't offended. "It's not like before. It hurt last time, but only when the baby came." Her eyes moistened. Her daughter, a precocious, delightful blonde elf, had died mysteriously soon after the civil war. That had been one of Fiana's great sorrows. Another had been the passing of her husband, the old King, an event which had precipitated the civil war.

"Come on. Stay."

He couldn't refuse her. The look in her eyes…

"Now," she said after he slipped in beside her, "tell me what happened."

"Nothing. Don't worry."

She was persistent. And he didn't need much encouragement. He had to loose the grief sometime.

She cried with him. Then they slept.

And no one disturbed them. Her people were discreet.

It was afternoon when Ragnarson wakened. Fiana immediately asked, "You think it's Shinsan again?"

"Who else? Wish I had a way to hit back. If it weren't for you, and Kavelin, I'd head east right now, and not stop till I had my sword through O Shing's heart." Someday, he thought. Maybe with Varthlokkur's help. The wizard had his own grudge against Shinsan.

He hadn't mentioned Varthlokkur. What he had revealed had troubled Fiana enough. And had done her good. Worrying about Kavelin distracted her. Knowing her condition had drawn Varthlokkur from his eyrie might crack what control she retained.

"Darling, I've got to go downstairs. Ragnar will think I abandoned him. And Wachtel is probably dancing in the hall, trying to decide if he should stick his nose in."

"I know. Come back. Please? As soon as you can?"

"I will."

And he did, with Varthlokkur and Wachtel. Varthlokkur had conjured sorcerer's devices from Fangdred—and had frightened half the Queen's staff out of Karak Strabger.

What wild rumors were afoot in Baxendala?

Ragnarson kept his promise, but Fiana never knew. Her siege of agony had resumed. She screamed and screamed while Bragi and the doctor held her so she wouldn't hurt herself.

"It's worse this time," said Wachtel. He was a kindly old gentleman who winced with every contraction. He had been Royal Physician for longer than Fiana had been alive, was one of those rare Kaveliners of whom Ragnarson had heard no evil at all. Like Michael Trebilcock, he was unacquainted with fear. Varthlokkur didn't impress him except as a respectable physician.

Wachtel knew the wizard's history. Varthlokkur had learned life-magicks from the Old Man of the Mountain, who was believed to be the master of the field.

"Hold her!" Varthlokkur snapped. "I've got to touch her…"

Bragi pressed down on her shoulders. She tried to bite. Wachtel struggled with her ankles. The wizard laid hands on her belly. "Never seen a woman this pregnant. You're sure it's only eight months?"

"That's what disturbs me," Wachtel said, nodding. His face was taut, tired. "You'd think she was delivering a colt."

"It's overdue. You're positive…? Oh!" He touched hastily, his face smeared with sudden incredulity. "Wachtel. You have anything to quiet her?"

"I didn't want to give her something and be sorry later."

"Give it to her. She'll need it. We'll have to cut. No woman could dilate enough to deliver this."

Wachtel eyed him—then released Fiana's ankles. The wizard assumed his place.

"Over twenty pounds," Varthlokkur murmured.

"Impossible!"

"You know it. I do. But that thing in her womb… Tell it, Doctor. Marshall?"

"Uhm?"

"I don't know how to tell you… I'm not sure *I* understand. This isn't your child."

A sneak attack with a club couldn't have stunned Ragnarson more. "But… That's impossible. She…"

"Wait! This's the part that's hard to explain."

"Go. I need something."

"Remember the plot hatched by Yo Hsi and the Captal of Savernake? As the Captal confessed it before you executed him?"

The Captal had been a rebel captain during the civil war. The Demon Prince had been his sponsor. Shinsan, to aid him, had put in the legions Ragnarson had defeated here at Baxendala. The plot had opened with the artificial insemination of Fiana, in her sleep, to create a royal heir controllable from Shinsan. To complicate their duplicity, the plotters had substituted another child for the newborn, ensuring a disputed succession.

Yo Hsi had made one grave error. Fiana's child had been a girl.

That had complicated matters for everyone.

Then Yo Hsi and Nu Li Hsi had been destroyed in Castle Fangdred. The plot lay fallow till Yo Hsi's daughter, Mist, resurrected it.

The ultimate failure of the rebel cause had brought the girl home to her mother. Then, during the winter, she had died of a spider bite.

"All right. Get to the point."

"This is the child meant to be born then."

"What? Bullshit. I ain't no doctor. I ain't no wizard. But I know for god-damned sure it don't take no fifteen years…"

"I confess to complete mystification myself. If this's Yo Hsi's get, then, necessarily, Carolan was your daughter."

Fiana's struggles lessened as Wachtel's drug took effect.

"Wizard, I can believe almost anything," Ragnarson said. "But there ain't no way I'll believe a woman could have my baby five years before I met her."

"Doesn't matter what you believe. You'll see when we deliver. Doctor. You agree we'll have to cut?"

"Yes. I've feared it all month. But I put off the decision, just hoping... It should've been aborted."

"When?"

"I'll have your help?"

"If I can convince the Marshall..."

"Of what?"

"That this isn't your get. And that you should let me have it."

Ragnarson's eyes narrowed suspiciously.

"I know what you're thinking. You don't trust me. I don't know why. But try this. We'll deliver the child. If you want to acknowledge it then, that's your choice. If you don't, I get it. Fair enough?"

Why would Varthlokkur lie? he wondered. The man was wiser then he... "Do it, damnit. Get it over with."

"We'll need some..."

"I've been at birthings before. Nine." Elana had had three children who had died soon after birth. "Wachtel, have what's-her-name get it. Then explain why it's not ready already."

"It is ready. Sir." Wachtel was angry. No one questioned his competence or dedication.

"Good. Get at it." Ragnarson settled on a chest of drawers. "The man will be here watching." He rested his sword across his lap. "He won't be happy if anything goes wrong."

"Lord, I can't promise anything. You know that. The mothers seldom survive the operation..."

"Doctor, I trust *you*. You do the cutting."

"I plan to. The man's knowledge I respect. I don't know his hand."

Wachtel began. And, despite the drugs, Fiana screamed. They bound her to the bed, and brought soldiers to help hold her, but she thrashed and screamed...

Wachtel and Varthlokkur did everything possible. Ragnarson could never deny that.

Nothing helped.

Ragnarson held her hand, and wept.

Tears didn't change anything either.

Nor did the most potent of Varthlokkur's life-magicks. "You can't beat the Fates."

"Fates? Damn the Fates! Keep her alive!" Ragnarson seized his sword.

"Sir, you may be Marshall," Wachtel shouted. "You may have the power to slay me. But, by damned, this's my field. Sit down, shut up, and stay the hell out of the way. We're doing everything we can. It's too late for her. We're trying to save the baby."

There was a limit to what Wachtel would tolerate, and the soldiers saw it his way.

Ragnarson's aide, Gjerdrum, and two men got between Ragnarson and the doctor.

While Wachtel operated Varthlokkur began a series of quiet little magicks. He and the doctor finished together. The child, brought forth from a dead woman, floated above the bed in a sphere the wizard had created.

Its eyes were open. It looked back at them with a cruel, knowing expression. Yet it looked like a huge baby.

"That's no son of mine," Ragnarson growled sickly.

"I told you that," Varthlokkur snapped.

"Kill it!"

"No. You said…"

Gjerdrum looked from man to man. Wachtel confirmed Varthlokkur's claim.

"Child of evil," Ragnarson said. "Murderer… I'll murder you…" He raised his sword.

The thing in the bubble stared back fearlessly.

Varthlokkur rounded the bed. "Friend, believe me. Let it be. This child of Shinsan… It doesn't know what it is. Those who created it don't know it exists. Give it to me. It'll become our tool. This's my competence. Attend yours. Kavelin no longer has a Queen."

Kavelin. Kavelin. Kavelin. A quarter of his life he had given to the country, and it not the land of his birth. Kavelin. The land of… What? The women who had loved him? But Elana had been Itaskian. Fiana had come from Octylya, a child bride for an old king desperately trying to spare his homeland the ravages of a succession struggle. Kavelin. What was this little backwater state to him? A land of sorrow. A land that devoured all that he loved. A land that had claimed his time and soul for so long that he had lost the love of the woman who had made up half his soul. What did he have to sacrifice to this land to satisfy it? Was it some hungry beast that ravened everything lovely, everything dear?

He raised his sword, that his father had given him when he and Haaken were but beardless boys. The sword he had borne twenty-five years, through adventures grim, services honorable and otherwise, and days when he had been no better than the men who had murdered his children. That sword was an extension of his soul, half of the man called Bragi Ragnarson.

He took it up, and whirled it above his head the way his father, Mad Ragnar, had done. Everyone backed away. He attacked the bed in which his Queen had died, in which he had lain with her, comforting her, her last night on earth. He hacked posts and sides and hangings like an insane thing, and no one tried to stop him.

"Kavelin!" he thundered. "You pimple on the ass of the world! What the hell do you want from me?"

Into his mind came a face. A simple man, an innkeeper, once had soldiered with a stranger from the north, whom he believed had come to set him free. Behind him were the faces of a hundred such men, a thousand, ten thousand, who had stood with him at Baxendala, unflinching. Peasant lads and hill-men, their hands virgin to the sword a year before, they had faced the fury of Shinsan and had refused to show their backs. Not many had been as lucky as that innkeeper. Most lay beneath the ground below the hill on which Karak Strabger stood. Thousands. Dead. Laid down because they had believed in him, because he and this woman who lay here growing cold had given them a hope for a new tomorrow.

What had Kavelin demanded of them?

"Oh, Gods!" he swore, and smashed that faithful blade against stone till it flew into a hundred shards. "Gods!" He buried his face in his hands, raked his beard with his fingers. "What do I have to do? Why must I endure this? Free me. Slay me. Keep the blades from going astray."

Wachtel, Varthlokkur, and Gjerdrum tried to restrain him.

He surged like a bear throwing off hounds, hurling them against the walls. Then he sat beside the torn body of his Queen, and again took her hand. And for a moment he thought he saw a tiny smile flicker through the agony frozen upon her dead face. He thought he heard a whisper, "Darling, go on. Finish what we started."

He threw himself onto her still form and wept. "Fiana. Please," he whispered. "Don't leave me alone."

Elana was gone. Fiana was gone. What did he have left?

Just one thing, a tiny mind-voice insisted. The bitch-goddess, the changeable child-vixen which he had come to love more than any woman.

Kavelin.

Kavelin. Kavelin. Kavelin. Damnable Kavelin.

His tears flowed.

Kavelin.

Henceforth there would be no other woman before her...

He lay there with his head on Fiana's breast till long after sundown. And when he rose, finally, with night in his eyes and tears dried, he was alone except for Gjerdrum and Ragnar.

They came to him, and held him, understanding.

Gjerdrum had loved his Queen more than life itself, though not with the love of a man for a woman. His was the love of a knight of the old romances for his sovereign, for his infallible Crown.

And Ragnar brought him the love of a forgiving son.

"Give me strength," said Ragnarson. "Help me. They've taken everything from me. Everything but you. And hatred. Stand with me, Ragnar. Don't let hate eat me. Don't let me destroy me."

He had to live, to be strong. Kavelin depended on him. Kavelin. Damnable Kavelin.

"I will, Father. I will."

TWELVE: SPRING, 1011 AFE
THE STRANGER IN HAMMERFEST

Hammerfest was a storybook town in a storybook land cozy with storybook people. Plump blonde girls with ribboned braids, rosy cheeks, and ready smiles tripped up and down the snowy streets. Tall young men hurried from one picturesque shop to another in pursuit of the business of their apprenticeships, yet were never so hurried that they hadn't time to welcome a stranger. Laughing children sped down the main street on sleds with barrel staves for runners. Their dogs yapped and floundered after them.

The thin man in the dark cloak stood taking it in for a time. He ignored the nibbling of a wind far colder than any of his homeland. It was warmer than those he had endured the past few months.

Tall, steep-roofed houses crowded and hung over the rising, twisting street, yet he didn't feel as confined as he had in towns less densely built. There was a warm friendliness to Hammerfest, a family feeling, as though the houses were cuddling from love, not necessity.

His gaze lingered on the smoke rising from a tall stone chimney topped by a rack where storks nested in summer. He watched the vapors rise till they passed between himself and a small, crumbling fortress atop the hill the town climbed. Peace had reigned here for a generation. The brutal vicissitudes of Trolledyngjan politics had passed Hammerfest by.

A sled whipped past, carrying a brace of screaming youngsters. The dark man leapt an instant before it could hit him, slipped, fell. The snow's cold kiss burned his cheek.

"They don't realize, so I'll apologize for them."

A pair of shaggy boots entered his vision, attached to pillars of legs. A huge, grizzled man offered a hand. He accepted.

"Thank you. No harm done." He spoke the language well. "Children will be children. Let them enjoy while they can."

"Ah, indeed. Too soon we grow old, eh? Yet, isn't it true that all of us will be what we will be?"

The man in the dark clothing looked at him oddly.

"I mean, we must be what our age, sex, station, and acquaintances demand."

"Maybe…" A beer hall philosopher? Here? "What're you driving at?" He shivered in a gust.

"Nothing. Don't mind me. Everybody says I think too much, and say it. For a constable. You should get heavier clothing. Ander Sigurdson could outfit you. That all you wore coming north?"

The stranger nodded. This was a real fountain of questions. Nor was he as full of good-to-see-you as the others.

"Let's get you up to the alehouse, then. You're cold. You'll want something warming. A bite, too, by the look of you." He danced lightly as a sled whipped past.

The stranger noted his deftness. This would be a dangerous man. He was strong and quick.

"Name's Bors Olagson. Constable hereabouts. Boring job, what with nothing ever happening."

"I took you for a smith." The stranger refused the bait.

"Really? Only hammer I ever swung was a war hammer, back in my younger days. Reeved out of Tonderhofn a few summers, back when. That's why they picked me for this job. But it's just a hobby, really. Don't even pay. My true profession is innkeeper. I own the alehouse. Bought with my share of the plunder."

They passed several houses and shops before he probed again. "And who would you be?"

"Rasher. Elfis Rasher. Factor for Darnalin, of the Bedelian League. Our syndics are considering increasing profits by bypassing the Iwa Skolovdans in the fur trade. I've begun to doubt our chances. I didn't prepare well. As you noticed by my outfit."

"And you came alone? Without so much as a pack?"

"No. I survived. The Kratchnodians and rest of Trolledyngja aren't as friendly as Hammerfest."

"Indeed. Though it was worse before the Old House was restored. Here we are." He shoved a tall, heavy door. "Guro. A big stein for a new guest. The kids just knocked him into a snowbank." He grinned. "Yeah. Those were my brats."

The stranger surveyed the tavern. It was all warm browns, as homey and friendly within as the Hammerfesters were outside. He sidled to the fire.

Bors brought steins. "Well, Rasher, I admire you. I do. You're one of the survivors. Weren't always a merchant, were you?"

The questions were becoming irksome. "My home is Hellin Daimiel. I saw the El Murid Wars. And I'm no countinghouse clerk. I'm a caravaneer."

"Thought so. Man of action. I miss it sometimes, till I remember drifting in a rammed dragonship with my guts hanging out on the oar bench…"

The stranger tried shifting the subject. "I was told Hammerfest was a critical fur town. That I might find men here who would be interested in making a better deal than the Iwa Skolovdans offer."

"Possibly. Those people are a gang of misers. I don't like it when they stay here. They fill the rooms and don't spend a groschen."

"When do they arrive?"

"You're ahead, if that's your idea. They're too soft to try the passes before summer. They'll be a month or two yet. But, you see, they'll bring trade goods. You've apparently lost yours."

"No real problem. A fast rider could correct that—if I find somebody interested. I'm the only foreigner in town now, then?"

The man's eyes narrowed. His mouth tightened. He wasn't much for hiding his thoughts. "Yes."

The stranger wondered why he lied. Was his man here? The trick would be to find him without bringing the town down on his head.

The best course would be to pursue his cover implacably, ignoring his urgency.

It had waited a year. It could wait a day or two more.

"Who should I see? If I can arrange something, I could get the goods through ahead of the Iwa Skolovdans. We've headquartered our operation at our warehouses in Itaskia…"

"You should get the frost out of your fingers first."

"I suppose. But I've lost my men and my goods. I have to recoup fast. The old boys who stay at home to tote up the profits and losses take the losses out of my pocket and put the profits in theirs."

"Oho! This's a speculative venture, then."

The stranger nodded, a quiet little smile crossing his lips.

"Gentlemen adventurers, perhaps? With the Bedelian League providing office space and letters of introduction, and you putting up the money and men?"

"Half right. I'm a League man. Sent to lead. I was supposed to get a percentage. Still can. If I find the right people, and make it back to Itaskia."

"You southerners. Hurry, hurry."

The stranger drew a coin from inside his cloak, then returned it. He searched by touch, found one which told no tales. It was an Itaskian half-crown, support for his story. "I don't know how long I'll stay. This should keep me a week."

"Six pence Itaskian, per day."

"What? Thief…"

The stranger smiled to himself. He had the better of the man for the moment.

Bors's wife brought ale and roast pork as they agreed on four pence daily. Pork! It was a difficult moment. But the stranger was accustomed to alien ways. He stifled his reaction.

"While you're making your rounds, could you ask that Ander to stop over?"

"His shop is just up the street."

"I'm not going out till I have to. I've had a couple months of snow and wind."

"It's a warm spring day."

"Well, all right then. But warm is a matter of opinion."

"I'll walk you up after you're settled."

"I'll need some other things, too. I'll be a boon to Hammerfest's economy."

"Uhm." The thought had occurred to Bors, apparently.

In the tailor's shop the stranger asked a few cautious questions. He had guessed right. No one would tell him a thing. This would take cunning.

Returning to the inn, alone because Bors was making his rounds, he had another sled encounter. He didn't see this one.

Its rider was a boy of six, scared silly that he had hurt the stranger. The dark man calmed him just enough to suit his purpose.

Then he asked, "Where is the other stranger? The one who stayed the winter."

"The man with black eyes? The man who can't talk?" The Trolledyngjan idiom meant a man who couldn't speak the language. "In the tower." He pointed.

The dark man stared uphill. The castle was primitive. It had a low curtain wall and what looked like a shell keep piled on granite bedrock. One step better than the motte and bailey. "Thank you, son."

"You won't tell?"

"I won't if you won't."

He continued staring uphill. A man who walked like Bors was coming down. He smiled his little smile.

He was in the common room, drinking hot wine, when the constable returned. "All peaceful?" he asked.

"Nothing changes," Bors replied. "Last trouble we had was two years ago. Itaskian got into it with a fellow from Dvar. Over a girl. Settled it before it came to blows."

"Good. Good. I'll feel safe in my bed, then."

"Peace is what we sell here, sir. Don't you know? Every man in Hammerfest is pledged to die fighting if trouble comes from outside. We need peace. Where else, in this land, can you find shops like ours? The outback people won't even plant crops, let alone work with their hands. Except to make trinkets they bury with their dead, to placate the Old Gods. Silly. If the New Gods can't get a man's shade safely to the heroes' hall, then they can't be much."

"I don't know much about religion."

"Most folks here don't. They give to the priests mainly so they'll stay away. By the way. I talked to a couple fur-dealers. They're interested. In talking. They'll be round tomorrow."

The stranger moved to the fire. "Good. Then I shouldn't have to stay long."

"Oh, I think your stay will be short. They're eager, I'd say." There was something in his tone…

The stranger turned.

His cloak was back. Bors hadn't seen him open it. But he saw the worn, plain black sword hilt and the cold dark eyes and cruel nose. That wicked little smile played across the man's lips. "Thank you. You're most kind, going out of your way. I'll retire now. My first chance at a warm bed for weeks."

"I understand. I understand."

As the stranger climbed the stairs he caught the flicker of uncertainty crossing the big man's face.

He arranged a spell for his door, then went to bed.

They came earlier than he expected, though he hadn't been sure they would come at all. The ward spell warned him. He rose sinuously, hefted his weapon, concealed himself.

There were three of them. He recognized Bors's hulking shape immediately. One of the others was shorter and thinner than the man he sought.

He took Bors with a vicious throat swing, then gutted the short man, shoving a rag into his mouth before he could scream.

The third man didn't react in time to do anything. A sword tip rested at his adam's apple the instant it took the stranger to decide he wasn't the man. Then he died.

The stranger shrugged. He would have to visit the castle after all.

But first he lighted his lamp and studied the dead men.

He found nothing unusual.

Why would they commit murder for no more excuse than he had given?

He dressed in his new winter boots and coat, donned his greatcloak, sheathed his freshly cleaned sword.

Bors's wife waited in the common room.

The stranger's dark eyes met hers. There was no pity in his. "I'll be leaving early. I have a refund coming."

Terror restructured her face. She counted coins with fingers too shaky to keep hold.

The stranger pushed back two. "Too much." His voice was without emotion. But he couldn't resist a dramatic touch. He fished a coin from his purse. "To cover the costs of damage done," he said with a hint of sarcasm.

The woman stared at the coin as he slipped out the door. On one side a crown had been struck. On the reverse there were words in writing she didn't recognize.

Once the door slammed she flew upstairs, tears streaming.

They had been laid out neatly, side by side. On each forehead, still smoking, was a tiny crown-brand.

She didn't know what it meant, but there were others in Hammerfest who had paid attention to news from the south. She would learn soon enough.

She and Bors had entertained a royal guest.

THIRTEEN: SPRING, 1011 AFE
REGENCY

Colonel Oryon had no idea what had happened at Karak Strabger. He did know he rode with a man possessed. His hard-faced, grim companion, closed of mouth, perpetually angry, wasn't the Ragnarson he had accompanied eastward. This Ragnarson was an avenger, a death-Messiah. There was the feel of doom, of destiny, about him.

Oryon watched him punish his mount, and was afraid.

If this man didn't mellow he could set a continent aflame.

He knew no pain, needed no comforts, wanted no rest. He plunged on till Oryon, who prided himself on his toughness, could no longer stand the pace. And still he rode, leaving his companions at an inn ten miles from Vorgreberg.

"Derel!" he roared through the Palace, as he stalked toward his office. "Prataxis! You south coast faggot! Where the hell are you? Get your useless ass up here on the double."

Prataxis materialized, partially dressed. "Sir?"

"The Thing. I want it assembled. Now."

"Sir? It's the middle of the night."

"I don't give a damn! Get those sons of bitches down there in two hours. Or they'll find out what it was like in the old days. We never threw out the hardware from the dungeons. And if you don't get it done yesterday, you'll be first in line."

"What's happened, sir?"

Ragnarson mellowed a little. "Yes, something happened. And I've got to do something about it before the whole damned house of cards falls in on us. Go on. Go, go, go." He waved a hand like a baker sending his boy into the streets, all rage gone. "I'll explain later."

He had arrived ahead of the news. And would stay ahead unless Oryon learned something, or Ragnar shot his mouth off. Ragnar had promised to say nothing, even to the ghost of his mother. Gjerdrum and Wachtel would keep everyone else locked up in Karak Strabger.

"Before I leave," Prataxis said, "there's a woman in town looking for you. She showed up the day after you left."

"A woman? Who?"

"She wouldn't say. She gave the impression she was *very* friendly with bin Yousif."

"Haroun? About time we heard from that… No. I won't say that. I think I understand him now. Go on. I'll see her after I talk to the Thing. How many of those bastards are in town, anyway?"

"Most of them. It's getting close to Victory Day and time to debate the Guild appropriations. They don't want to miss that."

"That won't be a problem anymore. I told Oryon to pack his bags. We'll pay them off. Thanks to you, Derel. You'll be rewarded."

"Service is my reward, Marshall."

"Bullshit. About two hundred Rebsamen dons fawning at your feet after you publish your thesis is what you're thinking about. You get the look a thief does when he sees loose gold whenever you talk about it."

"As you say, Lord."

"Get out of here. Wait! Before you go, send for Ahring, Blackfang, and Valther."

"The Queen, sir. She…?"

"Derel, don't even think about her. If they ask, say I need a vote of confidence on my army alert."

Blackfang and Valther arrived together.

"How're the kids, Haaken?" Bragi asked.

"Upset. You should see them."

"As soon as I can. Valther, you get anything yet?"

"Not a whisper. But there's a woman here…"

"Derel told me. Who is she?"

"Won't say. It looks like she wants us to think she's bin Yousif's wife."

"Wife? Haroun doesn't have… Well, he never admitted it. But Mocker thought he might. That'd be his style. They keep their women locked up in Hammad al Nakir. And he wouldn't want El Murid to know. Not after killing his son, crippling his wife, and masterminding the kidnapping of his daughter. Yeah. He might have a wife. But I don't think she'd turn up here."

"I'm watching her," Valther told him. "And I'm backtracking her. I put a girl into her hostel. She's just waiting for you."

"Good. Haaken, send messengers to Kildragon and Altenkirk. I want their shock battalions moved here."

"Fiana…?"

"Yes. Derel's getting the Thing together. I want to invoke martial law as soon as we're in session. Keep the Guild troops confined to barracks. Got that, Jarl?" he asked Ahring, who had just arrived.

"Uhm. Case Wolfhound?" Wolfhound was a contingency plan drawn up years ago, at Fiana's direction.

"Yes. Oh. Valther. Another problem for you. I met an innkeeper in Forbeck who said there's been men like our assassins going back and forth through the Gap. A gang went east right ahead of me. Catch a couple."

"And Maisak?"

"Better put somebody in."

The Savernake Gap, only good pass to the east for hundreds of miles north or south, controlled all commerce between east and west. Because Kavelin controlled the Gap, the kingdom and Gap-defending Fortress Maisak were constantly the focus of intrigue. Shinsan's plot to seize the Gap had been the root cause of Kavelin's civil war.

"You're spreading me awful thin," Valther complained.

"I'll try not to dump anything else on you. Wish Mocker was here. This's his kind of job… Anything on that yet?"

"I came up with a Marena Dimura who saw him with three men in Uhlmansiek."

"Ah?"

"But the men are dead."

"What?"

"My man asked the Marena Dimura to describe them. Instead, he showed my man their graves. Two of them, and that of a man who wasn't with them originally. He's a good man, that Tendrik. Dug them up."

"And?"

"He identified one as Sir Keren of Sincic, a Nordmen knight who disappeared at the right time, and another as Bela Jokai, the battalion commander who vanished with Balfour. Judging from the size of the third body, and from the list of friends of Sir Keren who're missing, the other one was probably Trenice Lazen. He was Keren's esquire, but had connections with the underworld. He and Keren ran a little swords-for-hire business. They were riding with that one-eyed Rico creature who sometimes worked for El Murid's people."

"Any sign of him? Or Mocker? Or Balfour?"

"No. The Marena Dimura down there aren't very friendly. Tendrik thinks it went something like this: Keren, Lazen, and Rico were taking Mocker to Al Rhemish. Jokai and Balfour waylaid them. They fought. Rico turned out to be Balfour's man. They killed Keren and Lazen, and lost Jokai, then made off with Mocker."

"End of story?"

"Apparently. Not a trace after that. I've got the word out on what's left of the merchant network, but that hasn't turned up anything. And the Guild still wants to know what happened, so they aren't having any luck either."

"Unless they're smoke-screening."

"They're not that subtle. They're like your mean moneylender who comes round demanding the deed to the old homestead."

"We'll see. I told Oryon we're paying him off."

"We've got the money?"

"Thanks to Prataxis. Jarl, watch the Treasury. Haaken, the same at the Mint. In case somebody tries something."

"You're getting paranoid."

"Because people are out to get me. You were at the house that night."

"All right. All right."

"Jarl, I want to see Oryon when he gets back. I'll tell him about Jokai. See how he reacts. Now, it's time I wandered over to the Thing."

The Thing met in a converted warehouse. Its members kept whining for a parliament building, but Fiana had resisted the outlay. Kavelin remained too heavily indebted from the civil war.

Ragnarson waited in the office of the publican consul. One of the Vorgreberger Guards stood outside. Another remained on the floor. He would inform Ahring when the majority of the members had arrived.

Case Wolfhound included sequestering the Thing. Several delegates, especially Nordmen, were suspect in their loyalty. They would happily precipitate another civil scrimmage.

The Nordmen had been stripped of feudal privilege for rebelling, then offered amnesty. They had accepted only because the alternatives were death or exile.

No one had believed they would keep their parole, though Ragnarson and Fiana had hoped for an extended reign during which recidivists would pass away and be replaced by youngsters familiar with the new order.

The soldier knocked. "Most of them are here, sir. And Colonel Ahring's ready."

"Very good. Have you seen Mr. Prataxis?"

"He's coming now, sir."

Prataxis entered.

"How'd it go, Derel? What feeling did you get?"

"Well enough. All but three of them were in town. And they suspect something. No one refused to come."

"You look them over downstairs?"

"They're nervous. Grouping by parties."

"Good. Now, I need you to take a message to Ahring. I'll tell you what happened later."

Prataxis wasn't pleased. This would be one of the critical points in Kavelin's history.

"Here. A pass so you can get back in."

"All right. Stall. I'll run."

Ragnarson chuckled. "I'd like to see that." Prataxis, though neither handicapped nor overweight, was the least athletic person Ragnarson knew.

Bragi went downstairs slowly. Ahring would need time. His bodyguard accompanied him. The man was jumpy. A lot of hard men would glare at them from the floor, and debate there sometimes involved the crash of swords.

Pandemonium. At least seventy of the eighty-one members, in clusters, were arguing, speculating, gesturing. Ragnarson didn't ask for silence.

Word of his arrival gradually spread. The delegates slowly assumed their seats. By then Ahring's troops had begun to fill the shadows along the walls.

"Gentlemen," Ragnarson said, "I've asked you here to decide the fate of the State. It *will* be a fateful decision. You'll make it before you leave this hall. Gentlemen, the Queen is dead."

The uproar could have been that of the world's record tavern brawl. Fights broke out. But legislative sessions were always tempestuous. The delegates hadn't yet learned to do things in a polite, parliamentary manner.

The uproar crested again when the members became aware that the army had sealed them in. Ragnarson waited them out.

"When you're ready to stop fooling around, let's talk." They resumed their seats. "Gentlemen, Her Majesty passed on about forty hours ago. I was there. Doctor Wachtel attended her, but couldn't save her." His emotion made itself felt. No one would accuse him of not feeling the loss. "Every attempt was made to prevent it. We even brought in a wizard, an expert in the life-magicks. He said she's been doomed since the birth of her daughter. The breath of Shinsan touched her then. The poison caught up."

His listeners began murmuring.

"Wait! I want to talk about this woman. Some of you did everything you could to make her life miserable, to make her task impossible. She forgave you every time. And gave her life, in the end, to make Kavelin a fit place to live. She's dead now. And the rest of us have come to the crossroads. If you think this's a chance to start something, I'm telling you now. I won't forgive. I am the army. I serve the Crown. I defend the Crown. Till someone wears it, I'll punish rebellion mercilessly. If I have to, I'll make Kavelin's trees bend with a stinking harvest.

"Now, the business at hand."

Prataxis hustled his way in burdened with writing materials. He *had* run. Good. Ahring and Blackfang would be sealing the city perimeter against unauthorized departures.

"My secretary will record all votes. He'll publish them when we make the public announcement."

He grinned. That would give him an extra ten votes from fence-sitters. He should be able to aim a majority any direction.

"Our options are limited. There's no heir. The scholars of Hellin Daimiel have suggested we dispense with the monarchy entirely, fashioning a republic like some towns in the Bedelian League. Personally, I don't relish risking the national welfare on a social experiment.

"We could imitate other League towns and elect a Tyrant for a limited term. That would make transition smooth and swift, but the disadvantages are obvious.

"Third, we could maintain the monarchy by finding a King among the ruling Houses of other states. It's the course I prefer. But it'll take a while.

"Whichever, we need a Regent till a new head of state takes power.

"All right. The session is open for arguments from the floor. Mind your manners. You'll all get a say. Mr. Prataxis, handle the Chair."

Someone shouted, "You forgot a possibility. We could elect one of our own people King."

"Hear hear," the Nordmen minority chanted.

"Silence!" Prataxis bellowed. Ragnarson was startled by his volume.

"Let me speak to that, Derel."

"The Marshall has the floor."

"'Hear hear' you shout, you Nordmen. But you can't all be King. Look around. You see anybody you want telling you what to do?"

The point told. Each had, probably, considered himself the logical candidate. Kavelin's nobles were never short on self-appreciation.

"Okay. Derel?"

"The commons delegate from Delhagen."

"Sirs, I think the Barons missed the point of the suggestion. I meant the Marshall."

That precipitated another barroom round. Ragnarson himself denied any interest. His denial was honest. He knew what trying to break this rebellious bronc of a kingdom had done to Fiana.

He understood the delegate's motives. There was a special relationship between himself and Delhagen and Sedlmayr, the city there. They operated almost as an autonomous republic federated with Kavelin, under a special charter he had urged on Fiana. In return the commons there had remained steadfastly Royalist during the civil war. Sedlmayr, with the similarly chartered "Sieges" of Breidenbach and Fahrig, were nicknamed "The Marshall's Lap Dogs."

Ragnarson smiled gently. The man had made the suggestion so he could gradually back down. Relieved, some opponent would propose the Marshall as Regent instead.

And that task he would accept. He had, in reality, been Regent since Fiana's seclusion. He could handle it. And a Regent could always get out.

Once, years ago, Haroun had tried to tempt him with a kingship. The notion had been more attractive then. But he had seen only the comforts visible from the remote perspective.

The moment gone, he fell asleep in his chair. It would be a long session. Nothing important would get said for hours.

Kaveliners were a stubborn lot. The arguing lasted four days. Weariness and hunger finally forced a compromise. The Thing named Ragnarson Regent by a fat majority—after every alternate avenue had been pursued to a dead end.

Ragnarson left the hall physically better than when he had entered. He had made a vacation of it, getting involved only when delegates threatened to brawl.

Vorgreberg anxiously awaited the session's end, sure the news would be bad.

When it came out Kildragon and Altenkirk were on hand. Vorgreberg was secure. Loyal troops were poised at the kingdom's heart, ready to smash rebellion anywhere.

FOURTEEN: SPRING, 1011 AFE
LADY OF MYSTERY

"Show him in," Ragnarson told Prataxis. He rose, extended his hand. "Colonel. Sorry I took so long with the Thing."

"I understand," Oryon replied. "Congratulations."

"Save it for a year. Probably be sorry I took the job. I wanted to talk about Balfour. My people came up with something."

"Oh?"

Ragnarson hoped Oryon's response would betray something about Guild thinking. He related the tale Valther had told. "Will you want Captain Jokai's body?"

"I'd have to ask High Crag. What the hell was Balfour doing in Uhlmansiek? His log says he was taking the week to go hunting around Lake Berberich. Something's going on here. And I don't like it."

"I've been saying that for a long time. Any idea why he'd kidnap my friend?"

"No. This Rico creature… The whole thing baffles me. I'll ask High Crag, of course."

"I still won't renew the commission."

Oryon's thick lips stretched in a grin. "I noticed the guards at the Treasury."

"I get some strange ideas sometimes."

Oryon shook his head. "Wish I could understand why you're scared of us. Maybe I could change your mind."

"Wish *I* understood it. Just an intuition, I guess. Victory Day is coming up, by the way."

"My staff is planning the evacuation. We'll move out come sunrise Victory Day. We expect to be out of Kavelin within five days. Because of the confinement to barracks, I haven't informed High Crag or made transit arrangements. I doubt there'll be any problems."

"Good enough. We'll put on a going-away party for your boys."

"Can't bitch about that."

"Don't want any hard feelings."

"Keep me posted about Balfour. Or our agent after I leave."

"Will do. Thanks for coming." He followed Oryon to the door. "Derel, want to find that woman for me? The one who wants to see me?"

"All right."

Ragnarson selected one of the mountain of requests that already had appeared on his desk. Everything held in abeyance during the Queen's indisposition was breaking loose. Every special interest was trying to get his attention first. "Hey, Derel. Get me a big box."

"Sir?"

"So I can file the stuff I want to 'put aside for further consideration.' Like this one. Guy wants me to come to the opening of his alehouse."

"Sir? If I might? Act on ones like that if you have time. Chuck the ones where some Nordmen insists on his right to collect ford tolls. Giving breaks to important people and cronies is a deathtrap. It's Wessons like that soldier-turned-innkeeper who are your power base. Keep them on your side. I'll get that woman. Half an hour?"

He took ten minutes. The word had reached her. He encountered her downstairs.

"Marshall? The lady."

"Thank you, Derel." He rose, considered her. She wore traditional desert costume. Dark almond eyes peered over her veil. There were crow's feet at their corners, though cunningly hidden. She was older than she liked.

"Madam. Please be seated. Kaf? I'm sure Derel could scare some up."

"No. Nothing is necessary." She spoke a heavily accented Itaskian of the Lower Silverbind.

"What can I do for you? My secretary says you hinted it has to do with Haroun bin Yousif."

A sad little laugh stirred her veil. "Excuse me for staring. It has been so long… Yes. Haroun. He is my husband."

Ragnarson settled into his chair. "I never heard of any wife."

"It is one of the unhappy secrets of our lives. But it is true. Twenty-three years… It seems an eternity. Most of that I was wife in name only. I did not see him for years at a time."

Ragnarson's skepticism was obvious. She responded by dropping her veil. It was an act which, in her culture, was considered incredibly daring. Women of Hammad al Nakir, once married, would rather have paraded nude than reveal their naked faces.

Ragnarson was impressed. He didn't have Derel throw her out.

"You do not recognize me still?"

"Should I? I never met a woman with a claim on Haroun."

"Time changes us. I forget that I'm no longer the child you met. She was fourteen. Life has not been easy. Always his men run—when they do not ride the desert to murder my father's men."

Ragnarson still didn't understand.

"But you *must* remember! The day the fat man brought me to your camp in Altea? When I was so much trouble you pulled up my skirts and paddled me in front of your men? And then Haroun came. He scared me so much I never said another word."

Why couldn't women just say things straight out? He tried to remember Mocker dragging a tart into some wartime camp—

"Gods! You're Yasmid? El Murid's daughter? Married to Haroun?" He strangled a laugh. "You think I'll swallow that?"

"So! You call me a liar? You had my skirts up. You saw." She bent and raised her skirts.

Ragnarson remembered the winestain birthmark shaped like a six-fingered baby hand.

"And this!" Angrily, she bared small, weary breasts. Over her heart lay the Harish tattoo worn by El Murid's chosen.

"All right. You're Yasmid."

Incredible. The daughter of El Murid, missing twenty years, appearing here. As Haroun's wife.

The marriage was the sort of thing Haroun would do to drive little knives into his enemy's heart. Why hadn't he ballyhooed it over half the continent?

"I did not expect you to be easily convinced. I made that my first task. I brought these." She showed him jewelry only Haroun could have given her and letters he couldn't read because they were in the script of Hammad al Nakir, but which bore Haroun's King Without a Throne seal.

"I believe you. So why're you here?" He decided to check with Valther. Men of the desert didn't let their women roam free. Not without an uproar.

"My husband has disappeared "

"I know. I've been trying to get in touch."

That startled her. "He has sworn to kill my father."

"Not exactly the news of the century."

"No. Listen. Please. After he came back, after the war in your country, after he started to attack my father, but turned north against your enemies instead…"

"That hurt him. He had it in his hands. Al Rhemish. But he let love for friends sway him. He surrendered his dream to help you."

Haroun had come out of nowhere with thousands of horsemen to harry O Shing through the Savernake Gap and into the plains east of the Mountains of M'Hand. Bragi hadn't understood Haroun then, nor did he now. For friendship? Haroun would murder his mother for political expedience.

"So?"

"When he came home, a year later, he was so tired and old… He didn't care. I made him promise he wouldn't hurt my father if my father didn't harm him."

"Ah! That's why he's been laying low. Been a long time since he's done anything. Just skirmishing to keep his people interested."

"Yes. That's my fault."

"He's changed his mind?"

"Yes. He told Beloul and Rahman to prepare the final offensive. He sent El Senoussi and El Mehduari to collect the wealth and fighters of the refugees in the coastal states. He ordered the deaths of my father's agents wherever they are found. It will be bloody."

"It's been that for years. It'll go on till Haroun or your father dies."

"Or longer. We have a son. Megelin. The boy is filled with hatred."

"I don't see what you're after. Or why Haroun made this about-face. He keeps his word."

"He thinks my father broke the armistice. My father's men here, Habibullah and Achmed, kidnapped your fat friend."

"Mocker. What's become of him? I sent him to see Haroun a year ago. He disappeared." He wouldn't say more till he heard her version.

"I'm not sure. Maybe Haroun is. The Marena Dimura told him what happened.

"Habibullah was one of my guards when Mocker kidnapped me. What they called kidnap. I wasn't very smart then. And he could talk, that fat man. I came willingly. I thought I could make peace. Anyway, your friend almost killed Habibullah that night. I suppose he's wanted revenge ever since."

"Derel," Ragnarson called. To Yasmid, "Could you face Habibullah now?"

"But why? Won't that make trouble? They have all forgotten me now. If they knew... It would just make trouble."

"Sir?" Prataxis asked.

"See if Habibullah what's-it can come over."

"Now?"

"As soon as possible."

"I don't think..." But Prataxis went.

"I'm running that man half to death," Bragi muttered. "Wish Gjerdrum would get back." Prataxis was supposed to be arranging appointments for ambassadors and factors for the caravan companies.

"Pardon me," Ragnarson said. "You needn't reveal yourself. You think Habibullah had Mocker kidnapped because Mocker embarrassed your father? Because of it Haroun plans to start fighting again?"

"One operation. One planned for years. All or nothing. He thinks the tribes will rise to support him."

"Yes. So. But El Murid doesn't have Mocker. And Haroun knows it. The Marena Dimura down there are his spies."

"I'll tell you what I know. Some men killed Habibullah's men. They handed the fat man over to a man in black. Haroun believed the killers went into the north to hide."

"Wait. The man in black. Tell me about him."

"The Marena Dimura say he was tall and thin. He wore a mask."

"Mask?"

"A metal mask. Maybe gold. With jewels. Like those creatures on the walls of the temples in the jungle cities. The killers were afraid of him."

Ragnarson buried his face in his hands.

"Haroun has vanished. I fear he will try to murder my father so there'll be confusion when he invades Hammad al Nakir. I came here because I hoped you could do something."

"What?"

"Stop him."

"I don't understand."

"I love my father. He was a good father. He's a good man. He means no evil..."

"Nearly a million people died during the wars."

"My father didn't do that. He didn't want it. That was the fault of men like Nassef. His generals were brigands."

Ragnarson didn't contradict her. She was partly right. But her father had given the order to convert the west, and to slay anyone who didn't accept his faith.

"What could I do? I don't know where Haroun is. I've only seen him once in the last ten years."

She wept. "The Fates are cruel. Why do the men I love spend their lives trying to kill each other?

"I shouldn't have come. I should have known it was useless. All that planning, that trouble getting away, hiding from Haroun's men... All for nothing."

"Maybe not. There's a possibility... The old story of the enemy of my enemy."

"Excuse me?"

"There's a greater enemy. One your husband and your father could agree to be more dangerous than one another."

"You're being mysterious."

"I hate naming the name. I've seen the men in black before. I've fought them. They call themselves Tervola."

The color left Yasmid's face. "Shinsan! No."

"Who would impersonate a Tervola?" But then, why would Shinsan grab Mocker? What was the connection between Balfour and Shinsan? Did that permeate the Guild? And this Willis Northen, who used a Marena Dimura name, was a Kaveliner Wesson... Had Shinsan penetrated Kavelin?

"Derel!"

But Prataxis was gone. Ragnarson wrote names. Oryon. Valther. Mist. Trebilcock. It was time he found out if Michael had learned anything.

"Does anybody know where Haroun went?"

"No. He just disappeared. He didn't even tell Beloul or Rahman. He does that. Everybody complains. He promises, but keeps doing it. I think he will try to get my father."

"If I could contact him, this war might be averted. Your father. Would he listen to you?"

"Yes."

How confident she was after all these years. "He's changed. He's a fat old man now. They say he's crazy."

"I know. People come from the desert to Haroun. They all say that. They say he's betraying the ideals he seized the Peacock Throne for... Men like Nassef changed him."

"Nassef died a long time ago. I killed him."

"A bandit named Nassef is dead. But there are more Nassefs. They have walled my father off and taken control."

"He still has his voice. The Faithful would support him if he spoke publicly. Disharhûn is coming, isn't it?"

Disharhûn was the week of High Holy Days celebrated in Hammad al Nakir. Pilgrims went to Al Rhemish to hear El Murid speak.

Ragnarson was thinking only of Kavelin. If Haroun launched an incursion from Kavelin and Tamerice, and failed, El Murid would have a legitimate case for counteraction. It might initiate a new round of wars.

"Don't I have trouble enough?" he muttered. "Haroun, Haroun, maybe I should've cut your throat years ago."

He still considered Haroun a friend. But he had never really *liked* the man much. A paradox.

Haroun had always been too self-involved.

"Marshall?"

"Derel? Just a minute." To Yasmid, "Will you reveal yourself?"

She replaced her veil. "I'll decide after I see him."

Bragi went to the door. "Ah. Ambassador. Glad you could come."

"I need to speak with you, too, Marshall. Our intelligence…"

"Excuse me. Derel, send for Valther, his wife, and Colonel Oryon."

"He just…"

"I know. Something came up. On Balfour. I need to see him again. And see if anybody knows where Trebilcock is."

"On my way." Prataxis wasn't pleased. His own work suffered more and more while he handled tasks Gjerdrum should have done.

"Thank you, Ambassador. Come in."

Habibullah cast a suspicious glance at the woman.

"Yes. That bandit bin Yousif…"

"I know. And you know why, too, don't you?"

"What?"

"There's an interesting story going around. About a man who paid to have a friend of mine kidnapped. Who also happens to be a friend of the bandit you mentioned."

Habibullah refused to react.

"You've probably heard the story yourself. Especially the part about the kidnappers failing to deliver their goods." He retold Yasmid's tale.

"Where did you hear this fairy tale?"

"Several sources. Today, from this lady."

Habibullah eyed her again. "Why would Shinsan kidnap a fat fakir?"

"Good question. I've even wondered why El Murid's agents would try it."

Habibullah started to make excuses.

"Yes, I know. But these days we're pretending to have forgiven and forgotten.

Doesn't El Murid say that to forgive is divine?"

"What the fat man did was a crime against God Himself…"

"No, Habibullah."

The ambassador turned.

Yasmid said, "You hate him because he made a fool of you." To Ragnarson, "The men of my people can forgive a wound, an insult, a murder. Habibullah has. But he can't forget the pain of being made a fool before his friends in the Invincibles. No. Habibullah, admit it. He told you those stories and showed you those tricks, and you believed he was your friend. You spoke for him to me. And he tricked you. That's why you risked another war to get him."

"Who are you? Marshall?"

Ragnarson smiled, licked his lips. "Mr. Habibullah, I think you suspect already."

Yasmid dropped her veil.

Habibullah stared. And it wasn't her boldness that astonished him. "No. This's some trick, Marshall. Have you leagued with the minions of Hell? You call up the dead to mock me?"

"I think Habibullah was in love with me. I didn't realize it then. I think a lot of them were."

"My Lady."

Ragnarson gaped as Habibullah knelt, head bowed, and extended his arms, wrists crossed. It was an ultimate gesture, the surrender to slavery.

Ragnarson could no longer doubt her genuineness.

"Rise, Habibullah." She replaced her veil.

"What would My Lady have of me?"

"Speak honestly with the Marshall."

"I've gotten what I needed. Except this: Can you escort the Lady to her father? More successfully than you did my friend?"

Habibullah became El Murid's ambassador once more. "Why?"

"I've got no use for your boss. I wouldn't shed a tear if somebody stuck a knife in his gizzard. The world would be better off. That's why I don't bother bin Yousif any more than I have to to keep the peace with Hammad al Nakir.

"But that peace is critical to me now, with Shinsan sticking its nose into Kavelin. I'm grasping at straws. I need my flanks free. Yasmid implies that she'll be the go-between in arranging a truce between her father and her husband."

"Her husband?"

"Bin Yousif. You didn't know?" Got him now, Ragnarson thought.

"It's true," Yasmid said. "And it was my choice, Habibullah." She explained how she had engineered the recent peace.

"Unlike the Marshall, I'm not concerned with Shinsan. But I'll play his game to keep my men from murdering each other."

"Are there children?" Habibullah asked. "He mourns the fact that he has no grandchildren. The wars cost him that hope."

"A son. Megelin Micah bin Haroun."

"That would please him." El Murid's name had been Micah al Rhami before the Lord had called him.

"It would make more sense to send your son," Ragnarson observed. "That way each principal holds the other's child hostage."

"No. Megelin would murder his grandfather."

"The risks should be equalized."

"I've decided, Marshall. I'll take the risks."

"Ambassador?"

"Yes?"

"Will you escort her? Or are you committed to this war you've made almost inevitable?"

"I haven't kissed the Harish dagger. I didn't realize the results would be so grave. One fat man. A nothing, from the slums. Who'd notice? Who'd care? I still don't understand."

"And I don't understand why you want him after so long."

"I'll do it. For the Lady Yasmid."

"Good. Let me know how it goes. Oh. A favor. Whenever you get another wild hair, get approval from Al Rhemish."

Habibullah smiled thinly. "My Lady?" He offered a hand. "Is there anything else?"

"No." She rose.

"Then we'll go to the embassy. We'll leave as soon as guards can be assembled."

Ragnarson saw them past the door of Derel's office. Already they were playing remember when.

He settled in to wait for Oryon, Valther, and Mist. He should get at that paperwork... Instead, he closed his eyes.

It was strange, the twists fate could take. So Haroun had a wife. Amazing.

FIFTEEN: SPRING, 1011 AFE
THE STRANGER'S APPOINTMENT

They jumped him when he left the inn. There were three of them again, and this time he wasn't ready. But they weren't professionals.

He was.

The plain-hilted sword made a soft *schwang* sound as it cleared his scabbard.

One of them nicked his arm, but that was it. They weren't very good. Peace had reigned for a long time in Hammerfest. He cut them up and laid them down in twenty seconds, before they could scream for help.

Then he stepped inside. "Guro."

He spoke softly, but his voice brought the woman rushing downstairs. She looked at him, and her face became a study in horror.

He tossed a coin. "Three more. In the street."

"You… You…"

"I didn't draw the first blade, Guro. I came to see a man. I'll see him. Why did they die? Must I slay every man in Hammerfest? I will. Tell them. I'm leaving now. I hope I won't have to pay for any more funerals."

He stepped over the neatly ranked bodies. Each bore a small crown-shaped brand on its forehead.

He strode uphill, his blade sheathed once more. He doubted that anyone would be bold enough to attack him now. He had already killed the best men in town.

When he passed the last building he looked back. Storybook town, storybook houses, filled with storybook people—till the sun went down.

Hammerfest would lose its fairy tale luster as the news spread.

Hell had visited this night.

He lifted his gaze to the crumbling little castle.

His man was there.

Was he awake? Waiting?

Certainly. *He* would be, in the man's position. Waiting for word of success—or of failure. Or for the intended victim to come asking questions.

A thin, cruel little smile crossed his lips.

It was a cold, chill walk. Each time he glanced back more windows showed light. Guro was busy.

Would they have the nerve to come after him? To save a man who had sent six of them to their deaths?

He came within bowshot of the curtain wall. His guerrilla's sensitivities probed for another ambush. Senses beyond the human also reached out. He detected nothing outside the keep. Inside, there were three life-sparks.

Just three? Even a tumbledown, cruddy little shed of a castle rated a bigger garrison. Especially when one of the sparks was female.

He paused, thought. There seemed to be a numerological relationship… Three assassins in his room. Three outside the inn. Three here.

Woman or not, she was part of it.

How? Women seldom bore swords in Trolledyngja.

A witch. That had to be the answer.

Then they knew he was coming.

Though he knew where they waited, he poked around like a man carefully searching. They knew a hunter was coming, but not who.

He used the time to prepare himself for the witch.

He readied his most powerful, most reliable spells. Though these Trolledyngjan wild women had little reputation, he hadn't survived thirty years under the sword without being cautious.

He probed. Still all in one room. And nothing sorcerous waiting anywhere else.

Whatever, it would happen there.

Again, they couldn't know who he was, only that he had come from the south. They would want to know who and why before they killed him.

They were going to be surprised.

He approached their room with right hand on sword hilt and left protruding from his greatcloak. He had the position of the woman fixed clearly in mind.

Now!

His left forefinger felt as though he had jabbed it into fire.

The woman screamed.

He stepped inside. The thin, cruel smile was on his lips. He tipped back his hood.

The woman kept screaming. She was strong. She had survived.

The others stared. The fat one with the mane gone silver had to be the Thane of Hammerfest.

"Bin Yousif!" the other gasped.

"Colonel Balfour. You seem surprised." He threw back his cloak. "He was my friend."

Balfour didn't reply.

"He has other friends," said Haroun. "I'm just the first to arrive." His left forefinger jabbed again. The woman stopped screaming. Another cruel smile. "You. Do you want to see the sun rise?"

The heavy man nodded. He was too frightened, too shocked, to speak.

"Then get up—carefully—and go down to Bors's inn. They need someone to tell them what to do. And don't look back."

The man went out like a whipped dog.

"He'll find his courage," Balfour predicted.

"Possibly. Having a mob behind you helps. Now. We talk."

"You talk."

"You have one chance to get out of this alive, Balfour. It's remote. It requires the leopard to change its spots. It requires you to tell me the truth despite your training. You want to be stubborn, you won't live out the night. And I'll get what I want anyway."

"You'll starve up here before you can break me."

"Perhaps. If I restrict myself to the physical." Haroun shifted to the tongue of ancient Ilkazar, now used only liturgically in Hammad al Nakir and by western sorcerers. He made a lifting gesture with his left hand.

The dead woman stood.

Haroun's fingers danced.

The witch took a clumsy step.

"You see? I master the Power now. The King of Hammad al Nakir is also his people's chief shaghûn."

The shaghûn belonged to a quasi-religious sorcerer's brotherhood. He served with military units, aided priests, advised leaders. He seldom was powerful.

Haroun had been born a fourth son. Distant not only from the Peacock Throne but from his father's Wahligate, he had started training to become chief shaghûn of his father's province.

Time and the efficiency of El Murid's assassins had made him chief claimant to the Peacock Throne. He had been smart enough, quick enough, murderous enough, to stay alive and maintain his pretense to the crown. After a two-decade interruption he had resumed his studies, and now he bent the Power to pursuit of his usurped Throne.

Balfour didn't respond.

"You see?" Haroun said again.

Balfour remained firm.

Haroun again spoke the tongue of emperors.

A dark umbra formed round the witch's head. She spoke.

She hadn't much to tell. This was a minor Nine, its only noteworthy member the man who had come north to hide.

Haroun squeezed his fingers into a fist. The woman dropped, tightened into a fetal ball.

"Colonel? Must I?"

Despite the draft in that old stone pile, Balfour was wet with sweat. But he was a hard man himself. Suddenly, he sprang.

Haroun expected it.

Below, villagers filled Hammerfest's streets, their torches painting the storybook houses with terrible, crawling shadows. They watched the castle, and shuddered each time it reverberated to one of those horrible cries.

They were being torn from a throat which couldn't respond to the will trying to control it.

Balfour was stubborn. He withstood Haroun's worst for hours. But Haroun's torments weren't physical, which a stubborn man could school himself to ignore. These were torments of the mind, of the soul. Witch-man Haroun bin Yousif conjured demons he sent into the soldier. They clawed through mind and soul and took control of his mouth, babbling both truth and lies. Haroun repeated his questions again and again. In the end he thought he had gotten everything to be had. He thought there were no more secrets…

He finally used his sword.

Then he slept, with corpses to frighten off evil dreams.

Haroun bin Yousif had lived this way for so long that it hardly disturbed him.

He wakened shortly before nightfall, finished what needed finishing, went down the hill.

The Hammerfesters remained in the streets, frightened. The fat man stood before them, shaking.

Haroun drew back his cloak. "You may return to your castle, Thane. I have no need of it now. Wait." He tossed a coin. "Bury them."

That cruel smile crossed his lips.

Nearly twenty men faced him, but eased out of his path. His unrelieved arrogance assured them that they had no choice. This dread man would pay for their funerals too if they argued.

"Thane."

"Yes?"

"Forget your game of Nines. It brings on the dire evils."

"I will, sir."

"I believe you will." Smiling, Haroun went to Bors's inn, took a room. He paid his due, as ever he did—be it in silver or evil.

He fell asleep thinking this Nine had been a puerile little conspiracy, fit for nothing but hiding men who had grown too hot elsewhere. But there were other Nines that might shake the roots of mountains.

Next morning he purchased a horse and rode southward. Traveling alone.

He knew no other way. Even in crowds this dread, deadly man traveled alone.

SIXTEEN: SPRING, 1011 AFE
DEATHS AND DISAPPEARANCES

Ragnarson woke with a start. "Eh?"

"Colonel Oryon, Marshall."

"Thank you, Derel."

His dream had been grim. He had been trapped at the heart of a whirling mandala with good and evil chasing one another around him, the champions of one as vicious as those of the other. The struggle had consumed everything he loved.

Fiana. Elana. Two children. Mocker. Already gone. Who would be next?

Rolf? What had become of Rolf, anyway? Bragi hadn't seen him since returning from Karak Strabger. Commanding the Palace Guard wasn't much, but it was a job, with its duties.

Would it be Haaken? Or Reskird, a friend of two decades? Haroun?

The Haroun he knew and loved was an idealization of the Haroun with whom he had adventured. He didn't know the Haroun of today. Today's Haroun was a different man.

Who else? His children. Especially Ragnar, in whom he saw his immortality. Ahring. Altenkirk. Gjerdrum…They were friends, but they hadn't gotten the grip on his soul the others had, perhaps because he had met them later, after the world had hardened him. Likewise Valther and Mist. Nepanthe, though… He had a soft spot for Nepanthe and Ethrian, his godson.

And for Kavelin. Kavelin had its claws in him. And he couldn't comprehend it.

"Marshall? You wanted to see me?"

"Oh, I'm sorry." Ragnarson's hair had grown shaggy through inattention. He brushed it from his eyes. "Grab a chair. Derel, bring something to sip."

"Your secretary says you've got something new on Balfour."

"Yes. But hang on a minute. There's a couple people I want to sit in."

Valther and Mist were a long time arriving. More than an hour later than he expected. He tried to make small talk, reminiscing about the El Murid Wars, the civil war, basic training at High Crag, whatever he and the Colonel had in common. Oryon waited it out. But he got antsy. He had his evacuation to prepare.

"Derel, what's taking them so long?"

"I don't know, sir. I was told they'd be here as soon as possible."

"Must be a family crisis," Ragnarson told Oryon. "Pretty sickly, their kids. Derel, have you seen Captain Preshka?"

"No sir. I've been meaning to mention it. He hasn't turned in his pay sheets. He's gone to pieces the last week."

"I'll talk to him."

"Here's Valther now, sir."

Valther and Mist filed in, Valther slump-shouldered, pale.

"What happened? You look like death warmed over."

"Trouble. Nepanthe and Ethrian are gone."

"What? How?"

"I don't know. Gundar was the only one who saw what happened. He doesn't make much sense. Says a man came. Nepanthe went away with him. She packed for herself and Ethrian, and went. Gundar thinks the man said he was supposed to take her to Mocker, who's hiding because you and Haroun want to kill him."

"I'll talk to him later. There's got to be more. Derel. Put out the word. How long have they been gone?"

Valther shrugged. "Since this morning. They've got at least four hours' start."

"Another move against us?"

"Probably. This's starting to look big, isn't it?"

"Yeah. I found a new angle, too. That's why I wanted you.

"I had a visitor. Right after you left, Colonel. Bin Yousif's wife."

Bragi let them settle down before adding, "She's also El Murid's daughter. That's not as important as what she told me. About why Haroun has been so peaceful. And about Mocker and Balfour."

He told the story. It elicited a covey of questions.

"Look, I don't have any answers. Valther, fit the pieces into your puzzle. Mist. The man in black. Tervola?"

"He must be. But the mask isn't familiar. It sounds like Chin's, but the black and gold are wrong— We could check. Didn't you capture Chin's mask at Baxendala?"

"There was a mask. I don't know whose."

"Chin. I remember. Get it for me. I'll tell you if it was Chin."

"Derel. See if you can dig the thing up. It's in the Treasury vault. We were going to display it when the army got rich enough to afford its own museum."

Prataxis bowed and departed. His writing materials he left lying in a sarcastic scatter.

"I'm getting that man's goat," Bragi observed. "If Gjerdrum don't get back pretty soon, he'll quit on me. I don't think I can manage without him. Colonel. You haven't said anything."

"I don't know. I don't like it. Our people conspiring with Shinsan? If that came out it could destroy the Guild's credibility."

"Yet you don't dismiss the possibility. How come?"

Three pairs of eyes fixed on Oryon.

"Because of something my adjutant told me. We talked a long time, after this morning."

"Ah?"

"He didn't know what it was about, but he once found a message to Balfour, from High Crag, partially destroyed in the Colonel's fireplace. The little he made out violated standing orders. The message was signed 'The Nine.' I'd heard rumors before that Balfour might be one of the Nine."

"What's that? I've never heard of it."

"Not many people have, even inside High Crag. It's a story that's been going around for several years. It says there's a cabal of senior officers trying to grab control. Whenever one of the old boys dies, you hear somebody say the Nine murdered him.

"The rumors started maybe three years ago. Jan Praeder claimed he had been invited to join the plot. To replace a member who had died. He said he looked into it, didn't like what he saw, and refused. He didn't say much, though, before he was posted to Simballawein, to replace Colonel Therodoxos, supposedly the member who had died. There was no mystery about Therodoxos's passing. He was killed when he interrupted a gang rape. Killed most of them before they finished him. But there were a lot of questions when Praeder died. He was supposedly poisoned by a jealous husband two weeks after arriving."

"Strong circumstantial evidence," said Ragnarson.

"Yes. Circumstance two: there have been eleven deaths in the Citadel since Praeder went down. That's a lot even for old men. Those guys are tough old geezers. Hawkwind is up in his eighties now. Lauder is right behind him. And they're as mean as ever. They go on like they're immortal. The others usually do, too.

"The name, the Nine, I guess, comes from the fact that that would make a majority in Council. To grab control you'd have to have nine conspirators at Councilor level. Balfour was a prime suspect because he was close, despite his youth, and because he was so damned impatient with the traditional mysteries."

"That I can understand," Ragnarson observed. "That was always hokey to me. But I only made the Third Circle. Maybe there's more to it later. I'm supposed to be a general now. Maybe I could go find out."

"You'd start where you left off. You don't short-cut the Seven Steps. Your Guild rank wouldn't mean much inside the Order."

"Why not? Why would they promote me, then?"

"The same reason you don't turn them down. It makes people think you've got the Guild behind you. They want your success to reflect on High Crag.

"I'll never get into the Citadel myself. I can't master the Mysteries of the Sixth Circle. Oh, well. The organizational table is top-heavy anyway."

"Valther? Mist? What do you think?"

Valther shrugged.

His wife replied, "Colonel Oryon sounds honest. He may even sympathize a little. He has stretched his conscience today." She flashed a smile that could melt hearts of bronze. Oryon responded.

She was, simply, inarguably, the most beautiful woman in the world. Before her fall from power in Shinsan she had spent ages engineering her perfection.

"What action will you take. Colonel?" Ragnarson asked.

"I don't know. If I inform High Crag, I'll either start worse rumors or warn the conspiracy—depending on who gets my letter. I'll have to investigate myself, when I get back."

"Well, I've done what I could. Wish we could lay hands on Balfour. Valther. I've given you a whole list of things. Got anything yet?"

"No. I sent a couple men to that inn just before we came over. Told them to grab the next bunch of riders."

"Mist. We need your help. First, locate Nepanthe. Then see if you can call in Visigodred and Zindahjira, and get Varthlokkur cracking."

For an instant the woman's cold beauty gave way to pique. "You can't trust a woman? You don't think I can handle…"

"No. Because you don't want to be involved in this sort of thing anymore. And because I don't think one wizard will be enough. Not when we're toe to toe with Shinsan… Ah. Derel. Well?"

"It's not there."

"It's got to be."

"You find it then. I took the place apart."

"Hey, cool off. I believe you. Mist?"

"Someone took it."

Ragnarson snorted. He needed an expert to tell him that? "Another job for you, Valther."

"I know. Find out who. When am I going to get some sleep?"

"Any time I'm in bed, you steal all you want. I won't be there to raise hell. Mist can help you. Can't you? At least to find out where the mask is now?"

"Yes."

"All right. Derel, I've got two more jobs for you, then I'll leave you alone. One I think you'll like. First, scare up Haaken. Have him meet me at the cemetery. It's time I saw what he did for Elana." He spoke with a throat suddenly tight. "Then write Gjerdrum. Tell him to quit farting around and get his ass back here." He signed a blank piece of paper. "That do you?"

Prataxis's smile was wicked. "Perfect, sir. Absolutely perfect. Oh. I couldn't find Trebilcock."

"Probably whoring around. He runs with a strange crowd. He'll turn up." But Ragnarson was worried. Too many people were out of sight. Michael might have found something and been silenced.

"I'll look for him, too," Mist offered.

"You want to find me someone, find Haroun. Valther, you be home later?"

"I imagine."

"Okay. I'll be out to see how the house is coming. And to talk to Gundar."

"What?"

"I told you to take the house apart to find this Tear of Mimizan, didn't I?"

"Yes."

"Well?"

"Haven't made any headway. My people are all in the field."

"Uhm." Valther was going to have to show more initiative. "Borrow them from Ahring. Or Haaken."

"All right. All right."

"You needn't destroy the house," said Mist. "I'll find it if it's there. I know it well…" Her eyes clouded as she remembered a cruel past, when she had been mistress in Shinsan and warring with the Monitor of Escalon.

She must be getting restless, Ragnarson thought. Being a housewife isn't what she thought. She might need watching, too.

This was getting touchy. The people he *knew* he could trust were being stripped away. Those who, potentially, could help most he didn't dare trust. Wizards. Witches. Mercenaries. People whose prime loyalties were to themselves.

And somebody wanted him dead. He didn't doubt for an instant that the false Harish Cultists' primary mission had been to murder him.

"Enough. There're a thousand things we can discuss. But not now. I'm going to the cemetery. Derel?"

"I'll have a horse readied."

"Someday you'll be rewarded."

"Thank you, sir."

To the others, "Sorry I ran you all over. I'm getting desperate, trying to make sense out of things. I feel like a fly in a spider web, and can't make out the spider."

He strapped on his new sword, donned a heavy coat. The nights were still chilly. He left ahead of his guests.

The cemetery lay on a hill north of Vorgreberg, beginning about a mile beyond the city gates. It was large, having served the city since its founding. All Vorgreberg's dead were buried there. Rich or poor, honored or despised, they lay in the same ground. There were divisions, family areas, parts set off for different religions, ethnic groups, and paupers put down at city expense, but all bodies ended up there somewhere. There were graves in the tens of thousands, mostly marked by simple wooden wands, but some in vast and ornate mausoleums like that of the family Krief, Kavelin's Kings. It was there that, before long, Fiana would be laid to rest.

The sun was on the horizon. A chill wind had come up. Ragnarson entered the open gate. Time and weather seemed appropriate.

"Bigger than I remembered." He had forgotten to ask where Elana lay. He spied gravediggers working in the paupers' section, asked them.

It was near the top of the hill. Haaken had gone all out.

The three new graves were easily spotted. There were no markers yet. Ragnarson decided to keep them simple. Ornateness didn't suit Elana.

He didn't see the leg till he tripped. He felt around.

He had found his missing Commander of the Palace Guard.

Preshka had been dead for hours. At least since morning. Ragnarson rose. His anger was indescribable.

There were flowers under Rolf, wild flowers, the kind Elana had loved. It must have taken him hours to gather them. The season was early... Someone had cut him down on his way to respect the dead.

Ragnarson tripped again.

He found another corpse.

This one he didn't recognize.

He scrambled around in the gloaming, searching amongst the headstones and decorative bushes.

"What're you doing?" Haaken asked.

Ragnarson jumped. He hadn't heard his brother come up. "Counting bodies."

"Eh?"

"Somebody jumped Rolf here, last night or this morning. He did a job on them before they finished him. I found three already."

Haaken searched, too. "That's all you'll find," he said a minute later.

"Why?"

"He was crawling toward her grave when he died. If there'd been any of them left, they wouldn't have let him."

"I wonder."

"What?"

"If they'll run out of assassins before we run out of us." He paused. "Let him lie where he fell."

Haaken understood. "It'll cause talk."

"I don't care. And I won't be buried beside her. I'll die on a battlefield. She always knew that. She should have someone... And he was more true than I."

"He was a tough buzzard," said Haaken. "Lived ten years longer than he had any right. And crippled he takes three of them with him."

"They'd sing him into the sagas at home. I'll miss him."

"You don't seem very upset."

"I halfway expected it. He was looking for it. Anyway, there's been too much. They got Nepanthe and Ethrian this morning."

"What?"

"Somebody talked her into going off with them. Gundar saw them. I'm going over there from here. Why don't you come, too? We've got things to talk about."

"Okay."

"Wait down the hill a minute, then."

Haaken moved off a short distance.

Ragnarson wept then. For his wife and children, and for Rolf. Rolf had been both a true friend and a loyal follower. No one could have asked more of the man than he had given voluntarily. Again Ragnarson affirmed his determination to avenge the dead.

Then he joined Haaken.

"The first thing I need," he said, "is a plan for partial mobilization. I want to start after Oryon crosses into Altea and there's nobody left to argue with me."

Haaken commanded the Vorgreberger Guards, a heavy infantry regiment begat by the force Ragnarson had commanded during the civil war. He was also Bragi's chief of staff.

Jarl Ahring commanded the Queen's Own Horse Guards, consisting of one "battle" of heavy cavalry and two of light. The army Ragnarson was building included another five regular regiments, each numbering six hundred to seven hundred and fifty men organized in three battles. Each regiment regularly drilled twice its number of volunteers, who could be integrated in case of mobilization. The volunteers, in turn, were responsible for training their neighbors. Counting Nordmen and retainers, Marena Dimura scouts and mountain troops, and regular garrisons and border guards, Kavelin could muster a field army of twelve thousand five hundred overnight, and be assured of a steady supply of partially trained replacements.

"How broad a mobilization?" Haaken asked.

"Just alert the ready people at first. But don't bring them in. Let them finish planting. Step up the training."

"You'll scare hell out of our neighbors."

"If they've got guilty consciences... No. The enemy is Shinsan. Let that leak when you issue the orders. No more leaves. Training in full swing from now on. And reinforce Maisak and Karak Strabger. We've got to hold the Gap. I'll do what I can diplomatically. We'll have a first class plenipotentiary."

"Who?"

"Varthlokkur. If they don't listen to him, they won't listen."

"You won't get much backing. I mean, I can take your word that Shinsan is moving again. But you'll have to produce hard evidence to convince other folks."

"I'll work on it. And about two thousand other things. You know, Haroun wanted me to take over as King here. The bastard is crazy. And look what *he* wants to be king of. Hammad al Nakir is a hundred times bigger than Kavelin."

"Hammad al Nakir runs itself. It's got a whole different tradition."

"Could be."

They reached Valther's home. "Any news?" Bragi asked.

"Not much. Nepanthe, Ethrian, Haroun, Rolf... She couldn't find a trace. They're either shielded, or..."

"Or?"

"Dead."

"Rolf's dead. Definitely. We found him in the cemetery. He took three of them with him."

"Three of who?"

"Ones like we had at my house."

"Harish?"

"No pretense this time. But they were the same breed. What about the jewel?"

"It's not there."

"Where'd it go?"

"She doesn't know."

"It keeps piling up, and that's the best we can come up with? Nobody knows anything for sure? But I do. I'll get them if they don't get me first."

"That goes without saying," Haaken remarked sarcastically.

"Eh?"

"They knew that before they started. That's why they tried to kill you first."

"Oh. Where's Gundar? Let's see what he's got to say."

Gundar didn't tell them anything new. His description of Nepanthe's visitor fit the six dead assassins.

"Guess we can kiss her off," Haaken whispered.

"Quiet!" Bragi muttered. "This'll give Valther a bigger stake. Maybe get some action out of him." He felt that Valther was dragging his heels. Why? His brother-in-law kidnapped, his brother murdered... That should have been motivation enough. If Nepanthe didn't move him, Ragnarson reflected, he would have to find a new chief spy.

His paranoia had reached the point where he suspected everyone. Anyone he didn't see working as hard as he—regardless of how hard they hit it when out of his sight—was somehow betraying him.

That, too, may have been part of the enemy plan. A cunning adversary operated on many levels.

SEVENTEEN: SPRING-SUMMER, 1011 AFE
MICHAEL'S ADVENTURE

Michael Trebilcock lay as still and patient as a cat. His gaze never left the house across Lieneke Lane.

He had stumbled onto the foreigners while visiting his friend Aral, whose father had known his own in their younger days. Aral's father was a caravan outfitter fallen on hard times. He survived on military supply contracts given because the family had remained loyal during the rebellion.

The three had left an inn down the block, looking so much like the men Michael had seen at Ragnarson's that he had felt compelled to follow them.

His investigation had been luckless till then. Even with Aral's help he hadn't discovered anything of interest.

Everybody in Vorgreberg believed something was afoot. But anyone who *knew* anything was keeping quiet. There was an undercurrent of fear. Knives had flashed by moonlight; bodies had turned up in rain-damp morning gutters. Few people were interested in risking a premature visit from the Dark Lady.

"Aral!" he had yelled, and they had followed the three here.

One was inside. The others were out of sight, hiding.

Aral Dantice was a short, wide, tough little thug, tempered in the streets during his father's hardship. He didn't look bright. Scars complemented his aura of thuggishness. His problem, his weakness, was a lack of patience. He wouldn't have taken half his scars if he had had enough self-control.

"Let's grab them," Dantice whispered. "If they're the same gang…"

"Easy. Let's find out what they're up to first."

"What they're up to is no good. Let's just cut them up."

"Suppose they're all right? You want to hang?"

Aral was straightforward, Trebilcock thought. You always knew where he stood.

Michael didn't understand their friendship. They had little in common but curiosity and itchy feet, and the past friendship of their fathers. They were opposites in virtually everything.

But Trebilcock didn't understand himself. He was a man without direction. He didn't know why he had come to Kavelin. Friendship for Gjerdrum? Plain wanderlust? Or just his intense need for an excuse not to take over his father's business? He had turned that over to the family accountants to manage and followed Gjerdrum to this incredibly complex little kingdom, never knowing what he was seeking.

There had been few of the adventures he had anticipated. Life had been pretty dull. But now… It had begun to move. His blood, finally, was stirring.

Aral started to rise.

Trebilcock pulled him down. "Hey! Come on!"

"One of them just left."

Michael peered at the house. The man who had gone inside was on the porch, watching the lane. One of his henchmen was running toward town.

"Okay. Follow him. But don't bother him. Let him do whatever he wants. I'll stick to this one."

"Where should we meet?"

"They'll get together again. When they do, so will we. If they don't, I guess we'll meet at your place."

"Right." Dantice scampered along the backside of the hedge where they had hidden. He was built so low that keeping down wasn't difficult.

A woman and boy joined the man on the porch.

The fat man's wife, Michael thought. The boy must be his son.

The woman said something. She seemed nervous. The man nodded. She ducked inside, returned with a bundle. All three hastened along the lane.

Trebilcock crept along behind the hedge, waiting for the third man to act. Nepanthe seemed extremely upset, though she was accompanying the man by choice. She was sneaking away, and was afraid someone would notice.

"That dark guy must've done some fancy talking," Trebilcock muttered.

The third man then followed Nepanthe and her escort once they rounded a bend. When he had made the same turn, Michael went back to the road. He kept his head down. He was passing the Marshall's home. A half-dozen soldiers were there, and might…

"Hey! Michael!"

"Damnit!" It was one of the Horse Guards he bummed with. For once in his life he wished he didn't have so many friends. "'Lo, Tie. How goes it?"

"Fine. Except I think they're getting carried away trying to find things for us to do. Squaring away the Marshall's house, you know what I mean? He's got a wife, he's got a maid and butler and all. Don't seem right…"

So. The word wasn't out. "That's a shame. But you could be out riding around the Gudbrandsdal in the rain."

"You got it. I don't complain to the sergeant. He'd come up with something like that."

"I'd like to hang around and see what's happening, Tie, but I've got a job."

"You?"

"Sure. Not much. Running messages for the Marshall's secretary. But he expects me to get them moved."

"Yeah. All right. Catch you later. Why don't you plop in at the Kit 'N Kettle tonight? Got some girls from Arsen Street coming down… But don't bring that chunky guy. What's his name? Dantice. He busted the place up last time."

"Okay. I'll see. If Prataxis don't keep me running."

"What's with that guy anyway, Mike?"

Trebilcock glanced up the lane. How far ahead were they? "Aral? Don't mind him, Tie. He isn't so bad when you get to know him. Hey. I've got to go."

"Sure. See you later."

Trebilcock walked briskly till his soldier friend could no longer see him. Then he jogged, glancing down the cross lanes to make sure they hadn't turned aside.

He hoped they were headed back to their inn. In Aral's part of town they would be easier to trail.

Luck was with him. That was their destination, and he picked up the rear guard in West Market Street, which was packed with shoppers.

He found Dantice lounging around outside his father's place. That, for Aral, was a near career. "What happened?"

"Not a damned thing. The guy came back to the inn. The others just showed up."

"What're they up to?"

"Mike, I don't know. You're the one playing spy. Ho! Hang on. Here's the first one again."

A dusky man had come to the inn door leading a half-dozen horses.

"Oh-oh," Trebilcock muttered. "What do we do now?"

"How should I know? You're the brains."

"Aral, they're leaving town. I never thought of that. I just thought... Never mind. Here." He slapped a gold piece into Dantice's hand. "Get us a couple horses. Some food and stuff. I'm going to talk to your father."

"Are you crazy?"

"Come on. Why not?"

"You're nuts. All right. You straighten it with the old man."

"Right. Yes. Come on. Hurry. We'll lose them."

"I'm going."

Trebilcock slammed through the door of the Dantice establishment, knocking the bell off its mounting. "Mr. Dantice! Mr. Dantice!"

The older Dantice came from the little office where he kept his accounts. "Hello, Michael. How are you?"

"Mr. Dantice, I need some money. All the money you can give me. Here." He seized pen and paper. "I'll write you a letter of credit. You can take it to Pleskau Brothers. They handle my finances in Vorgreberg."

"Michael, boy, calm down. What's this all about?"

"Mr. Dantice! Hurry!" Trebilcock raced to the door, peeped out. Nepanthe, Ethrian, and the dark men were mounting up. "There's no time. They're leaving. I'm doing a job for the Marshall. I've got to have money. I'm going out of town."

"But…"

"Isn't my credit good?"

"The best." The old man scratched the back of his head. "I just don't understand…"

"I'll explain when we get back. Just give me what you can." He wrote hastily, leaving a blank for the amount.

Puzzled, but wanting to help his son's friend—whom he thought a bit strange, but felt to be a good influence—Dantice retrieved his cash box from hiding.

"Michael, I don't have much here today. 'Bout fifteen nobles, and change."

"That's good. Whatever. We'll only be gone a couple days. It's just so we can eat on the way." He flung himself to the door again. "Hurry. They're almost gone. Come on, Aral. Where are you?"

"Twelve and seven. That's all I can spare, Michael. I have to keep some just in case…"

"Fine. Fine. Ten is plenty, really. If I can't get by…." He signed the credit for ten nobles, scooped coins as fast as the older man could count them out. "Thanks, Mr. Dantice. You're a gem." He kissed the old man.

"Michael!"

"Hey, we'll see you in a few days."

He whipped out the door. Aral was just coming with the horses. "They're all Trego had left."

"We'll switch later. You see where they headed?"

"Up the street. If they leave town, they'll have to use a gate. Different than the west one, right? From here that means the east or south."

"But which? Never mind. Let's see if we can catch up."

They made no friends that day, pushing through the streets the way they did, as if they were the Nordmen of old. They caught Nepanthe's party as it turned into the Palace Road, which ran straight to the east gate.

"Got them now," Trebilcock enthused. "We can swing around and get ahead."

"Why not just pass them?"

"The woman knows me."

"Whatever. You're the boss. What'd the old man say when you told him?"

"What?"

"That I'm going off with you. He's still trying to dump those account books on me."

"Oh, hell. I clean forgot, Aral."

"You didn't tell him?"

"I was too busy trying to get some money."

"Well, he'll live. He's used to me taking off for a couple days whenever I find me a new slut."

But this adventure would last longer than either expected.

Their path wound eastward, through Forbeck and Savernake provinces, often by circuitous routes. The group they tracked avoided all human contact. The two expended a lot of ingenuity maintaining contact while escaping notice.

"They're sure in a hurry," Aral grumped the third morning.

He hadn't complained yet, but his behind was killing him. He wasn't accustomed to long days in the saddle.

"Don't worry. They'll slow down. You'll outlast the woman and boy."

Michael picked the right note. There was no way Aral Dantice was going to be outdone by a kid and a broad in her forties.

Michael finally realized they were getting in deep after they passed Baxendala at night and were approaching Maisak, the last stronghold of Kavelin, high in the Savernake Gap.

There, between Maisak and Baxendala, stood several memorials of the civil war. It was said that broken swords and bones could still be found all through the area.

Two weeks after sneaking past Maisak, Michael and Aral reached a point from which they could see the eastern plains.

"My God! Look, Mike. There's nothing out there. Just grass."

Trebilcock grew nervous. How did people keep from getting lost out there? It was a green grass ocean. Yet the caravans came and went…

They met caravans every day. Traders were racing to get through with early loads, to obtain the best prices. Sometimes the two overhauled an eastbound train and encountered someone they knew. Thus they kept track of their quarry. Later, when they reached the ruins of Gog-Ahlan, they would have to close up. The other party might strike out toward Necremnos, or Throyes, or any of the cities tributary to them. And who knew where they would go from there?

They traded for better horses, foodstuffs, equipment, and weapons along the way, and always got a poor deal. Trebilcock had no mercantile sense whatsoever. He finally surrendered the quartermaster chores to Aral, who was more intimidating in his dickering.

It was in potentially violent confrontations that Michael Trebilcock was intimidating. Men tended to back down when they saw his eyes.

Michael didn't understand, but used it. He felt it was his best weapon. He had trained in arms, as had everyone at the Rebsamen, but didn't consider himself much good. He didn't consider himself good at anything unless he was the best around.

They reached Gog-Ahlan. Aral found a man who was a friend of his father. With Michael's help he wrote the elder Dantice, and wrote a credit on House Dantice, which Michael promised to repay. And they learned that Nepanthe's party was bound for Throyes.

There was no holding Aral to an unswerving purpose that night. Old Gog-Ahlan lay in ruins, a victim of the might of Ilkazar four centuries earlier. On the outskirts, though, a trading city had grown up. Vices were readily available. Aral had energies to dissipate.

It took him two nights. Bowing to the inevitable, Michael tried to keep up. Then, heads spinning, they rode on.

Their quarry moved more leisurely now, safely beyond the reach of Kavelin's Marshall.

The two overhauled them within the week, a hundred miles from Throyes. "Now we go ahead," Michael said. "We'll swing around, too far away to be recognized." That was what two riders overtaking a larger party would do anyway. Out on those wild plains no one trusted anyone else.

Throyes was a sprawl of a city that made Vorgreberg look like a farming village. Most of it wasn't walled, and no one cared who came or went.

Here, for the first time in their lives, they felt like foreigners. They were surrounded by people who were different, who owed them no sympathy. Aral behaved himself.

Four days passed. Their quarry didn't show. Dantice began fretting.

Michael had begun to consider hitting their back trail when Aral said, "Here they come. Finally."

Only one man remained. He was wounded. The woman and boy, though, were hale if still a little frightened.

"Bandits," Trebilcock guessed. "Let's stay behind after this. In case we need to rescue the lady."

"Hey, Mike, I'm ready. Let's do it. My old man must be out of his head by now. You know how long we've been gone?"

"I know. And I think we should stay gone until we find out what's happening."

"We won't get a better chance. That guy's bad hurt."

"No. Let's see where he goes."

The wounded man went to a house in the wealthiest part of town. There he turned the woman and boy over. The man who received them wasn't happy. Neither eavesdropper understood the language, but his tone was clear, if not his reasons.

"What now?" Aral asked.

"We see what happens."

They watched. Aral daringly climbed the garden wall and listened at windows. But he heard nothing of importance.

Two days later the woman and boy returned to the road with a new escort.

"Oh, no," Aral groaned. "Here we go again. We going to follow them to the edge of the world?"

"If we have to."

"Hey, Mike, I didn't sign on for that. A couple days, you said."

"I'm not dragging you. You can go back. Just give me half the money."

"What? You'd be in debtor's prison by tomorrow night. And I ain't riding around out here without nobody to talk to."

"Then you'd better stick with me."

"They can't go far anyway. Argon is the end of the road."

"How do you know?"

"They're heading for the Argon Gate. If they were headed east, they'd go to Necremnos. So they'd head for the Necremnos Gate."

"How do you know where they're heading?"

"You know my old man."

"So?"

"His stories?"

"Oh. Yeah."

Dantice's father bragged endlessly about his youthful adventures, before the El Murid Wars, when he had made a fortune in the eastern trade. Aral, having heard the tales all his life, had a fair notion of where they were.

They reached Argon two weeks later.

Argon, in summer, was an outpost of Hell. The city lay in the delta of the River Roë. That vast river ran in scores of channels there, through hundreds of square miles of marshland.

The city itself, twice the size of Throyes, had been built on delta islands. Each was connected by pontoon bridges to others, and some had canals instead of streets.

The youths' quest took them to the main island, a large, triangular thing with its apex pointing upriver. It was surrounded by walls rising from the river itself.

"Lord, what a fortress," Trebilcock muttered.

Aral was even more impressed. "I thought Dad was a liar. That wall must be a hundred feet high." He pointed toward the northern end of the island, where the walls were the tallest. "How did Ilkazar conquer it?"

"Sorcery," Michael replied. "And there weren't any walls then. They thought the river was enough."

Aral looked back. "Rice paddies. Everywhere."

"They export it to Matayanga mostly. We studied it at school, in Economics. They have a fleet to haul it down the coast."

"Better close it up. We might lose them in the crowd."

The pontoon was crowded. They couldn't find anyone who spoke their language, so couldn't ask why.

The trail led to a huge fortress within the fortress-island.

"The Fadem," Aral guessed. The Fadem was the seat of government for the Argonese imperium, and was occupied by a nameless Queen usually called the Fadema or Matriarch. Argon had been ruled by women for four generations, since Fadema Tenaya had slain the sorcerer-tyrant Aron Lockwurm and had seized his crown.

The men escorting Nepanthe were expected.

"Don't think we'd better try following," Michael said. Nobody had challenged them yet. The streets were full of foreigners, but none were entering the inner fortress.

Trebilcock led the way round the Fadem once. He could study only three walls. The fourth was part of the island wall and dropped into the river. "We've got to get in there," he said.

"You're crazy."

"You keep saying that. And you keep tagging along."

"So I'm crazy, too. How do you figure to do it?"

"It's almost dark. We'll go down there on the south end where the wall is low and climb in."

"Now I know you're crazy."

"They won't expect us. I'll bet nobody ever tried it."

He was right. The Argonese were too much in dread of those who dwelt within the Fadem. They would have labeled the plan a good one for getting dead quick. Suicides traditionally jumped from the high point of the triangular outer wall, where the memorial to the victory over Lockwurm stood.

Trebilcock and Dantice chose the Fadem, though. About midnight, without light, during a driving rain.

"No guards that I can see," Michael murmured as he helped Aral to the battlements.

"Must be the weather."

It had been raining since nightfall. They would learn that, in Argon, it rained every night during summer. And that by day the humidity was brutal.

It took them two hours of grossly incautious flitting from one glassless window to another, attending only those with lights behind their shutters, to find the right room.

"It's her," Aral whispered to Michael, who had to remain behind him on a narrow ledge. They had clawed eighty feet up the outside of a tower to reach that window. "I'll go in and…"

"No! She'd turn us in. Remember, she came because she wanted to. Let's just find out what's up."

Nothing happened for a long time. After resting, Michael slipped a few feet back down and worked his way across beneath the window so he could reach the ledge at the window's far side.

Three hours dragged through the stuttering mills of time. Neither man had ever been more miserable. The rain beat at them. Hard stone below dared them to fall asleep. There was no room to move, to stretch…

Someone entered the room.

Trebilcock came alert when he heard a woman say, "Good evening, Madame," in heavily accented Wesson. "I'm sorry you had to wait so long."

Trebilcock and Dantice peeked through the slats of the shutters. Why the hell don't they put glass in these things? Michael wondered. But Castle Krief, too, had unglazed windows, and weather in Kavelin was more extreme.

Glass was a luxury even kings seldom wasted on windows.

Nepanthe rose from a bed. Ethrian lay sleeping on a couch. "Where is he? When can I see him?"

"Who?"

"My husband."

"I don't understand."

"The men who brought me to Throyes… They said they were taking me to my husband. He sent for me. They had a letter."

"They lied." The woman smiled mockingly. "Permit me. I am Fadema. The Queen of Argon."

No "Pleased to meet you" from Nepanthe. She went to the point. "Why am I here?"

"We had to remove you from Vorgreberg. You might have embarrassed us there."

"Who is us?"

"Madame." Another visitor entered.

"Oh!"

Trebilcock, too, gasped.

He had never seen a Tervola, but he recognized the dress and mask. His heart redoubled its hammering. The man would discover them with his witchery…

"Shinsan!" Nepanthe gasped. "Again."

The Tervola bowed slightly. "We come again, Madame."

"Where's my husband?"

"He's well."

Nepanthe blustered, "You'd better send me home. You lied to me… I have Varthlokkur's protection, you know."

"Indeed I do. I know exactly what you mean to him. It's the main reason we brought you here."

Nepanthe sputtered, fussed, threatened. Her visitors ignored her.

"Madame," said the Tervola, "I suggest you make the best of your stay. Don't make it difficult."

"What's happened to my husband? They told me they were taking me to him."

"I haven't the faintest idea," the Fadema replied.

Nepanthe produced a dagger, hurled herself at the Tervola.

He disarmed her easily. "Fadema, move the boy elsewhere. To keep her civil. We'll speak to you later, Madame."

Nepanthe screamed and kicked and bit, threatened and pleaded. The Tervola held her while the Fadema dragged Ethrian away.

Michael Trebilcock suffered several chivalrous impulses. He didn't fear the Tervola. But he did have a little common sense. It saved his life.

After the Fadema left, the Tervola said, "Your honor and your son are our hostages. Understand?"

"I understand. Varthlokkur and my husband…"

"Will do nothing. That's why you're my captive."

In that he was mistaken. Varthlokkur ignored extortion, and Mocker just became more troublesome. It was in the blood.

"*Your* captive? Isn't this *her* city?"

"She seems to think so. Amusing, isn't it?" His tone grew harsh. "One year. Behave and you'll be free. Otherwise… You know our reputation. Our language has no word for mercy." He departed.

Michael waited five minutes, then crept forward to whisper to Aral… And found Dantice dead asleep.

The idiot had slept through almost the whole thing.

"Ssst!"

Nepanthe responded to his third hiss by approaching the window fearfully.

"What? Who are you? I… I know you."

"From Vorgreberg. My name is Michael Trebilcock. My friend and I followed you here."

"Why?"

"To find out what you were up to. Those men were the same sort who killed the Marshall's wife. And your brother."

She became angry anew. He had a hard time calming her.

"Look, you're in no real danger while they think they can use you to blackmail the wizard and your husband."

"What're you going to do?"

"I thought about bringing you out the window. But they've got your son. You probably wouldn't go…"

"You're right."

"There's nothing I can do for you, then. I can only go home and explain what happened. Maybe the Marshall can do something."

Nepanthe leaned out the window. "The rain's stopped. It's getting light."

Trebilcock groaned.

He and Aral would have to spend the day on that ledge.

Then the Fadema returned. But she stayed only long enough to taunt Nepanthe.

Michael thought he would die before daylight failed. That ledge was murderous. The sun was deadly… Damnable Aral simply crowded the wall and snored.

Trebilcock waited till the rain cleared the streets, then wakened Aral. He spoke with Nepanthe briefly before departing, trying to buoy her hopes.

"We'll ride straight through," he promised. "It won't take long."

Aral groaned.

"Wait," she said. "Before you leave. I want to give you something."

Her captors hadn't bothered searching her effects even after the dagger episode. That arrogant confidence led to a crucial oversight.

She gave Michael a small ebony casket. "Give this to Varthlokkur. Or my brother if you can't find the wizard."

"What is it?"

"Never mind. Just believe that it's important. No matter what, don't let Shinsan get their hands on it. Turran called it the last hope of the west. Someone gave it to me to take care of because she was thinking about… Never mind. Get it to Varthlokkur or my brother. Make sure it doesn't fall while you're going down." She checked his shirt to see if it was safely tucked in. "Oh, was I stupid! If he'd just stay home like normal people… Those men knew just what to say to me. I'm lucky I've got friends to look out for me."

She gave each man a little kiss. "Good luck. And remember about the casket. It's easy to forget."

"We will," Trebilcock told her. "And we'll be back. That's a promise."

"You're bold." She smiled. "Remember, I'm a married lady. Good-bye." She left the window. There was a bounce to her step that would puzzle her jailors for months.

Michael and Aral returned home. And the worst of their journey was getting down that eighty feet of tower.

Exhausted, they reached Vorgreberg during the first week of August. They had been gone nearly three months.

EIGHTEEN: SPRING, 1011 AFE
THE UNBORN

For a week no one dared enter the chamber where Fiana lay, where her child-of-evil was being nurtured by one of the older wickednesses of the world. Even Gjerdrum lacked the courage to intrude. He carried meals to the door, knocked, retreated.

Varthlokkur was indulging in those black arts which had made him so infamous. By week's end he had terrorized both Karak Strabger and Baxendala.

During the day the castle was obscured by a whirling, twisting darkness which throbbed like a heart beating. Its boundaries were sharply defined. The townspeople called it a hole through the walls of Hell. Some claimed to see the denizens of an Outer Domain peering out at the world with unholy hunger.

That was imagination. But the darkness was real, and by night it masked the stars over Karak Strabger. Eldritch lights from within sometimes cast red shadows on the mountains surrounding castle and town. And always there were the sounds, the wicked noises, like the roar of devil hordes praising some mighty demon-lord…

On the floor of the little chamber the sorcerer had laid out a pentagram which formed one face of an amazing construct. Eight feet above the floor floated another pentagram, traced in lines of fire. Rising like the petals of a flower, from the luminescent design on the floor, were five more pentagrams, sharing sides with five pentagrams depending from the design above. The whole formed a twelve-faced gem. Every apex was occupied by a silvery cabalistic symbol which burned cold and bright. Additional symbols writhed on the surfaces of the planes.

The dead Queen lay on a table at the construct's heart. Upon her breast lay the monster she had died to bring into the world. Outside, the wizard worked on.

He called his creation the Winterstorm, though it had nothing to do with weather or season, but, rather, a dead magician's mathematical way of looking at sorcery. It was a gate to powers undreamt even in Shinsan. It had enabled the destruction of the Princes Thaumaturge in times of yore.

Like so many evils, it was terribly beautiful.

For a week Varthlokkur had labored, taking no rest, and little food. Now his hands trembled. His courage wavered. His sense of morality recoiled. The thing he was trying to create would be more evil than he. Darker, possibly, than the incalculable evils of Shinsan. What it did to the world would be determined by his ability to control it—especially in the critical moments approaching. If he failed, he would be just the first to die a grisly death. If he succeeded only partially, it would be but a matter of time till he lost control.

Success had to be complete and absolute. And he was so tired, so hungry, so weak…

But he had no choice. He couldn't stop now. Nor could he turn back. He was committed.

On the edges of his consciousness, out where his heightened senses met the Beyond, he heard the Lords of Chaos chuckling, whispering amongst themselves, casting lots for him… He wasn't that kind of wizard. He refused to make deals. He increased the might of the Winterstorm and *compelled* them to respond to his will. He ordered, and they performed.

They hated him for it. And forever they would wait, tirelessly, patiently, for his fatal slip.

His fiery wand touched several floating symbols. Those beings on the edges of his senses screamed. Agonized, they awaited his commands.

The symbols blazed brighter. Colored shadows frothed over the barren walls. The dark cloud shuddered and swirled round the stronghold. The people of Baxendala locked their shutters and doors. The handful of castle servants huddled downstairs. They would have fled if Gjerdrum had let them.

The Marshall had told him not to let anyone leave till he heard otherwise. The news was to be stifled till Ragnarson had stabilized the political response.

Gjerdrum was devoted to his Queen and Marshall. Though wanting nothing more than to flee himself, he kept his flock inside. Now, with the howl above redoubling, he again prepared to block a rush toward freedom.

Varthlokkur raised his arms and spoke softly to the denizens of the netherworlds. He used the tongue of his childhood.

Those things would respond to any language. But the old tongue, shaped by the wizards of ancient Ilkazar, was precise. It didn't permit ambiguities demons could exploit. He commanded.

The things on the Other Side cringed, whined—and obeyed.

The Queen's corpse surged violently. The terrible infant, englobed in a transparent membrane, still in a fetal curl, levitated. Its head turned. Its eyes opened. It glared at Varthlokkur.

"You see me," the wizard said. "I see you. I command you. You are my servant henceforth." For seven days he had been shaping its hideous mind, teaching it, building on the knowledge of evil stamped on the thing's genes. "Henceforth you shall be known as Radeachar, the Unborn."

The name, Radeachar, meant only "The One Who Serves," without intimations of actual servitude. It had overtones of destruction, of sorcery held ready as a swordsman holds a ready blade. In olden times those sorcerers who had marched with Ilkazar's armies had been entitled Radeachar. The nearest modern equivalent was the shaghûn of Hammad al Nakir.

It fought him. The things he compelled to aid him battled back. He pitted his will and power against the Unborn…

He had to win beyond any shadow of compromise. It lasted thirteen hours. Then he collapsed.

But not before Radeachar had become his lifelong slave, virtually an extension of his own personality.

He slept, unmoving, on the cool stone floor for two days. And, though the blackness had freed the castle, and spring silence reigned, no one dared waken him.

The distraction of Varthlokkur's undertaking allowed Nepanthe, and those who followed her, to slip through the Gap during the time the wizard slept.

Varthlokkur never sensed the nearness of the woman who meant more to him than life itself.

She was married to his son now, but he and she had an agreement. When Mocker died—unless Varthlokkur himself were responsible—she would become his wife. The bargain, woven on the looms of Fate, had made it possible to destroy Nu Li Hsi and Yo Hsi.

He awakened almost too weak to move. From amongst his paraphernalia he secured a small bottle, drank it dry. A warm, temporary strength flooded him. He lay down again, let it work. A half hour later he went downstairs.

"You can turn them loose now," he told Gjerdrum. "What needed doing is done. And Ragnarson has finished in Vorgreberg."

"I haven't had word from him yet."

"You will."

Gjerdrum considered. Varthlokkur was probably right. "Okay. I won't tell them they can leave. But if they get away while my back is turned, that's all right."

"They won't go far. They won't be welcome in Baxendala. They'll stay around till you're ready to leave for Vorgreberg."

Varthlokkur insisted on showing Gjerdrum his masterwork.

Eanredson took one look and retched.

Varthlokkur was hurt. "I'm sorry." He had been proud, forgetting that it took a peculiar breed to appreciate his artistry.

"Come, then," he said. "We'll be needed in Vorgreberg."

"You're going to take that… that… with us?"

Puzzled, Varthlokkur nodded.

"Better do it on the quiet. The very damned quiet, else you'll start a revolution. The black arts aren't popular with the man in the street."

Varthlokkur's feelings were bruised again. His greatest work had to remain hidden? "All right. I'll leave it here."

"Good." Gjerdrum glanced at the Unborn. This time he forced his gorge down.

"You'll get used to it."

"I don't want to. It should've been killed when Wachtel saw what it was."

"You're being very narrow…"

Gjerdrum refused to argue. "If we're going, let's go. I've been away too long. That foreigner, Prataxis, has probably screwed everything up."

They left that afternoon. Gjerdrum kept going through the night. They reached Vorgreberg the next evening, exhausted. Gjerdrum had to invoke the wizard's reputation to keep the servants from scattering with their horror stories.

Gjerdrum and Varthlokkur got no rest. Prataxis dragged them to the Marshall's office immediately.

"About time," Ragnarson said. "You got Derel's letter?"

"No," Gjerdrum replied.

"Must've crossed paths. Just a note telling you to get your butt home."

"I was waiting on him."

"Everything taken care of?"

"I still have to make the servants forget," the wizard replied.

"Won't be necessary. The news is out. The Thing elected me Regent. They're already forming a committee to consider royal candidates."

"There're some things he *should* make them forget," Gjerdrum growled.

Ragnarson glanced at Varthlokkur.

"I performed a few sorceries. They upset him. Before we left, I performed a divination. Very unclear, but two names came through. Badalamen. The Spear of Odessa Khomer."

"Meaning what?"

"I don't know. Badalamen may be a person. The Spear sounds like a mystical weapon. It isn't one I've heard of. And that's unusual. Those things are pretty well known."

"Neither means anything to me," Ragnarson said. He related recent events in Vorgreberg, concluding, "I've prepared for mobilization."

"Before the mercenaries leave?" Gjerdrum asked. "They'll come at you twice as hard…"

"No problem. Oryon wants to go. To poke around High Crag for the connection with Shinsan. Meanwhile, we're going to turn Kavelin upside down. These assassinations and kidnappings have got to stop."

Varthlokkur glowed. "I have the perfect device. The perfect servant, the perfect hunter…"

"Gjerdrum? What's the matter?"

"I saw his perfect hunter."

Ragnarson looked from one to the other.

"The baby," Gjerdrum said. "The demon thing. He kept it alive."

Ragnarson leaned back, closed his eyes, said nothing for a long time. Then, softly, suppressing his revulsion, "Tell me about it."

"I merely salvaged it," the wizard replied. "I did what was necessary so it survived, bound it to me, taught it. It's not as bad as your friend thinks."

"It's horrible. You should have killed it."

"I go with Gjerdrum emotionally. How can it help?"

"It can find the men you want found. And kill them, or bring them to you."

"How'll it tell enemies from friends? When can you begin?"

"I could call it right now. It detects enemies by reading their minds."

The hairs on Bragi's neck bristled. Read minds? In all likelihood it would read everyone, friend or foe. "Let me think about it. Gjerdrum. You brought Fiana?"

Eanredson nodded.

"Good. Set up the funeral. Big as a coronation. With open house here. The works. Vorgreberg is restless. It's time we distracted it some. I've got a feeling there won't be time for fun much longer." He turned to Varthlokkur. "Can we possibly hit Shinsan first?"

"A spoiler? No. They're moving. The old destiny call is echoing from border to border. They've recovered from the war with Escalon and the feud between O Shing and Mist. They're ready. They're short just one element. An enemy. The Tervola want us."

"How do you know?"

"It's no secret. Baxendala shattered the myth of their invincibility. They want to regain that. You just said a Tervola was seen in the Kapenrungs. They're doing the obvious. Softening up. Eliminating men who would resist. Trying for a sure thing. I suggest we loose Radeachar now—before they reach anyone else who shapes the power. Did you find the Tear?"

"Gjerdrum, would you step outside please?" Once Eanredson left, "It hasn't turned up. Mist can't find a trace. She and Valther can't find our enemies, either.

They're either well shielded or gone."

"Why did you ask the boy to go?"

"They got Nepanthe."

The sorcerer rose slowly, face darkening.

"Wait! She's not dead. They kidnapped her. So to speak. My son Gundar heard a man tell her he could take her to Mocker. She and Ethrian went with him. Mist couldn't locate her, though."

"Excuse me. I've got work to do. I'll summon Radeachar. He'll begin bringing your enemies in soon. Then I'll gather the Brotherhood. And see if anyone will loan troops for another Baxendala. This time, I think, we'd better keep after O Shing till he's done for."

He dropped back into the chair. "I'm tired. Weary unto death. This constant struggle with Shinsan has got to end. Us or them, for all time."

Ragnarson countered, "Would that settle anything? Permanently? Aren't there always more evils? If we destroy Shinsan, won't something else arise? Somebody once said that evil is eternal, good fleeting."

"Eternal? I don't know. It's relative. In the eye of the beholder. The Tervola don't think they're evil. They feel we're wicked for resisting destiny. Either way, though, I want rid of Shinsan. A force of equal magnitude isn't likely to rise in my lifetime."

"Wizard, I'm tired too. And emotionally exhausted. I have trouble caring anymore. I've lost so much that I'm numb. Only Kavelin is left. Till we find a new king… Well, I'll keep plugging."

The wizard smiled. "I believe you've found a home, Marshall."

"What? Oh. Yes. I guess. Yes. I still care about Kavelin. But I don't know what to do."

"Trust me. Not forever, but for now. Our interests are congruent. I want peace. I want to escape the machinations of this pestilence in Shinsan. I want Nepanthe…"

"Did *you* grab Mocker?"

"No. I promised Nepanthe. My promises are good. And he's my son…" There was no resentment in his response.

"What?"

"It's true. It's a long story, that doesn't matter now. But he is."

"Uhm. That explains why he isn't afraid of you… Does he know the other thing?"

"No. And he'd better never find out. But back to our congruency of interest. You have my pledge to remain a steadfast ally till Shinsan falls. Or destroys us."

"All right. Destruction seems most likely."

"Maybe. They have the advantages. Unity. Power. A huge army… Why dwell on it? The die is cast. The doom is upon us. The Fates speed us from their bows. I'll go now. You may not see me for a while."

This was the point, according to Prataxis, when the First Great Eastern War began. He selected it primarily because histories need milestones. First causes could be traced back, and back, and back. And heavy, massed combat didn't occur till the Second Great Eastern War. Some authorities argued that Baxendala should be called the First Great Eastern War, and seen separately from Kavelin's civil war. Though the rebels accepted aid from Shinsan, Shinsan's objective in intervening was eventual mastery.

Whatever, this was the moment when, irrevocably, Ragnarson and Varthlokkur committed themselves to destruction of the Dread Empire.

NINETEEN: SUMMER, 1011 AFE
FUNERALS AND ASSASSINS

Haaken rode at his brother's side. Gjerdrum and Derel trailed them. It was the morning after the day following Eanredson's return. He had arranged the funeral quickly, for Victory Day, for whatever symbolic value that might have.

Behind them, Dr. Wachtel rode in a small carriage. He was too fragile for a horse. He would be an important speaker. His honesty was beyond question. His testimony would dispel rumors surrounding the Queen's passing—though he wouldn't tell the whole truth.

The word had spread quickly. The streets were human rivers flowing northward.

Ragnarson told Haaken, "Keep a sharp watch. This mess is perfect for an assassination."

"I'm watching." He glanced around. "Something we should talk about. Ragnar."

"Oh?"

"He's bound for trouble. And he won't listen."

"What is it?"

"A girl."

"That all? Well. The little devil. Ain't fifteen yet… You remember Inger, Hjarlma's daughter, back home? I was about his age when…"

"If you won't take it serious either…"

"Wait. Wait. I do. These southerners worry about that crap. Never understood why. She somebody's daughter?"

"No. Her father's one of Ahring's sergeants. It wouldn't be a political thing. I'm just thinking we've got trouble enough already."

"Okay. I'll talk to him. Where is he, anyway?"

"With Valther and his bunch."

"Maybe I'll keep him closer."

"You keep saying that."

"I get distracted. Damn, I miss Elana." He sagged in his saddle, momentarily overwhelmed by past emotions.

They encountered Valther on the road. Ragnarson asked, "You found anything, Valther?"

"No. Except that there were three men involved in Nepanthe's disappearance. I found their hostelry. The landlord thought they were guards off a caravan from Throyes."

"Ah. And Throyens look pretty much like desert people."

"Same stock. But they wouldn't have told the truth, would they?"

"Why not? Still, even if they were, they were just hired blades. Anything else? Mist?"

"I can't find much. No Nepanthe. No Haroun. No Mocker. Nothing here in Kavelin…"

"Trebilcock," Valther said.

"I'm getting to it."

"What about him?"

"I located him. He and a man named Dantice are in the Savernake Gap. Apparently following Nepanthe."

"What the hell? I told him to keep his ears open, not to… Following? You sure?"

"No."

"I hope so. This could be a real break."

"You want I should send a squadron after them?" Haaken asked. "In case they need help?"

"Let them run free. Trebilcock don't attract much attention. They might lead him to the guy running the assassins. But I'm not doing this right. Valther. She's your sister. What do you think? Should we risk it?"

The spymaster pondered, looked to his wife for support, thought some more. "She seems safe, doesn't she? If they meant her harm, they'd have done it already… I don't know. Using your own sister…"

"You've done it before. For smaller stakes."

"All right. Let it ride. We have Turran to avenge. And my other brothers. Brock. Luxos. Ridyeh. Okay. But I hope this Trebilcock is competent."

"I think so. There's a man under that weird facade."

"I'm trusting you. Now, what about Oryon? He going peacefully?"

"Yes. He's in a hurry to find out what's up at High Crag. I don't like him, but he's okay. He believes in the Guild. Which's a plus now. If someone in the Citadel is conspiring with Shinsan he'll root them out. He'll leave at sunrise. Which reminds me. Gjerdrum. What's planned for tonight?"

There was little festivity this Victory Day, despite Ragnarson's proclamation asking Vorgreberg to give the Guildsmen a good send-off.

"Won't be much," Gjerdrum replied. "Nobody's interested. This." He indicated cemetery and mob. "And politics."

Ragnarson had been elected Regent but his position wasn't unshakeable. The Nordmen already were accusing him of dictatorial excess. And he *had* been high-handed occasionally, especially in preparing for mobilization. He had explained to a handful of supporters in the Thing, but hadn't yet taken his case to the opposition.

He would have to make time. The sympathy generated by his announcement of Elana's murder wouldn't last.

They went up to the Royal Mausoleum. "Everybody in town must be here," Haaken observed. Crowds packed the hillside.

Trumpets sounded in the distance.

"Jarl's coming," Gjerdrum said.

The procession could be seen clearly from the hilltop. The Queen's Own Horse Guards, in full dress, rode ahead of the hearse, behind the heavy battle of Haaken's Vorgrebergers. Immediately behind the hearse were scores of knights in gleaming armor, many of them carefully chosen Nordmen barons. Behind them, afoot, came the leaders of the other ethnic groups, including chieftains of the Marena Dimura. Bringing up the rear was another battle of light horse. So that the glory of the knights wouldn't be eclipsed, no regular heavy cavalry had been included.

This wasn't just a send-off for a monarch, it was a major political event, with shows of unity and fence-mending. Key men had to be honored. Selected loyalists from each ethnic group would deliver eulogies. Members of the diplomatic community would contribute remarks—and watch closely for weaknesses.

Ragnarson's heart throbbed with the measured beat of Vorgreberger drums. "Derel, Gjerdrum, I appreciate this. What would I do without you?"

"You'd make do," Prataxis replied. "You got along without me before I came." Yet he was pleased. His employer tended to take for granted the competence of his associates.

It was a beautiful morning. The sky was intensely blue. A few stately cumulus towers glided sedately eastward. A gentle, chilly breeze teased through the graveyard, but the morning promised a comfortable afternoon. It was that sort of spring day which made it hard to believe there were shadows in the earth. It was a day for lying back in the green, courting cloud castles, thinking how perfect life was. It was a day for dreaming impossible dreams, like the brotherhood of man, world peace, and freedom from hunger.

Even a funeral that was a national enterprise couldn't blunt spirits sharpened by the weather.

The blunting came later, with the endless speeches already wearing the edge off.

Ragnarson had made his speech earlier. Like every speaker before and since, he had been windier than necessary. He had discarded the unification theme prepared by Derel, speaking instead of Fiana and her dreams, then of the threat Kavelin faced. He revealed almost everything, which unsettled his associates.

"Just trying to warn them," he told Valther. "And let them know it's not hopeless."

Secrecy was a fetish with Valther. He didn't tell anybody anything the person didn't absolutely have to know.

The crisis came during acting ambassador Achmed's strained praise of Fiana.

Three men plunged from the crowd, short swords in hand. One went for Valther, one for Mist, the third for Ragnarson. Bragi, arguing with Valther, didn't see them.

Haaken threw himself in front of his brother. He took a stroke along his ribs while dragging Bragi's assailant down. He also tripped the man going for Valther.

Gjerdrum and Derel tried to intercept the third assassin. Both failed.

Mist's eyes widened. Surprise, fear, horror plundered her beauty. The sword bit deeply...

Something like a shouted song parted her lips.

Thunder rolled across the blue sky.

Haaken, two assassins, Gjerdrum, and Prataxis stopped rolling across the hillside. Ragnarson gave up trying to smash heads. Valther stumbled, flung headlong from the impetus of his charge toward his wife. The crowd stopped yelling.

For an instant Mist was enveloped by fire. Then the fire stepped away, leaving behind a feminine silhouette in thick fog. The fire wore Mist's shape.

The assassin screamed and screamed, thrashing like a broken-backed cat. The fire-thing was merciless. It grew brighter and brighter as its victim became a wrinkled, sunburned husk sprinkled with oozing sores.

Finally, it left him.

And turned to the man who had tried for Valther.

The crowd began withdrawing, threatening panic.

"Wait!" Ragnarson bellowed. "It's the enemy of our enemies. It won't harm anybody else."

Nobody believed him. Common folk didn't trust anything about sorcerers and sorcery.

The man who had attacked Haaken ran for it. He and his comrades had been pledged to die, but not like this.

The fire-thing caught him.

"You all right?" Bragi asked Haaken.

"In a minute. He kneed me."

Bragi examined the sword cut. Haaken would need new clothes, and his hauberk the attention of an armorer, but his only injury would be a bruise.

Mist's fire avatar finished the third assassin, floated up thirty feet, hovered. Ragnarson again tried to calm the crowd. A few braver souls listened. The panic began dying.

The fire avatar drifted, hunting enemies.

"Mist," Ragnarson growled, "stop it. You might nail somebody we don't want to lose."

The fire-thing seemed interested in the Nordmen knights. With Nordmen, sedition was a way of thought.

It drifted to the shadow-Mist. They coalesced.

Ragnarson ordered the ceremonies resumed, joined Valther.

Mist was badly wounded, but didn't seem concerned. "I'll heal myself," she gasped. "Won't be a scar." She touched Valther's cheek. "Thank you for trying," she told Gjerdrum.

Then Ragnarson noticed Prataxis. He rushed to the man. What would he do without Derel's steady hand directing the everyday work of his offices?

But Prataxis wasn't dead. He had the same problem as Haaken.

Those who spoke after Achmed gave short speeches. Crowd noise settled to a buzz.

Then the Unborn made its public debut.

It followed the road from Vorgreberg, floating twenty feet high. Beneath, three men marched with jerky steps, frequently stumbling.

The people didn't like what they saw.

Neither did Ragnarson.

The thing in the milky globe was a malformed fetus thrice normal birth-size, and it radiated something that drove people from its path. Its captives, strutting like the living dead, wore faces ripped by silent screams.

Straight to Ragnarson they came. Haaken's Guards interposed themselves. They had seen the Gosik of Aubochon at Baxendala, had seen fell sorceries, but they were frightened. Yet they stood, as they had stood at Baxendala, while facing the terrible might of the Dread Empire.

"Easy," Ragnarson said. "It's on our side."

Unhappy faces turned his way. Men muttered. It wasn't right to form alliances like this.

The automaton-men halted five paces away. Ragnarson saw no life in their eyes.

One's mouth moved. A sepulchral voice said, "These are your enemies. Ask. They will answer."

Ragnarson shuddered. This *thing* of Varthlokkur's... Powerful. And terrifying.

The crowd began evaporating. Fiana had been popular, especially with the majority Wessons, but folks weren't going to bury her if it meant suffering a constant barrage of unpleasant surprises. All they wanted was to run their homes and shops and pretend, to hide from tomorrow.

"What's your name?" Ragnarson demanded.

"Ain Hamaki."

"Why are you here?"

"To slay our enemies."

"Who sent you?"

No response. Ragnarson glanced at the Unborn.

Another captive replied, "He doesn't know. None do. Their leader brought them from Throyes."

"Find the leader."

"He lies behind you."

Ragnarson glanced at the withered bodies.

One husk twitched. Its limbs moved randomly. Slowly, grotesquely, it rose.

The more bold and curious of the crowd, who had waited to see what would happen, also left for town. Even a few soldiers decided they had seen enough.

"Ask," said the dead man.

Ragnarson repeated his questions. He received similar answers. This one had had orders. He had tried to carry them out.

He collapsed into the pile.

Another spoke. He was a leader of Nine. He believed there were eight more Nines preparing Kavelin.

"Preparing Kavelin for what?"

"What is to come."

"Shinsan?"

The Unborn replied, "Perhaps. He didn't know."

"Uhm. Scour the kingdom for the rest of these… Whatever they are."

The three collapsed.

The Unborn whipped away so rapidly the air shrieked.

"Grab them," Ragnarson ordered. "Throw them in the dungeons."

He worried. Their organization had the earmarks of a cult like the Harish, or Merthregul, being used politically. He didn't recognize it, though he had traveled the east in his youth.

"Derel. Gjerdrum. You're educated. That tell you anything?"

Both shook their heads.

"We keep getting information, but we're not learning anything. Nothing fits together."

"If that thing really is going to help," Valther said, "I'd say we've taken the initiative. It should free us of assassins."

Ragnarson smiled thinly. "And save you some work, eh?"

"That too. It dredges up all those people, I'll have time to concentrate on my real job. Keeping tabs on home-grown troublemakers."

"How's Mist?"

"Be like new in a week." Softly, "I'd hoped she wouldn't get involved. Guess our enemies don't see it my way."

"O Shing owes her."

"I know. Nobody ever believes a wizard has retired. We'd better be careful," he added. "When they realize they're doomed, they might try to do as much damage as they can."

He was right. Before week's end Ragnarson had lost Thom Altenkirk, who commanded the Royal Damhorsters, the regiment garrisoning Kavelin's six westernmost provinces, plus three of his strongest supporters in the Thing, his Minister of Finance, the Chairman of Council in Sedlmayr, and a dozen lesser officials and officers who would be missed. There were unsuccessful attacks on most of his major followers. His friend Kildragon, who commanded the Midlands Light in the military zone immediately behind Altenkirk's, established a record by surviving four attacks. The bright side was that the enemy wasn't overly selective. They went for Ragnarson's opponents too. For anyone important.

Many of the assassins taken were native Kaveliner hirelings.

Terrorism declined as the Unborn marched foreigner after foreigner into imprisonment. He captured sixty-three. A handful escaped to neighboring states. Radeachar followed. When its actions couldn't be traced, it amused itself by tormenting them as a cat might.

Kavelin soon became more peaceful than at any time in living memory. When Radeachar patrolled the nights, even the most blackhearted men behaved. A half-dozen swift bringings-to-justice of notorious criminals convinced their lesser brethren that retribution was absolute, inevitable, and final.

It was a peaceful time, a quiet time, but not satisfying. Beneath the surface lay the knowledge that it was just a respite. Ragnarson strove valiantly to order his shaken hierarchy and prepare for the next round. He trained troops relentlessly, ordered the state for war, yet pressed the people to extend themselves in the pursuits of peacetime, trying by sheer will to make Kavelin strong militarily and economically.

Then Michael Trebilcock came home.

Twenty: The Years 1004-1011 AFE
The Dragon Emperor

Shinsan had no recognized capital. Hadn't had since the murder of Tuan Hoa. The Princes Thaumaturge had refused to rest their heads on the same pillows twice. Life itself had depended on baffling the brother's assassins and night-sendings.

The mind of Shinsan's empire rested wherever the Imperial banner flew.

Venerable Huang Tain constituted its intellectual center. The primary temples and universities clustered there.

Chin favored Huang Tain. "There's plenty of space," he argued. "Half the temples are abandoned."

They had been in the city a month, recuperating from the flight homeward. "I'm not comfortable here," O Shing replied. "I grew up on the border." He couldn't define it precisely. Too refined and domesticated? Close. He was a barbarian prince amongst natty, slick priests and professors. And Huang Tain was much too far west...

Lang, Wu, Tran, Feng, and others shared his discomfort. These westerners weren't their kind of people.

While touring Tuan Hoa's palace and gardens—now a museum and park—O Shing paused near one of the numerous orators orbiting the goldfish ponds.

"Chin, I can't follow the dialect. Did he call the Tervola 'bastard offspring of a mating of the dark side of humanity and Truth perverted'?"

"Yes, Lord."

"But..."

"He's harmless." Chin whispered to a city official accompanying them. "Let him rave, Lord. We control the Power."

"They dare not challenge that," said Feng. A sardonic laugh haunted his mask momentarily.

"They call themselves slaves—and enjoy more freedom than scholars anywhere else," Chin observed. "Even in Hellin Daimiel thinkers are more restrained."

"Complete freedom," said Wu. "Except to change anything."

Both O Shing and Chin wondered at his tone.

The official whispered to Chin, who then announced, "This's Kin Kuo-Lin. A history teacher."

The historian raved on, opposing the wind, drawing on his expertise to abominate the Tervola and prove them foredoomed. His mad eyes met O Shing's. He found sympathy there.

I'm incomplete, O Shing thought. As lame in soul as in body. And I'll never heal. Like my leg, it's immutable. But none of us are whole, nor ever will be. Chin. Wu. Feng. They've rejected their chance for wholeness to pursue obsessions. Tran, Lang, and I spent too much time staying alive. Our perspectives are inalterably narrowed to the survival-reactive. In this land, in these alum-flavored times, nobody will have the chance to grow, to find completeness.

Some lives have to be lived in small cages. Tam was sure the walls of his weren't all of others' making.

He chose to show the Imperial banner at Liaontung. He was comfortable with that old sentinel of the east. And Liaontung was a long, long way from the focus of the Tervola's west-glaring obsession.

"I swear. Wu rubbed his hands in glee when Tran told him." Lang giggled. "Chin like to had a stroke. Feng sided with Wu. Watch Wu, Tam. I don't think he's your friend anymore."

"Never was," Tran growled. He still resented Tam's having trusted Tervola expertise before his own.

"That's not fair, Tran. Wu is a paradox. Several men. One *is* my friend. But he isn't in control. Like me, Wu was cut from the wrong bolt. He's damned by his ancestry, too. He has the Power. He yields to it. But he'd rather be Wu the Compassionate."

Tran eyed him uncertainly. The changed, more philosophical, more empathetic Tam, tempered in the crucible of the flight from Baxendala, baffled him. Tran's image of himself as a man of action, immune to serious thought, became a separating gulf in these moments.

To defend his self-image Tran invariably introduced military business.

"The spring classes will graduate twenty thousand," he said, offering a thick report. He still hadn't learned to read well, but had recruited a trustworthy scribe. "Those are Feng's assignment recommendations. Weighted toward the eastern legions, but I can't find real fault. I'd say initial it."

No one could fault O Shing and his Tervola for reinforcing the most reliable legions first.

"Boring," Tam declared five pages in. "These reports can be handled at subordinate levels, Tran. Sometimes I think I'm being swamped just to distract me."

"You want to rule these wolves, you'd better know everything about them," Lang remarked.

"I know. Still, there's got to be a way to get time for things I *want* to do. Tran. Extract me a list of Tervola and Aspirants linked with legions being shorted. And one of Candidates I don't know personally. Lang, arrange for them to visit Liaontung. Maybe I can pick the men who get promoted."

"I like that," said Tran. "We can move the Chins out."

About Chin, Tran had developed an obsession. He *knew* their former hunter remained a secret foe. He went to absurd lengths to make his case. Yet he could prove nothing.

O Shing already pursued a policy of favoritism in promotions. He was popular with the Aspirants. He became more so when he pushed the policy harder. The machinery of army and empire drifted to his control. His hidden enemies recognized the shift, could do little to halt it.

One thing Tam couldn't accomplish. He couldn't convince one Tervola to repudiate the need to avenge Baxendala.

It was a matter of the honor and reputation of an army unaccustomed to defeat.

Feng, in a rare, expansive mood, explained, "The legions had never been defeated. Invincibility was their most potent weapon. It won a hundred bloodless victories.

"They weren't defeated at Baxendala, either. We were. Their commanders. To our everlasting shame. Your Tran understood better than we did, not having had the shock of losing the Power to impair his reason. Our confusion, our panic, our irrational response—hell, our cowardice—killed thousands and stigmatized the survivors."

A moment of raw emotion burned through when Feng declared, "We sacrificed the Imperial Standard, Lord!

"While Baxendala remains unredeemed, while this Ragnarson creature constitutes living proof that the tide of destiny can be stemmed, our enemies will resist when, otherwise, they'd yield. We're paying in blood.

"Lord, the legions are the bones of Shinsan. If we allow even one to be broken, we subject the remainder, and the flesh itself, to a magnified hazard. In the long run, we risk less by pursuing revenge."

"I follow you," O Shing replied. Feng spoke for Feng, privately, but his was the opinion of his class. "In fact, I can't refute you."

Tran, who disagreed with the Tervola by reflex, supported them in this. Every Tervola who managed an audience had a scheme for requiting Baxendala. Stemming the tide devoured Tam's time, making his days processions of boring sameness only infrequently relieved by change or intrigue.

Yet he built.

Five years and six days after the ignominy of Baxendala, Select Fu Piao-Chuong knelt and swore fealty to O Shing. Not to Shinsan, the Throne, or Council, but to an individual. His emperor assigned him an obscure post with a western legion. He bore, under seal, orders to other Aspirants in posts equally obscure.

The night-terrorist Hounds of Shadow struck within the week.

After a second week, Lord Wu, maskless, agitated, appealed, "Lord, what's happening?" He seemed baffled and hurt. "Great men are dying. Commanders of legions have been murdered. Manors and properties have been destroyed. Priests and civil servants have been beaten or killed. Our old followers from the days of hiding are inciting rebellion around the Mienming and Mahai. When we question a captured terrorist he invariably names an Aspirant as his commander. The Aspirant cites you as his authority."

"I'm not surprised."

"Lord! Why have you done this? It's suicide."

"I doubt it."

"Lord! You've truly attacked your Tervola?"

Lang and Tran were surprised, too. They weren't privy to all of O Shing's secrets either. He was developing the byzantine thought-set an emperor of Shinsan needed to survive.

"I deny attacking *my* Tervola, Lord Wu. You'll find no loyal names among those of the dead. The evidence against each was overwhelming. It's been accumulating for years. Years, Lord Wu. And I reserved judgment on a lot of names. I indicted no one because he had been an enemy in the past. Lord Chin lives. His sins are forgiven. The Hounds will pull down only those who stand against me now."

"Yes, Lord." Wu had grown pale.

"It'll continue, Lord Wu. Until it's finished. Those who remain faithful have nothing to fear.

"My days of patience, of gentleness, of caution, have ended. I *will* be emperor. Unquestioned, unchallenged, unbeholden, the way my grandfather was.

If the Council objects, let it prove one dead man wasn't my enemy. Till then the baying of the Hounds of Shadow will keep winding on the back trails of treachery. Let those with cause fear the sound of swift hooves."

Wu carefully bowed himself out.

"There goes a frightened man," Tran remarked. His smile was malicious.

"He has cause," Lang observed. "He's afraid his name will come up."

"It won't," said Tam. "If he's dirty, he's hidden it perfectly."

"Chin's your ringleader," Tran declared.

"Prove it."

"He's right," Lang agreed.

"Is he? Can I face the Council with that? Bring me evidence, Tran. Prove it's not just bitterness talking. Wait! Hear me out. I agree with you. I'm not asleep. But he *looks* as clean as Wu. He doesn't leave tracks. Intuition isn't proof."

Tran bowed slightly, angrily. "Then I'll get proof." He stalked out.

Tam *did* agree. Chin was a viper. But he was the second most powerful man in Shinsan, and logical successor to the empire. His purge would have to be sustained by iron-bound evidence presented at a perfectly timed moment.

Chin would resist. Potential allies had to be politically disarmed beforehand.

The Council, increasingly impatient with O Shing's delay in moving west, were growing cool. Some members would support any move to topple him.

It was a changed Shinsan. A polarized, politicized Shinsan. Even Wu admitted his suspicion that the empire had been better off under the Dual Principate. It had, at least, been stable, if static.

While Tran obsessively rooted for evidence damning Chin, Tam healed old wounds and opened new ones. He studied, and quietly aimed his Hounds at their midnight targets. And futilely persisted in trying to draw the venom of the Tervola's western obsession.

Then, without Tran there to advise them otherwise, he and Lang began riding with the Hounds.

Select Hsien Luen-Chuoung was a Wu favorite, a Commander-of-a-Thousand in the Seventeenth. Such a post usually rated a full Tervola. The evidence was irrefutable. O Shing had, for the sake of peace with Wu, avoided acting earlier.

The unsigned, intercepted note sealed Chuoung's doom.

"Go ahead. Deliver it," Tam told a post rider who was one of his agents. "We'll see who his accomplices are. Lang, start tracing it back." The note had come to his man from another post rider, who in turn had received it at a way station in the west.

The message? *Prepare Nine for Dragon Kill.*

O Shing was the Dragon. It was his symbol, inherited from his father. The sign in the message was his, not the common glyph for dragon, nor even the thaumaturgic symbol.

So, Tam thought. Tran was right, after all, in mistrusting learning. His advice about suborning the post riders had paid off.

"Lang, I want to go on this one myself. Let me know when the wolves are in the trap."

Chuoung, unsuspicious, gathered his co-conspirators immediately.

"It looks bad for Lord Wu," Lang averred as he helped Tam with his armor. The conspirators were all officers of the Seventeenth or important civilians from Wu's staff.

"Maybe. But nobody contacted him. He hasn't shown a sign of moving. And the message came from the west. I think somebody subverted his legion."

"Chin somebody?"

"Maybe. Remembering their confrontations back when, he might want Wu more vulnerable if there was a next time. Come. They'll be waiting."

Twelve Hounds loafed in the forest near the postern. Tam examined them unhappily. These scruffy ruffians were the near-Tervola he had recruited? He had insisted on having the best for this mission. These looked like they were the bandits the Council accused them of being.

Chuoung occupied a manor house a few miles southwest of Liaontung. As Commander-of-a-Thousand he rated a bodyguard of ten. And there would be sorcery. Most of Chuoung's traitor-coven were trained in the Power.

O Shing sent a black sleeping-fog to those guards in barracks.

Thus, six would never know what had happened. To distract the conspirators themselves he raised a foul-tempered arch-salamander...

They were guilty. He listened at a window long enough to be sure before he attacked.

Pure, raging hatred hit him then. Nine men squawked in surprise and fear when he lunged into the room, his bad foot nearly betraying him.

Their wardspells had been neutralized unnoticed by a greater Power.

The salamander blasted through the door.

They weren't prepared. The thing raged, fired the very stone in its fury. Screams ripped through melting Tervola-imitative masks. Scorched flesh odors conquered the night. O Shing retched.

Chuoung tried to strike back.

Lang, from over Tam's shoulder, drove a javelin through a jeweled eye-slit.

"Keep some alive," O Shing gulped as the Hounds swept in.

Too late. The surprise had been too complete, the attack too efficient. In seconds all nine were beyond answering any questions ever. The salamander didn't even leave shades which could be recalled.

O Shing banished the monster before it could completely destroy the room, then searched Chuoung's effects.

He found nothing.

He interrupted his digging an hour later, suddenly realizing that the screaming hadn't stopped. Why not? The conspirators were dead.

He went looking for his Hounds.

They were behaving like western barbarians, murdering, raping, plundering. And Lang was in the thick of it.

Tam spat, disgusted, and limped back to Liaontung alone.

Lang became addicted. He was a born vandal. He began riding every raid, ranging ever farther from Liaontung, using his fraternal ties to acquire ever greater command of the Hounds.

O Shing didn't pay any heed. He was happy to have Lang out of his way.

Lang did love it, making the Hounds his career…

The men attacked didn't accept their fates passively. O Shing lost followers. Yet every raid encouraged recruiting.

A plague swept Shinsan. Rejection of the established order became endemic. And O Shing didn't see the peril, that rebels are always against, never for, and rebellion becomes an end in itself, a serpent devouring its own tail.

It got out of hand. His tool, his weapon, began cutting at its own discretion.

Lords Chin and Wu came to O Shing. Backing them were Ko Feng, Teng, Ho Lin and several other high lords of the Council of Tervola. They were angry, and didn't bother hiding it.

Their appearance was message enough, though Wu insisted on articulating their grievance.

"Last night men wearing the Hound Badge invaded Lord Chin's domains. You challenged the Council to prove you in error. Today the Council insists that you produce proof of Lord Chin's perfidy."

O Shing didn't respond till he had obtained absolute control of his emotions. He had authorized no action against Chin.

He didn't dare be intimidated. "Those were no men of mine. Were they once, I repudiate them now. I said before, I bear Lord Chin no malice. Till he gives me cause otherwise, his enemies will be mine. I'll find these bandits and punish them." He doubted that that would mollify the Council, though.

"They have been punished, Lord," Chin replied. "They're dead. All but one." He gestured.

Soldiers dragged a chained Lang into the presence. The bravado of the night rider had fled him. He was scared sick, and more terrified of Tam than of his captors.

O Shing stared, tormented. "I'll issue orders. Henceforth any who raid, any-where, any time, will be outlawed. They'll be my enemies as well as the enemies of my enemies." Tran misbehaving he would have believed more readily than Lang. "The Terror ends. Henceforth, the Hounds will course outlaws only. Lord Chin, restitution will be made."

"And this one?"

"His actions convict him. I gave my word. The Hounds would strike only where the proof was *absolute*." He didn't flinch from the Tervola's gaze. He wanted Chin to *know* he dared make no mistake.

Lang, Chin, and Wu all seemed astonished because he didn't ask for the gift of a life.

It hurt, but he meant it. To bend these people to his will he was going to have to stop being indecisive and vacillatory. The future demanded a demonstration. Lang had convicted himself. Tam could ache with temptation, but O Shing dared reveal no weakness. The vulture wings of chaos shadowed his empire. He had to take control.

"Lang. Do you have something to say?"

His brother shook his head.

Tam was glad Tran was absent. The hunter's accusatory stare might have withered his resolve. He needed time to develop the habits of autocracy. "Your judgment, Lord Chin. You're the injured party."

Ruby eye-crystals tracked brother and brother. Then one gloved hand removed the cat-gargoyle mask. "It ends here, my Lord. I yield him to you. There's been enough unhappiness between us."

"A good thought, Lord Chin." You guileful snake. "Thank you. Is there anything else?"

"When do we avenge the Imperial Standard?" Feng snarled.

Wu took Feng's elbow. Chin said, "Nothing, Lord. Good day."

The door closed behind Chin. Lang whined, "Were you really going to…?"

"Yes." Tam limped to his communications devices. "I won't tolerate disobedience from anyone. Not even you. I didn't ask to be emperor. I didn't want to be. But here I am. And emperor I'll be. Despite all of you. Understand?"

The following week he ordered the deaths of seventy Hounds. His revolution had to end.

This was the inevitable blood purge of the professional rebels, men for whom the raiding, the fighting, was cause enough. Now the insurrectionists had to give way to the administrators. All Shinsan, he vowed, would become as steady and responsive as it had been during Tuan Hoa's reign. If he could just remain decisive…

Lang's indiscretion precipitated the Change, the Day, the Final, Absolute Decision.

Henceforth Tam would *be* O Shing. Completely, in the manner pioneered by Shinsan's founding tyrant. He would yield, minimally, only to absolute political necessity.

Shinsan's First Nine met in extraordinary session. Every member made sure he could attend. The Nines themselves were imperiled.

The last was still in the doorway when the cat-gargoyle said, "O Shing suspects. His Hounds weren't indulging in random violence. There was a pattern. He was trying to get a fix on who we are and what we're doing. He's suddenly a liability instead of an asset. Tally against him, too, his unremitting resistance to western operations. And his popular support. Question: Has he outlived his usefulness?"

The man in a fanged turtle mask (Lord Wu's current Nine disguise) countered, "I disagree. He's young. Still malleable. He's been subjected to too much pressure in too little time. Remember, he's risen to emperor from slavery in a few short years, without benefit of Tervola time-perspective. We're being too hasty. Ease the pressure. He'll mellow. Don't discard this tool before it's finish-forged. We're close to him. Eliminate his companions so he becomes dependent on our guidance."

Wu argued from the heart, from the identical weak streak that had earned him the sobriquet "the Compassionate." He felt more for O Shing than the youth had ever suspected.

Wu had no sons of his own.

He also argued from ignorance. He didn't know that Lord Chin had to conform to the timetable of a higher Nine.

Chin knew Wu's blind spots.

"I shouldn't have to admonish our brother about security discipline. Yet what he says deserves consideration. I propose a week's recess for reflection before we redefine our policies and goals. Remain available. In the name of the Nine."

One by one they departed, till only Chin and a companion remained. "Do we need another promotion?" the companion asked.

"Not this time, Feng. He spoke from his heart, but he won't desert the Nine. I know him that well."

Chin couldn't say that Wu, probably, couldn't be killed anyway. Mist had failed. And Chin himself, fearing future confrontations, had made several more serious attempts, in Mist's behalf, than his Ehelebe role had demanded. Wu could be slippery, and a terrible, determined enemy.

"As you will."

The bent man appeared after Feng left. "Delay action," he ordered. "But lay the groundwork. O Shing will have to go sometime. He'll resist when the Pracchia's hour arises."

Chin nodded. He needed no orders to do what he planned anyway. Hadn't he sniffed the breeze with Select Chuoung already? The cretin had muffed everything… "And his replacement? He has no heir, and the Pracchia dares not operate openly."

"Shall we say someone with direct responsibility to the Pracchia? Someone seated with the High Nine?"

Chin bowed. He hoped he put enough subservience into what, really, was a restrained gesture of victory. Soon, Shinsan. Later, perhaps, Ehelebe.

"Step up your western operations. The hour of Ehelebe approaches."

This time Chin bowed with more feeling. He enjoyed the intrigues he was running out there. They presented real challenges, and provided genuine results. "I'm handling it personally. It proceeds with absolute precision."

The bent man smiled thinly. "Take care, Lord Chin. You're the Pracchia's most valuable member."

The man in the cat-gargoyle didn't respond. But his mind darted, examining possibilities, rolling the old man's words around to see how much meaning dared be attached. They were playing a subtle, perilous game.

The armies had begun gathering. The storm was about to break upon an unsuspecting west. O Shing had exhausted the tactics of delay. His excuses had perished like roses in the implacable advance of a tornado. The legions had healed. Shinsan was at peace with itself. The Tervola were strong and numerous.

Liaontung bulged with Tervola and their staffs. O Shing had chosen Lord Wu to command the expedition. Wu was putting it together quickly and skillfully, abetted by hungry, eager, cooperative Tervola. Their obsession was about to be fulfilled.

O Shing could no longer back down.

Sometimes he wondered about the consequences of another Baxendala. More often, he worried about those of victory. For a decade, anticipation of this war had colored the Tervolas' every action and thought. It had become part of them. After the west collapsed, what? Would Shinsan turn upon itself, east against west, in a grander, more terrible version of the drama briefly envisioned in the struggle with Mist?

And sometimes he wondered about that eldritch lady. She had given up too easily. For the well-being of Shinsan? Or because she wanted him to play out some brief, violent destiny of his own before renewing her claims?

Neither Tran nor Lang had unearthed any nostalgic sentiment surrounding Mist, but in this land, with its secrecies, sorceries, and conspiracies, anything was possible.

She would have to be eliminated. Merely by living she posed a threat.

Tran returned from the Roë basin, where he had been watching the progress of a curious war. He brought some unusual news.

"It's taken me years," he enthused, bursting into Tam's apartment still filthy from the road. "But I've got Chin. Not enough to prove him your enemy, but enough to nail him for insubordination. Acting without orders. Making policy without consulting the Throne."

Lang arrived. "Calm down. Start from the top. I want to hear this." He gave Tam a wicked look.

O Shing nodded.

"The war in the Roë basin. Chin is orchestrating it. He's been busy the past couple years. Look. Here. He's been skipping all over the west. Chaos followed him like a loyal old hound dog." He offered several pages of hastily scribbled report.

"Lang? Read it. Tran, watch the door. Chin's out of town, but he and Wu are getting like that." He crossed his fingers.

Lang droned through Tran's outline of an odd itinerary. There were numerous gaps, when Chin's whereabouts simply hadn't been determinable, but, equally, enough non-gaps to damn the Tervola for violating his emperor's explicit orders.

They fell to arguing whether action should wait till after the western campaign. O Shing felt Chin would be valuable in that.

Tam dogged the relationship between Wu and Chin, wondering if, for so slight a cause, Lord Wu ought to be put to the question…

They forgot the door.

Lang's eyes suddenly bulged.

O Shing looked up. The moment at The Hag's hut flashed through his mind.

"Wu!" they gasped.

TWENTY-ONE: SUMMER, 1011 AFE
THE KING IS DEAD. LONG LIVE THE KING

The lean, dark man came like a whirlwind from the north. Horses died beneath him. Men died if they tried to slow him. He was more merciless with himself than with anyone else. He was half dead when he reached his headquarters in the Kapenrungs.

Beloul let him sleep twelve hours before telling him about his wife.

He hardly seemed to think before replying, "Bring Megelin."

The boy was his father reflected in a mirror that took away decades. At nineteen he already had a reputation as a hard and brilliant warrior.

"Leave us, Beloul," Haroun said.

Father and son faced one another, the son waiting for the father to speak.

"I have made a long journey," Haroun said. His voice was surprisingly soft. "I couldn't find him."

"Balfour?"

"Him I found. He told me what he knew."

Which wasn't strictly true. Balfour had answered only the questions asked, and even in his agony had shaded his answers. The Colonel had been a strong man.

All during his ride Haroun had pondered what he had learned. And he had planned.

"I didn't find my friend."

"There is this that I cannot understand about you, my father. These two men. Mocker and Ragnarson. You let them shape your life. With victory at your fingertips you abandoned everything to aid Ragnarson in his war with Shinsan."

"There is this that you have to learn, my son. Into each life come people who become more important than any crown. Believe it. Look for it. And accept it. It cannot be explained."

They stared at one another till Haroun continued, "Moreover, they have aided me more than I them, often when it flew in the face of their own interest. For this I owe them. Question. Have you ever heard Beloul—or any of my captains—complain?"

"No."

"Why? I'll tell you why. Because there would be no Peacock Throne for anyone, even El Murid—may the jackals gnaw his bones—if Shinsan occupied the west."

"This I understand. But I also understand that that was not your motive for turning north when you were upon the dogs at Al Rhemish."

"One day you will understand. I hope. Tell me about your mother." Pain marred his words. His long love with the daughter of his enemy made a tempestuous epic. Her defection seemed anticlimactic.

"That, too, I try to understand. It is difficult, my father. But I begin to see. Our people bring scraps of news. They draw outlines for a portrait."

Eyes downcast, Megelin continued, "Were she not my mother, I would not have had the patience to await the information."

"Tell me."

"She means to forge an armistice with the Beast. She went to your friend, Ragnarson. He sent her."

"Ah. She knows my anger. My other friend vanished. She knew I would swoop on the carrion at Al Rhemish. She knew I would destroy them. They have no strength now. They are old men with water for bones. I can sweep them away like the wind sweeps the dust from the Sahel."

"That, too."

"She is his daughter."

"The head understands, my father. The heart protests."

"Listen to your head, then, and do not hate her. I say again, she is his daughter. Think of your father when you think to judge her."

"So my head tells me."

Haroun nodded. "You are wise for your years. It is good. Summon Beloul."

When the general returned, Haroun announced, "I am leaving my work to my son. Two duties war for me. I pass to him the one that may be passed. The one that came upon me in Al Rhemish, so long ago, when Nassef and the Invincibles slew all others who had claim to the Peacock Throne."

"Lord!" Beloul cried. "Do I hear you right? Are you saying you abdicate?"

"You hear me, Beloul."

"But why, Lord? A generation, more, have we fought... We have it in our grasp at last. They are waiting for us, shaking in their boots. They weep in the arms of their women, wondering when we will come. Ten thousand tribesmen have buried swords beneath their tents. They await our coming to dig them up and strike. Ten thousand wait in the camps, eager, knowing the tree of years is to bear fruit at last. Twenty thousand more stir restlessly in the heathen cities, awaiting your summons. Home! A home many have never seen, Lord!"

"Beseech me not, Beloul. Speak to your King. It is in his hands. I have chosen another destiny."

"Should you not consult with the others? Rahman? El Senoussi? Hanasi?…"

"Will they oppose me? Will they stop me?"

"Not if it is your will."

"Have I not said so? I am compelled in another direction. I must discharge old debts."

"Whither, my father? Why?"

"The Dread Empire. O Shing has my friend."

"Lord!" Beloul protested. "Sheer suicide."

"Perhaps. That is why I pass my crown before I go." He knelt before a low table. His hands went to his temples. Immense strain clouded his face. His neck bulged.

Beloul and Megelin thought it a stroke.

Haroun's hands rose suddenly. Something hit the table with a thud.

Lo! A crown materialized.

"The crown of the Golmune Emperors of Ilkazar," Haroun said. "The Crown of Empire. And of what survives. Our Desert of Death. It is incalculably heavy, my son. It possesses you. It drives you. You do things you would loathe in any other man. It's the bloodiest crown ever wrought. It's a greater burden than prize. If you take it up your life will never be your own—till you find the strength to renounce it."

Megelin and Beloul stared. The crown seemed simple, almost fragile, yet it had scored the table.

"Take it up, my son. Become King."

Slowly, Megelin knelt.

"This is best for Hammad al Nakir," Haroun told Beloul. "It will ease the consciences of men of principle. He is not just my son, he is the grandson of the Disciple. Yasmid's story should be well known by now."

"It is," Beloul admitted. The return of El Murid's daughter was the wonder of the desert.

Megelin strained harder than had Haroun. "My father, I cannot lift it."

"You can, have you but the will. I couldn't lift it my first try either."

His thoughts drifted to that faraway morning when he had crowned himself King Without a Throne.

He, at fifteen, with the man for whom Megelin had been named, and a handful of survivors, had been fleeing El Murid's attack on Al Rhemish.

His father and brothers were dead. Nassef, El Murid's diabolical general, called Scourge of God so terrible was he, was close behind. Haroun was the last pretender to the Peacock Throne.

Ahead, in the desert, the ruin of an Imperial watchtower appeared. Something drew him. Within he found a small, bent old man who claimed to be a survivor of the destruction of Ilkazar, who claimed to have been charged with protecting the symbols of Imperial power till a proper candidate arose among the descendants of the Emperors. He begged Haroun to free him from his centuries-long charge.

Haroun finally took the crown—after having as much difficulty as would Megelin later.

Though he was to encroach upon Haroun's life many times, bin Yousif never again encountered that old man. Even now he had no idea whom he had met then, and who had defined his destiny.

Nor did he suspect that the tamperer was the same "angel" who had found a twelve-year-old desert wanderer, sole survivor of a bandit raid on a caravan, had named him El Murid, and had given him his mission.

That old man meddled everywhere, more often than anyone suspected. He often added a twist on the spur of the moment. He remembered, kept his plot-lines straight, and got found out only in retrospects of a century or more.

Things didn't always go his way, though, because he worked with a cast of millions. The imponderables and unpredictables were always at work.

Haroun wouldn't give up his crown just to rescue a friend. Would he?

Beloul's feeling exactly. He became quite difficult while Megelin wrestled the crown.

"Enough!" Haroun declared. "If you won't accept it, and follow Megelin with the faith you've shown me, I'll find an officer who will." Haroun wasn't accustomed to having a decision debated.

"I'm just concerned for the movement…"

"Megelin will lead. He is my son. Megelin. If you feel the need, go to my friend in Vorgreberg. Explain. But tell no one else. Westerners have tongues like the tails of whipped dogs. They wag all the time, whether there is need or not."

With that a barrier broke. Though Megelin's strain remained herculean, he raised the crown, stood, hoisted it overhead, crowned himself.

He staggered, recovered. In a minute he seemed the Megelin of old. The Crown was no longer visible.

"The weight vanishes, my father."

"It's only a seeming, my son. You will feel it again when the crown demands some action the man loathes. Enough now. This is no longer my tent. I must rest. Tomorrow I travel."

"You cannot penetrate Shinsan," Beloul protested. "They will destroy you ere you depart the Pillars of Ivory."

"I will pass the mountains." When Haroun said it, it sounded like accomplished fact. "I will find the man. I have mastered the Power."

He had indeed. He was the strongest adept his people had produced in generations. Yet that had little real meaning. The practice of magic, except in the wastes of Jebal al Alf Dhulquarneni, had been abandoned by the children of Hammad al Nakir. He had become the best for lack of competition.

Varthlokkur, O Shing, Chin, Visigodred, Zindahjira, Mist—they could have withered him at a glance. Excepting O Shing, they were ancient in their witchcraft. He would need a century to overtake the least and laziest.

Haroun still suffered from his ride, yet when he chose a place to rest, he sat and sharpened his sword instead of sleeping again. Sometimes he considered Mocker, and sometimes wandered among his memories. Mostly, he longed for his wife. The peaceful years hadn't been bad.

He hadn't been much of a husband. If he came through this maybe he could make it up to her.

He left before next dawn, slipping away so quietly that only one sentry noticed. The man bid him a quiet farewell. There were tears in both their eyes.

That was why he had chosen to depart stealthily. Some of his men had been fighting for twenty years. He didn't want to feel their grief, to see the accusation in their eyes.

He knew he was betraying them. Most were here for him. They were his weapons. And he was yielding them to an unfamiliar hand…

He wept, this dark, grim man. The years had not desiccated that faculty.

He rode toward the rising sun, and, he believed, out of the pages of history, a free man at last, and less happy than ever.

TWENTY-TWO: SUMMER, 1011 AFE
EYE OF THE STORM

Protected by the Unborn, Kavelin became bucolic. The common folk accepted that happily.

At the Palace they smelled the electricity of the calm before the tempest, yet couldn't keep an edge on. The quiet became possessive.

Even problems like Altea's refusal to permit Oryon passage didn't alter the atmosphere of well-being. Ragnarson quietly arranged transit through Anstokin and Ruderin, and asked caravaneers headed west to follow Oryon. Altea's mercantile houses depended on the eastern trade as much as Kavelin's. The new Altean leadership quickly became less obdurate.

The swift-flying rumor that Haroun had abandoned his armies to his son disturbed no one either. Ragnarson didn't believe it. He felt it a ploy to lull Al Rhemish.

The Thing did little to find a new King. Their one candidate, Fiana's baby brother, fourteen-year-old Lian Melicar Sardygo, didn't want the job. He and his father were downright rude in their refusal of the committee's invitation to visit Kavelin. They said they would come only to visit Fiana's tomb.

Ragnarson, often with Ragnar and Gundar, made a daily pilgrimage to the cemetery. He had the boys pick wild flowers along the lane. Then, till after dark, he would sit by Elana's grave. Too often, he counted headstones. Elana. Inger. Soren. Rolf. And two earlier children who had died soon after birth, before they could be named. He had had them moved here.

Sometimes he took a few flowers to the Royal Mausoleum, to Fiana's plain, glass-topped casket. Varthlokkur's artifices had restored her beauty. She looked as though she might waken… The old, secret smile lay on her lips. She looked peaceful and happy.

There were times, too, when he would visit Turran's grave, his face clouded. Once they had been enemies, and had become allies. He had considered the man almost a brother.

Yet strange things happen.

He felt no resentment, except against himself.

The days passed into weeks and months. He spent ever more time on his morbid jaunts. Prataxis, Gjerdrum, Haaken, Ahring assumed more of his duties. Ragnar began to worry. He had idolized his mother, and, though a little frightened by him, loved his father. He knew it was unhealthy to spend so much time mourning.

He went to Haaken. But Haaken had no suggestions. Blackfang remained steadfast in his belief that the family should return to Trolledyngja. The political compulsion for exile no longer obtained. The Pretender had abdicated—by virtue of a dagger between his ribs. The Old House had been restored. Heroes of the resistance were collecting rewards. Lands were being returned.

Bragi never considered returning, neither when the news first came down, nor now.

Someday he would go. He had family obligations there. But not now. There were greater obligations here.

Except that he was getting nothing accomplished.

Then Michael Trebilcock returned.

Trebilcock finally sought Haaken at the War Office. He had waited hours with Prataxis, and Ragnarson hadn't shown.

Haaken listened. An evil, angry smile invaded his face. It exposed the discolored teeth that had given him his name.

"Boy, this's what we've been waiting for." He strapped on his sword. "Dahl!" he called to his adjutant.

"Sir?"

"It's war. Spread the word. But quietly. You understand? It'll be a call-up."

"Sir? Who?"

"You wouldn't believe me if I told you. Get on it. Come on, man," he told Trebilcock. "We'll find him."

Dantice had remained to one side all afternoon. Now he said, "Mike, I'd better see my father."

"Suit yourself. He could wait another day, couldn't he? If you want to see the Marshall…"

"Marshall, smarshall. What's he to me? My Dad's probably half-crazy worrying."

"Okay."

After they parted with Aral, Haaken observed, "I like that boy. He's got perspective." He didn't elaborate, nor did he speak again till they reached the cemetery. Blackfang was no conversationalist.

Trebilcock replied, "The trip changed him."

They found Bragi, Ragnar, and Gundar at Elana's grave, with the usual flowers and tears. Haaken approached quietly, but the boys heard him. Ragnar met his gaze and shrugged.

Haaken sat beside his foster brother. He said nothing till Bragi noticed him.

"What's up, Haaken?" Ragnarson tossed a pebble at an old obelisk. "More bureaucratic pettifoggery?"

"No. It's important this time."

"They've got it made, you know."

"Huh? Who?"

"These people. Nothing but peace under the ground."

"I wonder."

"Do you? Damnit, when I say…"

"Father!"

"What's your problem, boy?"

"You're acting like an ass." He wouldn't have dared had Haaken not been there. Haaken always took his part. He thought.

Ragnarson started to rise. Haaken seized his arm, pulled him back.

Bragi was big. Six-five, and two hundred twenty-five pounds of muscle. His years at the Palace hadn't devoured his vitality.

Haaken was bigger. And stronger. And more stubborn. "The boy's right. Sit down and listen."

Trebilcock seated himself facing them. He wrinkled his nose. He was fastidious. He picked dirt and grass, real and imagined, off his breeches the whole time he told his tale.

Ragnarson wasn't interested, despite Michael's rending the veils of mysteries that had plagued him for months.

"Why didn't you bring them out?" Haaken asked. Michael hadn't told it all earlier.

"They separated her from Ethrian. She wanted to stay. And they had a man there, who wore black, and a golden mask… He would've found us in minutes if he'd known we were there. Probably before we could get out of town."

Ragnarson looked thoughtful when Michael mentioned the man in the mask, then lapsed into indifference again.

"I never saw a city that big… It made Hellin Daimiel look like a farm town. Oh. I almost forgot. She said to bring you this. Well, Varthlokkur, but he isn't around. It might not wait till he finds me." He handed Ragnarson an ebony casket.

Bragi accepted with a slight frown. "Elana's thing." He turned it over and over before trying to open it.

The lid popped up…

The ruby within was alive, was afire. It painted their faces in devil shades.

"Please close it."

They jumped. Swords whined out. They looked upward.

"Close it!"

Ragnarson kicked the lid shut.

Varthlokkur descended from the sky, his vast cloak flapping about him. Above him floated the Unborn.

Trebilcock, Ragnarson thought, at least had the decency to be surprised. Hopefully, someday, he would be afraid, too.

"Where the hell did you come from?" Haaken demanded.

"Afar. Radeachar came for me when he saw the pale man and his companion coming through the Gap. You were hard to locate. What're you doing here?"

Haaken made a gesture which included Ragnarson, Elana's grave, and the Royal Mausoleum.

Meantime, Bragi lost interest again. He sat down, reopened the casket.

"Damnit, I said close it!" Varthlokkur growled.

Ragnarson quietly drew his sword.

High, high above, a tiny rider on a winged steed spied another red flash. He circled lower, passing over unseen because he was invisible from below. He recognized three of the men. "Damn!" he spat. He soared, and raced northward. He didn't notice the great bird which circled higher still.

Varthlokkur shuddered and glanced around, feeling something. But there was nothing to see.

The Unborn darted this way and that. It had felt the presence, too. After a moment it settled into position above Varthlokkur's head.

The others felt it, too. Bragi lowered his blade, looked around, realized what he was doing. Attacking Varthlokkur? With simple steel?

It was getting dark. Ragnar lighted the torches he always brought because his father so often dallied till after nightfall.

The flames repulsed the encroachment of night…

Something shifted, made a small mewling sound beyond the light.

Weapons appeared again. A soft, hissing voice said, "Enough. I come in friendship."

Ragnarson shuddered. He knew that voice. "Zindahjira."

That sorcerer's life-path had crossed his before. The first time had been once too often. Zindahjira wasn't even human—or so Bragi suspected. When this wizard went abroad by daylight, he wrapped himself in a blackness which reversed the function of a torch.

Varthlokkur was the more powerful, the more dread magician, but, at least, came in human form.

Must be what we sensed, Ragnarson thought.

Something else moved at the edge of the firelight. Bragi had the satisfaction of seeing Michael Trebilcock startled.

Two more *things* appeared. One went by the name the Thing With Many Eyes, the other, Gromacki, the Egg of God. Each was as inhuman as Zindahjira, though not of his species.

They were sorcerers of renown and had gathered from the far reaches of the west. With them were a half-dozen men in varied costume. Not a one spoke. Each seated himself on the graveyard grass.

"This's the right place," Haaken muttered.

"Who are they?" Ragnar asked, terrified. Gundar, luckily, had fallen asleep during Michael's story.

Trebilcock kept his sword ready. He was wondering, too.

"The Prime Circle. The chief sorcerers of the west," Haaken whispered.

Cold steel fingers stroked Ragnarson's spine. Fear stalked his nerves. It was a dark day when this group covened, putting their vicious grievances in abeyance. "One's missing," he observed.

When last they had gathered it had been for Baxendala, to greet the eastern sorcery with their own.

An implacable enmity for the Tervola was the one thing they had in common.

"He comes," said the mummylike being called Kierle the Ancient. His words hung on the air like smoke on a still, muggy morning.

An inhuman scream clawed the underbelly of the night. Torchlight momentarily illuminated the undersides of vast wings. A rush of air almost extinguished Ragnar's brands. Anxiously, he lighted more.

The flying colossus hit ground thunderously. "Goddamned clumsy, worthless, boneheaded... Sorry, boss."

A middle-aged dwarf soon strutted into the light. "What the hell is this? Some kind of wake? Any of you bozos got something to drink?"

"Marco," said a gentle voice.

The dwarf shut up and sat. Ragnarson rose, extended a hand. The newcomer was an old friend, Visigodred, Count Mendalayas, from northern Itaskia. Their lives had crossed frequently, and they almost trusted one another.

"We're all here," Varthlokkur observed. "Marshall..."

"Who was that on the winged horse?" Visigodred asked.

Everyone looked puzzled. Including Varthlokkur, who should have understood.

Ragnarson caught it, though. He remembered seeing a winged horse over

Baxendala missed by everyone but himself. He remembered thinking the rider was a mystery which needed solving... But by someone else. Even this convocation couldn't excite him for long.

Varthlokkur went on. "Marshall, I tracked bin Yousif into Trolledyngja, where he had overtaken Colonel Balfour. He's back in the south somewhere now."

Since Bragi didn't ask, Haaken did. "What happened?"

"I don't know. Bin Yousif was thorough. He didn't even leave a shade I could call up. But he got something, fast as he rode south."

"Michael," said Haaken, "tell the wizards your story."

Varthlokkur was in a state before Trebilcock finished. "Shinsan, Shinsan," he muttered. "Always Shinsan. They've done this to force me to obey. How is it that they always cloud my mind? Must be something they did while I studied there... Was she well? Was she safe? Why Argon? Why not Shinsan? Marshall, what'd you do with the jewel? That we must unravel if we're to repulse O Shing again. It won't be just four legions this time."

His words gushed. The man in the golden mask—he must be one of O Shing's craftiest Tervola—had conjured one hell of a dilemna for Varthlokkur.

Dull-eyed, staring at Elana's grave, Ragnarson handed him the casket. Varthlokkur frowned, not understanding Bragi's lassitude.

Haaken touched his cloak diffidently. He beckoned Visigodred, led both a short distance away, explained Bragi's problem.

Behind them, having grown bored, Zindahjira created balls of blue fire, juggled them amongst his several hands. He threw them into the air. They coalesced into a whirling sphere which threw off visible words like sparks flying from a grindstone.

He was a show-off. A loudmouth and a braggart. For some quirky reason, he liked being called Zindahjira the Silent.

The blue words were in many languages, but when they queued up in sentences they invariably proclaimed some libel on Visigodred's character.

Their feud was so old it was antique. What irritated Zindahjira most was that Visigodred wouldn't fight back. He simply neutralized every attack and otherwise ignored the troglodytic wizard.

Visigodred ignored him now, though his assistant, the dwarf, made a few remarks too softly to reach his master's ears. Zindahjira became furious...

This sort of thing had driven Ragnarson to distraction in the past. It symbolized the weakness of the west. The wolves of doom could be snuffling at the windows and doors and everyone would remain immersed in their own petty bickerings. Right now Kiste and Vorhangs were threatening war. The northern provinces of Volstokin were trying to secede to form an independent kingdom, Nonverid. The influence of Itaskia was the only stabilizing force in the patchwork of little states making up the remainder of the west.

It was hard to care about people who didn't care about themselves.

Visigodred and Varthlokkur came to an agreement. The former returned with Haaken. The other went to the Mausoleum of the Kings.

The Prime Circle watched in silence.

The necromancy didn't take long. Neither woman had been dead long.

Even now, with ghosts walking, Michael Trebilcock showed no fear. But Ragnar whimpered.

That alerted Bragi. He drew his sword. What devilment…?

He recognized the wraiths, saw the sadness in their faces, their awareness of one another. "Have you no decency?" he thundered, whirling his blade.

Invisible hands seized him. His weapon slipped from numbed fingers, falling so that it stuck in the soft graveyard earth. The hands compelled him to face the ghosts.

A voice said, "Settle it. Finish it. Make your peace. Slay your grief. A kingdom can't await one man's self-pity." It was no voice he knew. Perhaps it was no voice at all, but the focused thought of that dread circle.

Both women reached out to him. Hurt crossed their faces when they couldn't touch him.

He was compelled to look at them.

There was no hatred, no accusation in his Queen. She didn't blame him for her death. And in Elana there was no damnation for his having failed her, in life or in death. She had known about Fiana. She had forgiven long before her death. In each there was a stubborn insistence that he was doing himself no good with his morbid brooding. He had children to raise and a kingdom to defend. All Elana asked was that he try to understand and forgive her, as she had done for him.

He had forgiven her already. Understanding was more difficult. First he had to understand himself.

He believed he had always done poorly by women. They always paid cruel prices for having been his lovers…

He tried to tell Elana why he had buried Rolf Preshka near her…

She began fading back into her new realm. As did Fiana. He shouted after one, then the other, calling them back. Fiana left him with the thought that the future lay not in a graveyard. He had maneuvered himself into a Regency. Now he must handle it.

Kavelin. Kavelin. Kavelin. Always she thought of Kavelin first.

Well, almost. She had allowed Kavelin to come second occasionally, and had paid a price, her belly ripped by the exit of a thing conceived in the heart of darkness. That darkness was responsible for Elana, too. And two dozen others. His friend Mocker…

Something could be done.

Tendrils of the anger, the outrage, the hatred which had driven him during his ride from Karak Strabger insinuated themselves through his depression. He glanced round, for the first time fully grasped the significance of this gathering.

Kavelin's peace was a false peace behind which darkness marshaled. This mob would not be here were the confrontations not to begin soon.

Nepanthe. Argon. It was all he had to work on. He would pick it up from there...

"Michael. Walk with me. Tell me about Argon." He recovered his sword and strode from the circle, eyes downcast but mind functioning once more.

Early next morning, as the sun broke over the Kapenrungs, he figuratively and literally followed an innkeeper's advice. He went onto the ramparts of Castle Krief and stomped and yelled. This was no quiet alert to the army and reserves, this was a bloody call to a crusade, an emotional appeal calculated to stir a hunger for war.

That innkeeper had been right about the mood of the country folk, the Wesson peasants and Marena Dimura forest-runners.

TWENTY-THREE: SUMMER, 1011 AFE
THE HIDDEN KINGDOM

The winged horse settled gently into the courtyard of Castle Fangdred. The fortress was even more desolate and drear now that Varthlokkur had departed. The small, bent man stalked its cold, dusty halls. When he came to them, he had no trouble passing the spells that had kept Varthlokkur from the chamber atop the Wind Tower.

He paused but a moment there, apparently doing nothing but thinking. Then he nodded and went away.

The winged horse flew eastward, to the land men named Mother of Evil when they didn't call it Dread Empire. From there he flew on to a land so far east that even the Tervola remained ignorant of its existence. The bent man believed it time to employ tools named Badalamen and Magden Norath.

It was morning, but light scarcely penetrated the overcast. Great shoals of cloud beat against the escarpments, piled up, and were driven upward by the Dragon's Teeth. From their dark underbellies they shed heavy, wet snow.

The air stirred in the chamber atop the Wind Tower. Dust moved as if disturbed by elfin footfalls.

A single muscle twitched in the cheek of the old man on the stone throne. Varthlokkur had said his former friend neither lived nor was dead. He was waiting. And his next passage through the world would be his last. He had been burned out in a life extended beyond that of any other living creature (excepting the Star Rider), and by the things he had had to do.

He had even died once and, a little late, been resurrected.

It remained to be seen how much the Dark Lady had claimed of him.

An eyelid, a finger, a calf muscle, twitched. His naked flesh became covered with goose bumps.

His chest heaved. Air rushed in, wheezed out. Dust flew. Minutes passed. The old man drew another breath.

One eye opened, roved the room.

Now a hand moved, creeping like an arthritic spider. It tumbled a glass vial from the throne's arm. The tinkle of breakage was a crash in a chamber that had known silence for years.

Ruby clouds billowed, obscuring half the room. The old man breathed deeply. Life coursed through his immobile limbs. It was a more powerful draft than ever he had wakened to before, but never before had he been so near death.

He heaved himself upright, tottered to a cabinet where his witch tools were stored. He seized a container, drained it of a bitter liquid.

He operated almost by instinct. No real thoughts roiled his ancient mind. Perhaps none ever would. Lady Death had held him close.

The liquid refreshed him. In minutes he had almost normal strength.

He abandoned the room, descended a spiral stair to the castle proper. There he drew waiting, ready food from a spell-sealed oven and ate ravenously. He then carried a platter up to the tower chamber.

Still no real thoughts disturbed his mind.

He went to a wall mirror. With sepulchral words and mystic gestures he brought it to life.

A picture formed. It showed falling snow. He placed a chair and small table before it. He sat, nibbled from his tray, and watched. Occasionally, he mumbled. The eye of the mirror roamed the world. He saw some things here, some there. Like a navigator taking starshots he eventually got enough references to fix his position in time. Bewilderment creased his brow. It had been a short sleep. Little more than a decade. What had happened to necessitate his return?

Thoughts were forming now, though most were vagaries, trains of reasoning never completed. The Dark Lady had indeed held him too tightly.

Much of what he had lost could be called will and volition. Knowledge and habit remained. He would be a useful tool in skilled hands.

The hours ground away. He began uncovering events of interest. Something mysterious was happening at the headquarters of the Mercenaries' Guild, where soldiers ran hither and yon, parodying an overturned anthill. Smoke billowed and drifted out to sea. Curious debates were underway at the Royal Palace in Itaskia, and in the Lesser Kingdoms princes were gathering troops. The tiny state called Kavelin was a-hum.

Something was afoot.

A footfall startled him. He turned, A tall, massive man in heavy armor, in his middle twenties apparently, dark of hair and eye, met his gaze. "I am Badalamen. You are to come with me."

The absolute confidence of the man was such that the old man—his only name, that he could remember, was the Old Man of the Mountain—rose. He took three steps before balking. Then, slowly, he turned to his sorcery cabinet.

The warrior looked puzzled, as if no human had ever failed to respond to his commands.

He had been born to command, bred to command, trained from birth to command. His creator-father, Magden Norath, Master of the Laboratories of Ehelebe and second in the Pracchia, had designed him to be unresistible when he issued orders.

His amazement lasted but a moment. He revealed the token Norath had given him. "I speak for he who gave me this."

That medallion changed the Old Man. Radically. He became docile, obedient, began packing an old canvas bag.

There was an island in the east. It was a half-mile long and two hundred yards at its widest, and lay a mile off the easternmost coast. It was rugged and barren. An ancient fortress, erected in stages over centuries, rambled down its stegosaurian spine. The coast to the west was lifeless.

It had been built during the Nawami Crusades, which had broken upon these shores before Shinsan had been a dream.

This land and its ancient wars were unknown in the west. Even the people of the so-called far east were ignorant of its existence. A band of lifeless desert a hundred miles wide scarred that whole coast.

No one remembered. There were few written histories. But the Crusades had been bitter, enduring wars.

The great ones always were. The man who orchestrated them made certain....

The born soldier led the Old Man from the transfer portal to a room where a man in a gray smock leaned over a vast drawing table, sketching by candlelight. Badalamen departed. The man on the stool faced the Old Man.

This was the widest man he had ever seen. And tall. His head was bald, but he had long mustachios and a pointed chin-beard. His facial hair and eyes were dark. There was a hint of the oriental to his features, yet his skin was so colorless veins showed through. Dark lines lurked at the corners of his eyes and mouth, and lay across his forehead like a corduroy road. His head was blockish. He was a gorilla of a man. He could intimidate anyone by sheer bulk.

The Old Man wasn't dismayed. He had seen many men, including some who had exuded more *presence* than this one.

"Hello." Any other visitor might have snickered. The man's high, squeaky voice was too at odds with his physique.

There was a scar across his throat from an attempt on his life.

"I'm Magden Norath." He flashed the medallion Badalamen had shown before. "Come." He led the Old Man to the battlements.

The Old Man began remembering. The near past was gone, but, like a senile woman reliving her childhood, he had no trouble recalling remote details. He had been a player in the drama of the Crusades.

"It's changed," he said. "It's *old*!"

Norath was startled. "You've been here before?"

"With Nahamen the Odite. The High Priestess of Reth."

Norath was puzzled. He had been led to believe that no one knew who had built the fortress.

He knew nothing about it himself, nor did he care. He saw it only as a refuge where he could continue the researches that had caused him to be driven from his homeland, Escalon, a decade before it fell to Shinsan.

"There is no need, then, to explain where we are."

"K'Mar Khevi-tan. It means 'The Stronghold on Khevi Island.'"

Norath eyed him speculatively. "Yes. So. It's that for the Pracchia." A smile bruised his lips. "If Ehelebe has a homeland, this is it. Come. The others have arrived by now."

"Others?"

"The Pracchia. The High Nine."

Enfeebled though his mind was, the Old Man didn't like what he saw.

They had gathered, sure enough, and most wore disguises. Even the bent man, whom he recognized instantly.

Only Badalamen and Norath didn't hide. They had no need.

Norath was the creative genius of the society. Beside Badalamen, he had filled the fortress with the products of other experiments. Most had to be caged.

There was a Tervola in a golden mask. A woman of middle-eastern origins. A masked man clothed as a don of the Rebsamen. A masked general from High Crag. Two more, whose origins the Old Man couldn't place. And one empty seat.

"Our brother couldn't join us," said the small man. "He couldn't leave his bed. It behooves us to consider replacements. He has cancer of the blood. No one survives that—though he whom I have summoned, had he his whole mind, might have arrested it. Sit, my friend."

The Old Man took the empty chair.

The Tervola spoke. "Question. How do we deal with this monster created by Varthlokkur? It betrays our agents everywhere."

Others agreed. The Mercenary added, "It's demoralized the working Nines. We're on the run. Our people are cowering in the Hidden Places to escape the Unborn. In Kavelin it merely collected them. Now that it haunts the entire west, it's killing. Cruelly. It's kept us from moving for weeks. I've lost touch with what's going on in Kavelin. Maybe our brother from Shinsan, with his sight, has seen."

Golden Mask shook his head. "Not only the Unborn is there. Varthlokkur is. Mist is. They've veiled the country. Only the living eye itself can see there."

And a certain mirror, but the Old Man volunteered nothing.

He who was first said, "I was there last night. In the evening. I was bound toward High Crag when I noticed a red light. Descending, I saw Varthlokkur, the Regent, and three more men gathered over the Tear of Mimizan…"

A susurrus ran through the room. Norath growled, "I thought it had disappeared."

"It reappeared. In a cemetery, with five men. And, about to join them, every wizard of consequence in those parts."

The susurrus ran round again.

"They're forewarned. And forearmed. We'll have to move fast," said the general.

"That will require the strength of Shinsan. And Shinsan is not yet ours," said Golden Mask. "O Shing remains reluctant."

"Then we have to buy time."

"Or convince O Shing."

"I can't overcome the Unborn," said Golden Mask. "We can't buy time without that."

"We could," said the bent man. "Unless O Shing moves, they have the edge—while their sorcery holds. But they're not united. My Lady," he said to one woman, "prepare your army. General, move your Guild forces east. Find a provocation. Secure that pass and hold it till O Shing arrives. Itaskia won't interfere. El Murid's no threat either. He's fat and weak. We may use him to add to the confusion."

"And their wizards?" Golden Mask asked.

"They'll be neutralized."

The Tervola peered intently. "And ourselves? Will we be deprived, too?"

"There are cycles of Power. We're entering an epoch of irregularity. My contribution is the ability to predict the shifts. Unfortunately, the effect isn't localized. But we can take advantage. It becomes a plain military matter, then, for the general and Badalamen. Why worry so?"

"Because things are happening that surpass my understanding. I feel forces working and can't control them. There're too many unpredictables."

"That gives it spice, my friend. Spice. There's no pleasure in the sure thing."

The man in the mask said no more. But spice didn't interest him.

"Enough," said the other. "Return home, to your assignments. We'll meet monthly after this. Quickly, now. The Power will wane soon."

When the last had departed, the bent man shed his disguise, approached the Old Man. "Well, old friend, here we are again. Am I too secretive? Would they tear me apart if they knew? You say nothing. No. I suppose not. You're not the man you were. I'm sorry. But there's too much to keep up with. It seems the scope of things, to be successful, has to be bigger each time. And the bigger, the harder to control. And these days there's ever less time to plan, to prepare. Now I have to keep several currents running, have to anticipate next stages before present ones are finalized. The Shinsan era is still a-building toward climax, and already I have to input Ehelebe. Time was, we had centuries. We had almost four between the Ilkazar and El Murid epics. The birth epic of Shinsan lasted two generations. The Nawami Crusades spanned five hundred years. Remember Torginol and The Palace of Love? A masterwork, that was… Old friend, I'm tired. Old and tired. Burned out. The sentence, surely, must be near its end. Surely *They* must free me if there's nothing left when this's done."

He whispered in the Old Man's ear. "This time it's the holocaust. There are no more ideas. No more epics to play out on this tortured stage.

"Old friend, I want to go home."

The Old Man sat like a statue. A handful of memories had been cast into the turgid pool of his mind. He struggled to catch them.

He had lost a lot. Even his name and origins.

The bent man took his hand. "Be with me for a time. Help me not to be alone."

Loneliness was a curse that had been set upon him ages past.

Once, in some dim, unremembered yesterday, he had sinned. His punishment was countless corporeal centuries, alone, directing diversions which would please *Them,* and possibly move *Them* to forgive…

He had said it himself. Things had become too complex to control.

The Guild general stepped from the portal into his apartment—and the cauldron of an unbelievable battle. He had no opportunity to learn what had happened. Two elderly, iron-hearted gentlemen, to whom the Guild meant more than life itself, awaited him.

"Hawkwind! Lauder! What…?"

They said nothing. Sentence had been passed.

They were old, but they could still swing swords.

TWENTY-FOUR: SUMMER, 1011 AFE
KAVELIN A-MARCH

The volunteers poured in. Campfires dotted every patch of unused land.

"They must be coming out of the ground," Ragnarson observed.

Haaken stood beside him on the wall. "It is hard to believe. So many. Who's doing the work?"

"Yeah. Some will have to go home. You sorted out the ones we want?" Haaken, Reskird, and his other staffers had found trebled work dumped upon them. Kavelin, preparing for war, could no longer proceed on inertia.

Ragnarson had to devote his entire energy to being Regent. He had to browbeat the Thing into accepting this venture, and to prepare a caretaker regime for his absence. Gjerdrum had gotten that job, primarily because his father, Eanred Tarlson, had been a national hero trusted by every class.

Gjerdrum thought being left behind worse than being accused of treason.

Haaken, Reskird, and the other zone commandants had selected six thousand men for Ragnarson's expeditionary force. On a backbone of regulars they had fleshed a corpus of the best reserves and most promising volunteers. A force of equal strength would be left with Gjerdrum.

It would be essentially an infantry force. The venture had raised little enthusiasm among the Nordmen, whence the trained knights came. Ragnarson would take a mere two hundred fifty heavy cavalry, counting those of the Queen's Own. Fleshed out, Ahring would field a thousand men, only half of whom were real horse soldiers. Most were light horse, skirmishers, messengers, and the like.

The infantry would be the Vorgrebergers, the Midlands Light, the South Bows, a battle each from the Damhorsters, Breidenbachers, and Sedlmayr Light, plus a hodgepodge of engineers, select skilled bowmen, and Marena Dimura auxiliaries.

Ragnarson was an inveterate tinkerer. He would have fiddled till he had his force balanced to the last billet. Only Haaken's nagging got him moving.

Ragnarson understood what few of his contemporaries did. That training and discipline were the critical factors in winning battles. That was why little armies whipped big ones. Why Shinsan was so dreaded a foe. Her army was the most disciplined ever formed.

Ragnarson's plan depended on trickery and surprise, and his cabal of wizards.

"I'm nervous," he told his brother. "We're not ready for this."

"We'll never be ready," Haaken countered.

"I know. I know. And it pains me. All right. Get them moving. I'm going back to the Palace."

He soon joined Gjerdrum in the empty War Room. Every available map of the east was posted there. Scribes directed by Prataxis had made copies for field use. His intended route was sketched in red on a master.

He kept worrying. Could he make it without being detected? Could he feed his men on the wild eastern plains?

What about water? Could he trust the maps to show genuine creeks and water holes?

I've got to stop this, he thought. What will be will be.

There was no turning back. If nothing else, even failure would startle Shinsan. His spunk might make O Shing back off awhile, giving the west time to respond to Varthlokkur's warnings.

This was the second time Kavelin had had to be the bulwark. It wasn't fair.

Varthlokkur arrived. He was a pale imitation of the wizard of a week earlier.

"It's still dead?" Bragi asked.

"Absolutely. Even the Unborn is weakened."

For no reason the wizards could determine, the Power had ceased to function six days past. Only the Unborn retained any vitality, and that because it drew on the Winterstorm, partially tapping different sources of energy.

The weakened Radeachar was busy. A spate of enemies had pelted against Kavelin's borders after the Power's failure. Visigodred's assistant, flying the huge roc, was as pressed, scouting beyond the borders.

Radeachar would stay with Gjerdrum. His presence would keep the Nordmen in line.

"Marshall," Prataxis called from the door, "you have a minute? There's a man here you should see."

"Sure. Come on in."

Derel's man wore a Guild uniform. Ragnarson frowned, but let him have his say.

"Colonel Liakopulos, General. Aide to Sir Tury."

Ragnarson shook his hand. "Hawkwind, eh?" He was impressed. Hawkwind was the most famous of High Crag's old men, and justifiably so. He had performed military miracles.

"Colonel Oryon asked me to come. The General approved."

"Yes?"

"Oryon was my friend."

"Was?"

"He died last week."

"Sorry to hear it. What happened?"

"Trouble at High Crag. Oryon was in the thick of it. You know how he was."

"Yes. I know." The main message wouldn't register. Guildsman fighting Guildsman. It couldn't happen. "What?... Explain."

"He threw some wild charges around after he got back. Not at all in character. He always kept his mouth shut before. So people listened. And started digging. I believe he mentioned rumors of a junta trying to take over?"

"He did."

"There was one. We cleaned it out. The leader, General Dainiel, had disappeared from his apartment just before Oryon's return. Hawkwind and Lauder moved in. Six days ago Dainiel reappeared out of thin air. A transfer. It had that Shinsan smell. They cut him down. None of his intimates knew for sure, but thought he'd been to Shinsan to meet with other cabal heads. Dainiel had hinted that they were ready to grab control of the west."

Ragnarson looked for someone to tell "I told you so." Derel was the only one handy. Telling him wouldn't give any satisfaction.

"Thank you for your courtesies. Thank the General. I feel better about the Guild now. Oryon probably mentioned my suspicions."

"He did. The General apologizes for the pressures. The Citadel never planned to force its protection on anyone. That's Dainiel's doing. He wanted a strong force kept near the Savernake Gap.

"We can't offer much restitution right now. It's not much, but Hawkwind offers *my* talents."

Ragnarson raised an eyebrow. "How?"

"Training soldiers is my forte, Marshall. You appear to be mounting an expedition. Yet your men aren't ready. It'll take imaginative leadership to teach on the march."

"It's my biggest headache."

"I can handle it."

There was no arrogance in his manner.

"All right." Ragnarson made the snap decision based on Hawkwind's reputation. "Derel, take Colonel Liakopulos to Blackfang. Tell Haaken to put him in charge of training, and don't bother him."

He remembered the name Liakopulos now. The Colonel had a reputation equal to his self-confidence.

"Thank you, Marshall."

"Uhm." He returned to his maps.

Too late to turn back. Advance parties were already in the Gap. A force had occupied Karak Strabger, to stop eastbound traffic at Baxendala so word wouldn't cross the mountains. Maisak backed the play. No one not authorized by the Marshall traveled east of that stronghold.

The cessation of eastbound trade would itself be a warning that something was happening in Kavelin. Bragi had sent loyal mercantile factors through to hint that another civil war was brewing. The trade community expected something savage to follow Fiana's death.

He had run himself and everyone else ragged. What more could he do?

Go, of course. And hope.

He went.

A post rider overtook him slightly east of Maisak. He brought news from Valther.

"Haaken, listen to this. That kid of Haroun's has invaded Hammad al Nakir." He hadn't anticipated that. "Twenty-five thousand men, Valther says, in six columns. Headed for Al Rhemish."

And Ragnarson had expected Haroun's movement to collapse without him.

This Megelin bore watching.

"What about it?" Haaken asked.

"Will it affect us?"

"How? Unless people think we closed the Gap to cover his rear."

"Possible." His friendship for bin Yousif was well known.

"I hope Megelin makes it. This'll give El Murid an excuse for war."

"Should I turn back?"

"Go on," Varthlokkur advised. "Megelin will hurt him even if he loses. El Murid won't be able to do anything. Cooler heads will prevail before he recovers."

"The numbers worry me," Ragnarson told Haaken. "I didn't realize Haroun could scare up that many men." He turned to Visigodred. "Could Marco fly down there occasionally? To keep track?"

"Too damned much trouble," Marco protested. "Got me hopping like the one-legged whore the day the fleet came in now. What do you think I am? I need to sleep, too. You guys think because I'm half-size I can do twice the work?"

"Marco," said Visigodred.

The dwarf shut up.

"Skip some of your visits to your girlfriends."

"Boss! What'll they do? They can't manage."

Haaken rolled his eyes. Bragi whispered, "He's for real. I've seen him in action.

"So," he said aloud, "we continue. Ragnar, let's catch Jarl."

Ahring commanded the vanguard, a day ahead. He filtered westbound caravans through, then kept anyone from turning back.

The entire Gap was confusion. This was the height of the caravan season. In places several were crowded up nose to tail, their masters muttering obscenities about being shoved around. Ragnarson saw more than one wound. Jarl had had trouble here and there.

He asked questions. Kaveliners returning home answered.

His advent in the east remained unanticipated.

After riding with Ahring a day he took Derel, Ragnar, Trebilcock, and Dantice and forged ahead, to overtake the scouts. In time he passed them, too.

He knew the risk was wild, yet his spirits soared. He was in the field again. Political woes lay a hundred miles behind. He let his beard go feral. Boldly, he took his friends to Gog-Ahlan. He and Ragnar spent a day prowling the ruins and ramshackle taverns and whorehouses.

Rumors of unrest in Kavelin were thick. Less daring traders were staying put till they knew what was happening.

Kavelin's army turned north twenty miles short of the town, following a side valley. It debouched on the plains away from routes frequented by caravans. A screening force broke contact and began herding cognizant caravaneers westward.

Ragnarson tightened his formation. He allowed his light horse troops to roam only a few miles. Marco would watch the plains nomads. Bragi increased the pace, and turned away whenever Marco reported riders approaching.

Marco also patrolled their back trail, to frighten off any nomads threatening to discover it.

A hundred miles east of the ruins of Shemerkhan, following marches of forty miles per day, the Power reasserted itself. The wizards scrambled to take advantage, but it faded before they could get organized.

The Power quickened again next afternoon, and again it faded rapidly.

The sorcerers debated its meaning for hours.

Ragnarson suspected that little man on the winged horse. In the lonely, quiet hours of riding he tried to think of ways to capture the man, to find out who he was and what he was up to. If legends were to be believed, that would be impossible. It had been tried a thousand times. Anyone who attempted it came to grief.

Nearing lands tributary to Necremnos, the army turned south. Bragi took Varthlokkur, Prataxis, Trebilcock, Dantice, and Ragnar into the city. He left Haaken with orders to move to the Roë halfway between Necremnos and Argon, in the narrow zone beholden to neither city.

People lived there. He counted on Marco and the horsemen to cut their communication with Argon.

He didn't plan on staying long. Just while he visited an acquaintance, a Necremnen wizard named Aristithorn.

He wasn't sure the man still lived. His own wizards had heard no reports of Aristithorn's death, though the man had seemed on his last legs back when Bragi had helped him make Itaskia's King Norton honor a debt.

Necremnos hadn't changed in twenty-some years. Varthlokkur said it hadn't since his own last visit, centuries earlier. Old buildings came down and new ones arose, but the stubborn Necremnens refused to borrow from foreigners. New buildings were indistinguishable from those demolished.

Aristithorn maintained a small estate outside the city proper. A miniature castle graced its heart. Continuous moans and wails echoed from within.

"He's very dramatic," Bragi told Varthlokkur. The wizard didn't know Aristithorn.

Aristithorn's door was tall and massive. Upon it hung a knocker of gargantuan proportions. It struck with a deep-voiced boom. That was followed by a sound like the groan of a giant in torment.

"Is this the man who married that princess?" Ragnar asked. "The one that you…."

"Tch-tch," Bragi said. "You forget I told you that story. He's old and retired, but he's still a wizard. And a cranky one."

The massive door swung inward. A voice which could have been that of the tormented giant boomed, *"Enter!"*

"He's changed the place some," Ragnarson observed.

They stood in a long, pillared chamber done in marbles. The only furnishings were several dozen suits of armor. Even whispers echoed there, playing around the chuckling of a fountain at the center of the hall.

Varthlokkur stood at Ragnarson's left. Trebilcock and Dantice remained a step behind, to either flank, facing the walls, their hands on their weapons. Prataxis and Ragnar tucked themselves into the pocket thus formed. The place was intimidating.

"Cut the clowning and get your ass out here," Bragi yelled. "That'll get him in here," he whispered. "He's got this thing about scaring people. Bet you he runs a bluff about turning us into frogs."

He was right, though newts were the creatures mentioned. Decades had passed, but Aristithorn hadn't changed. He had become more of what he had always been. Older, meaner, crankier. He didn't recognize Ragnarson till the third time Bragi interrupted to explain who he was.

And then Aristithorn wasn't pleased. "Back to haunt me, eh? Ye young ingrate. Thought ye got away with it, didn't ye? I tell ye, I knew it all along…" He was speaking of a woman. One of his wives.

Ragnarson had had even less sense about women when he was twenty.

"Let me introduce my companions. Michael Trebilcock. Aral Dantice. Soldiers of fortune. Derel Prataxis, a don of the Rebsamen. Ragnar, my son. And a colleague, Varthlokkur."

"… saw ye two and yere wickedness… Eh?"

"Varthlokkur. Also called the Silent One Who Walks With Grief and the Empire Destroyer."

Varthlokkur met Aristithorn's gaze. He smiled a smile like the one worn by the mongoose before kissing a cobra.

"Eh? Oh, my. Oh. Oh my god. Pthothor preserve us. Now we know. The visitation of Hell. I recant. I plead. Give me back my soul. I should have known when the Power failed me…"

"Was he always like this?" Trebilcock asked. "How'd he stand up to that King Norton?"

"Don't pay any mind. It's all act. Come on, you old fraud. We're not here to hurt you. We want your help. And we'll pay." To the others, "He's got a lot of pull here. I don't know why. Guess they haven't figured out he's ninety percent fake."

"Fake? You… You… Young man, I'll show you who's fake. Don't come croaking in my pond when you're a frog."

"You admitted the Power deserted you."

"Ha! Don't you believe it!"

Varthlokkur interrupted. "Marshall, can we get to the point? Seconds could be critical now. You! Be silent!"

Aristithorn's lips kept moving but no sound came forth. He was doing as directed while indulging an old vice. He had to talk, but didn't have to say anything.

"Old friend," said Ragnarson, "I've risen in the world since our adventure. I'm Marshall and Regent of Kavelin in the Lesser Kingdoms now. I'm marching to war. My army lies just beyond Necremnen territory. No. No worry. Necremnos isn't my target. I'm going to Argon. Yes, I know. Argon hasn't been invaded since Ilkazar managed it. But nobody has gone about it seriously… Why? Because they attacked me. On orders from Shinsan. They murdered my wife, two of my children, some of my friends. And they kidnapped a friend of mine's wife and son. And maybe the friend, too. They're locked up in Argon's Royal Palace. I'm going to punish Argon."

Aristithorn's gaze flitted to Varthlokkur whenever the urge to verbalize became strong. Varthlokkur merely stared.

Aristithorn seemed a mouse, but that was pure show. He was a mortal danger to his enemies.

"What I want is boats. All the boats I can lay hands on. And don't forget, we'll be in your debt. Varthlokkur's ability to meet his obligations has never been questioned."

Ragnarson smiled to himself, pleased with his double entendre. A threat and a promise in one simple declarative sentence—which meant little. Varthlokkur was accepting no obligations himself. This wriggling in the worm pile of politics was making a politician of him, too.

Aristithorn changed. He sloughed the pretense, stood tall and arrogant. "You say Shinsan has its hooks in the Fadem? That would explain some strange things."

"Fadem?" Bragi asked.

"What they call their Royal Palace in Argon," Trebilcock reminded.

"Yes," Aristithorn continued, "Argon has behaved oddly the past few years. And I've heard that a man resembling a Tervola visits there frequently, and came here once. Pthothor gave him short shrift, the story goes. This's bad—if it's true. This's a sad enough earth without Shinsan creeping into its palaces like some night cancer. Yes. This explains things that puzzle the wise. Particularly about the Fadema."

"Queen of Argon," said Trebilcock.

"Boats? Did I hear right?"

"Boats, yes. As many as possible. Big, little, whatever can be had. But quickly. So I can arrive before they know I'm coming, before the Power returns and they can see me with their inner eyes."

"Ye might work it. Argon's defenses be meant to stop land-bound armies."

"Told you he was sharp. Figured it without me telling him a thing."

"Yes, this must be stopped. And Pthothor, with his fear of things Shinsan, and his lust to be remembered as a conqueror... He may join ye."

The old coast reever in Ragnarson became wary instantly. Somebody was hinting about divvying the plunder. Before the booty was gained. "That might be useful," he said, trying to sound noncommittal. "As later support. But the enemy has agents everywhere. We dare not risk ourselves by including anyone in our plan just now. In a week...?"

"My sense of rectitude compels me to assist ye. But there must be balance."

"Derel. The man's ready to dicker. Don't give him the Royal silverware."

Prataxis was a master. With Varthlokkur to handle the intimidation he soon got Aristithorn to agree to what Ragnarson considered bargain terms. A modest amount of cash. A few items believed to be in possession of the Fadema. Kavelin to sponsor his children's educations at the Rebsamen. The university's fame had spread far and wide, and a man from these parts who could honestly claim to have been educated there was guaranteed a high, happy life.

What Ragnarson didn't realize was that Aristithorn had children in droves. His wives were always pregnant, and often bore twins.

Later, as they strolled to the waterfront with the babbling wizard, they were spotted by a chunky brown man who scrambled into shadows and watched them pass. His face contorted into a mixture of surprise and bewilderment. Only Aral Dantice noticed him. He had no idea who the man was. Just another curious easterner...

TWENTY-FIVE: SUMMER, 1011 AFE
THE ASSAULT ON ARGON

Aristithorn did better than Ragnarson expected. His reputation locally was as nasty as Varthlokkur's worldwide. Boat owners, merchant captains, no one refused him more than once. No one quibbled over the vow of silence he extracted. Boats and ships departed, fully crewed, without question of payment being raised, though Ragnarson promised owners and crews a portion of the loot of Argon.

Aristithorn claimed that didn't matter. This was war. If Ragnarson failed, Pthothor would take over. There were old grievances between Necremnos and Argon. The cities were overdue for one of their periodic scrimmages.

So Ragnarson led an armada down the Roë and met Haaken. Three thousand men boarded the vessels, more than he had hoped. His spirits rose. If he remained unnoticed he had a chance.

Aristithorn virtually guaranteed that the Necremnen army would be right behind him. Ragnarson soon hoped so. Argon was huge. A million people lived in its immediate environs. Six thousand men could disappear quickly if the populace fought back.

As Argon drew closer, Bragi found ever more reasons for forgetting the whole thing. But he went on. Worrying was his nature. Haaken had chided him for it since childhood. Sometimes you had to ignore potential difficulties and forge ahead. Otherwise nothing got done.

The first wave consisted of the smallest boats, carrying Marena Dimura mountaineers, attacking at two points. One group drifted down to where the walls of the Fadem rose from the river. The other remained at the apex of the island.

The Marena Dimura scaled the rough walls and established bridgeheads. Their boats returned upriver to Haaken, whose men, weary from slogging through marshes and swimming delta channels, awaited their turns to ride. One battle of the Queen's Own had taken the horses and train back into the plains, to erect a fortified camp a few miles above the Argon-Throyes road.

Ragnarson traveled aboard a galley which served Necremnos's trade in the Sea of Kotsüm. He had filled a dozen such with Haaken's Vorgrebergers, Reskird's Damhorsters, and bowmen. The assault captains were ex-mercenaries who had come to Kavelin with him years ago. They were the shock troops who would expand the bridgeheads.

It went so smoothly he suspected he had a friendly god perched on his shoulder. The Argonese were expecting nothing. As always, when the evening rains came, the wall sentries had scurried for cover. Argon lay as defenseless as a virgin thrown by her protectors to barbarian raiders. Two thousand men were over the walls before they attracted any attention.

The fighting broke out, as Ragnarson had hoped, at the apex of the island. Kildragon, in charge there, immediately began raising the biggest fuss possible.

Ragnarson took his party into the second bridgehead.

There the troops were lying low. The Fadema maintained a personal guard of a thousand, and had regular army units quartered in the Fadem, too. Ragnarson wanted to be as strong as possible before the Argonese counterattacked.

He cleared the top of the wall, scuttled out of the way, gasped, "Didn't think I'd make it. Getting old for this. Jarl? How's it going? You spreading out yet?"

Here the Marena Dimura were doing what they did best, skulking, stabbing in the dark, occupying strongpoints by stealth.

"We've taken everything you can see from here. This's the sloppiest defense I ever saw. We haven't found anybody awake yet. It's too bad Reskird's raising hell up there. We might've grabbed the whole damned place before anybody knew we were here."

"Uhm. Keep moving. Grab what you can while you can. Gods, it's big."

The Fadem alone seemed as big as Vorgreber. Trebilcock said it had thirty thousand permanent residents.

"Michael. Aral," Bragi whispered. "Where's this tower?"

"The squarish one yonder, with the spire sticking up from the corner," Dantice replied.

"Let's see if she's still there."

They descended to street level and slipped through narrow passages between buildings, making of a two-hundred-yard crow flight a quarter-mile walk. They won the distinction of being first to face wakened opponents.

It was over before Ragnarson realized what had happened. The parties stumbled into one another at a sharp turn. Trebilcock disposed of the Argonese in an eye's blink.

Ragnarson's eyebrows rose. Michael could handle a blade damned well.

"It's sixty feet to the first ledge," Trebilcock whispered. "And twenty more to the one by her window. I'll drop a line from the first one..."

"Kid, if you and Aral can make it, so can I." Bragi sheathed his sword, felt for hand and toeholds.

He quickly regretted his bravado.

Trebilcock and Dantice went up like rock apes. Ragnarson had thirty feet to go when they reached the first ledge. His muscles threatened cramps. His fingers were raw when he heaved himself onto the ledge. Looking down, he muttered, "Bragi, you're a fool. You've got men who get paid to do this."

A clash of arms sounded here and there. The defenders still weren't reacting except locally.

Reskird had a good fight going. The uproar reached the Fadem, and the bellies of the rain clouds glowed with firelight.

The last twenty feet were worse. Now he was conscious of how far he could fall. And of his age. And his sword kept beating the backs of his legs.

"We're going down by the stair," he muttered when he rolled onto the upper ledge.

Trebilcock smiled, a thin, humorless thing in the reflected firelight. "Would've been easier if we'd gotten here before the rain."

Ragnarson's stomach flip-flopped as he realized how easily he could have slipped.

Dantice crept back from the window. "Can't tell if there's anybody inside."

A head popped out. Bragi recognized Nepanthe. She didn't see them. "Inside," he growled. "Quick."

Dantice went. They heard his sword clear its scabbard. Trebilcock and Ragnarson plunged after him.

Sounds of struggle, of steel against stone. Dantice cursed. "She bit me!"

"Nepanthe!" Bragi snapped. "Settle down!"

"She started to yell," Dantice said.

"Michael, find a lamp." Ragnarson moved the other way. "Damn!" He bruised his shin on something low.

Someone crashed to the floor. Metal skittered across stone. "Marshall, I'm going to clout her!"

"Easy, son. Nepanthe! It's me. Bragi. Behave yourself."

Cang-chang. Sparks flew. A weak light grew, illuminating Trebilcock's face. As the flame rose, it revealed Nepanthe and Dantice on the floor. Aral had one hand on her mouth, his legs scissored around her. He was fending a dagger with his free hand. Bragi kicked the weapon away.

He grabbed handfuls of Nepanthe's hair and forced her to look at him. "Nepanthe. It's me."

Her eyes widened. Her fear subsided. She relaxed.

"Can you keep quiet now?"

She nodded. He grinned as Dantice's hand bobbed with the motion. "Let her go, Aral. Michael, look at his hand."

Dantice winced when he put weight on that hand while rising. Ragnarson helped Nepanthe up.

"Take a minute," he said as she started babbling. "Get yourself together."

After she calmed down, she explained how the stranger had come to Valther's house and convinced her that Mocker had gone into hiding because Haroun had tried to murder him. He feared Bragi was in on it. The messenger had brought Mocker's dagger as a token. And she had always suspected Haroun of the worst.

"He could do it if he thought he needed to," Bragi observed. "But how would Mocker have been a threat to him?"

"I never thought about it. Not till I found out they tricked me." She started crying. "Look what I got you into. What're you doing here, anyway? Who's watching things at home? I heard about Fiana. They tell me all the bad news."

"I'm here because you are. Because Argon seems to be behind all our trouble."

"No. It's Shinsan. Bragi, there's a Tervola… He controls the Fadema… I think. Maybe they're partners."

"I mean to find out."

"But… You're only one man. Three men." To Michael she said, "Thank you. Did you get the casket to Varthlokkur? And you. I'm sorry. I was scared."

Dantice smiled. "No matter, ma'am." He sucked his injured hand.

"He brought the Tear back, yes. Tell me about the Tervola. Does he wear a golden mask?"

"Yes. How'd…?"

"He keeps turning up. Must be O Shing's special bully boy. And I didn't come by myself. That's our army kicking ass out there."

"But… *Argon!* They took me out once. I think the Fadema wanted to show me what a hick I was. Bragi, you can't get in a war with Argon. Not over me…"

"Too late to back off. The boys are probably too loaded with loot to run." He chuckled. "I don't want to take the city. Just the Fadem. Just to spoil whatever they're up to. I'm no conqueror."

"Bragi, you're making a mistake…"

"Somebody coming," Trebilcock said. He had one ear against the door. "Sounds like a mob."

"Get out of sight. Aral! Your sword."

Dantice scampered back for the weapon.

"Nepanthe, pretend we're not here. They must be coming for you. They'll want their prize counter safe. Get by the window. Make them come to you. Michael, Aral, we'll hit them from behind."

Dantice was a street fighter. He understood. But Michael protested.

"We're here to win, Michael, not get killed honorably."

Ragnarson concealed himself just in time. The door creaked inward. Six soldiers entered, followed by the Fadema.

"Well, Madam," said the woman, "your friends are more perceptive and less cautious than we anticipated. They're here."

"Who?" Nepanthe asked, cowering against the window frame.

"That bloody troublesome Marshall. He's attacked Argon. What gall!" She laughed. It was forced.

Things must be going good, Bragi thought.

"You stay away," Nepanthe told the soldiers. "I'll jump."

"Don't be a fool!" the Fadema snapped. "Come. We have to move you. The tower is threatened."

"I *will* jump."

"Grab her."

Four soldiers advanced.

"Now," Ragnarson said. Leaping, he took out a man who had remained with the Fadema.

Dantice went for the man on her far side instead of the four. Trebilcock got another, but quickly found himself in trouble.

Ragnarson smacked the Queen to shut her up, turned to help Michael.

Somebody hit him from behind.

He turned as he fell, looked up into a golden mask.

The Tervola had hit him with a wooden statuary stand. "Finish them!" he ordered. "This's the man we want. The Marshall himself."

Trebilcock was fencing a man who was good. Dantice rolled across the floor with one of the others. The third soldier pranced around looking for a chance to strike a telling blow.

Ragnarson kicked the Tervola's legs from beneath him, dragged him nearer. The stand rolled away.

The Tervola had the combat training of every soldier of Shinsan. And he had staying power, though Ragnarson was stronger. They rolled and kicked and gouged, and Bragi bit. He kept trying to yank the man's mask off so he could go for his eyes.

That usually put a superior opponent on the defensive. And this Tervola was a better fighter than he.

The extra soldier almost got Dantice. But Nepanthe stabbed him from behind, turned on Aral's antagonist, stabbed him too. Aral muttered, "We're even, lady," recovered his sword, took a wild chop at the head of Michael's opponent.

Meanwhile, the Fadema recovered and fled.

Ragnarson got a thumb under the golden mask. By then he was sure he was dead. The Tervola had a hold of his neck and he was losing consciousness.

Dantice and Trebilcock closed in. The Tervola saw them. The Power was dead. There was nothing he could do. He threw himself after the Fadema. His mask remained in Bragi's hand.

Dantice helped Ragnarson up. "That was close. Mike, better make sure of those guys."

"But…"

"Never mind. I'll do it." While Nepanthe and Trebilcock supported Ragnarson, he cut throats. "I don't understand you, Mike. It ain't beer and skittles. It ain't no chess game. You want to come out alive, you got to be meaner than the other guy. And you don't leave him alive behind you."

Ragnarson groaned. Nepanthe massaged his neck. "See if any of our people are outside. We'll have half an army on us in a minute."

Dantice leaned out the window. "Nope. They're all down the street."

"You and Michael pile stuff in front of the door. No. Let me go! I'm okay. I'll make something to lower Nepanthe down."

"Wait!" she protested. "What about Ethrian?"

Bragi hurt. It made him cranky. "What do you want me to do? We've got to get out of here first. Then we'll worry about Ethrian."

She kept arguing. He ignored her. There was a racket in the hall already.

A party of Marena Dimura came up the street as he dropped his rope of torn blankets. "You men. Hold up. It's me. The Marshall. Aral, hand me that lamp." He illuminated his face. "Hang onto the end of that down there, and stand by."

Several Wesson bowmen joined the Marena Dimura. They stood around watching.

"Nepanthe, come here."

Still complaining, she obeyed. He turned his back. "Put your arms around my neck and hang on."

"You'd better let me do that," Dantice offered.

"I can handle it. I'm not all the way over the hill." He did leave his sword belt, though, remembering what a hazard it had been coming up.

Going down was a pain, too. He hadn't made it halfway before he wished his pride had let him yield to Dantice.

"Hurry up," said Trebilcock. "The door's giving."

Dantice started down the instant Bragi's feet hit pavement. He came like a monkey.

"Boy, you'd make a good burglar."

"I am a good burglar." They watched Trebilcock lever himself over the window sill.

Someone yelled inside. Michael stared, then threw himself aside, barely managing to cling to the ledge.

Men appeared in the window.

"Bowmen," said Ragnarson. "Cover him."

Arrows streaked through the window. The Argonese withdrew, cursing. Ragnarson asked the Marena Dimura captain, "Where's Colonel Ahring?"

The man shrugged. "Around."

"Yeah. Michael, hurry up." Trebilcock had reached the lower ledge. Someone upstairs was throwing things out the window. A vase smashed at Bragi's feet.

Trebilcock kicked away from the wall and dropped the last fifteen feet, grunting as he hit cobblestones. "Damn. I twisted my ankle."

"Teach you to show off," Aral growled.

"Come on," said Ragnarson. "Back to the wall. You men. Go on wherever you were going."

Ahring had left. His men had penetrated the Fadem deeply in several directions. Runners said some defenders were fleeing the fortress for the city.

Haaken had arrived. He was directing operations now.

"What's happening?" Ragnarson asked.

"They're running. All our people are in now. But we've got a problem. Most of those Necremnens are heading out. We'll be in big trouble if we don't win this."

"Michael, where's the nearest causeway?"

Trebilcock leaned over the battlements. "Upriver a quarter-mile."

"Haaken, scare up some men and grab it. Michael. Is there a causeway Reskird could use?"

"Inside his area. Shouldn't be any problem."

Ragnarson stared northward. The entire apex of the island seemed to be burning. The rain had let up. Nothing held the flames in check.

"Getting bad up there," he observed. "Could be as rough for Reskird as the Argonese."

"Bragi." Haaken had unrolled a crude map atop a merlon. He shaded an area with charcoal. "This's what we've taken. Half." Dark salients stuck out like greedy fingers. There were white islands throughout the area already captured.

"How're they fighting?"

"Us or them?"

"Both."

"Our guys are having fun. Theirs... Depends on the unit. The officers, I guess. Some are tromping each other trying to get away. Some won't budge. I'd say our chances of carrying it are better than even. But then we'll have to hold off counterattacks while we mop up."

"Keep after them. Any Necremnens have balls enough to stick?" He leaned over the wall. A dozen smaller boats rocked against the base of the wall.

"Why?"

"I want to go get Reskird. Watch Nepanthe. And keep an eye out for Ethrian. They've got him here somewhere."

TWENTY-SIX: SUMMER, 1011 AFE
BATTLE FOR THE FADEM

Reskird had an overachievement problem. "Bragi, I've got them whipped. I could clean up on them. Only I can't get to them. Damned fire..."

A curtain of flame thwarted Kildragon's advance. It spanned the base of an acute isosceles triangle. Whole blocks were infernos, drawing a strong breeze. Neither side could get close enough to combat the blaze.

"I can't leave you here while it burns itself out. Might be days."

The devastation was stunning. Even during the El Murid Wars Ragnarson had seen nothing to equal it. "Jarl and Haaken need help."

"Those damned Necremnens took off like rabbits afraid of a fox."

"You taken that causeway there yet?"

"The gatehouse guards won't give up. But we'll get it. It's all we've got to work on anymore."

"Michael. Does it hook up to the same island as the one by the Fadem?"

"I think so."

"You see?" Bragi asked Kildragon.

Reskird's sandy hair flew as he nodded.

Bragi laughed.

"What?"

"Look at us. Me, you, Haaken. We've gotten civilized. We never cut our hair short before we came to Kavelin. And we didn't shave, except you."

"It's a strange country. I'd better go get things moving before it's light enough for them to see what we're up to."

They didn't join Haaken before dawn. The causeways didn't connect to the same island. They had to cross three. There were skirmishes. And then the right causeway turned out to still be in Argonese hands.

Haaken hadn't had a chance to grab it. The garrison had counterattacked.

Bragi's old veterans carried the bridge in a short, brisk battle, only to find Argonese troops forming up beyond. The melee lasted several hours. Haaken's bowmen, when they could, plinked from the Fadem. Ragnarson advanced till he screened the Fadem's main gate, which remained in enemy hands.

"Who's got who trapped?" he wondered aloud. "How long before the whole city turns on us?"

Tactically, it was going magnificently. Yet the strategic situation looked worse and worse.

Kildragon considered the houses and shops facing the fortress-palace. "A lot of wood in those places. Maybe another fire…"

"Go to it."

Kildragon's fire masked their flank. Bragi had men climb the wall where Blackfang and Ahring were already established. They took the main gate from behind.

Weary, he joined Haaken at another merlon. The map now showed only a few white islands.

"The gate completes the circuit," said Blackfang. "The whole wall is ours."

"Think that's smart?" Ragnarson asked. "They'll fight harder if they can't get away."

"If they could, the Fadema might get out. Shouldn't we get a hold of her?"

"She'd be a good bargaining counter if things got hairy. You found Ethrian yet?"

"No. Else I'd say let's get out now."

"Another reason to get our hands on the Lady. They'll chase us all the way home if we don't."

"Those wizards want to see you."

"They come up with something?"

"I don't know. They've been everywhere, getting in the way."

"How are the men? Any problems?"

"Not yet. Still think they can lick the world as long as you're in charge. But it's daytime now. They've seen how big the place is. I'm scared they'll start thinking about it."

The western soldier was flighty, and totally unpredictable. One day he might, if inspired, stand against impossible odds and fight to the death. Another day some trivial occurrence might spook an entire army.

"Keep them too busy to think. These pockets. What are they?"

"Citadels within the citadel. They've locked themselves in. Don't look like it'll be easy digging them out."

"Where's the Queen? Keep the others from sallying. Go after her. On the cheap."

"Been doing that. Lying about Pthothor's intentions. Got more prisoners than I can handle. Reskird showed up just in time. We'll need men on the wall."

"Keep the fires going. What about casualties?"

"Not bad. Mostly new men, the way you'd expect. Enough to be a problem if we have to fight our way out."

"Where're those wizards?"

Haaken was skirting the question of leaving the wounded. Ragnarson didn't want to think about it, let alone verbalize it. It always gnawed at his guts, but sometimes it had to be done.

"Wherever you find them. Just prowl around till one bites your ankle."

He did. Trebilcock and Dantice followed, playing their bodyguard role to the hilt.

Ragnarson found a courtyard where a thousand prisoners sat in tight ranks on the cobblestones, heads bowed, thoroughly whipped. In a second courtyard he found his dead and wounded, in neat rows on mattresses looted from a barracks room. The dead and mortally wounded were pleasingly few.

On one mattress lay the innkeeper met during the ride to Baxendala.

"Hey, old man, what're *you* doing here? You should be home minding the tavern."

"Old? I'm younger than ye are, sir."

"My job. I get paid for being here."

"My job, too, sir. It's my country, ye see. My sons, Robbie and Tal, have ye seen them, sir? Are they all right, do you think?"

"Of course. And heroes, too. Be taking home a double share of loot." He hadn't the faintest idea where they were. But the innkeeper hadn't many hours left. "When it lets up a little, I'll send them down."

"Good, sir. Thank ye, sir."

"Get better, innkeeper. We'll need you again before this's done."

"Be up and around in a day or two, sir. These Argonese can't cut ye bad when they're showing their backs."

Ragnarson moved on before his tears broke loose. Again and again he saw familiar faces, men who had followed him so long they were almost family. The same men were always at the forefront, always where the killing was worst.

He couldn't help himself. More than once he shed a tear for an old comrade.

Three wizards handled the doctoring. The Thing With Many Eyes, strange though he appeared, was a sympathetic, empathetic soul. He hated watching pain. He, Kierle the Ancient, and Stojan Dusan were performing surgery on an assembly line. With the Power they would have defeated Death and pain more often.

"Michael, our species is a paradox," Ragnarson observed as they departed. "All sentience is paradoxical."

"Sir?" The hospital court hadn't fazed Trebilcock. Dantice, though, had grown pale.

"Those wizards. They get mad, they can rip up a city, wipe out twenty thousand people, and never bat an eye. But look at them now. They're killing themselves for men they don't even know."

"That's part of being human. We're all that way, a little. I saw you weep in there. Yet you'd destroy Shinsan to the last babe in arms. Or reduce Argon to ashes."

"Yes. Is a conundrum, as my fat brown friend would say. What's the difference between the innkeeper and the man I killed last night? Each did his duty… No. Enough. Let's find Varthlokkur."

The downhill side of, and aftermath of, battles always pushed him into these moods. If he didn't catch himself, didn't become otherwise preoccupied, he would plunge into a nihilism from which he wouldn't recover for days.

Night threatened before they tracked Varthlokkur down. He and Visigodred were in a library, searching old books. Zindahjira was there, too, though Ragnarson never saw him. From back in the stacks he fussed and cursed and tried to get Visigodred's goat.

"What's that all about?" Trebilcock asked.

"I don't know," Ragnarson replied. "It's been going on as long as I've known them."

Ragnar materialized from the stacks. "Dad!"

After hugging him, Bragi held him at arms' length. The boy was festooned with loot. "Somebody been breaking plunder discipline?"

"Aw, Dad, I just picked up a couple things for Gundar and the kids."

"What if everybody did that? Who'd do the fighting?"

Ragnar posed cockily. "Varthlokkur's still alive."

To keep him out of trouble Ragnarson had convinced him the wizard needed a bodyguard. An amusing notion. Varthlokkur, Visigodred, and Zindahjira all were damned formidable even without the Power.

"He's been invaluable," said Varthlokkur. "How goes the fighting?"

"So-so. We're on top. But we've got to lay hands on the Fadema. Haaken said you wanted to talk to me. Problems?"

"Not sure," Visigodred said. "I heard from Marco this morning. He visited Hammad al Nakir."

"So?"

"El Murid hasn't collapsed. For a while Haroun's boy won everywhere but at Al Rhemish. He had help from the tribes. After that last surge of the Power, though, things turned around."

"How?"

"Rumor says El Murid appealed to the angels. Because he claims a direct commission from Heaven, I guess. The angels apparently responded. They sent him a general. The Royalist offensive bogged down."

"Only a matter of time before weight of numbers tells."

Varthlokkur took it up. "Megelin learned from the best. But he's losing. Three battles last week, all to inferior forces. This angelic general is superhuman."

"And?"

"Two points. What happens if Megelin loses? Another round of El Murid Wars? The man is old and fat and crazier than ever. He'll want to get even with everybody who helped Haroun. Second point. The general calls himself Badalamen."

"Badalamen? Never heard of him."

"You have. In a divination, remember? So cloudy, but the name came through as dangerous…"

"Yeah. Now I remember."

"We've reasoned thus: Badalamen was furnished by O Shing, to reverse El Murid's fortunes because Shinsan isn't ready to move. This business with Argon was probably geared to an attack next summer. But we've wrecked that.

"Oh. I heard about your fight with the Tervola. He's still here. With the Fadema. Haaken gave me the mask. I didn't recognize it. It does look a lot like Chin's. He might have changed it after Baxendala. If it is Chin, he's as dangerous as Tervola come. We'd save a lot of grief by killing him. But to the matter in Hammad al Nakir.

"It's my guess that your reaction has been more effective than O Shing expected. And there's Radeachar. So he's put this Badalamen in to threaten your flank."

"He another Tervola?"

"No. Marco says he's pretty ordinary. You've seen the eastern martial arts artists? The way they use an opponent's strengths against him? That's the way Badalamen operates.

"I don't think he's human at all. Nu Li Hsi and Yo Hsi both tried to breed superhuman soldiers. O Shing was the result of one experiment. I'd guess Radeachar is another. I doubt the work stopped with the passing of the Princes Thaumaturge."

Ragnarson pursed his lips, sucked air across his teeth. "There's not a lot we can do about it, is there?"

"No. I just wanted you to know. I'd say it makes it imperative that we kill the Tervola here. He's bound to be one of O Shing's top men."

"And the Fadema," Ragnarson added. "Whoever takes over might think twice about being Shinsan's stalking horse."

"Marco went to Necremnos, too," Visigodred said. "Pthothor has gathered an army. But he's in no hurry to get here. Waiting to hear how we did. Doesn't want to throw live men after dead."

"Can't blame him. Well, I'd better tell Haaken we've got to get that tower."

Having admonished Ragnar again, Bragi departed. Zindahjira resumed fulminating in the stacks. Bragi chuckled. Someday he'd have to find out what had started that.

The Fadema stubbornly refused to surrender. Days passed. The impasse persisted. Ragnarson worried.

The city garrisons recovered. Troops from out of town reinforced them. Ragnarson had to lock his force into the Fadem. His men stayed busy defending its walls. He expected a major assault.

There could be no escape, now, without victory. And that appeared to be slipping away—unless Necremnos came.

The first week ended. Except for the Queen's stronghold, the Fadem was his. Outside, the Argonese seemed content to wait, to starve him out. Their probes he beat back with heavy losses. Necremnos was moving, but slowly, willing to let Kavelin do the heavy dying.

The stalemate persisted, though Ragnarson didn't sit still. His engineers worked round the clock to tunnel into the Queen's tower. He battered its walls with captured engines. He tried sending Marena Dimura up its wall by night.

The sappers completed the tunnels the last day of the second week.

Ragnarson chose his assault teams carefully. Haaken and Reskird each led one, and he took the third. Ahring mounted a vicious diversion outside.

The bailey was a cylindrical tower with thick walls and little room inside. The easiest entry, once the single door had been sealed, was over the top—almost a hundred feet above the encircling street.

Unless one penetrated its basements. An obvious and anticipated tactic. The defenders would be waiting. It would be rough.

Bragi didn't doubt the outcome. His concern was keeping costs down.

His engineers tested to see if the basements had been flooded. They hadn't. Some other greeting waited.

Bragi expected fire.

It didn't materialize. Again, Argon's initial lack of readiness told.

It was a savage melee, fought through dim passages and narrow doors, Ragnarson's men advancing by sheer mass. The defenders remained stubborn despite the hopelessness of their situation.

It went floor by floor, hour by hour.

"Why the hell don't she give up?" Bragi asked Kildragon. "She's just wasting lives."

"Some people keep hoping."

"Marshall! We're at the top."

"Okay! Reskird, Haaken, this's it. Send for Varthlokkur."

The wizard appeared immediately. Ragnarson and his friends forced themselves into the Fadema's last redoubt.

She had but two soldiers left. Both were wounded, but remained feisty.

And the Tervola was there. Ethrian, bound and gagged, stood behind him.

"My Lord Chin," said Varthlokkur. "It's been a while."

Chin bowed slightly. "Welcome to Argon, old pupil. You learned well. Someday you'll have to teach me the secret of the Unborn."

"I have no taste for teaching. Is there anything you'd care to tell us, My Lord? So we can avoid the rough parts?"

"No. I think not." Chin glanced at an hourglass. He didn't seem worried.

Ragnarson grew wary. These people always had something up their sleeves…

He collected a fallen javelin, pretended to examine it. "Something's going to happen," he whispered to Reskird. "Start moving the men out."

Chin responded to the withdrawal with the slightest of frowns and a touch of nervousness.

"My Lord," said Ragnarson. "Could you tell me why you killed my people? My wife never did anything to you." Iron and pain tinged his voice.

Chin glanced at the hourglass, brought his sword to guard. "Nothing personal. You're in the way. But we'll correct that soon enough. The hour has come."

For an instant Ragnarson thought that the Tervola meant it was his moment to die. Then, when Varthlokkur gasped and staggered, he realized Chin had been warning his companions.

The Power had come alive. A portal had opened behind Chin and the Fadema.

The Tervola attacked. Haaken and Michael met him, prevented his blade from reaching the Marshall. The Fadema came at Bragi with a dagger identical to that he had taken off the leader of the assassins who had killed Elana. A trooper savaged her knife hand with a wild swing, kicking the dagger toward his commander. He tried to follow up. Bragi grabbed his arm, yanked him away from Chin's blade.

"Thanks." He slapped the dagger into the soldier's hand. It was rich booty, a spell-blade worth a fortune.

Chin hurled the two Argonese soldiers, the Fadema, and Ethrian into the portal's black maw, chanting a hasty spell. Varthlokkur responded with a warding spell.

Chin jumped for the portal. His magick roared through the chamber.

Bragi hurled the javelin, then dropped to the floor, rubbed his eyes. He couldn't see. His skin felt toasted.

He moaned.

"Easy," said Varthlokkur. "You'll be all right. I blocked most of it."

Ragnarson didn't believe him. "Did I get him?" he demanded. "Did I get him?" Chin's life almost seemed worth his eyes.

"I don't know. I'm sorry. I don't."

TWENTY-SEVEN: SUMMER, 1011 AFE
MOCKER RETURNS

The brown man watched from the shadows. He shivered, sure Varthlokkur would notice him. But only one man glanced his way, a squat, hard looker he didn't recognize. The youth didn't react to his stare.

His breath hissed away. Relieved, he waited till they rounded a corner, then followed.

What were they up to? Bragi and Varthlokkur had no business being in Necremnos. And who was the Necremnen? Everyone seemed to know and fear him.

The brown man interrupted a street cleaner.

"Self, beg thousands pardon, sir. Am foolish foreigner, being ignorant of all things Necremnen. Am bestruckt by puzzlement. Am seeing man pass, moment gone, ordinary, with foreign companions, and people hide eyes from same. Am wondering who is same?"

"Huh?"

Necremnen was one of the languages of Mocker's childhood. He could reduce any tongue to unintelligibility.

He tried again.

"Him? That's the high and mighty Aristithorn, that is. Him what makes himself out to be a little toy god, out in his little toy castle… Here now. Where're you going already?"

Mocker had heard enough. He had never met Aristithorn, but he knew the name. Bragi had mentioned it often enough.

So the big bastard was recruiting old accomplices into his schemes, eh?

He slid hurriedly through the crowds. But he had wasted too much time with the street cleaner. He had lost them.

He traced them to the waterfront. Again he was too late. He did learn that they had visited shipping firms and the master of the Fishers' Guild.

Boats. A lot of them. That had to be it.

Why would Bragi be in Necremnos trying to build a navy? It didn't make sense—unless he was on some adventure with Kavelin's army.

It seemed possible, with Argon a probable target, but reason failed him at that point. He could conceive of no cause for Kavelin to attack Argon. Nor could he figure how Bragi hoped to get away with it. Bragi had pulled off military miracles before, but this was unrealistic.

Mocker knew Argon. Ragnarson didn't. The brown man knew that the city boasted a population greater than that of Kavelin. The biggest force Kavelin could muster would simply vanish into the crowds…

But Bragi had Varthlokkur with him. That could make all the difference. It had for Ilkazar.

He might be guessing wrong. Bragi might need boats to ferry across the Roë.

He kept on the trail. This needed investigation.

It was time he started moving. He had been here for a month and a half accomplishing nothing. He had gambled away almost the entire fortune Lord Chin had provided him before transferring him here. He knew what he was supposed to do, but old habits, old thought patterns, died hard.

Chin would throw a fit next time they met. He should have been in Kavelin by now.

Hunger taunted him. He touched his purse. Empty again. It was a long walk to his room, where his final emergency reserve lay hidden. He considered stealing, didn't try. He wasn't as quick as he used to be. Age was creeping up. Soon he'd be able to commit robbery only by the blade. He hadn't lost his skill with a sword.

Cursing all the way, he trudged across town, retrieved his poke, bought a meal twice too big, downed it to the last drop of gravy. Overindulgence was his weakness, be it in food, gambling, or drink.

He finally overtook Aristithorn three days later. Bragi and Varthlokkur were long gone. Their visit had caused little public comment.

But something was happening.

The half-ruined stone pile palace of Necremnos's King had come alive. The captains of Necremnos's corrupt, incompetent army swarmed there, coming and going with ashen faces. They were hobby soldiers, allergic to the serious practice of their craft. They hadn't signed on to die for their country, only to bleed its treasury. In the taverns soldiers patronized, there was both grumbling and anticipation.

Mocker was there, listening.

The subject was war with Argon. No one seemed to care why. Pessimists argued that penetrating Argon's defenses was impossible. Optimists verbally spent the booty they would bring home.

Regiments mustered at the Martial Fields south of the city, slothfully, in the tradition of all Necremnen state activity.

Mocker was there, too. He wasted no time insinuating himself into the camp following. He recruited a half-dozen young, enthusiastic, attractive girls capable of drawing the big-spending officers. He put them to work. And listened.

He quickly determined that the high command was stalling. The generals would never admit it, but they knew they were incompetent. They knew they couldn't manage forces like these against Argon. That city's army was poorly trained and equipped, and its officers as corrupt as they, but it did take war seriously.

Finally, sluggishly, like a bewildered amoeba, the Necremnen host stumbled southward, following the east bank of the Roë. A hundred thousand regulars, levies, allies, and plunder-hungry auxiliaries had responded to the raising of Pthothor's war baton. The movement went forward in dust and confusion. Despite Aristithorn and the King, the mass never did quite sort itself out.

Its first skirmish nearly resulted in disaster, though the enemy numbered no more than ten thousand. The regulars and levies almost panicked. But hard-riding auxiliaries from the plains tribes finally harried the Argonese border force into retreating, then swept ahead, burning and pillaging.

After the near-disaster the army began suffering seizures of near-competence. Pthothor hanged fifty officers, dismissed a hundred more, and demoted scores. When someone grumbled about losing traditional prerogatives, Pthothor referred him to Aristithorn.

No one challenged the cranky old wizard.

The army eventually blundered into the Valley of the Tombs, where countless generations of Argonese nobility lay with their death-treasures. The Argonese came out to forestall looting and vandalism.

An unimaginative battle raged among the tombs and obelisks from dawn till dusk. Thousands perished. The thing came to no conclusion till the steppe riders broke free, circled the valley, and began plundering Argon's suburbs. They captured the pontoons to a dozen outlying islands. During the night the Argonese command brought up thousands of hastily mobilized citizens, and might have turned the tide had the news not come that the Queen's bastion had fallen.

Mocker whooped when he heard that Bragi's banners flew everywhere over the Fadem.

The Necremnens took courage. The Argonese began melting away, running to salvage what they could from their homes.

Pthothor pushed on, occupying islands which had failed to destroy their pontoons and bridges.

Mocker couldn't believe the confusion on both sides. This had to be why Bragi believed he could best Argon. Kavelin's troops were superb compared to these, and the quality of their leaders was incomparable.

Haaken and Reskird would be here, he knew, with the Vorgreberger Guards and the Midlands Light. Ahring and Altenkirk, too, probably with the Queen's Own and the Damhorsters. And, knowing Bragi's fondness for archers, TennHorst and the King's Memory Bows… Maybe even the Breidenbachers and the Sedlmayr Light, and who knew what from the Guild…

The more Mocker thought, the bigger the army he conjured from imagination, till he pictured the Fadem crawling with the entire adult male population of Kavelin…

His depression began receding. He showed flashes of the Mocker of old, amazing his girls with his lighthearted nonsense. For a time he forgot the pressure…

The officers he entertained knew little about Bragi. Aristithorn and Pthothor were tight-lipped, trusting none of their staff. Mocker wished he could get the wizard into his tent.

His girls went along most of the time, but that they wouldn't tolerate. Aristithorn had a reputation. He took home girls who caught his fancy. They were never seen again.

So Mocker just tagged along, the officer's best friend, and awaited the opportune event.

His moment came soon after the Valley of the Tombs.

A Necremnen barge came meandering up a delta channel. Aboard were Bragi, his son, Varthlokkur, Haaken, Reskird, Trebilcock and his squat friend, and—Nepanthe!

They were hunting Aristithorn and Pthothor, allegedly to arrange coordinated action against Argon, most of which remained unconquered.

Mocker spotted Nepanthe long before she saw him. And couldn't believe what he saw. She was laughing with Haaken and Reskird about the clown army of their allies. The immaculate, perfectly disciplined troopers of the Queen's Own made the ragtag Necremnen loafers at Pthothor's headquarters look pathetic. Like poorly organized bandits.

Mocker eased as close as he could without revealing himself.

Nepanthe was supposed to be in the dungeons of Castle Krief.

He didn't see Ethrian, and that disturbed him more than his wife's presence. The boy seldom strayed from his mother's side. She wouldn't let him.

She was going to make Ethrian a mama's boy in spite of himself.

He was so intrigued by his wife's presence, and by trying to eavesdrop, that he ignored everything else—especially the others in Bragi's party.

Beyond being able to get into trouble anywhere, Aral Dantice had one noteworthy talent. He remembered. Now he remembered a dark face seen only momentarily in Necremnos when he noticed the same face peeping from an ornamental hedge. He whispered to Trebilcock.

It didn't occur to them that they shouldn't nab suspects on Necremnos's turf. They decided, they split, they drifted round till they could take the watcher from behind.

Mocker's first warning was a grip of iron closing on his shoulder.

He squealed, "Hai!" and jumped, kicked, sent Dantice sprawling—and found himself staring into the cold, emotionless eyes of Michael Trebilcock, along the blade of a saber.

He whipped out his own blade, began fencing. In silence, which was one of the most un-Mocker-like things he had ever done.

The clash of steel drew a crowd.

He had meant it to be a quick passage at arms, perhaps wounding the boy as he whipped by and fled across the yards and hedges...

But Trebilcock wouldn't let him.

Mocker's eyes steadily widened. Trebilcock met his every stroke and countered, often coming within a whisker of cutting him. Nor did the younger man give him any respite in which to calculate, or regain his wind.

Trebilcock was *good*.

Mocker's skill with a blade was legend among his acquaintances. Seldom had he met a man he couldn't best in minutes.

This time he had met one he might not best at all. He managed to touch Trebilcock once in ten minutes, with a trick never seen on courtly fields of honor. But Trebilcock wasn't daunted, nor did he allow the trick a second chance.

Trebilcock couldn't be intimidated. Mocker couldn't perturb him. And that scared Mocker...

"Enough!" Ragnarson shouted. "Michael, back off."

Trebilcock stepped back, lowered his guard. Perforce, Mocker did likewise.

He was caught.

Wham!

Nepanthe hit him at a dead run. "Darling. What're you doing? Where've you been?" And so on and so on. He couldn't get in a word.

"Come on," said Ragnarson. "Back to the barge. It's time we moved out. Nepanthe, keep a hold of him."

Mocker looked everywhere but at Bragi. He could feel Bragi searching his face.

He considered pretending amnesia, rejected it. He had given himself away by responding to Nepanthe. Some fast thinking was in order.

As he clambered aboard the barge, Ragnarson said, "Michael, you handle a blade damned good."

"Sir?"

"I've never seen anybody go to draw with Mocker."

"Wasn't a draw. He was tiring."

"That's why I stopped you. Where'd you learn?"

"My father's fencing master. But I'm not that good, really. At the Rebsamen..."

"You impressed me. You men. Get this sonofabitch cast off. We've got to disappear before they find out I told them a pack of lies."

Nepanthe slackened her fussing. Mocker took the opportunity to look around.

He didn't like what he saw.

Haaken leaned against the deckhouse, a piece of grass between his dark teeth, staring. Varthlokkur stared from the bows. Reskird, directing the bargemaster, stared. They didn't have friendly eyes.

The safest course would be to tell ninety percent of the truth.

He was confused. Nepanthe was babbling all the news since his capture. It piled up dizzyingly. She and Ethrian had been kidnapped by agents of Shinsan? Possibly by Chin, his supposed rescuer. Though he tried, he couldn't make the evidence of his own kidnapping indict Chin. If the Tervola had stacked it against Haroun, he had stacked it perfectly. The accusation against Bragi could be due to misinformation…

When it came to question time he told the exact truth. All he held back was his feeling that it hadn't ended, that he still had to make up his mind which way to jump.

For the moment he leaned toward his old companions, despite bin Yousif's apparent perfidy. He could be on Bragi's side without being on Haroun's.

"Get those lazy bastards rowing," Bragi yelled at Reskird. "Damn." He slapped at a mosquito. It was everybody's hobby. "Let's get some miles behind us before those clowns change their minds."

Mocker frowned puzzledly.

"Stealing a march, old buddy. One from Haroun's book. Kind of hate doing it to Aristithorn. He's not a bad guy. The others… They deserve whatever they get."

"Self, am wondering what old friend blathers about. Is getting more governmentalized all time, till cannot speak with meaning."

"I made a deal with the junta that took over when we got rid of the Fadema. We finished what we came for. We got Nepanthe. Only reason we've been hanging around is we couldn't get out. So I told them, let us go home, we'll leave without bothering you anymore. If they didn't, I'd whip on them from behind the whole time they were trying to handle Necremnos. Argon's in a bad way. They'd didn't have much choice. My boys have been turning them every way but loose. They didn't have any stomach left for storming the Fadem, against my bows, with the Necremnens behind them. So they agreed. Ahring and TennHorst are moving out already.

"Of course, if they saw a chance to plunder us back, they'd jump on it. So hurry, damnit, Reskird."

"What about Necremnens?" Mocker asked.

Ragnarson grinned. "Their bad luck. They didn't show up because we needed help. They came to plunder. And they'd jump us, too, if they thought they could get away with it. Old Pthothor hedged every time I tried to pin him down about designating plunder areas."

"Old friend is right. Trick is worthy of Haroun."

"Think they'll report to Pthothor?" Haaken asked after they debarked and joined the escort Ahring had left for them. The Necremnen rivermen were wasting no time heading upstream.

"Not unless he heads them off," Bragi replied. "Those boys are scared. They're homeward bound."

Later, as they hurried along a road raised above rice paddies, Visigodred's roc made a clumsy landing a few hundred yards ahead. Marco tumbled off, landed with a hearty splash and heartier cursing. He came boiling up the embankment, blood in his eye. He fell back. Sputtering, he tried again.

"Goddamned overgrown buzzard, you did that on purpose. We're gonna bring this pimple to a head. You're lower than snake puke, you know that, you big-ass vulture?"

He slipped again. Splash!

"Throw him a rope," Ragnarson suggested.

The bird quietly preened, ignoring everyone.

"I'm gonna carve out your gizzard and make me giblet stew," Marco promised. Soldiers helped him dry off. He bowed mockingly toward Ragnarson.

"Got a word for you, chief," he said. "And that's get your butt home. That creep Badalamen is kicking ass all over Hammad al Nakir. And El Murid told him to whale on Kavelin next." He snatched a lance from a trooper, rushed the bird, whacked it between the eyes. "Listen, bird, if I wasn't allergic to walking…"

Ragnarson waved his companions past and hurried onward. Marco was still cursing when they passed out of earshot.

The army gulped huge distances daily. Ragnarson walked himself, to demonstrate that anyone could manage. The column became strung out. Plains riders came for a look, but withdrew when they saw the Thing and the Egg prowling the column's flanks.

Ragnarson halted near Throyes, sent a party to the city for supplies, and to inform the Throyens of Varthlokkur's presence. The Throyens might have been tempted otherwise. The loot of the Fadem was considerable.

Mocker went along.

He had been given plunder money and he knew Throyes of old. He knew its gaming houses well.

It was in one of those that the Throyen Nine contacted him.

The emissary was fatter than he. Sweat rolled off him in rivers, and he smelled. Flies loved him. Yet men made way for him when he approached the table where Mocker, having an apparent run of luck, was amazing the house with his bets.

The man watched during three passes of the dice. Then he whispered, "I would speak with you, fat man."

"Hai! Is case of kettles calling pot black. Begone, ponderous interrupter of…"

"You want these people to check your dice?"

Mocker rattled the bones slowly, wondering if he could resubstitute without the fat man noticing.

"Come. We have to talk."

Mocker collected his winnings, apologized to the onlookers. The house didn't object, which was surprising. He was into it deep.

He did manage to switch dice before departing.

He followed the fat man outside and into an alley...

He grabbed the fatter man, laid a dagger across his throat. "Self, being old skulker of alleys, take steps first, before trap springs," he murmured. "Speak. Or second, redder mouth opens under first."

The bigger man didn't seem perturbed. "I speak for The Hidden Kingdom."

Mocker had wondered if the contact would ever come. He hadn't done much to please Lord Chin.

"Speak." He didn't relax.

"The message comes from the Pracchia. A directive. Dispose of the man named Ragnarson."

"And in case of possibility former adherent, self, has changed mind?"

"They have your son. You choose which dies."

"Pestilential pig!" He drew the blade across the fat man's throat.

But when he turned to flee he found someone blocking his path. The man threw dust into his face.

He collapsed.

Endlessly repetitive, droning voices told him what he had to do...

"Here he is," Haaken called. Several Kaveliners joined him in the alley. "The fat guy must be the one he left with. Poul, look out for the Watch. This other one looks like Mocker nailed him before he went down."

A soldier knelt beside Mocker. "He's alive, Colonel. Looks like he got knocked in the head."

"Check his purse."

"Empty."

"Funny. It's not like him to get caught this easy. Here. Blood. Looks like he hurt a couple more, but they got away." He stirred a third body with his foot. Mocker's sword still pierced its heart. "What the hell was he doing down an alley with somebody he didn't know? With that much money on him? And why the hell didn't they kill him?"

"Colonel..." Poul shouted too late.

The Watch identified the man with Mocker's blade in him as a notorious cutpurse. The fat man was an important magistrate. They took detailed depositions. Their mucking around enraged the managers of the gaming house. The police wanted to hold Mocker. Blackfang fumed and stormed and threatened to have Varthlokkur roast their tongues in their mouths. They finally released

Mocker on condition that his deposition would be presented as soon as he recovered.

When Mocker came round he found Bragi, Varthlokkur, Nepanthe, and Haaken waiting over him.

"What happened?" Bragi demanded.

"Give him a chance," Nepanthe pleaded. "Can't you see... ?"

"All right. Get some of that soup down him."

Mocker took a few spoonfuls, desultorily, while trying to remember. Voices. Telling him he had to... To what? Kill. Kill these men. Especially Bragi. And Varthlokkur, if he could.

He felt for his missing dagger.

The compulsion to strike was almost too much for him.

Varthlokkur eyed him suspiciously. He had been doing so since the island encounter. This would take cunning. He had to get himself and Nepanthe out alive.

He had to do it. For Ethrian.

His friend of more than twenty years, and his father... Already the necessities gnawed his vitals like dragon chicks eating their ways out.

Varthlokkur was the illegitimate son of the last King of Ilkazar. He had killed his father, indirectly. It was the curse of the Golmune line. The sons slew the fathers... Mocker had slain Varthlokkur once already, long ago, over Nepanthe... But that spooky little man with the winged horse had revived him.

Mocker told his lies, and his mind strayed to his own son. Ethrian. Would he, too, someday, be responsible for the death of his father?

TWENTY-EIGHT: SUMMER, 1011 AFE
A FRIENDLY ASSASSIN

Marco brought the news to Ragnarson at Gog-Ahlan. Megelin had retreated to the Kapenrungs. The blood of half his followers stained the desert sands.

El Murid had suffered as bitterly. Nevertheless, he had ordered Badalamen to lead the ragged, war-weary victors into Kavelin.

Ragnarson increased the pace again.

As the army entered the Savernake Gap, Varthlokkur told him, "We have a problem. Mocker. Something was done to him. He's lying..."

"He's acting strange, yeah. Wouldn't you if Shinsan had had a hold of you?"

"Shinsan has had a hold of me. That's why I'm suspicious. Something happened in Throyes that he's not admitting."

"Maybe."

"I know what you're thinking. The spook-pusher is getting antsy about moving in on Nepanthe. Keep an eye on him anyway."

Later, after the army had passed Maisak and started eagerly downhill into its homeland, Varthlokkur returned. "Nepanthe is gone," he announced.

"What? Again?"

"Your fat friend did it this time."

"Take it from the beginning." Ragnarson sighed.

"He left her at Maisak."

"Why?"

"You tell me."

"I don't know."

"To remove her from risk?"

"Go away."

He didn't like it. Varthlokkur was right. Something had happened. Mocker had changed. The humor had gone out of him. He hadn't cracked a smile in weeks. And he avoided his friends as much as possible. He preferred remaining apart, brooding, walking with eyes downcast. He didn't eat much. He was a shadow of the man who had come to the Victory Day celebration.

Challenging him produced no answers. He simply denied, growing vehement when pressed. Haaken and Reskird no longer bothered.

Ragnarson watched constantly, hoping he could figure out how to help.

Kavelin greeted them as conquering heroes. The march lost impetus. Each morning's start had to be delayed till missing soldiers were retrieved from the girls of the countryside.

"I don't like it," said Haaken, the morning Bragi planned to reach Vorgreberg.

"What?" There had been no contact with Gjerdrum. Vorgreberg seemed unaware of their approach.

"How many men have you seen?" Haaken's way was to let his listeners supply half the information he wanted to impart.

"I don't follow you."

"We've been back for three days. I haven't seen a man who wasn't too old to get around. When I ask, the people say they've gone west. So where are they? What happened to the garrison Gjerdrum was supposed to send to Karak Strabger?"

"You're right. Even the Nordmen are gone. Find Ragnar. And Trebilcock and Dantice. We'll ride ahead."

Varthlokkur joined them. They reached Vorgreberg in midafternoon. The city lay deserted. They found only a few poorly armed old men guarding the gates. Squads of women drilled in the streets.

"What the hell?" Ragnarson exploded when first he encountered that phenomenon. "Come on." He spurred toward the girls.

Months in the field had done little to make him attractive. The girls scattered.

One recognized Ragnarson. "It's the Marshall!" She grabbed his stirrup. "Thank God, sir. Thank God you're back."

The others returned, swarmed round him, bawled shamelessly.

"What the hell's going on?" Ragnarson demanded. "You!" he jabbed a finger at the girl at his stirrup. "Tell me!" He seized her wrist. The others fled again, through quiet streets, calling, "The Marshall's back! We're saved."

"You don't know, sir?"

"No, damnit. And I never will unless somebody tells me. Where're the men? Why're you girls playing soldier?"

"They've all gone with Sir Gjerdrum. El Murid… His army is in Orthwein and Uhlmansiek. They came through the mountains somehow. They might be in Moerschel by now."

"Oh." And Gjerdrum had little veteran manpower. "Haaken. …"

"I'll go," Ragnar offered.

"Okay. Tell Reskird to pass the word to the men. One night is all we'll spend here. Nobody to wander. Go on now."

He watched his son, proud. Ragnar had become a man. He was nearly ready to fend for himself.

"Thank you, miss. To the Palace. We'll fill in the gaps there. Varthlokkur, can you reach Radeachar?"

"No. I'll have to wait till he comes to me."

"Damn. Ought to take ages to cross those trails. How did they get through? Without Radeachar noticing?"

They hadn't. Badalamen had, simply, moved more swiftly than anyone had believed possible, and Gjerdrum, unsure if he were attacking Megelin or Kavelin, had waited too long to respond. Then, thoughtlessly, he had ordered his counterattacks piecemeal. Badalamen had cut him up. He had taken to Fabian tactics while gathering a larger force in hopes of blocking the roads to Vorgreberg.

Two days had passed since there had been any news from Gjerdrum. Rumor had a big battle shaping up. Gjerdrum had drawn every able-bodied man to Brede-on-Lynn in the toe of Moerschel, twenty-five miles south of the capital.

Ragnarson had passed through the area during the civil war. "Gjerdrum smartened up fast," he told Haaken. "That's the place to neutralize big attacking formations. It's all small farms, stone fences, little woods and wood lots, some bigger woods, lots of hills… And a half-dozen castles within running distance. Lots of places to hide, to attack from if he loses, and no room for fancy cavalry maneuvers. Meaning, if that's the way this Badalamen wants to fight, he'll have to meet our knights head on."

Varthlokkur observed, "He'll refuse battle if the conditions are that unfavorable."

"He wants Vorgreberg. He'll have to fight somewhere. Us or Gjerdrum. The maps. They'll tell us." They moved to the War Room, set out maps of Moerschel and neighboring provinces. "Now," Ragnarson said, "try to think like Badalamen. You're here, over the Lynn in Orthwein. There's a big mob waiting at Brede. The ground is bad. What do you do to get to Vorgreberg?"

"I might split my strength," Trebilcock replied. "Hold Gjerdrum at Brede and circle another group around. If he has enough men. Gjerdrum couldn't turn even if he knew what was happening."

"Till we hear from the Unborn, or the dwarf, we're guessing. I'd bet he's outnumbered. Gjerdrum's probably mustered twenty, twenty-five thousand men. But Badalamen's soldiers are veterans."

Trebilcock fingered a map. "If he circles, he'll go east, up the Lynn." He traced the stream which formed the southern boundary of Moerschel. It ran toward Forbeck and the Gudbrandsdal Forest, approaching the Siege of Vorgreberg, emptying into the Spehe. As a river it wasn't much, yet it formed a barrier of sorts. An army crossing would be vulnerable.

Ragnarson joined Trebilcock. "Yeah. The hills and woods are rough in Trautwein. The roads would be easy to hold. But that don't mean he won't go that way. He's never been to Kavelin."

Haaken snorted. "You think Habibullah and Achmed were sleeping the last five years? He probably has maps better than ours."

"Yeah. Well. I agree with Michael. I'd come up the south bank of the Lynn, too. So we'll get lost in the Gudbrandsdal. He should cross the Lynn at Norbury, where it runs into the Spehe. There're bridges both sides of town. We'll hit his flank while he's crowded up to cross. The woods aren't a hundred yards from the one bridge. They run right down to the banks of the Spehe."

The arguments continued. Ragnar returned, bringing Mocker.

"We're fussing too much," Bragi declared later that evening. "We can't plan to the last arrow. We shouldn't. We'd get too set on a plan. We'd try sticking to it no matter what. Sleep will do us more good. Mocker, the room you and Nepanthe used before should be empty. Make yourself to home."

Jarl Ahring arrived, drew Haaken aside. A moment later they approached Ragnarson. "Sir," said Ahring, his steely eyes evasive.

"Well?"

"A problem."

"What?"

"One of my sergeants wants to talk to you. A personal matter."

"Important enough that I should see him?"

"I think so," Haaken said.

"All right. Bring him up."

"I warned you," Haaken muttered as Ahring departed.

"Oh-oh. Ragnar and that girl…"

"She's pregnant."

"Get Ragnar back here. He know?"

"Probably. I expect he made time to see her."

Sergeant Simenson was a tough buzzard Bragi wouldn't have wanted to face in a fracas. His scars showed he had been in the thick of it throughout his service, which had begun before Ragnarson's appearance in Kavelin. Nevertheless, he was as nervous as a child asked to explain a broken vase.

Haaken brought Ragnar. Ragnar nearly panicked when he saw Simenson.

Bragi growled, "Boy, you've been aping a man. Let's see if you can be one. You and the sergeant have some talking to do. Do it. I'll just listen—till somebody acts like an ass. Then I'll crack heads." Simenson he admonished, "It's too late to change anything. So confine yourselves to the future. Sergeant, did you talk to your daughter?"

Simenson nodded. He was angry, but was a good father, mainly worried about his daughter's welfare.

Ragnarson exited that confrontation admiring Ragnar. His son hadn't tried weaseling. He was truly enamored. He got down to cases and worked out a marriage agreement. Bragi couldn't have handled it as well himself. He hadn't with Fiana.

That was that. Except that the story leaked, and eventually won support for Ragnarson's Regency. Prataxis-generated tales showed Bragi as incorruptible. He wouldn't bend to benefit his own son.

It was late when he retired, a return to the field awaiting him beyond the dawn. He fell asleep hoping his men wouldn't waste themselves drinking and skirt-chasing, and knowing the hope vain.

Something wakened him. It wasn't a sound. The intruder moved with the stealth of a cat.

Dawn would soon break. The slightest of gray lights crept through the window.

He sensed rather than saw the blow, rolled away. The knife ripped through the bearskins and slashed his back, sliding over ribs and spine. He bellowed, pulled the covers with him to the floor.

The assassin pitched onto the bed.

Ragnarson staggered to his feet. Warm blood seeped down his back. He whirled the bearskins into the killer's face, wrapped him in his arms, bore him off the far side of the bed.

He was a short man, heavy, yet agile as a monkey. His knee found Bragi's groin as they hit the floor. Bragi grunted and clung, smashed the man's knife hand against the bed post. The blade skittered under a wardrobe.

The assassin kicked, gouged, bit. So did Ragnarson, and yelled when he could.

His antagonist was tough, skilled, and desperate. He began getting the best of it. Bragi grew faint. His wound was bleeding badly.

Where the hell were the guards? Where was Haaken?

He stopped blocking blows, concentrated on getting an unbreakable hold. He managed to get behind the assassin and slip an arm around the man's throat. He forced his hand up behind his own head. He arched his back and pulled with his head.

"Now I've got you," he growled.

It was a vicious hold. Applied suddenly, to an unsuspecting victim, it could break a man's neck.

The assassin kicked savagely, writhed like an eel out of water. He slapped and pounded with his free hand. Bragi held on. The assassin produced another dagger, scarred Ragnarson's side repeatedly.

Where the hell was Haaken? And Varthlokkur? Or anybody?

The murderer's struggles weakened.

That, Bragi suspected, was feigned.

Slowly he dragged the man upright…

The assassin exploded, confessing his fakery.

Enough, Bragi thought. He leaned forward till the man was nearly able to toss him, then snapped back with all the strength and leverage he could apply.

He felt the neck go through his forearm and cheek. He heard the crunch.

The door burst inward. Haaken, Varthlokkur, and several soldiers charged in. Torchlight flooded the room. Bragi let the would-be murderer slide to the floor.

"Oh, my gods, my gods." He dropped to his bed, wounds forgotten, tears welling.

"He's alive," said Varthlokkur, touching the pulse in Mocker's throat.

"Get Wachtel!" Bragi ordered.

Varthlokkur rose, shedding tears of his own. "Stretch out," he told Ragnarson. "Let me stop that bleeding. Come on! Move!"

Ragnarson moved. There was no resisting the wizard's anger.

"Why?" He groaned as Varthlokkur spread the cut across his back.

"This will lay you up for a while. Wachtel will use a mile of thread. Cut to the bone. Side, too."

"Why, damnit? He was my friend."

"Maybe because they have his son." The wizard's examination wasn't gentle. "I had a son once…"

"Damnit, man, don't open me up."

"… but I think he died in an alley in Throyes. The Curse of the Golmunes again. But for Ethrian he wouldn't be lying there now."

Wachtel bustled in. He checked Mocker's pulse, dug in his bag, produced a bottle, soaked a ball of wool, told Haaken, "Hold this under his nose." He turned to Bragi.

"Get hot water. Have to clean him before I sew." He poked and probed. "You'll be all right. A few stitches, a few weeks in bed. It'll be tender for a while, Marshall."

"What about Mocker?"

"Neck's broken. But he's still alive. Probably be better off dead."

"How come?"

"I can't help him. No one could. I could only keep him alive."

While Wachtel washed, stitched, and bandaged Bragi, Varthlokkur reexamined Mocker carefully. Finally, he ventured, "He won't recover. He'll stay a vegetable. And I don't think you'll keep him that healthy long. You'll have trouble feeding him without severing his spinal cord." His tone betrayed his anguish, his despair.

Wachtel also reexamined Mocker. He could neither add to nor dispute Varthlokkur's prognosis.

"He'd be better off if we finish him," the wizard said. His eyes were moist. His voice quavered.

Bragi, the doctor, and Haaken exchanged looks.

Ragnarson couldn't think straight. Crazy notions kept hurtling through his mind...

Mocker twitched. Weird noises gurgled from his throat. Wachtel soaked another ball of wool, knelt.

The others exchanged glances again.

"Damnit, I'll do it!" Haaken growled. There was no joy in him. He drew a dagger.

"No!" Varthlokkur snapped. His visage would have intimidated a basilisk.

"I'm the doctor," said Wachtel.

"No," the wizard repeated, more gently. "He's my son. Let it be on my head."

"No," Ragnarson countered. "You can't. Think about Nepanthe and Ethrian." He struggled up. "I'll do it. Let her hate me... She's more likely to listen if it was me... Doctor, do you have something gentle?"

"No," said Varthlokkur.

"It has to be done?" Bragi surveyed faces. Haaken shrugged. Wachtel agreed reluctantly. Varthlokkur nodded, shook his head, nodded, shrugged.

"You men," Ragnarson growled at the soldiers who had come with Haaken and the wizard. "If you value your lives, you'll never forget that he was dead when you got here. Understood?"

He knelt, grunting. The cuts were getting sensitive. "Doctor, give me something."

Wachtel reluctantly took another bottle from his bag. He continued digging.

"Hurry, man. I've got a battle to get to. And I'm about to lose my nerve."

"Battle? You're not going anywhere for a couple weeks." Wachtel produced tweezers. "Lay one crystal on his tongue. It'll take about two minutes."

"I'll be at the fight. If somebody has to carry me. I've got to hit back or go mad."

He fumbled the little blue crystal three times.

Ragnarson stared across the Spehe at Norbury. Tears still burned his cheeks.

He had scourged himself by walking all the way. His wounds ached miserably.

Wachtel had warned him. He should have listened.

He glanced up. It might rain. He surveyed Norbury again. It was a ghost town. The inhabitants had fled.

He fretted, waiting for his scouting reports. The Marena Dimura were prowling the banks of the Lynn.

Again he considered the nearer bridge. It was a stout stone construction barely wide enough for an ox cart. A good bottleneck.

Behind him archers and infantry talked quietly. Haaken and Reskird roamed among them, keeping their voices down. Up the Spehe, Jarl and the Queen's Own waited to ford the river and hit the enemy's rear.

If he came.

Not today, Ragnarson thought as the sun settled into the hills of Moerschel. "Ragnar, tell the commanders to let the men pitch camp."

He was still standing there, ignoring his pain, when the moon rose, peeping through gaps in scurrying clouds. It was nearly full. Leaning on a spear, he looked like a weary old warrior guarding a forest path.

Trebilcock, Dantice, and Colonel Liakopulos joined him. No one said anything. This was no time to impose.

Mostly he relived his companionship with Mocker and Haroun. They, with the exception of Haaken and Reskird, had been his oldest friends. And the relationship with his fellow Trolledyngjans hadn't been the same. Haaken and Reskird were quieter souls, part-time companions always there when he called. There had been more life, more passion, and a lot less trust with the other two.

He reviewed old adventures, when they were young and couldn't believe they weren't immortal.

They had been happier then, he decided. Beholden to none, they had been free to go where and do what they pleased. Even Haroun had shown little interest in his role of exiled king.

"Somebody's coming," Trebilcock whispered.

A runner zipped across the gap between village and stream. He splashed into the river.

"Get him, Michael."

Trebilcock returned with a Marena Dimura. "Colonel Marisal, he comes, The Desert Rider, yes. Thousands. Many thousands, quiet, pads on feets of his horses, yes."

"Michael, Aral, Colonel, pass the word. Kill the fires. Everyone up to battle position. But quietly, damn it. Quietly." Of the scout, "How far?"

"Three miles. Maybe two now. Slow. No scouts out to give away."

"Uhm." Badalamen was cunning. Bragi looked up. The gaps in the clouds were larger. There would be light for the bowmen.

"Ragnar. Run and tell Jarl I want him to start moving right away." Ahring's task would be difficult. His mounts wouldn't like going into action at night.

The men had barely gotten into position. Shadows were moving in the town. El Murid's horsemen came, leading their mounts. Soon they were piling up at the bridge.

Ragnarson was impressed with Badalamen. His maneuver seemed timed to reach Vorgreberg at sunrise.

A hundred men had crossed. Ragnarson guessed three times that would have crossed upriver. Five hundred or so had piled up on the south bank here.

"Now!"

Arrows hit the air with a sound like a thousand quail flushing. Two thousand bowmen pulled to their cheeks and released as fast as they could set nock to string.

The mob at the bridge boiled. Horses screamed. Men cursed, moaned, cried questions. In moments half were down. Fifteen seconds later the survivors scattered, trying to escape through brethren still coming from the town.

"Haaken!" Bragi shouted. "Go!"

Blackfang's Vorgrebergers hit the chill Spehe. Miserably soaked, they seized the far bank, formed up to prevent those already over the bridge from returning. Once bowmen joined them they forced it, compelling the horsemen to withdraw upstream or swim back.

Badalamen reacted quickly.

Horsemen swept from the village in a suicidal, headlong charge, startling the infantrymen screening Haaken's bridgehead. Arrows flew on both sides. More horses went down by stumbling than by enemy action.

Another force swept up the north bank of the Lynn, against the Kaveliners there.

The south bank riders hit the thin lines protecting the Spehe crossing, broke through. The arrows couldn't get them all.

The struggle became a melee. Ragnarson's troops, unaccustomed to reverses, wavered.

"Reskird!" Bragi called. "Don't send anyone else over. Spread out. Cover them if they break." With Liakopulos, Dantice, and Trebilcock helping, he scattered his forces along the bank, made sure the archers kept plinking. Victory or defeat depended on Ahring now.

Across the river Haaken Blackfang bawled like a wounded bull, by sheer thunder and force of will kept the Vorgrebergers steady. He seemed to be everywhere.

Something drifted down from the north. It glowed like a small moon, had something vaguely human within it…

The fighting sputtered. Both sides, awed, watched the Unborn. Here, there, El Murid's captains silently toppled from their saddles.

Haaken started bellowing again. He took the fight to the enemy.

A huge man on a giant of a stallion cantered from the village. In the moonlight and glow of the Unborn, Ragnarson saw him clearly. "Badalamen," he guessed. He was surprised. The man didn't wear Tervola costume.

His appearance rallied his men. Ragnarson yelled at his bowmen. Some complained they were short of arrows.

"It's in the balance," he told Trebilcock. "Tell Reskird to send more men over."

Radeachar and Haaken cleared the west bank again. The Midlanders didn't have to fight their way ashore.

"Wish I could get my hands on that bastard," Ragnarson said of Badalamen. The reinforcements hadn't made much difference. Badalamen's men were, once more, confident of their invincibility, of their god-given destiny.

For Radeachar had attacked the eldritch general with no more effect than a bee stinging the flank of an elephant. Badalamen had hardly noticed. His only response was to have archers plink at the Unborn's protective sphere.

Soon, despite their numbers, the Kaveliners were again on the verge of breaking.

Then Ahring arrived.

Not at the point of greatest danger, but up the Lynn, at the other bridge.

He led with his heavy cavalry. His light came behind and on his flanks. The knights and sergeants in heavy plate were unstoppable. They shattered the enemy formation, leaving the survivors to the light horse, then came against Badalamen from behind. The news reached him scarcely a minute before the charge itself.

Here Ahring had more difficulty. He was outnumbered, faced an inspired leader, and had little room to gain momentum. Nevertheless, he threw the desert riders into confusion. Haaken and Reskird took immediate advantage.

Ahring and his captains drove for Badalamen himself, quickly surrounding the mysterious general and his bodyguard.

Ragnarson laughed delightedly. His trap had closed. He had won. While his men slaughtered his enemies, he planned his march down the Lynn to relieve Gjerdrum.

In the end, though, it proved a costly victory. Though the last-gasp might of Hammad al Nakir perished, Bragi lost Jarl Ahring. Badalamen cut him down. The born general himself escaped, cutting his way through the Queen's Own as though they were children armed with sticks.

Radeachar was unable to track him.

His entire army he abandoned to the untender mercies of Kavelin's soldiers.

TWENTY-NINE: WINTER, 1011–1012 AFE
A DARK STRANGER IN THE KINGDOM OF DREAD

The dark man cursed constantly. The Lao-Pa Sing Pass, the Gateway to Shin-san, penetrating the double range of the Pillars of Heaven and the Pillars of

Ivory, had no visible end. These mountains were as high and rugged as the Kratchnodians, and extended so much farther…

He was tired of being cold.

And damned worried. He had counted on using the Power to conceal himself in enemy territory. But there was no Power anymore. He had to slip around like a common thief.

His journey was taking longer than he had expected. The legions were active in the pass. He had to spend most of his time hiding.

When the Power had gone, he had learned, turmoil had broken loose in Shinsan, rocking the domains of several despotic Tervola. Peasants had rebelled. Shopkeepers and artisans had lynched mask-wearers. But the insurrections were localized and ineffectual. The Tervola owned swift and merciless legions. And, in most places, the ancient tyranny wasn't intolerable.

Haroun made use of the confusion.

He traveled east without dawdling, yet days became weeks, and weeks, months. He hadn't realized the vastness of Shinsan. He grew depressed when he reflected on the strength pent there, with its timeless tradition of manifest destiny. Nothing would stop these people if O Shing excited them, pointed them, unleashed them…

O Shing, it seemed, had hidden himself so far to the east that Haroun feared that he would reach the place where the sun rose first. Autumn became winter. Once more he trudged across snowy fields, his cloak pulled tight about him.

His horse had perished on the Sendelin Steppe. He hadn't replaced it. Stealing anything, he felt, would be tempting Fate too much.

He had entered Lao-Pa Sing thinking the journey would last a few hundred miles at most.

His thinking had been shaped by a life in the west, where many states were smaller than Kavelin. Shinsan, though, spanned not tens and hundreds, but thousands of miles. Through each he had to march unseen.

In time he reached Liaontung. There, based on the little he understood of Shinsan's primary dialect, he should find O Shing. And where he found O Shing he should find Mocker.

In happier circumstances he might have enjoyed his visit. Liaontung was a quaint old city, like none he had seen before. Its architecture was uniquely eastern Shinsan. Its society was less structured than at the heart of the empire. A legacy of border life? Or because Wu was less devoted to absolute rule than most Tervola? Haroun understood that Wu and O Shing were relatively popular.

O Shing's reputation didn't fit Haroun's preconceptions. The emperor and his intimates, Lang and Tran, seemed well known and accessible. The commons could, without fear, argue grievances with them.

Yet O Shing was O Shing, demigod master of the Dread Empire. He had been shaped by all who had gone before him. His role was subject to little personal interpretation. He had to pursue Shinsan's traditional destinies.

He was about to move. Liaontung crawled with Tervola and their staffs. Spring would see Shinsan's full might in motion for the first time since Mist had flung it at Escalon.

The holocaust was at hand. Only the direction of the blow remained in doubt.

O Shing favored Matayanga. Though he realized the west was weak, he resisted the arguments of the Tervola. Baxendala had made a deep impression.

Haroun hid in a wood near the city, pondering. Why did O Shing vacillate? Every day wasted strengthened his enemies.

He scouted Liaontung well before going in. Hunger finally moved him.

His eagerness for the kill had faded.

He hadn't heard one mention of Mocker yet.

He went in at night, using rope and grapnel to scale a wall between patrols. Once in the streets he took it slow, hanging in shadows. Had it been possible, he would have traveled by the rooftops. But the buildings had steeply pitched tile roofs patched with snow and ice. Stalactites of ice hung from their ornate corners.

"Getting damned tired of being cold," he muttered.

The main streets remained busy despite the hour. Every structure of substance seemed to have its resident Tervola. Aides rushed hither and yon.

"It's this spring," he mumbled. "And Bragi won't be ready."

He stalked the citadel, thoughts circling his son and wife obsessively. His chances of seeing them again were plummeting with every step.

Yet if he failed tonight, they would be trapped in a world owned by O Shing.

It didn't occur to him that he *could* fail. Haroun bin Yousif never failed. Not at murder. He was too skilled, too practiced.

Faces paraded across his mind, of men he thought forgotten. Most had died by his hand. A few had perished at his direction. Beloul and El Senoussi had daggers as bloody as his own. The secret war with El Murid had been long and bloody. He wasn't proud of everything he had done. From the perspective of the doorstep of a greater foe the Disciple didn't look bad. Nor did his own motives make as much sense. From today the past twenty years looked more a process of habit than of belief.

What course had Megelin charted? Rumors said there was heavy fighting at home. But that news had come through the filter of a confused war between Argon and Necremnos which had engulfed the entire Roë basin, inundating dozens of lesser cities and principalities.

Argon, rumor said, had been about to collapse when a general named Badala-men had appeared and gradually brought the Necremnens to ruin.

Haroun wondered if O Shing might not be behind that war. It was convenient for Shinsan, and he had heard that a Tervola had been seen in Argon.

He could be sure of nothing. He couldn't handle the language well.

Liaontung's citadel stood atop a basaltic upthrust. It was a massive structure. Its thirty-foot walls were of whitewashed brick. Faded murals and strange symbols, in places, had been painted over the whitewash.

The whole thing, Haroun saw after climbing seventy feet of basalt, was roofed. From a distance he had thought that a trick of perspective.

"Damn!" How would he get in? The gate was impossible. The stair to it was clogged with traffic.

The wall couldn't be climbed. After a dozen failures with his grapnel he concluded that the rope trick was impossible, too. He circled the base of the fortress. There was just the one entrance.

Cursing softly, he clung to shadow and listened to the sentries. He retreated only when certain he could pronounce the passwords properly.

It was try the main entrance or go home.

He waited in the darkness behind the mouth of a narrow street. In time a lone Tervola, his size, passed.

One brief, startled gasp fled the man as Haroun's knife drove home. Bin Yousif dragged him into the shadows, quickly appropriated his clothing and mask.

He paid no heed to the mask. He didn't know enough to distinguish Tervola by that means.

The mask resembled a locust.

In complete ignorance he had struck a blow more devastating than that he had come to deliver.

Haroun hadn't known that Wu existed. Nor would he have cared if he had. One Shinsaner was like another. He would shed no tears if every man, woman, and child of them fell beneath the knives of their enemies.

Haroun was a hard, cruel man. He wept for his enemies only after they were safely in the ground.

He mounted the steps certain something would go awry. He tried to mimic the Tervola's walk, his habit of moving his right hand like a restless cobra. He rehearsed that password continuously.

And was stunned when the sentries pressed their foreheads to the pavement, murmuring what sounded like incantations.

His fortune only made him more nervous. What should his response have been?

But he was inside. And everyone he encountered repeated the performance. He remained unresponsive. No one remarked on his behavior, odd or not.

"Must have killed somebody important," he mumbled. Good. Though it could have its disadvantages. Sooner or later someone would approach him with a petition, request for orders, or…

He ducked into an empty room when he spied another Tervola. He dared not try dealing with an equal.

His luck persisted. It was late. The crowds had declined dramatically.

He stumbled across his quarry by accident.

He had entered an area devoted to apartments. He encountered one with its door ajar and soft voices coming through…

A footfall warned him. He turned as a sentry entered the passage, armed with a crossbow. For a moment the soldier stared uncertainly.

Haroun realized he had made some mistake. The crossbow rose.

He snapped the throwing knife underhand. Its blade sank into the soldier's throat. The crossbow discharged. The bolt nipped Haroun's sleeve, clattered down the hallway.

"Damn!" He made sure of the man, appropriated his weapon, hurried back to the open door.

To him the action had seemed uproarious. But there was no excitement behind the door.

He peeped in. The speakers were out of sight. He slipped inside, peeped through a curtain. He didn't recognize the three men, nor could he follow a tenth of their argument. But he lingered in hopes he could learn the whereabouts of his target, or Mocker.

O Shing told Lang and Tran, "I'm convinced, Tran. There's too much smoke for there not to be fire. Chin's it. And Wu must be in it. You identify anyone else, Tran?"

"Feng and Kwan, Lord." He used the Lord of Lords title.

Haroun stepped in.

"Wu!" the three gasped.

Haroun was the perfect professional. His bolt slew Lang before his gasp ended. He finished Tran a second later, with the knife he had thrown before.

O Shing hobbled around a bed, pulled a cord.

Haroun cursed softly.

"You… You're not Wu."

Haroun discarded the locust mask. The cruel little smile tugged his lips as he cranked the crossbow.

"You!" O Shing gasped. He remembered who had harried him through the Savernake Gap. "How did you…?"

"I am the Brother of Death," Haroun replied. "Her blind brother. Justice."

Running feet slapped stone floors.

Haroun fired. The bolt slammed into O Shing's heart.

The dark man drew his sword and smiled his smile. Now there might be time for Bragi and the west. He was sad, though, that he hadn't found Mocker. Where the hell *was* that little tub of lard?

He couldn't know that his bolt had removed the only obstacle to Pracchia control of Shinsan. His action would have an effect exactly opposite his intent.

He fought. And broke through, leaving a trail of dead men.

He stayed to find and free Mocker.

He remained at liberty long enough to bloody the halls of that fortress, to learn that Mocker wasn't there, and had never been. Long enough to convince his hunters that he was no man at all, but a blood-drinking devil.

THIRTY: SUMMER, 1011-WINTER, 1012 AFE
THE OTHER SIDE

The Old Man watched dreamily as the Star Rider reactivated the Power and opened a transfer stream.

A gang tumbled through immediately. A bewildered boy and a maskless Tervola followed. Curses pursued them. Then a javelin flickered through, smashed into the Tervola's skull.

The Old Man and Star Rider froze, stunned. Then, cursing, the bent man scuttled after the boy. Catching him, he demanded, "What happened?" Panic edged his voice.

Everything was going wrong. The leukemia victim had expired. The Mercenaries' Guild had cleansed itself. There had been no time to replace Pracchia members. Now Chin, his most valuable tool, lay dead at his feet. "Help him!" he roared at the Old Man, before the Fadema could answer his question.

The Old Man knelt beside the Tervola. It was hopeless. The javelin had jellied Chin's brain.

"Ragnarson," the Fadema whined.

"What? What about him?"

"He crossed the steppes. He made an alliance with Necremnos. He came down the Roë and attacked from boats. He captured the Fadem. We barely held on till transfer time."

The others began arriving. They milled around, trying to comprehend the latest disaster.

"Move along! Move along!" the Star Rider shouted. "Get to the meeting room." Badalamen came through. He looked dashing dressed as a desert general.

"Who's this?" the bent man demanded, indicating the boy.

"The fat man's son. His wife got away."

"Take him to the meeting room." He kicked Chin's corpse. "Incompetent. Can't get anybody to do anything right. Argon was supposed to be ready for war." Pettily, viciously, he used the Power to murder the Fadema's soldiers.

He asked the Old Man, "How will I ever get out of here?" Then, "Drag the bodies to Norath's pets." He kicked Chin again.

While working, the Old Man slowly put together the thought that he had never seen his master behave this irrationally.

He wandered to the meeting room once he finished, arriving amidst a heated discussion.

The setbacks were gnawing at Pracchia morale. The stumbling block, the man responsible for the delays, was O Shing. He wouldn't move west. Nor would he be manipulated.

"Remove him," Badalamen suggested.

"It's not that simple," the Star Rider replied. "Yet it's necessary. He's proven impossible to nudge. If he weren't more powerful than Ehelebe-in-Shinsan... Most of the Tervola support him. And we've lost our Nine-captain there. He died without naming a successor. Who were the members of his Nine? We must locate them, choose one to assume his Chair. Only then can we take steps against O Shing."

"By then he may have moved west voluntarily," Norath observed.

"Maybe," the bent man replied. "Maybe. Whereupon we aid him insofar as he forwards our mission. So. We must proceed slowly, carefully. At a time when that best serves our western opponents."

"What about Argon?" the Fadema demanded.

"What can we do? You admit the city is lost."

"Not the city. Only the Fadem. The people will rally against them."

"Maybe. Badalamen."

The born general said, "Megelin has been stopped. It was difficult and expensive. It will continue to be difficult and expensive if El Murid is to be maintained. The numbers and sentiment oppose him. But it can be done."

"The point was to weaken that flank of the west. That's been accomplished. Continued civil war will debilitate the only major western power besides Itaskia."

"There will be nothing left," Badalamen promised.

"Win with enough strength left to invade Kavelin," said the bent man. "Seize the Savernake Gap. Make of yourself an anvil against which we can smash Ragnarson when we come west."

After the meeting the Star Rider went into seclusion, trying to reason how his latest epic could be brought back under control. At last he mounted his winged steed and flew west, to examine Argon.

He drifted over the war zone and cursed. It was bad. Not only had Ragnarson done his spoiling, he had extricated himself cheaply. The Argonese were too busy with the Necremnens to pursue him.

He fluttered from city to city, hunting Chin's little fat man. He finally located the creature in company with Ragnarson. He raced to Throyes, gave instructions to order the fat man to eliminate Ragnarson before Kavelin's army returned home. When Badalamen finished Megelin he could move north against limited resistance...

Then he butterflied about the west, studying the readiness, the alertness, of numerous little kingdoms. Some, at least, were responding to Varthlokkur's warning.

He was pleased. Western politics were at work. Several incipient wars seemed likely to flare. Mobilizations were taking place along the boundaries of Hammad al Nakir, too, in fear that El Murid might reassume his old conqueror's dream.

The raw materials for a holocaust were assembling.

He nudged a few places, then returned to his island in the east. He began hunting Chin's replacement.

Lord Wu was initiated into the Pracchia minutes before Badalamen announced his defeat in Kavelin. Wu showed no enthusiasm for his role. Badalamen blamed a lack of reliable intelligence. Both men, supported by Magden Norath, petitioned the return of the Power.

"What can I do about it?" the bent man demanded. "It comes and goes. I can only predict it… Fadema. Are you ready to go home?"

"To a ruin? Why?"

"It's no ruin yet. Your people are still holding out. Necremnos's leaders are too busy one-upping each other to finish it. A rallying point, a leader, a little supernatural help, should turn it around. Badalamen. Go with the Fadema. Destroy Necremnos. They're too stubborn ever to be useful. Then head west. Seize the Savernake Gap. Throyes will help."

Badalamen nodded. He had this strength, from the viewpoint of the bent man: he didn't question. He carried out his orders. He was, in all respects, the perfect soldier.

"What supernatural aid?" the Fadema demanded. "Without the Power…"

"Products of the Power, my lady. Norath. Your children of darkness. Your pets. Are they ready?"

"Of course. Haven't I said so for a year? But I have to go with them, to control them."

"Take a half-dozen, then." He buried his face in his hands momentarily. To the Old Man, who sat silently beside him, he muttered, "The fat man. He failed. Or refused. Throw the boy to Norath's children."

A pale vein of rebellion coursed through the Old Man as he rose.

The boy gulped, shivered in the Old Man's grip. He stared across the mile-wide strait. A long swim. With desert on the farther shore.

But it was a chance. Better than that offered by the *savan dalage.*

Shaking, he descended to the stony beach.

It was the turning of the year and, the bent man hoped, the shifting of luck to the Pracchia. Wu would have finalized plans for the removal of O Shing. Badalamen's report on the war with Necremnos would be favorable…

The Pracchia gathered.

Badalamen's report could have been no better. Norath and his creatures had turned it around. When Shinsan marched, the Roë basin would be tributary to The Hidden Kingdom. The holocaust had swept the flood plain and steppes. Argon was closing in on Necremnos.

But Lord Wu didn't show. The Pracchia waited and waited for Locust Mask to come mincing arrogantly into the room.

Later the bent man wearily mounted his winged steed. His flight was brief. It ended at Liaontung.

THIRTY-ONE: SPRING, 1012 AFE
BAXENDALA REDUX

"Man, I don't know," said Trebilcock. He surveyed Ragnarson's captains.

"What's that?" Kildragon asked. Reskird was still gray around the gills from wounds he had received at Norbury. His left arm hung in a sling. Badalamen had overcome a dozen champions in fighting free.

"Might as well wait for everybody. Save telling it twice." Trebilcock approached Ragnarson.

"Where's your shadow, Michael?"

"At his father's. Learning bookkeeping."

"Last summer took the vinegar out of him, eh?"

"His father claims it gave him perspective. What I wanted to say... I should tell everybody. Old friend of Aral's dad showed up while I was there. First man through the Savernake Gap this year."

"Oh? News?"

Ragnarson didn't ask if it was bad. There wasn't any other kind these days.

"Go ahead. Latecomers can hear it from somebody else." He pounded his table. "Michael has got some news."

Trebilcock faced the captains, stammered.

"I'll be damned," Bragi muttered. "Stage fright."

"I just talked to a man from Necremnos." Michael eyed his audience. Half he didn't know. Many were foreign military officers. Most of his acquaintances were recovering from wounds. Gjerdrum still couldn't walk without help. He'd had a savage campaign of his own.

"He says Argon is kicking Necremnos all over the Roë basin. The Fadema reappeared with a general named Badalamen and a wizard named Norath. Since then everything's gone her way."

A murmur answered him.

"Yes. The same Badalamen we whipped a couple months ago. But Norath, even without the Power, was the real difference." He glanced into the shadows where the Egg of God lurked. It seemed excited. Did it know Norath?

"Magden Norath?" Valther asked.

"Yes."

"I heard about him in Escalon. The Monitor exiled him for undertaking forbidden research. Everybody thought he was dead."

"He's running some nasty creatures ahead of the Argonese army," Trebilcock continued. "The worst is called a *savan dalage*."

"Means 'beasts of the night' in Escalonian," Valther interjected.

"They're supposedly invulnerable. They prowl at night, killing everything. Aristithorn has only found one way to control them. He lures one into a cave or tomb and buries it."

"I hope our friends from the Brotherhood can find a better solution," said Ragnarson. "I expect we'll get a look at them ourselves. Anything else, Michael?"

"Necremnos probably won't last through spring."

"Anything about our friend in the mask?"

"No. But the man said there's been a palace revolution in Shinsan. O Shing was killed. The Tervola are feuding."

"Varthlokkur. That good or bad?"

The wizard stepped up behind Ragnarson. "I don't know enough about what's happening to guess."

"Mist?"

The woman sat in an out-of-the-way seat. When she rose, the foreigners gawked. Few had encountered a beauty approaching hers.

"It's bad. They'd overthrow him only if he were too timid. The Tervola have grown anxious to grab Destiny. They're tired of waiting. As soon as they've decided who'll take over, they'll be here. The shame of Baxendala."

"Michael, bring this Necremnen to Varthlokkur. Varthlokkur, if you can get in touch with Visigodred, ask him to send Marco to see what's going on around Necremnos."

Visigodred had returned home after Badalamen's defeat in Moerschel. He was a genuine Itaskian count and couldn't abandon his feudal duties forever.

"I'll have Radeachar tell him." The wizard left with Trebilcock. Varthlokkur was developing a liking for Michael simply because the man wasn't afraid of him.

Varthlokkur had lived for centuries in a world where mere mention of his name inspired terror. He was a lonely man, desperate for companionship.

Ragnarson peered after them, frowning. An hour earlier Varthlokkur had asked him to be best man at his wedding.

The pain hadn't yet eased. Thoughts of Mocker made him ache to the roots of his soul. And in the wounds his friend had inflicted.

Wachtel insisted he had healed perfectly, yet he often wakened in the night suffering such agony that he couldn't get back to sleep.

The temptation to drink, to turn to opiates, was maddening, yet he stubbornly endured the pain. Other voices whispered of his mission.

He turned to the Nordmen baron who was the Thing's observer here. "Baron Krilian, haven't you people found a candidate yet?"

Ragnarson hadn't visited the Thing since his eastern expedition. There hadn't been time. Derel Prataxis handled all his business with the parliament now.

"No, Regent. We've gotten refusals from everyone we've contacted. Quite offensive, some of them. I don't understand."

Ragnarson grinned. Men like Baron Krilian were why. "Anybody interested?"

"The Kings of Altea, Tamerice, Anstokin, and Volstokin have all hinted.

Volstokin even tried to bribe old Waverly to push him in committee."

"Good to hear you and the old man agree on something." Waverly, a Sedlmayr Wesson, was the Regency's whip in the Thing.

"We're all Kaveliners, Marshall."

That truism had faltered during the civil war. Previously, the tradition had been to close ranks against outsiders. The Siluro minority had plotted with El Murid and Volstokin. The Nordmen had been in contact with Volstokin and Shinsan.

The Queen's side hadn't been above it either. Fiana had received aid from Haroun, Altea, Kendel, and Ruderin. Ragnarson himself had come south partly at the urging of the Itaskian War Ministry.

Itaskia wanted a strong, sympathetic government controlling the Savernake Gap and lying on the flank of Hammad al Nakir. The then War Minister had been paranoid about El Murid.

Ragnarson turned to the agenda, finally got his neighbors to lend him token forces. As the group dispersed, he asked, "Derel, what'd we get?"

"Not much. Fifteen thousand between them." Prataxis leaned closer. "Liakopulos said the Guild will contribute. If you're interested. He says Hawkwind and Lauder are still angry about Dainiel and Balfour."

"I'll take whatever help I can get."

He didn't expect to best Shinsan this time. Not without a hell of a lot more help than he was getting.

That evening he visited his home in Lieneke Lane, where Ragnar and his new wife were staying with Gundar and Ragnarson's other children. The real ruler of the household was a dragoness named Gerda Haas, widow of a soldier who had followed him for decades, and mother of Haaken's aide. Bragi didn't visit his children much, though he loved them. The little ones exploded all over him, ignoring his guilt-presents to sit in his lap. Seeing them growing, seeing them become, like Ragnar, more than children, was too depressing. They stirred too many memories. Maybe once the pain of Elana's loss finally faded…

Marco arrived two weeks later. He had overflown the middle east. He brought no good news.

Necremnos had fallen. The Roë basin was black with Shinsan's legions. Tervola had allied with Argon and Throyes. The Throyens were camped at Gog-Ahlan.

O Shing *was* dead. And, apparently, Chin as well. The latest master of the Dread Empire was a Ko Feng. Varthlokkur spoke no good of him. Mist called him a spider.

"How did they get out?" Bragi demanded. "Marco says the Lao-Pa Sing is still snowed in."

"Transfers," Varthlokkur replied. "The Power has been coming and going, oscillating wildly, for months. They must be sending people through with every oscillation. They seem random, but maybe Feng can predict them."

"They'll come early, then. Damn. We might not get the crops planted."

He planned to meet Shinsan as he had before, at the most defensible point in the Savernake Gap west of fortress Maisak. Baxendala.

Work there had been going forward all winter, when weather permitted. Civilians had been removed to Vorgreberg. Karak Strabger was being strengthened. New fortifications were being erected. Earthen dams were being constructed to deepen the marshes and swamps which formed a barrier across part of the Gap. A major effort was being made to construct traps and small defensive works which would hold the enemy while bowmen showered them with arrows, and siege engines bombarded them from their flanks.

Farther east, at Maisak—unreachable now—the garrison were striving to make the Gap impassable there. The fortress had fallen but once in its history, to Haroun, who had grabbed it by surprise while it was virtually ungarrisoned.

Ragnarson didn't expect it to survive this time. He did hope it would hold a long time.

Every minute of delay would work to Kavelin's advantage. Every day gained meant a better chance for getting help.

Wishing and hoping...

It wasn't the season of the west. Already Feng's Throyen allies were at the drudgery of opening the Gap road. They brought Feng to Maisak a week early.

Ragnarson stood in the parapet from which he had directed the first battle of Baxendala. His foster brother leaned on the battlements. General Liakopulos snored behind them. Varthlokkur paced, muttering. Below Karak Strabger, soldiers worked on the defenses. Fifty thousand men, half Kaveliners. Five thousand Mercenaries, Hawkwind himself commanding. Nineteen thousand from Altea, Anstokin, Volstokin, and Tamerice, the second-line states. The remainder were Itaskian bowmen, a surprise loan. They would make themselves felt.

Wagons swarmed behind the ranked earthworks, palisades, traps, incomplete fortifications. Long trains labored up from the lowlands. Baxendala had been converted to a nest of warehouses.

Bragi meant to compel Feng to overcome an endless series of redoubts in close fighting, under a continuous arrowstorm. Attrition was his game.

Marco said there would be twenty-eight legions supported by a hundred thousand auxiliaries from Argon, Throyes, and the steppe tribes. Ragnarson couldn't hope to turn such a horde. He aimed only to cut them up so badly they would have bitter going after they broke through.

Bragi wasn't watching the work. He stared eastward, over the peaks, at a pale streamer of smoke.

It was a signal from Maisak. While it persisted the fortress held.

Ragnarson used mirror telegraphy and carrier pigeons, too.

Shinsan had learned. The Tervola brought dismantled siege engines. For a week they pounded Maisak. The Marena Dimura reported encounters with battered patrols which had forced the Maisak gauntlet. They finished those patrols.

Those little victories hardly mattered. The patrols were forerunner driblets of the deluge.

"Smoke's gone!" Liakopulos ejaculated.

The mirror telegraph went wild.

"Damn! Damn-damn-damn! So soon." Ragnarson turned his back, waited for the telegraphists to interpret.

It was a brief, unhappy message. *Maisak betrayed. TennHorst.*

The last pigeon bore a note almost as terse. *Enemy led over mountains into caverns. Last message. Good luck. Adam TennHorst.*

It spoke volumes. Treachery again. Radeachar hadn't rooted it all out.

"Varthlokkur, have Radeachar check everybody out again. A traitor in the right place here would be worth a legion to them."

The weather was no ally either. A warm front accelerated the snow melt. Bragi's patrols reported increasingly savage skirmishes.

Then Ko Feng attacked.

Two things were immediately apparent. Shinsan had indeed noted the lessons of the previous battle. And the Tervola hadn't understood them.

Cavalry had ruined O Shing. So cavalry came down the Gap, steppe riders who had come for the plunder of the west.

Ragnarson countered with knights. Though grossly outnumbered, they sent the nomads flying, amazed at the invincibility of western riders.

Three days later it was an infantry assault by the undisciplined hordes of Argon and Throyes. Again the knights carried the day. The slaughter was terrible. Hakes Blittschau, an Altean commanding Ragnarson's horse, finally broke off the pursuit in sheer exhaustion.

Feng tried again with every horseman he could muster. Then he used his auxiliary infantry again. Neither attack passed Blittschau. The troops in the redoubts grumbled that they would never see the enemy.

When knights fought men untrained and unequipped to meet them, casualty ratios favored the armored men ridiculously. In five actions Blittschau killed more than fifty thousand of the enemy.

Ravens darkened the skies over the Gap. When the wind blew from the east the stench was enough to gag a maggot. After each engagement the Ebeler ran red.

Blittschau lost fewer than a thousand men. Many of those would recover from their wounds. Armor and training made the difference.

"Feng must be crazy," Ragnarson mused. "Or wants to rid himself of his allies."

Liakopulos replied, "He's just stupid. He hasn't got one notion how to run an army."

"A Tervola?"

"Put it this way. He's not flexible. The pretty woman. Mist. Says they call him The Hammer. Just keeps pounding till something gives. If it doesn't, he gets a bigger hammer. He's been holding that back."

"I know." Twenty-eight legions. One hundred seventy thousand or more of the best soldiers in the world.

When Feng swung that hammer, things would break.

The legions came.

The drums began long before dawn, beating a cadence which shuddered the mountains, which throbbed like the heartbeat of the world.

The soldiers in the works knew. They would meet the real enemy now, dread fighters who had been defeated but once since the founding of the legions.

Ragnarson gave Blittschau every man and horse available.

The sun rose, and the sun set.

Hakes Blittschau returned to Karak Strabger shortly before midnight, on a stretcher. His condition reflected that of his command.

"Wouldn't believe it if I didn't see it," Blittschau croaked as Wachtel cleansed his wounds. "They wouldn't give an inch. Let us hit them, then went after the horses till they got us on the ground." He rolled his head in a negative. "We must've killed twenty… No, thirty, maybe even forty thousand. They wouldn't budge."

"I know. You can't panic them. You have to panic the Tervola." Ragnarson was depressed. Feng had broken his most valuable weapon. Blittschau had salvaged but five hundred men.

The drums throbbed on. The hammer was about to fall again.

It struck at dawn, from one wall of the canyon to the other. Stubbornly, systematically, the soldiers in black neutralized the traps and redoubts, filled the trenches, demolished the barriers, breached the palisades and earthworks. They didn't finesse it. They simply kept attacking, kept killing.

Ragnarson's archers kept the skies dark. His swordsmen and spearmen fought till they were ready to drop. Feng allowed them respites only when he rotated fresh legions into the cauldron.

The sun dropped behind the Kapenrungs. Bragi sighed. Though the drums sobbed on, the fighting died. His captains began arriving with damage reports.

Tomorrow, he judged, would be the last day.

The archers had been the stopper. Corpses feathered with shafts littered the canyon floor. But the arrows were nearly gone. The easterners allowed no recovery of spent shafts.

Mist was optimistic, though. "Feng has gone his limit," she said. "He can't waste men like this. The Tervola won't tolerate it. Soldiers are priceless, unlike auxiliaries."

She was correct. The Tervola rebelled. But when they confronted Feng they found…

He had yielded command to a maskless man named Badalamen. With Badalamen were two old-timers: a bent one in a towering rage, and another with dull eyes. And with them, the Escalonian sorcerer, Magden Norath.

The bent man was more angry with himself than with Feng. His tardiness had given Feng time to decimate Shinsan's matchless army.

Feng grudgingly yielded to the Pracchia. The transition was smooth. Most Tervola chosen to come west were pledged to The Hidden Kingdom.

At midnight the voice of the drums changed.

Ragnarson exploded from a restless sleep, rushed to his parapet. Shinsan was moving. No precautions could completely squelch the clatter.

Reports arrived. His staff, his wizards, his advisors crowded onto the parapet. No one could guess why, but Shinsan was abandoning positions they had spent all day taking. Sir Tury Hawkwind and Haaken attacked on their own initiative.

"Mist. Varthlokkur. Give me a hint," Ragnarson demanded.

"Feng's been replaced," Mist said.

"Yeah? Okay. But why back down?"

"Oh!" Varthlokkur said softly.

Mist sighed. "The Power…"

"Oh, Hell!"

It was returning. Ragnarson decided he was done for.

The Unborn streaked across the night. Beneath it dangled Visigodred. After delivering the shaken wizard, it communed with Varthlokkur. "Gather the Circle!" Varthlokkur thundered. "Now! Now! Hurry!"

The monster whipped away too swiftly for the eye to follow.

Visigodred said, "Something is coming down the Gap. Creatures this world has never before seen. The ones Marco said turned Argon's war around. We can't stop them."

"We will!" Varthlokkur snapped. "The Unborn will! We have to." He, Visigodred, and Mist staggered. "The Power!" they gasped.

"Clear the parapet," Varthlokkur groaned, handling it more easily than the others. "We need it."

Kierle the Ancient arrived, followed by the Thing and Stojan Dusan. Radeachar rocketed in with the Egg of God. Ragnarson hustled his people downstairs.

He didn't want to stay either. There was little he dreaded so much as a wizard's war. But his pride wouldn't let him turtle himself.

Screams erupted from the canyon.

"They're here. The *savan dalage*," said Visigodred. "Varthlokkur. Unleash the Unborn before they gut us." He threw his hands overhead, chanted. A light-spear stabbed from his cupped hands. He moved them as though he were directing a mirror telegrapher. The earth glowed where the light fell. "Too weak," he gasped.

Here, there, Ragnarson glimpsed the invaders. Some were tall, humanoid, fanged and clawed, like the trolls of Trolledyngian legends. Some were squat reptilian things that walked like men. Some slithered and crawled. Among them were a hundred or so tall men who bore ordinary weapons. They reminded him of Badalamen.

And there was something more. Something shapeless, something which avoided light like death itself.

Radeacher swooped and seized one, soared into the night. Ragnarson saw an ill-defined mass wriggling against the stars.

"*Savan dalage*," Visigodred repeated. "They can't be killed."

Radeachar departed at an incredible speed.

"He'll haul it so far away it'll take months to get back," Varthlokkur said.

"How many?" Ragnarson asked.

"Ten. Fifteen. Be quiet. It begins."

A golden glow began growing up the Gap.

All the Circle had arrived. They babbled softly, in their extremity even welcoming Mist to their all-male club. This was no time for masculine prerogatives. Their lives and souls were on the gaming table.

Radeachar reappeared, undertook another deportation.

Ragnarson briefly retreated to the floor below, where a half-dozen messengers clamored for his attention.

His formations were shambled. His captains wanted orders. The troops were about to panic.

"Stand fast," he told them. "Just hang on. Our wizards are at work."

Back on the parapet he found the human sorcerers all imitating Visigodred, using light to herd the *savan dalage*.

The Egg, Thing, and Zindahjira concentrated on the remaining monsters.

"The men-things," Zindahjira boomed. "They're immune to the Power."

Ragnarson remembered Badalamen's indifference to Radeachar.

"They're human," he observed. "Sword and spear will stop them."

True. His men were doing so. But, like Badalamen, the creatures were incredible fighters, as far beyond the ordinary soldier of Shinsan as he was beyond most westerners.

"Arrows!" he thundered from the parapet. "Get the bowmen over there!" No one heard. He ducked downstairs to the messengers.

The struggle wore a new face when he returned. The Tervola had unleashed a sorcery of their own.

At first he believed it the monster O Shing had raised during First Baxendala. The Gosik of Aubochon. But this became a burning whirlwind with eyes.

Mist responded as she had then. A golden halo formed in the night. Within its confines an emerald sky appeared. From that a vast, hideous face leered. Talons gripped the insides of the circle.

The halo spun, descended. The ugly face opened a gross mouth, began biting.

The screams of the ensuing contest would haunt Bragi's dreams forever. Yet the struggle soon became a sideshow. Other Tervola-horrors rose. Ragnarson's sorcerers unleashed terrors in response.

Through it all the Unborn pursued its deportations in a workmanlike manner.

The whirlwind and halo rampaged up and down the Gap, destroying friend and foe. Once they crashed into Seidentop, the mountain opposite Karak Strabger. The face of the mountain slid into the canyon. In moments the defense suffered more than in all the previous fighting.

Shinsan tasted the bitterness of loss, too. Stojan Dusan conjured a seven-headed demon bigger than a dozen elephants, with as many legs as a centipede. Each was a weapon.

"It's the battle for Tatarian all over again," someone murmured. Ragnarson turned. Valther had come up. He had served Escalon in its ill-fated war with Shinsan.

The mountains burned as forests died. Smoke made breathing difficult.

"Pull out while you can," Valther advised. "Use this to make your retreat."

"No."

"Dead men can't fight tomorrow. Every death is a brick in his house of victory." Valther stabbed a finger.

High above, barely discernible, a winged horse drifted on updrafts.

"That damned old man again," Bragi growled.

Visigodred's apprentice suddenly struck from even higher. The winged horse slipped aside at the last instant. Marco kept dropping till Bragi was sure he would smash into a flaming mountainside. But the roc whistled along Seidentop's slope, used its momentum to hurl itself into the updraft over another fire.

Surprise gone, Marco tried maneuver. And proved he had paid attention to his necromantic studies. His sorceries scarred the night air. The winged horse weaved and dodged and fought for altitude.

Ragnarson asked Valther, "Who's winning? The battle."

"Us. Mist and Varthlokkur make the difference. Watch them."

Oh? Then why the admonition to get out?

They were holding the Tervola at bay and still grabbing moments for other work. Varthlokkur developed the Winterstorm construct. Mist opened and guided another, smaller halo. It cruised over the defensive works, snatching the creatures of Magden Norath. It even gobbled one *savan dalage.* Just one.

"Must have a bad taste," Ragnarson muttered sardonically.

Radeachar returned from a trip east and was unable to find another unkillable. He joined the assault on the Tervola.

"We've got them now," Valther crowed, and again Bragi wondered at his earlier pessimism.

The Tervola went to the defensive. Above, Marco harried the winged horse from the sky.

But, as Valther had meant, that old man *always* had another bolt in his quiver.

Fires floated majestically in from the eastern night, from beyond the Kapenrungs, like dozens of ragged-edged little moons.

Mist spied them first. "Dragons!" she gasped.

"So many," Valther whispered. "Must be all that're left."

Most dragons had perished in the forgotten Nawami Crusades.

Straight for the castle they came. The glow of their eyes crossed the night like racing binary stars. One went for Marco. He ran like hell.

The Unborn took over for him.

The leaders of those winged horrors were old and cunning. *They* remembered the Crusades. They remembered what sorcery had done to them then, when they had served both causes, fighting one another more often than warlocks and men. They remembered how to destroy creatures like those atop the castle.

"Get out of here!" Valther shouted. "You can't handle this."

Bragi agreed. But he dallied, watching the saurians spiral in, watching Radeachar drive the winged horse to earth behind Shinsan's lines.

The Unborn turned on its dragon harrier.

The beast's head exploded. Its flaming corpse careened down the sky, crashed, thrashing, into a blazing pine grove. Flaming trunks flung about. A terrible stench filled the Gap.

Varthlokkur completed his Winterstorm construct as a dragon reached the tower.

Ragnarson dove downstairs, collecting bruises and a scorching as dragon's breath pursued him.

"Messengers, Valther," he gasped. "You were right. It's time to cut our losses."

Ragnarson's army, covered by the witch-war, withdrew in good order. By dawn its entirety had evacuated Baxendala. Shinsan had redeemed its earlier defeat.

The wizard's war ended at sunrise, in a draw. Kierle the Ancient, Stojan Dusan, and the Egg had perished. The others scarcely retained the strength to drag themselves away.

Radeachar had salvaged them by driving the dragons from the sky.

The Tervola were hurt, too. Though they tried, they hadn't the strength or will to follow up.

The bent old man ordered Badalamen to catch Ragnarson, but Badalamen couldn't break Bragi's rear guard.

Ragnarson had bought time. Yet he had erred in not trying to hold.

As he debouched from the Gap he encountered eastbound allies from Hellin Daimiel, Libiannin, Dunno Scuttari, the Guild, and several of the Lesser Kingdoms. Auric Lauder commanded about thirty thousand men. Ragnarson borrowed Lauder's knights to screen his retreat.

He didn't try correcting himself. Baxendala was irrevocably lost. Shinsan still outnumbered him three to one, with better troops.

Lauder followed the example of previous allies and accepted Bragi as commander.

In thought, Ragnarson began laying the groundwork for the next phase, Fabian, accepting battle only in favorable circumstances, playing for time, trying to wear the enemy down.

THIRTY-TWO: SPRING-SUMMER-AUTUMN, 1012 AFE
DEFEAT. DEFEAT. DEFEAT.

Fahrig. Vorgreberg. Lake Turntine. Staake-Armstead, also called the Battles of the Fords. Trinity Hills, in Altea. The list of battles lost lengthened. Detached legions, supported by Magden Norath's night things, conquered Volstokin and Anstokin. Badalamen, by slim margins, kept overcoming the stubborn resistance of Ragnarson's growing army.

He reinforced his northern spearhead. It drove through Ruderin and curved southward into Korhana and Vorhangs. Haaken Blackfang, with a hasty melange of knights, mercenaries, and armed peasants, stopped the drive at Aucone. Ragnerson extricated himself from envelopment in Altea. Badalamen ran a spearhead south, through Tamerice, hoping eventually to meet the northern thrust at the River Scarlotti, behind Bragi.

Reskird Kildragon harried the Tamerice thrust but refused battle. Tamerice's army had been decimated in Kavelin.

Then Badalamen paused to reorganize and refit. He faced Ragnarson across a plain in Cardine just forty miles short of the sea and cutting the west in two.

In the Kapenrungs, Megelin bin Haroun chose to ignore the threat behind him. He launched another campaign against Al Rhemish and El Murid.

"Damn! Damn! Damn!" Ragnarson swore when the news arrived. "Don't he have a lick of sense?" He had counted on Megelin thinking like his father, had anticipated that the Royalists would conduct guerrilla war behind Badalamen's main force.

He sat before his tent with Liakopulos, Visigodred, his son, and officers from most of the nations which had sent troops. This ragtag army was the biggest gathered since the El Murid Wars.

"I think we've done well," said Liakopulos. Hawkwind and Lauder nodded. "We've managed to keep from being destroyed by the best army in the world."

Lord Harteobben, an Itaskian observer, agreed. "The persistence of your survival continues to amaze everyone."

"Uhm." Bragi surveyed his army.

It wasn't especially dangerous, despite its size. The demands of constant retreat hadn't given him time to organize and integrate. New contingents had to be thrown in immediately. Often his captains didn't speak the language of their neighbors in the line.

"Why shouldn't he?" Ragnar asked. "El Murid *is* Shinsan's client now." He stirred the fire with the tip of a crutch. He had been injured at Aucone. Haaken had sent him south to keep him from getting himself killed. He was too impetuous.

"Maybe. But I wish he'd helped us instead. Haroun would've seen that getting El Murid ain't worth a damn if the rest of the west goes."

At least the west now believed an eastern threat existed. But mobilizations hadn't helped yet. A battalion arrived now, a regiment then. Too little relative to the task.

The political question of who should be the supreme commander hadn't yet been posed. That the generals of major nations should be commanded by the Marshall of a country village-state like Kavelin seemed implausible to Ragnarson. He considered Hawkwind the best man. But his allies remained impressed with his ability to evade disaster.

Hawkwind didn't want the job anyway. He had had enough of command politics during the El Murid Wars.

"When'll we see help from Itaskia?" Bragi asked Visigodred. The wizard had been home several times and been able to produce just Lord Harteobben and another thousand bowmen. Itaskia was husbanding her resources to fight on home ground.

Ragnarson had rebuilt his cavalry advantage. He pressed it mercilessly, compelling the legions to remain close and their allies to stay within the protective umbrella of Badalamen's genius.

Marco and Radeachar hunted and exterminated the creatures of Magden Norath—excepting the *savan dalage,* the disease without a cure. The Tervola transported them back almost as fast as Radeachar hauled them away. Varthlokkur and the Unborn tried burying them in caverns on islands in the ocean, but even there the Tervola found them.

Shinsan's sorcerers had to be exterminated before the *savan dalage* could be solved permanently.

The Tervola wouldn't permit that.

For the time being, then, there was a thaumaturgic impasse.

At least, Bragi thought, if defeated, he would fall to force of arms.

The nearest town was Dichiara. The battle took its name.

It was the nadir of Ragnarson's career.

Badalamen announced himself with drums. Always Shinsan marched to the voice of drums, grumbling directions to legion commanders.

Bragi had had two weeks to prepare, to plan. He was as ready as time permitted.

Varthlokkur, privately, told him, "Back off. The omens aren't right."

Ragnarson remained adamant. "This far and no farther. This's the best position for leagues around. We'll hurt him here."

His army held a rough hill facing a plain on which cavalry could maneuver easily. His bowmen could saturate climbing attackers who survived the horsemen. Once Badalamen came to grips and drove him back, as was inevitable, he would withdraw into woods on the west slope, where Shinsan's tight formations would become less effective. He would re-form beyond the trees.

Attrition. That remained the game. Quick victory was out of the question. He worked against the day the power of the north took arms. Till then he had to stay alive.

His espionage was poorer than he thought.

Badalamen started his first wave.

Bragi, as always, responded with knights. That had worked well in every confrontation. He saw no reason to change.

Badalamen counted on that.

The knights swept over the plain—and into destruction ere striking a blow. Badalamen had cut a trench across his front, by night, and had camouflaged it.

The legions hit the tangle before the riders could extricate themselves. Half the knighthood of the coastal states and the Lesser Kingdoms perished.

Badalamen circled the debacle, rolled toward the hills. Ragnarson began falling back.

"I warned you," Varthlokkur said.

"Warned me, my ass! You could've been specific. Damned wizard never says anything straight out. Come on, Klaust. Get those men moving." He studied a map. "Hope we can ferry the Scarlotti. Else we're trapped at Dunno Scuttari."

The sun hadn't been up an hour. Radeachar, till now occupied deporting *savan dalage,* brought his first scouting report.

The legions in Tamerice weren't. They were racing north, having begun at sunset, and now were just ten miles away. They might beat him to the far side of the woods.

The withdrawal became a rout. Bragi desperately tried to keep control, to blunt the legions from Tamerice. The Guildsmen and his Kaveliners responded, but hadn't enough strength.

Their effort prevented total disaster. Most of the army escaped. Half reached the Scarlotti, where Ragnarson regained control and ferried them over.

Thousands of escapees joined Kildragon, who fled toward Hellin Daimiel.

Legions pushed south as far as Ipopotam, leaving enclaves at Simballawein, Hellin Daimiel, Libiannin, and Dunno Scuttari. The garrisons hadn't the strength to sally. The Itaskian Navy ran supplies in, as it had done during the sieges of the El Murid Wars.

Badalamen brought reinforcements through the transfers. Valther identified elements of seven legions not seen at Baxendala.

Badalamen beefed up the force in Vorhangs while facing Ragnarson across the Scarlotti near Dunno Scuttari. Blackfang strove valiantly, but hadn't the resources for success. He lost a battle at Glauchau, just three miles from Aucone. Agents of the Nines betrayed him. Haaken led the survivors westward.

Weeks passed. Late summer came. Though Badalamen drew heavily on transfers, most of his supplies and replacements came through the Gap. Again Ragnarson fought for time, trying to survive till winter isolated Badalamen.

The born general gathered boats and exchanged stares with Ragnarson. His Vorhangs expedition hammered Haaken back toward his brother.

The holocaust had come. Badalamen's auxiliaries erased towns, villages, crops. Winter's hunger would decimate the survivors.

Then Varthlokkur and Mist came to Ragnarson.

He stared guiltily across the broad Scarlotti, repeating, "This's my fault."

"Marshall, we've made a breakthrough. The biggest since Radeachar."

Bragi could imagine nothing capable of brightening the future. "You've compelled Itaskia to move?" Itaskia's noninvolvement stance was a bitter draught.

Varthlokkur chuckled. "No. We've found a way to scramble the transfer stream. We can intercede whenever they send."

"Oh? How long before they figure out how to stop you?"

"When they create their own Winterstorm."

"Maybe tomorrow, then. They're working on it. Because of the Unborn."

Varthlokkur smiled dourly. "He has orders to obliterate anybody research-ing it."

"Do whatever you want. Got to play every angle." Bragi turned, stared across the gleaming brown back of the river. How long till winter closed the Gap, giving him a chance to regain the initiative?

The Battle for the Scarlotti Crossing began with a massive, surprise thau-maturgic attack at midnight. The western army got badly mauled before Ragnarson's wizards reestablished the sorcerous stalemate.

By then legionnaires had landed. That, too, was a surprise. Bragi had antici-pated Badalamen shifting his emphasis toward Haaken. Coming straight into his strength seemed suicidal.

It was. For a time. But superior training, superior skills, gradually told. Earthen ramparts grew around the beachheads. Ragnarson's counterattacks, hampered by a haphazard command structure and language barriers, fell short.

Haaken, just four leagues upriver, reported himself under heavy pressure. Several legions had crossed above him, marching into Kuratel.

Daylight exposed the grim truth. The frontal attack was a feint. Badalamen's main force had moved upriver.

Ragnarson saw the trap. The bridgeheads. They were weak enough to destroy, but strong enough to last days. If he yielded to the bait, a pocket would close behind him. He had been outgeneraled again.

He offered his resignation. His allies and associates just laughed. Hawkwind suggested he get moving before Badalamen reaped the fruit of his maneuver.

Badalamen hadn't wanted to attack. Not here. The old man had been adamant. Failure of the transfers had made quick victory imperative. Winter was a foe he could neither manipulate nor coerce.

Bragi took command. He set Hawkwind and Lauder to confine the bridgeheads. He sent help to Haaken to secure his flank, and flung his remaining horsemen after the spearhead plunging into Kuratel. His vast, confused mass of infantry he led in retreat again, up the Auszura Littoral, out of the pocket.

He adopted the Fabian strategy again. The Porthune crossings he cleared and abandoned without contest. Itaskia became his goal, winter his weapon of choice.

Legions caught him near Octylya. In the absence of Badalamen, Ragnarson proved he had *some* talent. He sucked them into a trap, beneath his bows, and annihilated twenty-five thousand legionnaires. But he didn't grow heady. He persevered in his strategy.

In early October he crossed the Great Bridge into Itaskia the City, where he, Mocker, and Haroun had spent much of their earlier lives.

Reskird Kildragon had problems. Some of the Rebsamen faculty were agitating for accommodation with Shinsan. It surpassed him.

Hellin Daimiel had withstood years of siege during the El Murid Wars. Those defenders had never lost spirit. And that enemy hadn't planned to obliterate them.

Kildragon couldn't convince the dons that Badalamen was truly destroying everything and everyone outside.

Chance had separated Prataxis from Ragnarson at Dichiara. Now he was Kildragon's assistant. He came to Reskird one autumn evening, pale as old sin.

"I've found the answer. Our own people…"

"What?" The inevitability of failure had eroded Reskird's patience, making him a small, mean man, all snarl and bite.

"A Nines conspiracy. Here. At the Rebsamen. I stumbled on it… I was on my way to see my antiquarian friend, Lajos Kudjar, about the Tear of Mimizan. I overheard an argument in the Library, in the east wing, where they keep…"

"Skip the travelogue. Who? Where? How do we nail them?"

"In time, my dear man. This has to be handled properly. They have to be exposed carefully, every one identified. Else we risk turning Hellin Daimiel against us."

Kildragon stifled his temper and impatience. Survival instinct reminded him that a politically satisfactory outcome was critical.

A perilous month passed. Three times traitors opened the city gates. One quarter was irrevocably lost.

Then the member of the Pracchia, tricked with false directives, made his misstep. Prataxis made certain the right people were witnesses.

The mob destroyed the Rebsamen Nine.

Searching at Ragnarson's insistence, Radeachar uncovered a conspiracy in Itaskia.

The Greyfells group, an opposition party, had used treason as a political tool since the El Murid Wars. Radeachar destroyed every conspirator.

Itaskia's semineutral stance ended instantly.

Political victories, tactical defeats.

The big battle loomed. The bent man gathered his might on the south bank of the Silverbind. The contest, if he won, would shatter the west. Heads bent together. Famous men, old enemies from smaller wars, shared the map tables.

They dared not lose.

Yet winning would prove nothing. Not against Badalamen, armed with Shinsan's resources.

THIRTY-THREE: WINTER, 1012-SPRING, 1013 AFE
ITASKIA

"When?" Ragnarson asked Visigodred. He and the lean Itaskian watched Badalamen's army from the Southtown wall. Southtown, a fortified bridgehead of Itaskia the City, stood on the south bank of the Silverbind. It was the last western bastion below the river, excepting Hellin Daimiel and High Crag. Simballawein, Dunno Scuttari, Libiannin, and even Itaskian Portsmouth, had fallen during the winter.

The wizard shrugged. "When they're ready."

For months the armies had stared at one another, waiting. Bragi didn't like it. If Badalamen didn't move soon, Ragnarson's last hope of victory would perish. Each day the opening of the Savernake Gap drew closer. Marco said hordes of reinforcements were gathering at Gog-Ahlan. Shinsan's new masters were stripping their vastly expanded empire of every soldier.

Ragnarson also feared an early thrust through Hammad al Nakir. There were good passes near Throyes. The route was but a few hundred miles longer, though through desert. Megelin couldn't thwart the maneuver.

Megelin had taken Al Rhemish and declared himself King. But El Murid had escaped to the south desert, round Sebil el Selib, where his movement had originated. He would keep making mischief. Yasmid remained in his hands.

"We've got to get him going," Ragnarson growled, kicking a merlon.

Visigodred laid a gentle hand on his arm. "Easy, my friend. You're killing yourself with caring. And the auguries. Consider the auguries."

The wizards spent hours over divinations and could produce nothing definite.

Their predictions sounded like the child's game of knife, paper, and rock. Knife cuts paper, paper wraps rock, rock breaks knife. Every interpretation caused heated, inconclusive arguments among the diviners. Identical arguments raged amongst the Tervola.

Factions in each command insisted any attack would, like rock, knife, or paper, encounter its overpowering counter.

Drums throbbed. Their basso profundo was so old it bothered no one any longer. Several legions left Badalamen's encampment, making their daily maneuver toward Southtown.

It had been the coldest and snowiest winter in memory. Neither side had accomplished much. Each had weathered it. Shinsan had the force to seize supplies from the conquered peoples. Ragnarson's army had Itaskia's wealth and food reserves behind it. Badalamen had tried two desultory thrusts up the Silverbind, toward fords which would permit him to cross and attack toward Itaskia the City from the northeast. Lord Harteobben, his knights, and the armies of Prost Kamenets, Dvar, and Iwa Skolovda had crushed those threats.

Itaskia's fate would be decided before her capital, by whether or not Badalamen could seize the Great Bridge.

The structure was one of the architectural wonders of the world. It spanned three hundred yards of deep river, arching to permit passage of ships to Itaskia's naval yards, established upriver long before bridge construction began. Construction had taken eighty-eight years, and had cost eleven hundred lives, mostly workmen drowned in collapsed caissons. Engineers and architects had declared the task impossible beforehand. Only the obsession of Mad King Lynntel, who had ruled Itaskia during the first fifty-three construction years, had kept the project going till it had looked completable.

Despite a barbarian upbringing, Ragnarson cringed when he thought he might have to destroy the wonder.

The possibility had stirred bitter arguments for months, dwarfing the debate over supreme command. *That* had ceased when Varthlokkur had declared Ragnarson generalissimo. Nobody had argued with the slayer of Ilkazar.

The Great Bridge touched every Itaskian's life. Its economic value was incalculable.

Economics weren't Bragi's forte. He admired the bridge for its grandeur, beauty, and because it represented the concretization of the dream of The Mad Builder and his generation.

There were few sins in Bragi's worldview. He felt destroying the Great Bridge would be one.

His had been a lonely winter. He had seen little of his friends. Even Ragnar had been away most of the time, dogging, hero-worshiping, Hakes Blittschau. Haaken Bragi seldom saw, though his brother roomed just two blocks away. Gjerdrum came more than most, often slighting his duties. Michael, Aral, Valther, and Mist had disappeared, pursuing some mysterious mission at

Varthlokkur's behest. Few others had survived.

Bragi spent his time with the Itaskian General Staff, aristocrats who considered him down a yard of nose. They acquiesced to his command only because it was King Tennys's will.

They were above petty obstructionism, for which Bragi was grateful. They were professionals meeting a crisis. They devoted their energies to overcoming it. Their cooperation, though grudging, was worth battalions.

Varthlokkur sensed Bragi's alienation. A wizard, usually Visigodred, accompanied him everywhere, always providing a sympathetic ear. Ragnarson and Visigodred grew closer. Even pyrotechnic Marco acknowledged their relationship by according Bragi a grudging respect.

"Damn, I wish it would start," Bragi murmured. It was an oft-expressed sentiment. Even action leading to defeat seemed preferable to waiting. Plans and contingency plans had been carried to their limits. There was nothing more to occupy a lonely mind—except bitter memories.

His emotional lows outnumbered highs, and had since his return from Argon. Without Elana he couldn't be positive. Nothing could jack his spirits, get his emotions blazing.

Too, his children, and Ragnar's wife, were still in Kavelin. He couldn't stop brooding about that. They were hostages to Fate…

Badalamen he found puzzling. On the Scarlotti the man had kept several threats looming. Here he seemed to be doing nothing—and the Brotherhood watched closely.

"He's not loafing," Ragnarson declared. "But what's he up to?"

Again he wondered about his children. He had had no news. Were they alive? Had they been captured? Would they be used against him?

His Kaveliner soldiers had had no news either. They were a glum, brooding lot.

Radeachar and Marco seldom brought pleasant tidings from the south, save that Reskird and High Crag remained unvanquished. Reskird couldn't be reached because of patrolling dragons.

Winter had been hard in the occupied kingdoms…

A roar jerked his attention to the wall a quarter-mile eastward. "What the…?" A huge cloud of dust reached for the sun.

Another roar rose behind him. He spun, saw a section of wall collapsing, flinging into shallow snow.

"Miners!" he gasped. "Trumpets! Alert! Visigodred…"

The thin old wizard was in full career already. Bragi's shouts were drowned by a change in the song of the drums. More sections collapsed. Friendly horns screamed, "To arms!"

There were no civilians in Southtown. Its quickly busy streets contained only soldiers.

The maneuvering legions rushed toward the fortress.

Ragnarson's face turned grim. Badalamen had surprised him again. But what sane man would have sapped tunnels that long? How could he believe it would go undetected? How *had* he managed it?

Sections of wall kept crumbling.

"Too many breeches," Bragi muttered. More legions double-timed toward Southtown. A glow grew over Shinsan's camp. Bragi smiled. Sorcery. He had a surprise for Badalamen, too.

The first legionnaires hit the rubbled gaps. Arrows flew. The world's best soldiers were in for a fight this time. They were about to meet the soul of Itaskia's army, bowmen who bragged that they could nail gnats on the wing at two hundred yards. In the streets they would face the Iwa Skolovdan pikes who had dismayed El Murid's riders during those wars, and a host of crazy killers from Ragnarson's Trolledyngjan homeland, overpowering in their fearlessness and barbarian strength. They were Tennys's praetorians, selected for size, skill, and berserker battle style.

Bragi smiled tightly. His defense was reacting calmly and well. Rooftop bowmen made deathtraps of the gaps in the wall.

Yet he was about to be cut off.

A sound like the moan of a world dying rose from the enemy camp. The glow became blinding. Bragi ran.

Something whined overhead. He glimpsed the Unborn whipping southward.

He saw little after that. The invaders forced a band of defenders back upon him. He escaped that pocket only to become trapped in a bigger one.

Badalamen's sappers hadn't ended their tunnels at the wall. They had driven on into deep basements.

"Treason," Ragnarson muttered. "Can't ever root it out." Somebody had done the surveying…

Southtown decayed into chaos. Ragnarson just couldn't reach his headquarters. His rage grew. He *knew* his absence meant defeat.

The southern skyline flared, darkened. Thunders rolled. *Things* rocketed into view and away again. The Tervola were putting on one hell of a show. Varthlokkur's surprise must have fizzled.

He encountered Ragnar near the Barbican, the final fortification defending the Great Bridge.

"Father! You all right?"

"I'll make it." He was an ambulatory blood clot. A lot was his. "What's happening?"

"Covering the evacuation."

"What? Bring in…"

"Too late. Southtown's lost. You're about the last we'll save. They ran two tunnels under the river. They've closed the bridge twice. We reopened it, and closed one tunnel."

"Drown the sons of bitches." He turned. Southtown was burning. Fighting was waning. A ragged band of Trolledyngjans hurried their way, grim of visage. They had been stunned by their enemies. No soldiers should be that good.

"Save what you can. Don't let them take the Barbican." He started for the city. Two soldiers helped. He had lost a lot of blood.

He paused at the bridge's center. The Silverbind was alive with warships, each loaded with Marines. "What now?"

It was the first thing Haaken explained. "They've launched a fleet from Portsmouth, across the Estuary."

"Damn. That bastard don't miss a shot."

Ragnarson quickly counterattacked through the underriver tunnels. Zindahjira and Visigodred spearheaded. Badalamen's assault on the Barbican petered out.

"Your spook-pushers are whipping theirs," observed Lord Harteobben, recently appointed Itaskian Chief of Staff. "That Unborn… It won't let the Tervola direct their legions."

"We've got to hurt them while we can," Ragnarson averred. His wounds were worse than he would admit. Willpower couldn't keep him going. He collapsed.

Blackfang took charge, stubbornly pursued prepared plans.

The woman wore black. He couldn't see her clearly. She seemed ill-defined, haloed.

"Death," he sighed as she bent. The Dark Lady bringing her fatal kiss.

Her lips moved. "Marshall?" It tumbled down a long, cold tunnel littered with the bones of heroes.

The equalizer, the great leveler, had turned her gaze his way at last. The last narrow escape lay behind him, not ahead…

She wiped his face with a cold, wet cloth.

He saw more clearly.

This was no Angel of Death. She wore the habit of a lay helper of the Sisters of Mercy. The halo came of window light teasing through wild golden hair.

She had to be the daughter of an Itaskian nobleman. No common woman had the resources to so faithfully maintain her youth, to dress richly even in nursing habit.

He guessed her to be thirty… Then realized he was nude, and tendering a halfhearted male salute.

"The battle…" he babbled. "How long have I?"

"Four days." Her glance flicked downward, amused. "The fighting continues. Your Blackfang is too stubborn to lose." She bathed him, enjoying his embarrassment.

"The situation, woman, the situation," he demanded weakly.

She bubbled. "Admiral Stonecipher caught their fleet two days ago. They were seasick. He forced them onto the rocks at Cape Blood. The Coast Watch finished them. A historic victory, Father says. Greater than the Battle of the Isles."

"Ah." He smiled. "That'll warm Badalamen's heart." The fleet from Portsmouth had counted every seaworthy vessel captured along the western littoral. Tens of thousands of easterners must have drowned. "What about Southtown?"

She pushed him down. He was too weak to resist.

"The enemy who crossed over are cut off in Wharf Street South, west of the Bridge…"

"Crossed? To the city?" He tried to rise.

She pushed. "Father says it's still bloody in Southtown, but going our way. When Lord Harteobben attacked from the Fens…"

Bragi's head swam. He hadn't planned any operation from upriver.

"… and half the Tervola are dead. The Power went away for a while. It didn't save them." She made a sign against evil. "That thing… The Unborn… They say it melts their bones… The Power is back. Really, I don't know who'll win. I just know I'm not getting much sleep. The wounded… It's sickening. So many…"

"We're winning," he whispered, awed. "If Haaken's grabbed the initiative…"

Her fingertips brushed his stomach. Perhaps it was accidental. But Itaskian women, when their menfolks weren't looking, could be damned bold. And he was a celebrity. He had had some interesting offers, offers he wasn't emotionally ready to accept.

He was too weak this time. He drifted off cursing a missed opportunity.

There had been a change. A psyche as well as a body had begun healing.

Her name was Inger. He thought that a delicious irony. His first love had worn that name.

They had been pledged till Trolledyngjan politics had led to conflict between their parents. Inger's father had slain his. And now, so quickly, he was getting involved with a family he had fought from his arrival in Itaskia following the El Murid Wars.

She was a Greyfells, of a branch that had remained neutral in the Dukes of Greyfells's periodic assays at seizing the Itaskian throne. One of those Ragnarson himself had thwarted through the expedient of assassination. His arranging the murder had sent him flying to Kavelin…

That Duke had been Inger's father's eldest brother.

It's a bloody strange world, he thought, lying beside her, concern about the war briefly forgotten.

Possibly there was a more efficacious therapy, but neither Wachtel, Visigodred, nor Varthlokkur could name it. A week of Inger wrought miracles.

Ragnarson even stopped suffering from the wounds Mocker had dealt him. He left that hospital renewed, with plans, with a destination, a goal for after the war.

He had broken another resolve. Another woman had penetrated his soul.

Only Inger updated him during his convalescence. No one came for his advice. His pride was bruised—till he heard that Varthlokkur had ordered his isolation. He had, like an athlete, been off his form. The wizard, selfishly, wanted to give him time to find himself.

Haaken managed well enough, both at battering Badalamen and cowing aspirants to supreme command. Adopting Haroun's style, he jabbed from every direction, avoiding haymakers, fading when the enemy turned to fight. In Southtown he succeeded on stubbornness, knowledge of his men, and devotion to Bragi's planning. He, like Bragi, respected the Itaskian bow. Plied from housetops, it gave him mastery of the streets. He used them as killing zones, letting Badalamen commit ever more men to Southtown's capture. He buried the pavement in corpses.

Now, Bragi saw from the Great Bridge, Southtown was so grim even the vultures shied away.

Visigodred's and Zindahjira's tunnel attacks had taken them to the heart of Shinsan's camp. They had started a few fires, then had withdrawn. The damage was more moral than physical.

Attacked from every direction, mundanely and magically, the Tervola were in disarray. Blittschau and Lord Harteobben harried all but the largest foraging parties. They made occasional forays against the main encampment.

The dismay of the Tervola communicated itself to the Pracchia. Badalamen argued that victory couldn't be attained in present circumstances. Soon his superior force would be leagued up in its own camp. Forcing the Great Bridge was plainly impossible. Attempts to outflank it had failed. He urged a staged retreat calculated to draw Ragnarson into the open. There, hopefully, he could be lured into pitched battle and obliterated. Magden Norath backed him.

The bent old man was impatient. He wanted the holocaust now. He demanded another try at the river. Or, if Badalamen had to move, he should take the entire army up the Silverbind, to Prost Kamenets, Dvar, and Iwa Skolovda, depriving Itaskia of her allies, returning south after fording the river's upper reaches.

The Tervola refused. They wanted to escape Varthlokkur's fury long enough to develop a counter to the Unborn. And Norath wanted to rearm with his own special weapons.

"It's good, Haaken," Ragnarson kept saying. "The only sane course."

"You'd think so. You did the planning."

"The trouble with nibbling is we have to finish before the Gap opens."

"How?" Ragnar demanded. "He'll treat us like a stepchild if we try to take him heads up."

Despite Badalamen's severe losses recently, that remained immutable. Shinsan couldn't be beaten on the battlefield. Quiet, gentle, loving Visigodred offered an answer.

It was disgusting. It turned Bragi's stomach.

Visigodred said, "Remember when Duke Greyfells brought the plague from Hellin Daimiel? With the ships filled with rats?"

Ragnarson remembered. He, Haroun, and Mocker had foiled that cunning play for Itaskia's throne and had won the eternal gratitude and indulgence of the Itaskian War Ministry.

Volunteers returned to the fetor and horror of Southtown, trapping rats. Radeachar scattered them through the enemy camp.

The inconclusive fighting continued. Bragi applied more pressure, trying to keep the legions crowded so plague would spread swiftly if it got started.

Only sorcery could stop the disease.

Could Varthlokkur protect his allies? Plague ignored artificialities like national allegiance. Itaskia, packed with refugees and soldiers, made fertile disease ground.

The wizard didn't know.

Days passed. Then Badalamen suddenly came alive. He narrowly missed luring Lord Harteobben to his destruction near Driscol Fens. Later the same day Hakes Blittschau rode into an ambush Marco had missed seeing from above. While they licked their wounds, Badalamen moved.

Nighttime. Ragnarson galloped across the Great Bridge, answering Visigodred's summons. The wizard was directing the cleansing of Southtown.

He showed Bragi a southern horizon aflame. Badalamen had won his argument with the bent man. "What's happening?" Ragnarson demanded.

"They're pulling out. He summoned his dragons at dusk, fired everything."

"Marco. Radeachar. Where are they?"

"Staying alive."

The dragons had rehearsed handling the two. Marco was impotent against their ganging tactics. He remained grounded. The Unborn could go up, but under pressure could accomplish nothing.

Dawn came. Still the fires raged. Forests, fields, Shinsan's camp. The dragons kept them burning.

A lone masked horseman waited near the empty camp. The bones of burned corpses lay heaped behind him. He bore a herald's pennon.

"Looks like plague got some," Ragnarson observed. "Who is he?"

"Ko Feng," Varthlokkur replied. Jeweled eyes tracked them coldly. "Easy. He won't try anything under the pennon."

"A message?" Ragnarson asked.

"Doubtlessly."

Feng said nothing. He dipped his pennon staff till it pointed at Bragi's heart. Ragnarson removed the note. Feng rode stiffly into a narrow avenue through the flames.

"What is it, Father?" Ragnar asked.

"Personal message from Badalamen." Gaze distant, he tucked it inside his shirt.

Another meeting. A reckoning. An end. Softly, gentlemanly, dreadfully, Badalamen promised. Kings on the chessboard, Badalamen said. Played like pawns. Endgame approaching.

"Beyond the fire…" Ragnarson murmured, looking southward. Then he turned and hurried toward the city.

An army had to march.

Even in retreating Badalamen had surprised him. He would get a week's lead from this…

It would be a bittersweet week, he thought, filled with impassioned good-byes.

His thing with Inger was getting serious.

THIRTY-FOUR: SPRING, 1013 AFE
THE ROAD TO PALMISANO

"Goddamnit, lemme alone!" Kildragon snarled. He pulled his blanket over his head.

The cold, thin fingers kept shaking him.

"Prataxis, I'm gonna cut you."

"Sir?"

Reskird surrendered, sat up. His head spun. His gut tried to empty itself again. It had been a hard night. A lot of wine had gone down. He fumbled with his clothing. "I said don't bother me for anything but the end of the world."

"It's not that." But it was earthshaking.

"They *are* pulling out," Reskird whispered, awed. He hadn't believed Derel. The sun hadn't yet risen and already the besiegers were moving. Engines and siegeworks burned behind them. A rearguard awaited the inevitable recon-naissance-in-force.

"Got to be a trick," Kildragon muttered. That Shinsan should give up, and liberate him from the interminable political hassle of this walled Hell, seemed too good to be true.

A dragon glided lazily overhead. It was a reminder that Shinsan wasn't de-parting in defeat.

"Something happened up north," Prataxis reasoned.

"What was your first clue?"

There had been no communication with Itaskia since the fall of Portsmouth. Marco had, occasionally, tried to, and had failed to, penetrate the dragon screen. The Unborn, apparently, wasn't doing courier duty.

"We better get moving," Kildragon sighed. "Bragi will need us. Tell the Re-gents they can join us—if they'll stop fussing about money long enough to give the orders."

Kildragon had spent eons listening to complaints about the cost of defending the city.

Ragnarson sent a few companies across the Scarlotti. They met no resistance. Light horse scouts followed.

"I don't understand him," he told Haaken. "Why didn't he try to stop us here?"

Badalamen served the Pracchia. And the Pracchia were divided. Receiving conflicting orders from the old man and Norath, Badalamen could do nothing adequately. Each failure deepened the split between his masters.

The once invincible army of Shinsan now twitched and jerked like a beheaded man.

"Palmisano," Ragnarson mused, finger on a map. There was a fateful feel to the name. It sent chills down his spine.

The Pracchia closed ranks temporarily. Badalamen turned to fight.

Palmisano, in Cardine, lay close to the Scarlotti. The survivors of thirty legions waited there, an ebony blanket on a rolling countryside. Tens of thousands of steppe riders, Argonese, and Throyens guarded river-girdled flanks.

"We have to go to him this time," Ragnarson muttered. He had scouted the region. The prospects didn't look favorable.

He didn't need Badalamen's letter to tell him this would be their last meeting. He didn't need the prophecies of Varthlokkur and his cohorts. He knew it in his bones. The winner-take-all was coming. This would be the *Götterdämmerung* for Bragi Ragnarson or the born general. One war chieftain wouldn't leave this stage…

He had little hope for himself.

Just when he had found new reason to live.

Each morning the armies stared at one another across the ruins of Palmisano. The captains, generals, and kings with Ragnarson howled at the delay. Badalamen's incoming occupation forces swelled his army. The snows in the Savernake Gap were melting.

Two quieter voices counseled delay. Varthlokkur and Visigodred had something up their sleeves.

News came that Reskird was approaching. His ragtag army had skirmished its way up from Hellin Daimiel, preventing several thousand foemen from rejoining Badalamen. Ragnarson and Blackfang rode to meet their friend.

When they returned, next day, the sorcerers were abuzz.

Visigodred and Varthlokkur were ready.

Valther, Mist, Trebilcock, and Dantice had reappeared.

The Council was a convention of Kings and Champions. Twenty-seven monarchs attended. Hawkwind, Lauder, and Liakopulos attended. Harteobben and Blittschau, Moor and Berloy, Lo Pinto, Piek, Slaski, Tantamagora, Alacran, Krisco, Selenov… The list of renowned fighters ran to a hundred names. The old companions, wizards' and Ragnarson's, were all there, too. And his son, and Derel Prataxis with the inevitable writing box. And near Iwa Skolovda's King Wieslaw, an esquire, unknown and untried, whose name had puzzled wizards for years.

Varthlokkur announced, "Valther and Mist have returned." He indicated Dantice and Trebilcock. "Protected by these men, they visited The Place of A Thousand Iron Statues."

"Nobody ever got out alive," Zindahjira protested. "I used to send adventurers there. They never came back. The Star Rider himself animated the killer statues."

"The Star Rider came and went at will," Varthlokkur replied.

"Armed with a Pole of Power."

"As were my friends." Varthlokkur smiled gently. "The Monitor of Escalon wasn't lying." He held up the Tear of Mimizan, so bright no one could gaze upon it. His fellows babbled questions.

"It was the supreme test. And now we know. We go into battle perfectly armed."

Ragnarson held his peace. Point, he thought. Do you know how to use it? No. Point. The old man over there does.

Getting him, too, had become an intense personal goal. The man had shaped his life too long. He wanted to settle up on the one-to-one.

"The Tervola who remain," Varthlokkur continued, "can be rendered Powerless. My friends accomplished that. They exceeded the Monitor. We control the thaumaturgic game. But let them tell it."

Michael Trebilcock did the talking. He didn't embellish. They had crossed Shara, the Black Forest, the Mountains of M'Hand, and had hurried to The Place of A Thousand Iron Statues. They had penetrated it, had learned to manipulate the Tear and living statues, had discovered secrets concerning the Star Rider's involvement in the past, then had reversed their course, reaching Itaskia soon after Ragnarson had begun pursuing Badalamen. Michael skipped dangers, ambushes, perils that would have become an epic on another's tongue. His stage fright compelled brevity. He communicated his belief that they now possessed the ultimate weapon.

Ragnarson shook his head. Softly, "Fools."

The crowd demanded action. They were tired of war. They weren't accustomed to prolonged, year-round campaigns, dragging ever on. The exiles were eager to return home and resume interrupted lives.

Varthlokkur, too, was eager. He had left Nepanthe in Kavelin.

"Not yet," he shouted. "Tomorrow, maybe. We have to plan, to check the auguries. Those legions won't roll over."

Ragnarson nodded grimly. The Tear *might* disarm the Tervola. But soldiers had to be beaten by soldiers. What Power remained to Varthlokkur and the Unborn, through the Winterstorm, would be devoted to the creatures of

Magden Norath.

Badalamen had anchored his flanks on a tributary of the Scarlotti and the great river itself, footing a triangle. He couldn't withdraw easily, but neither could he be attacked from behind. Refusing to initiate battle himself, he had repeatedly demonstrated his ability to concentrate superior force at any point Bragi attacked.

Ragnarson knew there would be no finesse in it. The terrain didn't permit that. The armies would slaughter one another till one lost heart.

He and Badalamen were sure which would break. And that, with the pressures received from his masters, was why Badalamen had opted for this battle.

Why he had chosen the imperfect ground of Palmisano remained a mystery, though.

Ragnarson attacked at every point, his probes having revealed no weaknesses. His front ranks were the stolid pikemen of Iwa Skolovda, Dvar, and Prost Kamenets. Behind them were Itaskian bowmen who darkened the sky with their arrows. While the legions crouched beneath shields, suffering few casualties, otherwise unemployed westerners scuttled between pikemen to fill the trench preventing Ragnarson from using his knights. Badalamen's men countered with javelins. It was an innovation. Shinsan seldom used missiles.

Here, there, Badalamen had integrated Argonese and Throyen arbalesters...

Ragnarson's men crossed the ditch several times, and were hurled back.

That was the first day. A draw. Casualties about even. Ultimate point to Badalamen. He was a day nearer the moment when the Savernake Gap opened.

The witch-war was Varthlokkur's. His coven gathered over the Tear and round the Winterstorm, and taught the Tervola new fear.

The bent old man could have countered with his own Pole. He didn't. His situation wasn't so desperate that he was willing to reveal, undeniably, his true identity.

The night was Shinsan's. *Savan dalage* in scores stalked the darkness, trying to reach the Inner Circle and Bragi's commanders. Captains and a wizard died...

Now Bragi knew why Badalamen had chosen Palmisano.

A half-ruined Empire-era fortress crowned a low hill beside the eastern camp. Within it, after coming west, Magden Norath had established new laboratories. From it, now, poured horrors which ripped at the guts of the western army.

The second day was like the first. Men died. Ragnarson probed across both rivers, had both thrusts annihilated. His men filled more of Badalamen's ditch.

Again the night belonged to the *savan dalage,* though Varthlokkur and his circle concentrated on Norath's stronghold instead of the Tervola.

Marco predicted the Gap would be open in eleven days.

The third day Ragnarson sent up mangonels, trebuchets, and ballistae to knock holes in the legion ranks so Itaskian arrows could penetrate the shield-walls. His sappers and porters finished filling the ditch.

That night the *savan dalage* remained quiet. Ragnarson should have been suspicious.

Next morning he stared across the filled ditch at lines of new chevaux-de-frise. There could be no cavalry charge into those.

The fringe battles picked up. The bent man threw in his surviving dragons. Norath's creatures, excepting the light-shunning *savan dalage,* swarmed over the chevaux and hurled themselves against the northern pikes.

"The tenor is changing," Bragi told Haaken. "Tempo's picking up."

Haaken's wild dark hair fluttered in the breeze. "Starting to realize the way the wind's blowing. Their day is over. Them spook-pushers are finally doing some good."

It looked that way. Once Norath's monsters disappeared, Varthlokkur could concentrate on Shinsan's army…

Ragnarson's heavy weapons bombarded the chevaux with fire bombs. Behind the western lines, esquires and sergeants prepared the war-horses. Above, Radeachar and Marco swooped and weaved in a deadly dance with dragons.

Bragi waved.

"What?"

"There." Ragnarson pointed. Badalamen, too, was observing the action. He waved back.

"Arrogant bastard," Haaken growled.

Bragi chuckled. "Aren't we all?"

Ragnar galloped up. "We'll be ready to charge at about four." He had spent a lot of time, lately, with Hakes Blittschau, enthralled by the life of a knight.

"Too late," Bragi replied. "Not enough light left. Tell them tomorrow morning. But keep up the show."

Badalamen didn't respond. He recognized the possible and impossible.

That night he launched his own attack.

Savan dalage led. As always, panic surrounded their advance. Radeachar swept to the attack. Above, Marco tried to intimidate the remaining dragons. Following the *savan dalage,* unnoticed in the panic, came a column of Shinsan's best.

As Haaken had observed, Badalamen had sniffed the wind. This move was calculated to disrupt Ragnarson's growing advantages.

The attack drove relentlessly toward the hill where the captains and kings maintained their pavilions, and where the war-horses were kept.

Kildragon and Prataxis woke Ragnarson, Reskird shouting, "Night attack! Come on! They're headed this way."

The uproar approached swiftly. Norath had committed everything he had left. Panic rolled across the low hill.

Ragnarson surveyed the night. "Get some torches burning. Fires. More light.

We've got to see." And light would turn the *savan dalage.*

Ragnar, Blittschau, and several knights ran past, half-armored, trying to reach the horses. If the enemy scattered those…

"Haaken?" Bragi called. "Where the hell's my brother?"

He looked and looked, couldn't find Haaken anywhere.

Blackfang hadn't been able to sleep. For a time he had watched Varthlokkur work, marveling both at the Winterstorm and Mist, who manipulated some symbols from within the construct. He shook his head sadly. He had never had a woman of his own, just chance-met ladies for a night or a week, their names quickly forgotten. No doubt his own had slipped their minds as quickly.

He had begun feeling the weight of time upon him, his lack of a past. His life he had devoted to helping Bragi build Bragi's dreams. Now he realized he had never spun a dream of his own.

The noise from the front was different tonight. Badalamen was up to something. He rushed toward the clamor, torch in one hand, sword in the other. He didn't fear the *savan dalage.* He had met them before. A torch could hold them at bay till Radeachar arrived.

Badalamen drove through the juncture of Iwa Skolovdan forces with those of Dvar, into the Itaskians behind. Men of all three countries shrieked questions, got no intelligible answers. Some fought one another in their confusion.

A solid, single black column poured through.

Blackfang, through sheer lungpower, assembled company commanders, calmed panic, gave orders, led the counterattack.

Pikemen and arrows. A deadly storm tore at the legions, opening gaps. The Iwa Skolovdans insinuated themselves, broke the unity of the column. Blackfang, howling, brought more men to bear. That part of Shinsan's advance devolved into melee. Haaken, with a woodcutter's axe, inspired those near enough to see. Always, when not shouting other orders, he called for torches and fires.

Forty-five minutes later the gap was gone. The line was secure. He turned his attention to the thousands who had broken through.

The headquarters hill was aflame. It looked bad for its defenders.

Though near exhaustion, Blackfang ran to help his brother.

The *savan dalage* caught him halfway. There were three of them. He couldn't swing his torch fast enough. He went down cursing his killers.

The dwarf kicked the roc into a screaming, sliding dive. Fear and exhilaration contested for his soul. One dragon side-slipped winging over, the air rippling its wings. They fluttered and cracked like loose tent canvas in a high wind. The monster vanished in the darkness.

"One away," Marco crowed. "Come on, you bastards."

The other two held the turn and took the dive, wingtip to wingtip, precisely, their serpentine necks outthrust like the indicting fingers of doom. They were old and cunning, those two.

The fire and fury of the battlefield expanded swiftly, rocking and spinning as the roc maneuvered. To Marco it seemed someone had hurled him at a living painting of the floor of Hell. The roar swelled. His heart hammered. This was his last chance. A do or die game of chicken. *They* had to pull up first...

They were old and wise and knew every molecule of the wind. They stayed with him. Their wings beat like brazen gongs when they broke their fall.

Marco glimpsed startled faces turned suddenly upward. Screams. A dragon shriek when one pursuer's wingtip dipped too low and snagged a tent top.

"Eee-yah!" Marco screamed over his shoulder. "Let's go, you scaly whoreson. You and me. We got a horse race now." One on one he could outfly the grand-daddy dragon of them all.

He didn't see the winged horse quartering in. He didn't see the spear of light.

He felt pain, and an instant of surprise when he realized there was nothing but air beneath him.

The stars tumbled and went out.

Six columns of two thousand men each followed scattered trails, captained by old killers named Rahman, El Senoussi, Beloul. A seventh's path defined their base course.

It was tired, deserted country they rode. The few survivors vanished at the sound of hooves.

The young King had led his tired, grumbling old terrorists through night-march after night-march till, now, they saw dragons scorching the northern sky.

"It's begun," Megelin sighed. He planted his standard and waited for his commanders.

He fell asleep wondering if his gesture had merit, if his father's ghost would approve.

The night stalkers pursued the creature calling himself the Silent, who for centuries had been anything but. He hated light almost as much as they, but in his terror spelled anything to keep them at bay. Balls of flame floated overhead. He flailed about with swords of fire.

The long span of his arrogant bluster was scheduled to end. The Norns had scribbled-in Palmisano as the destination that ended his life-road.

The nearness of *savan dalage* stampeded a herd of war-horses. In the fractional second while they distracted him, Zindahjira died.

The stampeding mounts battered Ragnar. He scuttled beneath a haywagon. It nearly capsized in the equine tide.

The smell of *savan dalage* overrode that of horse fear and manure. Sweat soaked Ragnar's clothing. He had no torch. "Hakes!" He heard Blittschau bellowing, but the Altean didn't hear him. The clang of metal on metal rose against the drumming of hooves.

Shinsan's men had reached the horses.

The last screaming, lathered stallion hurtled past…

Ragnar rose slowly, his palm cold and moist on his sword hilt. A tiger-masked Tervola and three dark soldiers advanced with scarlet swords.

The wagon frame ground into his back…

The western line bent, bowed, withdrew a hundred yards under Badalamen's predawn general attack. But he committed auxiliaries and allies, spending their lives to tire and weaken his foes. They didn't break through. The panic of the night hadn't gotten out of hand.

Ragnarson, having shed his tears, rose from beside his dead. He shook off Reskird's sympathetic hand. "I'm all right." His voice was cold and calm. He glanced at the crown of the hill where, till last night, his headquarters had stood. The surviving attackers were heightening their earthworks.

They had completed their mission. Now they would await relief from their commander.

Visigodred departed the tent concealing the remains of his oldest and dearest antagonist. Mist held him momentarily, whispering. Radeachar had just found Marco.

Like scenes were occurring everywhere. A dozen national ensigns flew with hastily stitched black borders. Death had shown few favorites during her midnight rampage.

Bragi glimpsed a winged horse settling into the remains of the Imperial fortress. He growled, "We begin."

Trumpet voices filed the air. Drums responded. The knights advanced. Their pennons waved bright and bold. Their spirits were high. King Wieslaw of Iwa Skolovda had made a speech to stir the souls of veterans as old as and cynical as Tantamagora and Alacran.

This would be their finest hour, the battle remembered a thousand years. The greatest charge in history.

An infantryman walked at each stirrup. Some were the knights' men. Most were doughty fighters Ragnarson had assigned: Trolledygnjans, Kaveliners, Guildsmen, veteran swordsmen who had been withheld from the front. They were rested and ready.

Aisles opened through the pikes and bows. Arrows darkened the air. Mangonels and trebuchets released.

The Iwa Skolovdan battle pennon dipped, signaling the charge.

How bright their crests and pennons! How bold the gleam of their armor! How brilliant their countless shields! The earth groaned beneath their hooves.

The sun itself seemed to quake as the army shouted with a hundred thousand throats.

The drums changed voice as Wieslaw spurred his charger. Lockstep, the men in black marched backward.

Not many pits appeared, but enough to blunt the charge.

"Damn!" Ragnarson growled, watching the gleaming tide break on the black wall, slow, and swirl like paints mixing.

The knights abandoned their lances, flailed with swords or maces. The men who had run at their stirrups guarded the horses.

The bowmen, unable to ply their weapons without killing friends, grabbed swords, axes, hammers, mauls, rushed into the melee.

Bragi had kept no reserve but the pickets round last night's raiders, and the pikemen, who would screen any withdrawal.

From river to river the slaughter stretched, awesome in scale.

"Even the Fall of Tatarian wasn't this bloody," Valther murmured.

Derel Prataxis, without glancing up from his tablet, observed, "Half a million men. The biggest battle ever."

He was wrong, of course, but could be pardoned ignorance of the Nawami Crusades.

"Need to fall back and charge again," Ragnarson grumbled. But there was no way to order it. He could only hope his captains didn't let their enthusiasm override their sense.

Not that time. Wieslaw, Harteobben, and Blittschau extricated themselves, returned to their original lines. The easterners pressed the pikemen hard till the Itaskians again hid the sun behind arrows. Then the knights and stirrup men charged again.

Ragnarson and his party talked little. Grimly, Bragi watched Harteobben and Blittschau, on the wings, begin to be devoured. Only Wieslaw's echelon maintained momentum.

Ragnarson considered fleeing to Dunno Scuttari. He could take ship to Freyland and rally the survivors there… No. Inger wouldn't be there. He had left too many dear ones behind already. His role in this war had been to leave a trail of his beloved. There had to be an end. He would share the fate of his army. He would fulfill the letter of Badalamen's message.

He saw to his weapons. His companions watched nervously, then did likewise. Prataxis rode through camp collecting cooks, mule-skinners, grooms, and the walking wounded.

THIRTY-FIVE: SPRING, 1013 AFE
PALMISANO: THE GUTTERING FLAME

It seemed he had been chopping at black armor for days. He had trained and trained, but his instructors hadn't told him how arduous it would be. Here, unlike the practice field, he couldn't rest.

"Almost through!" Wieslaw screamed, gesturing with his bloody sword. Only a thin line screened the open ground beyond Shinsan's front.

The esquire glanced back. The hundreds who had followed Wieslaw now numbered but dozens.

The youth redoubled his attack.

The line broke. They were through. Wieslaw cavorted as though the battle itself had been won. His standard bearer galloped to his side. More knights surged through the gap, rallied round, congratulated one another weakly.

The respite lasted but moments. Then a band of steppe riders attacked. While the westerners turned that threat their bolt hole closed behind them.

"Badalamen," said Wieslaw. "We have to plant a sword in the dragon's brain."

The esquire stared across the quarter-mile separating them from the born general. Badalamen's bodyguards had sprung from the sorcerous wombs of the laboratories of Ehelebe. And crowds of Throyens masked them.

Wieslaw assembled his people to charge.

The Throyens put up little fight. In minutes the knights reached the tall, expressionless guards surrounding Badalamen.

Ragnarson cursed as his mount screamed and stumbled. Her hamstrings had been cut. He threw himself clear, smashed a black helmet with his war axe while leaping. He continued hacking with wild, two-handed swings, past pain, rage, and frustration, exploding in a berserk effort to destroy Shinsan single-handedly.

He knew no hope anymore. He just wanted to hurt and hurt until Badalamen couldn't profit from winning.

His companions felt the change. Morning's optimism was becoming afternoon's despair. The invincible legions were, again, meeting their reputation. Soldiers began glancing backward, picking directions to run.

Varthlokkur, too, despaired. He had recognized his antagonist at last. Shinsan, Tervola, Pracchia, Ehelebe, all were smokescreens. Behind them lurked the Old Meddler, the Star Rider. He knew, now, because someone was negating his manipulation of the Tear. Only the other Pole's master could manage that.

The devil had come into the open. He needed anonymity no more.

It seemed but a matter of time till the tide turned and the Power became Shinsan's faithful servant once more. Not even Radeachar, frantically buzzing the old fortress, would help. The Tervola had learned to neutralize the Unborn.

How long? Two hours? Four? No more, certainly.

Varthlokkur watched Mist and longed for Nepanthe.

Four still lived. The esquire. Wieslaw. His standard-bearer. A baronet of Dvar. Bodies carpeted the slope.

Badalamen fought on, alone, surrounded.

The born soldier struck. The esquire fell, a deep wound burning his side. Hooves churned the earth about him. He staggered to his feet. The baronet fell. The standard-bearer cried out, followed. The esquire seized the toppling standard, murmuring, "It can't fall before His Majesty."

Badalamen seemed to strike in slow motion. The youth's thrust with the banner spear seemed even slower.

Wieslaw collapsed. Badalamen, speartip between his ribs, followed. The esquire, Odessa Khomer, fell across both.

A mystery long pursued by sorcerers of both sides consisted of a youth with makeshift weapon. Thus the Fates play tricks when revealing slivers of tomorrow.

Megelin whipped his horse, surged out of the river. Fighting greeted him, but Beloul quickly routed the Argonese pickets. Megelin surveyed the battleground. Nothing barred him from reaching the main contest. Shinsan's encampment appeared undefended. Only the few pickets weren't in the battle line.

He gathered his captains, gave his orders. Wet horsemen, tired-eyed, formed their companies.

"Three hours, Beloul," the young King remarked, glancing at the westering sun.

Beloul didn't reply. But he followed. His mind had stretched enough to see the national interest in a defeat of Shinsan.

Their charge swept through the eastern camp and round the hill where the old fortress stood. Megelin and a handful of followers invaded the stronghold. They found nothing, though in a courtyard they so startled a winged horse that it took flight and vanished into the east. Puzzled, Megelin left, led his men against the enemy rear. He swept past the drama of Badalamen and Odessa Khomer only minutes after its completion, and never learned what had happened there.

A centurion informed the Tervola.

Only a dozen survived. Each had pledged himself to Ehelebe in times gone by. The Star Rider had saved each from the Unborn. But command was devolving on unready Aspirants and noncoms.

They repudiated their oaths, reelected Ko Feng commander.

"That's all. We're done here," Feng said. "Though the cause isn't necessarily lost, I propose we withdraw."

The Tervola agreed. Shinsan's destiny could no longer be pursued through the fantasy of Ehelebe. Nor could it without legions which, pushed to win today, might be pushed too far. The army's skeleton had to be salvaged so Shinsan could rebuild against tomorrow.

The bloody mind-fog lifted. For a moment Ragnarson stood amidst the carnage, shield high, axe dragging, puzzled. The pressure had eased. His men had stopped backing up. An army tottering at the brink, already disintegrating, had stiffened unexpectedly...

Or had it?

He caught a hobbling, distraught horse, mounted for the instant needed to discover that Shinsan was disengaging. As always, in good order, evacuating the wounded first, still attacking along a narrow aisle to relieve the force waiting on the hilltop.

Desert-garbed men flew about behind them. The easterners ignored them, having already taught them the cost of getting too close.

The sun was nearing the horizon. In an hour it would be too dark to see...

Bragi swore, shouted, cajoled. His men leaned on their weapons, staring with eyes that had seen too much bloodshed. They didn't care if the foe were vulnerable. He was going. That was enough.

Bragi caught another horse, raged around looking for men who would fight on.

He glimpsed movement near the fortress. Someone with white hair scuttled toward a band of legionnaires. Megelin's riders chased him back inside.

A wild, evil glee captured Bragi's soul. He walked his mount toward the battered stronghold.

He passed the remains of Badalamen and hardly noticed. A mad little laugh kept bubbling up from deep in his guts.

The bent man watched the barbaric rider cross that field of death as implacably as a glacier. He studied Feng, a mile eastward, directing assembly of the pontoons Badalamen had prepared. He searched the sky. Nowhere did he see his winged steed.

He spat. A potent tool, the Windmjirnerhorn, the Horn of the Star Rider, from which he could conjure almost anything, remained strapped to the beast's back. He was naked to his enemies, defenseless—except for cunning and foresight.

And his Pole.

The rider loomed huge now, subjectively growing larger than life as their confrontation approached.

He scuttled into the fortress's cluttered recesses, through the shambles of Magden Norath's laboratories. What had happened to the Escalonian? The first rat to desert the ship, he thought. No guts. Lived his dreams and fantasies through his creations.

The Fadema, though, remained where he had left her, sitting with his ancient, mindless accomplice.

"Is it over?" she asked.

"Not yet, my lady. But nearly." He smiled, stepped past her to a cluttered shelf, selected one of Norath's scalpels.

"Good. I'm tired of it all."

"You'll rest well." He yanked her head back, cut her throat.

The Old Man frowned.

"The Fates have intervened, old friend. Our holocaust becomes a country fair. Hold this." The Old Man accepted the scalpel. The Star Rider began extinguishing lamps. When one remained he produced his golden token, placed it over his "third eye."

"The Tervola have decided to cut their losses. I should have known. Their first loyalty will always be to Shinsan. A foul habit. Ah! I can hear *Them*. *They're* laughing. My predicament amuses *Them*."

He pocketed the medallion. "That'll scare hell out of somebody." He cocked his head, listening. The measured tread of boots echoed from a darkened passage.

"He comes." He selected an unconsecrated kill-dagger from the shelf. "The final scene, old friend."

Varthlokkur, Visigodred, and Mist, only survivors of the Inner Circle, sat, exhausted, watching the Winterstorm. Outside, dull-witted, disarmed, weary, the Unborn bobbed on the breeze, abiding Varthlokkur's command.

Valther burst in. "We've done it!" He was blood-filthy. A battered sword trailed from his hand.

They didn't respond.

He planted himself before them. "Didn't you hear? We've won! They're retreating…"

The Winterstorm exploded.

Valther shrieked once as flames consumed him.

Mist wept quietly, too drained to move.

Visigodred held her, softly observed, "If he hadn't been there…"

"We'd have burned," Varthlokkur said. "It was time. He had been redeemed. The Fates. They weave a mad tapestry… He was the last Storm King. They had no further use for him." He didn't seem surprised that his enemy, suddenly, was able to overpower his creation.

Ragnarson paused. There was a wrongness about the dimly lighted chamber. Yet the entire fortress had that taint. The evil of Ehelebe?

He entered, knelt by the corpse. "Fadema. Thus he rewarded you." Blood still oozed from her ruined throat. She stared up with startled dead eyes.

Sensing something, Bragi whirled.

The blade slashed his already ruined shirt, turned on his mail. He drove hard with his sword. The old man groaned, clutched his belly, hurtled toward the remaining lamp as if yanked by puppet strings. It broke. In seconds the room was ablaze.

"Burn forever, you bastard." One of those mad chuckles escaped him. "You've hurt me for the last time."

A bone-weary Trebilcock met him beside his mount. "Valther's dead," Michael said. "We thought you should know." He described the circumstances.

"So. He got in one last shot. Where's your shadow?"

"Aral? Him and Kildragon went around the sides. In case you came out over there. Why?"

"I think I might need somebody to carry me back."

"Mike!" Dantice's shout penetrated the remaining clamor of the battlefield. "Hurry up!"

They found Dantice kneeling beside a dying man.

"Reskird!" Bragi swore. "Not now. Not here."

"Bragi?" Kildragon gasped.

"I'm here. What happened?"

"My boy. Look out for my boy."

Reskird had a son who was a fledgling Guildsman. Bragi hadn't seen him in years.

"I will, Reskird." He held his friend's hand. "Who was it? What happened?"

The silver dagger had missed Kildragon's heart, but not by much. It had severed the aorta. Reskird gulped something unintelligible, shuddered, went limp in Bragi's arms.

He wept. And, finally, rose to assume command of the fields that were now his. Later Varthlokkur would suggest that Madgen Norath, unaccounted for, owed them a life.

"He was the last," Bragi mused. "None of us are left but me." And, after a while, "Why am I still alive?"

THIRTY-SIX: SPRING, 1013 AFE
HOME

Feng didn't go peacefully or quietly, with his tail between his legs. He went in his own fashion, in his own time, underscoring the fact that he was leaving by choice, not compulsion. He wouldn't be pushed. In Altea, when the Itaskian became too eager, he gave Lord Harteobben a drubbing that almost panicked the western army. In Kavelin, with Vorgreberg in sight, Feng whirled and dealt the overzealous pursuit ten thousand casualties they need not have suffered.

Ragnarson got the message that time. His captains, though, had trouble digesting it.

Feng was going home. But he could change his mind.

The Gap was open. Bragi put his commanders on short leash. Feng was no Badalamen, but he was Tervola, bitter, unpredictable, and proud. He could still summon that vast army at Gog-Ahlan.

The west had no new armies. Feng had to be let go with his dignity intact.

"Nothing's changed," Prataxis sighed their first night back in Kavelin's capital. "In fact, they've shown a net gain. Everything east of the mountains."

"Uhm," Ragnarson grunted. He had other problems, like learning if his children had survived.

Vorgreberg had been deserted. But as Feng withdrew beyond the eastern boundary of the Siege, people began drifting in. Sad, haggard, emaciated, they came and looked at their homes like visitors to a foreign city. They had no cheers for their liberators, just dull-eyed acceptance of luck that might change again. They were a shattered people.

There were, too, the problems of putting the prostrate nation onto its feet, and of driving Feng *through* the Savernake Gap.

The first faced every nation south of the Silverbind.

The latter task Ragnarson surrendered to Lord Harteobben. Derel, he hoped, would manage the economic miracle...

And a miracle it would be. Shinsan now bestrode the trade route which, traditionally, was Kavelin's major economic resource.

It was too much. "I'm going walking, Derel."

Prataxis nodded his understanding. "Later, then."

Bragi had never seen Vorgreberg so barren, so quiet. It remained a ghost city. Dull-eyed returnees flittered about like spooks. How many would come home? How many had survived?

The war had been terrible. Derel guessed five million had lost their lives. Varthlokkur deemed him a screaming optimist. At least that many had been murdered by Badalamen's auxiliaries. The small villages round which western agriculture revolved had been obliterated. Few crops had been sown this spring. The coming winter would be no happier than the past.

"There'll be survivors," Bragi muttered. He kicked a scrap of paper. The wind tumbled it down the street.

From the city wall he stared eastward. Distantly, dragon flames still arced across the night.

He lived.

What would he do with his life? There was Inger, if their hospital romance hadn't died. But what else?

Kavelin.

Still. Always.

He stalked through the lightless city, to the Palace, saddled a horse. A sliver of moon rose as he neared the cemetery gate.

He visited the mausoleum first.

Nothing had changed. The Tervola hadn't let their allies loot the dead. He found an old torch, after several tries got it sputtering halfheartedly.

Fiana looked no different. Varthlokkur's art had preserved her perfectly.

She still seemed to be asleep, ready to rise if Bragi spoke the right words. He knelt there a long time, whispering, then rose, assured his service to Kavelin hadn't ended.

He would persist. Even if it cost him Inger.

He almost skipped visiting Elana's grave. The pain was greater than ever, for he had failed abominably at the one thing she would have demanded: that he care for the children.

The torch struggled to survive the eastern wind. It was, he thought, like the west itself. If the wind picked up…

He almost missed them in the weak light.

The flowers on Elana's grave were, perhaps, four days old. Just old enough to have been placed there as Feng came over the horizon.

"Ha!" he screamed into the wind. "Goddamned! Ha-ha!" He hurled the torch into the air, watched it spin lazily and plunge to earth, refusing to die despite dwindling to a single spark. He grabbed it up and, laughing, jogged to his horse. Like a madman, by moonlight, torch overhead, he galloped toward Vorgreberg.

They arrived two days later. Gerda Haas, Nepanthe, Ragnar's wife, and all his little ones. They had been through Hell. They looked it. But they had grown. Gerda told him, "The Marena Dimura were with us. Even the Tervola couldn't find us."

Ragnarson bowed to the chieftain who had brought them, an old ally from civil war days. "I'm forever in your debt," he told the man in Marena Dimura. "What's mine is yours." He spoke the language poorly, but his attempt impressed the old man.

"It is I who am honored, Lord," he replied. In Wesson. "I have been permitted to guard the Marshall's hearth."

There was much in the exchange that went unspoken. Their use of unfamiliar tongues reaffirmed the bond of the forest people to the throne, a loyalty adopted during the civil war.

"No. No honor. The imposition of a man unable to care for his own."

"Nay, Lord. The Marshall has many children, of the peoples. It was no dishonor needing help with the few when he cared for so many."

Bragi peered at Prataxis. Had Derel staged this?

The Marena Dimura's remarks were a taste of things to come. Despite Bragi's conviction of his incompetent conduct of the war, he became a hero. Those he considered the real architects of victory went unheralded. People and wizards alike preferred it that way.

The real surprise arrived ten days after Vorgreberg's liberation.

He was at home in Lieneke Lane, busting his tail helping clean the place, wondering how Inger would respond to his message. Yes? No? Gjerdrum brought a summons from the Thing. Bragi hugged his children, and grandson (whom his daughter-in-law Kristen had named Bragi), and went.

Kristen had soared in his regard. It was she who had maintained her husband's family graves. She, Nepanthe said, had been strong for all of them, optimistic in the darkest moments. She had lost her husband and parents and still could smile at her father-in-law as he departed.

He met Prataxis outside the warehouse parliament. "Damned Nordmen trying to pull something already?" he snarled. "I'll kick the crap out of the whole damned Estates right now." The noble party had begun calling itself The Estates during the exile.

"Not yet." Prataxis gave Gjerdrum a secretive smile. "I think it's news from the Gap."

"Aha! Harteobben grabbed Maisak. Good! Good!" He strode inside, took a seat on the rostrum.

The Thing was a raggedy-assed comic imitation of a parliament now. Only thirty-six delegates were on hand. Most of those were self-appointed veterans. But it would do till some structure could be created for Kavelin's remains.

Assuming the chair, Derel immediately recognized Baron Hardle of Sendentin.

Ragnarson loathed Sendentin. He had a big mouth, and had been involved in every attempt to weaken the Crown since the civil war. Yet Bragi grudgingly respected him. He had served uncomplainingly against Badalamen, and had been a doughty fighter. In the crunch he had stuck to Kavelin's traditions and had closed ranks against the common enemy.

"News has come from Maisak," the Baron announced. "The Dread Empire has abandoned the stronghold. Not one enemy occupies one square foot of the Fatherland. The war is over."

Ragnarson wanted to protest. The conflict could never end while the Tervola existed. But he held his peace. Hardle's remarks had drawn unanimous applause.

Hardle continued, "I suggest we return to the task we faced before the invasion. We need a King. A man able to make decisions and stick to them. The near future will be harrowing. All parties, all classes, all interests, *must* repudiate the politics of divisiveness. Or perish. We need a leader who understands us, our strength and our weakness. He must be fair, patient, and intolerant of threats to Kavelin's survival."

Bragi whispered, "Derel, they wanted me to hear self-serving Nordmen campaign speeches?" Hardle, when wound up, could talk interminably.

Hardle spent an hour describing Kavelin's future King. Then, "The Estates enter a consensus proposition: that the Regency be declared void and the Regent proclaimed King."

Bragi's dumbfoundment persisted while the Wesson party seconded the proposal.

"Hold it!" he bellowed. He realized that all this had been orchestrated. "Derel… Gjerdrum…"

Both feigned surprise. "Don't look at me," said Prataxis. "It's their idea."

"How much help did they have coming up with it?" He glared at Varthlokkur, who lurked in the shadows, smiling smugly.

The Siluro and Marena Dimura minorities accepted the proposal, too.

"I don't want the aggravation!" Bragi shouted an hour later, having exhausted argument. "With no war to keep you out of mischief you'd drive me crazy in a month."

He now suspected the motives of The Estates. A King was more constrained by law and custom than a Regent.

They out-stubborned him. They were planning the coronation before he yielded. His election, Derel insisted, would be lent legitimacy by the attendance of the Kings with the western army.

"You know," he told Prataxis, "Haaken never wanted to come south. He wanted to fight the Pretender. If I'd known leaving would lead to this, I would've stayed."

Prataxis grinned. "I doubt it. Kavelin was always your destiny."

Kavelin. Always Kavelin. Damnable, demanding little Kavelin.

A sweating courier rushed in. He bore Inger's response. Bragi read it, said, "All right. You've got me. Gods help us all."

In his rags, with sores disfiguring his hands and face, the bent man didn't stand out. He was but one of tattered thousands lining the avenue. The King's Own Horse Guards pranced past, followed by Gjerdrum Eanredson, the new Marshall, then the Vorgrebergers.

The King and his wife approached. The Royal carriage wasn't much. Fiana's hearse converted. Kavelin had few resources to waste.

The old man hobbled away on feet tortured by hundreds of miles. He stared at the flagstones, hoped he wouldn't catch Varthlokkur's eye.

He squeezed the Tear shape in his pocket.

The wizard had been singularly careless, leaving it unattended.

But that was the nature of the Poles. To be forgotten. His own was the same.

Varthlokkur might not check on it for years.

He hobbled eastward, gripping the Tear with one hand, tumbling his gold medallion with the other. An hour outside Vorgreberg he began humming. He had had setbacks before. This one hadn't been so terrible after all. The Nawami Crusades had gone worse.

There were countless tomorrows in his sentence without end.

Night Shade Books Is an Independent Publisher of Quality SF, Fantasy and Horror

ISBN: 978-1-59780-148-5,
Mass Market Paperback; $7.99

Glen Cook delivers a masterpiece of galaxy-spanning space opera. For four thousand years, the Guardships ruled Canon space with an iron fist. Immortal ships with an immortal crew roamed the galaxy, dealing swiftly and harshly with any mercantile houses or alien races that threatened the status quo. But now the House Tregesser believes they have an edge; a force from outside Canon space offers them the resources to throw off Guardship rule. Their initial gambits precipitate an avalanche of unexpected outcomes, the most unpredicted of which is the emergence of Kez Maefele, one of the few remaining generals of the Ku warrior race—the only race to ever seriously threaten Guardship hegemony.

ISBN: 978-1-59780-119-5,
Mass Market Paperback; $7.99

The ongoing war between Humanity and the Ulant is a battle of attrition that Humanity is losing. Humans do, however, have one technological advantage—trans-hyperdrive technology. Using this technology, specially designed and outfitted spaceships —humanity's Climber fleet—can, under very narrow and strenuous conditions, pass through space undetected. *Passage at Arms* tells the intimate, detailed, and harrowing story of a Climber crew and its captain during a critical juncture of the war. Cook combines speculative technology with a canny and realistic portrait of men at war and the stresses they face in combat. *Passage at Arms* is one of the classic novels of military SF.

Find these Night Shade titles and many others online at http://www.nightshadebooks.com or wherever books are sold.

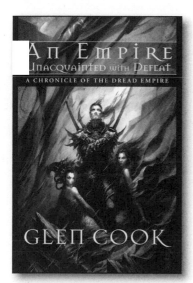

Night Shade Books Is an Independent Publisher of Quality SF, Fantasy and Horror

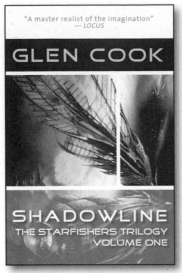

ISBN: 978-1-59780-167-6,
Trade Paperback; $14.95

From Glen Cook, the master of modern heroic fantasy, comes *Shadowline*, the first novel in the Starfishers Trilogy, a seamless blend of ancient myth, political intrigue, and scintillating futuristic combat action.

Mercenary warlord Gneaus Julius Storm surveys his domain from the Fortress of Iron, his citadel among the stars. Surrounded by the mementos of his centuries of conquest, his hand-picked soldiers, and his sons, Gneaus has grown weary of warfare and his artificially extended life. But far away, on the burning half of the planet Blackworld, the armies of the galaxy are about to clash, battling for wealth unimaginable along the Shadowline.

ISBN: 978-1-59780-168-3,
Trade Paperback; $14.95

Coming in October 2010
Stars' End
Volume Three of the Starfishers Trilogy
ISBN: 978-1-59780-169-0,
Trade Paperback; $14.95

From Glen Cook, *Starfishers*, the second novel in the Starfishers Trilogy.

Known as Starfishers, the High Seiners defy Confederation rule and Sangaree attack alike to skirt the dangerous boundaries of Stars' End, gathering their priceless cargo.

It is with the Starfishers of the harvestship *Danion* that Confederation agents Mouse Storm and Moyshe benRabi now fly and fight, probing the mysteries and myths of Stars' End, a strange fortress planet beyond the galactic rim, bristling with automatic weapons programmed to slaughter anyone fool enough to come into range. And where benRabi, a man of many names, must surrender his dreams and his mind itself to the golden dragons of space.

Night Shade Books Is an Independent Publisher of Quality SF, Fantasy and Horror

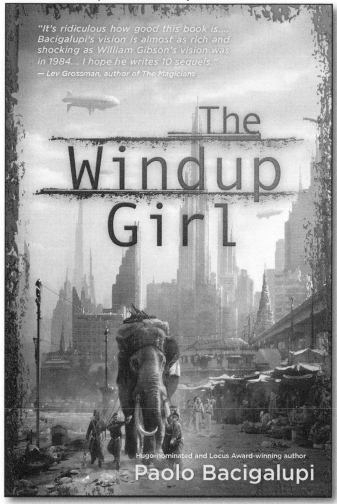

"It's ridiculous how good this book is.... Bacigalupi's vision is almost as rich and shocking as William Gibson's vision was in 1984... I hope he writes 10 sequels."
— Lev Grossman, author of The Magicians

The Windup Girl

Hugo-nominated and Locus Award-winning author
Paolo Bacigalupi

ISBN: 978-1-59780-158-4, Trade Paperback; $14.95

Anderson Lake is a company man, AgriGen's Calorie Man in Thailand. Undercover as a factory manager, Anderson combs Bangkok's street markets in search of foodstuffs thought to be extinct, hoping to reap the bounty of history's lost calories. There, he encounters Emiko...

Emiko is the Windup Girl, a strange and beautiful creature. One of the New People, Emiko is not human; she is an engineered being, crèche-grown and programmed to satisfy the decadent whims of a Kyoto businessman, but now abandoned to the streets of Bangkok. Regarded as soulless beings by some, devils by others, New People are slaves, soldiers, and toys of the rich in a chilling near future in which calorie companies rule the world, the oil age has passed, and the side effects of bio-engineered plagues run rampant across the globe.

Night Shade Books Is an Independent Publisher of Quality SF, Fantasy and Horror

ISBN: 978-1-59780-187-4, Trade Paperback; $15.95

Dragons: fearsome fire-breathing foes, scaled adversaries, legendary lizards, ancient hoarders of priceless treasures, serpentine sages with the ages' wisdom, and winged weapons of war. *Wings of Fire* brings you all these dragons, and more, seen clearly through the eyes of many of today's most popular authors, including Peter S. Beagle, Holly Black, Orson Scott Card, Mercedes Lackey, Charles de Lint, Diana Wynne Jones, Ursula K. Le Guin, George R. R. Martin, Anne McCaffrey, Garth Nix, and many others.

Edited by Jonathan Strahan (*The Best Science Fiction and Fantasy of the Year, Eclipse*), *Wings of Fire* collects the best short stories about dragons. From writhing wyrms to snakelike devourers of heroes; from East to West and everywhere in between, *Wings of Fire* is sure to please dragon lovers everywhere.

Night Shade Books Is an Independent Publisher of Quality SF, Fantasy and Horror

ISBN: 978-1-59780-189-8, Trade Paperback; $15.95

The Devil is known by many names: Serpent, Tempter, Beast, Adversary, Wanderer, Dragon, Rebel. No matter what face the devil wears, *Sympathy for the Devil* has them all. Edited by Tim Pratt (*Hart & Boot & Other Stories*), *Sympathy for the Devil* collects the best Satanic short stories by Neil Gaiman, Holly Black, Stephen King, Kage Baker, Charles Stross, Elizabeth Bear, Jay Lake, Kelly Link, China Miéville, Michael Chabon, and many others, revealing His Grand Infernal Majesty, in all his forms.

Thirty-five stories, from classics to the cutting edge, exploring the many sides of Satan, Lucifer, the Lord of the Flies, the Father of Lies, the Prince of the Powers of the Air and Darkness, the First of the Fallen... and a Man of Wealth and Taste. Sit down and spend a little time with the Devil.

Glen Cook is the author of dozens of novels of fantasy and science fiction, including *The Black Company*, *The Garret Files*, Instrumentalities of the Night, and the Dread Empire series. Cook was born in 1944 in New York City. He attended the Clarion Writers' Workshop in 1970, where he met his wife, Carol. "Unlike most writers, I have not had strange jobs like chicken plucking and swamping out health bars. Only full-time employer I've ever had is General Motors." He currently makes his home in St. Louis, Missouri.